ALSO BY WILLIAM EASTLAKE

THE BAMBOO BED

CASTLE KEEP

3 BY EASTLAKE

SIMON AND SCHUSTER · NEW YORK

For Martha

CONTENTS

Go in Beauty

The days and nights were long before it came time for us to go to our homes. The day before we were to start we went a little way toward home, because we were so anxious to start. We told the drivers to whip up the mules, we were in such a hurry. When we saw the top of the mountain from Albuquerque we wondered if it was our mountain, and we felt like talking to the ground, we loved it so, and some of the old men and women cried with joy when they reached their homes.

MANUELITO, Navaho chief,
upon returning from exile at Fort Sumner

1

Once upon a time there was time. The land here in the Southwest had evolved slowly and there was time and there were great spaces. Now a man on horseback from atop a bold mesa looked out over the violent spectrum of the Indian Country—into a gaudy infinity where all the colors of the world exploded, soundlessly.

"There's not much time," he said.

The young man was confiding things to no one beneath a single buzzard witness sailing in patterned concentric rounds without tracings in the hard, perfect New Mexico blue, way up. Now the young man swung the horse and walked it slowly along a ledge that looked down on the geological southern end of the Rocky Mountains above an unknown wash called the Rio Salado. The Rockies finished in a flaring red Morrison formation set off by a dwindling stripe of white gypsum. The long, giant, heroic Rockies died here in a crumpled flag motion where few people knew.

Closer to the young man but still blued by the distance was the trading post. The post appeared to be set down in the middle of nowhere and surrounded by no one but it was the exact center and capital of the world for the Navahos who called themselves The People and shaped domed houses named hogans that matched the feel and color of the country. The post was big and sprawling and built of enormous logs chinked with adobe and it lay between two mushroom-shaped and bright-colored mesas in the dry heart of the Indian country. Nearby was a low, native-type house made of petrified wood which the young man's ancestors had built. The spread of the buildings was cut off from the outside world, or from what one Indian named Quicker-Than-You called "the violent pretense of reality," by the quiet long mountains and the weird huddled mesas and the blue deep arroyos and total indifference.

Below at the post, the exact center and capital of the world for The People, two Indians crouched at the massive stone root of the petrified-wood house where it made its way into the ground.

"This crack—" Tom-Dick-and-Harry said, tracing it with his brown finger.

"They can fix it," Rabbit Stockings said.

"No," Tom-Dick-and-Harry said, both Indians still crouching outside under the log overhang and beneath the high voices within. He traced the crack again with his brown finger close to the red earth where the stone root entered the ground. "No," Tom-Dick-and-Harry said again. "And perhaps even The People cannot stop something coming apart and beginning here at the center of the world."

Still above and at the edge of the gay and loud-striped mesa, the rider allowed the horse to move up over a beginning sharp and purple butte away from the post and everything below.

The horseman, Alexander Bowman, ran the trading post

with his brother George and his brother George had recently got a beautiful wife. The trading post had been with the Bowman family almost one hundred years. It had passed down through many generations, and when the Indians first saw the new white woman they thought it would get nicely through another. The Indians did not sense anything wrong in the fact that there was only one wife; neither did George Bowman, whose wife she was. George Bowman, like his brother Alexander, was tall, lank, high cheek-boned and black haired, which would have made them look perfect and banal if all these qualities had not been exaggerated. Alexander was older than his brother George and it was he who got his education first, leaving the post with George, and then, of course, George went and got his. And now that George had got a wife the Indians reckoned that it would not be long before Alexander went and got his. That's what George thought too.

But Alexander did not think this. Alexander was a writer and he thought many strange things. But Alexander did not call it thinking, he called it knowing. He knew that George's wife was not happy in the Navaho country. He knew she had been to Paris and when she saw one of the Indians' sand paintings she did not think of The People, she thought of Picasso. He knew she had been to Vassar and when one of the Navaho People talked to her she did not listen to what he said but wondered what went on in his subconscious. Still, she was beautiful and she was not the only one who felt hemmed in by the mesas.

Alexander felt hemmed in by the mesas himself. He was hemmed in by the mesas, the blue mountains and by circumstances. He felt that George's wife had a great deal of

3

understanding along with her great deal of beauty. Together Alexander and Perrette could be with the whole world. Together they could see and feel everything a writer must see and feel, and a writer who is going to be any kind of a writer must see and feel everything.

Alexander Bowman was as certain that he knew this as he was certain that George's wife, Perrette, was in love with him, Alexander. Love was a word that was used loosely and no one seemed to know the meaning of the word but that was one of the discoveries he might make as a writer. But Perrette used the word anyway and with her it meant that now the word "writer" sounded more romantic than the word "trader" had sounded seven months ago. It meant that Paris and Rome and Cap-d'Ail would be exciting to see again and that the romantic idea of living in nowhere with the Indians had worn off. The word love also evidently meant to her that Alexander should play the beautiful joke on his brother of running off with his wife.

No, Alexander thought, a man couldn't rightly do that. Alexander pushed the stick, prodded it into the jaws and sprang the trap. It was a big Victor trap and it went off with a loud clack. The trap had been concealed on a narrow path on the mesa where the big cats had been moving down. A man could just walk out on the whole business, Alexander thought, but then she will leave him anyway. Alexander pushed the big trap with his stick off the ledge so that it hung down on its heavy chain over the sandstone rock of the mesa. Alexander climbed up now over the sheer face to the wide ledge above where his horse waited. He picked up the reins and the horse followed.

Alexander had sprung four traps in the last hour and

picked up two saddle bags of poisoned meat the government had placed. The government policy at the moment was to make coyotes and big cats extinct because the ranchers complained. When the animals that these animals preyed on increased to overrunning proportions, then the farmers would complain and the government would make these animals extinct.

Alexander had spent the morning making traps and poisoned meat extinct. Let nature take care of keeping a population in balance. Once you destroy that balance you would be overrun with something which you have to make extinct too. Eventually everything would be extinct. Alexander already missed the howls of the coyotes that he had grown up with. Nothing else much had changed in the mesa country. The government trapper had come in silently with poisoned meat and taken away the coyote, that was about all that had changed. They were beautiful animals, and clean, he thought, and part of the country and they belonged. With their noises and their swift running and their shadows in the moon, they belonged. But she does not belong, he told himself. With her beauty even, she does not belong.

He had reached a wide basin in the yellow sandstone that was strewn about with concretions, pieces of bowl-shaped soft stone that had once formed around hard objects and were now freed by erosion. They made good ashtrays. There were giant hunks of petrified wood too, and he sat down on one of these. The wood had weathered out of the rocks above and had gotten down to this basin. Soon a loud flood would push it over the cliff and it was at this point below this cliff that they had gathered most of the petrified wood for the house. And it was on this basin, where all the eroded-out objects were scattered neatly about on the surface of the smooth floor, and plainly visible, that he had always searched for fossils. If all those millions of tons of wood had fossilized why had no animals? A good question, a scientist named Cope who had horse wandered from his expedition, based at Gallina, had told old Bowman in 1869. Keep looking.

The Bowmans had looked ever since. Cope would have been proud of their tenacity. Cope, who had discovered the first fossil horse on the same venture, would or should strike off a medal for persistence. And Darwin had written of similar rocks when they tumbled in flood in South America. "The thousands and thousands of stones which, striking against each other made one dull uniform sound, were all hurrying in one direction. The ocean is their eternity and each note of that wild music spoke of one more step toward their destiny." Alexander had memorized that and thought about it each time it rained rocks off the cliff. It would be nice to be able to write as exactly as that.

He had come to this basin which looked out over the wide Indian Country to write ever since he was a boy. It was just at the ponderosa line in back of the basin, in creative revery over a stroke of genius (which he tore up in the clear revealing light of another day), that he had tumbled into a mine shaft, an abortive project that the courageous Conquistadores in the name of God and at the price of fifty heathen Indians, had sunk in vain. Alexander had spent three days there until George had got him out.

Alexander pulled on the reins of the horse now from his seat on the petrified palm trunk. The palm trunk was an exactly preserved anachronism from the days before the land pushed up when this dry, empty country was dense and lush and steaming, hanging with monkeys, primordial and rife. His horse, Fireboy, standing awkward in front of him, had picked up some cactus burs on the dry slope and complained by whinnying as Alexander pulled them out.

"No, this isn't a very nice thing to do to a brother, is it?" Alexander repeated to the horse. "Run off with his wife? No. I don't think anybody woud give us a medal for that. I'll tell you what we'll do. Let's just write it out of us, write a story about it and let it go at that. Let's not spoil everything; let's anchor ourselves here; let's make this place our eternity, not make any wild music toward any destiny with any ocean. Let's just write about it." And then he made a low throat noise when he thought of Perrette and decided after all it wasn't, like a stock Western movie, a matter you could be philosophical about with a horse. Perrette was very real and—well, Perrette was very real. There wasn't anything about Perrette that could be anchored by scenery or a horse. But with a brother, that's different, he thought. That could be very rough.

He got up now and mounted the horse and watched carefully all the gentle color of the distant folding hills.

That's right, he thought. Try to get away from George and Perrette for a while and back to the plans for the novel. A person can always lose himself in a good novel. His book would be about the mountain men working their way south from Bent's Fort and their meeting and joining Carleton's army from California. The idleness and boredom of the army with no South to fight in New Mexico. Their fighting and exterminating the Indians in Carleton's need for glory. The gradual degeneration of the mountain men that makes them finally accept Colonel Carleton's plan to place the remaining

7

Indians in a concentration camp called Bosque Redondo, where most died.

And Kit Carson would be the hero. It was not a bad plan for the novel. He knew the country well enough and the descendants of those involved including reds and whites. But what was he trying to prove? Maybe that evil is a permanent thing in any country among any group of people, even the nicest. Once there was nowhere a more generous and understanding man than Kit Carson. Maybe he was trying to prove that heroes must exist in the long periods of boredom because in the period of hysteria all heroes are victims. And words like "evil" and "good" must be avoided because they are abstract and do not exist. A gradual twisting process exists, that bends men into animals.

But the novel would have a strong surface movement of the bang-bang of the cowboys and Indians, then if somehow the writer could get this across there was—there should be—there must be put in an even greater, bigger, but quieter bang-bang beneath all this, an attempt to keep the beast human. But that would take some writer. To avoid being pretentious, to avoid making a speech, to keep the entertainment there and the reader always there would take some writing.

The buzzard witness, now borne on an updraft, laid his slow circles cleanly against the flat blue, higher and higher, as the horse dropped off the ledge and began the steep climb down and Alexander's mind got back to George and Perrette.

This dependency, this hero worship, George had for him, wasn't it bad for George? Wouldn't it be best for him to shock George out of it? Everything was always getting back to George and Perrette. George he knew in his youth had made a short catalogue in writing of everything he had wanted in a wife. It had begun with the usual platitudes digested in every digest and consisted of all those rationalities that ignore the deep and undying need for everyone to know his true individual self which is so different from another it frightens us. Perrette must have made a mental catalogue too, that was now breaking up on these mesas of reality. And what about his own? All he knew was that he had a loyalty to George and the Indian Country and his forefathers and particularly to George, and that was all breaking up now too and all he could do each day was fight it and watch the inevitable destruction of something valuable grow into a bigger destruction. Why not finish it now—go off with her now, before it, the inevitable end, got even more tragic?

Alexander had arrived at the corral now and he slung the saddle in the corner and started to say why the hell not. When he got to the bridle and slung that in the corner instead of hanging it properly as was his custom he did say, "Why the hell not?" But he dismissed the thought now and finally hung up the saddle and the bridle properly.

"That's better," Rabbit Stockings said.

"What's better?" Alexander said.

"That you don't take it out on things."

"Oh," Alexander Bowman said, and he walked out into the hard light of the corral and got on the top rung and sat there where he could see her. He could see too the long spell of emptiness covered by the one gray of the chico, chamise and sage that hid the arroyos from this height, but the desert growth did not hide the mountains that circled round it, did not hide the occasional Indian pony nor the adobe and log post nor the petrified-wood house. He could also see the

9

Indian hogans way out there in the distance and the three Indians driving out a sheep. But mostly he could see her.

Perrette Bowman was painting on a picture. She had studied in Paris under Lhote and she was painting it the way he had said. She was organizing it the way he said and using the colors he said and she had set herself up a still life of apples and pineapples and roses the way he had said. She had had George bring her the apples and pineapples and roses especially from Gallup. It was the kind of a still life Lhote would have liked. As a matter of fact the painting was a weak Lhote. Next she wanted to paint three dead fish all in a row alongside three lively baseballs. Alexander would be going to Albuquerque tomorrow and he would get them for her although it would be nice to go and pick out the three dead fish personally because there are Braque fish and Matisse fish and the kind you eat. Alexander would get the kind you eat although he would certainly do a better job of selecting fish with a feeling than his brother, her husband George.

"His brother, my husband, George." She repeated this feebly out loud, glancing over her still life but not seeing the Indian Country all around. Yes, she would definitely go to town tomorrow with Alexander when he went to the whole-sale ring to buy cattle. And what was Alexander doing wasting his time buying cattle when he should be writing? There was no one in the whole world who had his talent. There was not too much here to write about. Nothing ever happened. The country was blank and unexciting, it was part of that long stretch of land between Hollywood and New York, or better, between Carmel and Paris. It separated Texas from California so their incredibilities did not interfere with each other. It was that endless nothingness beneath the clouds when you are going to Los Angeles. Still, at one time it had been an exciting idea. The country as it had been described by the Santa Fe writers was romantic and awe-inspiring with picturesque and spiritual Indians and sunsets with poetry, described by Lawrence, where a woman could find herself. To be taken here by George when she had met him in New Haven had been her dream, and now her dream, she thought, touching her brush into one of Lhote's roses, had not turned into a nightmare. No. It had turned into a long, quiet bore. And it was not George's fault. Nothing would ever be George's fault. George was dedicated to the Indians and what could be more noble, more altruistic, more—how could she put it?—more depressing, than to be dedicated to the Indians? She admired him and respected him but she did not see him now as he came over a salt mound on his horse Ute. She was mixing some exciting things on her pallette.

George Bowman was trying to bring the horse into a walk. He had been recovering some breachy steers that had wandered into Apache country and he had told his wife he could not wait till morning to get them. They were branded fine but the Apaches did not seem to mind the brand when they ate. He had left Rabbit Stockings and Quicker-Than-You in charge of the post so he had not thought about that much on the way back—things could not be in worse hands. He had thought some about the salt blocks that were stolen, the wool that must be bought and the tuberculosis among the Indians that refused to yield to government statistics. He had thought, too, about the dream of cheap feed, the illusion of weight when the Indians rolled their wool in sand before they traded it to him expensively, the low price of beef on

11

the hoof, beautiful horses, fat cows, heavy sheep, and he wondered aloud that the country had changed none since his grandfather's time in 1863. Alexander would put all this beauty into words, all the beauty of the land, the mesas, the mountains and the pure sky and his white wife. Perhaps Alexander could put into words, and make acceptable by arranging the words properly, the fact that a Navaho, a man in Indian Country is, within, the same man as in any country. No, Alexander could not write that well. No one could ever write well enough to make truth acceptable to some people. But Alexander would write well enough to be number one and if the Indian Country ever fell to the advancing ravages that civilization called progress it would all be set down. The shock of a simple naked country would be set down. The shock of a simple naked country shot quietly in the morning with poles of purple light bending through the cliffs, and in the evening the same light shattering the whole world in spectrum violence would be set down. The Indians would be set down. Everything would be set down. George hoped he himself would not be set down but he hoped that Alexander would take an interest in Perrette. He wanted Perrette to be happy. George pulled up his horse on the top of the mesa. From here he could see Perrette painting and Alexander watching her. Good, he thought. Everything is going well.

"Lousy. Things have been going lousy." Rabbit Stockings grabbed the bridle as George Bowman got off for the gates. The Indian was dressed in yellow-and-black tall boots and blue jeans and he moved easily as he caught the horse.

"They haven't spoken to each other all day," Rabbit Stockings said as he brought the horse through the gate.

George Bowman dropped the hoop on the gate and followed toward the barn.

"I'll get the saddle," Rabbit Stockings said.

George Bowman broke away and walked over to the corral and sat on the top rail next to his brother Alexander.

"I got those steers," he said.

"Apache country?"

"Yes," George Bowman said.

"Fence cut?"

"Hard to tell."

"It was cut all right."

"I got the steers."

"Those people got nice habits."

"It's a custom," George Bowman said.

"Those people got nice customs."

"My Indian spy tells me you two haven't talked all day."

The two brothers from their high perch on the rail were staring out over the head of George's easel-crouching wife, their eyes not focusing on anything, just taking all the big emptiness in.

"Your Indian spy is right." Alexander removed a pack of Camels from his shirt pocket, pounded one out and lit it deliberately and talked into the smoke.

"I hoped you two would get along fine," George Bowman said. "You got a lot in common."

Alexander watched the tip of his cigarette carefully. "Yes," he said. "Yes."

"Painting and writing and everything."

"Yes."

"How is the writing going?"

"Fine. Fine."

"I put those Angus steers over in the Largo pasture. They're not putting on weight."

"Angus don't do well in this country. We should stick with Herefords."

"It was an experiment."

"And was she an experiment?"

George now too took out a cigarette and lit it from Alexander's cigarette that was handed to him.

"You think we should stick with Indians?" He handed the cigarette back.

"I don't think she is doing too well here, George."

"Not if she gets the cold treatment," George said.

Alexander took one foot off the rail. George now, too, swung one foot over the rail so he faced his brother.

"If you'll talk to her about the things that excite and interest her—she's concerned about your work, Alex, as I am—we can be three happy Indians."

There was a silence as both brothers studied the railing.

"By God," George said finally in recognition. "I've got it. You think I don't trust you. You think complicated like a writer. You'll do fine. But this is real and you're my brother."

Alexander got down off the fence. "You're my brother," he said to himself as he walked alone to the post. As he lifted the latch he said aloud, "Three happy Indians."

2

Inside the post Quicker-Than-You, an intelligent and delicate-faced Indian, was explaining the medicine man's business to the medicine man to whom the trader's father had given the extra name of Paracelsus. The medicine man, who was taller than any other Indian, was resplendent in sheep-suede trousers and a dark velvet jacket; white seashells circled his neck twice and silver coins circled his waist once.

Quicker-Than-You was behind the counter but as he talked he pointed out the inadequacies of the medicine man's medicine to the medicine man with the aid of his finger.

"We cannot accept your word that a man is going to steal something and that this will cause an endless drought."

Alexander leaned against the gun rack and listened.

"Tell him he's crazy," Alexander said.

"Tell him yourself," Quicker-Than-You said. "You speak Navaho as well as the People."

"I can be as stubborn about speaking the Navaho that I know as he can be about speaking the English that he knows."

Quicker-Than-You turned to the medicine man.

"He says he can be as stubborn about speaking The

People's language as you can be about speaking the foreign language."

"It is no ordinary theft," the medicine man said, slowly in The People's language. "The theft that will cause the great drying up will be no ordinary theft of things."

"Tell him he's crazy," Alexander said quickly in Navaho, ignoring the medicine man.

Alexander turned and went into the back room where the hides were kept and sat on a pile of hides in the dim airless room and looked out the slot window at his brother who still sat on the fence.

"Those Indians," he thought, rubbing his face, "they know too much. He calls it medicine but he knows too much."

He felt and then heard the door open and she came in and sat down beside him on the pile of hides.

"The medicine man knows," Alexander said, still watching out the window.

"How could he know?" she said quietly, her voice meeting the dim quiet of the room.

"That's why he's the medicine man," Alexander said.

"Will he talk?"

"No. He won't talk. Even after it's over he won't talk, but now they will know that he always knew and they will think him some medicine man when it's over."

"When is it going to be over?" Her voice was still gentle.

"Never," Alexander said, watching his brother through the slit window. "Maybe never."

"But when are we going to leave?" Her voice was still gentle and smooth.

"Maybe never," Alexander Bowman said. "The medicine man predicts a drying up of everything."

16

"And if we don't there will be a drying up of everything."

"Yes, yes," Alexander said. "All the medicine is bad."

"Listen," she said. "There is no medicine. This is the twentieth century and people do what we have to do because we are still animals no matter what century. Nice animals."

"Nice animals." Alexander caressed her arm that now lay across him. "Nice animals. Nice brother. Three happy Indians. It's a circle with no medicine."

"Three happy Indians. He likes to say that. He is a wonderful person. We must not hurt him, Alex. How can we do it without hurting him?"

"Call it off," Alexander Bowman said.

"Can you call it off?"

"No."

"We can no more call off love than we can call off our own hands or feet." Perrette was silent against the incredible silence of the big hide room. "Quickly," she said. "We must do it quickly."

"Quickly," Alexander said, watching his brother. "The medicine is to do it quickly, to hit Albuquerque and keep right on going."

"Yes, quickly, quickly," she said. "Quickly."

"But the medicine man said the land would dry up."

"We are in the twentieth century."

"But the Indians are not in the twentieth century. I do not know what century they are in but it is not this one. I only spent four years away from here at that university myself. Anyway the medicine man has never been wrong. He never says too much but when he talks he has never been wrong. That's why he's the medicine man."

Then she said, not listening, "We must move quickly."

"Quickly, quickly," he agreed, turning toward her alive beauty, her warmth now. "Tomorrow. Quickly."

They rose now as George dropped off the fence and came toward them. She went outside to collect her easel and Alexander went into the post. He thought "quickly, quickly, quickly" as he saw his brother through the leather of the harness he dragged toward the counter. Now he saw the medicine man standing alone with a quiet dignity amid the babble of the Indians and he thought, that's why he's the medicine man. But he forced this out of his mind and went back to the phrase "quickly, quickly, quickly."

Rabbit Stockings, who was one of the Indians left in charge of the post, was standing straight in the attitude he assumed when he was going to make a report to the trader George Bowman.

"That mission Indian, Tom-Dick-and-Harry, has been hanging around here all day. Every time a white rancher comes in he makes fun of him by singing one of their songs like 'I'm Dreaming of a White Christmas.'"

"They don't know they're being made fun of," Quicker-Than-You said.

"Just the same he shouldn't do it when they're our guests," Rabbit Stockings said.

"He thinks the whites are too vulnerable," Quicker-Than-You said.

"Yes, if that means the whites are silly. Yes," Rabbit Stockings said. "But maybe we believe things that seem odd to them too."

"Maybe we do," George Bowman said, not thinking.

"I don't think so," Quicker-Than-You said. "The whites don't think much. They got a lot of important things to do."

"They got books as far as you can see," Rabbit Stockings said.

"Did you ever read one?" Quicker-Than-You tried on four turquoise rings for size.

"No," Rabbit Stockings said. "I can't. I would if I could."

"But you can't." Quicker-Than-You did not like any of the rings. Now he tried the necklaces. "I can and did but I don't now. I tell you, let Tom-Dick-and-Harry have his fun."

"Do you think we should allow Tom-Dick-and-Harry to make fun of the whites' beliefs, Sansi?" Rabbit Stockings asked.

"No," George Bowman said.

"You think they're too vulnerable to be fair game," Quicker-Than-You said.

"Yes," George Bowman said.

"Be that as it may," Quicker-Than-You said, trying the turquoise rings again, "and I am in partial agreement with you, be that as it may, they ask for it." Quicker-Than-You held the ring at arm's distance to see it.

"Let's get on with the rest of the business," George Bowman said.

"Okay. Number two," Rabbit Stockings said. "Quicker-Than-You read all your and Alexander's mail and threw it all away."

"I saved a few relevant pieces," Quicker-Than-You said.

"That's nice," George Bowman said.

"I saved a bill for three dollars and seventy-five cents you owe the University of Oklahoma Press and another from Albuquerque Grain and Feed for seven hundred and thirty-two dollars."

"That's nice," George Bowman said.

"I saved two rejection slips that came for Alexander and that I don't think he should see until later when he's finished his writing."

"Considerate of you," George Bowman said.

Quicker-Than-You put all the pieces of jewelry back in the case.

"Alexander's writing damn well about us Indians. Of course some would think his Indians are atypical, but all Indians are atypical. People are atypical."

"What does atypical mean?" George Bowman asked and Rabbit Stockings agreed with the question with his eyes.

"You know what it means. It's Alexander's pose not to know what it means. He's the writer."

"Yes. But could I coax the rest of my mail out of you?"

"There's that usual letter from that girl you met at college. I burned it."

"Thank you," George Bowman said. "Like our great President you are indispensable."

"I function," Quicker-Than-You said.

"With my mail you function beautifully." George placed his hands broadly on the counter. "The next time I leave the post I am going to tie you up."

"I quit," Quicker-Than-You said.

"You're always quitting," George said.

"And you're always hiring me back. You come to the hogan. I don't come here."

"Okay, so I don't tie anybody up. By God, I hope I didn't hurt your feelings about a tiny thing like plundering my mail and running my life."

"Everyone can see there's an equity on your side," Quicker-Than-You said.

20

"Thank you. You're noble," George Bowman said. "By God, I hope I didn't hurt your little Navaho feelings."

"Without further facetiousness or racial prejudice on your part," Quicker-Than-You said, "I'd like to consider the incident closed."

"Thank you," George Bowman said. "By God, I'm lucky today."

Rabbit Stockings, who spoke a great deal of the foreign language, English, heard almost nothing of this except the last words of Sansi's, that he was lucky today—words with which, after what the medicine man had said, he could not agree.

"Okay. Number three. The medicine man has made a prediction. The prediction is that something important and valuable is going to be stolen. We better lock up double tonight."

"Valuable things can't be locked up," Quicker-Than-You said.

"That's Indian talk," George Bowman said. "Let's get back to white man's talk. We will lock up everything double tonight. The medicine man has never been wrong. He has an excellent grapevine of information."

"Now the second part of the prediction. After the theft there will be an endless drought."

"If we cope with the theft we won't have to cope with the drought. Lock up everything double tonight," George Bowman said, moving off to where there was something waiting to eat.

"Go in beauty," Quicker-Than-You called after him in Navaho.

The house Indian had set three places at the plank table.

Perrette sat in the middle in a costume that was fresh and chic and certainly the thing on the Riviera but odd in the Indian Country. She sat in the middle, her rope-soled espadrilles perched on the top rung of the chair, her bright, billowing peasant skirt covering the whole chair so that she might have been sitting on a studio floor in Cannes. The two brothers sat on either end of the table with their wide-brimmed Stetsons set alongside them.

"Three happy Indians," George Bowman said, looking into his pinto bean soup as he spooned it.

Alexander and Perrette looked up from their pinto bean soup and over at each other.

"How goes the writing?" George asked, still concerned with the soup.

"Okay."

"How many pages this morning?"

"Five and a half."

"Not bad. Is it good?"

"I've read worse."

"Prejudiced?"

"Yes."

"All us Indians are prejudiced," George said, still involved with the soup. "Even Quicker-Than-You likes it. He doesn't like much."

"Why don't you go in and pick up those cattle tomorrow, George?" Alexander said.

George looked up from his soup abruptly.

"That's been arranged. You're going in with Perrette. It will be difficult to drive all the way to Albuquerque and back without speaking to each other."

"Yes," Alexander said. He had not started his soup and neither had Perrette.

"I've got to bury those two TB victims at Star Lake, then they can burn down the hogans. It's all been arranged," George said eating.

"Yes," Perrette said. "The white man has an obligation to the Indian. He can learn from the Indians as well as steal from the Indians. The white man has got to work with the Indians instead of for the Indians. That has been the Bowmans for three generations now, ever since the white man came and it has been a happy life. It's all been arranged," Perrette said in a rote tone as though repeating something.

"But Alex will put that into believable language," George said. "He'll get a lot of fine books out of the country. But look, you two Indians haven't started to eat."

Alex and Perrette both looked down at their soup and then, as though at a signal and together, they began to eat.

"That's better," George said.

They all went through the soup and the salad without saying anything but when they got to the beef that the Indian woman brought George said: "The medicine man said something big was going to be stolen."

"Paracelsus is crazy," Alexander said.

"Then he said there'd be a big drought."

"He can have crazy ideas," Alexander said.

"He doesn't say much but he's generally right. That's why he's the medicine man."

"Then lock everything up double."

"That's what I figured," George said.

"I'd rather you went to Albuquerque tomorrow, George."

"Listen, it's all been arranged," George said.

"Everything is arranged," Perrette repeated.

"And if the medicine man has it from the grapevine that there will be a theft it's better that you two are gone and I am here."

"Perfect," Alexander said. "You think your arrangements will work against the medicine."

"I'll be trying," George said.

"I believe that," Alex said.

"I'll lock everything up double."

"But you say the medicine man is always right."

"Well, I'll be trying," George said.

"You are trying all right," Alex agreed.

Outside, after lunch, there were three horses saddled waiting for them.

"I'm not going," George said.

"But we're all going," Perrette said. "We planned yesterday to check that new gate we paid for."

"That was before I had to ride all morning looking for those cows. I'll stay here and get in some target practice with the Indians."

Alexander and Perrette swung onto the horses and made toward the cross fence, four strands anchored to cedar posts, that swept along the arroyo before it ran over the mesa. Alexander rode in advance on Fireboy and Perrette followed closely on a paint she had named Abstract. As they swung away from the arroyo and began to climb the mesa Perrette pulled Abstract even with Fireboy. They rode now in absolute silence through the diminishing chico and sage and beginning grama up the gentle slope that began the climb to the quiet mesa.

"Of course," Alexander said finally, "I must tell George."

"After it's done," Perrette said.

They eased the horses through the last of the cactus and grama and among a scattering of piñon, still climbing.

"The Indians," Alexander said, "call this hill The Long Blue Mesa. It's sacred. On top of it they gather stones for medicine." Alexander rubbed the neck of his horse. "But I must tell George."

"After it's done," Perrette said.

Alexander turned his head. "I think we're being followed," he said. "I heard something back there."

"Nerves," Perrette said.

The trail became nothing now as they climbed up through the loose rock, the horses feeling their way carefully.

"What medicine do they collect medicine for on this mesa?"

"Marrying Way, Shooting Way, Prostitution Way. Which one interests you?" Alexander said.

"Let's try the last one," Perrette said.

"Well, there's a disagreement," Alexander said. "The Jesuit school at Window Rock is generally a good authority but one priest writes in his book that the ceremonies are to discourage and another says in his book that they are to encourage prostitution."

"And how do you vote?" Perrette said.

"I vote to turn around and see who's following us."

"Nerves," Perrette said.

Now they came up to a round platform of rock and stopped their horses.

"Down there," Perrette said, pointing to the base of a distant, gay-colored cliff. "The road. We could reach it in one hour, follow it into Cuba, take the bus to Albuquerque. Now."

"Now," Alexander repeated, "we'll get behind this overhang and find out who's following."

Alexander dismounted and he led both horses back of the concealing rock and they waited.

"No one," Perrette said, still atop her horse. "No one."

"Quiet," Alexander said.

"No one, Lover," Perrette said.

"Listen."

"No one."

"Listen."

"The wind."

The almost noiseless, moving horse came around the cliff now, ridden by the medicine man. He pulled up alongside them.

"You just happened to be out for a ride," Alexander said, annoyed. "You weren't following us."

"I was following you," the medicine man said.

"Thanks," Alexander said. "Dangerous country. We need your protection."

"I wasn't protecting you," the medicine man said.

"Forget it," Alexander said, and he slid onto his horse and swung it around. "Let's get home."

At the post between the two mesas they had the targets set up and the Indians were sitting one hundred yards away while one of them was standing shooting the seven shots that their Marlin or Winchester lever-action carbines held. They each had brought, or found at the post, a one-pound coffee can and at the end of the shoot the one with the most holes in his can was the winner. They preferred the Hills Brothers cans because they were red but today most had settled for the blue Maxwell House cans because that's all the post had got.

"Shoot this cigarette out of my mouth, Gee," Alexander said toward George.

Perrette, the medicine man and Alexander had dismounted at the corral and walked over to the shooting. It was George's turn to shoot and Alexander had lit a cigarette and walked over to the target.

"Go ahead and try it, Gee. Shoot the cigarette out of my mouth."

George had already begun to raise the gun on the coffee can that Alexander stood in front of, but now he lowered it.

"No," he said. "It's silly. It was all right when we were kids, but now it's silly."

"Very silly," Perrette agreed.

Alexander tossed away the cigarette and walked toward the house. The others went back to watching the shooting. Soon Alexander came out of the petrified-wood house with a gun. All the others were watching the shooting. George had lit a cigarette and was watching the shooting carefully.

Now there was a shot that did not come from the gun of the Indian who was shooting at the coffee can and George's cigarette exploded.

Alexander lowered the gun and placed it against the house, then he walked to the target and lit a cigarette.

"Go ahead and try it, Gee. Shoot the cigarette out of my mouth."

George's face was all white as he raised the gun quickly

and then began to squeeze off the trigger carefully. The gun went off as Perrette hit it. "No!" she called as she hit the gun and the gun went off.

All of the Indians watched Alexander when the gun went off. The cigarette had not been touched. They could all see the cigarette and now they could all see the stream of blood that was very red against the white kerchief Alexander wore. Alexander went down on one knee.

Perrette got to him first.

"You damn damn fool," she said, taking his head in her arms. "Did you have to give him the chance? Did you have to ask him whether—?"

The others came up now and George examined Alexander's chin. The medicine man was the only Indian who was not concerned.

"It's just a crease," George said. "It will bleed a little but it will be all right. Have the doctor take a look at it when you take the semi into Albuquerque tomorrow."

Early the next morning Alexander and Perrette were in the cab of the great semi-truck and trailer. They were waiting for the Indians to finish putting the stake body on the trailer. They had taken the stake body off the trailer to haul sand from the Puerco Wash and now they were putting the stakes on again for the cattle Alexander was going to bring back. The medicine man, Paracelsus, was watching everything, standing alone on a dry hill above them. George Bowman was leaning against the cab directing the Indians and talking to his brother.

"Don't bid against the packers, Alex, and don't go over twenty-three cents on anything. And don't bid against Cass.

He stopped his bidding the last time I bought a bunch."

"And no Angus," Alexander said.

"That's right."

"They don't do well in this country."

"I thought we were going to forget that."

"Okay," Alexander said and he started up the engine and looked over at Perrette.

When the engine started the medicine man walked down the hill and stood in front of the truck. The stakes were all in place now and Alexander touched the horn. The medicine man did not move.

"Nashda, nashda, nashda!" Alexander hollered to the medicine man and then he hollered in English, "Out of the way!"

The medicine man still did not move. Alex raced the engine and sat on the horn. No luck. George went up and grabbed Paracelsus by the shoulder.

"Can't you see it's my brother?" he said low and in Navaho. No luck. Alexander raced the engine and hit the horn again. It was an air horn and it echoed big through the canyons and across the mesas, but there was still no luck. Tom-Dick-and-Harry came up and grabbed the other shoulder and together with George they pulled him along but the medicine man did not help with his feet so he was an awkward burden and his head hit the gate post causing a small trickle of blood, but he was quiet now and out of the way.

Alexander put the truck in gear and George jumped on the side of the cab.

"He's okay," George said. "These medicine men get a crazy streak once in a while. It's an occupational disease. I guess he figured you were the one that was going to steal something."

"Yes," Alexander said, racing the engine.

"I'll have the government doctor check him when he comes through."

"Yes," Alexander said, and he began to move the giant truck forward.

"And don't worry. I'll lock everything double. Enjoy yourselves. It will be raining when you get back."

The great truck was moving along good now and George had to drop off quickly. Alexander raced her into second gear as soon as he could. It will be raining when you get back, Alex thought as he double-clutched the giant and eased her into high. That was the nicest thing anyone could say in the Indian Country. But Quicker-Than-You had not come out to say his usual "Go in beauty." No one at all had told them to go in beauty. Alexander tramped down hard now on the gas as they hit the long straight stretches of sand road that dropped away from Indian Country.

"We're off," Perrette said toward him.

"Yes," Alexander said aloud and he said to himself as he checked the air and fuel gauge with his eye, "But not in beauty."

When George dropped off the truck he walked through all the silent Indians until he got hold of the medicine man and then, arm in arm, he led him into the back room away from everyone and sat him comfortably on the hides. Then he got out some cotton and dabbed at the slight cut.

"The white man's world is built on faith and confidence and understanding," George said.

It seemed that Paracelsus would still say nothing out of a stolid, implacable expression that could go through infinities saying nothing, but then he said finally in a voice that was deep and grating, and at last in foreign English: "But supposing that the white man does not understand himself. I think that's what's happening here."

George stopped dabbing at the cut and sat down alongside the medicine man. He needed to sit down.

As the huge semi rocked along through the Indian Country Alexander took one more good last look. It was, he thought, what you are supposed to see when you are dying. Everything that has been of you for such a long time is going by you fast before the book is closed. Now he was, he thought, having the privilege of putting the final chapter first. As they hit a switchback he could see the petrified-log house each generation of Bowmans had worked on to make right for Indian Country. He could see the horses too that each generation of horses had worked on to make right for the terrain and altitude of the Indian Country, and all the outbuildings and the hogans the Indians had made right for the Indian Country, and ahead and all around were the cliffs, sage and rock and wide mesas the world had made right for Indian Country. The only thing that had gone wrong was himself. He felt the big weight of the enormous truck and trailer hurtle forward through the pass and knew that somewhere, somehow, something had happened that made him wrong for Indian Country. Anyway now it was true and when it was no longer true, when he, like the petrified logs his ancestors had sweated over and like the horses the stallions had plunged and sweated over and the hogans and the cliffs, when he too was made right for Indian Country then he could return—return.

His leg reached forward to touch the air brake and met hers

and then his eyes met hers and the great truck plunged on below the gay and loud-colored cliffs at greater speed, shot on big and lumbering and fast through the weird and simple Indian Country, dim and fading now with his memories of childhood, and the immemorial rocks rising enormous that had witnessed the first coming of the white man and would be there to see the last—all of the great dumb land, all of Indian Country, witnessing now this small chapter.

"Quickly," she said.

Now the big red truck and trailer wound down the long hill going much too fast as it entered the Pueblo country with the Navaho country well behind them and Perrette said, "Keep to the left. It will take us around Albuquerque."

"Yes," Alexander said. "Yes," and he gave it more gas as they approached the big curve.

"What are you trying to do?" she said. "Commit suicide? We'll never make that curve."

"We'll see," Alexander said and he hung on the wheel and gave her all the gas she would take. Perrette had her arms around him now as the big truck and trailer tried to make the curve. It began to rock and it tried to go over to the left and then it tried to go over on its right side, the whole rig, truck and trailer tried to jack-knife into the arroyo as Alexander pulled it out on the straightaway. But the wheels held and they were running level now and Alex laid his foot off the accelerator to take it down from eighty miles an hour.

"We made it," she said.

"Yes," Alexander said. "Maybe They want to see how far we can go. I guess it will be some trip."

He straightened out the big rig now and kept her at a constant speed with his eye on the long road ahead.

"No one told us to go in beauty."

"Quickly," she said.

Later that night on the long flat stretch between Albuquerque and El Paso the big outfit pulled up in front of a motel and Perrette and Alexander got out.

Inside the motel room after the fat proprietor had left them finally alone with the Gideon Bible and the Sears, Roebuck rancho décor Alexander began to fumble with his necktie.

"Let me help you, you damn genius," Perrette said, and she removed the necktie deftly and began to unbutton his shirt.

"Quickly," she said.

3

In Mazatlán, Mexico, Alexander wrote his novel quickly and the publishers rejected it quickly. It occurred to him then that they had set up wayside stations in the middle of continents to anticipate and return all those objects that looked dangerously like manuscripts for it seemed that he was getting the book back before he sent it. However, by persistence or confusion of his name with another's, there at last arrived a note borne to their room by Perrette saying that if all the characters were changed somewhat and the locale, say (we do not want to presume), were switched to Bombay where the editor witnessed a similar scene—well, who knows. they might be able to use it.

With this encouragement Alexander mailed it out again to another and another and another, and finally (as a friend, an unrealized author turned bitter, remarked), in error or through mistaken identity or drunkenness in the publisher's office—it was accepted.

"There," Perrette said, looking up from her easel. "It's easy."

The book was about Alexander's early childhood among the Indians and at the post. About his grandfather who had, in the Civil War and in the territory of New Mexico, volunteered to defend the Union, decency, the blacks from the wisdom of Southern gentlemen. About his grandfather who was forced instead to fight, or better, slaughter, the Navaho Indians and concentrate the women and children at Fort Sumner where most died. About his grandfather who finally sickened, quit, resigned, "tendered his resignation in, got shut of murdering Indians at water holes, concentrating the women and children. I, who innocently, unconsciously, youthfully, volunteered to defend the Union, the blacks, decency, from the wisdom of Southern gentlemen, quit and took to trading with the Indians, just traveling around trading, without a gun, among the brutal, warlike savages who must be killed or concentrated in a camp." (It is our opinion at the office that this is propaganda, the personal prejudice of the author, that no believable . . .)

It was about his grandfather who, when he quit the Northern army, worked his way into the Cuba country and founded a post, began to build it of the petrified wood of the Eocene cliff, of his being caught by Kit Carson, the hero. No, maybe it wasn't Kit Carson who was the hero. Carson was a mountain man doing a job he didn't understand. Maybe Colonel Carleton, Carson's commander who was supposed to be fighting the Civil War, was the hero, he who gave orders like this: "I have been informed that there is a spring called Ojo de Cibola about fifteen miles west of Limitar where the Navahos drive their cattle. A cautious, wary commander, hiding his men and moving about at night might kill a good many Indians at this point."

It was about his grandfather who refused to exterminate the Indians, to whom, when he "tendered his resignation in"

35

Carson said, "We'll have to draft you as a private."

"If you can find me," Bowman had said.

It was about his grandfather whom Carson found three months later building his petrified-wood house. Carson, after thinking a while, but still sitting atop his horse, said, "But, well, I guess you killed your share of Indians."

"More," Bowman said.

"But we will have to concentrate or exterminate these Indians who are helping you build this house. Orders."

"Orders?" Bowman said.

"Yes," Carson said and he got down off the horse. "Unless you and me can think of something different about your Indians we'll have to take them in."

"They live in a petrified-wood house," Bowman said.

"Well," Carson said, kicking the petrified-wood foundation and then getting on the horse and riding off. "Then they can't be real Indians."

The petrified-wood house became just another rock, another outcropping of the land in the Indian Country where not Indians or whites, but human beings could—

"Yes," Perrette had said over his shoulder. "It stood there as a rock, a bulwark, a testament that people can get along together in the Indian Country, that they don't have to kill and steal from each other."

"Maybe that was it," Alexander said.

"And then there was your father, but did I ever tell you—" Perrette was staring out over the town of Mazatlán. "Did I ever tell you about my father?"

"He had a lot of money," Alexander said.

"Has," Perrette said. "And you should accept some of it."

"I didn't marry your father," Alexander said.

"Oh, Daddy wouldn't mind giving us a stack of it," she said. "It's just a game. Did I tell you that Daddy was a Socialist? One night in 1919 when he was eighteen he was beaten up by the Communists. He didn't mind that, it kind of made him proud, but two weeks later, and for his politics again, he was jailed by the New York police. When he got out he said he wasn't going to be serious anymore, he was going to play games. He said he was going to play the American game of making money. Oh, occasionally now he'll give twenty or thirty thousand to some do-gooder cause but his heart is not in it now and he always goes back to the game of making money."

"Where are the old ennobling dreams? But I didn't marry your father," Alexander said. "I married you. What effect did your father have on you?"

"I don't know," Perrette said. "Except he was very strict. He said he didn't want me getting any silly ideas or ways he had when he was young. If I was a boy I guess he would have sent me to military academy. I was a girl so he sent me to a convent school. Which was all right," Perrette said, "except that I had his blood in me, his bone, and when I looked at those walls I said, When I bust out of here watch me go."

"Watch me get back to the rewrite on this novel," Alexander said. "This part is about my father."

"Go," she said.

And it was about his father and not about his mother, who died young having George—not too uncommon in the Indian Country with doctors two hundred miles away—mothers dying. It was about his father, who was away a good deal of the time trading with the Indians. So the two boys grew up kind of like wild Indians. That is, they played with the Indian kids but the Indians had a hogan, a family, so it was more like wild animals. But wild animals have a cave and a family too, so it was more like—

"Oh God, you've made your point!"

And mostly the book was about the two brothers. With his father gone trading with the Navahos, with everyone gone except the Indians, George, the youngest, fastened onto Alexander. When all the Indian kids would begin to circle the post on their ponies, getting ready to attack the whites, it was Alexander who organized the defense, barricaded the doors and windows with George following him around goggle-eyed and taking orders. It was Alexander who saved the day in George's boy eyes, saved the candy and kept them from getting chucked in the pond, till their father got back. And when they were ambushed by the Indian kids in the back country George always had Alexander. It was the big brother, Alexander, who bluffed the Indian boys by charging them with a big noise and then retreating fast before the Indians knew what it was, Alexander who got them quickly home, losing the horse's tracks in streams and dead-ending the Indians up box canyons. It was Alexander who always won. George always had Alexander.

Of course the proper names were left out and something else was left out too. Alexander had spent three days at the bottom of a mine shaft. It was the most important thing that had happened to Alexander. That was left out. Perhaps it was because he was not absolutely certain of how it ended. Diamond Jack was one of the very few who knew absolutely how it ended but he was not around when Alexander wrote the book.

This Jack had come early to the Cuba country when it was all open range, no fences, when you could run your cattle anywhere. Somewhere, way back there someplace, someone had stolen, or maybe borrowed, a cow. That victim then had to steal or borrow one to live. When they stole Jack's, Jack went right on getting even for years. They called him a rustler. Diamond Jack was a good friend to the Bowmans but they had fine cattle and Jack did not object to stealing them if they were conveniently around. Jack was conveniently around when the mine episode ended but he was not conveniently around when Alexander wrote the book. Perrette was conveniently around and she said, "You got in everything, didn't you?"

"Almost everything," Alexander said.

"You did not get in the part that George must have hated you, must have been jealous."

"Jealous?" Alexander said. "About what?"

"Sibling rivalry. Freud."

"Vassar," Alexander said.

"Well, his resentment of your taking over, dominating?"

"I don't think so," Alexander said, thinking. "George is a very gentle man."

"But underneath all that," Perrette said, "I felt something else, some kind of resignation, bitterness."

"Yes, I know what you mean," Alexander said. "I have sensed it too, but it was never that—jealousy. Would he alone, among all those people, have rescued me from the mine shaft? Would—?"

"You didn't put the mine shaft incident in the book," Perrette said.

"Because I'm not certain of all the facts," Alexander said. "If it were all known it might make a book in itself. But this book is finished."

And when it was published a film company recognized the book's success, bought it for fifty thousand dollars, and ended with an excellent picture. Better than the book, Alexander thought.

From Mazatlán they went to the Varadero Beach in Cuba, close enough to the name sound of his own little town in New Mexico to make him feel less dispossessed. The second book, still about Indian Country, was judged better than the first. The film company, alerted and awake now, paid a small fortune and really ruined this one with a perfect director and four million dollars. Alexander never saw this one but everyone else had to suffer it, as well as the TV version. But the book was in hard covers and Alexander was made.

"Not only made," Perrette said, "but I was right."

Perrette, who had begun life with ambition and wealth and the finest of convent schools and who finished at Vassar, had to be right. She was much too clever in her attested-to cleverness at Vassar to marry, finally, after one admitted mistake, anything but a genius. For an excellent reason she had never told anyone that she had attended, for one year, a public school in Tacoma. It was, she knew, because she had hated everyone there, all those "qui n'étaient pas de son monde," all those who had never appreciated her cleverness in the least. Now she would get even, now that she was the wife of a genius. In her life now the public school never existed. The convent schools that had marked her indelibly must be allowed to exist and Vassar would be allowed to exist too. Vassar approved depth.

Now they would leave the Varadero Beach. Now they would go to Europe. Soon Alexander must write about some-else than Indian Country. Soon there would be nothing more to write about Indian Country. One day it would be written out—so they went to Europe.

Everything that happened those long years in Europe seemed later to be only a searing powder flash of light, a series of brief hallucinations quickly caught and never allowed to be forgotten, sudden pictures of a brittle expatriate world survived sometimes by those with a real and hard and unprotected past. There was in Perrette's past nothing to protect her future. She was born into that kind of middle-class wealth that demands a greater outward show and inward certainty of nothingness called sophistication than Perrette or any human might mentally survive. There was no rock of family, and, beginning with her convent education, there was no rock of love. There was discipline for the sake of discipline, Latin for the sake of Latin, religion for the sake of religion, which so easily evolves into Marx for the sake of Marx, Bohemianism for the sake of Bohemianism, art for art's sake, but never love for any human sake at all. There was never that human kind of love, for that love is a normal, wretched thing, achieved without discipline, wealth, cleverness or kinds of sophistication at all. That kind of love, Perrette thought, is a many suburbaned thing.

"Yes," Perrette said aloud now from her deck chair on the Ile de France. "But it suddenly could become the thing. It could become chic."

"What?" Alexander said staring, watching a man named Bentley disappear.

"Nothing," Perrette said. "What did that man want?"

"Moral support," Alexander said. "He has plans for an avant-garde magazine in Europe. *The Joiner* or *The Booster*, he can't make up his mind. I half promised him something and he threatened to look us up. I figured you knew him. Ezra Pound is considering him and Ernest Hemingway has already knocked him down."

"I know no Charles Bentley," Perrette said.

"Tea?" the deck steward said, balancing his world against the north sea.

"No, thank you very much," Perrette said.

Bentley came back now threatening to let them in on the ground floor of the magazine. Bentley ran to tweeds and a heavy pipe and an Ivy League face and manner that would have been more at home, Alexander thought, in the Oak Room of Merrill Lynch Etcetera than under some gable on the Left Bank, more at home with the solidity of Continental Can and Miami Copper at 25 bid, 27 asked than with the airy instability of Zero, *transition*, *Tomorrow* or the name that Bentley had now finally decided upon—*The Joiner*.

"The name has a wholesome, contemptuous feel about it," Bentley announced to the Atlantic and his two captives bound in blankets as he paced in front of them on the leaning deck.

"Splendid," Perrette said from somewhere deep among her weight of blankets, sun goggles and books. "I think it's splendid."

Bentley did not know how to take this. He stopped his pacing and went over to the rail and looked down on the tourist class below, while he thought it over. Some of the tourist class have interesting heads, he thought.

"Don't bait him," Alexander said to Perrette from his

deck chair and from deep within the same mummy trappings that Perrette wore. "A writer has enough natural enemies without killing each other off. If we start a fight among ourselves on the wagon train we'll be a cinch for the Indians. An old frontiersman by the name of Bill Williams said that," Alexander said. "Don't insult Bentley. We may need him when the going gets rough."

"You've got it made," Perrette said.

"A writer is as successful as his last paragraph." Alexander said. "You might not like what some of the boys on the wagon train are up to but one day they might save your scalp. No one else is liable to."

"Old Bill Williams," Perrette said.

"He could have said it," Alexander said. "He said a lot of things like that that he didn't practice. The boys could always tell when there would be trouble because Old Bill would always disappear before an attack."

"A smart man," Perrette said.

"They found him one day," Alexander said, "standing at attention, his rifle standing straight alongside him, alone and frozen to death."

"But I wasn't baiting him," Perrette said. "I thought it was a good title for a magazine. I really did."

Bentley had at last decided that Perrette had not meant ill by her remark and he ceased examining the heads of the tourist passengers on the deck below and went back to pacing up and down in front of Perrette and Alexander.

"Let's say we price the magazine," Bentley said, "at one dollar a copy. I just picked that out of the air. Now let's say we sell, well, ten thousand copies. I picked that out of the air too. I have no idea what the circulation will be

43

but that's a theoretical ten thousand dollars per month."

"If you charged five dollars a copy," Perrette said, "you'd have a theoretical fifty thousand dollars a month."

"I see your point," Bentley said. "Well, let's say we charge fifty cents for the magazine and we cut the circulation down too."

"Yes," Perrette said. "Well, if you sold one copy each to your contributors you'd be taking in four dollars and a half a month. I'm afraid there's nothing theoretical about that."

Bentley went back to the rail, not because he was annoyed with Perrette or the low figures. He knew his break-even point on the magazine would be about five thousand copies and there must be some law that operates against your selling less than the break-even point. He did not go back to the rail to examine the heads of the tourist passengers either, but to examine the ocean, which he found intellectually stimulating.

"Lay off," Alexander said to Perrette. "Let him peddle his papers."

"He's mad," Perrette said.

"Anyone who has anything to do with writing is mad," Alexander said. "The editors, the publishers, all of us. If Bentley seems a little crazier than the rest of us it may be because he's younger."

"I have an intellectual spitball I'd like to try out," Bentley said, coming back. "I have a young genius in his teens and in my stable, a poet, Alfred Marlowe. He should get the credit for this."

"If we're going to give him all the credit," Perrette said, "who is he?"

"A very deep young man."

"If your deep young man's too deep for me what a very very deep young man your deep young man must be."

"Alfred's very aware of his limitations," Bentley said. "He realizes he's operating on the third layer of consciousness. That is, he's still being understood. He figures when he reaches the fifth layer he will break off contact and be on his own, then without the ropes of tradition holding him it will be an unrestricted search for the pure essences of poetry. Without those ropes holding him he figures he will catch it, or at least glimpse it down there someplace, which is sufficient for him."

"Supposing there is a cave-in? Perrette said.

"He has resources to withstand almost anything," Bentley said. "Intelligence, character, insight . . . He's a Texas Tech man."

"Resources?" Perrette said.

"I just told you."

"Money," Perrette said.

"Oil," Bentley said. "He was brought up in oil. But he's not happy. He's looking for new horizons. Truthfully, he's put some money in the magazine with no strings attached except, well—"

"Except he wants to run it," Perrette said.

"You could kind of say that," Bentley said.

"Unfortunately he apparently kind of said it," Perrette said. "But you go ahead. What's his idea for the magazine?"

"Yes. Well, the gimmick on the magazine is that there is no gimmick. All the stories are square. They all have a beginning, a middle and an ending, with all the commas and periods in the right places. They all have an up-beat ending. The editorials will be written by a U.S. Congressman or a Member of Parliament. There will be no dirty words. And the thought for the day will be written by a Methodist minister. We will run editorials against modern art, close dancing, divers forms of fornication up to and including sexual intercourse where reproduction is not indicated. We will have editorials upholding and in praise of the Hawley-Smoot Tariff Act and Mrs. Smoot, George Horace Lorimer, the Republican Party, the Boy Scouts, the Epworth League, the American Legion, Carrie Jacobs Bond and the editors at Doubleday's."

"It's been done before," Perrette said. "When we were in school we got out a mimeographed thing like that."

Bentley stopped pacing.

"Why don't you get out a magazine," Perrette said, "in which all of the writing is a masterpiece, each one a classic, every story better than has ever been done before or will ever be done again, then set your price and the circulation will be enormous."

"Yes," Bentley said, but this time he did not go back to the rail but retreated down the passageway.

"Don't ever kill dreams, even silly dreams, weird dreams. People with shuttered minds will attack them soon enough," Alexander said, removing his dark glasses. "Do you know what I was thinking about while Bentley was talking? I was wondering how many head George would be running this year and I was wondering about George."

"Ole Hoss, you need a drink," Perrette said.

Below in a bar, camouflaged, it seemed, to appear a brothel, they had drinks. They talked about things that did not matter and then Alexander, after being quiet for a few long moments, said, "Perhaps it would be nice to have some kids. Two boys, say."

Perrette thought it would be nice to have another Manhattan. Alexander finally had a Martini.

"What else would you like?" she said.

"To go back to Indian Country."

"There will be plenty of time for that," she said, "after you see the world. I don't want to go back to anywhere particularly. Vassar maybe? Home? At home we had a nice butler. At home Mommy and Daddy were always a little frightened of me. Daddy used to hide from me in the *Wall Street Journal* and Mommy hid from me by giving me presents."

"Tell me more," Alexander said.

"All right," she said. "I will tell you that when you run out of Indian Country material you don't have to worry. You can have a lot of experiences and write of them."

"Experiences?" Alexander said.

"Yes," Perrette said. "Waiter! Where's the waiter?"

They had some more drinks and then they went on top to their stateroom. The clerk at the steamship office had sold them the finest suite of rooms on the boat for mere money. All of the fixtures in the bathroom were silver except the bathtub faucets.

"These are gold," Perrette said, turning on the hot water, and it steamed heavy into the bedroom where Alexander was getting undressed.

"Everyone," Perrette said, "cannot travel like this. It's only writers, corrupt or lucky, a few millionaires and kings."

"I'll make a note of that," Alexander said. "And what am I, corrupt or lucky?"

"Now you are lucky," Perrette said.

A steward tapped on the door and Alexander threw on a robe against his lank and awkward nakedness and let in the steward with the bottle of champagne Perrette had ordered.

"Merci."

"De rien."

"Did it arrive?"

"It's arrived," Alexander said.

The steward had set the bottle of Mumms in a silver bucket on a teak tray between the twin beds and left.

"Ole Hoss, I reckon you ain't seen nothing like this before," Perrette called from the room that billowed with steam.

"Not rightly, ma'am," Alexander said, watching her.

"The champagne, I mean," Perrette said.

"Yes, ma'am," Alexander said.

"It ain't the homestead," she said.

"Not rightly, ma'am," Alexander said.

"I'm just a cowgirl myself," she said, coming into the room naked.

"I reckon," Alexander said.

"What do you think the critter would weigh, Ole Hoss?"

"One ten. One twenty. I wouldn't rightly know, ma'am."

Perrette put on a robe and sat on the bed.

"What are you going to write about in Europe, Ole Hoss?"

"I don't know. What am I going to write out of now?"

"New experiences, Ole Hoss."

"And why?"

"Money, Ole Hoss."

"That's all?"

"Art, Ole Hoss."

"That man has put up with a lot," Alex said.

"Well, he'll have to carry us too," Perrette said. "Let's drink to Art."

"That's all?"

"No. This," Perrette said and she sat on his lap and put her arm under his robe. "This," she said.

The ship made a bad list and the champagne, glasses, teak tray, silver and everything not nailed ended up in a silk-draped corner on top of Alexander and Perrette. There was a long silence as the big ship evened and until Perrette said weakly, "What's happening to us, Ole Hoss?"

4

All the time they were on the boat going over Bentley continued to appear and disappear suddenly. It seemed that all those lonely, long years in Europe he continued, as on the ship, to appear suddenly and with a look of bewilderment as though surprised to see them still alive.

Although he did not come when they were in Paris, Biarritz or Venice he came again when they were in Ischia and Alexander was half dead, blue-green and white as though he had been in the water four days. There were nurses working over him, kneading him, rolling him over like dough.

At the dock where Bentley landed from Naples there was still a lot of commotion, flags and color. Bentley learned soon that Alexander had swum from Capri to Ischia, an impossible swim that had probably never been done before, no one knew exactly.

Alexander and Perrette were living up in a castle that overlooked the town and the harbor. It had belonged to King Emmanual or some dispossessed royalty who must now settle for their picture on a sardine can. A big wedding cake of a castle, or château, glaring white over the small pink tile roofs of the town, a place that only an American can

50

afford, which is justice, Bentley thought, because no one else would take it for free.

There were two sets of marble stairs that climbed up in back of the town to the front entrance and when Bentley got to the top of one of these stairs a lackey in uniform let him in. There was Perrette, crouched over an easel, painting a picture in the middle of the entrance hall or place where the ancients took off their armor and helmets. It was that old. Perrette was painting Indians.

Bentley told her he had come for the story.

"Story?" she said, looking up puzzled from her easel.

"Yes," Bentley said. "Alexander tentatively promised me a story."

"Oh, I am sorry," she said. "Won't you follow me?"

Bentley followed her into a small, high, marble room with onyx columns, just off Alexander's bedroom.

"It's not much of a story," Perrette told Bentley leaning forward in one of those small gold chairs. "He swam from Capri to Ischia. You think that would impress his brother?"

"I guess so," Bentley said.

"Good," she said. "First it's climbing mountains, then hunting impossible animals in Africa, and now this. As a child he could always impress George, always win him over when he was mad by—"

"But this is not the story I came for," Bentley said.

"Oh," she said. "The money then. Well, we sent him part of the money. We sent him part of it to finish that petrified-wood house, or burn or throw away. It's Alexander's guilt, although he says the story was about George, partly about their childhood, so George should get part of it—but it was because of me. Yet I was twenty-one."

"But I came for part of the new novel. Fiction," Bentley said.

"Fiction?" she said.

"Yes," Bentley said and he named the magazine.

"Fiction," she said. "Then treat everything I said as fiction." She sat watching Bentley with her big open eyes, leaning perched forward on the small gold chair.

"What Alexander says is true," she said. "Soon, particularly now that he's not there, can't be there—soon there won't be anything more to write about Indian Country. What real experiences can you have when you live in this vacuum? You've got to make experiences, make things happen. So maybe it's for his books, maybe it's for his brother, I don't know." She went back in the small gold chair. "It's this awful business that happened today," she said. "We rowed alongside in a boat feeding him. When it got bad we tried to get him to quit but he's stubborn like a small boy, like all the Bowmans. Then they brought him out and up here all blue and almost dead, so is it any wonder that I am talking about things that should not be talked about? But unless they revive him soon I will go out of my head. I went out there to paint hoping that would get my mind off it. But you said you did not want an article but something to do with fiction."

"Yes," Bentley said and he named the magazine again.

"But that's not the same magazine."

"No. *The Joiner* went bust. We had a fight over the word 'exist' and Alfred ran out of patience before he ran out of genius. But we've got another backer now who still has both. His name is Wendwood Hopgood, Jr., and he likes the name *Nothing*."

"And he's probably awfully right," Perrette said. "Oh, you poor slob. I'll see if Alex is any better."

He was and she said Bentley could look in. Alexander looked very green. Bentley waited out in the onyx room until they called him, and this time everything was splendid. Alexander was sitting in the big chair in a smart robe with a drink but he looked very alert and interesting, as though he had just finished a book. He shook hands and he motioned Bentley into a velvet chair by a cathedral window that looked over the town.

"We had a sheep camp on the Largo," Alexander said finally. "You could see the snow on the Sangre de Cristos all the year around. I always get a place with a view if I can." He took a drink and then continued. "You wouldn't by any chance remember whether they black-topped that trail from Aztec to Dulce? I was just thinking about it."

"Dulce?" Bentley said.

"Yes. That's the Apache Indian headquarters. There was a lot of talk of surfacing it when I left."

"Dulce?"

"I'm sorry," Alexander said and he pulled a big gold-covered rope and the same flunkey who opened the door brought Bentley a drink.

"George would get a kick out of all these gold and marble halls. George was great for adobe floors, claimed it was hard as marble. The trick in adobe floors is light on the straw and heavy on the blood."

"Blood?"

"Sheep's blood. But you came about the story. Well, it's not much. People have swum from Capri to Ischia before, but not in this century. You think George might get a kick out of it?"

"Who?"

"Yes," Alexander said. "Yes. Well, I see you have never been to Indian Country. Still it's not important. What story do you want?"

"A part of the novel you're working on," Bentley said.

"What magazine?"

Bentley told him and Alexander said, "Let's eat. You must be starving."

While they ate Alexander said, "I came out of the small magazines myself, so I help them when I can, if they want it. Anyway we feed everyone who comes to the post now. But we're not just knocking around the world, living in these marble tents. We have a plan."

"Listen to this," Perrette said.

"Yes," Alexander said. "When we make this swim, climb those mountains, hunt those animals in Africa, it's all experiences out of which a person can write. When the Indian Country gives out, when there's no longer a novel there, then I've got these experiences."

"Notebooks upon notebooks full of them," Perrette said. "The only thing he hasn't done against the day when he can't write about his own country is jumping from a plane without a chute."

"And it could be done too," Alexander said. "Those wings they strap to you—what do they call them?—batmen."

"Or fight a bull," Perrette said. "He hasn't done that yet."

"Another writer takes care of that and very well too," Alexander said.

"And there's one more experience we haven't thought of," Perrette said.

"Yes," Alexander said.

"Suicide," Perrette said.

Now fireworks began to burst around the castle, shot from the square below. Bentley did not know what the occasion was; it could have been that they were celebrating Alexander's swim. They would explode outside the window in red, green and purple streams of fire, spinning and hissing, stars exploding within stars, a pleasant nightmare in technicolor.

"Suicide," Alexander repeated. "I suppose," he said, "we commit suicide by living, by getting older."

"Yes," Perrette said. "But the whole thing can be cushioned with drink, which makes it a lot easier for me to wait while you're up there about to fall off a mountain or get run over by an elephant."

A big rocket exploded outside the château with a terrific noise. All the lights went out. Bentley waited around awhile drinking with them in the dark. When he left early in the morning the lights were still out and they were still sitting in the dark drinking, but the fireworks, the celebration, had ceased.

It was in Constantinople the next time Bentley saw Alexander and Perrette. They were staying in another one of those castles. This one was white too but it had a minaret, a tower. They were guests of the Emir, Alexander said—or Caliph. Bentley saw them on the Bosporus. They were driving a white carriage, huge, with gold wheels. That is, a big black Negro in costume, who must have belonged to the friend, the Emir or the Caliph, was driving it. Four golden horses with black tails, purple plumes over their necks. Perrette and Alexander were sitting behind this costumed black on white cushions all dressed to kill with a small boy at their feet playing what might have been a dulcimer.

Bentley waved and hollered to them but they didn't hear. Maybe it was the noise of the dulcimer. Bentley expected any moment they would throw a gold coin. He followed them all the way to the castle, where there was a crowd, and again he expected them to throw gold coins. When they got to the castle someone belonging to the Emir or Caliph closed the big, wide, iron-grilled carriage gate in his face, and that was the end of that.

Bentley did not see them again until he had to take a temporary job as a correspondent and ran into them in Israel during the Arab war. They were all staying in the Hayarkin Hotel in Tel Aviv, where the correspondents were housed. Alexander was quite famous now and some magazine was paying him tons of money to write some opinions about the war. Bentley didn't feel good in Tel Aviv. He saw the war the way the Arabs saw it. Alexander? Well, the Israelis were losing at the time so he saw it the way they saw it. Finally he saw it so much that way that he disappeared.

Perrette would sit in front of his typewriter all day in the correspondent's room, the lobby of the Hayarkin, where they had the desks set up. Just sit there looking out at the ocean, past that wrecked ship that was always there. At four o'clock the Israeli information colonel would come in and tell what appeared to Bentley a pack of lies about the glorious victories of his heroic Israeli armies, then the colonel would pass this out in mimeographed form and Perrette would take Alexander's and add it to the growing stack that already hid the ship if not the ocean. Then she bought a parrot, took to feeding it and teaching it to say something patriotic to please the colonel. It wasn't until later, not long before they discovered Alexander, that she began to bring a bottle.

They found Alexander in a hospital in Beersheba. He had joined up as a private and finally got hit badly; shrapnel. The hospital had overflowed so they had him in a captured Arab house. It had a dome ceiling, done in mosaic tile, no windows, just a door. Bentley drove Perrette down there in an old German jeep. Alexander was very bad. Bentley stayed there as long as he was still very bad. Perrette was with him three weeks. Alexander raved most of the time, turning over on the army cot, whispering into the dirt floor on one side and then turning over and talking to the dirt floor on the other.

"Go, George, and get help. Get the Indians. Get Father. Get a rope. Lower the rope and pull me out of the mine. I see a hole of light. It must be a mile above me. The side of the mine is slippery. I gain a few feet and sink back again. I have to go up a little way once more but until the daylight comes I dare not move. To keep my sanity I make up stories. Here at the bottom of the world I wait."

Bentley joined Perrette at the door of the arched hut.

"It's a symbol," Bentley said. "The mine is a word for everything outside of Indian Country."

"Symbol, no," Perrette said. "He really spent three days at the bottom of a real mine shaft, buried one hundred feet deep, lost. You don't know all the facts and maybe neither does he. All the facts," Perrette said. "There seemed to be a feeling at the post among some of the Indians that the whole story never got out."

"But I got this out of his raving," Bentley said. "It was George who rescued him, brought him back to Indian Country, the world, life again."

"Maybe we don't know all the facts," Perrette said. "And neither does he."

"What were the facts?" Bentley said. "What are the facts about Alexander's entombment, his first burial, his being resurrected, snatched from certain death by his brother?"

"Plucked," Perrette said. "But I don't know. Ask George."

"Who's George?"

"His brother," Perrette said.

Alexander got well and they began to travel again and all those final years in Europe were images of those first sad desperate years in Europe. Their's was the way of expatriates, all those people who wander. But Alexander wrote another very successful Indian Country novel, his fourth, and had many new experiences against the day when the Indian Country material would be exhausted. And Perrette waited at the foot of the mountain or the edge of the jungle with her heart in her mouth, then drinking.

He finally had to write that book about his experiences, adventures, and it was silly. Maybe it was that his public had gotten to expect a great deal of him. Maybe it was as good as any adventure story but for him the verdict was that he was making up heroics. Sometimes a critic will wait a lifetime for a friend to write a book as bad as Alexander's. One of the nicest things they said was that "our boy has run out of gasoline."

Then Alexander and Perrette went back to Mazatlán

to get as close to Indian Country as they could get. In Mazatlán, as close, he figured, as his brother would let him.

The last time Bentley saw them in Europe, before they went back to Mazatlán, they had finally moved out of castles—marble hogans Alexander called them—discovered that you did not have to live in suburbia or a castle. There was something else. There were villas on the Mediterranean. It was in Cros-de-Cagnes and joined the hotel. It was very impressive. People thought he was renting half the hotel. Alexander would work in the morning, then in the afternoon they would hike up the stream to Cagnes-sur-Mer; they even had the courage sometimes to climb up the mountain to Haut-de-Cagnes. It took courage because it was full of rats—artists who lived like rats. The painters had burrowed into this old medieval fortress called Haut-de-Cagnes, built about the tenth century, lived there certainly without food, encouragement or even hope. Then Perrette and Alexander began buying their pictures.

"This one, that one and the one over there," Perrette would say. The outcasts would take their money in unbelief and haste as though expecting any second someone from the twentieth century would come and lock up Alexander and Perrette.

Going down the mountain they talked intimately so Bentley thought it best to lag behind, pretending an interest in the hovels. The steps were in tiers, about fifteen steps and then a platform. Bentley always stayed an echelon behind but he could still hear them. And then they drifted into a café halfway down the mountain. Bentley stopped at the bar while they went into the back room but he could still see and hear them. Alexander looked tired, empty, and he rested his chin on the roll of canvases, looking over at Perrette, who was still young with that kind of youthfulness that will, someday, suddenly collapse under its own tricks.

"We've got to get home," she said.

"We're going," Alexander said.

"I mean home to the States," she said.

"And live in one of your father's marble tents on Long Island? I don't think so."

"Then I could try Indian Country again," she said. "George is here all the time with us anyway. And he may have forgotten or married or something by now."

"I've written him," Alexander said. "Nearly twenty or thirty times, and no answer." They had a drink. "I was thinking," he said, "the only thing that separates us from the rats, those people, is success."

"You look terrible," she said.

"I got the book off this morning," he said.

"Good," she said. "Then you won't have to write about Indian Country—ever. We can forget it."

"Yes," Alexander said.

"Jesus, you look terrible," Perrette said.

"The book can't help but be successful," Alexander said. "It's got everything—everything but Indian Country. I'm off the hook."

"Then let's celebrate," Perrette said. They touched glasses.

"To the future," Alexander said.

"My God, you look ill," Perrette said. "I'd better call a doctor."

"There's nothing wrong with me," Alexander said, grabbing her arm, "that any doctor, any white doctor, can treat. You remember a fool, an unscientific fool, on the reservation called Paracelsus? He could help me," Alexander said. "And you remember a man called George Bowman, a brother, a husband? He could help me," Alexander said. "I've got to get home, the Indian Country, the ranch, something I know—interests me—I can write about, live about. And don't worry, George won't carry a grudge all his life. He'll come through when he's really needed. I was three long dying days at the bottom of an old mine shaft in the Largo country and George found me. George never let me down. We have got to have patience and hang on. George will—"

"You're hurting my arm," Perrette said.

"To the past, then," Alexander said, and he dropped her arm and raised his glass.

"Yes, to the past," Perrette said. "To those happy first four months when we thought we could find some kind of happiness in running away, to the first day I saw you, to the first night in Albuquerque, to our last night in Europe and our first night back in the States."

They got back to Mexico. That's as far as they got.

5

The Chevvy pickup made its way around the point of the dry mesa. The pickup was all blue and so was the sky. The rocks were orange here, further on they were yellow and jutted out over the trail so that soon the golden rock would form a roof over the blue pickup. There was a big splash of red in the back of the blue pickup because that was the color of the blankets the Pendleton people were showing this season in the checkerboard area. There were two Navaho women in the back of the truck facing each other. They were not saying anything but this was their custom. That they rode in the back and the men in the front was a custom too. The women were being driven from the post of George Bowman, the white trader, where they had had nothing but talk because they were without credit, back to their hogans which were without food, to put an edge on their knives. The long drought had given their hunger a splendid edge. This was becoming a custom too.

George Bowman and the husbands of the two Indians in the rear were going to drop the wives at a hogan to rig a pole and sharpen their knives to dress out a buck. The people in front were going to kill a buck. They had their guns hidden under a blanket above the floor board. They were going hunting out of season. This wasn't a custom at all. But this hunger was becoming a custom and, among many other and more painful words, one Navaho found it a bore.

"I tell you, Sansi," Quicker-Than-You said to George Bowman, "it's becoming a big bore."

Once upon a time in the Indian Country there was rain but now the Indian Country had gone through fifteen years of drought. The great petrified-log house had been boarded up for fifteen years. Alexander Bowman had stolen George's wife fifteen years ago. To the Indians the drought made sense. It was brutal but it made sense. The medicine man in his prediction had been right. The medicine man was always right. George Bowman and Quicker-Than-You were certain that the theft of the wife had nothing to do with the drought (we are convinced after many consultations with many wise men that the drought is caused by insufficient rain). But the cruel drought continued as did the prestige of the medicine man, and the best of the Indian Country continued to blow away.

The Indians wanted George Bowman to write a letter to his brother, Alexander, to bring him back. They thought this might stop something. George was certain this would not stop the drought on the land.

George had an excellent reason for not writing his brother. All the Indians knew this but the drought continued and they tried. George believed, too, that he had a perfect excuse for never answering the letters he got from his brother, but the drought continued in his heart and he tried.

"Anybody but a human being could do it. It would be easy," the Indian next to the door said.

"What?" the Indian in the middle said.

"Forgive what we are doing today. My wife can't see it."

The two Navahos were wearing blue Levis, black-and-yellow boots, and each had a red cotton band around his forehead. George wore a leather jacket and a large and very worn Stetson. They wore the same thing in any season.

George said nothing but continued to watch the road. He was trying to drive the blue pickup and compose a letter in his mind.

"I tell you, Sansi," Quicker-Than-You kept up, "it's become an awful bloody bore." George still said nothing and the Navaho said, "I got that from a book, Sansi. Tell me, is that the way they talk at your Yale during the cocktail hour? That is, you can't possibly play football all the time even at your Yale. There must be a cocktail hour. Did you know that Sansi went to Yale? Alexander went to Yale too. It must be about fifteen years since he went away to be with the whole world. His last book was not so good. I wonder if he has reached the end of the world."

Rabbit Stockings was the other Indian in front of the blue pickup with the guns hidden and he said, "Shut up, Quicker-Than-You."

They arrived now at the hogans of the Navaho. George stopped the blue pickup and the wives who were riding in the back got off. They would erect a pole to hang the buck on and sharpen their knives and wait for the men to get back. The hogan was octagonal shaped and made of vertically placed cedar posts chinked with adobe. The roof was conical and of mud, laced underneath with piñon. There was a hole in the middle for the smoke to come out when they cooked but there was no smoke from any of the hogans.

There was a green-and-orange wagon parked outside the hogan with an enormous lever that was a hand brake and the big letters INDIANA written on its side. The trader's name appeared in smaller letters underneath. Between the gaudy wagon and the mud-colored hogan two skeletal paint horses refused to get off the trail for the blue pickup, just staring at it as it came up with their feral, stupid and beautiful eyes. Each of the paint horses had a ragged patch of white over his left eye, which gave them the appearance of having only two eyes between them. George was forced to go around the paint horses, knocking down the thick olive chamise brush, the pickup thumping heavily. The horses looked at each other as if they had won something.

They were on the trail tracks again now, their fenders brushing against the wide, heavy, head-high, olive-colored chico and chamise bushes and the rabbit brush that, from a distance, made the country all appear yellow.

"Tell us one of the stories your brother wrote about us Indians, Sansi," Rabbit Stockings said.

"I never read one."

They had to cross an arroyo now and there were two crossings, one a tender-looking bridge made of number five lumber, and a road that wound down the arroyo and up the other side for the heavier wagons. George tried it across the bridge and made it okay with the Indians not breathing.

"Didn't you tell us about the law of the brotherhood of man, Sansi?" Quicker-Than-You said. "Doesn't that apply to your own brother?"

"There are other laws too," George said.

"Like not stealing wives when the husband is around or not

hunting out of season," Quicker-Than-You said.

"I suppose so," George said and he swore at the Indian under his breath.

The earth in the badlands all had wide cracks and was in waves. It was encrusted with alkali. Sometimes there was a big barranca where the scientists hunted and the government soil people looked and which the Navahos found difficult to cross.

"And our paintings aren't supposed to look like anything."

The driver didn't say anything.

"Check, Sansi?" Quicker-Than-You insisted.

"I said they need not look like something familiar."

"They have other laws, Sansi, like—"

"Shut up, Quicker-Than-You," Rabbit Stockings said.

The pickup was crawling in compound over a great mound that looked like a dome of salt and the land was without anything except the distant dry blue mesa as far as they could see.

"Okay, Sansi, I'm going to lay off it," Quicker-Than-You said. "I'm going to be a heap good tourist Indian. Tell me, Sansi, do you like my wife's pictures on the rugs she makes where the men's bodies are like a pencil? Are they unfamiliar enough?"

"I like them very much, very much," George said.

"Okay, Sansi, I believe that. You buy them even now when you can't sell them. But do you think my wife is beautiful?"

"Yes," George said.

"Okay, we better change the subject," Quicker-Than-You said. "And speaking of women, you know we Navahos haven't raided the Pueblo People for a little while now."

"Almost two hundred years," Rabbit Stockings said.

"I wonder if their women miss us," Quicker-Than-You said.

George had to shift down again to get over a bad place.

"Before the whites the Navaho could take what he wanted," Quicker-Than-You said slowly. "That went for the wives and the game too. Nothing was out of season."

George was hoping that the very-bright-indeed Indian would drop it for a while. He was trying to compose the letter.

The Navaho was still cricling in the attack and he came in now fast and under the cover of something else.

"You going to hit me with a writ, Sansi, on my wagon that isn't paid for?"

"No," George Bowman said. "Because it wouldn't do any good."

"That comedian from the used-car lot in Gallup hit me with a writ on my former Cadillac, Sansi. I tell you, Sansi, a Cadillac is not much of an automobile for this country."

"Especially when they hit you with a writ," George said.

Rabbit Stockings was not following anything. He always found Quicker-Than-You sharper than anything he had ever felt before. It cut him when he touched—understood him—which was not very often, but he could not put down Quicker-Than-You. Quicker-Than-You would not allow himself to be dropped. Quicker-Than-You had begun his campaign several days ago, when the hunger got bad, to go hunting out of season. Today he had succeeded.

Rabbit Stockings was not silent only because he found Quicker-Than-You too sharp but because Rabbit Stockings had nothing to say. Rabbit Stockings had just gone through a period when he had plenty to say; his wife had to have a kidney stone removed and the clan had had many sings for her to pull her through and Rabbit Stockings was very popular. It was the biggest thing that had happened to his clan for two years. Even when the stone turned out to be much smaller than supposed, "and, of course, of no intrinsic value."

One thing you could credit to Quicker-Than-You was that he was not a professional Indian. They were passing two professional Indians. From this hill they could see the heart of Cuba city, which was worth about two professional Indians dressing as the Babbitts insisted they should dress and jumping the way the Babbitts insisted they should jump. Today the professional Indians walking toward Cuba were Tom-Dick-and-Harry and Silver Threads. The Indians in the pickup did not wave to them as they went by.

One credit you could *not* give to Quicker-Than-You, Rabbit Stockings thought, was that he knew when to keep his mouth shut.

"When the regular hunting season was on we were scared," Quicker-Than-You said. "I tell you, Sansi, I went through the war. It never bothered me very much, but I tell you, Sansi, when those shooting people from the city were here I was scared. What was the word they used, Sansi? Safari? What does it mean? Sansi says safari means they're trying to prove something."

"I did not," George said and shifted her into second, slowing her to go over a steel cattle guard.

"Well, say it now," Quicker-Than-You said.

"Okay, it's been a long time. Certainly I should write him, answer his letters."

"What?"

"Oh, all right," George Bowman said, looking over at

the Indian now. "I will say the safari people are trying to prove they've got more money than you."

"That's my boy," Quicker-Than-You said, clapping George Bowman on the knee.

"Speaking of writing, my wife's reading a book," Quicker-Than-You said. "What do you think, Sansi? You think that can be dangerous?"

They waited alongside the trail now for a wagonful of Navahos to pass.

"Sansi, it's called *The Power of Positive Drinking*, or *Thinking* I guess it is. I read parts of it. You know, Sansi, I think they're trying to fool us Indians."

"I think so too," George said, starting the car again. "But they're sincere." And then he wished he had said nothing.

"Everybody's sincere, Sansi. The game warden's sincere. Everybody's sincere, Sansi. We're sincere about killing a buck out of season. But we're hungry, Sansi."

"Half the world is hungry," George Bowman said.

"But the other half isn't as close to the deer as this half, Sansi."

"For an illiterate Indian you do all right," George said.

"I stayed out of Yale," Quicker-Than-You said. "That's more than a lot of the Indians who live this close to the mission did. I stayed out of Yale."

"But you can't live on that," Rabbit Stockings said. "You've got to accomplish something else. Your wife stayed out of Yale."

"True," Quicker-Than-You said. "But Sansi didn't."

"Okay," George said. "But can't you drop everything for a while?"

"Sure, sure," Quicker-Than-You said. "And I will accomplish something else today. I will kill that big buck. Five hundred yards, right between the eyes."

George Bowman winced.

They had passed through the great city of Cuba now and were going past the ranches of the white people. There were not many of them in these thousands of square miles of New Mexico and these were between the Navaho and the Apache Nations. Alexander, the writer, had called the white lands a buffer state. What Quicker-Than-You called them was not printable. Rabbit Stockings was patient and completely without heavy weapons to support his opinions so he was patient. Most of the other Indians were patient too.

They went by Red Feeder's place and Red Feeder with Cass Goodner and Whitey Johnson, all in identical wide black hats and sharp-pointed boots, were trying to pour a corralful of mixed white-faced and Brahma cattle up through a chute and into a huge semi-truck and trailer that would hold thirty-six. They wanted to get started back to the sale ring in Albuquerque, and the sharp-faced, city-dressed driver was swearing and trying to erect a center section in the semi to keep the cattle from going down in the hills above San Ysidro, but the cattle were pushing and he wasn't doing any good, and as they went by the people in the blue pick-up could hear the city man swearing.

They continued down the trail which had become a road now that went to Aztec and they began to count the gates. They would turn off at the third forest gate. The Indians had spotted the big buck some time ago and knew he ran with two does at a logged clearing near the center of the Cuba mesa. They had to get the trader in on it because he would furnish the shells, now that they were without credit, and the pickup with a tarp to put the buck under, which would create no suspicion as they went by the ranger station in Cuba. They had nothing to worry about, the nearest game warden was one hundred miles away. The scheme was absolutely fool-proof.

"You have nothing to worry about but your thoughts, Sansi. And I tell you your thoughts are absolutely wrong." Quicker-Than-You counted the second gate and continued as he had been continuing for the last week. "It's not that I am bitter, Sansi. I am willing to let lost wars be lost wars and lost land remain forever lost. But remember, in this you're in the same position as the Navaho, Sansi. You are frightened as any non-institutionalized person would be to venture your head above ground while the city whites are banging away at each other during the hunting season to celebrate the next Du Pont Powder Company's dividend. You have seen the deer starving in the winter snows because of overpopulation since the wise policy of the Great White Father to kill off the big cats. You see the starving weak deer get killed every winter by the few remaining cats. I ask you, Sansi, are the mountain lions more privileged than us?"

"How many gates was that?" George Bowman asked.

"Two. We turn at the next one, Sansi."

"And if you keep it up," George said, "we will go back to the post."

"I'm not saying anything, Sansi. I apologize for being born."

They turned into the third forest gate now and Rabbit Stockings got out to pull the fence. There was a small clearing of logged country before they entered the forest. At the edge of this there was a Spanish family from La Ventana cording firewood. The Indians, who did not have to get along with these people, called them Mexicans. The Anglo ranchers, who did, called them Spanish-Americans. Alexander had called them people. These people bent upright again and waved as the blue Chevvy pickup went by. The trader waved back. They had on red baseball caps.

The pickup entered the dark forest now and nobody said anything, even while they traveled for fifteen minutes and until George stopped the truck near an old abandoned mine shaft, and then they talked in whispers and signaled to each other with their arms.

This hunt had been carefully planned and they all knew very much what to do. They started off with Rabbit Stockings, who was probably better than anyone in the world at this sort of thing, leading, then came the trader followed quickly by Quicker-Than-You. They began to travel in a big circle in a direction that always kept the moving air coming into their faces, and up wind from the deer, and which would bring them soon to the point in the jut of the mesa where they would no longer walk in file but all make a half turn and sweep the mesa. The buck and the two does, if he still had them, could not outflank the hunters and double back, which is an old wisdom of theirs, because there was a sheer cliff on either side of this jut in the mesa. And soon the deer would have to make a break in the logged clearing the hunters were pushing them toward. This maneuver was a memorable startegy of the Navaho long before it was a classic strategy of the British Navy.

The hunters had made their simultaneous turn now and were combing the mesa. A big, gentle, wafer-soft snow began to come down as they made their turn but it did nothing to their plans; if there was enough of it they could even use it for tracking. The great drought that had had the Navaho People down on one knee for a very long count might be breaking. On the way up George had noticed the fat gray cumulus building up to the cirrus and now, as the flat gentle flakes came into his face on a long downward curve, so individual, big and spaced apart that maybe you could count them, he was not surprised at all. He could still see the Navahos in a quiet white haze through the sparse piñon as the line moved forward.

The big dark gray buck with a white belly and great puzzled eyes beneath ten fine spreading points of antlers, who must easily go three hundred or more pounds, had his two does working a stretch of grama grass just above the logged clearing when the buck picked up the man smell. The buck felt toward the direction of the man smell with his square black nose that was shining wet, until he was certain there were three of them and that there was no hope of getting around their flank and coming in behind them. But he took several tentative but graceful and light, for his heaviness, quick steps toward the hunters to make certain he could not bring his does through them before he went with them toward the clearing he knew he must avoid.

The great buck with the large puzzled eyes who nuzzled the does now into movement had, in his wisdom and ten years of experience, gotten through eight hunting seasons, subtracting those years when he was illegal game. Now he had to get through an extra season. He had only last week finished weathering a month-long war which came each year at the same time when the man smell shot at everything that moved, including, not only each other, but, in some strange rite, themselves (the great buck had watched from a crag with his two does a hunter stumble as he left his car and shoot himself, and as the pool of red spread, these three witnesses had fled into the Largo country, to return only three days ago to this part of the mesa on which he had, until now, been able to successfully maneuver and triumph).

Rabbit Stockings made an arm signal to the others that he had picked up the almost noiseless sound of the buck pushing his wide spread of antlers through the drought-dry ground suckers of the dwarf oak. The Navaho must have picked up other gentle sounds too because he pumped his left arm three times to indicate the number and then, with the same arm, made a great circle in the air to signify that the buck was moving in front toward the open clearing up ahead.

George signaled now to increase the pace, knowing they must press the deer and close the range—be able to take advantage of that moment's hesitation the deer would have before they broke across the clearing. The hunters clicked off their safeties. The deer would have to go any second now.

The does broke first, pushed out by the buck. They made their run fast and bounding. Then the buck came out but slowly as though to draw the fire on himself. He made an unnecessary turn and looked back straight at the trader, and George Bowman had never had an easier shot in his life. He raised the gun and squeezed off two shots. Rabbit Stockings on his right, who had an even easier shot, pounded off two more. The big buck turned, pivoted slowly again, his white tail flashing before he decided to bound off fast in the direction of the aspens where the does were already safe. They watched him go with no one firing. Quicker-Than-You had not fired at all.

74

They all converged on the trader now, but they said nothing until they had each lit up one of George's cigarettes. They all stood with the butt of their carbine alongside their left foot.

"Son of a bitch. I missed him twice," Rabbit Stockings said.

"I missed him twice," George Bowman said.

"I never got off a shot," Quicker-Than-You said. "I knew you boys had him."

"Son of a bitch. I missed him twice," Rabbit Stockings said.

When they finished their cigarettes it was beginning to snow very heavily and as they made their way back to the pickup they crossed the tracks of the buck where he had joined the does. They could tell by the size of the tracks he was as beautiful as they remembered.

"Too late to track," Rabbit Stockings said.

"Much too late," George said.

When they got back to the blue pickup it was already cased in white and George scraped the snow off the windshield before he started her up. He thought the snow would be heavy on the poles the Indian women had prepared.

There was a heater in the cab of the blue pickup and they were plenty warm going back. They did not hide their guns now; the Navahos kept them between their knees. They were short carbine twenty-inch lever-action Winchesters, pointing at the roof. George's big and old Clabrough-Martin, which had been the property of his father, was pointing at the floor. He had emptied it. All the guns were empty. When they got to the edge of the dark forest and came out into the light the Navahos waved to the people gathering wood. The Spaniards looked up surprised but they waved back. One of them took off his red cap.

After they got through the forest gate there was a wagonful of Apaches pulled by two starving small Indian ponies, getting ready to camp for the night against the driving snow. The Navahos in the pickup waved to these people too. The wagonful of Apaches did not seem to know how to take it but they waved back. They were probably going to Zia for a sing. There must be, Rabbit Stockings thought, fourteen of those red Apaches piled in that green wagon being pulled by those two splashed-white and sorry horses.

At Red Feeder's the men had emptied the semi and were trying to load it again, properly this time. The men with wide black hats and pointed boots were waving at the mixed Brahma and white-faced cattle with sticks, and the sharp-faced city driver was on top of the red semi cursing and waving a stick too. None of them were waving at the Navahos in the pickup who were waving at them. The Navahos did not seem to mind.

In the heart of Cuba they stopped in front of Bart Montoya's New York City Bar and allowed the two professional Indians to get in the back of the pickup. Going out of town they waved to the small, thin, college-boy forest ranger in green uniform and Boy Scout hat sitting in the window of the ranger station reading a book of DeVoto's on the Wild West. He looked a long way from home. He wasn't waving to anyone.

Soon they were back in the checkerboard area and there wasn't any more waving. The snow was piling up on the north side of the hogans and there was no smoke from the holes in the dome-shaped roofs. All the chimneys were quiet. They went by the petrified-log house that had been boarded up fifteen years now. This one was especially quiet.

When they got to Rabbit Stocking's hogan the snow was thick on the poles the women had erected to dress out the buck. George didn't stop; he kept right on going.

"Wait," Rabbit Stockings said. "I live here."

"I know," George said. "But first we must go to the post."

Inside the dark, great room of the adobe-and-log trading post George pumped up the Colemans and lit them and from underneath the bare shelves he managed to assemble two boxes of groceries.

"But," Rabbit Stockings said, "what are you going to eat?"

"I got plenty," George Bowman said.

Quicker-Than-You went around in back of the counter where he did not belong and then he stuck up his head and said, "There's nothing left but a case of beans."

"You cannot live on a case of beans," Rabbit Stockings said.

"I can live on a case of beans if an Indian can live on nothing," George said, and he lit up a cigarette and offered them each one which they did not accept.

"We can work up a credit at Johnson's," Quicker-Than-You said. "There's no need to rob you."

"Johnson's post is finding it impossible to carry their own Indians through this period. He absolutely could not carry you."

"I know," Rabbit Stockings said. "Our credit is worthless."

George was looking out the window toward the hogans and beyond these to the blue mesa. The snow had stopped. It wasn't much of a snow after all. It wouldn't do much good.

"After today we all maybe draw a little fresh credit," George said finally and he pushed the boxes off on his friends and they left silently.

After they had left George took one of the cans of beans, the Coleman lantern and a pen and piece of paper into a small back room he used as a kitchen since he had boarded up the big house, and opened the can of beans.

Yes, George thought, when you had inherited all of the downs and ups of three generations, then maybe you could take one more bad year. Just one more year, he had been telling himself for fifteen years now, and now he told it to himself again. Just maybe one more year, he said. Just one more year finally adds up to eternity but I do not find eternity with The People too hard to take. Even with Quicker-Than-You. Perhaps it is only the Quicker-Than-Yous that make eternity bearable, he thought. Anyway you take it as it comes. George was feeling pretty good about the day's happenings. In the last fifteen years he had learned to be satisfied with being a small winner.

Yes, after today everyone deserves some credit, he said aloud slowly and to no one. Now he got down to the business of trying to write a letter to Alexander. He couldn't do any good so instead he would try to eat the beans. He was sick of beans.

After he finished the beans he got back to the letter again. "Dear Alex," he wrote. And then he wrote, "It has been a long time." And then he crossed this out and started again.

"Dear Alex: Today we went deer hunting but didn't get a deer but we talked about you. The country has changed a lot. It is getting drier all the time and they are beginning to drill for oil all over the place. Fortunately they have not found any and soon they may leave. There was a Malco engineer here yesterday testing. He told me a foreign car club he belongs to intends to hold a rally here. As the Indians have just planted I will do my best to stop it. But I am writing around something, Alex. Backing into saying what I want to say to you—what I must say to you which is—"

George put the pen down and looked out the window. The snow wasn't falling any more. How, he thought, after fifteen years—? Then he thought, he's doing fine. Why should I bother. Forget. Then he said, against the window pane that was rough with ice, "Sure, why not? If it's impossible to write, to say all the things you must say, you can't say, then say this. George went back and picked up the pen.

"Tonight I am writing you for the first time in fifteen years. Why tonight? Because today we talked about you on the mesa where the old mine shaft is. You remember Rabbit Stockings and Quicker-Than-You? Well, today they talked about you on the mesa where the mine shaft is. Quicker-Than-You is always talking about you, reading your books and telling me about them. But today he made me realize that for twenty-five years, since we were boys, I have been avoiding that part of the mesa. I did not want to go up there but I went up there because the Indians were hungry. Fifteen years have passed since you and Perrette went away. Fifteen years of drought. The medicine man was right on all counts. Fifteen years of bad crops and not enough food for my Indians. Fifteen years of tearing up your letters. In fifteen years a man should forgive—forget."

George threw the pen down then took it up again and wrote: "I do not think I can do any real good for myself or the Indians until we settle this thing between us. I was thinking the best thing—" George scratched this part out. He would get back to it later. "The Indians blame me for the drought. They say it would stop if you came home. They say you would come home if I wrote 'I for—' "

Now George picked up the letter. He walked across the small room and out into the great room of the post. It was dark and heavy with the cold in the big room and when he opened the front door even the night outside seemed bright. He tore the letter up now and allowed the pieces to flutter out of his hand in the cold wind. An Indian was huddled there someplace, against the wind, beneath the log overhang, watching the night and now the bits of white paper streaming past.

"Love letter?"

"Yes," George Bowman said.

6

Alexander had taken a room high in the hotel in Mazatlán so that he could look out over things and catch all the breeze there was.

The fifteen years that he had spent in Paris and Bombay and London and Nairobi and especially Paris and all the other splendid places that the expatriates go because they cannot go home, had, along with his inner longings, aged him on the outside more than fifteen years will. But on the inside it had been much more than this. It felt much closer to one hundred years since he had seen the country and people he loved because he knew and understood them. Now, after fifteen years, he knew that he must write about them again because everything else was written out of him. Certainly his last book proved that. Not as much as they said, he thought, but it certainly proved I have come to the end of something. But this is about as close as I can get to Indian Country now. Quicker-Than-You tells me in his seldom letters that I am responsible for the drought. I wonder if that medicine man holds me responsible for the Treaty of Versailles. I wonder if George will ever write.

As he thought these thoughts he was looking out over Mazatlán, Mexico, which rose sad across the gulf from the tip of Baja California at a point on the Tropic of Cancer where the quiet desert ends and the poisoned jungles begin. It's on a flat, ocean-jutting peninsula, but along the land base rises a bald mountain. On its dome they had erected a radio mast and beneath this a wild red-and-yellow transmitting shack, now disintegrated. Once upon a time, and on a good day, and before something complicated had decomposed, the tower could send a signal almost to Tepic.

Today a herd of cattle grazes the dry brown grass of the dome. At some distance from the others stands an older seed bull; short ugly scars gouge his once brilliant flank, the horns are shattered and the eyes have begun to go dull. He is muscle-hurting and looking down at the town which he can't see sharply. Yet he would not have to see sharply to notice the sudden slab of ferro-concrete hotel that rises, alien, from among the aged red-tiled roofs at the deepest swing of the crescentric, eye-hurting white beach. Up on about the tenth floor, in a corner room, all of the windows are open but the curtains are catching no breeze.

Alexander, in a long-billed fishing cap and shorts, was sitting at the typewriter near the window but he was not looking at the machine that had been silent all morning, but looking up the dry, hot road that ran along the edge of the beach. The large modern, sanitary room in which he sat hung out over the sea and, from an angle way back in the room, it might have been the prow of a ship over the water; but even up here with the windows on both sides there was not any breeze at all. It was real Mazatlán weather. And right now he saw it all the hard way. But he had not seen Perrette. And now he looked through the heavy heat all the way up to the big rock at the end of the peninsula that marked the end of the bay for the fishing ships. If she had gone to the post office she would be coming back soon. Alexander still hoped, after so many years of silence, that there might be that certain letter for him.

He could see the post office clearly through the heat and he could see the people walking on the streets but he could not see the Hawaiian red shirt splashed with gaudy yellow Perrette had worn. And Alfred was certain to be with her again. The Genius and the Child—he had been calling them that for several days now. And it had not started when the fishing went bad—it had started before that. He would have to give this some thought. He had been giving things like this much thought all morning and he felt like hell.

There was a knock on the door and the tall man leaning over the typewriter, looking thoughtfully out of the window, said: "Come in." The door opened but no one came in. A man stood at the open door dressed in a careful business suit, his white hair brushed immaculately over his forehead.

"I am from the Chamber of Commerce," the man said in pretty good English. "We did not discover until this morning that you were the famous American writer. We would have had a deputation at the airport if we had discovered it earlier."

Alexander, sitting at the typewriter said nothing, not even looking toward the clean man standing in the door.

"Now that we have discovered it," the man standing in the door said, "we are waiting on your pleasure. Is there something we can do for you?"

"Yes," Alexander said finally, not looking at the door, still looking out the window. "Go away."

"I have been chosen," the man standing in the door said, "to speak for the others, for the press. We did not want to bother you when we know you would be busy composing so they are all waiting downstairs and they nominated me as a party of one. Do you have something for the press?"

"No," Alexander said.

The well-pressed Mexican fidgeted at the doorway now, brushing his flat Indio face with his small delicate hand.

"Someone below said you might belong to the Kiwanis but I did not think so," the man said.

"Yes, I belong to the Kiwanis," Alexander said, "and I have a hole in my head."

"An Elk then?" the Mexican asked sympathetically.

"Tiger," Alexander said.

"We have quite a Rotary here," the business Mexican said, "of which I have the privilege to head, although I suppose you would not be interested in that."

"Fascinated," Alexander said.

The man at the doorway looked confused and searched for something different to say. "Your article on Mexico I enjoyed very much," he said finally. "It should bring tourists."

Alexander said nothing, still looking out of the window.

The booster was reassured, thinking he had gotten something going. "Your last book I could not follow," he said. "It seemed quite bitter. I thought that—"

"If you're going to give a talk we will sell tickets," Alexander said.

"But I must have something for the press," the man almost insisted.

"The press in this town must be quite an operation," Alexander said, not thinking about it.

84

"We have one paper," the Mexican said, "And then the man from the paper at Tepic is here. Soon, with a personage such as yourself, there should be someone from the big dailies of Mexico City."

"Do you have a pair of fieldglasses?" Alexander said at last, turning his face away from the window.

"Yes," the Mexican said. "There is a pair at the desk. They use them for spotting fish. I suppose you want to see if there are any fish breaking at the islands."

"Yes," Alexander said. "I want to spot some fish."

The Mexican closed the door quietly. Alexander did not move from his hunched position over the typewriter until the Mexican came back with his gentle knock. The door barely opened and the fieldglasses came in first.

"Thank you very much," Alexander said, taking them.

"I hope you see many fish running," the Mexican said.

"I hope I see some, but they will probably not be running."

"Still nothing for the press?" the Mexican said hopefully.

"Nothing for the press of Mazatlán, Tepic or even New York. Did you know," Alexander said, "that there is someone here from New York, a Mr. Alfred Marlowe, a famous young man from a famous literary publication? Few people have heard of the famous literary publication and only my wife has heard of Mr. Marlowe."

"I have not heard of a Mr. Marlowe being here," the Mexican said, confused, thinking.

"No one has," Alexander said. "But yet he is a big something. According to my wife he is a genius." Then Alexander knew that he had pushed it too far, but he noticed that the Mexican was not following it, wasn't putting anything together. But he thought he had better break it off before he began putting it together. "You can go now," he said. "And thank you very much for the glasses."

"Perhaps you will have something to say later," the Mexican said, turning.

"Much later," Alexander said as the door closed. He went back to his seat at the window and hiked the glasses over the typewriter. He looked carefully and long at the horizon. There was nothing there but he was thinking about something else. Then he pointed the glasses down the oily road that wound out finally past the steep cliffs above the sea. He scanned the street along the hill that ran up to the beach road, focusing the big glasses. There was the gold and neon, once Spanish Colonial, now almost Hollywood, cathedral in front of the market place. The market place sprawling in back of it was big and dirty he knew, and yet how clean and orderly it looked from here. The federal school alongside the Plaza looked very hot in its red paint, and then there was the broken monument to Benito Juarez on the square in front of the cathedral. On each of the streets there was always one good building, usually placed conveniently in the middle, on which all the other buildings on the street could lean. On Angel Flores there was no good building on which they could lean so the angle on these buildings was a little frightening. There were very few people moving in the heat of this time of day and she was not one of them. Nowhere on any of the visible streets could he see her familiar gaudy clash of color.

Now he tried searching the outdoor cafés along the beach front at the foot of the hotels that only the Americans could afford. He tried the Corizo Café. There were only two elderly American women waiting over a lemonade for their husbands to return from fishing. He tried the front of the Utrillo Hotel and as he did so he wondered if it was named after the painter. There was her splash of red and yellow in the middle of the café and she was sitting with someone else. He got a better focus.

He screwed the glasses until he removed her double image for she had never been a double image. Since the first few months after they had left together he had seen her quite clearly, when he wanted to see her at all. Watching her at this great distance reminded him that he had been watching her at a great distance for a long time now. This distance was surely not his fault and it was not her fault but each day there seemed to be more distance.

Still screwing the eye pieces she came abruptly into sharp picture now and he could see all the things that had not changed about her. She was still young, the fifteen years did not seem to have aged her a day. The hair still fell big and loose in a gentle swing to her shoulders and as she talked it vibrated and caught the sun. Her lips were full and not too short and her large light blue eyes must be very large and very blue down there in the sun and close to the water. Her heavy, firm, uptilted breasts jutted over the iron table with only the negative lines in the glasses outlining them. A wondering smile that was almost amazement flickered across her face now as she talked; he liked to call it youth and it flickered across her face now as she talked with eagerness across the small iron table to the man who was not himself. He shifted the glasses over to the man who was Alfred Marlowe, a rising poet, and young.

He had in his glasses now the man who was sitting across from his wife. In his book he might have begun to describe him in a first draft and then quit. The face, Alexander thought, ran a little too closely to the face in the Boy Scout ads, nothing interestingly there with all its human contradiction, but something conceived in the high sterile clatter of a typewriter and the firm commercial arm of a firm commercial artist. He shifted his glasses slightly as the man moved—he could move and he could speak, the lips in the glasses revealed a cold whiteness of teeth as the man spoke—and as he speaks now he might even be saying something.

"You could look into it," the young man called Alfred said.

"I don't know what to do but I couldn't do that," she said.

"How do you know it won't work out?" The young man was thinking about something else. "Anyway you know what I mean."

"You mean you were thinking about your poetry. All right, if you want to think about your poetry then what shall we think about your poetry?"

"I don't think it matters a damn what we do," Alfred said slowly, and getting back to it. "He is going to punish himself no matter what we do."

Alfred had never seen Perrette's pretty face tense before, it seemed to give the face an illusion of insight.

Perrette crushed out a cigarette she had just lit but she was not watching the ceramic tray, just looking straight ahead.

"He doesn't work now," she said mechanically, as though telling something to herself. "He says there's nothing worth writing about."

Alfred thought he should not mix in anything at all, just wait for her to come out of it.

"All right," she said at last, removing another cigarette from the flat tin she had in front of her. "All right, Alfred," she said, fixing on him as though trying to recall his face. "I don't think it's a bad title; you go ahead and use it. 'Sounds of Phallic Cymbals.' It isn't as bad as we said it was. It isn't too bad."

"It's bad enough," Alfred said. "I don't like it any more."

" 'Sounds of Phallic Cymbals'," Perrette said as though considering it from every angle. Then she said definitely, "I wouldn't abandon the title, Alfred. It represents a whole morning's work."

"Thank you," Alfred said. "But as a matter of fact it's not a bad title. It's a satire on the sixteenth-century virelai ancien poetry. With a title like 'Sounds of Phallic Cymbals' my thought was to use the nada motif in a contemporary Dijon bistro setting in which the feeling is imposed of there being a brothel upstairs. Below the dialogue the poetry is a contradiction of the life process, a mere banal statement of the everyday questions and answers. Do you think Alexander could see it?"

"Well, *I* can't see it, Alfred. I'm sorry but I can't. You know since it's been going the way it's been going between Alex and me, I've been thinking that you and I—"

Alfred interrupted by taking one of her cigarettes. Alfred thought she had done a decent job in holding it in all these months since things had begun definitely to fall apart. But the fact that she could take it for so long without discussing it did not make Alfred feel any better now.

"I'm sorry. I didn't mean to say anything, Alfred. It just came out. I'm like Alex's Indian who did not want to retreat, his legs just moved toward the rear. Can I get you something, Alfred? You look faint. Should you be drinking those tequila cocktails in the sun, Alfred?"

"I'm all right," Alfred said. "I'm plenty all right."

"Very well, we'll discuss your poetry, Alfred," she said in a kind voice.

"Leave my poetry alone. I don't want to discuss my poetry," Alfred said.

"How about the weather then, Alfred?"

"All right. We'll get back to my poetry," Alfred said. "But I don't want any subjective reaction. I want you to relax and get our talk out of your mind so you will have a spontaneous objectivity. This is a little corny," Alfred said, "but are you ready?"

"I'm ready," Perrette said, trying to change her expression.

"Okay," Alfred said, slowly turning his head toward her. And then suddenly—" 'Sounds of Phallic Cymbals'!"

"Splendid, Alfred. I think it's absolutely splendid."

Above them in the room that jutted over the water like a stateroom Alexander in the long-billed fishing cap and holding the binoculars arched over the typewriter thought; and now she is telling him how much she does not love me any more and what a pity it is that all the books we have with us bore her. But I do not know what she is saying because I cannot read lips. Once I thought I could read lips pretty well but perhaps it was only my writer's imagination working. There was a rummy rancher near the reservation that I found very interesting. After he had drunk away his hair and his teeth and his cattle and his ability to walk he began to drink away his ability to talk and when it got very bad I used to think I could read his lips and I put what I imagined he said into some short stories. And what writer's imagination can I use on those two down there? It's that they're going to kill me and run away with all the money or all the love, depending upon which lousy writer handles it. And what did I run away with when I ran away fifteen years ago? Perhaps that's what I should write about. But I can't. If I could then I would have nothing to worry about. If I could write it all down it would probably go like this. . . . Like what? No, you can't do it. Maybe it would go like it's going with those two down there. Maybe this is a repeat performance. Maybe it's a remake of the old film with different actors. People go on performing the same script. They get a new set of actors—faces anyway. I wonder if they'll change the lines much. I wonder if people are beginning to talk like the second- and third-rate writers who write imitation people; with all the television they've got going if people will begin to imitate imitations of man. All right, but if you tried to do it correctly how could you get those two down there on paper? In the rough draft Alfred would have to go down as an incredible idealist, big-blown with a plot to perfect the world, to perfect it all with love and art. And Perrette? Love and art too. Adolescent too. But in the meantime, while things are building, they must eat, not too well but very well enough. In the meantime, while things are building, they must starve to get the proletarian feel but then reject this as a capitalist myth. In the meantime, while things are opening out, they must love, honor and obey Jean-Paul Sartre, or some other substitute for God, assuming that they no longer had him, Alexander Bowman, as a substitute for God. How could he explain to those two down there that the challenge is to grow, that youth is for the young. Love is for all but youth is for the young. And now down there the young man must be talking about love and if he was, what was the attitude

91

toward love now? If he could read lips perhaps he could find out. He focused his glasses on their faces.

Below, the young man was watching the gaudy birds, three Mexican yellow heads and two beebees, on top of the sea wall side of the patio crawling stupidly around in circles. Inside the wall and seeming bright against the dull brick, a big awkward English-speaking, heavy-billed parrot with dirty white-blue wings, who kept looking down at Alfred and Perrette with yellow eyes, climbed the decomposed wall crookedly all the way almost to the top.

"Do you think," Alfred asked, "Do you think Alexander would consider a thing like this?"

"Why don't you ask him?" she said.

"The last time I showed him my work he said, it's not my pitch, Alfred. I can't help you. But then you must go ahead and make your play, you're entitled to make a mess of it, but I can't help you, Alfred. You're not fishing in my ocean. Jesus, does everybody have to swear in his key before he'll look at your stuff?"

"Why don't you do a story based on him, Alfred?" Perrette asked softly. "He might like that."

"Because at times I think he's a son of a bitch," Alfred said.

"Buenos días, caballeros y señoritas." The parrot had gained the top of the broken wall now and was strutting over the sharp, bottle-topped barricade. "Drink Carta Blanca. She's good for you all alone."

Alfred leaned over and took a cigarette out of the broad flat tin she had arranged in front of her breasts. She helped him by turning the box. "And so?"

"And so he's my SOB," Alfred said.

"That's sweet of you, Alfred."

"No, it isn't," Alfred said. "It's just that he's almost the best writer around."

"And that precludes—?"

"That precludes almost everything," Alfred said.

"You're sweet, Alfred. Look at the parrot, he's scolding us. I suppose that we should order something."

"Well, I won't order any of his beer."

"Tell me," Alfred said finally, looking up. "Couldn't we do something, you and I, that would open him out? This trip since we got to Mazatlán has turned into a parade of the dead. Couldn't we do something, you and I, something warm and generous? The last book was very bad but his next book will be a good book. We should do something to jolt him out of this."

"We probably will," she said.

"You want some more drink?" The waiter had intruded a dirty white shirt sleeve.

"No," Alfred said. The white arm hesitated and then remained. "No, no, no," Alfred repeated. "You said something, Perrette?"

"I see there's a man at our window." She was looking up at the hard UN façade of the hotel. "He has binoculars but he's probably only looking toward the Indian Country. Do you know, when I got up this morning he was staring out the window and he said: Out there beyond the border and hidden carefully by the horizon is the drought-ridden Indian Country." But Perrette seemed nervous. She closed her cigarette box and sat more erect. Alfred noticed her movement and got up.

"I've got to finish the poem. It's important that when you

start something you finish it while you're still in the mood."

"Very important," Perrette said, not looking up. "Very important that when you start something you finish it while you're still in the mood."

Alfred started to say something, decided against it and turned and left quickly.

The parrot repeated again by rote from high on the rotted wall, "Drink Carta Blanca beer. She's good for you all alone." Perrette looked out at the big, flat, empty ocean and up at the wide vacant sky, blue and without any clouds at all, but she did not look again toward their high window where her husband must be looking toward the Indian Country. She started to call the waiter but then she decided that what the parrot said was meaningless too.

"All right, bring me a Carta Blanca." Alexander said. Perrette looked up at Alexander as he sat down.

"I was looking out the window up there toward La Paz," Alexander said. "It can't be more than fifty miles. I think a person could swim it."

"Remember what happened in Ischia?" she said. "And remember why they didn't take you in the army."

"Bad heart," Alexander said. "But it's only fifty miles. I think it could be done. I was talking with an interesting wreck called Mimi Jimenez this morning. He's got an old harbor and pier that's going to ruin since they built the new wharf. He wants to sponsor the swim, furnish the boat and food, if we arrive at his place."

"Well, you have come to the final experience," she said.

"What's that?"

"Suicide," she said.

Perrette took out her pad and began sketching. "I don't

want to be throwing cold water on everything," she said, "but—but well, let's talk about something pleasant. Alfred was just here."

"I don't think anyone ever swam to La Paz. It could be interesting," Alexander said.

"Alfred," Perrette said, continuing to sketch, "has just written a new poem."

"Now the world can breathe again," Alex said. "What does he call it?"

"What difference does it make?" Perrette said, rubbing her forefinger now into the charcoal sketch she was making. "A title isn't important. It could still be a good poem. But," she said, taking up a new stick, "as a matter of fact he calls it 'Sounds of Phallic Cymbals.' "

"Splendid," Alexander said. "Still, it's one thing I suppose I won't have to take the blame for."

"Well, you could help him some," she said.

"He's never asked me."

"Well, you frighten him, Alex. You give him the impression—"

"That children should grow up."

"But he does admire you—your work. You know, Alex, I think he writes somewhat like you did when you were young."

"Oh," Alexander said. And then he said, "What are you sketching?"

"A picture of Alfred," she said and she held it up. "Do you like it?"

"Splendid," Alexander said. "I think it's—"

The waiter came up now with the beer and Alexander looked around the empty café and then out over the shimmering water to La Paz. The waiter left now. They both continued silent but the trained parrot knew it was time for the commercial and croaked, "Drink Carta Blanca beer. She's good for you all alone."

Alexander looked toward the horizon again now but not toward La Paz.

"That's right," he said to the parrot. "Indian Country, she's good for you all alone. I think there's a story up there that I might write and maybe George's writing it. It will start with 'Once upon a time' and will end with George's tearing it up. People destroy an awful lot."

All over the world people will see a sign, a portent in something big that happens to all of them. The day began now with a green sky and the sun rising orange and starting slow through the interstices of the log window. After the day was over an Indian said that this was the trouble the medicine man had predicted a long time ago. But that would have ignored these fifteen years of drought in the Indian Country since Alexander had stolen George's wife.

"Nothing can ignore the drought," George Bowman said. "It won't let you."

And whether he was speaking of the drought on the land or the drought in his heart was not important, for in both cases all that had been good for so many generations was drying up and blowing away and the homeless sand was moving in. But the Indians had cause to speculate and theorize and make big talk about this day. Nothing much like it had happened since they lost to the white man.

Now, fifteen years after the theft and the beginning of the drought and sixty-three years after they had lost to the white man, Kurt Heinitz, in absolute command of the third foreign car rally of the Southwest, watched the gaudy cars pull into the rendezvous place at La Ventana, ten miles below the trading post at Tonatai, and he didn't approve of anything at all. Kurt Heinitz had begun his career with Rommel, achieved full command under Von Modell before he was switched to Guderian for the big push to Moscow. That the genius of Heinitz, Rommel and Guderian had failed was a monument to the insanity of a corporal trying to run things from Berlin. Heinitz had to remind himself occasionally that that was why he was playing with these toy bright cars that were streaming into La Ventana now, instead of doing something real, and he blamed it all on insanity in a politician.

But it was not insanity that annoyed him with the Van Esters and the Johnsons, the Jag and the Porsche that were closest to him now. It was plain stupidity which, along with naïveté, seemed to nail down Americans. Heinitz advanced toward the Johnsons.

The Johnsons in the canary-yellow-and-red Jaguar with blown-up fenders looked splendid in identical pink-and-white checked caps with purple poms, Red Ryder shirts, blue jeans and cowboy boots, and they were both worried about the same thing—Kurt Heinitz. Mrs. Johnson preferred to be known as Helen Hooyar and her husband as Lonesome Johnson. He had a TV show that went on when everybody went to bed. The Platter Parade King of the Southwest, Lonesome Johnson. Mrs. Johnson thought that her maiden name should not be allowed to die, that it kept her from being thought of as a housewife. She had records pressed in Albuquerque under the name of Helen Hooyar; her husband played them and she had a feeling they were beginning to catch on. Her husband was kind and never showed her the mail. She was kind and didn't tell him she was having an affair with his biggest account. Everyone was kind except Kurt Heinitz. Why doesn't he pick on the Van Esters?

Heinitz hesitated between the two cars and walked toward the Van Esters. Mrs. Van Ester had a thin long face that never relaxed from that set, tight, holding-on-to-the-door-handle look—"Isn't this fun!"—that she achieved at that climactic, bone-shaking moment that passes for high speed in a noisy car. Raoul Van Ester had a round, cherubic face for a man who drove such a formidable machine. They were again accoutered in those identical checkered and pomponned caps that seemed to be the thing. They did not affect the cowboy get-up of the Lonesome Johnsons but ran to Tattersal vests and jodhpurs and King Alfonso boots, mail ordered from the Country Store in Aspen.

The Van Esters had a tape recorder with them in the car and were going to record cultural Indian chants and play these at the next Great Books meeting in their home town of Truth or Consequences. But right now they were afraid; they were afraid of Heinitz, who was coming up. They had turned up the speedometer in their car so they could compete for the Concours d'Elégance prize for cars with over sixty-thousand miles, and they were afraid of Heinitz.

Heinitz came over and touched the scooped door of the Porsche, gentle and relaxed. He wore a nondescript American suit on his long frame that made anything hang with a military assurance. He had emerged from a large, standard American car that was the color of dirt. When Heinitz selected a car he wanted to be inside when he was inside and outside when he was outside and no "Isn't this fun" foreign-car nonsense.

"Are you enjoying yourselves?" Heinitz said, quietly, looking down on the Van Esters' purple pompons.

"Swell! Exciting first pass," Mr. Van Ester said eagerly, his round face dancing up at Heinitz.

"Yes," Heinitz said slowly, hitting the door a quick bop with his palm and moving away.

"By God, I know when I'm being patronized, Skeets," Mrs. Van Ester said tightly toward her husband. "I'm not strictly Truth or Consequences. I grew up with a set in Santa Fe and I know when I'm being patronized, Skeets."

Mr. Van Ester clasped the purple wheel tightly, looking straight ahead out through the tinted windscreen and over the yellow bonnet.

"You're imagining things, Bullet," he said toward his wife. "We're out to have fun. Don't ruin everything by imagining things."

"Imagining things, Skeets? Swell! Exciting first pass! Jesus, must you grovel every time that Kraut shows? I mean, let's face it, Skeets, we're people."

Heinitz had placed his hands in back of him and walked up to the Johnsons' Jaguar as though he were thinking of something far away. The Johnsons seemed to scrunch a little closer to the gear shift on the floor and waited.

"I've been thinking," Heinitz said without any preliminaries to the Lonesome Johnsons, "how could the Van Esters have put sixty-thousand miles on their car in so short a time? I thought from the air scoop it was a '55. Still I could be wrong."

"I remember it was a '55," Lonesome Johnson said, excited. "November, '55. They drove it up to our house, nonchalant, as though they still had the Gordini, as though nothing had happened, said they wanted to borrow a Miracle Cloth, pretending that's what they came for, as though nothing had happened. So I gave them the Miracle Cloth and pretended that's what they came for, as though nothing had happened. They got sore."

"Thank you," Heinitz said and thumped the car before moving away.

"Poor show, Loney," Helen Hooyar said without looking at her husband. "Did you have to squeal on those chaps? I think it was a very poor show."

"Those snobs," Lonesome Johnson said. "And don't forget we're interested in that thing ourselves. How do you pronounce it?"

"Concours d'Élégance," his wife said. "And all the more reason it was a poor show. We've all heard of a little noblesse oblige and it would be inverted snobbery to pretend we hadn't." Helen Hooyar removed something from her nose with her pinkie finger. "A bloody lousy show, Loney. Nothing resembling cricket at all."

"Bull," Lonesome Johnson said.

"That's what I mean by inverted snobbery, Loney. If you can't see it can't you feel it?"

Lonesome Johnson said one word preceded by "Oh." The word was short and obscene and the Navahocade moved off from an abrupt command by Heinitz and Helen Hooyar laid down her long cigarette holder on her Apache snake-skin bag and dabbed at her eyes with her handkerchief.

"It's Heinitz," she said. "There was nothing like this before Heinitz. He's making us into brutes."

The Navahocade was headed for an allotment or checkerboard area known as Tonatai. The Aspencade to Jemez had been brilliant under Heinitz' leadership and so had the Atomcade to Los Alamos. No one could organize like Heinitz.

And Heinitz enjoyed himself. It allowed him to keep his hand in. The club selected Tonatai because they said it was not just a big hole like Grand Canyon or Carlsbad where the tourists and tract dwellers came by the thousands to gawk and erect platitudes but a place made famous by the writer, Alexander Bowman. Another nice reason for having the Navahocade at Tonatai was that there were no roads.

Kurt Heinitz had two MGs working the point, scouting about two miles ahead. The MGs had army-surplus walkie-talkies installed and their tall whip antennas were in touch with Heinitz. Heinitz brought up the rear of the main body of cars and he was using two Siatas to cover the flank. When the MGs spotted any trouble or difficulty in the terrain they were to contact Heinitz.

Heinitz got a message now that the trail had ended at an arroyo and he answered back that he was coming forward on the double. The long string of garish and odd cars parted for Heinitz as he moved forward with his hand on the air horn. Some did not move quickly enough and Heinitz was forced to run them into the ditch, but there were no complaints. They realized that they had been quite stupid and were turning the Navahocade into a poor show.

When Heinitz arrived at the front his scouts were alongside their pink and chartreuse MGs looking vacantly into a thirty-by-thirty flood erosion, and making perfect targets, Heinitz thought absently. The wife in the pink MG, whose husband had a black eye patch, herself wore a pink snood and plaid-rimmed, very dark glasses which, along with her posture in the bucket seat, and despite the fact that she was straddling a case of Schweppes, gave her the appearance of a holy woman being patient at Benares. The wife in the chartreuse MG had a chartreuse snood and a chartreuse alligator bag and very dark glasses trimmed in rhinestones and appeared out of the same litter except that she was suffering from a bad case of exposure and wished she had never left Tucumcari.

Heinitz assessed the situation immediately and sent the chartreuse to scout the left and the eyepatch to scout down the right bank and contact him when they discovered a crossing.

The sky over the Indian Country reminded him of no sky he had ever seen before, a sea of almost green shot with orange and long strokes of black. And what kind of people would live in this land that looked like the bottom of the ocean after the water had been removed?

Heinitz received a message now that chartreuse had made contact and Heinitz threw his car forward toward the scout. When Heinitz reached chartreuse an Indian was destroying a crude bridge across a low point in the arroyo and damned if chartreuse wasn't arguing with him. Heinitz grabbed a wrench with quickness of mind and hit the Indian across the skull just in time to save the Navahocade from an embarrassing wait.

The Indian had been trying to explain in Navaho that his farm on the other side was just planted to winter rye. He had also tried to explain to the Moving People in his small Spanish but the Moving People did not seem to speak any language at all. But fortunately Heinitz had arrived just in time to save the situation and Mr. Van Ester had wondered aloud where the hell the club would be without Heinitz and Mrs. Van Ester had said, "But a spanner, Skeets! It's not quite playing the game to hit one of their chaps on the head with a spanner." And then in a low voice that was more her own,

"We're not animals, Skeets." Mr. Van Ester seemed to think about this a minute before he said profoundly, "Biologically I suppose we are, Bullet. Yes, and by the bye, who's got the tonic?"

"I don't want to play any more," his wife said in a tired voice. "I don't want to play any more with all this rich man's junk. I hate quinine tonic and I hate jodhpurs and boots and I hate open foreign cars and I hate Heinitz and I feel sorry for that poor damn Indian who got hit with a wrench."

Her husband said, reaching down and chucking her under the chin, "We've got to carry on, old girl." And then, when he got no response but a sob, he grabbed the wheel and said in his own voice, "Jesus, I guess we have to go through with it now."

The Indian who had been hit with the wrench had fallen down into the bottom of the arroyo. There was a dead black-and-white feist dog at the bottom of the arroyo and the body of the Indian rolled until it almost touched the dead feist dog. The side of the arroyo was too steep for them to get to the Indian with succor so they fixed the bridge and watched while three Indians came down the arroyo with one other Indian leading a spare mount. They watched while the Indians hung the Indian who was hit on the spare mount, and one of the Indians who had not helped with the loading held the hit Indian on, leading both horses, as they went up the far bank and toward the log trading post and the great, boarded-up house they could all see in the distance. The Indians did not look at them once.

Felix Mount Royal, Lord Rundle and Rabbit Stockings had discovered the wounded Indian and with the help of

Tom-Dick-and-Harry, who was out chasing sheep with a spare mount, they lugged him up to the post of George Bowman, on into the back room heavy with the smell of sheep hides and brilliant with the blankets of their wives. George put some white man's medicine on the head of Coyotes-Love-Me and the Indian opened his soft dark eyes on the blankets that hung down too bright and turned his head until his soft eyes lighted on the hides that stank.

"Why really, he will be fine, he is better. Why really, everything will be all right." The Indians did not believe or disbelieve this that they told George Bowman but they wanted him to feel good about his religion, about his magic. The Indians always allowed him to try his magic first because, after all these years, they had grown to respect him and this was one of the ways they showed their appreciation. Sometimes it even did some good and they did not have to have a sing, did not have to use their own religion. For Coyotes-Love-Me they all knew that tonight they would have a chant. It was a terrible wallop. The white man's magic was not enough against the white man's blow; it would take serious medicine not only for the head of Coyotes-Love-Me but against the spirit of the man who had done it.

George Bowman motioned them all into the front room and sat down on a small Victorian stool covered with perfect velvet. There was something regal about it, sitting there surrounded by all the turquoise and silver jewelry The People had pawned against the flour and tobacco you could not see. It had an effect.

"Why really," George began in their own language, "why really, the jails of Gallup are full of The People who war on the white man. I have some medicine to use against this man, this man and his spirit, if you will permit me."

"Why really, no," Lord Rundle said quickly, raising his fiery-jeweled hand to a brown face that was heavily dark-lined like a contour map beneath a red cotton band across his forehead. He was dressed in the Levis and boots of the others.

Some velvet-clad squaws came in now to watch the talk and sat on the floor sucking Pepsi and Royal Crown Colas.

"Why really, no," Lord Rundle repeated. "With this man we deal in our own custom."

There was a silence with George Bowman saying nothing, tipping a silver and turquoise pawn in front of him.

"Oh, but really, it is true," Felix Mount Royal said. "The Gallup jails are full of us."

Felix Mount Royal's squaw congratulated him with her eyes and switched her cold bottle of Royal Crown Cola to her other hand.

"Why really, maybe I will listen to your plans, Sansi," Lord Rundle said.

"Hokka-shai. Thank You," George said. "My plan is to make him lose face. That is complicated to explain but excellent for permanent cure if I have luck."

"May you have luck," Rabbit Stockings said.

All of the squaws banged their Pepsi and Royal Crown Colas on the floor in agreement and approval and to make a noise which they liked too.

Tom-Dick-and-Harry, a short, white-appearing Indian with bandy legs and a clean scar under his right eye, came in now from the back room and gave them permission to put the hurt Coyotes-Love-Me in his hogan as was his custom. It was not only that Tom-Dick-and-Harry was not convinced of the truth of the Navaho belief that the bad spirits would return to haunt a hogan in which one of The People had died, it was also that he was certain that he had all the bad luck there was in this world right now and that no spirit could add much more to what was coming his way in the future.

All of the Indians helped carry out the body of the victim, with Tom-Dick-and-Harry leading the way and Rabbit Stockings bringing up the rear carrying a large economy-sized box of corn flakes and a pint of Sloane's liniment.

The squaws remained on the floor to finish their drinks. The squaws are not moved easily to excitement, which is probably good, George felt, because they carry the entire wealth of The People around their necks and waists in the form of coral, silver and turquoise jewelry of expensive and good taste and it costs nothing to giggle but with excitement you never know. They would pawn the jewelry with the trader when the winter was deep and win it back when they sold the sheep. The jewelry was shown off well against the billowing bright skirts of calico and velvet, cut in the manner of the American army officers' wives at the stockade of Fort Sumner where all The People were imprisoned from 1864 to 1868.

George Bowman put the velvet stool away on its shelf back of the counter where his father had kept it and took a piece of jewelry off the counter and put it back in the case, beneath the books of his father, *Ivanhoe*, *Burke's Peerage*, *The Lady of the Lake* and others his father had used to name the Indians away from some of the names that were too long for the ledger, like Son-of-the-Man-Who-Got-Kicked-in-the-Stomach-by-a-Deer-on-the-Other-Side-of-the-Mountain.

There was a Bible on the shelf too, a present from the

mission that had made a short and dull stand in the vicinity before it disappeared, to have immortality only in a sign which read: TRADITION IS THE ENEMY OF PROGRESS. When the sign was completed the missionary asked George to come and have a look and George had said that if the missionaries believed it the church would collapse in the morning. Nevertheless George was sorry when the mission folded. They brought food and clothing in winter. And if they were rude enough to insist their religion was superior to The People's religion, they knew not what they did.

But George was concerned now about the invasion of the Moving People. Maybe this too was some form of Progress. George was not a romantic who was opposed to the word but, although inevitable, he did not believe it could not be selective, and although Progress has many aspects, this would never be: the destruction of the rye and the winter wheat, the busting of The People on the head with wrenches. George had decided to make his stand here at the store. Later he might use The People but first he would meet the leader of the Moving People here alone.

When George had been tipped off to the invasion by an engineer from Albuquerque who had come up to check on the seismograph crews, George had told him to lay off because the Indians had most of the flat areas planted to rye and winter wheat that was beginning to show green in spite of the drought and it would be impossible to stay off it. The engineer said it was his duty to report possible scenic rally points to the club, and if Kurt Heinitz decided on this area there was nothing he could do, or anyone else for that matter. And if the trader and the population were going to be difficult and the terrain impossible, well, that was what

Heinitz was looking for—enjoyed. The engineer would get a brush on the back from Heinitz instead of a slap on the car and Heinitz did not give his favors lightly or often. He told George Bowman the date.

George had then gone into the vast back room to direct the sorting of the hides and think. When he had thought of something acceptable he wrote a message out on his father's desk and gave it to the sorter of the hides, Lord Acton, with instructions to ride full gallop to the trader at La Ventana. Then he drained the gasoline from his own Sears gravity-feed tank on stilts into his tractor and gave the last remaining two gallons to the medicine man, Paracelsus, to use for bright fires. He had busied the remaining interval of time until today with the organization of treating the Indians' sheep against blue-tongue. As he looked out the window now he saw the advance scouting pink and chartreuse MG's pull up. They circled the post three times, each time in a smaller circle until they finally stopped. One of the women got out and walked toward the post and the others remained behind to contact the main force over the walkie-talkie.

The woman in chartreuse with the huge chartreuse alligator bag walked up to the post and looked in the window, then she went to the door and opened it and looked in to see if what she had seen through the window was true. Then she closed the door and hollered to the others, "My god! The boy in here is a loveboat. He looks exactly like young Lincoln."

The others looked up from their sending equipment in surprise as she opened the door again and went in. She entered a room lined with silver and turquoise and food under a ceiling draped with saddles and boots, lanterns and harness, so that she had to move among them carefully until she reached the

109

counter laden with pawn. She pretended an interest in this but all the while she was staring at George Bowman, who was writing something, and working her way up the counter toward him, and now she was at the elbow of his heavy leather jacket.

"I don't like to be rude but did anyone ever tell you you looked exactly like young Lincoln?"

George put down his pen and looked at her carefully. "No, ma'am, they never did."

"No, but seriously, I don't say these things," she said. "You do look exactly like young Lincoln."

Helen Hooyar came in now and the lady in chartreuse said, "Don't you think he looks exactly like young Lincoln?"

Helen Hooyar was fiddling with the edge of one of the blankets and staring out at them between two saddles that hung down.

"By God, I think he looks like Alexander Bowman," Helen Hooyar said. "I never met Alexander Bowman but I've seen his pictures and he looks like Alexander Bowman. He's a real man, not one of these city creeps. Living out here alone develops the soul, and something else too. I bet I could write poetry if I lived out here. And that boarded-up beautiful petrified-log house—I bet there's a story there, an eternal mystery. I bet that's where Alexander Bowman wrote those books."

George went back to the sheep ledger.

Lonesome Johnson and Mr. Van Ester came in now and they noticed the squaws lined along the counter on the floor sipping their drinks with the decorum of any DAR chapter. Lonesome Johnson wandered down the shelves until he found a certain brand of soap. Putting this on his shoulder he walked up to the trader.

"Does this do anything to you?" he said. "Strike any bell at all? No? Twelve o'clock every night I merchandise this product. Still, way out here you're out of touch, kind of, with reality. You probably don't even have a TV set."

"No," George said.

"I certainly could use a character like you just to sit alongside me on the show and shill my pitch. You wouldn't consider it?" Lonesome Johnson said.

"No," George said.

"You know, you're right," Lonesome Johnson said and, turning to the others, "No, but he's right. My God, I wish I could live out here myself. The air! Notice the air," Lonesome Johnson said, taking a deep breath of sheep hides. "By God, this country makes a man of you. I might chuck everything some day and come out here and start again. I could paint pictures. If Alexander Bowman could write books here I could paint pictures."

Skeets Van Ester was looking through the window out at the mesa country. His wife wasn't playing any more. She was in the car reading T. S. Eliot. Soon she would wander to have a look at the latest thing in hogans.

"It's spectacular," Skeets Van Ester said, still staring through the window. "It's like something out of Cecil B. de Mille. It makes you feel close to God. Imagine what a man like Kurt Heinitz could do with a place like this. Why, he'd organize it into the greatest tourist spectacle in the world. All these beautiful possibilities wasting away for a man like Kurt Heinitz."

"Everybody outside." Kurt Heinitz was standing inside the door waiting for them to file out. They filed out.

Kurt Heinitz closed the door gently and walked quickly

111

toward George Bowman, pausing to examine a piece of jewelry on the way. "You have fine workmen," he said, putting the concha belt down. George didn't say anything. "I've come to apologize for that accident to one of your men." George still didn't say anything but he took the concha belt and put it under the counter before he went back to the sheep ledger.

"We want to be correct," Kurt Heinitz said. "We are not a mob. We are very well organized and I am the leader. We want to be correct if you will simply tell me what—"

"I think you had better go home," George said quickly, without looking up from his ledger.

"Before we can discuss that we will need some gasoline," Heinitz said.

"No gasoline," George said.

"Perhaps we can make a deal," Heinitz said quickly, picking up the edge of a blanket.

"No deal. No gasoline," George said.

"But I told them," Heinitz said, his voice loosening, dropping the edge of the blanket. "I told them when there was no gas in La Ventana that they need not go on to Cuba and waste their time. I told them there was gas here. I had it on good authority. If we had to walk out of here they would think me a fool."

George Bowman dropped his pen and looked at Kurt Heinitz for the first time.

"We will see what we can do to get you out of here. I gave the medicine man two gallons of fuel for bright magic. Maybe you can talk him out of it. It will take you to Cuba, where you can bring back enough to leave here."

"Good," Heinitz said, confidently. "I'm kind of a medicine

man myself. Have you ever seen my rockets over Alamogordo? That is, I'm a twentieth-century medicine man. Countries bid for me. Where is this other medicine man? I hope he speaks something recent."

"There's an interpreter outside the door. It has been arranged."

"Thank you very much," Heinitz said, turning.

"You have nothing to thank me for," George said.

"You Americans are all alike," Heinitz said, going out the door and smiling. "All alike."

George Bowman went back to his ledger with his pen but actually he wrote only one word in a clear hand and then he tapped the pen against his nose in thought before he reached down and crossed it out. He got up now and stared out the window. The odd cars of the Moving People looked strange against the hogans.

Tom-Dick-and-Harry was outside. He was a mission Indian and he spoke a little of everything. Tom-Dick-and-Harry was kind of a mess. He didn't fit in with the whites and now he didn't fit in with The People. Tom-Dick-and-Harry didn't believe anything any more. But he would be a good interpreter.

The medicine man that George's father had named Paracelsus was dressed like the other Indians except that the quality of his clothes was better, his hogan was bigger and his horses were fatter, just like most doctors on the outside except that the payoff was in sheep—but he had knives and herbs and such that go with the business. And besides all this the medicine man had sings, he was part of the religion, he treated the whole person. He had a lot of luck.

Was Heinitz going to get the gas? "Why really, of course,"

the medicine man told him, but first there were a few things he must do for a cure. Heinitz was desperate and willing and he tried to make some sand painting while the medicine man corrected him and the Moving People laughed. Now the medicine man explained the whole thing very carefully to Heinitz through Tom-Dick-and-Harry in one-syllable words. But Heinitz was still all thumbs and his Moving People laughed. He jumped on hot rocks while the Moving People laughed and he made signs to the sun while the Moving People laughed again.

But nobody laughed at the next medicine. Heinitz didn't have to do anything, The People took care of everything, and nobody laughed. No one laughed at all.

George Bowman was still busy with the sheep ledger when Rabbit Stockings came in and got some matches. George had some bad thoughts about the matches at first but then consoled himself with the guess that they were probably for Lady Blessington's pipe. She smoked a home-made mixture that was put together by Paracelsus which was marvelous except that it was non-combustible. Sometimes it took two boxes of the matches to get a good fire going. Lady Blessington had smoked a pipe long before cancer became a fad, but she smoked it for her health and, not counting TB and a few other things she had in her own right, it seemed to work.

George Bowman smelled gasoline. He could be wrong but the wind was right and he thought he smelled gasoline. He put down the saddle.

"No more medicine," George said, cutting the ropes.

114

"Why really," the medicine man said, "I was right in the middle of an operation."

"You certainly were," George said, taking the rope from around Heinitz' shoulders. Heinitz' face was perfectly white.

"Why really, he is not cured," the medicine man said.

"I promised you he is cured," George said.

"Thank you, Sansi," Paracelsus said. "I do the best I can with the little I have."

"Is there any gas left?" George asked, feeling the clothes of Heinitz soaking with it.

"We had to use it all in the medicine, Sansi. But you didn't think we were going to burn him?"

"It was just a scare," George said.

"That's right, Sansi. Just a scare."

"Well, you scared me," George said.

"Sometimes it is necessary to treat everyone," Paracelsus said. "Evil is that kind of sickness."

Now there was the beginning of the sing. As the strangers sweated to get their cars back across the arroyo, as George Bowman said they must, they could hear the thin, high wail of an alone singer re-echoing off the dark mountains. Then the singer was joined by all of The People and it became a deep low-cadenced chant like a part of the bright-banded cliffs and the mushroomed mesas, the big flat lands and the arroyos enormous with nothing. Perhaps, too, tonight the sing was deep and sad with the now quickened remembrance of things that must always be forgotten—the Navaho Nation was once the greatest of all the Moving People.

"The Navaho Nation was once the greatest of all the

115

Moving People," George said aloud now, and then he picked up the pen and wrote:

"Dear Alex: All these silly and cruel people that I saw here today made me think that maybe I made the right decision in getting away from the world and living here with The People, for The People and nothing more."

"The Navaho Nation was once the greatest of all the Moving People," George repeated aloud. Where had he heard that? It must have been in one of Alexander's early stories. And what about Alexander's later stories, those he had written in the last fifteen years? He had read none of them, which was exactly as it should be. And yet—? And he began to write now.

"Early this morning I took the trail up on the mesa on the horse and with my binoculars to see if I could see the Moving People coming. I did not see them, they came another way, but I saw the mine shaft—I made myself go there. If it had been dark and I had stumbled in the hole I was all alone, there would have been no one to get help. Are you and Perrette out there all alone now? The people who came here today seemed desperately alone. They have soothed their loneliness in their bright sparkling foreign things. You should have seen them against the hogans. But these things are maybe not enough against the loneliness because they tried to take something out on us. There was a great beating of wings against us here today before they drifted on to a greater loneliness. Alex, what are you doing against the loneliness? Who is the victim of your loneliness? What has the loneliness cost you until now? The Indians are the victims of my loneliness. I'm with them but separate. They must feel it. It has cost me until now the knowledge that I try to protect, help, the Indians—while condemning a brother to another country—and yet the Indians knew what to do against the evil today, I did not. Right now they are—"

The chanting of the Indians rose high now and then lowered abruptly to a steady, endless chanting that would weave far into the morning. Now George felt sleepy. Sleep, he thought, is a better way of avoiding things, of not finishing something, than alcohol. He felt tired and sleepy. He rested his head on his arms on the big roll-top desk. Since the petrified-log house was closed, boarded up, this would be as good a place to sleep, to hide, as any. The small back room of the post was dark. Here, in the back room, at the roll-top desk of his grandfather, would be as good a place as any. Now he thought he heard someone try the door and then the window, but he was very sleepy. Maybe it was someone with a message, someone to help him. And what help could he be? No, sleep was the thing for brothers. Soft sleep.

8

When George awoke the chanting had ceased and the great room was coming to light. The noise of someone breaking in had wakened him, he was certain of that and yet who would want in? He went over and turned on the red plastic battery radio that was on the counter and from his seat over the roll top he listened to the news. Now he rose, shutting off the radio and went back to the letter he had been working on the night before. As he was busy over the desk a young Indian with a gun entered quietly from the rear room and came up in back of George.

George dropped the pen and began to sort the Navaho pawn which was in a large box on the desk, examining each piece carefully until he said finally, and while holding a hunk of turquoise up to the light, "How did you get out?"

The young Indian's name was Four Thumbs. When he was in the army the other soldiers had called him Chief Tom Thumb, but his name was Four Thumbs and he had just escaped, by killing a man, from a psychiatric cell, where he had been placed for killing another.

"You're my prisoner, Captain," the Indian with the gun said.

118

George repeated, still holding the hunk of turquoise up to the light, "How did you get out?"

"Yesterday about noon I . . ."

"I know when," George said. "The radio is full of it. I expect they're right about that, but how about the other?"

"What other?" the young Indian still holding the gun on the trader said.

"The other man you killed."

"You believe everything you hear on the radio and read in the papers?"

"Most everything," George said. "For example," the trader said, "I believe this."

"You'd believe them before you'd believe a man who served under you, a man, for example, that was in your outfit in France?"

George, who wore a cowhide jacket and a bemused expression beneath his worn, wide Stetson, did not remember who had started this "for example" business but he would try and finish it. "For example, yes," he said.

"You think we got started on the habit of killing people over there and we keep it up here? We got a habit?"

"You have," George Bowman said.

The young Indian grabbed the pistol he was carrying by the wrong end in his wrong hand and walked over to the front door and locked it as he had already locked the back. As he walked back toward George he dropped the gun in his pocket.

"You wouldn't turn me in," he said.

"Can't do anything else," George said. "Unless you leave."

"I got no place to leave to, Captain."

119

George went back to his letter.

"I came back to this part of the reservation because—"
The young Indian hesitated. He had on a white man's blue
serge coat that fitted as though it had been taken at the point
of a gun. "Listen, he said. "I knew you'd help me. You
always have."

"Always have," George repeated and he looked at the
young Indian now.

"Yes. That patrol you organized got through just in time.
Cut off for six days. Fought off a whole Kraut platoon for
six days. But I couldn't have lasted a minute longer. You
got through with relief just in time."

"I got through one day too late. I'm sorry," the trader
said.

And he thought: When I got there he was all that was
left of his outfit. He was the only one alive, if you can call
what he was alive. He was giving orders to an outfit, to a
platoon of men that did not exist any more. He was giving
all the orders and carrying all the orders out. It must have
been that, like his forefathers, like the old ones who defended
this final mesa above us here in Indian Country against the
whites, he did not know how to say "surrender." When his
outfit was surrounded in France he too did not know how to
say the word. When they were without food and water he
did not know how to say it and when all of his comrades
were dead he still could not bring himself to say it. He did
not know how to say "They shall not pass" or how to say
"Nuts" to the Germans either, or any other historically
remembered simplicities. He only knew that the mesa—this
position somewhere on the flank of Bastogne—must be held.
He did not know that his mind must be held also, and, after

the sixth day of the German breakthrough, after six days of bludgeoning artillery fire and no food or water, he did not notice that his mind had deserted the action and left his body all alone defending the position.

"I got through one day, maybe two days too late. I'm sorry," the trader said.

"What? Are you crazy?" Four Thumbs said quickly. "Look, you're not crazy, are you?"

This was a favorite word of Four Thumbs for a long time now. Lots of people were crazy.

"Look, Captain. I'm here. Feel me. You got through just in time."

"One, maybe two days late," George said, but he was not talking to Four Thumbs now. He was looking out the window. There was a big, and seemingly much longer than it actually was, silence with some horse noises coming through the heavy piñon log corral on the south side of the post. The silence made the gentle horse noises very loud.

The young Indian had both hands jammed into some white victim's blue serge coat and he stared at George as though it were George's move, as though George had the gun. The young Indian very much had the gun. It made an awful bulge in the blue serge coat.

"For an Indian a quiet padded cell is no place to die," Four Thumbs said finally.

George continued to look out the window at the endless country of the Navaho. Actually it was less endless even than George's people had promised in the Treaty of 1865 but George thought it had the beauty of endlessness with the sudden violent-colored mesas you could always see beyond. The big blue spaces make the Navaho country a part of everyone and of everything else. From here you feel you are almost there. It might make a passing safe and easy—almost acceptable.

"A quiet padded cell is no place for anyone to die," George said, still watching the country. "And some foreign castle, some marble tent, is no place for a Bowman to die."

"Then you don't—"

"I don't know yet," George said, turning, looking at the young Indian. "Anyway, give me the gun."

Four Thumbs gave him the gun although he had some trouble locating it. He was used to being armed with an army Garand rifle.

George walked around and put the gun beneath the counter in a case alongside The People's pawn.

Someone tried the door now. The young Indian felt for his gun.

"You better let him in," George said.

The Indian continued to feel in the white man's too big blue coat for his gun. He looked worried.

"You're back in my outfit. You've got to take orders," George said. "I take all the responsibility, give all the orders around here."

The young Indian stiffened. "Yes, Captain."

"Please open the door."

"Yes, Captain," and the young Indian opened the door and let in Rabbit Stockings.

"Why really, have you heard the news?" Rabbit Stockings said to George Bowman.

George was busy.

"That psycho from Window Rock broke out, killed another man, ditched his car in the Chijuilli. They figure he's headed this way."

Rabbit Stockings had begun his talk in Navaho and then switched to English when he noticed the other Indian. There is no damage in impressing another Indian.

"We better be ready."

"We are very ready," George said. "Rabbit Stockings, I want you to meet One-of-Us. One-of-Us, I want you to meet Rabbit Stockings."

The young Indian called Four Thumbs who had just had his name changed to One-of-Us yatayed Rabbit Stockings pleasantly and Rabbit Stockings yatayed One-of-Us pleasantly too.

"If he was headed this way I could begin to put my knowledge into motion," Rabbit Stockings said. Rabbit Stockings was not referring to any mere doctorate degree; Rabbit Stockings had taken a special FBI course by mail. George figured that this was the knowledge Rabbit Stockings was going to put in motion although he had taken a body-building course, a pedicure course, an airplane Diesel engine course and another one the government had stopped coming through the mails. But maybe, George thought, he is going to put the airplane Diesel engine course into motion; a Navaho will fool you.

"One-of-Us," Rabbit Stockings said, "I am about to take my final exams. I think I'll bone up. Would you care to take a look at some of the latest crime-stopper bulletins?"

"No," Four Thumbs said.

George was watching out the window someone in a uniform coming up the trail.

"I think, One-of-Us, you had better go with Rabbit Stockings," George said to Four Thumbs.

"Yes, Captain," Four Thumbs said and he left with Rabbit Stockings for a secret place where all of the FBI and airplane Diesel engine knowledge was hidden from the other Indians.

George was watching Arturo Trujillo, the state trooper, who was responsible for the one hundred and fifty miles between Bernalillo and Aztec, get out of old man Curry's four-wheel-drive Willys pickup. He had been forced to leave his red-flashing, black-and-white, insigniaed Ford, with a radio that was in touch with headquarters in Santa Fe, at the Gallegos' garage in Cuba. The state did not want to buy him a new front end for a red-flashing, black-and-white Ford every time he had to chase an Indian.

Old man Curry stayed outside in the Willys pickup while the state trooper came over to the door of the trading post. The trader let him in.

"George," the state trooper said, walking over where the tobacco was kept, "we got Indian trouble. How about a pack of English Ovals?"

"How about a pack of Camels?" George said, taking them out.

"Okay. And a Milky Way," the trooper said. "And I'm supposed to be watching my figure."

"How's the wife?" George asked.

"Watching her figure," the trooper said.

"And Curry's boy, is he still watching her figure?"

"Not any more, he isn't," the trooper said and he tried to toss the Milky Way wrapper into an Indian basket and missed.

"Where you hiding that Indian?" The trooper put both blue-uniformed elbows on the counter and studied the trader.

"That's why I pay my taxes," George said. "To pay you to find out where they hide."

"In New Mexico they don't collect much taxes," the trooper said, still studying George. "We need your help."

"Don't ask any questions," George said. "Don't ask me any questions, Arturo," George said, taking up a pencil and tapping it on the pawn counter.

"Okay," the trooper said. "But don't make me look bad."

George walked to the window and looked out at the country, still thinking.

"Can you imagine an Indian dying in a quiet padded cell, a billion times removed from everything?"

"I don't like it," the trooper said. "But don't make me look bad. Just promise me you won't make me look bad."

George went back to the counter. "All right," he said. "If you don't want to be a hero."

"I don't want to be a hero," the trooper said. "It's tough enough with the wife."

"You have a very attractive wife," George said. "Take her some of this candy." He put a stack of Powerhouse bars in front of the trooper. The trooper put them in his pocket, looking puzzled at George.

"All this time I never suspected you," the trooper said.

"You should spend more time at home, Arturo," George said.

"I know," the trooper said. "That's where I'm going now. But first I have to take a look around. I got to make a report. A citizen, old man Curry, is outside. I got to take a look around and make a report."

"Just so it's only for a report," George said.

"Listen," the trooper said, standing erect now, his pockets bulging with the Powerhouses. "You got sixty thousand Indians around here. You think I want to be a hero with those kind of odds? You promised me about the boy that I wouldn't look bad."

"All right," George said. "I'll get someone to show you around for the report. Is that citizen still watching?"

"Yes," the trooper said, looking at old man Curry through the window.

"Then I'll get someone to show you around for the report."

"Thank you. Take care of me when I'm gone too," the trooper said and he took out one of his beautiful wife's Powerhouses and began to eat it.

Two Indians entered, Felix Mount Royal and Lord Rundle. They had two bags of turquoise and silver jewelry that they wanted to pawn. They wanted to hang onto their lamb crop a while yet because the present price interested but did not concern them. Try sometime to bargain with a Navaho for his sheep and win something. With his wife's jewelry, George knew, he has a lot of staying power.

The two Indians, Felix Mount Royal and Lord Rundle, did not much like the looks of the policeman so they did not open their bags of jewelry yet. They talked to each other in low Navaho about this unexpected situation, with the trader, George Bowman, listening. Finally, between them, and with no help from the audience, they decided on one answer which took the form of a question. Coming up to George Bowman and planting their bags of jewelry on the counter they asked in classical Navaho, "Sansi, what in the hell is the cop doing here?"

"He's perfectly safe," George said. "He's got to make a report. We don't want to make him look bad."

The two Navahos, still without opening their bags of jewelry, had a short conference in Indian about this before they asked, "Sansi, we don't want to be rude, but what is it he doesn't want to look bad about?"

"That psycho boy, Four Thumbs, who was in my outfit during the war and came back to the States and killed two extra white men during the peace. They think he escaped into this officer's territory. They want to put him back in the padded cell."

The two Navahos thought about this for a while without consulting each other but both tapping their bags of jewelry before Lord Rundle said in Navaho, "Why really, Sansi, what can we do not to help?"

"Why really, not to help," George Bowman answered in their own language, "go find me a boy named One-of-Us, who is with Rabbit Stockings, so he can show this officer around so this officer can make out a report and not look so bad that they will send someone who is thinking in terms of heroic actions, or worse, someone who is sincere."

"Good. As you say, we will find the boy and do our very best not to help and if this young gentleman is not sincere I guess it is safe to leave our jewelry here on the counter."

George told them where Rabbit Stockings' FBI and airplane Diesel secret hiding place was and they left.

"I don't think they trust me," the young Spanish trooper said, between bites on his beautiful wife's Powerhouse.

"They don't trust people who are what they call sincere. They feel their Navaho Nation has been cheated out of almost all it ever owned by those who are sincere."

127

The trooper looked confused and opened another Powerhouse, tossing the wrapper at the Indian basket and hitting it this time.

"Just don't make me look bad," he said.

Up the rincon in the Largo Canyon where a big cavity had been caused by the loss of a large tree of petrified wood that had imbedded itself in the sandstone sixty million years ago and had recently departed, Rabbit Stockings and One-of-Us had now more recently arrived. They had to go back to the roots, which had made a large room deep within the Eocene sandstone, through a five-foot-wide, fifty-foot-long tunnel caused by the absence, the weathering out, of the very old and tropic trunk. They had to climb over the silica remains of the actual tree getting up the cliff. George had explained about all this to the Navaho People and the Indians pretended to believe him. "Of course, Sansi. What else, Sansi?" All white men had a few beads missing.

"It's darker in here than a whore's dream," One-of-Us said, speaking army language. He spoke three languages.

"Let's try and keep it clean," Rabbit Stockings said, lighting an FBI bulletin to find his cache of candles. He lit a candle now and set it on one of the fragments of the very old tree.

"Sixty million years old," Rabbit Stocking said.

"Who's crazy now?" One-of-Us said.

"You want to be a dumb Indian all your life? Don't you want to have a white man's diploma in something?"

"No, because I'm not crazy," One-of-Us said.

"I just can't believe that one does not seek to better himself," Rabbit Stockings said slowly and as though he had read it someplace.

"Listen, you're being taken in by a bunch of white con artists. Who's crazy now?"

Rabbit Stockings looked hurt and he looked down at the sheaf of correspondence courses he held.

"Well," Rabbit Stockings said, "maybe all of us are a little bit crazy but most of us don't hurt other people."

Four Thumbs began to tense up. He began to work his mouth and a bit of saliva ran down that he did not wipe off. It was cold in the cave but One-of-Us was sweating.

"I could kill you with Sansi's hunk of phony tree. I could smash your crazy head."

One-of-Us lifted a silica-glistening chunk of the lead-heavy wood.

"Hokka-shai." Lord Rundle said thank you in Navaho as he took the chunk that was poised over Rabbit Stockings' head.

"Interesting," Lord Rundle said, examining it in the dim light. "But Sansi's sixty million years—it's difficult even for an Indian to believe."

"Sansi's crazy," One-of-Us said.

"Of course," Lord Rundle said.

"You just saved my life," Rabbit Stockings, who had been too shocked to talk until now, said.

"He's crazy too," One-of-Us said.

"Of course," Lord Rundle said .

Lord Rundle turned the lead-heavy, silica-glistening rock in his jeweled hand, the candle catching all the highlights.

"But you'd better come back to the post. You are One-of-Us, are you not?"

"No. Four Thumbs."

"Come anyway," Lord Rundle said.

Back at the post the state trooper was trying to build a pyramid on the counter with the Powerhouse bars. George was watching and the Navaho women sitting on the floor with their babies stacked along the counter in cradle boards had been sucking Pepsi but now they were holding their breaths while the trooper tried to get the final Powerhouse on the pyramid.

"Don't bother me," the trooper said tensely, without looking up as the Indians entered.

The Navahos from the cave took places along the counter quietly. The leather-strapped Indian babies stacked along the base of the counter in their cradle boards could not see the pyramid that was being built but they could see the tense faces of their fathers who watched.

"Who's crazy now?" One-of-Us said.

The pyramid collapsed just as the final Powerhouse was about to be placed deftly by the state trooper to complete the impossible structure. One-of-Us spoke and everything collapsed.

The trooper turned suddenly on the Navahos along the counter. "Who said that?" he asked tightly.

"I did," One-of-Us said. "I think you're crazy."

The trooper stared at the Navaho hard and One-of-Us stared hard at the trooper. The trooper dropped his eyes.

"Maybe. I don't know. I was just having some fun."

"They tell me I'm the man who is supposed to show you around," One-of-Us said.

"Don't bother," the trooper said, still watching the floor. "I've seen plenty. I been here long enough to make a report," he said over to George. "I think that's old man Curry pressing the horn."

It was old man Curry pressing the horn. The trooper left but not before saying to George from the door, "Don't forget what you promised me."

"One-of-Us, I promised him," George said when the door had closed, "that you would not be caught by somebody else on his territory and that you would always be a good soldier and not cause any more trouble so you would not die in a padded cell—that you would remain here and be a good soldier. I sent for you to show him around so you would not be discovered hiding."

"Yes, Captain." One-of-Us stiffened to attention.

"Rabbit Stockings will take you back to the cave where you will remain until it is safe to take a hogan."

"Yes, Captain."

The door opened again now and One-of-Us grabbed quickly at the trooper's gun that was on the counter next to the candy where the trooper had laid it down and forgotten it. One-of-Us fired two shots quickly at the crazy enemy before George yelled, "Cease fire." The trooper went down on one knee at the door. The Indians picked up the trooper, who was bleeding from the thigh, and carried him out toward Curry's pickup.

"I came back for—" The trooper was shocked and couldn't complete the sentence.

They got him in the front of the pickup and Curry started her up.

"I think you can make it back all right. How do you feel?" old man Curry said. The trooper was feeling better now and felt he could finish his sentence.

"—back for the candy," he said.

George had taken Four Thumbs outside.

"I think you and I had better go up on the mesa," George said.

"Yes, Captain. But I thought I was going back to the cave."

"A new situation has arisen since then. I must give new orders."

"Yes, Captain."

When they had climbed steadily upward for fifteen minutes George remembered that Four Thumbs, who was following, still had the gun. Never mind. Let him take it with him like a good soldier. He heard Four Thumbs come up alongside him now.

"Captain."

"Yes, Chief?"

"I've still got the gun."

"On a patrol you always need a gun."

They were winding up the high sheer mesa, along a path that had been hacked out by Four Thumbs' forefathers one hundred years ago. By rolling down boulders the old Indians had felt they could keep the whites away forever. They almost did, but, defending this final fort, the top of this dry mesa, they ran out of water. No one quit. They were all still up there.

Here, on one side of the narrow rock path, was a slick wall of deep-colored sandstone to the top of the high mesa and a drop-off of almost six hundred feet to the desert rocks on the other. Soon, on the next switchback, they would be in the clouds and a fall would seem to be into infinity.

George felt the young Indian come up on him again now, as close as he could get, about as close as a small dog will follow on the heels of his master.

"Captain."

"Yes, Chief?"

"You ever hear of an officer being shot in the back by one of his own men?"

The trader wanted to stop and rest now, he was sweating and the sweat was not warm, but he knew he must go on. They had made the switchback and soon they would be in the clouds. The trader was using his handkerchief and now he put it back in the breast pocket of his cowhide leather jacket before he answered.

"Yes, Chief," George said. "We all hear stories like that in back of the lines. Up front—well, I suppose it depends on what kind of a leader a man is."

George steadied himself now. The path was getting very narrow as they entered the white clouds.

"He takes his chances," George said. "And listen," George said. There was a big silence within the clouds as the Indian listened. "When a soldier comes back and begins to kill his own outfit and there is nothing that anyone at all can do to help him, then the soldier himself, in one of those moments when his mind comes back to him, must think of some way of saving the outfit he is destroying. But the command decision is with you," the trader said. "We are cut off from everything and you can do with the rest of us what you will. You got the gun."

Now George felt suddenly that the Indian was no longer

with him. And then he heard a voice that was much further to his left than the path say quietly, "Yes, Captain."

George froze, the gray mist swirling around him. There was nothing on all sides except the steady, long shriek of an Indian falling to eternity.

The next day at the post Rabbit Stockings was seated on a high stool alongside the counter. He had all the airplane Diesel engine books on the stool so he could reach the burial prayer stick he was working on. He was looking in the corner now where the trader always kept his Clabrough-Martin rifle.

"That's the first time I never saw your rifle in that corner," Rabbit Stockings said.

"You never will again," the trader said.

"Isn't it kind of primitive," Rabbit Stockings said, "burying a rifle with a man? That was a valuable gun."

"My people believe the man was much more valuable," George said. "And we respect your ancient customs."

"Thank you and thank your people," Rabbit Stockings said. "It must have been quite a climb, carrying that body to the top of the mesa."

"That's the way I figure he would have wanted it—back up there with the other warriors."

"Those old people," Rabbit Stockings said, "cut off up there without water, must have gone crazy before they died."

"Yes," George said. "No one could get through until it was too late."

"But they stuck it out when they could have quit," Rabbit Stockings said.

"Indeed they did," George said. "And he was their son."

Both of them looked out through the adobe-and-log-rimmed window at the blue mesa that concealed the bones of the very brave Old People—at the bright blue and orange-banded and yellow-lensed mesa that in turn was concealed now within the swirling purple and red refractions of a dying sun—stared up at the long mesa within the mirror cloud which shot the whole sky above the desert with a clear and gaudy light. When you had to go neither George nor Rabbit Stockings could think of a better, a more altogether fitting place to make it across.

George swung around in his oak chair and looked up at the heavy logged ceiling of the room. And where is Alex going to make it across? George thought. In another country, I suppose. And who cares? No one. Well, that's the way he wrote it, wanted it. That's what he asked for.

George let his eyes drift back to the desk and he stared at the piece of paper there a long time.

This soldier who came back . . . I am always, George thought, taking part in something that sounds like an early story of Alexander's. I wonder what the moral would be if Alex were writing it. Alex would probably write it as it happened and let people draw their own moral if any. And my moral would be, George thought, and he wrote:

"Dear Alex: By God, we have got a situation between us we can solve if we would only stop acting like white people. An Indian you must remember by the name of Four Thumbs showed me how like the boy I was twenty-five years ago I have been acting. Four Thumbs became a psycho in the war and when he got back here he continued to kill people. Today in one of his short moments of sanity he killed himself. He came back home to where the brave Old People are, and with courage. I suppose we've all got a different way of killing ourselves. Mine is to retreat and retreat from my life into the life of the Indians. What is your way, Alex? We have got somehow to get around this hardness that stands between us. We have got somehow to stop one of us from killing himself. Hold on, Alex, and I will think of something yet. Hold on and I will write 'Come home.' Until now 'Come home' is too simple and powerful to write but hang on and I will write it, sign it, seal it, stamp it and mail it. Hang on."

"What are you writing?" Rabbit Stockings asked.

"Words," George said. George put down the pen and swung in his chair until he looked out the window. He looked past all the beauty and down to the long scar of dirt road that led to Albuquerque and the world beyond.

"Yes, words," George said. "Words."

9

Yes," Alexander said. "A person could swim to La Paz nicely."

The others around the iron table made no comment at all. Finally Perrette, who was sitting next to Alfred and watching Mimi Jimenez, the owner of the rotted wharf, three tired sports fishing boats and the marlin record, her voice non-committal and playing it safe, said, "You mean, Alex, you're going through with this—?"

"I reject the idea absolutely," Alfred said. "If you're just trying to prove something there must be some other way of proving whatever it is that you want to prove."

"Suppose I want to prove," Alexander said, his voice rising a bit now, "supposing I want to prove that if a man can't go back to Indian Country, if a man can't go home, then he can make things happen he can write about?"

The small smile on Mimi's face had become a big one. They were speaking slowly enough so that he could about follow it. He had been trying to cultivate English but he realized he was making little progress when they spoke rapidly; when they spoke slowly and the subject was of interest to him he understood enough to give this big smile.

Mimi had a huge lizard neck capped by almost no head in which there could have been concealed no brain—a Mexican dinosaur smiling.

"And if he was serious?" Perrette asked, speaking to Mimi Jimenez. "Would they allow it? Would he have a chance?"

Mimi hesitated, feeling for the words, spreading his fat hands in front of him, speaking slowly. "A swimmer no has to be rápido. No es importante ser joven."

"He does not need to be young," Alexander helped.

"In catching the big fish you need to be young," Mimi went on carefully, looking at Alexander, who had helped him. "A sports fisher, yes, he needs to be young. He must have the courage—"

"And stupidity," Alexander helped again.

"Of youth," Mimi went on. "It is muy necesario, but for swimming the presteza of youth no is necesario," Mimi insisted. "A long time ago, before there were automobiles," Mimi said, "on the Day of the Gobernadores, the mayor offered one hundred reales to anyone who could swim to La Paz. On that very day two completed the swim. It was necessary to divide the money between them. Es toda en la resistencia."

"It's all in the endurance," Alexander said.

"Sí. Endurencia," Mimi said, holding up his arms.

A waiter in degrees of dirtiness came from behind a plane tree, examined the fat, small lizard arms that Mimi was holding out and wanted to know what they were going to have.

"Nothing," Alexander said.

The waiter retreated again behind the plane tree.

"Why did you send him away, Alex?" Perrette said. "We

are going to need a drink."

"Drink?" Alfred said, moving forward. "I don't see anything to celebrate in the writer, Alexander Bowman, risking his life."

"Oh," Alexander said dramatically. "Get thee hence, thou cream-faced loon. Those linen cheeks of thine are counsellors to fear. Shak-es-pee-ray," Alex said to Mimi, pronouncing it as a Mexican might.

"Yes. Shakespeeray," Mimi said. And then in Spanish, "I would rather have him make the swim but he's not around."

"You think my making the swim from your old boat harbor would do your ruin some good?" Alexander said.

"Sí. Mucho publicidad. Sí," Mimi said.

"And if we go ahead with the plans and I walk out on you would you kill me, Mimi?"

"Sí. Cómo no? Sí," Mimi said.

"He didn't understand you," Perrette said.

"They tell me you've killed three people, Mimi," Alexander said.

"Sí," Mimi said. "Tres."

"I don't think he understood you," Perrette said.

"Le comprendo perfectamente," Mimi said.

"What was that?" Perrette said.

"Confusion," Alexander said. "But we can have something to eat. I hear there is a cantina, a place called the Del Mar, that is not a bad place. Let's try that."

"When you leave the big hotels," Alfred said, "you run the danger of getting the turistas and spending most of your time in the bathroom. The Cantina Del Mar is a native place and one would certainly get the turistas there."

"Young man," Alexander said, "I am a walking monument

to the fact that in any of the Latin countries you get the turistas wherever you go—at the Del Prado, at the Havana-Madrid, at the Utrillo—anyplace you go. It's a question of time. A few days sooner at the cantinas than at the big tourist hotels."

"The Del Mar has good camarones," Mimi said.

"Well, then," Alexander said, "we will all go down to the Del Mar and have some shrimp. I will arrange for the carriage," Alexander said, standing up.

"Let Mimi order the carriage," Perrette said. "Let Mimi make the deal for the carriage. Speaking the language perfectly well he will arrange a better price."

"I can speak Navaho," Alexander said. "And that should confuse them into giving me a good price. We will take two carriages; that will spread the act and make the war party look big."

Alexander moved toward the edge of the Malecón de las Olas Altas, looking up and down the broad spray-swept street for another carriage. There was one immediately by them at the curb but he could see no other.

"We will give your four pesos to take us to the Cantina Del Mar," Alexander said in Spanish to the defeated and old Mexican driver who stood at the head of his skeletal horse. The cab driver looked at him and said quickly in English, "Okay, boy."

"This is the only carriage," Alexander said back to the others. "If you people want to pile in the back I'll get up in front with the driver."

Alexander hiked into the hard, high, forward seat with the driver and the others came slowly from the table, Alfred remaining to pay the bill.

Alfred could not locate the waiter so he dropped a few pesos on the table and got into the carriage.

"Arre, burro!" Alexander called to the horse.

The driver took the reins and they started slowly down the broad Malecón.

"Do you work this poor horse all day?" Alexander asked the driver.

The old man crouching over the reins did not look up.

"Sí, señor," he said. "My patron owns the bullring. That is, he manages it as he manages all the livestock in town, including the horse that is pulling us today. When the horses get so they cannot pull us then we use them in the ring against the bulls."

"Oh," Alexander said. "And do they bring good bulls here? Bulls that charge straight and are brave?"

"If you substitute the word stupid for brave I might see it," the old man said, still following the horse.

"Oh," Alexander said, smiling faintly. "You have ruined a few paragraphs already. I write books and I was supposed to dominate these early pages. I asked the right questions, I did my part, but you gave all the wrong answers."

"I'm sorry," the old man said, addressing the horse. "But I thought I was being paid to take you to the Cantina Del Mar."

Alexander was silent.

"This book," the driver flopped the reins in annoyance, "will it be mostly about your home country?"

"No," Alexander said. "Not now because I can't go home again. But the people I write about now can but won't because of self-inflicted wounds."

"And people will pay to read about that? About people

who feel sorry for themselves?" The old man was inquiring of the horse again.

"Yes, some will pay for that," Alexander answered. "Because I guess some Americans suffer from self-inflicted wounds."

"You have no relatives?" the old man asked.

"Yes, a brother. Now," Alexander said hopefully, "the conversation in this part is going much better. It is going as it should go."

"Well," the old man said, shifting himself on the hard seat, "you can always cut out the pieces of the story that I ruined. And perhaps I can give you something," the old man said, looking up. "You see that café over there?" He pointed with his stick of a whip. "The one with the red and yellow front marked Tequila y Something? Well, a long time ago, before there were automobiles, the Spanish gobernador was here on the Day of the Gobernadores. The mayor offered one hundred reales to anyone who would swim to La Paz. Sixteen people entered the water and two made it."

"You mean," Alexander said, his voice rising, "that two men who had never swum that distance before, two men with little experience, swam from here to La Paz?"

"Yes," the old man said quietly, going back to his horse. "But the fourteen who drowned had never swum it before either."

At the café they all tumbled out in front of the weather-ravaged shack on the edge of the water. The entrance side was hidden by a thick growth of coconuts and palmettos. Alex bargained the driver into waiting so that he could take them to the wharf after they finished eating. "Or better," he told the old man, "come in with us and have a drink."

Inside there were no lighting and no windows, but the seaward side of the café was without a wall and opened out on a wooden pavilion for dancing, although it would be quite a trick with the heavy boards and wide gaps in between. In the big inside room there was an American jukebox of horrendous size and frightening color. The people in the café were grouped around this, drinking beer out of the heat of Mexico—the four young girls were out of this world.

"They're gone, Jackson!" Perrette hollered to Alexander.

Outside on the pavilion there was a four-piece Mexican orchestra: guitar, accordion, another guitar and another accordion, playing to no one, bravely making a noise against the indifference. The group went out there and quartered themselves around a table that had not yet collapsed.

"Siéntese, señores," a waiter who had followed them said. "You speak English?"

"Of a kind," Alexander said.

The waiter got them some hard extra chairs and they made themselves uncomfortable.

"But we're Indians," Alexander said, "who are still bitter and will not concede defeat to the white man. But let's have camarones all round."

The waiter seized on the word camarones and got back into Spanish quick. "Sí, señor. Pronto," he said, backing off.

The people at the jukebox had stopped their intense interest in the machine and were staring over at Mimi. They had followed him with their eyes as he came in and now were looking over at him and talking it up among themselves. Also another party had come in looking like tourists from the States and they too were interested in the table.

"Pardon me for breaking in on this chapter," Alexander

said, "but while we were quietly camping here I think we have been surrounded by our compatriots. They are going to lay siege to us, but it's four of them against five of us. As unprepared as we are I think we can do all right. They've already spotted us so there's no use keeping quiet. I place them as two dentists and their wives. Both of them are joiners. A couple of years ago they were reduced to pulling each other's teeth, but now, since the inflation, they think five thousand dollars will buy them some happiness in Mazatlán. They have had the great sports fisherman Mimi Jimenez pointed out to them, and now they've tracked the inestimable one to his lair where they can watch him from as close as ten feet. But what lies in store for them on this exciting trip? What will happen to their children yet unborn after their encounter with the dashing Mimi Jimenez? Read the next exciting installment of Alfred Marlowe's great novel of tenderness and brutality. You can have that story, Alfred," Alexander told the young man. "You can have it if you have not already used it."

"I think we can tell many stories and have quite a time," Alfred said. "Yes, I think everything could be quite amusing if you would give up your idea of swimming to La Paz."

"Ugh," Alexander grunted. "You tellum story and I swim to La Paz."

"Well, I don't see the humor in it," Alfred said.

"No, you couldn't see the humor in it, Alfred. No, you couldn't be funny," Alexander said. "You couldn't be funny, Alfred. Even when you're stealing something, you couldn't be funny, Alfred."

"Stealing?" Alfred asked. "What am I stealing?"

"It is a good day," Mimi said, trying his English. "Do you

144

not think, everybody, that it is a good day?"

"Yes," Perrette said. "It is a good day. But what does Alex' wise old scout think about it? Certainly, Alex, you brought him along for his aged wisdom. Will he give us some wise words? Will you translate for us, Alex?"

"A long time ago," the old man began, "before there were automobiles, the Spanish gobernador was here on the Day of the Gobernadores. The mayor offered one hundred reales to anyone who would swim to La—"

"Yes," Perrette said. "But let's not be serious. Let's dance, Alex," she said.

The orchestra began with a high wail.

"You can't even do a war dance on this prairie," Alexander said, looking at the floor.

The Americans had seated themselves at a table near the orchestra and now the two women got up and advanced toward Bowman's table. They were dressed in Jalisco print dresses and a-jangle with tourist silver bracelets.

"You better duck," Perrette said to Mimi Jimenez. "Here come a couple of your aficionados."

Women not quite middle-aged advanced, eager-looking, holding what might have been a bullfight manual for tourists that they sell outside the Plaza de Toros for three pesos.

"Yes," Perrette said. "Now you can explain to them exactly how you catch the big fish and autograph their tourist guides for them."

Mimi blinked nervously and slid in his chair a little, but anxious.

"How old are they?" he said in Spanish. "Quantos años tienen?"

The two women advanced all the way to the table and then

leaned over toward Alexander, extending the books that were novels of Alexander Bowman's that, although good, had become popular enough to get into the paper-backed edition.

"Will you kindly autograph these for us?" the taller one said to Alexander. "We heard that you were in town and went down to the Pan American hoping that we would be lucky enough to catch you."

"Yes, madam," Alexander said. "I will autograph them for you."

She extended the books together with the pen and Alexander autographed both of them quickly.

"We don't know how we can thank you," she said, picking up their books.

"There's no way you can thank me, madam," Alexander said, looking at both of them carefully.

"Just the same it was a thrill to see you," she said, both of them beginning to back off toward their table.

"It was a thrill to see you, madam," Alexander said.

"Oh, I don't see how you could be thrilled by American girls like us." The woman stood hesitating, still standing near the table.

"I am quite thrilled," Alexander said.

"Our husbands sell oil-drilling machinery," the woman said, "and we came down here to join them, but they travel all over Mexico selling oil-drilling machinery."

"That sounds quite thrilling," Alexander said.

"You talk just like you sound in your books." She giggled and the other woman touched her.

"Madam," Alexander said at last, "when I start sounding like that in my books I am finished."

"Oh," she said, still lingering at the table, embarrassed,

the other woman even pulling on her now. "You sound just like the he-man you are in your books. Oh, but you don't want to talk to nobodies like us." She started to giggle again, becoming audible.

"You are somebody who buys my books. That's important to me," Alexander said.

"Oh, go on," she said.

Alexander gave up and stared at Mimi Jimenez.

"Well, good-by now. We're going," the woman said. "Pleased to have met you."

Alexander had given up now and did not acknowledge her, staring across the table at Mimi. The women giggled off back to their table just as a man came over from the same table.

"Is that the way you talk to my wife?" the man said. He was a square, wide man built so that he looked shorter than he actually was. He had been doing quite a lot of drinking and he wiped his face with his hand as he spoke.

"Is that the way you speak to my wife—call her madam? You think she's running a joint down here or something?"

Those at the table remained silent and Perrette winked over at Alfred.

"Don't you say good-by when she says good-by? What's the matter, is she dirt or something?"

"Listen," Alfred said, the only one to look up at the man. "Listen, drop it before something happens."

"Something has already happened," the man said, wiping his face again. "My wife has been insulted. I want satisfaction."

"I should think you would," Perrette said.

"Jesus, that's so funny. Jesus, you people are so funny I'm going to bust a gut. Is that how you people get so famous,

147

being so funny?" the stocky man said, working his shoulders. "Famous people can go around insulting other men's wives, is that it?"

"You only heard part of the conversation. Nobody insulted her. You better go home now," Alfred said, standing up white-faced and trembling.

"You asked for it. By God, he is asking for it," the man said as he hauled back his big arm and lunged at Alfred. Alex stood up but his movement stopped in midair as the kick that Mimi Jimenez threw at the short man caught him in the groin and dropped him where he had stood. The man now lay quietly on the floor. Two waiters came up and pulled him back to his own table. Alfred sat down, still shaking badly.

"White man never should have crossed river," Alexander said, folding his arms. "White man should never have come to Little Big Horn without better general. White man all dead now so we can eat."

"He never should have done that," Alfred said, clenching and unclenching his hands, his voice high and nervous. "Mimi should never have hit him there," he said. "It isn't fair. It isn't—"

"Oh," Alexander said, "nobody asked white man to come into our prairie looking for fight. When white man do that, anything fair. Anyone fooling with Mimi Jimenez lucky not to get killed."

Alfred continued in his high voice, insistent. "Certainly the man is entitled to an explanation when his wife—"

"White man should keep his squaw home when he comes to our country," Alexander said. "Squaws who can read, very dangerous. Particularly dangerous, squaws who can read.

That's a quotation from a famous Indian named Quicker-Than-You, Alfred."

"But certainly Mimi didn't do it fairly," Alfred said, talking almost intimately now. "It wasn't fair the way he—"

"When white man cross river looking for fight we no ask for everything fair. Particularly when he pick on defenseless poet. That's all, Alfred," Alexander said, going back to his normal voice.

Alfred held his eye for a moment and Alexander looked straight into his and Alfred broke it off and went back to twitching his white fingers between his hands.

The waiters had gotten the other party into an automobile cab that was waiting outside. They laid the short, wide man in gently but then part of him, part of his leg, was still sticking out. One of the waiters pressed the leg in with his own foot and then tried to close the door. Some of his pants leg was still stuck so he opened the door again and pushed the man's leg in heavily with a shove and closed the door and the bright car started off back to the hotel.

"Living abroad," Alexander said, "getting off the reservation, teaches you how the white man lives, makes you able to write about—to see—"

"And feel the whole wide world," Perrette said.

10

"I've got to get home," Perrette said, frightened.

"Here. You can go here," Alexander said.

"No. I've got to get home to the Pan American," Perrette said.

Alexander got her out and into the carriage, leaving Alfred and Mimi at the table arguing mayhem.

Soon they were going as fast as they could go and Alexander was leaning far forward and tense and Perrette was much too relaxed and the color of jade.

The high, two-wheeled Mexican horse-drawn carriage, fiery circus red with yellow wheels, tilted into the rutted dirt narrowness of Guillermo Nelson. Now they left the choking Guillermo Nelson for the broader Twenty-First of March, which led into the Fifth of May, which became the Benito Juarez and the openness of the Plaza de la Revolución with its wide-spreading acacia tree, its dedicated stone benches, its ugly marble fountain and its romantic, delicate iron-flowered bandstand of the Díaz regime. Then a short, bone-jolting tilt down the Plaza Hidalgo, which became the Street of the Boy Heroes of Chapultepec with its commerce and its hotels of the later day, the Alcazar and the Central with their lush tropical patios concealing dank, airless rooms.

"Oh dear, oh dear!" Perrette called sharply.

"Here. Right here," Alexander said. "We can stop at the El Central."

"Oh, no," Perrette said, thinking that the romantic façade concealed an antique and rotted bathroom. "No, no, no. We must get to the Pan American."

"A place is a place," the driver said, spreading his hands but starting the horse off on a trot again down the Boy Heroes of Chapultepec.

The carriage careened a little wildly now down to the turn for the Angel Flores. On the left the whole distance was flanked by a grim flat wall of the Barracks of the Revolution with one long scrawl of whitewashed, childish lettering—VIVA GENERAL HENRICO. Then they were on the Malecón de las Olas Altas, a concrete-paved, broad esplanade running past the grand hotels. The street facing the hard, glinting Pacific was suddenly like another country: no press of people, no monuments, vacant lots, streets proclaiming revolution, no one dying in a doorway, no poison colors or desperate music, no garish, shrieking signs. Only an occasional drift of soft, uninspired foreign music from an unseen room.

"Oh oh oh," Perrette cried softly.

"Here is the Utrillo," Alexander called, looking at a mass of brick on the right. "There's no decomposed plumbing there."

The driver slowed but when he got no encouragement he jerked the horse on again.

It was only a wild minute to the Pan American and then another minute to make the U turn in front of the Escuela Oficial Josepha Ortiz de Dominguez and then they pulled up in front of the fresh, clean, modern shaft of the Hotel Pan

American and the two bright-silk-shirted boys hurried down the steps to assist them.

"Oh, I don't think I should move," Perrette said. "I really don't think I should move."

Alexander reached in with his long body and took her in his arms, lifting her by bracing his stomach against the side of the carriage. He rushed her through the lobby and into the waiting elevator—where they waited.

"Isn't there anyone to run this thing?" Alexander hollered.

A workman stepped in, cement-caked and grizzled, carrying everything of his business in his arms.

"Someone runs this thing?" Alexander asked in Spanish.

"Quién sabe? Who knows?" The workman settled in a comfortable position against the side of the car.

Alexander jumped out of the elevator and started going up the stairs fast, Perrette bouncing. At the top of the first flight was the office with the clerk, facing across from the elevator.

"The elevator boy—where is he?" Alexander asked.

"It's an interesting subject," the clerk said with an air of deep thought.

Alexander turned.

"But have you tried the Bodega of Ortega on the Plaza Madera? His brother—"

But Alexander was already halfway up the second flight, jumping up the stairs in twos and threes, carrying his weight easily. As they turned for the fifth floor Alexander was dragging badly.

"I can't make it," Perrette gasped. Perrette's face was a mild shade of green. "I must go in there," she said, pointing to an open door.

The door opened onto a disheveled bedroom and through another door onto the pristine white sanctuary of an American bathroom.

"There," Perrette pointed.

Alexander bolted through the open door, through the stranger's cluttered bedroom on into the bathroom, and deposited her there. Closing the bathroom door after him he went back into the stranger's bedroom and collapsed on the low bed.

"I must be in the wrong room." It was a thick, heavy, dry voice behind Alexander.

Alexander turned and saw an American Negro sitting at the writing desk in a gray-striped, visitor's baseball uniform with the red lettering GUAYMAS written across his shirt. He had a wide, spreading face.

"No, you're in the right room," Alexander said between gasps. "It's that my wife has the sickness and the elevator isn't running and I had to get her in here quickly."

"That your wife you just ran through here with? That young girl your wife?"

"Yes," Alexander said.

"You picks 'em young," the Negro commented slowly, placing his shoeless feet up on the bed.

"I didn't come into your bathroom to be insulted," Alexander said.

"Out of the hundred rooms in the hotel you just happened to pick ours?" the Negro asked carefully.

"Yes," Alexander said. "It happened that this is as far as we got."

"With the hundred rooms in the hotel it happened that this is as far as you got," the Negro repeated.

"Yes," Alexander said. "That's the way it happened and I apologize for the intrusion."

"You apologizes for the intrusion," the Negro continued, speaking with a neutral voice out of a neutral face. "Of the hundred rooms in the hotel you just happened to pick me and Howard's room. It wasn't that you knew that this was me and Howard's room and that anybody can walk in me and Howard's room whenever it's convenient."

"No, I didn't know it was me and Howard's room," Alexander said, his breath coming more slowly now.

"If you choose to mock me," the Negro said, a little lower and a little tenser and dropping his shoeless feet silently on the floor, "if you choose to mock me you can get out until you have gone through the proper amenities of being admitted into the room."

"But I must wait for my wife," Alexander said.

"You can wait for your wife in the hall," the Negro said with formal quietness.

"Very well," Alexander said, getting up and moving toward the door.

"Plan to attend the game?" the Negro asked as Alexander moved across the bedroom.

"No," Alexander said, his hand on the knob. "Will it be interesting?"

"It could be," the Negro said. "Good day."

Alexander stepped out and closed the door after him. A second later the door opened and the broad face of the Negro appeared again.

"Won't you step in and wait in our room?" he said.

Alexander came inside.

"This chair is not too copesetic," the Negro said, pushing

him the one he had been sitting on. "But it is the best we have. Make yourself comfortable. Your wife should be out in a moment."

The Negro removed his spiked shoes from under the chair, brought them around with him and sat on the bed. He was silent a moment adjusting a pillow under himself.

"It's better now this way. I don't like the idea that people think they can bust in on me and Howard any time they want. We paid our money for this room just like anybody else. That is, the club paid it in our name. Anyway, it's our room."

"It's your room," Alexander admitted.

"I'm Leroy," the Negro said. "I'm the third baseman. Howard is the first baseman for Guaymas. He's out now getting a bite but he'll be back shortly. And you're the writer," Leroy continued. "Your entrance made quite a commotion the other day. Howard and I were on the balcony watching you come in. Howard is a fan of yours." Leroy touched a worn, paper-bound copy of Alexander's book that was on the bedside table.

The door opened and a big burnt Negro, broad-shouldered and with a continuous defensive smile, entered the room, stood holding the door with his hand, staring at Alexander Bowman, and then looked over at Leroy.

"Where did you find him?" he asked.

"He brought his wife to use our bathroom," Leroy said from the bed.

"That's cozy," Howard said, and then he added slowly, thinking it over, "The elevator's not running and your wife got the Aztec's Revenge.

"That's right," Alexander said.

"And did he give you a bad time?" Howard asked, closing the door, speaking to Alexander.

"What do you mean, give him a bad time? Of course I didn't give him a bad time," Leroy said.

"Okay, okay," Howard said, watching Alexander Bowman now. "How is the writing going?"

"It ain't," Alexander said.

"It isn't," Howard repeated. "Well, that is disconcerting. Perhaps a change is indicated. We're going fishing, that is if we win today and don't have to practice, we're going fishing. We'll share the boat with you," he said toward Alexander, "if you'll pay half. They want three hundred and fifty pesos. That's pretty steep for Leroy and I."

"How are they running?" Alexander asked.

"Marlin and sail running pretty good," Howard answered with interest. "You pay half and you can use one of the two fishing chairs all of the time."

"Whose boat?" Alexander asked.

"Louis Peron's. Those hulks of Mimi Jimenez' won't float too good. Louis's got a twin universal with beer, Cokes and bait on the boat for three hundred and fifty pesos, you pay half."

"Okay," Alexander said. "But no family. Last time I shared a boat out of La Paz with an Englishman he brought his whole family along—a passel of kids that drank all the beer, ate all the sandwiches before we were out of the harbor, spent the rest of the time playing cowboys and Indians over my body."

"Last time we was on a fisher," Howard said, "we went out with some whores from the Siete Monos. They was down below with the crew drinking our beer and we went aground on the Tres Marianas."

"I'm topped," Alexander admitted. "Your fishing stories are better than my fishing stories."

Howard got up and paced the floor as though anxious to put on his uniform. He looked over toward the closet and then he walked over to the table beside the bed and picked up the worn paper-bound copy of Alexander Bowman's book and hit it against his hand.

"Good book," he said.

"Thank you," Alexander said. "Did you like the last one?"

The Negro hedged, hesitated a moment and then put the book down.

"Are you ready?" Alexander said, standing up and calling toward the bathroom.

"I think I can make it now."

The slight shade of green in her face had changed to a pale yellowish tinge. Alexander grabbed her around the waist and helped her across the room. Leroy had gotten up and walked across to the door.

"I'm sorry," Leroy said. "But do you think you can make the game today?"

"Thanks for the use of your bathroom," Alexander said and Leroy closed the door.

Alexander helped Perrette up the last flight of stairs, not needing to carry her now, just gripping her under the shoulder of the right arm. In the long white room he helped her undress while she sat on one of the low side-by-side beds. When he got her between the covers he took two of his pillows and put them under her head and then he went into the bathroom

157

and turned on the shower to see if there was any hot water. There wasn't any hot water and there wasn't any cold water either. He went over to the table that faced the window in the main room and sat down at the typewriter.

He took a clean sheet of yellow paper and put it in the typewriter and looked at it for a while, then he turned around and picked up the Mazatlán paper and looked at that for a while. It was full of today's ball game with pictures. He let it slide to the floor.

"They're awfully bright, those Negro boys downstairs," Alexander said. "Clever."

"It was nice of them," Perrette said, "to let me use their bathroom."

"They're awfully smart," Alexander said.

"Did you get into an argument with them?" Perrette said.

"No. They were just telling me how to write my books," Alexander said.

"That's cute of them," she said. "What did they say?"

"They said an Indian evidently couldn't write about white people, that he should leave the white people alone. They said I was beginning to act and write like an expatriate, that I should get back to the hogan fast."

"They couldn't have said anything as sophisticated as that," she said.

"They said that I knocked myself out on the last book. They said I threw everything at them, they said I tried so hard there wasn't any stuff on the ball and that I didn't have any control, and that it was a very bad performance."

"I don't think they said anything as sophisticated as that," she repeated.

"They said I sounded like a writer who was coming apart,

that I've got to get hold of myself."

A blast of salted air off the bay ballooned the monk's-cloth curtain high against the ceiling. It streamered out now, flapping in mid-room. As the wind slackened it slowly fell down over the typewriter. Alexander did not bother to remove it, just sat watching the spot where the keys should be.

"A child," Perrette said, her voice weak, from the big bed. "Why don't you have a child?"

"Because I'm incorrectly built," Alexander answered.

"I mean you and me," she said, eager.

"You and I," Alexander said.

"You and I," Perrette said, still excited.

"Because we use contraceptives," Alexander said.

"If we had a child then there would be the three of us, that would be a creation more and bigger and more mystifying than any creation," Her voice rang high and clear in the long flat, modern, sanitary room.

"Think of it," she said. "A creation of ours, a warm-blooded, throbbing, full creation of ours. It would be original. It would have a beginning, a beautiful middle and an exciting end."

"Yes," he said. "Maybe you have been reading one of my old books."

"But isn't it exciting?"

"In the first place," Alexander said quietly, folding his hands, "now the idea runs into the reality of the dangerously increasing birthrate factor, and in the second place the idea runs into competition with TV. TV has handled the idea much better, better even than the comic books or the church."

"I am trying to help you," she said. "I am trying to make things different. It could build your interest in life—give you something to write for."

"Yes," Alexander said, lifting the monk's cloth off the typewriter. "I think you have a touch of genius, Perrette."

"I only wanted to help," she said.

"I only want to write a book," he said in her same tone.

"Yes," she said. "That's what we want to do. That's what we must do—help you write the book. That is the important thing. We must help you to remain great."

"We?" Alexander repeated, going back in the chair. "Who else is in on the act?"

"Well, you know Alfred wants to help you," she said confidently.

"Does he figure in the end of the book too?" Alexander asked.

There was a pause. "I don't know yet," Perrette said finally. Then she said quickly, "But he is a wonderful critic."

"Did he tell you I was an Indian son of a bitch?" Alexander asked.

"No," Perrette said. "No. You know he didn't. Of course he didn't."

"Then maybe he isn't much of a critic," Alexander said.

Perrette pulled the covers tighter toward her small head, her long blond hair spread out over the blue blanket.

"If we left each other then perhaps you could go back home to Indian Country."

Alexander unrolled the yellow sheet out of the typewriter, wadded it into a neat ball in the palms of his hands and then tossed it for the wastebasket and missed it.

"What about a parrot?" he said. "I saw some nice red and blue and green parrots on Gomez Street."

Perrette was quiet and made a pattern of the blanket, folding and refolding it.

"Sure you wouldn't want a red, green and yellow parrot? Yellow beaks I think they call them."

"No, I don't want a parrot," she said.

"A monkey?"

"I don't think I want a monkey."

"I am in need of a drink," Alexander said, getting up. "What would you like? An aspirin?"

"No," she said. "I don't think I want anything."

Alexander got up and put on his battered jacket.

"You know what I would really like?" she said. "You know what I think would be awful fun?"

"What?" Alexander asked, putting on his coat.

"An airplane," she said, watching him, her mouth big and smiling. "Wouldn't it be fun? You and I—just you and I all alone up there with just the moon and the stars and the big white heavy clouds, with the entire world spread out beneath us."

"Yes," Alexander said, buttoning his coat. "I think it's double peachy. Are you sure you don't want any aspirin?"

"You could get me two before you go," she said, tired, her voice low again.

Alexander went into the bathroom, took down the bottle of aspirin, knocked out two on the palm of his hand, got a glass of water, set it along with the two pills on the small stand beside her bed and then he leaned over and kissed her on the cheek. She smelled of My Sin and Chase Me, but there was always something there that took him back to that first night in the airless motel room outside Albuquerque.

"Kiss me, Alex."

He kissed her and then touched her lightly.

"Later," he said. "White man go now and get firewater."

He waved to her from the door as he closed it. She did not look pathetic there in this last look. She had begun to gather herself up and was preening herself like a young Ute or a young Navaho, Alexander thought as he closed the door.

In the hall Alexander paused and looked at himself in the big mirror alongside the elevator.

The danger is, he thought, that you begin to feel sorry for yourself, that you cease to expect twice as much from yourself as from other writers, that you cease to become hard with your work, cease to become truthful with your work, and that gives other people a chance to be hard and truthful with it. He pointed to the man in the mirror. Fifteen years is such a long time, he said, you should be a grown boy by now. Try to respect yourself and love others. It's important not to love yourself but respect yourself. And loving others at least means not hurting them. If only, he thought, we could cure something by recognizing it. "I don't like that man in the mirror."

He turned away from the man in the mirror.

That man in the mirror, Alexander thought as he pressed the elevator button—back on the reservation I think I could whip him.

11

Alexander stepped into the elevator and Howard and Leroy, the Negro ballplayers, were there and an eager, white-haired man was on the elevator too and he said, "Fellow Americans, eh? Congressman Willborne. I'm down here investigating—"

"Listen," Howard said to Alexander from the corner of the elevator. "I tell you what. You come to the ball game and I'll finish reading your last book."

Alexander continued quiet and Willborne said, "Investigating—"

Howard said, "Still nothing, eh? Well, I tell you what. I think your writing is it. I think it could be very it."

"Listen," Willborne said. "Investigating—"

"So we lost a bunch of ball games," Howard said. "You write a couple of bad books. Is that the end?"

"Let this man speak," Leroy said, touching the eager, white-haired, red-faced man.

"It's not important," the eager man said importantly.

"Say it, man," Leroy said, "and get shut of it."

"Well, I'm actually on vacation," the white-haired man said. "But I'm keeping my eyes and ears well open, you can bet on that."

"Thank you," Leroy said. "Keep everything well open. I

163

feel safer now."

"Thank you," Willborne said and he drew in a big breath and said, "It has been my now crystallized observation from a former incontrovertible fact that—"

"Yes," Leroy said. "But it ain't your turn."

"Simply that Alexander Bowman," Howard said, "is it and that Alexander Bowman could be very it."

"Listen," Willborne said quietly, "there's a section of town— Only as an official observer, you understand."

"Seven blocks straight right," Leroy said. "Tell them that Reginald—"

"Seven blocks," Willborne whispered.

"I feel safer now," Howard said.

"Thank you," Willborne said stepping out of the elevator. "Thank you very much."

Getting out of the palm-cluttered lobby Howard touched his arm to Alexander's. "Can we give you a lift?"

"No," Alexander said. "I'm just going over and sit on the bench. And I hope you win."

"Thank you," Leroy said to Alexander and then, watching Willborne scurrying, "Thank you very much."

Alexander went over and sat alone on the big stone bench that faced the ocean. He was immediately surrounded by a flight of shoe-shine boys.

"You want a shoe shine, Joe?"

"No."

After Alexander had had his shoes shined twice and paid three times he tucked his feet under the bench and watched the ocean.

"You want to see some pictures, Joe?"

Alexander got rid of that one and went back to watching

the ocean. She was going out still booming but dirty and tired and heavy with foam.

"Where you live, Joe?"

Alexander started to tell him and then realized that the boy didn't care. He lived, he thought, in a land that took in two townships or seventy-two sections with six hundred and forty acres to the section. About one section was deeded, the rest leased, most from the government, some privately. A land where in winter you drove out fifteen miles in the snow and spread cake in a circle. Where you spread the soybean cake pellets, one circle within another circle so that the cattle, flinging themselves out of the low, concealing dwarf piñon and cedar could all get to it. The cake, dung-colored droppings against the very white snow, beginning, as you worked, to form a great rosette in the big draw. The cattle grouped themselves in bold and formal pattern joined soon by elk (the Bowmans allowed no hunting) and then the whole country was a stage full of big dancers neatly arranged against a white world for some wild ballet.

"You want a girl, Joe?"

And Sunday afternoons in town, the men driving their women in to church, the wives' religion having even survived each Sunday's assault by the preacher, the men's not so, as they dawdled, whittling, politicking, in the square, excepting old man Minter, emerging from the church, hand-shaking with the minister. And didn't Minter think in view of the small turnout the preacher had spoke mightily, given it his all? Minter stared at the preacher, coining some answer. Well, Minter answered finally, maybe. But on second thought, when he, Minter, drove out a wagonload of cake to feed, if only three cows showed up he wouldn't pitch out the whole damn load.

"You want to know a good place, Joe?"

Alexander already knew a fairly good place. It was on top of the Jemez now, in the summertime, where they had government permits for three hundred head. You had to start pushing out the cattle very early to make the drive from the ranch to the mountaintop in one day. It was nice in the years when you had plenty of Indian cowboys who could dive into the brush for a stray and the others could keep the main bunch moving. You had to make it in one day; there was no water on the trail and you risked losing a bunch of water-crazed cattle in the rock and almost impenetrable brush if you had to make camp. Moving them down was easier. The snow was beginning to threaten and the cattle wanted down badly, lowing at the forest gate and bellowing, wanting off the fast-yellowing, aspen gold-turning, autumn-cold, whistling mountain before she closed in. Sometimes there was an animal who would not join the bunch, who would wander alone and higher and stranded, rather than join the others. Sometimes this one they would find alive in the spring, sometimes dead. He took his chances wandering alone and higher but he would not join the others. Alexander lit a cigarette and tossed the match at the foam that retreated down the beach.

"They're all gone, Joe."

Alexander focused on the boy who remained and decided he looked like the others and allowed his eyes to drift over to Mrs. O'Flynn's restaurant (A Home away from Home) and to another tourist trap, Captain Fleet's Oasis (English Spoken, American Understood). The two expatriates had set up their heavens between the only two decent hotels in town so they would catch the Americans coming and going and falling down. Mrs. O'Flynn was a refugee from Iowa. She had twice been closed by the sanitary authorities, which takes a lot of talent in Mexico. But Mrs. O'Flynn was a genius. The captain was a bore ("Old soldiers trade away") who had come to this small town in Mexico and set up a stand where the Americans could not avoid him. The captain had served under MacArthur in the Rainbow Division and Doug and he and he and Doug. Alexander had not returned after Alexander had told the Captain "I shall return."

Alexander looked on up the spray-swept street where there was no one. The few tables in front of the Belmar were empty and the kiosks were doing business with no one at all. He thought he saw the doorman in general's uniform outside the Siesta but it might have been a flag. Now a gull floated in, lonely and airborne, and lighted on the nose of Cortes leading his bronze troops across the asphalt of the Twenty-first of September toward the concrete boulevard of the Fifth of May.

"Everybody gone, Joe."

Yes, Alexander thought, everyone is gone.

"They tell me you going to swim the ocean, Joe."

Alexander remained silent.

"When Colombus cross the ocean he use three sheeps."

"Yes," Alexander said.

"You no afraid of esharks, Joe?"

Esharks and sheeps. What was the boy talking about?

"I'm wetback, Joe. I swim the Rio Grande all the time. I can give you pretty good tip."

"Yes?"

"Don't."

"Thank you."

167

"I swim to your country all the time, Joe. You have very good country."

"Thank you."

"When they catch me up there they no give me rough time. They just turn me around and put me on bus. But by that time I got lots of money. It's a good country."

"Yes."

"You know, Joe, this time I make pretty good money, all the money there is in the world. And you look very sad, Joe. I think I give you some for the bus. You want to go home, Joe?"

"Yes."

"How much you want, Joe? Five, six, seven dollars? How much you want, Joe?"

Alexander looked at the boy now. He had a round, dark, smooth peasant face, the kind Goya used in his backgrounds.

"I get this from your people, Joe. I can give a little."

"I too have all the money there is in the world," Alexander said.

"Good, Joe. Then as one millionaire to another we can relax. We can have a talk. We won't have to sell each other anything. We can discuss the future—"

"As equals," Alexander said.

"And our success stories," the boy said. "Mine began one dark night when I was tending the sheep in the fields and I heard a voice say twelve to one, twelve to one."

"Twelve to one?" Alexander said.

"Yes, Joe. This twelve to one, twelve to one meant nothing to anyone in our village. It was when I came to town here, to Mazatlán, that I saw an American exchange, one dollar for twelve pesos, that I saw the great luz. So I sold all my worldly goods, parted with my family and innumerable relatives and made the journey to the promised land of twelve to one. At the border they tell me I need a passport to get in. Just this side of the border they tell me I can get through the needle's eye if I am rich."

"How rich?"

"One hundred and fifty dollars rich, Joe. For one hundred and fifty dollars a Juarez taxi company would deliver me through all of the immigration traps to Denver, Colorado, for one hundred and fifty dollars. But all my worldly goods in Mexico had amounted to only one dollar. So I swam underneath the camel. Was caught on the other side of the Rio Grande in El Paso the next day and marched back across the bridge. Seven times I tried and seven times el paradiso fué perdido."

"Paradise was lost," Alexander said.

"Yes," the boy said. "One time they put me on a train that did not stop till it got to Guadalajara. Another time they flew me almost to Mexico City, almost dos thousand kilometers de paradiso."

"Two thousand miles from paradise."

"Sí," the boy said. "But the eighth time I got through Texas" (he pronounced it Tay-hass) "and into the promised land. I worked for a month for one hundred and fifty dollars for promised money. The day before payday the man called the immigration and said, 'Come and get him.' There was another man there who had come to buy some cattle and he was standing near the phone and he said, 'Red, you son of a bitch,' and he didn't buy no cattle. Later, outside, he told me where to hide and where to come to him. I did and he paid me one hundred and fifty dollars a month, every month."

"Yes," Alexander said. "And there was a house there that was sealed, a house made of wood that was not wood, that was sealed."

"Yes," the boy said. "Did you work there too?"

"Yes," Alexander said.

"Then we can talk as equals."

"We can talk as equals," Alexander said.

Yes, with the boy, Alexander thought, watching the big green ocean go backward, he could talk as equals. But not with anyone else now. Certainly not with Perrette. To talk as equals you were relaxed, relaxed in such a way you feel you must have known the person well before life began. Perrette's name was Perrette Marin but this knowledge did not help much. He did not even know the name of the boy and yet he felt he had known him even before life began. For example, Perrette knew all there was to know about the fringes of art and the boy did not know what the word meant. Perrette was sexually attractive, came from a family on Long Island with tons of money, had been to all the right schools, which could mean the wrong schools, but the boy had been to nothing, knew nothing about all the things that are supposed to be important, and yet this feeling that he had known him before life began.

The boy snapped his fingers. He was in a crouching position between Alexander and the ocean looking up at Alexander and now he snapped his fingers and said, "Are you thinking of someone you love?"

If he was thinking of the land that was his home then, yes, he had been thinking of something he had openly said he loved. If he had been thinking of Perrette, well then he would have something to tell her. If that was maybe the most important thing in the world, perhaps the most important beginning would be to tell her. It had been on his tongue many many times but always something small and hard from way way back someplace would get in the way. He thought he realized now, looking out over the bay at the low, roiling, timeless, dirty sea, that he had neglected people except those that were in his books. This boy and this ocean and all the loneliness of a hundred thousand expatriate nights could bring a person to the fact that the land cannot respond, only people, only Perrette. And the responses must be relaxed, between equals. There had always been this tension that a cliché could cut like a clean knife. Alexander had never used a cliché in his life. Tonight he would use one, but as a clean knife.

"Tonight I could tell her," he said.

"Good," the boy said. "You can never tell a woman too much. It is a discovery I have made."

"Perhaps then I would not have to swim that ocean." He looked at the big eyes of the boy now. "Even in three sheeps. Maybe it is a discovery I have just made that between two people nothing should get in the way, not books, not Indian Country, nothing should get in the way of having known a person well, even before life began."

"Yes, Joe."

Alexander thought, she is all I have left, and the boy said. "Yes, Joe."

Now that the boy was even reading his thoughts he would have to break this off. So the boy had gotten a job at the ranch. It was not too coincidental. There were only three big ones in the entire hundred miles north of Bernalillo. A lot of wetbacks had worked there before they were picked up by immigration.

"Did you like the ranch?"

"Very much, Joe,"

"Would you like to go back?"

"No. I've got my home, my own country, Joe."

Now that he has seen it all and has all the money there is in the world, all the experience, he wants to go home to his own country. And he can, too. Me too, I can too. To a hotel room, a bar—climb a mountain, swim an ocean. I can too. A hotel room, a bar. But is it true that Perrette who was slipping away is all that is left? It is about true. It is true.

"I go, Joe. I got to go."

"All right," Alexander said as he watched the boy rise and start down the street. The back of his head, Alexander thought, is Goya too. A friend too. There weren't many. Soon he would be alone.

"Good-bye," Alexander called. "Enjoy."

"Thank you, Joe." And then the boy turned the corner suddenly and disappeared.

Alexander spotted a speck of something way out on the enormous ocean and tried to concentrate on that.

"Your friend said seven blocks. Seven blocks to the right. We went there and there was nothing—nothing but a church. Oh, pardon me, this is a colleague—same committee. We are both investigating—"

"No, no, we're not," the other man said. "We're those congressmen abroad you read about. Kind of a roving assignment, expenses paid, for looking into things. No matter what, we try to keep our eyes and ears well open."

"Right is not the same in every country," Alexander said. "In Mexico you should have gone the other way, and tell them Reginald sent you. But I feel safer now."

"Thank you," the other man said, and they both disappeared.

But I don't feel safer about Alfred, Alexander thought. I should not have left him with that homicidal maniac Mimi, and I should not have left Perrette unhappy and alone. Alexander tried to concentrate on the speck he had spotted before, way out on the enormous ocean, but it was nowhere. We are all alone.

Some young Indios, almost naked, were playing dice in front of Alexander now but he did not see them. The waves were tilting in on him, blowing a fine spray, but he saw them as a series of small avalanches and the fine mist a powdery snow blowing off the long slopes of the Sangre de Cristos above the ranch.

A policeman came up and stopped in front of him. "You need help?"

"What?" Alexander said. Then at last in recognition, "No, I guess not."

The policeman hesitated, still wanting to be helpful until Alexander shook his head slowly and finally in a definite no.

The policeman walked on to the next bench before he looked back at the tall, angular, Norteamericano sitting alone and staring out at the sea.

From his seat at the bar of the Belmar Alfred could see Alexander sitting watching the ocean. He had gotten rid of Mimi Jimenez somewhere two or three bars back and he did not want to see Alexander right now. Not after what I have done, he thought.

"Experiences," Alfred said, watching the bartender through

his green drink. "I will give him the experience of Mimi Jimenez and stop him from making the swim at the same time. I personally called the American Consul and then he called the mayor and had him stop the whole thing. When Mimi finds out, I'm getting out of his way. I hope Alexander gets out of his way. I hope he does not have to have another experience. But when you are cut off from your origins, your roots, you have nothing really important that you know well enough to write about, you have to have experiences. Alexander knows that. We all know that, don't we?"

"Si, señor."

"I'm a poet. I don't need them. And perhaps if he has an experience I can have a little time with Perrette."

"Si, señor."

"It's not that I'm a villain." Alfred moved his green drink. "Those who understand people, the psyche, know that villains outside of books do not exist, so that, unless someone puts me in a book, I'm just a person who happened to be around when things began to fall apart between them."

"Si, señor."

"I don't know how it got started between Alexander and Perrette but I know how it began to fall apart. I don't know for sure but I think it got started between them this way." Alfred took a drink first. "There was a bunch of those Indians sitting around a fire one night on that ranch up there in New Mexico and one of those Indians had a wife. It was Alexander's brother who had the wife, but she got to talking to Alexander about Art. Art can be an enormous item for anyone, let alone a fire-watching Indian, so Alexander gave her her beautiful head and let her talk about Art while he watched. This Perrette comes from a rich family in the East.

Marin. Perrette Marin. Perrette's father manufactures something to cure athlete's foot which doesn't do much harm and comes in three-sized bottles including the large economy fraud. I think she had a normal, healthy, maladjusted childhood and was always beautiful—and she is beautiful."

Alfred pushed his glass for another green drink.

"It is hard to tell where she went wrong, why she married someone she didn't fit, like Alexander, but it must have been that she confused him with Art. Art is most attractive all of the time but few people recognize this until Art is dead. But she recognized Art too early in life which can be very dangerous too."

"Muy, muy interesante," the bartender said, setting down the fresh green drink.

"No, it's not interesting at all," Alfred said. "But it gives you some background, better than my damn symbols. I tell you what, another drink and I could go see Perrette. It's that I respect him as a writer. It's not that I am afraid."

"No, no. Of course not," the bartender said, mopping up in front of Alfred.

"You're not listening. You want your money."

"No, no. Of course not," the bartender said.

"Here," Alfred said, getting up unsteadily. "Ten pesos." He slammed them on the bar. "I go now to do my work."

"No, no. Of course not," the bartender said as Alfred went out through the swinging door.

Alfred came out of the Belmar Café and saw Alexander still sitting there staring out to sea. Oh, he thought, now would be a good time to see Perrette. He had intended to go to another café and work on his poem. But instead now he turned and walked toward the Pan American. Quickly.

175

12

At home, in Indian Country, George wrote down a Navaho's name in the yellowing sheep ledger—Opportunity Knox. George had corrupted this from the boy's given English name, Opportunity Knocks. He had made the change to lend the name some dignity in case the boy went to college. The mission, now defunct, had once promised Knox that opportunity which the Indian had construed as a threat and Knocks had left the checkerboard area for Flag only to return a few months ago. Nevertheless George entered him as Knox—this name and twenty-four dollars in pawn (a concha belt and two turquoise necklaces) against four boxes of eating groceries, a bridle and a paper-bound copy of *Think and Grow Rich*. George Bowman, having finished this business, put the big ledger to one side and began the letter to his brother. Now he would write that letter to his brother and nothing, absolutely nothing, would get in the way.

"Well, he's leaving," Quicker-Than-You said.

That Indian, George thought, is always coming up in back of me and making world-ending pronouncements.

"Don't bother me," he said.

After several lines of writing and rewriting, lines he kept

crossing out, he turned to the Indian with relief.

"Who's leaving?"

"Jack. Diamond Jack. He says an honest rustler can't make a living in this country any more. He's going to Mexico. The State Police are definitely going to pick him up if he's here next week."

"Mexico," George said, swinging in the chair, turning toward the Indian. "Why then he could deliver— He could tell him for me. I wouldn't have to write this impossible—"

"Certainly," Quicker-Than-You said. "But where you'll find him no one has ever been able to find out. Tso's clan has been missing some cattle so he's probably up on the big mountain someplace on his final job. He sent word by Tso's clan that he would shoot anyone on sight who tried to get the cattle back."

"We'll go and find him and get the cattle back too," George said. "Are you with me?"

"No," Quicker-Than-You said.

"You going to let him scare you?"

"Yes."

"Well, somehow it doesn't scare me."

"If I were you trying to write that letter it wouldn't scare me either."

George Bowman left the post alone but he had only got his horse up the far turn of the Penistaja Mesa when Quicker-Than-You pulled up alongside of him.

"Any time more than one white gets together there's bound to be a war. I think I'd better come along to bury the dead. You got a cigarette?"

They smoked and rode in deep silence up through the gradual, gray foothills; sometimes a jack rabbit looked at them and sometimes a deer watched. Now a buzzard floated close but they rode on in silence.

"What are we doing up here?" the Indian said finally.

"Catching a rustler."

They had to go through a bright narrow pass in the rocks now and when they came out on the other side the Indian said, "That's good because I thought we were avoiding something."

"We're catching a rustler."

"Like in the movies."

"Exactly like in the movies."

They rode now through a wide, gently waving and violent yellow plain of rabbit brush. Interspersed at intervals through the rabbit brush was the quiet, green, deadly milkweed that kills sheep. When the Indian herders hit this patch they drove the sheep hard to keep them from eating and dying, but George and Quicker-Than-You moved through it quietly.

"I haven't much time for pictures," the Indian said.

"Ever see a picture called *The Great Train Robbery?*"

"No."

"A good picture."

"I don't want to play words any more," Quicker-Than-You said. "You should be back at the post writing what you were writing. I'm sorry I interrupted you."

"That was okay," George said, taking off his Stetson and wiping his forehead against the sun. "We should keep our mind on what we're doing."

"You were doing a letter to your brother."

"Not now, I'm not. We're looking for that rustler." George quickened his horse.

"We're doing good works for the Indians," Quicker-Than-

You said, coming up again.

"We're changing the subject," George said quietly. "That's what we're doing."

"Okay," Quicker-Than-You said. "But you're taking the blame for the drought."

"They've got nothing to go on."

"No, but they can see what's happening."

George Bowman could see what was happening too. The Indian was putting on the pressure. Okay, George would get rid of the Indian. He had things to do. He pulled up his horse.

"Okay," he said, pointing. "You try the Chavez Canyon and I'll go up the Baca. Be sure you check all the side rincons and if you need my help fire three quick ones."

"And if you need any help—"

But George's horse was already moving away rapidly.

"If you need any help," the Indian continued to himself. "Jesus, can anyone help him?"

George was happy to get rid of the Indian. Now he could change the subject properly. He would think about the post. Now that Quicker-Than-You was away Tom-Dick-and-Harry would take over. Tom-Dick-and-Harry was brought up at the mission, which kind of lamed him for The People or the whites. That was why George had hired him. The other traders had a theory that you couldn't hire an Indian, based on an observation that they give the store away to the clan. Some of the traders, imitating the traveling salesman who picked a small town to leave his wife in, picked an Indian with a small clan to leave in the store. George picked Tom-Dick-and-Harry because when he got back from the mission school The People didn't think too much of his white ways. There wasn't anybody much who would take the store if

Tom-Dick-and-Harry made the offer.

Now George watched the mountains. George was impressed with the mountains, the heavy endless mass that piled all the way to the snow clouds. They would be his compass. With the wind and the water, a slow, infinite leveling process was reducing the mountains to the plains. In a few billion years, give or take a few millions from the professors, the mountains would be no more. But despite the professors, the mountains would be with us a little while yet. They would not be with us as long as the Diamond Jacks, but give them something. George gave them, not majesty because the word was worn out, he gave them a simplicity and an organization that is understandable to man and called beauty. How about the joy after traveling the low mesa country, the excitement after the monotony of threading up and down the gray arroyos in the badlands, the tingle and awe of an explosion of green and solid mass burgeoning and quick with water and the mountains all alive and all there?

No, beauty is plenty. And you do not have to take from the mesa country to give to the mountains. George lived with the Indians down here in the mesa country and now as the great dark hills came on solid ahead of him he gave the mountains beauty. The mountains gave George a compass.

George thought, I am thirty-seven years old. The horse is not too much younger and the mountains are quite old. The mountain here is named San Pedro. At Diamond Jack's, where I am heading, the mountain is named Sangre de Piedra, but it all belongs to the Jemez, which, of course, is a part of the Nacimiento. This family knowledge can be helpful when you are using it as a compass.

Somewhere, way back in one of the deep folds of the

180

mountain that was always dark, you could hide things in the inside of the mountain. The old-time bad men knew this, not popular movie boys like Billy the Kid, but unrecorded men who stole cattle—lots of cattle—kept the unheard, bawling longhorns deep near the dark heart of the old mountain until the brand was right, and the righteous indignation had channeled into the log church, and then rode herd over the back trails to Abilene and blew the take at faro before the girlies took them. Diamond Jack had been dipping into books.

George paused now to get his bearings along the mountain. Although he pretended not to, the aged horse appreciated this consideration. Banjo liked to give you the impression, prancing around the post, that he was a four-year-old, but he was older than his master, Silver-Threads-Among-the-Gold, twenty-five. The trader owned three horses of his own but Silver Threads, with the connivance of Opportunity Knox and possibly Tom-Dick-and-Harry, would chase George's horses up the Pierna Canyon each time they knew that he planned a ride. Silver Threads got one dollar in trade every time George used Banjo. Diamond Jack had twice stolen Banjo (the second time accidentally and in the dark) and twice, and in the daylight now, turned him loose. Each time Banjo would drag into the post until spotted and then he would go into his dance of the four-year-olds.

George gentled Banjo out of the wide San Juan into the Baca Canyon. Baca Canyon ran, lonely and heavy with brush, up to the snow on the great mountain. Here the big Baca was gray with chamise. Soon the olive would turn to the dying red of the scrub oak, then the heavy green of the piñon country before you wound into the great and towering ponderosas, fretted with snow, and the ice-cased aspens, scintillant.

Somewhere along the big Baca was Jack's canyon and now George began to track. Sometimes he would slide off Banjo and get down on his haunches and examine something closely before mounting again and spurring his horse.

George was all the way through the red country, part way through the green and approaching the painful white of the Nacimiento. He was not dressed for it. The fine hard sand granules of snow began to beat into his face off the de Piedra haunch. It was below zero and the wind was up and the long shadows were starting to lengthen into the heart of the canyon. Some one of the Indians certainly had logged up here and had a parka. George should have borrowed it. But he had not figured Diamond Jack for the white country; not the gray but probably the red, possibly the green, but never the white. That was George's first mistake; he had underestimated the courage or the stupidity of Jack.

Now George made his second mistake; he dismounted to examine something interesting in the snow and he dropped Banjo's reins ahead of him. You do this to any good cow horse and he will stand stock still till eternity, but Banjo belonged to Silver Threads, a professional tourist Indian, who corrupted everything he owned.

Banjo began to move off to the left away from the blowing cold and into the trees. George was down on his knees and did not see or hear, in the hard blowing snow, Jack move through the trees on horseback and seize the reins of Banjo and lead him down canyon.

Now George, suddenly and without sight of the disaster, became aware that everything had gone wrong and just at that moment too when he had picked up the trail of the Navaho cattle. He rose and retreated from the box canyon and toward the bunching of ice-clad and glaring aspen where his horse had finally wandered, only to see there the tracks of another horse and the series of tracks that were the leading away of his own. George knew there is no more immediate doom than to be stranded up mountain without a horse in a driving snow. The tracks were all gone now and so quickly too. The canyon was in complete shadow and the cross winds beat in, kicking the snow in all directions with tall spumes of it going straight up, and everywhere there was a bitter fog of it blinding any sense of direction. George began to move in what he hoped was a great circle, and at last his feet, not his eyes, stumbled upon what he sought, a huge long U of standstone he had observed before the wind had begun to kick and blind.

George had already made two mistakes and if the third was a blunder too it was to be conscious and of his own plan and making. He crawled now on all fours against the driving snow along the wind-swept sandstone to the end of the U and then went down on his belly and waited.

He was waiting for Diamond Jack to come back and finish him off in Jack's tradition of the Old West, or better, old films, old, thumbed and worn copy of the *Rider of the Silver Sage.* George had no alternative; even if he had known, even if the furies had lifted and he could tell which direction was desert, he could still not make it on foot and without clothing against the burning cold that was already beginning to stiffen him as he lay pressed against the sandstone. George would very much like to see and hear his mesa country once more.

The wind made a dull, high dissonant sound cutting through the deadly cold, but there were no sounds in all the noises of the winds of this last mountain that brought back the drums down there on the desert. George Bowman thought he would very much like to see and hear his mesa country once more.

There was a huge stillness within the noises of the wind and everything was becoming much too soft, much too pleasant, much too dulce—tqidajina, was the impossible Indian word for it—this ecstatic easiness after the first pain of freezing when everything begins to slip away. Oh, most certainly George Bowman would like to see and hear his mesa country once more.

And would he like to see his brother once more? Yes, certainly he would. And Perrette? To hell now with Perrette and to hell with his brother and this cold and the silly mountain and the crazy Indian Quicker-Than-You who kept interfering.

Things were even quieter now and softer and he wondered if there was any use struggling. Maybe he would write that letter. It was the only thing to do. He would be well again. He could see the letter written all signed and sealed and ready to put in the mail bag. Then he could walk in beauty.

Now for a split second and then gone again in a sudden kick of the wind, George saw Jack, a wraith figure within a dervish of swirling white, leaning into each new direction of wind, slack-jawed head down, and clutching a readied Winchester at port, still able to make out the quick-dissolving tracks of the trader. George waited for Diamond Jack to reach the center of the U before he made his dive for the horses. Diamond Jack had tracked him to the sandstone now and was coming out on the U. Soon the distance between Jack and the horses would be greater than the trader's on the other end of the U.

Suddenly George made a quick lunge to where he knew

the horses must be and felt as though something within his body had frozen and two shots went off in the time it takes to work the big lever beneath a Winchester 30-30 carbine. George tried again, this time not to run but to spring and fall forward, successfully now, and then again and again within the jerking bursts of the Winchester. He fell against something now—a horse—Banjo. He pulled himself up into the saddle, not having to use that part of his body that was dead with the cold. He turned Banjo in a quick circle, in the same motion picking up the reins of Jack's horse.

George spurred Banjo and dropped the reins and the old horse began to move in the direction that George hoped was the corral where Banjo did his dance. The Winchester somewhere around him was still snapping but wildly, directionless, a protest but impotent now against the blinding curtain of white darkness closing in around Jack.

Two days later and at the post George watched, interested, as Rabbit Stockings helped Tom-Dick-and-Harry stack the trade goods along the back counter. There had been an inventory and very little had been stolen—"taken" would be a better word. George hesitated, putting down the bridle he had been assembling. The Indians had taken, absconded, raided, any way you want to put it, and every chance they got, from every trader between here and Star Lake. Some of the traders were bitter; one of them at Rico had taken to beating the Indians until he himself was killed and the post burned down. All the traders had a defense. Some had bitterness, all had a system. The man at Rico had called his a system too.

George Bowman's system began in the mind and it was to

recognize that the Indians had a system and that their system had a priority over the itinerant whites. At length and in detail, the Indian system was to rob the traders blind. It was an old old system with all sorts of equities and legal tenures and had precedent way way back to the time when the first white man with a gun poked his first bald head over the first mesa. But the Indians were not ready to become extinct. They swam alongside the current, the long winding current of covered wagons. They picked them off one by one and divided the take. It amounted to kind of a tithe, a tax for the use of the land that was theirs. Sometimes they had had to follow the Moving People all the way to Needles, where the difficult crossing of the Colorado made it easier for the Navahos. Sometimes they collected scalps too, but this, George thought, was a reciprocal tariff for what that first white bald head, with a gun, over the first blue mesa, had begun long since. Then came the cavalry alongside the winding wagon trains of the whites and it became difficult and expensive for the Indians to collect. Then came the U.S. Army and it became impossible. But the Indians had within them the same stuff the whites were made of and they thought and they prayed, but mostly they had the instinct to wait, to survive. And it was not a very long long time before the whites, the Bowmans, came and laid everything right out on the counter without the cavalry or the United States Army anywhere in sight. The traders, the Bowmans, were a complete and unequivocal answer to their thoughts, their prayers, their instincts, their survival, their wildest peyote dreams. It was too good to be true and to this day George Bowman knew the Navaho People practiced fantastic and unbelievable restraint in their taxation. Then, too, after all, The

People knew that not even a white man can be made to work for absolutely nothing.

All this stealing business was in George's mind because he had been thinking about Diamond Jack. What would happen to Diamond Jack now—now that Jack no longer had a system? Would he too, like the profession he had chosen, become extinct as the Indians had failed to do? Was he already a victim of his Old West, his box canyon, his frozen mountains, his dreams?

George heard a commotion in the back of the store and then he heard a voice, Lord Acton's, who spoke no English, say in Navaho, "Why really, the Jack of Diamonds is dead."

George made his way back into the warehouse among the hanging and stinking hides. Lord Acton was talking with Silver Threads.

"Why really, what do you mean, dead?" George asked in Navaho as he came up. "You mean they found his body on the mountain?"

Lord Acton waved a dark weathered hand along the red sweatband across his forehead.

"No. I saw his body walking around Cuba but he told me Diamond Jack is dead."

"Why really," George said, "where is he now?"

"Now he is back of the corral. He asked for you yesterday and the day before but of course I told him you would not see him."

"I will see him," George said.

George went back to his office, to his grandfather's old roll top in the back of the warehouse, surrounded, almost buried, by hides.

He motioned Diamond Jack to a seat on a bale of raw

wool. Diamond Jack moved as though he had been hit in the back with a board, or as though he had been deep frozen.

"Listen," Diamond Jack said, "when I came back to that sandstone U I was looking for you—wanted to give you back your horse that had wandered. I fired only in the air to stop you running."

"Maybe. I don't know," George said. "But I couldn't take that chance. I didn't know what Wild West book— what moving picture you had just seen."

"You know I wouldn't shoot at you, George. But some of those cows you took off the mountain were mine," Diamond Jack said.

"They're in the corral in back of Rabbit Stockings' hogan. Take them," George said.

"Don't want them," Diamond Jack said. Jack spoke out of an uptilted face, petulant, inquiring, delicate. "I'm moving now," Diamond Jack said. "You see, you've got to move with the times, the frontiers."

"Yes," George said. "Especially when the police are after you. What business—?"

"Frontiers, that's the only thing that's certain, definite, the only thing that changes."

"Yes," George said. "This business is in Mexico?" He leaned forward. "Then you can take a message. No, never mind. As long as your business is nothing that will bring you back here," he said finally, lightly hesitating, swaying in the chair.

Diamond Jack advanced to the roll top and laid three halves of walnut shells on the oak surface along with a pea.

"This is my new business. I'm going to give up rustling. Doesn't pay."

"Get out," George said.

"Then you don't want me to—?"

"I want you to get out," George said. "But if it will help you to quit this idiot business too, the pea is under that shell," he said, pointing to the shell he had not seen it go under, knowing Jack, through conjuring, must have put it there.

"For the six cows," Diamond Jack said.

"Anything if you will go. The six cows," George agreed.

Diamond Jack swept the shells into his pocket. "Take my word for it, it wasn't there, it wasn't under any of them, it was between my fingers."

George thought now, staring at the ceiling.

"I'll take your word for it that you're just getting a start, that you're new at the business but that you'll always stay away from here, you'll always leave my Navahos alone."

"Agreed," Diamond Jack said with the sobriety and solemnity that would have served to conclude all the oil rights. "As a matter of fact the police will see to that. But how do we stand now on those six cows?"

This was getting too complicated for George and staring at the ceiling didn't help much this time.

"They're yours," Diamond Jack said. "For old time's sake." Diamond Jack got up. "I'm a busy man. I'm off for Mexico."

"Wait," George said. "I want you to tell something to my brother. He's staying at the Pan American in Mazatlán."

"Yes?" Jack hesitated, his hand on the door.

"Tell him to come— Tell him he— Tell him all is—"

"Yes," Diamond Jack said. "Yes."

"Tell him I—"

"Yes, yes," Jack said. "What language is this?"

"He's my brother. You tell him that I feel now after all these years—" George broke it off staring at the desk and looked at Jack. "You and I know the drought will break when it breaks. And the mine shaft—you know the truth about that."

"You all right in the head?" Jack said.

"Tell him," George said. "Tell him—"

"I got to go," Jack said. "People are after me."

"Tell him I will try to write a letter."

"Good. I'll tell him. And good-by," Jack said and he slammed the door.

"But tell him," George said to no one except his reflection in an Indian trade mirror he did not see, "tell him things keep getting in the way."

13

Approximately in the middle of that enormous stretch of emptiness that separated Alexander and George Bowman there were two young gentlemen in a large yellow car with THE WHEEL OF FORTUNE URANIUM COMPANY gold-lettered on the side, entering El Paso, Texas. There was a leather flap that could be dropped from the inside to conceal the sign. It doubled as an arm rest and obliterated the sign when there was a situation that the two gentlemen did not want to bring the Wheel of Fortune into.

The two young gentlemen in the Cadillac coupe de ville, Leland Hepburn III, who carried a letter addressed to George Bowman, and his friend Garry de Grasppe, were on their way to an almost non-existent place called Tonatai, near Cuba, New Mexico.

You could maybe say, to all purposes and intents, legally— anyway as far as uranium, which is do re mi, which is what makes the world go round (or are you one of those people who want to stop it and get off?)—you could safely say the Wheel of Fortune had discovered Tonatai. Perhaps New Mexico when all was said and done. No one at the Wheel of Fortune, not even these two young gentlemen from the

191

public relations department, claimed that the Wheel of Fortune had discovered the United States; but then again, where would the country be, would it truly be the United States, without their élan vital?

The traffic was heavy as they entered El Paso, as it had been heavy since they left Houston. They would have to go across the border to Juarez to get themselves in the right frame of mind to deal with the Indians. The Indians were backward around Cuba, and primitive, and did not know what was good for their own selves. So you might say that the two young gentlemen were going across to Juarez to help the Indians.

They paid their bridge fare and drove the coupe de ville across the border and then decided that this was no proper place to leave the Caddy so they drove back across the international bridge and left the coupe de ville in a parking lot in the United States, paid their fare again and walked back across the bridge to Mexico. They were going to a lot of trouble, you might say, to help those Indians who did not know what was good for their own selves.

Garry de Grasppe had regular, beautiful, clear-cut features, vacuous and emasculated. When he had completed his rise to stardom at the Dairy Dell Little Theater in Houston, Texas, Oveta Culp Hobby's newspaper's theatrical critic had promised "Garry de Grasppe will take Hollywood by thunderstorm." But he went into uranium instead because that's what all the smart boys were getting into. The future belongs to those who sense nuclear possibilities. Blow everything up. Leland Hepburn III had had an identical short and immature career except that the columnist had chosen him for television.

"No girlies," Garry said.

"On the way back then, after a successful venture," Leland said.

"After a successful venture, who knows," Garry said, "we may buy the town."

The two blond gentlemen from the public relations department of the Wheel of Fortune who had left their coupe de ville in the United States walked around Juarez, Mexico, to see, you might say, what they would get.

"No more either," Garry said, "than one or two drinks. You might say we are the spearhead of an expedition. There should be almost no drinking in the field."

"Almost none," Leland agreed. He always agreed with Garry de Grasppe because Garry de Grasppe had been with the company one month longer than he had. He did not think of himself as a sycophant in continuously agreeing because the company had already been in existence six months and if they continued to get a raise each month, even by the salary route alone, they woud soon each and all have a Caddy of their own and what man could ask for more? Uranium's got a wilder future than your dreams are made of. And whatever might be said by weird types against the young gentlemen from Houston, they knew their Horatio Alger.

"You got that letter you were asked to deliver to someone at Tonatai?" Garry asked.

"Right here," Leland said, touching his coat. "It goes to George Bowman. He's somewhere near where we're going. He's the brother of the writer, Alexander Bowman."

"Alexander Bowman," Garry de Grasppe said. "I liked his last book very much but the critics didn't. They don't like books you can't understand. If we don't have things we can't understand then there is no place for God. You got to have faith in the un-understandable."

"That's right," Leland Hepburn said seriously.

"They're a bunch of frightened Philistines."

"That's a good phrase, frightened Philistines."

"It's the title of a book by James Farrell."

"I bet it's a swell book."

"Show me a book that's un-understandable and you'll see me beneath it reaching for it with star mud in my eyes."

"Star mud is a good switch on star dust. I like it."

"Thank you," Garry said.

"But supposing that Alexander Bowman's book has no meaning?"

"All the better. Then you're striving for the unattainable, hearing the unutterable."

"Hearing the unutterable is a good phrase," Leland said. "I like it. You should be a writer yourself."

"Thank you," Garry said. "And this man who wrote the letter, is he a writer too? I never heard of him."

"No one has. Alfred's stuff is much too good. He writes a word here and a word there and no word bears a relation to the other words. It makes you think."

"I like it if it's well done," Garry de Grasppe said.

"Oh, Alfred does it very well," Leland Hepburn said, carefully. "He does it swell."

They were on a street now just off the international bridge. It was jammed with peep shows, missions, prostitutes, beggars, priests, Texas millionaires, a revivalist road show, burros, Cadillacs, weeping and laughing mujeres, Mexican gentlemen sleeping in the street and against decomposing stone walls that did not a building make.

"Those savages out there on the reservation," Leland said in the confusion, "they must really want to take their place in our civilization. It's the romantics among us that do all the damage."

"No, it's the Indian who's his own worst enemy."

"They've got to be protected from themselves."

"Check. But don't call them savages."

"Did I call them savages?"

"You did."

"Then I apologize."

They both felt tolerant and generous now and in need of a drink. But now they were being swept down the street by the flow of animals, people and things. They were wedged in between a woman and an old man trying to sell them something and a boy standing on a burro and holding a dog and trying to show them pictures. They were also being pushed along toward the river by a giant smell and tons of things that were being thrown out of windows and shoved out of doorways.

"Your letter," Garry de Grasppe said, picking it up out of the mud. Leland Hepburn shoved the letter back in his pocket. A piece of tin roof fell near them and a radio drifted close, advertising, in rapid machine-gun Spanish, a machine-gun. The tin roof sank. A long-boned man in a silk hat who said he was God drifted by announcing in a clear impartial voice the end of the world, followed by an English type who said he was left over from the revivalist road show and that the man in front of him, who must already be in the Rio Grande, was an imposter.

The two young gentlemen from the public relations department of the Wheel of Fortune Uranium Corporation of

195

Houston, Texas, made one final surge to free themselves from the swarming tangle and smell of six generations of the North American continent and they were assisted by a console TV set, seven reels of a recent spectacular and a pile of paperbacks that gave them a push so that they shot head first into the Amigos de los Americanos liquor store. There was an international brass band playing outside.

Inside the liquor store they demanded and got a straw, wicker-bound gallon bottle of Jamaica rum with a counterfeit label for almost no money at all plus no tax.

"It hits the spot," Garry said, drinking and then passing the bottle to his accomplice.

"It does, you know," Leland said after he took a drink.

"Please, thank you very much," the Mexican liquor-store owner, who was not running a funeral parlor, said. "It's against the law to drink in here."

The two young gentlemen took the wicker-bound gallon of rum with an interesting label back across the bridge and put it between them on the front seat of the Caddy. By taking drinks of it along the way it would help them to face the Indians at Tonatai.

By the time they got just outside Truth or Consequences, through no fault of the young gentlemen, it was impossible to tell which side of the road was which, and the blond driver was singing above the radio that was going too, "City gals they may be fine, but give me that squaw of mine, roll along, covered wagon, roll along."

It was now also impossible for either of the two blond gentlemen to remember the name of the tribe the Wheel of Fortune Uranium Company was going to emancipate. The Apaches? The Navahos? The New York Yankees?

196

"We got to get hold of ourselves, boy," Garry said as he took down a sign entitled "The Rotarians of Truth or Consequences Welcome You."

"You got zeal," Leland said. "Getting the Indians to sign will be pigeon soup."

The sky over the Indian country at Tonatai was black. The Indians had taken their accustomed place for the meeting and they were convinced that George Bowman was going to spoil everything. The women were seated on the floor in all their jewelry with their babies stacked in cradle boards along the flour sacks. The women too were concerned that the white trader might ruin their day. The babies, leather bound into the cradle boards, did not care much one way or the other but their serious, same faces looked up at their fathers' faces at the counter and mirrored their worry.

"Look, Sansi," one of their fathers said carefully to the trader. "Why do you want to ruin everything?"

George put down his pencil and looked up at More-Wives-Than-Anyone. (He only had two. He did not have more wives than anyone. He did not, for example, have more wives than A-Cover-for-All, who had four and his eye on another.)

"I don't want to spoil anything," George said quietly and for the seventh time to the dark and powerfully square-built Indian with the hair bun on the back of his neck called More-Wives-Than-Anyone. "I don't want to ruin anything. I just don't want you to sign something away that you would regret later."

"But put yourself in their hogan, Sansi. You come all the way from Houston, Texas, to see the miserable Indians. Can we be rude? Would that be nice?"

George had been over this many times this afternoon so he did not look up from the marks he was making in the sheep ledger to say anything.

"They come all the way from Houston, Texas, and you wouldn't cross the trail to give us hello."

"Maybe not." George was annoyed now and went ahead with his marking in the ledger seriously.

"I withdraw that, Sansi. You come with your bottled magic when we're sick and credit when we're hungry. But all the way from Houston, Texas, is quite a thing even if they are dishonest. It's a long way to come even to steal something."

"It is," George said without looking up.

"Then they think highly of us."

"Of what you've got," George said.

More-Wives-Than-Anyone turned now to the ladies seated on the floor. He had made the trader concede something and he felt entitled to some small applause. The Indian women gave it to him with their eyes and the jiggle of their heads and they looked over to the Coca-Cola box for their hero to buy them Pepsis all round. More-Wives-Than-Anyone nodded his head to George's flunkey, Tom-Dick-and-Harry, that he would pick up the tab and Tom-Dick-and-Harry began opening the bottles.

"One more victory and I'll be ruined," More-Wives-Than-Anyone said.

Paracelsus came in now. He was dressed in a finely tanned leather jacket and matching moccasins. He must have divined that the Indians were baiting George because he gave More-Wives-Than-Anyone an annoyed look before he sat on a pile of sheep hides in the corner where he could speak to everyone.

"Why really, I hate to say this but this section of The

198

People is so smart."

The others looked down on the floor.

"I hate to say this, but you think nobody has a culture but yourselves."

The People shuffled their feet.

"Why really, I hate to say this but you think everybody on the big reservation is crazy. You think their religion gives them no togetherness with nature, has nothing to do with medicine and is for the ignorant and the superstitious. You think their work is to go around in circles rapidly. You think their gods are the dollar, the big car and inspirational books. You think they think what is good for the big car is good for the country and what is bad for the big car is good for the enemy. Why really, I hate to say this—" The medicine man hesitated now, began again and hesitated and then said in a weak voice, "Why really, it is only in part true."

More-Wives-Than-Anyone was feeling set up. He half turned at the counter. He had won a great victory without even opening his mouth. The medicine man had come in to do battle with him and the medicine man had knocked himself out. The victory was so complete, enormous and sudden that More-Wives-Than-Anyone did not trust it; it might be pyrrhic. The medicine man might have laid an ambush. More-Wives-Than-Anyone said nothing, just rolled his body in the corner of the counter in front of the women on the floor and the babies at his feet and hoped the medicine man would hit himself again.

"Oh, you're so smart, oh so smart, making me do that to myself," the medicine man said. "And I hate to say this but it is true that The People feel themselves so superior to the white man. You make no allowances for the fact that the white man never had an opportunity to become civilized, no allowance for the fact that he has spent all his time learning and studying without any opportunity to think. To you a white man is just an animal with just enough brains—" the medicine man looked out toward the mountain that held Los Alamos—"to build something complicated to kill himself with."

The medicine man got off the stack of sheep hides. "But that's not the terrible thing," he said, pacing the floor in front of the brown and stiff-boarded babies. "The terrible thing is that you've got me believing it. But there is a salvation," the medicine man said carefully.

George dropped his pencil. The word, any word that dealt with absolutes, always scared him.

"Our salvation lies," the medicine man said, thinking carefully and in a low voice on which everyone hung. "Our salvation, our loss of arrogance" (he used the Indian word "asidisah") "lies in helping these two white men from Houston. If they want the uranium, give them the uranium. If they want to get rich rich rich, let them."

"You could use a few dollars yourselves," George said. All the Indians nodded in agreement.

"But, Sansi," the medicine man said with confidence, "we could all use a few hundred dollars but those people from Texas talk only of billions. What would a civilized Indian do with billions except perhaps become uncivilized." All of the Indians nodded in agreement.

"But those particular people," George said slowly to the medicine man, "are dishonest."

"Evil," Paracelsus said. "But I'm not their medicine man."

"But how do you know the whites will not put our uranium

to peaceful things?" More-Wives said.

"They never have," the medicine man said.

"They could change."

"But evil does not change. Sin changes; it is a way of looking at things. They punish sin. They allow evil to grow great."

The other Indians did not agree this time; they did not want to rub anything in, and Paracelsus too went back quietly and sat on the hides.

George Bowman thought: we live and we change big or we do not live, and maybe that is why, for the past fifteen years, I have been only half living. George let go of it with this and went back to his ledger, consoling himself with the knowledge that the Navahos in this allotment area, although it was not a true part of the reservation, could not lease the mineral rights to anyone without a tribal council okay, and the government Indian agency would not allow them to sign anything before a battery of Philadelphia lawyers looked at it. Nevertheless, if his Indians signed something it would tie the rights up in court for a long time with the Indians getting nothing.

"Look what I got." Silver Threads had come in the door with a piece of yellow something. He had been to town playing professional Indian for the tourists in a costume that amused the Indians and on his way back he must have discovered this. He placed it on the counter.

"I found it in the Puerco Wash," he said. It was a beautiful object, yellow and chrome and all sparkling.

The medicine man touched it gingerly with his brown, turquoise-ringed finger.

"It must have something to do with the white man's religion but perhaps I can use it at our next yebechai."

George had been examining the chrome and yellow object with the care of an archeologist. Now he stepped away from it and the Indians waited for him to identify it correctly.

"It is," George said slowly, with a scientific caution for the truth, "a left rear gas cap top, stop light and combination design treatment for the fender fishtail section of a late '55 or early '56 Cadillac Eldorado or coupe de ville."

The Indians were impressed by this careful classification of an unknown culture.

"Then I was wrong about it being something to do with their worship?" Paracelsus said.

George thought about this awhile and said, "You could be wrong."

The Indians were impressed by the scientific lack of certainty while George looked out at the dark, lowering sky.

"You say you found this in the Puerco Wash?" George questioned Silver Threads.

"Yes. Enormous wheel tracks going up the wash."

George looked out carefully at the sky now and with the same movement reached blindly for his large Stetson.

"We got to get going fast," he said. "Some white strangers are up the wash. They can't turn around in the Puerco and won't have enough knowledge to run before it's too late. The way the rain just broke on the mountain the water will come down in a flash flood with a fifteen-foot head."

George was already through the door with the Indians following. Outside, the sky above the Navaho country was very low, weighted down, black within a heavy dimension of black.

They got the taut, quick-dancing, wild-eyed horses pinned

along the corral and threw on bridle and saddle. Rabbit Stockings got off first, pulling his wild, paint horse within a tight circle outside the corral. George came out now and pulled his lashing horse into another small circle alongside, then they both broke toward the cloud-shrouded mountain where the water had collapsed.

Lord Acton, Paracelsus, Silver Threads and More-Wives-Than-Anyone shot out of the corral all at once, causing a storm of dust that enveloped them and the post and any sense of direction so that it was minutes before they caught Rabbit Stockings and George, long horsetails flowing, and leveled out, running easily and fast beneath the gay-striped flag rock of the Penistaja Mesa. Silver-Threads-Among-the-Gold flowed up in back of George, deepened his spur until he pulled up alongside, leaned out and over and shouted in perfect Hollywood English, "Ride 'em, Cowboy!"

At the Puerco Wash there was another tangle of gaudy, flashing horses within an explosion of dust before Rabbit Stockings picked up the trail and fled up the wash followed by all. The canyon rose, sudden bright and towering on both sides, the horses were diminutive, antlike and scurrying toward the wall of water they could all hear now, the horses panicked and charging toward the equally charging wall of death, bearing down with all speed on each other with the gentlemen from Houston, Texas, somewhere in between.

"This is a nice place," Garry de Grasppe said from his seat down on the running-board section of the yellow coupe de ville. "But I don't think it's the main highway." He passed the gallon of rum to the other.

"I don't think so myself," Leland Hepburn said, taking the bottle.

"Let me read that letter," Garry said. "I want to read everything Alfred ever wrote."

Leland passed him the letter.

"Can't read it," Garry said. "The type keeps moving." He tossed the letter on the ground. "It looks like there's a storm up ahead of us."

Leland picked up the letter and put it in his pocket. "It might be an important message. Anyway if Alfred wrote it it's important."

He paused now, the giant jug frozen in mid-air. "You hear something?"

"Yes! Yes! Yes! Look!"

Now they saw the wall of water like a sudden miracle in front of them as their extended, horror-risen arms were yanked almost from their sockets and their bodies flew behind the mad horses up the cliff. Everything was a giant roar and flashing of bright hoofs in their cut faces before they were deposited or thrown high on a pile of greasewood.

The horses, sobered now and thick-lathered, paced deliberately in 8's above the heavy flood, the riders still helpless yet to talk. The two gentlemen from Houston, thrown on the greasewood, were too shocked seemingly to talk ever.

They all had a furtive glance at the yellow-and-chromed coupe de ville poised at the top of a crested, pig-and-chicken-house-foaming mountain before it collapsed, the yellow-and-chromed monster sucked within the great curling lip of water and smashed down somewhere deep into the banded iron red earth from which it had so recently arisen.

"Sho'h. Sho'h. Sho'h," the medicine man said, dismounting and beginning a circle around the two whites which the others joined. They all seated themselves, none speaking, all still insensible from the sudden happenings. They all waited, deadened, for the medicine man to speak, to explain the happenings.

"You bring contract?"

"Yes, but after what happened we'll tear it up. We bring peace. Peace," the white man moaned low. "Peace. Oh yes, and this letter for a man named George Bowman."

George took the wadded letter that Leland extended. He noticed that it was from someone called Alfred Marlowe. He put it in his pocket. He would read it when he got home.

"Sho'h," the medicine man said to the Navahos. Sho'h, George knew, meant listen. He walked to the outside of the circle while the medicine man repeated again, "Sho'h."

"The gods have taken away the white man's magic and cast it into the earth again. Sho'h. Listen."

The Navahos leaned forward.

"It could be a sign to all the earth-surface people that we are responsible for the world."

"Sho'h. Sho'h," all the Navahos repeated.

"A sign that all the earth-surface people are responsible for the world, but soon the world will go back into the world and bright objects will be no more and earth will become earth again like it was when The People came."

"Like it was when The People came," the Navahos chanted.

And the Navahos continued to chant, "Like it was when The People came," weird, rich chanting that became a polyphonic sing above the heavy flood.

Even after George Bowman left and was working his horse back slowly and alone beside the bright-banded cliffs he could still hear their high sing above the steady, deep movement of the flood. They might have a sing far into the night, certainly until the loud, quick flood receded and the white men made their way back across the arroyo, back to the seething city, and all this quiet, sprawling land, shot with a fiery sky and empty with the weird, strange-shaped emptiness of the beginning, was again filled with the huge, awful silence—like it was when The People came.

George gentled his horse across a flat world of rock and sage, sharp and pungent with its perfume, alone, and the whole broad spread of the infinite land, still virgin from the oily chrome paw and smoke of civilization, still blessed—like it was when The People came. George was home now and he dismounted.

14

George dropped his horse at the corral and as he moved toward the post he noticed a purple convertible making its way over toward the buildings beneath the mesa. Ten minutes earlier and he would have been caught in the flash flood, George thought. But he dismissed the arriving car from his mind and went inside and over to the roll top desk to read the letter that simply had GEORGE BOWMAN on it, that the tall blond gentleman had handed him. He straightened it out and read.

My dear George Bowman:

As a friend of your brother's I write this because nothing he has written to you seems to get through. Perhaps when you suspected the source you tore them up. Perhaps you had good reason. I only write this to say that if Alexander does not get home he will die. That last obstacle to your allowing Alexander to come home again will be removed when you get this. I am leaving with Perrette. I meant Alexander will die not only literarily but literally too.

Sincerely,
ALFRED MARLOWE

P.S. After much thought and discussion with Perrette we have decided that the best way to leave a person like Alexander that she does not want to hurt would be to do it quickly.

"Well?" Quicker-Than-You said. He had come in silently and was standing over George Bowman's shoulder.

"I thought you were at the sing," George said.

"I left," the Indian said. "The medicine man is getting orthodox. What about the letter?"

"I will answer it."

"When?"

"As soon as I have some time. I have things to do for The People."

"He is one of The People."

George Bowman looked sadly around the post then up to Quicker-Than-You and then back to the letter on the desk.

"He is my brother," he said.

"That should make it easier."

"Supposing someone ran off with your wife."

"Which one?"

There wasn't any use talking about it to an Indian, George thought, fingering the letter, or a white. You couldn't talk about it to anyone. You couldn't talk about it to yourself. This is one of the things you bury. You forget it. You do good works for the Indians. Other people do good works for the Lord. You do good works for the Indians. You bury things in good works.

Some of the other Indians had come back from the sing now, probably to buy something. Then George Bowman noticed a white stranger coming through the door. He was probably out of that odd car George had seen when he was coming home. George got up from the desk and went behind the counter. There was something about the white man that set him apart from even white men. It was not the careful carelessness of his expensive clothes nor the shock of red hair above the typical wide, simple, open, honest face of a confidence man; the white stranger was set apart by some strong inner, spurious dedication that was scored in money or names and pictures in the papers and gossip columns and called success. He was, in all probability from Mars, and if George had reckoned incorrectly on his first guess, then it must certainly be Venus, New York City or Saturn.

"Hollywood," the man said, stopping in front of George Bowman. "I'm from Hollywood. Tell me," the man said, stroking his violent red hair and leaning forward on a pile of blankets toward the trader. "Did they even bother to deliver the letter up here that you did not answer?"

"Yes," George said and he began to make a geometric design out of the boxes of wool dyes that were scattered on the counter.

"And you did not bother to answer a personal inquiry from the director John Dykeman?"

"No," George said. He was stacking all the turkey-red dyes in a separate pile.

"John will get a big charge out of that," the Hollywood man said. "John Dykeman is outside now."

"Who is John Dykeman?" George asked.

The Hollywood man turned to the seated squaws who had arranged themselves in a line on the floor against the counter facing the babies who were thonged into private boards and stacked against the flour sacks.

"He asked who John Dykeman is," the Hollywood man said, smiling toward the squaws.

The squaws sympathized with something the turkey-red man was telling them, with an understanding nod of their heads toward him, and then they all looked at the trader with a stare that said he was impossibly dense. They spoke and understood no English.

"John will certainly get a charge out of this," the Hollywood man said, studying the trader. "Look, maybe you can see him out there. We're serious up here all by ourselves. No women. All the rest of the studios are around the world someplace making *War and Peace*. They'll shoot a million feet of film and five million dollars in Yugoslavia or someplace, then they'll come back to Hollywood, burn what they took and make the picture for a hundred thousand—all that's left in the budget. Not John. John will make *War and Peace* when he's in the mood to make *War and Peace* and he'll film it all in Russia. Look, you can see him through the window now. No women. I'm not kidding about the no women bit. We actually came all the way up here without any women at all. John will be in as soon as the notion strikes him."

The group of male Indians that had drifted in from the sing were watching the scene, leaning against the adobe-log wall alongside a stack of hides. One of the braves, More Wives, was mounted on his own saddle on a wooden sawhorse. He had pawned the saddle with the trader but he used it when he felt like it which was now. He was practicing leaning far out dangerously on the saddle and picking things off the ground. More Wives was upright in the saddle now after a swipe that pleased him. "Who in the hell is John Dykeman?" More Wives said.

"I like this. I like this. I like this very much," the Hollywood man said. "But I suppose we can carry it too far. The gag, the bit is good but don't milk it."

George went back to his business of arranging the rug dyes, More Wives went back to practicing (he was roping cattle now from the saddle), the babies went back to staring at the women and the women went back to staring at the men.

"I've got it! By God, I've got it!" the red-haired man said. He took out a beautiful handkerchief and wiped his face. "The bit is good, so good that it fooled me. The bit is that you never heard of John Dykeman. Let's play it that way."

"That should be easy," George said.

"That's a good line," the Hollywood man said. "But don't try to fool me any more. Remember I'm in on the bit now too. I'll go find John. John will get a charge out of this."

When the turkey-red-haired man with the very white skin had left More Wives got off his saddle, coiled his rope and came over and sat on the counter in front of George.

"I think maybe we go too far, Sansi," he said to George. "You were a genius not to answer the letter. It worked perfectly. It brought them down here on the double. But I do not think John Dykeman will get this charge out of not being famous here that Turkey Red thinks he will. I think he'll charge right back to Hollywood and we won't get a chance to wear feathers and holler, shoot white men and get overpaid for it."

The Indians in the shadows along the adobe back wall chanted an Indian word in agreement.

"Maybe," George said. "But if we want to build him up we won't recognize which one he is even."

"He'll be dressed in some clown costume," More Wives said. "And he'll act like God."

"All right," George said. "But what pictures did he make? You won't know what to tell him he is great about."

"Hollywood God is not interested in the particulars, Sansi. You worship with words like 'spectacular,' 'the greatest.'

Words like 'More-Wives-Than-Anyone,' " More Wives said.

"That's an Indian important word," George said.

"But you get the idea, Sansi."

"I get the idea," George said. "And I agree to try it. But don't overdo. Don't ham it up."

Outside the Hollywood man did not find the other Hollywood man for a time, then he saw the purple car parked on the edge of the yellow mesa. He was a while climbing and when he got there such a long minute had gone by that he couldn't hold it in any longer.

"John," the red-haired man said, "they've got a wonderful bit going on down there. I'm in on it now too. The bit is that they never heard of you, don't know who you are. To them you're just another white man."

"It's not bad," the other Hollywood man said thoughtfully. "As long as they don't overdo, as long as they don't ham it up."

The Hollywood white man, the director John Dykeman, who did not have red hair but a plaid cap, also wore a suede jacket with a fringe line along the chest, a black string tie and squaw boots.

"I cased the tip," the red-haired man, who was the assistant to the assistant producer and who was named Wiles Baedecker, said. "Like you thought, it's the real thing, John. A picture here would lose tons of money."

"Listen, Wiles," John Dykeman said, relaxing from his poetic pose, moving his suede squaw boots under him. "I don't want to lose tons of money."

"John, John," the other said.

"No, I mean it, Wiles," John Dykeman said. "No, Wiles. Just because the studio said I could do one of my own after the last smash I did for them, that doesn't mean necessarily that the thing I do now will lose tons of money."

"Oh?" Baedecker said.

"I simply want to make an honest Western picture of Alexander Bowman's first book right here where he wrote it."

"A sincere picture."

"That's right, Wiles."

"A germane picture."

"That's right, Wiles."

"Bust the studio."

"I don't follow your humor, Wiles."

"You won't get to shoot *War and Peace*." Baedecker's voice was edged hard now. "Remember they said no *War and Peace* for you if you lost a bundle on this one."

"I've got to have *War and Peace*, Wiles. And I've got to make this Alexander Bowman Indian picture honest, sincere and germane."

"You're getting me in the heart, John."

"I must say I don't follow your humor, Wiles," John Dykeman said.

Inside the log-and-adobe post the Indians were practicing a war dance. They had never done or seen a war dance before but Tom-Dick-and-Harry and Silver Threads had seen many movies and the other braves had seen some and they were all going up and down in a conga line and making war whoops when the director and Baedecker entered.

"Oh no," John Dykeman said. "Oh no."

"Aren't you John Dykeman?" George Bowman said.

"Oh no," John Dykeman said. "Oh no."

George took a long pipe and offered it to the director.

"They switched the bit on me, John," Baedecker said. "They're playing me for a patsy."

"Stop them," John Dykeman said.

"Cut!" Baedecker hollered.

The Indians halted the war dance, More Wives stopped shooting and the dead Indians were risen from the dead. When all the noise of the shooting ceased the babies and the squaws seemed disappointed.

"You people are not with it," Baedecker pronounced in a loud voice. "We're up here to get a story line on an honest, sincere, germane script on the contemporary Indian. Let's not have any more war dance."

"But they thought this was going to be fun," George said.

"No, let's get this straight, sir," Baedecker said carefully, but his voice still low. "John Dykeman is an artist, sir. Anyplace else in the world except right here they would recognize John for the artist he is."

"Don't overdo, Wiles," John Dykeman said, examining the beaded belts.

"No, I've got to say this," Wiles Baedecker said. "It's got to be said wherever false values threaten integrity. John Dykeman is the type of man that what Louella Parsons and Hedda Hopper and all the other movie columnists say in praise of him means nothing. He doesn't even read them. You know what he was reading on the way up here? Spinoza. Bennett Cerf and Leonard Lyons mention him every day."

"He knows they're just columnists," John said.

"See what I mean?" Baedecker said. "The *Saturday Review*, the best newspapers, to John they're nothing. He's in a class with George Bernard Shaw."

"Shaw is dead," John Dykeman said.

"You see?" Baedecker said. "To John even George Bernard Shaw is dead."

"I mean Shaw is really dead," John Dykeman said, putting down the belt.

"You see what I mean," Baedecker said. "With John Shaw is really dead."

"I think we've established the point, Wiles," John Dykeman said. "Let's get down to the business."

"Okay. Everyone line up along the wall."

The Indians had already resumed their former positions along the wall and were ready for anything.

"Okay," Baedecker said, going to the head of the line. "Now, after each of you answer the first thing that comes into your head I will place in your hand this crisp new five-dollar bill."

Baedecker removed a sheaf of new money from his inside coat pocket. "I guess we're ready to roll," Baedecker said. "Remember this has got to be spontaneous, we've got to find out what you Indians are really like. We can work better with you if we know what you're really like. No help from the audience. Say the first thing that comes into your head."

He stepped in front of Rabbit Stockings. "Okay," he said.

"Okay," Rabbit Stockings said.

Baedecker placed a five-dollar bill in his hand and stepped in front of More Wives. "Okay," he said.

"Okay," More Wives said.

Baedecker placed a five-dollar bill in his hand and stepped in front of the next Indian. "Okay," he said.

"Wait a minute. Wait a minute please," John Dykeman said. "Wiles, they only repeat what you say."

"Please, John, let me do this."

"I won't let you give them each five dollars to mimic you."

"It worked with the Esquimos, John."

"It didn't work with the Esquimos. They said okay too."

"They're both primitive people, John, so they both happen to say the same thing. Is that so strange? To me cogs are beginning to mesh. It traces the primitive pattern right down to here."

"I think they know we are the primitives by now," John Dykeman said.

"John," Baedecker said, running his hand hopelessly through his red hair and relaxing the sheaf of money to his side. "John, I don't think you meant to say that. I don't think you want to lose face this early."

"Okay, roll it," John Dykeman said.

Baedecker stepped in front of and got an okay from each of the Indians and when he had finished John Dykeman asked how much it had cost.

"Seventy-five dollars," Baedecker said.

"And we call the picture *Okay, Baedecker*," John Dykeman said.

"Please don't fight me, John."

"Gentlemen, gentlemen," George said, sliding over the counter. "What are the Indians going to think?"

"Young man," Baedecker said, rising up in all his small majesty. "We might spend one million dollars right here if John Dykeman is pleased. Now, after your speech, do you think John Dykeman is pleased?"

"Don't overdo, Wiles," John Dykeman said.

"But," George said, "do you have to act like a tribe from Hollywood? Can't you act like human beings at least?"

"No," Baedecker said, his voice rising. "Because we're not

from Hollywood and we're not human beings."

"We are human beings," John Dykeman's voice was insistent now. "And our residence *is* in Hollywood. That's true, Wiles. That's true."

"All right, it's true, John," Baedecker said. "But it's not true, John. You're not a human being. You're a great artist. There's a difference, John. You're not Hollywood, John. You happen to live there but you're not Hollywood. How many times has the *New Republic* said that? How many times has the *Nation* said that?"

"How many times?" George asked.

"You never heard of the *Nation* or the *New Republic*?" Baedecker said.

"No," George said.

"Then your inquiry was an attempt at levity."

"And humor too," George said.

"Well, we don't think it is funny, do we, John?"

"It wasn't a bad line, Wiles. But I think we're all hamming too much. Let's get back to the business."

"All right," George said. "The way I understand it you want to make a Wild West cowboy and Indian picture here and my Indians think it would be a big time, a lot of fun."

"I'm sorry, sir," Baedecker said. "But art is serious. There's nothing better that John would like to do than make the picture you describe."

"Oh, I would not. I would not," John Dykeman said.

"Will you wait for my punch line, John? Will you please wait for the punch line?" Baedecker turned back to George. "John would like to be human. He'd like to relax too and make Hollywood pictures but he's an artist. Can you understand that? Am I getting through?"

"No," George said.

"Then we're wasting our time with these feebs, John."

Quicker-Than-You pushed himself off the wall now and made his way through the squaws and babies and saddles. He was tall and broad-shouldered and he stopped annoyed in front of the talking people.

"Our trader, here," he said, touching George Bowman and looking down on the Hollywood people, "I don't like you strange people trying to—" The Indian hesitated and began again. "I don't like you people—"

"Patronizing him," George said. "But they're not, Quicker-Than-You."

"I think we were," John Dykeman said.

"I still don't think we were," Baedecker said.

"I think you'd better go out and wait for me outside, Wiles," John Dykeman said.

"No. I want to—"

"I said to get the hell out."

Baedecker crept out.

"I want to try now to make this clear," John Dykeman said.

"I think you've made it very clear," George said. "But we've all got to make a living."

"Yes, but we shouldn't fool ourselves," Dykeman said. "I'm beginning to believe what the columnists say about me. I think I've been believing it for a long time now."

"You've got to make a living," George said.

"But how low can you get?" Dykeman said.

"You don't hurt anybody," George said. "And I understand you have made some pictures that are better than most.

That must be difficult with the pressure and I respect you for it."

"Thanks," John Dykeman said. "We make one sometimes that I think might stand up. But I think this one is off."

"The Indians could use the money," George said. "Why is it off?"

"I've been looking around," Dykeman said, "at the country outside and the Indians here and I think it's too real. I think the landscape looks too real and the Indians too real. It's not convincing. I think it would lose money and, as Baedecker says, I can't afford to lose money on this one, not if I'm going to make *War and Peace*. True, the book was about this country but *Oklahoma!* was about Oklahoma and we made that in Arizona. *The Texan* we made in Utah and this one, I guess, we'll make in Hollywood."

"Well, I hope the red-haired man recovers all right," George said.

"Their feelings recuperate quickly when their swimming pool is at stake," Dykeman said. "I tell you, I would like to buy these Indians a drink."

George nodded to Tom-Dick-and-Harry to serve Pepsis all around, which he did.

Baedecker thought it might be safe now to creep back in again but he stayed well on the periphery of the room until he was absolutely certain.

"What's the picture now, John?" he called from a distance and from the protection of a row of saddles.

"The picture is we don't make this picture here," John Dykeman called back.

"Great. You mean we're going to make *War and Peace*?"

"Yes. We're going to make *War and Peace*," John Dykeman said.

"And we'll make it in the Ukraine, John?"

"Where else would one make *War and Peace*?" John Dykeman said.

"What about the Russians, John?"

"I think you can take care of the Russians, Wiles."

Baedecker was across the room now and had his arms around John Dykeman.

"Baby, baby. John, doll!"

"Don't overdo, Wiles."

"No, baby. I mean, I'm serious, doll," Wiles Baedecker said, pointing up to where the Indians could see the hanging hides. "I can see your name up there now in red neon half the length of Broadway. *War and Peace*, produced, directed and written by John Dykeman."

"Well, good-bye," John Dykeman said. "If he ever writes another book we'll be back."

"Who?" George said.

"Your brother," John Dykeman said. "You didn't think we came here by accident? We were here considering a remake of an old book of his, *The Big Rider*. We own the rights."

"It wouldn't cost us anything for the rights," Baedecker said.

"Why don't you buy his last book," George said, "and make that?"

Dykeman looked around the room and toward the door.

"Because it was terrible," Baedecker said.

"Well," John Dykeman said, "it wasn't that—"

"It was terrible," Baedecker said. "Terrible."

"We'll make the next one," Dykeman said.

"He's finished," Baedecker said. "Alexander Bowman is dead." Baedecker walked out the door and stopped under the log overhang, his small voice resolute now with satisfaction. "Alexander Bowman is not really dead. It's worse, much worse. Alexander Bowman is simply dead."

John Dykeman closed the door and faced George. "Don't believe him," John Dykeman said. "A man, as long as he's alive—"

"I know," George said.

"And don't judge us by people like Baedecker. This Baedecker is a clown, a hunker," John Dykeman said. "A Hollywood name for those who get our coffee, know the baseball scores and we strike matches on."

"Yes," George said.

"You'll see," Dykeman said. "Soon Alexander will be back here and in a position to see things as clearly—"

"Yes," George said. "Certainly."

"God," John Dykeman said. "You look awful."

George followed the visitors out and when they got in their car and drove away George kept right on walking. He walked for several hours, and he thought—I write you this to tell you that if he does not come home Alexander will die. I mean this not only literarily but literally too. Alexander Bowman is dead, the red-haired man had said. Not really dead but worse, simply dead. Dead and dying. Dead—

George walked until he was on top of the mesa and until his foot struck something. It was the old mine shaft.

"This," he said, touching the top of the mine shaft with his foot, "was my first attempt to win something or to get even with a person who always won, to become a person myself, to exist. And after he won the last one, after he won Perrette, then I did not want to play any more. Since then it has been a steady retreat, a withdrawal into the Indians in the guise of protecting the Indians from the Moving People and all the rest of it, including the drought and the uranium people and all the rest of it. But all along it was the Indians who were protecting me from life. Getting back into life again is not easy. Alexander had to lose everything. And does that make me win something?" He kicked the mine shaft. "Not a damn thing. Fifteen years trying to win. Not a damn thing. Fifteen years is a long time but it will never be more. You can't win because the other guy loses. It will never be fifteen years and one day more. You can't back into victory. You can't win because a brother loses."

George turned and, moving fast, stumbled down the mesa. He ran through the desert, the moon edging up now and the sage cutting him as he ran toward the boarded-up petrified-wood house. He made a big jump that landed him on the porch. He reached up and ripped off the two by six that was nailed across the door and then heaved all his weight into the door against the rusted lock whose key had been thrown down the mine shaft fifteen years ago. He heaved his weight again and the door splintered and George found himself in an enormous space. He went around lifting dry and dusty window shades, letting in some pale moonlight. The pallid light lit up the great fireplace, the oval rotogravure pictures of the Bowmans around the wall, the wide bear and Indian rugs along the floor; it lit up too a candle placed upon an oak desk above a drawer from which George extracted pencil and paper.

He sat down and wrote and when he had written it all he

signed it, sealed it and stamped it and wrote his brother's name and address on the envelope and got up and breathed easily and deeply and well for the first time since God knows when.

"Since eternity," he said, moving toward the window.

15

I tell you I seen her—Perrette," Jack said. "Or somebody who looked exactly like her. And there was a man there too, in the same place, with a book."

"And the man with the book, could it have been Alfred?" Alexander said. "Could it have been a poet?"

"Poet? I wouldn't say anything about a man that I wouldn't say to his face," Jack said.

The Mexican village was quiet and dark and the noise of the horses was very clear in the narrow street. The houses were joined together and made a wall so that it was like going down a dirt lane banded on both sides by the same dirt. Each house in the wall was marked by a piece of burlap door that was lighter colored in the darkness than the wall. On horseback you were higher than the low mud barricade and you could breathe and feel the cleanness of the quiet night. There wasn't any moon.

Alexander and Jack rode into the big square now, which had a fountain where the washing was done. At the far corner of the square, on the leaning mud wall, there was a green globe with the numerals 504. It was supposed to light up the sign *Casa de las Santas* but it didn't quite make it. On the street of the café were abandoned several tired cars in junk attitudes dangling Mexican license plates. Guarding the cars that, years before, had had everything stolen, was a sharp and yellow-faced man who might have done it. When they rode into the square the car watcher ignored them with the thoroughness of a used-car salesman during a war. The car watcher was stationed under the green 504 globe with a piece of somebody's sweat-rotted underwear in his hand. He was stationed also in front of the only car that looked as though it might run. It was a sparkling chrome-and-pink, bucket-seated, disk-wheeled sports MG with California plates. Along the fountain was a rusted iron rail where two wisely stupid-looking burros were hitched. The two men dismounted near the burros and tied up.

The sharp-faced car watcher abandoned his MG and scuttled over to them, only a dim shape now away from the light.

"Guardo los caballos para un peso," the car watcher chanted.

"No," Jack said.

"Cincuenta centavos?"

"No," Jack repeated.

Inside it all went very dim. There was a good-sized oval dance floor with orange and blue Chinese lanterns strung across it. It must have been intermission when they walked in because the orchestra wasn't making any noise at all. It sagged on a platform in the rear, all pomade and teeth and once red jackets. When it spotted them it made a noise, dismal and without hope. It became a loud inertia; a wild chrome trumpet went off alone, blown by a fat man and muted with rags.

They had to make their way along the edge of the dance

floor to get to the bar that ran the long length of the other side. The girls pulled in their legs for their passage. They had made their faces into the universal female mask of Hollywood so that they could not be separated from the *New York Times* society page or the girls working the Via Veneto. Their dresses ran from white, hand-sewn cambric with lace such as children wear for their first communion, to the latest J. C. Penney imitation of Dior and Mainbocher thrown out by some desperate drummer from San Diego.

When they got to the bar Jack said, "There he is, the man with the book."

"Hello, Alexander," the man with the book said. "I've been looking for you." It was Bentley.

Alexander and Jack sat down at the bar.

"Where's the girl?" Jack said.

"Oh, the girl," Bentley said. "I sent her back to Hasbrouck Heights. It wasn't Perrette," Bentley said to Alexander. "I was sorry to hear about it."

"Yes," Alexander said.

"I figured you'd be low," Bentley said, "with your last books and now this happening. Here, let's have a drink."

They had a drink.

"I have a proposition," Bentley said.

"Oh?"

"Yes," Bentley said. "I guess we never figured there in Europe when you were somebody and I was nobody that old Bentley would make it to the top and be able to help you the way you helped me. Top?" Bentley repeated. "Well, I guess some people would call it that. I got a big job at the studios. Top?" Bentley said again. "Well, let's call it that. Anyway I can help you."

"Help me?" Alexander took a sip of the drink.

"Yes," Bentley said. "I'm story editor and the studio wants big names. If it's a has-been it doesn't make any difference. Even though you haven't had anything good for five years I've convinced them that you still have a name."

Alexander looked around the room and then at himself in the back bar mirror.

"You've convinced them that I have a name," Alexander said.

"Yes," Bentley said. "It took a little doing."

"And if it's a has-been it doesn't make any difference," Alexander said.

"No," Bentley said. "You kind of coast. At the moment we have in mind an Indian Country story. We got a couple of young whiz boys at the studio. We've already cracked the story. All you have to do is leap-frog these boys, do every third scene. Then on the credits you get all the credit. The studio wants a name."

"In the credits I get all the credit," Alexander said. "All I have to do is leap-frog the boys and I get all the credit."

"And all the money too," Bentley said.

"All the money too," Alexander agreed. "And all the credit. Credit for what?"

"It hasn't got a name," Bentley said. "We'll think of something on the plane."

"Certainly," Alexander said. "How stupid of me. Why didn't I think of that? We can do the whole thing on the plane."

"Almost," Bentley said.

"And then when the plane lands I can leap-frog the boys," Alexander said.

"You mean you don't want it?" Bentley said.

"That's right."

"Think a bit," Bentley said.

A man came up and put his hand on Alexander's shoulder. It was the congressman who had been asking for directions back at the hotel, long days before.

"Well, I found it," Willborne said. "It took me a long time. I had been by it four or five times. If only I'd stopped to think a bit the first time I wouldn't have wasted so much time. All the time I thought it was a church, nothing but a church. But inside it's the real thing. How's about a drink?"

"No, but thanks," Alexander said.

"Oh, there's a man looks like an American," Willborne said, marching toward Jack.

"Who was he?" Bentley asked.

"The world is in his hands," Alexander said.

"Yes," Bentley said, "but let's get back to this important thing. It could be that you have had it. I'm not saying you've had it, but I want you to think about this offer for a while."

"It's no," Alexander said.

"I think you should think about it awhile," Bentley said.

"I've thought about it all my life."

"All right," Bentley said. "I'll tell you the way I see it. You people see a few writers like Fitzgerald get pushed around out there and defeated, but don't forget Scott was a rummy." There was a silence and Bentley ordered another drink. "That's the way I see it," he said.

"It's the way you see it," Alexander agreed.

"I'm offering you your last chance," Bentley said. "All right, so you go along with some box-office pictures, but if you make good you'll get a decent assignment, the chance to adapt something of your own."

"If I make good," Alexander said.

"Oh, this art bit," Bentley said. "This art kick. We all go through it. God knows I have more than anyone, but we grow out of it. We face reality."

"Do we?" Alexander said.

"If we're going to survive," Bentley said. "Where's the bartender? Yes, I can't quite follow you, Alex. You're the one writer I know, including those who are taking from them, who never panned the movies. And now they offer you what may be your last offer on a silver platter—and nothing?"

"Nothing," Alexander agreed.

"Well, I give up."

"Thank you," Alexander said.

"You just keep repeating," Bentley said, "everything I say."

"You say it so well."

"I was just trying to help you," Bentley said. "You know you helped me. God, back there in my naïve days I printed a lot of junk. If it wasn't for your stuff we would have collapsed long before we collapsed."

"Let's go," Jack said, attempting to escape Willborne.

"All right," Alexander said.

"Before you go, Alex," Bentley said, "how about a loan? I could let you have a thousand."

"No. No thanks," Alexander said.

"And don't worry about Perrette. She can take care of herself."

"I wish you were right," Alexander said, moving toward the door now.

"We must keep in touch," Bentley called.

"Yes," Alexander said as he closed the gold-leafed door for himself and Jack.

"Well, I guess we looked for her about every place that's likely," Jack said.

"Yes," Alexander said. "She's gone back to the States."

"With that fellow you spoke about. The poet."

Alexander sat down on the curb in the dimly lit street. "Yes," he said.

"Well, neither of us could follow her there," Jack said, still standing and commencing the business of a cigarette.

"True," Alexander agreed.

Alexander lit a cigarette and passed the light up to Jack, who had completed making his.

"Not until I hear from George," Alexander said. "But I should be hearing from him one of these days, especially now that Perrette has—"

"I've got to tell you something," Jack said. Jack sat down on the curb next to Alexander. "You know," Jack said, "back in Indian Country they call me a rustler but you people always got back what I took accidental."

"Yes," Alexander agreed.

"You remember as a kid," Jack said, "whenever some of your cattle was missing you two boys used to ride out to my place, used to carry a wooden gun to ambush me, launch attacks at me from the bushes, until I got off my horse and laid down and died for you. Then you'd go home and tell your father you couldn't find the cattle but you'd killed Jack the Rustler again. But your cattle always did show up cause we got along. Remember all those Wild West stories I told you?"

"Yes," Alexander said, "but what's that got to do with what you want to tell me?"

"Nothing," Jack said, "except I got to tell you a Wild West story this time that's true." Jack paused and went down on his haunches next to Alexander. "You've got to get back to Indian Country and you're waiting for a letter from George. And I got to tell you something."

"Yes."

"It's not coming," Jack said.

"There must be something more."

"Yes. He said he would try to write a letter."

"Nothing more?"

"No," Jack said. Jack's cigarette flared brightly. "You weren't thinking you'd hear from him because—?" Jack blew out a puff of smoke that Alexander waved away. "Well, because he got you out once before—the mine shaft?"

"Maybe," Alexander said.

"Well, there's nothing wrong about that. It adds up all right," Jack said. "Except—"

"Excepting what?"

"Except nothing," Jack said. "It adds up all right."

Alexander got up now. "Excepting what?"

Jack's hand-rolled cigarette had flamed briefly then collapsed. Now he thought he would roll another.

"The facts," Jack said. Jack mothered the makings of the cigarette into his chest.

"He got me out. That's enough," Alexander said.

"I didn't want to tell you this, but there's no use you wasting your life waiting for a stubborn brother. No, he got you in," Jack said. "Anyway he saw you fall in. I got it from an Indian that George swore to secrecy. George knew where you were the whole three days."

"Then why didn't he, the first day—?"

"Maybe it was because he was at last in the position of your not being the hero. Maybe for the first time he was the brother who was somebody, the brother, the somebody who was going to rescue you."

"Then why didn't he the first day?"

"Maybe because he enjoyed being important, enjoyed being a person for the first time without your shadow big over him." Jack paused and went back to his cigarette, then said, quietly, "He is gentle but he is stubborn. So maybe he will make you wait forever."

"But he did finally. It was him—"

"No it wasn't," Jack said. "It was Tom-Dick-and-Harry who was walking straight toward your hole—couldn't have missed it. It was only then that George decided he must find you."

Jack noticed the expression on Alexander's face and said quickly, "But I think he was about to do it, about to find you. Anyway just about to pull you back like he is now," Jack said.

"Now?"

"Yes," Jack said. "Something could happen back there to make him change. Time could make him change. Back there when I talked to him he almost got it out—almost said you could come home. You've got to hold on."

"But there's nothing now to hold on to," Alexander said, beginning to walk away.

Bentley came out of the café and walked toward them.

"You boys want to join me?" Alexander said, making toward another yellow café door. Jack and Bentley paused.

"This could be the final chapter," Alexander said, turning. "I'm not too bad at last chapters. Why don't you join me?"

"I—I guess not," Jack said as they both turned and moved off, leaving Alexander alone. They had seen his face beneath the dim café lamp. They were both frightened.

16

Alexander entered the café that was mirrored all round. He sat down at a mirrored table on a mirror-backed chair and had several drinks. Then he began carefully explaining to himself what a great old Indian fighter Kit Carson was. No one disagreed but he felt he should concede the point anyway that Kit Carson, the old Indian fighter finally had difficulty locating old Indians. Alexander broke away from his profound thoughts now and looked up from his drink.

"O Captain, my Captain!" Alexander called to a dim figure who had just entered the house of mirrors through the yellow door and now seemed to be trying to go through one of the walls. It was Captain Fleet, the bore that Alexander had been avoiding with all of his craft since his arrival, the one who owned the tourist mecca next to the hotel.

"O Captain, my Captain!" Alexander called. "The ship is in, the prize is won, oh come and have a drink."

The captain moved over to the table, seeming in the mirrors to be coming from all directions. His many heads were covered with a stiff crew hair cut that was gray and a stubble of beard the same shade so that his whole head seemed to be one bristle. His small dark eyes, almost no nose and weak mouth were the only alien matter in a perfect brush.

"Oddly enough I have news," the captain said with a British cut to his voice. "It's rather important too. I think you better leave and get back to the foreign quarter. Mimi Jimenez is looking for you."

"Sit down, O Captain," Alexander said, patting the mirrored chair back. "If there is a war party coming we may have to take to the hills. The captain must not be found sober. Now what is all this talk about getting back to the foreign quarter? You sound as if you spent too much time reading my lesser works. Where did you ever pick up dialogue like that? I've been bad but never that bad. Tell me, O Captain, have you been reading the opposition?"

"You are underestimating the situation," the captain said, taking the chair. "This chap can become very awkward." The captain had acquired British mannerisms of speech to, in the expatriate tradition, isolate himself more completely from himself.

"It seems," the captain said, "that you chaps arranged a do and now it's been called off and he's very drunk and he's got this machete and he's looking for you. It seems as though he holds you responsible for the whole mess."

"I didn't call it off," Alexander said drinking his tequila. "Alexander Bowman never call it off. Government call it off. Alexander Bowman is annoyed with Jimenez for co-operating so abruptly with government."

"Well, it's gotten most complicated," the captain said, fishing his eye around for a drink. "He's down in Louis' bar now, or he was a few minutes ago, explaining it to everyone who would listen. It isn't logical any more. You know it never is with a Mexican-Indian chap when he gets drunk. It seems as though it's boiled down now to the fact that he thinks you want to get yourself killed and he's going to oblige."

"Never should sell these Indians firewater," Alex said. "It's against the law in my country. Keeps them off the warpath."

"I don't think we should make a joke of it," the captain said, with thirsty seriousness, still casting his eye. "That old wharf of his you know, it's been in desperate circumstances for the last years. Since the tourist fishermen won't use his boats any more he's been up against it. What with the city condemning his firetrap and the local people not using his boats now he counted quite heavily on your name for the tourist publicity. It seems now that this thing has been called off the poor chap is ruined."

"That's too bad."

"After all it isn't his fault, old man, exactly, is it? After all if the government—" The captain interrupted himself to help himself to one of the drinks. "And don't forget that machete he's got," the captain pronounced, squeezing the lime directly into his tequila.

"Ever hear of Geronimo?" Alexander asked, finishing his drink and motioning an order for the captain too this time.

The captain shook his head as though he had never heard of any kind of an Indian.

"There are only supposed to be three great Indian warriors," Alexander said. "Unless you call that wild flurry of Sitting Bull's important. But there is another fighter, my boy Geronimo."

"Does your son actually fight?" the captain asked.

Alexander quit. The captain was not sharp today. The captain was never sharp. It was impossible to write lines for the captain and if you changed the captain's dialogue as much as it needed to be changed it ended up not being the captain,

not being any captain, not being anybody at all but some fig-
ment of some anoymous typewriter's imagination with all the
credibility of my last book.

"But why should you, Mon Capitaine, why would you not,
Mon Capitaine, make a decent last book?" Alexander asked
aloud through the brain fog of his ten tequilas, through all
of the cheroot soot and perfume stink, through all the whore-
dom and boredom of the Tres Bolitas. "Why would you not,
O Captain, make an admirable admiral, O Captain."

"You don't seem to realize this machete business is bloody
serious." The captain's voice was excited without any of the
inquisitorial dignity of Alexander Bowman's booze. "You
don't seem to realize, old man, that Mimi Jimenez is out to
give you what for, right here, tonight. You see," the captain
was intimate, sliding his glass forward for emphasis and hint,
"he's figured it all out. He's figured that only a man who's
reached the end, only a man who wants to commit suicide,
would swim to La Paz. So he's figured his last charitable act
in Mazatlán before he leaves this ingrate town for a brighter
land will be to oblige you. To kill you. This last auto-da-fé
will be made somewhat easier for him he claims by the suspicion that he does not love you."

"Does not love me," Alexander repeated, stroking his face
as though hand and face were frozen with alcohol. "I do not
believe it. I conclude," he said with his inquisitorial alcohol
voice, "that it is a plot to get back on the plot and I want to
live my life. I do not want to be a story book, I do not want
to become an adaptation for the movies, I do not want to
become another book club selection. I only want to get drunk
—that means irrelevant dialogue, that means no story line.
Can't you understand that people have a right to live, a right

to write, to be real, alive, irrelevant, irreverent and impossible?"

"Yes," the captain interrupted. "But you'd best get back to the quarter. You can get drunk, do what you like there, but it's bloody dangerous here."

And now Alexander noticed that the mirrored walls had twisted his face, distorted his whole body; all the objects in the room became rubberized. Things distended and then all crammed together in a ball. Mouths as wide as caves and feet on stilts as though they were all in some childish fun house of mirrors.

Perhaps I have been given a Michael Finn, Alexander thought. Why don't they get some air in this place. His body was turning all hot and then suddenly cold with the same rhythm that the multi-faces in the mirror switched from crouching gargoyles to giants. The thing to do, Alexander told himself, was to maintain his freedom of movement, not to fall down sideways into a lump under the table and become the prey of every cutthroat in the quarter. Alexander heaved onto his feet, not feeling his legs under him but feeling the higher altitude, feeling the change of air, the increased thickness of the swirling smoke, but still not focusing absolutely on anything. The strategy would be to work his way back to the bartender, to anchor his flank at the bar so that they would have to come at him frontally. Then too, the bartender would be directing the enemy and there at the corner of the bar, Alexander thought, he might be able to get in on their staff conferences. He floundered now, hitting a glass-top table, and listened to the crash, but always maintaining his mobility. He was going well; one more good step and it would be an orderly retreat. He made one last final lunge at the corner of the bar and made it, clutching, dangling there. And now I can regroup my forces, Alexander whispered to himself and wiped a sheet of cold sweat off his forehead with his numbed hand.

"Usted," Alex commanded the bartender in a gravel voice, "usted, bring me the bottle of tequila. Traígame la botella de tequila, por favor. Put down the bottle in front of me so I can pour it myself. And a glass of water."

The bartender did as he was commanded and Alexander congratulated himself that he had put the enemy to work bringing up his supplies.

Alexander observed now the squashed bulk of Bentley surrounded by Leroy and Howard with Guaymas still written across their chests, spearheading a flanking operation against his right wing. The mirrors multiplied them into a small army, elongating their foreheads into a hundred gleaming helmets. Don't fire until you see the whites of their ties, Alexander told himself. Bentley halted now to reconnoiter the position.

"Lay on," Alexander baited him.

Bentley and the same army of Bentleys leaned against the bar. "I want to buy you a drink," the spokesman for the Bentleys said.

"Yes, you want to poison the command. Are you afraid to fight it out in the open?"

"I want to buy you a drink," Bentley said. "I'm with you."

"With me? Then you should know what it's like to be me, to lose everything, your home and your work and everything that was close. But I'm just resting now. I'm planning a way back. I'm going to try and find where I did it wrong and try to do it right another time."

"Splendid," Bentley said. "I will help you."

"Yes," Alexander said, stalling, adjusting at the place at his neck where his tie should have been. "Yes," he said, and thinking now—the thing to do is to plunk him with an arrow as soon as he comes out. And if that doesn't work try not to fall for his peace offerings.

"Do you want a treaty of peace?" Alexander asked.

"I simply said that I wanted to buy you a drink," Bentley said, getting up on the green stool.

"Do you know who I was?" Alexander asked, turning the white bottle of tequila on its axis and studying the lettering.

"Yes," Bentley said, "you were The Writer."

"No. I was That Indian," Alexander said, but he mumbled "that writer" to himself a couple of times to figure if Bentley meant well or ill, then he suddenly progressed several jumps ahead in his thinking and decided that Bentley was trying to sell him something and he slammed the glass down upon the counter just as a man came up at his elbow and confided in a bartender voice, "Let the kid alone," glancing at the corpulent Bentley. "The kid's all right," the voice continued in a hushed whisper. "Let the kid perform. Let the kid ride. Don't rope his animal."

"I was just walking along minding my business when out of a Mexican sky this man—but that's all right, Jack," Alexander interrupted himself. "Just stop this place from going up and down, if you've got any interest in it at all. Stop these mirrors from squeezing everybody, stop my legs from going rubber so I can withdraw from this position in good order."

So Jack and Bentley had not deserted him and neither had Leroy and Howard, so there are good whites, including the blacks.

Alexander felt now for Jack along the bar as far as he could reach but he was gone and Bentley was gone and Leroy and Howard were gone too; the only thing that was still there was the recurrent waves of heat and cold, and all that was there was an awful mob of whores and bores squashed into one big blob spreading and contracting on the mirrors.

Alexander mopped his numbed hand across his forehead. Everything was icy and desolate and the cause was lost. Terry was all for turning back, Reno and Colonel Benteen were all for crossing the Little Big Horn. (Face the arrows, Custer, the beer people want to paint the picture.) But Reno was a fool and Benteen was ambitious and now Custer was forced to lean heavily on his Indian scout for advice. Under the weight of the leaning Custer Alexander slipped on the ice that darkened the swamp down to the Little Big Horn. The Indian scout sprawled heavily on the rubber ice. Reno and Custer reached down and grabbed the Indian scout and Jack whispered into Alexander's ear, "Steady, old man."

"The ice," Alexander mumbled.

"No ice in it at all," Jack told him. "You're drinking straight tequila."

Alexander got up into a position where he could hold onto the bar.

"Now get those Indians under cover and feed them properly. I'll address them in the morning. But as for now, let's have rum all around," he told the bartender.

"You've been drinking tequila, sir," the bartender said.

Alexander could see that the bartender was oily but a mere white boy, a mere white boy who had never played Indian.

"I said rum," Alexander said. "You pretend to speak English. Rum. Ron. Aguardiente. I know where I am and what I'm doing. I'm in Mexico and in a little town outside of

Mazatlán. Although I appear to be here alone on a scouting expedition there is more than meets the eye. I am actually reinforced by a visiting cattle rustler, a literary chap—and two friends. Now let's have rum all around."

"Yes, sir."

"And don't sir me," Alexander said. "I'm an egalitarian. I left General Custer there on the floor."

But Alexander was not thinking about that. He was thinking very much about how he was feeling, and he was feeling very much the way the people in his stories felt after they had been given a Mickey Finn. For certainly, Alexander thought, he had only had nine or ten drinks and he had always been able to go nine or ten drinks with the best of them without falling on the floor and fighting the war. Soon, he knew, if it continued to go like this he would be on the floor fighting the Civil War, assisting General Grant, or maybe on the floor with Georgie Patton, advising against a frontal attack on Metz, or on the floor with General MacArthur at the Republican Convention. Anyway soon, in here in this heat and with that knockout wallop in him, he knew he would be on the floor. Right now he knew he must get back to the Indian Country. But he must not, he thought, go out the front, he must not go any place or anywhere that anyone who might have had anything to do with harassing him could be. Even Bentley, who was obviously innocent, must be avoided. Certainly the bartender and even O Captain and quite decidedly Jack, who on the surface seemed decent enough but who, after all, was a white man. That left only Leroy and Howard. No, somehow he must back out the rear, covering his retreat with remarks about the arrival of the cavalry. Somewhere back there among the pileage of bottles, garbage, boxes and broken crockery there must be an exit, an escape to the Indian Country.

"Hold it," Alexander announced, holding his long arms over the heads of the others. "Everyone keep their seats and no one retreat until I get back."

When Alexander was safely away from their eyes, behind three stacks of Carta Blanca, he came to a sign marked CABALLEROS. He knew that to go in there, in the stink and airlessness of the small room, was to invite an immediate knockout plus a small session on the floor at Wounded Knee, and then to be searched and macheted and thrown in an arroyo to die with the dogs. Maybe that was building it up but he could not take any chances. He felt his way back now in the semi-darkness, past more cartons of cerveza, piles of broken chairs and shattered mirrors until he saw a piece of neon light falling through a busted door. Alexander got out the decomposed door, and even the hot tropical air, thick and humid, smelling of rotted flesh, iron roofs and alcohol—even this felt refreshing and sharp and gave him enough lift to be able to sit down on a nearby beer barrel without falling.

A harsh electric sign blared out now across the street—TOME PACIFICO—and somewhere a radio was going at incredible speed advertising sex hormones. The lights began going on down the alley, yellow electric weaknesses that lit the religious signs over fallen doorways. There was a faded bunting of purple and once-white over each hovel signifying the day of St. Teresa. A weak-kneed drunk trotted bandy-legged from a camouflaged and decomposed bodega and collapsed triumphant. Some parchment-old mestizos were making their way gently down the intersecting alleys toward the church, and above him and to the left angry flocks of birds were beginning to fight for the right to a night's refuge in an over-hanging jacaranda tree.

Alexander managed to get to his feet. It was not an easy thing to do. Although the dry retching had left him he was seized now with vertigo. The sign across the alley—TOME PACIFICO—bleared in a weird whir of color. The birds above seemed to dart with insanity and the obscene world about him tipped at an odd angle. Alexander leaned back heavily against the wall and grabbed at a molding of rotten brick. He would hang on here at the corral until his head cleared, until the awful belt he had received in the stomach was no longer trying to turn him inside out. If he could hang onto the corral long enough it would clear up.

Just when he had the plan all figured out, just when things were going to pan out all right if only he had the time, just when he was pulling out of his disgusting and abject helpless-ness—then Alexander saw him.

He came around the broken corner of the alley, the machete first, red and blue in the Tome Pacifico glare. Then the greasy and protruding belly, beneath a conical-shaped head, long Asiatic eyes and no neck. It was Mimi Jimenez come to see if Alexander had tried to beat it out the rear. Alexander could do nothing, his body still numbed and racked. His only sense of feeling was where his fingers dug into the rotted brick, his long form impaled against the decomposing and iron-shot wall. The only thing that could help him was that the Indian was borracho too. He seemed to be balancing himself with the silvery machete.

"Har you wanting to play, har you wanting to run away?" Mimi had a long silky mustache that would never need cut-ting; it seemed the only place on his face that hair would grow. He used a soft musical, almost gentle voice. He said, "Har you going to make goddamn fool of Mexican by not keeping word?"

"I keep word," Alexander said almost as though he were trying to reassure himself, not speaking aloud.

"Makes no difference anyway. Lose everything anyway. Goddamn writer sonabitches talk against my wharf. Now everybody go watch American bazaball. Condemn my wharf for firetrap."

So that was it, Alexander thought. Mimi was going to blame him for everything that had ever happened to the poor wreck.

Mimi sidled up to Alexander now with an arrogance born out of Alexander's helplessness. The top of his conical head did not come up to Alexander's shoulder. As he rubbed closely Alexander could smell the reek of cheap mescal and perfume. Mimi raised the machete with a gliding motion and then lowering it slowly ticked off the buttons of Alexander's jacket with the razor-sharp edge. "You will never more need these," Mimi whispered.

Alexander knew he had no strength left, not even enough to hold himself up without grabbing the wall. But he could drop all his weight on him—Mimi Jimenez was directly under him now, slithering the machete down his side slowly as though measuring Alexander and at the same time planning a quick insane run down the alley while Alexander bled away in the gutter.

Abruptly Alexander dropped all his tall hulk on Mimi and felt him beneath his body like a gigantic inner tube. Alexander tried to grab and hold him but his arms were useless, still numbed. Alexander got up with an effort of violence and with the same momentum began to run crazily down the narrow passage, careening from one hard wall to the other, feeling his hands and head scrape against the aged brick. And now he reached an intersection where there was no wall to career off and he fell face down on the cobblestones, where he could hear the scrape of the retrieved machete, and he knew that Mimi was close again.

Alexander made it up once more, not feeling his legs under him as he made another long drunken dash. This time it ended falling through an open doorway, smashing into some wooden benches. His head was against another wall beneath the flickering light of two candles. The noise following had ceased now as though this particular doorway afforded some invisible bar to the pursuer, as though the doorway he had fallen through were some taboo, some sanctuary.

Some church, Alexander thought and glanced up past waving candles to the waxen face of a carved saint. He tilted his head toward the five-and-dime festooned altar, garish with tinsel, paper flowers, bloody saints and varicolored votive candles. There was no service at the altar, no movement in the church save around the confessional booths that stood like sentry boxes down the aisle.

Despite his noisy entrance Alexander seemed to be going unnoticed. Not that this happened every day but their ignoring it seemed to be their technique of discouraging it. A young woman in rags dropped a coin in the box above Alexander and exited with the weightlessness of the starved.

Alexander's head was commencing to ache, a long throbbing steady beat, and he could hear above the pain a low, low murmur from the confessional boxes. Cuántos veces? The voice of the priest repeated quickly. The priest was confessing two people at once and Alexander noticed that there were cubicle holes for three so that the priest was only working at two thirds of his efficiency. Alexander wondered, watching the somber aquiline face, if the young Jesuit was not up to confessing the entire world—the universe. And if God Himself had walked up to the third cubicle, would not that unassailable face murmur, Cuántos veces?—How many times?

Just when things were clearing up again, just when he felt he had some control over his limbs, at this point he had a relapse and he could no longer make sense out of anything in the church. He could no longer see the things around him properly or think about them at all. He could think of Perrette and then he thought of Alfred and wondered what Perrette and Alfred were doing. What would become of George and his Indians? That would certainly be worth writing about and living about and that he would never know if this insane Mexican had some luck when he stepped outside the church.

Now he got back to Perrette, and Alexander was very very unhappy that he had said such unkind things about her in his last book, and no one could mistake who she was. He had done everything but mention her name. Yes, one of his big regrets, if the machete had any luck, would be that he had talked too much in his books about the things that he knew a great deal about, and although that was the way they told you at the universities, why had he been fool enough to do that? Why had he cheapened every experience in his last book by telling the whole world about something that was none of their business? He had not done it for money or fame because he had both of these things when he started telling the truth. No. He did it because he wanted to confound all those who admired him, to be alone and the big cock of the walk. Instead of that, near death now— Near death now. The thought hit hard even into his numbed, insensitive brain and there was a surge through him to regroup himself, to organize some sort of resistance back here in the rear and make some attempt to break through to the reality of the reservation. Near death on the steps of a small Mexican church in a red-light district was not the way he had written it in any of his books. His last book did not count. Expatriates always die of self-inflicted wounds. He was repeating himself, he had already told the cab driver that. But he had not told the cab driver that they were administered by a gentleman named Boredom. But in his books that counted his heroes met their death for other people. On the surface it was something else that was mixed up with war paint and banners and fate and circumstances but beneath it all they were in control, they were not victims, they were not men that things happened to. They were men who had a healthy respect and fear of death but preferred it to watching human beings become not human beings.

No, this kind of gutter death here would not read well. It would make a lousy ending. It would give too much satisfaction to too many writers that Alexander thought had sold themselves cheaply. The fact that his friend Tolstoy had died in a railway shack didn't help any. After all, a railway shack could be associated with the working man but a gutter is associated with dead dogs and drunks.

And what can I be associated with now, Alexander wondered. His head was spinning and diving, huge colors tearing all over, with no sight. He felt the church tilt under him and he thought he saw the black, moldering Pieta above him oozing blood and all of the altar seemed on fire, and before the blaze small men in black were struggling with a catafalque marked CIVILIZATION which in reality was only a horrendous emptiness that they were offering on the pyre. And their strugglings were a mere simulation of great effort to confuse the new arrivals that clustered around the now empty three cubicles of the Jesuit priest's inlaid sentry box for confessional. Now they all marched inside the box, first a man with his brother's wife, then they came two by two. Two wise men and two fools, two of everything and still they came. The inside of the box was neon lined and on the ceiling were the scalps of those that had been there before. Now they all began to dance around a hole in the floor that might have been a mine shaft. There was someone way down there at the bottom of the hole; they could hear him calling but they knew it was only a human being down there so they continued to dance. They did not seem to realize the scalps on the ceiling might be the scalps of the dancers who had been there before so they continued to dance. People dance. What's wrong with dancing? Let's all dance. Those scalps on the ceiling might be artificial and the people below us are different from you and me. Let's dance.

The priest had pulled Alexander now onto a hard wooden bench, had an altar cushion under his head and was administering convenient holy water.

"Usted está muy borracho," the young Jesuit said in a low voice.

"Cómo no en este país?" Alexander tried to answer to the dim voice that was coming through. "Why not drunk?" he said in English.

"It's a small matter," the priest said, following Alexander

into the new language.

"You turn a confessor out?" Alexander wanted to know, his heavy lips moving, his eyes still not open.

"We'll get you to a hotel," the priest said, ignoring the other's drunkenness.

"But I have come to confess," Alexander insisted with some roughness.

"We will get you some coffee and we will get you to a hotel." The young Jesuit continued to wipe Alexander's forehead with holy water.

"I want to confess that I never should have tried to live among the whites, be tough. It must be that I am really a gentle Indian."

"But you're white. You're white."

"You grow up with the Esquimos and you're an Esquimo. You grow up with the Indians and—" Alexander broke it off and then said, "His wife."

"Whose wife?"

"My brother's."

"Then you have something to confess."

"It's too late," Alexander said.

"There is one God," the young priest said.

Alexander got up, stumbled. "I got to see a medicine man," he said. "I need the whole treatment."

"But someone is pursuing," the priest said. "I saw someone with a machete."

"I can take him," Alexander said, standing up deliberately. "I feel good enough to take him."

"I'll call a taxi and get you to a hotel," the young priest insisted.

"I tell you I can take him," Alexander said. "Anyway it's

not whether I can take him or I can't take him. You just don't run away from things, that's all."

"You are being—what is the word?—silly," the young priest said.

"No. It used to be courage. I don't know what it is called now. In my youth in the Indian Country it went for courage. Maybe they use 'silly' now but I guess I just never grew up. I mean by that, that when people grow up they lose everything that it's convenient for them to lose when the going gets rough."

"Black coffee," the priest pronounced.

"No, I'm this way most of the time," Alexander said, leaning against the big wooden door now. Then he turned heavily away from the young priest and started going down the long low steps. He could hear the high voice of the implacable Jesuit call down, "Black coffee. Many times."

The soft night air across Alexander's face cleared the fuzz off his vision to the extent that he almost did not miss the step that he did miss, that sent him crashing down on the hard stone. He worked himself quickly into a sitting position on the standstone and wondered why he had been fool enough to trust his rubbery legs at this stage. He would need a little more of the night air before he tried it again. Perhaps the priest had a point with his black coffee.

"Har you tired, my fran? My goddamn sonabitch writer fran." It was the low intimate voice of the assassin, mi amigo Jimenez.

It wasn't fair, Alexander thought, that after he had built up characters in his books so carefully, so that everything they did and thought was well motivated and inevitable, he should have it out finally with a weakly drawn insane.

"Sit down and build yourself up," Alexander said, touching the still sun-warm, rough stone alongside him.

Alexander listened but heard no reply from behind him, no noise of movement or even sense of presence of his very good friend.

Alexander was feeling set up. This was the way to handle them—to ignore them or treat them with extreme lightness. Yes, he thought, Mimi would not even be worth a line in the book; he would reduce him to the myriad background; he would relegate him to one of those same anonymous faces that stared out at his war-painted hero from some continuous neon, burro alley saloon or bright banana patch. Why did I run from him at all? It was in the manner in which you would run from a bad odor, the reek wind of humanity, when all a person in my profession would have to do is slam the door with a few chosen words.

Yes, Alexander was feeling better. He even straightened himself a little on the hard steps in front of the cathedral. Alexander Bowman felt that soon he would be back in Indian Country. Then the full, heavy blow of the wide quick blade, going all the way, entered his back just to the side of his right shoulder and above his heart.

"Brother!" he whispered heavily into his big clenched wet hands.

There was an awful quiet in front of the dark cathedral as Mimi Jimenez stood straight a moment and took it all into his small, unsteady eyes before adjusting himself and then trotting softly across the alley to get on the winding street marked Boy Heroes of Chapultepec.

17

Indian country. That's what the train whistle blew, blasting out the syllables as clear as flame. When the train got going the big drivers picked up the rhythm—Indian Country—Indian Country—Indian Country. Now it stopped. It might never get going again. It was a very old train.

"It will get here any day now," Jack said, placing a nugget-studded watch back in his pants. "Like I said, I'm wanted back in Indian Country under the improbable name of Diamond Jack." Jack touched the long pine box. "He wasn't wanted back there under any name at all."

The six Americans were crowded in a bar, huddled around a box, waiting for the tired train, somewhere near the station in Mazatlán, Mexico. The man in the cowboy outfit, Jack, sat on the box. The two Americans closest to the box, Alfred Marlowe and Charles Bentley, asked the questions. Alfred's face was drained and poetic too, if he would remove the eagerness, which he never did, and Bentley was in tweeds and had graying hair above a too youthful face that was listening now.

"Yes," Jack said. "Man has bred hisself out of room and man is done finished. Indian Country's the only place left where a man can stretch his arms without breaking another's radiator."

"Yes," Charles Bentley said. "The Indian Country is even more, I suppose, then you presume it to be. But we want to know— Some of us, have come all this way—" He pointed to the others.

Jack looked at the others, then back to his drink, shifted his weight importantly on the box and then looked back to the others. It must be that they had all been Alexander Bowman's friends, Jack thought, except Perrette. She had at least been married to him. Perrette drank slowly and steadily, lifting her drinks with a regular rhythm to a superbly composed face, poised and invulnerable, all-wise and absolutely certain. Insane, Jack thought. Ready for the bughouse. Either that or the rest of us are. The others, Jack thought, were in some way connected with Alexander's business, or profession I guess they call it when you write. But not those two Negro ball players who were drifting with self-consciousness on the fringe of the group in the dim bar in Mazatlán, Mexico.

"A long way back to Indian Country," Jack said importantly and aloud and probably to annoy Charles Bentley and Alfred Marlowe. Jack shifted again on the long pine box, possessively and with a vanity as though he occupied a stage and the others were an audience.

"What do you two Negroes want?" Jack said.

"It's a public place," one of the Negroes said from the darkness he matched. "We don't have to want anything. Me and Leroy got the same rights as anybody else to be here or anyplace else. No one's goin' to push us—"

"Did you know him?" Jack said.

"Yes," Leroy said, the voice coming from back there

somewhere in the darkness he was mated to, the light as he spoke catching a gold highlight.

"Then I'm sorry," Jack said. "Perhaps one of these gentlemen will buy you a drink."

Alfred ordered more drinks and the Negro ball players pressed closer to the pine box. They still had their bright jackets on with GUAYMAS written across their chests.

Jack, Alfred thought, was maybe fifty-five, sixty or seventy years old. His age was hard to come by, concealed in a long and lank and wind-burnt and finely wrinkled face and a figure that had been horse-bent at nineteen. The Bull Durham string and label that dangled from his striped shirt pocket was impossible to come by in this part of Mexico so it was a badge, a kind of campaign ribbon, of the Indian Country, along with the boots and spurs too.

"So," Jack said, "first I'll fill you in on the—what do you call it?"

"Background," Charles Bentley said.

"That's correct," Jack said. "If you stand at one point in the Indian Country, say near Window Rock—well, I don't know. Say near—"

"Brooklyn." It was Perrette who spoke between the rhythm of raising the glass of straight American whiskey toward her youthful face. Youth—an age you grew out of except Perrette. She grew more into it. More into youth, excitement and new things. Youth, and finally now into this triumphant childishness, alone and absolutely dependent, sipping her whiskey like milk.

"Like I was saying," Jack said, "standing near Nargeezi." Jack rolled a cigarette with one hand as though a conjuring trick to pull them all closer, but the audience was listening anyway. Even Perrette paused now to get her bearings in this darkening Mexico.

"Of course this Indian Country's in New Mexico," Jack said. "All sage and mesquite, greasewood and dry, very dry. There is the Colorado mountains off to the north and east and that peak to the south and east is Sandia. After they concentrated the Indians in a camp and died off half of them they give them this plateau, dry, very dry, that was up for grabs with no takers. Alkali and such. No water. Kit Carson," Jack said.

"But we didn't come here for a historical—"

"No. To get the story," Jack said. "But there's no story without—what's the word you use?"

"Background," Charles Bentley said.

"Correct," Jack said. "Well, maybe Kit Carson wasn't the hero."

"I quit," Charles Bentley said. "But there is a story someplace in these woods and I will settle for your part in it."

"That's what he did—quit," Jack said. Jack had worked the cigarette up to his mouth finally and lit it with the same hand like a one-armed man. "Quit and took to trading with the Indians. Just traveling around trading without a gun among the brutal, warlike savages who must be killed or concentrated in a camp."

"That was in Alexander's book," Bentley said.

"Yes. Well, he finally settled down with a post and ranch in the Cuba country."

"All right," Alfred said. "That was in the book too. But how about the brothers now?"

"Now?" Jack said and he tapped the box.

"I mean," Alfred said, "did George and Alex get along all

right as brothers will? Did this thing happen quickly?"

"Nothing happens quickly," Jack said. "It never does. That's just the word they use out of laziness to explain what happened. When you're going to steal some fine cows you don't do it quickly. You study them a long time to figure if they're worth it. Maybe you are taken quickly by their beauty when you first see them, but after that the act itself takes a long time. Between the day you spot the animal you want and the day you cut the fence takes a long time."

"But how long did it take with them?" Bentley looked at the box and then over at Perrette. "She's not much help to us," Bentley said.

"You need a drink, Ole Hoss," Perrette said dully.

"But first you got to see it, how it was before she came there," Jack said. "Corn as high as an old shoe where people try to grow the stuff that don't belong there. Nothing belongs there that grows well anyplace else. Indian Country's the place for everything that the rest of the world's trying to get shut of—Russian thistle, chamise, grama grass, the Bowmans, myself."

"You don't think there was a place for them then on the outside?" Bentley nodded toward the box. "Among us?"

"No," Jack said. "They was Christians. I guess no place for them anywhere in the world. Leastwise not in any Christian country."

"But you knew his father," Alfred said.

"Yes. I used to steal quite a bit from him. A fine man," Jack said.

"But there was nothing in him that could have led to this?"

"Yes. He used to read," Jack said. The others waited patiently for him to begin again, studying over their drinks.

"By reading I mean that it got his sons in the habit of reading. It did no harm to him. He had lived long enough on the outside to be able to allow ample for the lies and prettifying of the men who wrote about the outside. And the stuff they wrote about Indian Country didn't confuse him either of course. But his son Alexander here," he tapped the box, "was ready to believe most anything he read about the outside. George, the other son, he went off to a war. That's where he found out. But Alexander never went anyplace except to a university before she came." He nodded toward Perrette. "I guess there's nothing more to unfit a man for life on the outside than a university."

"I used to teach in one," Bentley said.

"I figgered so," Jack said.

The two Negroes crowded toward the center now to where the others were grouped around the man who sat on the long pine box. The Negro named Leroy went down on his haunches alongside the box, then reached out and touched it.

"I knew him well enough," the Negro said. "He is titled to his privacy. If he wanted people on the outside to know about his life he would have written it. That's what he was, a writer, wasn't he?"

The big Negro still standing, said, "We didn't come for the story. We came for the funeral—the funeral of an artist."

"There ain't goin' to be one," Jack said.

The assembly moved over to the bar as the waiter set out the new drinks. They leaned over the drinks in an attitude of prayer.

"We just set it down in here awhile out of the sun," Jack said. "We're taking it to the train."

"No," Bentley said. "There couldn't be a funeral. I guess

258

all you would want the preacher to say would be. 'The poor son of a bitch.' I guess you couldn't hire one to say that and nothing more—not even that."

Bentley paused and someone went on. "How did he become a writer? I mean there must have been something honest—I mean plenty of opportunities—"

"He figured," Bentley said, "there had been so much dishonest sentimentality written about his country, the Southwest, by people all the way from dying Englishmen to those who gather in Santa Fe to read their gems to each other that he— Anyway he wanted to right wrongs."

"Oh, the poor son of a bitch!"

"No matter," Bentley said, "what original justification or cause he had for beginning writing, later on it can't be stopped. It becomes a habit, a disease."

"Like rustling," Jack said.

"Yes," Bentley said, not listening. "But about the Bowmans, I don't want to extrapolate—"

"Not near this box," Jack said.

"I mean," Bentley continued, "I don't want to put words in your mouth but was there something different—?"

"They was human," Jack said.

"Not really?" Bentley said.

"They was Bowmans," Jack tried again.

"But what was different about Bowmans?"

"Well, for one thing they had this peetrified-wood house."

"Then what happened to this one, Alexander? Did your damn petrified-wood house burn down?"

"Nope," Jack said.

"Then bring us up to date, to the brothers."

"This one's dead," Jack said.

"You're a big help, Jack," Bentley said, walking up to the bar with the others. Bentley took Jack to one side. "I'd like to get all the information I can on him. I'm planning a book—"

"He's gone," Jack said. "Someone's done made off with him."

"What?" Bentley said.

"The box," Jack said. "When we come up here to the bar I left the box back there. Now it's gone."

"No need to alarm the others," Bentley said. "Some fool Mexican saw you guarding it, thought it was something valuable, waited for his chance and made off with it. No need to alarm the others. We'll slip out the back here and have a look around. They'll abandon it when they pry it open and see it's worthless."

"Worthless?" Jack said.

"Yes," Bentley said. "Now we go right through this opening."

They stepped into an alley.

"Now here," Bentley said. They stepped into another bar.

"We'll wait them out," Bentley said. "Give them a chance to take it to their hideout, den, whatever word they use. Give them time to pry it open and discover it's worthless."

"Worthless?" Jack said.

"Yes," Bentley said. "Two beers, please."

"Por favor?"

"Two beers," Bentley said louder.

Bentley looked around the adobe, cool room, clean and empty, white-washed pink, then out into the hot street.

"Nothing doing now," Bentley said. "We'll keep our eye on the alley." Bentley watched Jack examine his watch with style and then begin a cigarette. He doesn't tell time or make cigarettes, he performs, Bentley thought, and then he said, "That Alfred, I guess he wants material too. Material for a story. And those two Negro ball player friends of his, they want—"

"A funeral," Jack said.

"Now, Perrette," Bentley said. "When I first saw her in Europe she was painting a picture. It was very bad and she was quite pleased with it. I was editing a small magazine in Paris. I was embarassed about asking Alexander for anything because the magazine paid very little for stories."

"How little?" Jack asked.

"Well, we didn't pay anything," Bentley said.

"That's little enough. Two more beers," Jack said.

"I scout around now," Bentley said, "for a movie company that pays plenty."

"Make that two whiskeys," Jack said.

"You want the beer or the whiskeys?" the bartender said.

Jack stared at the man, who wore a big mustache on a round red face with a conservative, gray Homburg hat that had had the brim torn off.

"Both," Jack said.

"Well, I guess I'm not going to get very far with my story," Bentley said.

"I apologize," Jack said and he drank the whiskey. "A movie company. I apologize. I take off my hat. A movie company." Jack tipped his hat and the bartender touched his too.

"Well, now," Bentley said, "about the book. There should be a market for memoirs by people who knew him, now that there's been this trouble."

"Trouble?" Jack said.

"Well, death," Bentley said.

"That's trouble enough," Jack said. "Go ahead."

"I first ran into them on the boat, then again in Europe—"

"But where is he now?" Jack asked.

Bentley watched Jack take out his nugget-studded watch again, examine it and return it to his pants.

"I don't know," Bentley said, without humor. "I'm not a religious man."

"But we're supposed to be looking for him," Jack said. "I've set myself to see that this box gets on the train and back to—" Jack waved away some of the smoke to find his position in relation to the brimless gray Homburg of the bartender.

"From here," Bentley said, "we can cover the alley and beyond that you can see the plaza. From a well-stocked, well-located bar one good man might cover the whole country."

"Yes," Jack said, "if the whiskey held out. You said you met him again in Europe."

"Hello, Alfred," Bentley said.

Alfred Marlowe had entered, taken a seat at the bar and ordered a crème de menthe.

"Oh, no," Jack said.

"It seems," Bentley said to Alfred, "it seems that Alexander here—"

"Where?" Jack said.

"Oh, incidentally," Alfred said. "We have found him."

"Where?" Jack said.

"Those two Negroes, the ones advertising Guaymas on their chests, they have taken him to a church."

"Church?" Jack said. "Come on," he said, touching Alfred. "We've got to rescue him, bring him back here, wait for the train, take him back home and save his damn soul."

"Soul?" Bentley said to the bartender when they were alone. "Words are my business, yet I never knew quite what that one meant."

"In Spanish, alma," the bartender said. He pushed down on his brimless gray Homburg and then gestured emptily in the air. "It means nothing."

"Exactly," Bentley said. "Won't you join me?" The bartender poured himself a tequila.

Bentley looked out into the alley and back to the bartender.

"He got back to Mexico. That's as far as he got."

Bentley looked around the clean adobe room, out into the hot alley and over to the plane-tree-shadowed plaza. He could see too the corner of the gold-striped brothel and beyond and above that the slightly leaning tower of the church.

"Yes," Bentley said. "But now he will go all the way."

Outside Alfred paused. "No, I can't face him again," he said.

"He's dead," Jack said.

"He has passed over to the ages."

"Well, I reckon we'll still have to do something about him," Jack said.

Alfred leaned against the adobe wall of the cantina.

"How about a funeral pyre on the beach? That's what Byron did for Shelley."

"That's what who did for what?" Jack said.

"They were men without a home," Alfred said.

"Well, Alexander's got one and I'm fixin' to get ready to take him back. Back to Indian Country," Jack said.

"Yes. Then take him home," Alfred said. "That would be nice. A home would be nice. I was brought up under the influence of oil myself. We had about five houses located any place in Texas that was close to a very large bank. But no matter. I will found another magazine and Perrette can do the art work. People who have four or five houses apiece should stay together I guess and found polo teams or magazines against homelessness. Your taking Alexander home would be nice. He has luck to have a home. Your taking him back would be very decent. I cannot face him again myself but tell him this for me. Tell him I'm damn sorry. Tell him I'm awfully, awfully sorry. But tell him he made it. Tell him he will last."

Alfred looked up. Jack was gone.

Yes, Alfred thought. Yes. Yes.

Jack walked toward the falling-down railway station that backed up on the plaza. The two huge black Negro ball players were carrying the coffin easily toward the tired, long train that had finally arrived.

"They wouldn't do any good at the church," the leading Negro, Leroy, said as Jack came up. "They said he did not have the right religion."

"That's what they all say," Jack said. "Slide it in here."

They slid the box through the car entranceway until it rested between the seats.

"I don't know what religion you two fine gentlemen have got," Jack said. "But more people ought to get it." Jack sat down on the old velvet car chair next to the box. "Yes," Jack said, "if we had more Americans like you scattered around the world we could get shut of our ambassadors."

"Thank you," the Negroes said, leaving.

Jack tapped some of the Bull Durham into the clean white paper and arranged himself for a long trip. "And a right smart idea," Jack said.

Jack leaned over and raised the worn green window shade as the the train began to jerk, trying to get off. Outside Jack could see no one at all across the bare plaza. No one at all had come to see the train leave. Finally a figure, a woman, emerged from a bar on the far side of the plaza and began running now obliquely across the square. The train was slow and soon she was running alongside the train. She raised her arm when the train picked up speed, and as she began to fall back now she cried, "Good-by, Ole Hoss."

18

The slow black train that was working its way up the aged, worn track that writhed like a pair of shaken steel ropes along the Gulf of Baja California paused each mealtime so that those riding and hanging on to the train could eat. They built fires alongside the train in the morning and at noon, with vendors carrying things on their heads and women with great baskets selling things and putting things on the train. At Mazatlán they put something big on the train and when the train paused that dark evening at Culiacán they lit the long string of miniature dancing fires; they reflected against the aquiline, slanting Indio faces and the glittering machetes. The glare lay somber now, then leapt up in sharp pennants and, like small fires of hell, they silhouetted everything in grotesque. It was raining.

At Mazatlán a long box had been put on the very slow old train with coaches that had been discarded a long time ago from the fast, bright trains in the United States. Some of the coaches still had the frosted glass light globes in the shape of tulips. One of the Victorian tulip light globes shone on the long box the two days it took to make the trip to the border at Nogales.

Jack sat on the outside aisle in a velveted, old-fashioned chair next to the long box. When the train was jammed with people, animals and fowl at Huatabampo, some of the lady Mexicans, carrying wicker baskets crowded with gay-plumaged roosters, sat on the long box and Jack fed them cigarettes and candy and Wild West stories to pass the time of day. At Guaymas Jack explained to them about the long box and no one would sit on it now. One Mexican lady had three red-headed Muscovy ducks tied together with cactus fiber inside her coat with their three bright heads sticking out watching the world go by between her breasts, also watching while the Mexican lady put a flower on the long box.

The border at Nogales was as far as Jack dared to go but he stood quietly with his enormous hat in his hand while they transferred the long box to the bright United States train and then he went quickly and got himself the drink he needed.

At the Nogales side there were some people who watched the transfer too. They had come from the Arizona towns of Twin Buttes, Tubac and Pomerene. There were not many of them but they were there and they all had a small bunch of flowers they placed on the long box. The same thing happened when the Super Chief pulled into Flagstaff and at every town where the Super Chief stopped. It was still raining.

There were some New York and Hollywood people on the train going back and forth, back and forth to New York and Hollywood and Hollywood and New York. When they discovered who the other passenger was some cried and some told reminiscences but they all got drunk. When the train approached Albuquerque a whisper ran through the long, gliding train that the passenger was getting off and no one seemed to have much more to say. There was a deep, still hush now above the clickety click, clickety click, clickety click of the Super Chief.

"A man steals his wife and he goes to all this trouble to take care of him after a man steals his wife."

"Sansi tells me that Alexander wanted to see the whole world."

"But he took the wife of Sansi and left Sansi all alone and lonely with nothing to provide for except us miserable Indians. He stole the wife of his brother."

"We cannot take without taking from our brother," the medicine man said.

Paracelsus, the medicine man, was talking to Coyotes-Love-Me, but there were as many Indians as could get in the trader's blue pickup waiting on the railway platform in Albuquerque—waiting for the Super Chief that was bringing the long box. The long box would make a seat for the Indians that had to sit on the floor of the pickup on the long trip down from the checkerboard.

"A man steals his wife and he writes the man a letter telling him it's all right now, it does not hurt as much as it used to hurt, anyway it does not hurt as much as your not coming home hurts, as much as it hurts you and hurts me and hurts The People, your having no home to come to. It must hurt until something breaks. . . ."

"He was a lot of years writing a letter like your letter."

"Yes, he was a lot of years but he finished it, his writing of the letter. He finished it three days ago. He must have finished it about the same time something broke in the other

268

country. And these last days he has been carrying it, switching it from one hand to the other, looking for a place to mail it, wanting to mail it but knowing there was no place to mail it to. He could have written it, finished it, mailed it maybe, a long time ago, when there was someplace, someone, a brother, to mail it to, but he was a Bowman, a white man, a human too. Things keep getting in the way," Quicker-Than-You said.

A group of the Indians were huddled in the corner near the ticket office because the wind, cutting with rain, was blowing across the platform. George Bowman was standing alone with a small white envelope in his big hand, in the middle of the platform, upright against the rain, waiting for his brother, Alexander Bowman, and the Indians were letting him alone.

"A man steals his wife and the other man spends all night digging a grave on top of an impossible mountain."

"A brother steals from a brother and the brother spends all night digging on the impossible mountain," Paracelsus said.

"It sounds worse the way you put it," Quicker-Than-You said.

"No, you can't steal another person. You can only make a chance they were waiting for. It's hard to get a white woman to live among the miserable Indians. If Alexander had not stolen Sansi's wife the miserable Indians might have lost Sansi."

"Isn't that kind of selfish of the miserable Indians?" the Marquis of Steyne said.

"It may have been," the medicine man said. "The all-knowing whites might have been able to use one like him."

The band of Navahos watched while the trader, standing

269

alone on the big platform, faced into the blowing rain as they could all make out the growing hum of the distant Super Chief.

"I rode down in front with Sansi," the medicine man said. "I rode down in front with Sansi and he didn't say much. But he said his brother was an artist. I said yes but even an artist cannot smash things and he said that was not too important. The important thing was the work. I said yes but you don't let people smash things. Not if they can't make something better you don't, he said."

As the Super Chief wound into the station it could not seem to make up its mind exactly where it wanted to stop. It went forward and backward twice with the bunch of Indians chasing the baggage car back and forth, back and forth. There was the danger of something becoming a comedy.

The Hollywood and New York people had their faces pressed against the glass of the club car watching to see their passenger get off. There was enough curve to the track and with the long make-up of the Super Chief they could watch the Indians chasing the baggage car.

"It would make a good shot," someone in the club car, holding a very dry martini, said.

The Indians had caught the baggage car now and they banged on the side of the train with a stick and waited for the great door to slide open. The tall white man with a huge black Stetson who was alone on the platfrom held onto his hat and leaned into the rain-heavy wind as he made his way to the freight window to clear the long pine box.

The Indians had made the door of the Super Chief open now and they all crowded forward as the whites inside pushed the long pine box to the edge of the car with their feet. The

Indians reached in and slid the long box until it pointed toward them. Then as they pulled it out a pair of Indians, one from either side, put their shoulders under it. Quicker-Than-You and Rabbit Stockings were first, then More Wives and Lord Acton, then the Marquis of Steyne and Coyotes-Love-Me, then Tom-Dick-and-Harry and Silver Threads. Paracelsus, the medicine man, led the way with Lord Rundle holding on and guiding the end of the box. When the white dispatcher tried to stop them, demanding a piece of paper, Tom-Dick-and-Harry hollered from beneath the coffin, "Go to hell, man, and get out of the way!"

When they got to the blue pickup the white dispatcher was still trying to hold up the parade and he kept interfering until the trader, the tall, lank man in the big black hat who had been standing alone on the platform, came up and handed him a piece of paper for the box.

Paracelsus dropped the tail gate and they slid the long box into the blue pickup, each pair of Indians letting go with their shoulders as their portion of the box reached the deck. When the long box was safely in, the Indians climbed aboard and took seats on either edge of the box so none faced each other and they could all see everything that happened.

The Super Chief began to blow a high message now that she was going to leave. The people in the club car still had their faces pressed against the glass of the window as she began to move.

"A damn good show," the man still holding the very dry martini said.

On the long trip back to the Indian Country Paracelsus and Rabbit Stockings sat in the front cab with the trader. There was a Montgomery Ward car radio beneath the dash and Paracelsus turned on the Indian station in Gallup.

"What does an Indian want most?" the announcer said. He let the audience think about that for a while as he played a chant on the turntable.

"Money!" The announcer was back on again now. "Money. And you can get all you want from the Indian's white friend, Lending Sam Sepowsky, 999 Welter Street, Gallup. 999 Welter Street, Gallup."

The announcer played another chant but first he gave the Indians something more to think about. "How would all you forward-looking Indians like a used Lincoln to make you feel like you belonged? The Indian's friend, T. Texas Taylor, has permitted me to say that this car will be given to the first Indian who arrives on the lot with nine hundred ninety nine dollars and ninety-five cents. Never forget the Indian's friend who makes this offer possible, T. Texas Taylor. I repeat, the Indian's friend, T. Texas Taylor."

"You going to stop at the Casino de Paree for some gas?" Rabbit Stockings said.

"I filled her up at the Gulf in Cuba this morning. I should have plenty," George said, watching the road and thinking about something else.

"The boys all gave me a little to pay for the gas. They'd like to pay for this trip. So if you'll stop at the Casino de Paree."

"Okay," George said.

It was a long way to the Casino de Paree and the announcer from the Indian station in Gallup did not help much. In the back of the pickup the boys were getting a taste of weather their wives had on every trip.

"I hope he stops at the Casino de Paree," Tom-Dick-and-Harry said.

The road from Albuquerque to the checkerboard area swings gradually but steadily up and up. You leave the flat country of the Pueblo people not long after you cross the Rio Grande at Bernalillo but you do not get to the country of The People for a long time. There is not much in between. First there is the ranch country where you can run one head to thirty acres, then there is the country where you can run one head to forty acres and then the country where you run one cow to sixty acres. Anyway, by the time you get to the checkerboard area you've got to cut way down on everything. But all the way up is beautiful. It is the country where those who are called paleontologists find fossils that prove things about the whole world, where the uranium hunters are certain they will find something to change that world. And here there is mostly beauty; beauty in the long, high, ever-running-alongside-you cliffs; beauty even in the deadly erosions that are killing the earth; and beauty in the pure blue distant spaces with the Brahma-bull-shaped, cloud-hung mountains rising like other countries in another land; beauty that the blue Chevvy pickup was chasing through with quickness up to the top of the blue mesa. Up to the high, sighting-clearly-everywhere top of the blue mesa to a grave a brother had dug.

Between every Navaho chant he played the announcer would never let the people in the blue pickup alone.

"How would all you Indians like a conservative drape-shape to show that you belong? When you go some place you want them to say, 'There goes somebody.' Be somebody. Show them that you belong. See Dress Up Sam, the Indian's

Indian. They will say, 'There goes somebody who belongs.' The secret medicine is Dress Up Sam, the Indian's Indian. Sam, spelled S.A.M. Sam remembers you. Remember Dress Up Sam, the Indian's Indian."

This went on for another hour between chants and then they were pulling into the Casino de Paree. The Casino de Paree was a two-story hogan that appeared to be strapped together, lashed tightly to keep it from falling down, with neon tubing. Their first and last floor show was given by a medicine man who lost so much face he left the reservation and tried acting in wrestling but was last heard from making a comeback leading an evangelist rally in Stockholm. The neon tubing had never lighted up since its construction a lot of moons ago but there had always been plans to replace the gasoline Colemans any day now. When they entered the place Liquor Joe was seated in back of the bar with his hair properly tied in a bun on the back of his neck. When they had all yatayed each other More-Wives-Than-Anyone asked what the floor show was going to be tonight.

"Greta Garbo," Liquor Joe said.

"Every night Greta Garbo," Lord Acton said.

"Popular acclaim," Liquor Joe said. "Anyway she's all we can afford."

The Indians went around the place examining and looking under things until Liquor Joe set a bottle of Old Moccasin on the bar in a spot where it had long since burned a ring.

"What you boys drinking?" Liquor Joe said.

"Pepsi-Colas all around," Silver Threads said, letting a picture slide back that he was looking under.

"Big-time Indians," Liquor Joe said, getting the Pepsis. "Did you strike oil on the checkerboard?"

"Uranium," Quicker-Than-You said. "Soon as you get lights in here we're going to make a big bang."

"Big-time comedian," Liquor Joe said, opening up the Pepsis. "You give the Indians a nice place like on the outside and they run it down with bad talk."

"Haven't you heard," Quicker-Than-You said, "we Indians are victims of a one-way stream of acculturization. The whites are forcing the worst of what they got off on us and accepting nothing of our culture in return. So we are both becoming poorer. What I am trying to tell you is your whiskey is lousy."

"Planning a book or are you going to run for something?" Liquor Joe said, stroking his bottle.

The Indians continued to drink their Pepsis and look under things at the same time.

Liquor Joe stared out of the window and then suddenly his head gave a little jerk.

"What's that you got on the pickup?" No one answered him and he said, "Indians shouldn't get too close to something like that."

"You better fill her up with gas," Tom-Dick-and-Harry said.

Liquor Joe put down his bottle and moved toward the door as George came in.

"I filled her up," George said. "Ten and a half gallons."

"You probably could use a drink," Tom-Dick-and-Harry said.

"Yes."

Liquor Joe made a movement toward a shot glass with his favorite bottle but the trader shook his head and Liquor Joe got out another bottle and filled the glass. George dropped a small white envelope into his pocket and drank the drink down with haste and allowed Rabbit Stockings to pay for it from the fund. This was their day.

When they got the Chevvy pickup going good again they were hitting her along at sixty miles an hour, which is about all the Aztec-Bernalillo road will take; with the highway right-angling through the Chinle purple formations and sharp twisting through the red of the Wingate you have to be able to cut her down quickly. Signs like SLOW TO 40 and SLOW TO 35 went by. Signs like SLOW CURVE and signs like DANGEROUS WINDING ROAD went by.

"He did not know when to cut her down," Rabbit Stockings said.

George Bowman pulled down his hat. "He was going someplace," he said.

"Fast."

"Fast."

"He had to see the whole world," Rabbit Stockings said.

"But things keep getting in the way," Paracelsus said.

The blue Chevvy pickup was going through the old Spanish grant of Ojo del Espiritu Santo. It ran flat on both sides of them forever; way back up there someplace it ran into the Jemez Mountains. The elk and the deer and the bear and the mountain lions came down when no one could see them and took what they could from Cass Goodner, who leased part of the grant. Cass Goodner's cattle came down to where everyone could see them if it was not branding time or herding time. Now as the Chevvy approached it was time for them to stand exactly in the middle of the road. Several older bulls seemed to have thought the idea up and stood in front of the four hundred head, their front legs planted apart, heads down, defiant, waiting for the Chevvy pickup to make the next move.

The Chevvy pickup crept up to them slowly, cautiously, and then began to feel its way between the forward bulls; one of the bulls pawed, tried to plant his feet within the asphalt as the blue fender touched him gently and shoved him to one side. As the rear of the pickup went by Silver Threads reached out and patted his great head. He let out an enormous bellow. The game was up now and the rest of the cattle drifted slowly to both sides of the black pavement.

"Cass Goodner should have made steer out of those bulls. They'll cause him a lot of trouble."

"You can't make them all into steers," George said.

"Certain ones you can."

"Let's drop it," George said.

"I didn't mean to be rough, Sansi."

"I know you didn't, boy. It's all right."

In the rear of the pickup all the Indians were perched forward watching everything go by. They were in the Indian Country now and they felt better except Tom-Dick-and-Harry, who did not know where he was.

Tom-Dick-and-Harry was sucking a bottle. He had borrowed some of the fund and bought a fifth from Liquor Joe when no one was watching. He did not know where he was now or what he had done now, but all the Indian Country and all the white country, no matter what, looked rosy; everything looked fine. He set down the bottle on the long box when they left the pavement for the checkerboard area. As they began to climb and twist up the final mesa that looked down upon their hogans, the bottle fell over and before he could retrieve it a lot of the precious stuff had bled down between the cracks in the coffin.

After much twisting and turning and shifting down into

compound low they were on top of the long high mesa finally and the pickup stopped. The Indians piled out of the pickup and slid the coffin out, each pair taking it on the shoulder as it came off; Silver Threads and Paracelsus were a pair; Coyotes-Love-Me and the Marquis of Steyne were a pair; Rabbit Stockings and Lord Acton were a pair; More Wives and Quicker-Than-You were a pair. Tom-Dick-and-Harry just sat alone on the tail gate of the pickup examining the bottle in which there was nothing more.

The Navahos walked the coffin with measured, synchronized step to the edge of the grave, then they lowered it gently to the ground, where they tied a leather thong and then they lowered it, still gently, beneath the ground until it touched.

As George had left the pickup something—a letter—dropped out of his pocket. He recovered it and now, as he stood alone above the grave, he kept switching the letter from one big, dry, hot hand to the other. There did not seem to be any place for it at all. He felt someone, the medicine man, take the letter gently from him and then he saw it flutter quietly into the grave of Alexander Bowman, his brother. It made no sound when it finally touched.

All of the Navahos stood in peace above the grave for a long minute before they turned and made their way on foot down the high, blue mesa. Now, and for the last time, they would leave the brothers alone.

When the Navahos reached the bottom of the mesa and started along the long flat prairie of the Indian Country, by turning and looking far far up they could see a spade working, brightly signaling in the rain that soon something would be all over. The Navahos knew that, from way up there with the wide clear sky of the Indian Country, Alexander could see and feel the whole world.

One of the Indians, before he entered his hogan, looked up one final time to the long blue mesa. Now he raised his turquoise-ringed arm to the sky and shouted into the deep, pure distance above, "Go in beauty."

The Bronc People

PART I

ONE The two quiet Indians, resting in Z shapes, could watch and hear the shots going back and forth, back and forth, as in a Western movie. But suddenly someone was hurt and it wasn't like a Western movie now.

The two Indians had been watching from the peak of a purple New Mexican butte ever since the big white rider had driven his cattle up to the only active water hole in thirty miles and asked for water.

For two days now this forward-leaning rider with bright silvered trappings that exploded in the sun had allowed his horse to weave slowly in back of the herd; the easily distracted calves bunching to the rear, loitering then leaping ahead suddenly; the mother cows bawling for their young, turning back within the herd only to be pressed forward again in the great shove; the steers sensing the great drought ahead, pausing, tongues hanging, necks sagging, pointing rearward, red-eyed in retreat against the long dry march, quizzical, hesitant and defeated on the flank of the herd, hoping to be bypassed. The white-faced, now dust black-masked, wild-eyed heifers watched the rider, then fled frontward as his rope sang. The insulted, pride-hurt, wide-shouldered, and ball-heavy bull, forced to go now where he had not dictated to go, abused and coerced, lashed and driven toward a mad man-destiny of no water, tolling his big bellow of protest and outrage at the lead of the harem, the cows plodding, patient now, the steers following hesitant, the calves coy, tumbling, skipping sometimes forward, quick

285

and lost—they all bore the brand of the Circle Heart and they had all been without water for two days now.

"Perhaps that's true," the Indian who was on the highest part of the butte said. "But it's the other man's water. And I know the Circle Heart."

"You seem to know everything about everything," the second Indian said.

"I know how the Gran Negrito got this place and I know the Circle Heart."

"Yes, you seem to know everything about everything," the other Indian said.

"And I know how the Circle Heart will get it. They're getting it now."

The two Indians had been right in at the start of everything. They had been there when the two men had begun by talking sensibly. They were right there when they began raising their voices and they were right there when they raised their guns.

"The one who owned the water fired first."

"But not last."

The Indians had seen the man who owned the water go back in the red adobe house. They had seen the other man raise the gate to let his cattle in and they had seen the man in the house break a pane and heard him fire through the window. Then they saw the cattleman drop behind a rock and fire back. The Indians had not seen the man who went in the adobe house take a child from off the bed and put him under the bed before he started firing.

"Is the man inside the adobe house hit badly?" the Indian who was lowest on the butte asked.

"Yes."

"How can you tell?"

"Well, he seems to be firing faster," the other Indian said.

The child under the bed in the house sensed this too. Both of the men were firing much faster now. The boy's father had a lever-action Winchester and he swung the new shells in with a herky-jerky motion of his right arm. The child could not see this from under the bed but he could see the sudden brass empties that dropped around his head and he could smell the acrid gunpowder smell. He could see his father's boots moving quickly from position to new position and the floor becoming slick with something red and bright.

"Somehow I don't want to get in this one," the taller Indian said.

"Do you usually?"

"Yes, I usually do."

"Have you noticed," the shorter Indian said, "that our seat is not too good now, that the war has moved to the other side of the house? Do you think we should move with it?"

"I don't see why not."

The two Indians moved off the butte and, using the very high gray-green sage and orange, bloom-waving Cowboys Delight for cover, got over to the other side of the rincon, where they found a good red rock to sit on. Their pants were very blue against it and their shirts were very yellow. Their wide Stetsons were so beaten up they weren't anything against anything. They both seemed tired.

"Are you bored?" the shorter Indian wanted to know.

"No."

"Have you noticed that the firing has become very irregular?"

"Yes, I've noticed that."

"Have you noticed the man on the outside seems to be winning?"

"Yes, I've noticed that."

"Do you think there'll be a result today?"

"Before the night, yes."

"Then it will be all settled today?"

"No, I don't think so."

"Can you see all right from your seat?"

"Perfectly."

The man who was supposed to be winning was firing from behind a sandstone concretion, almost round, that had come down from the Eocene cliff that circled around and made all of the firing echo. When the firing had started he told himself that all he was doing was answering back. That is, when someone insulted him he insulted back and when someone shot at him, if he had a gun, he shot back. Something like that, but actually without thought. Now he was only trying to pour enough fire, put enough shots, through the window so that he could get away with his cattle. This was the man who was supposed to be winning. He had been hit in the leg, not too badly; he could still move easily and it did not bother him at all. He had been in the last war, and in the infantry, too, but in this kind of fighting it did not help much. He had read some Western pulp stories that were supposed to be about things like this but they did not help at all. The thing he kept in mind was to fire back at the window that kept firing at him. That might stop it. Then he could trail back to the Circle Heart.

The man inside the house, who, according to the two Indians, was supposed to be losing, thought he was doing nicely. Actually, as the small boy under the bed noticed from watching the slipperiness on the floor increase, his father was not doing well at all. He had been hit seriously but did not feel it too much because he was feeling other things more. If only the intruder would leave. If only the first shot he had fired at the white man had had some effect. Now there was nothing to do except keep this up until something happened.

At the beginning he had tumbled a blue box of brass Remington 30-30 soft-point Kleen-Bore cartridges on the low oak table, and all during the fight he would pick them up in handfuls of six, which is what the lever action held, and jam them in the receiver. Now, near the ending, his wide black hand swept up the final six.

"One, two, three, four, five, six," the boy heard him say.

Actually it was the arm that had done the sweeping in of the shells. His hand did not seem to be working correctly any more. The long black arm had gathered the final shells in one big movement—sweep! At the same time a bullet hit into the adobe above the boy's head softly—thwang!

"Son? Son, it's going to be all right." The boy under the bed was too tensed to answer anyone.

The Indians had moved again and they were within a clump of sage on a small knoll now. The two Indians were Navahos and they remembered this place well from their fathers telling about it. This spring-fed, huge circle of green surrounded by mesa was where Many Cattle and Winding Water had hidden their band of

288

Navahos in 1884. This was the place where the whites were not supposed to reach them, the place that the whites would not find. But they found it and burned everything down, the crops and the houses, and they took Many Cattle and Winding Water and their people to the stockade when they caught up with them, starving, at the Canyon de Chelly.

"Can you see all right?" the tall Indian asked. The tall Indian's name was President Taft.

"Very well," the short Indian said. The short Indian allowed the trader to call him My Prayer. They both had Indian names, too—Water Running Underneath The Ground and Walking Across A Small Arroyo. They both wore hats that were not smashed in at the top like white men's hats and they had on army surplus shoes and they both rolled cigarettes without taking their eyes off the spectacle they were watching.

"We could move down a little now, get closer now, without any danger I think," the taller Indian said. The taller Indian had just completed the manufacture of a cigarette entirely by feel and now he placed it in his mouth without ever seeing it. "Yes, I think we could move down closer."

"I guess I'm perfectly happy here," the shorter Indian said.

Inside the cabin that the Indians could see perfectly, the man was beginning to pick his shots. He was trying to place them carefully and he was trying to make each one important, as though each one were his last, which it very nearly was. He had even ceased the herky-jerky movement of throwing the shells into the chamber with a short swing of his right arm and he now worked the lever action more deliberately and certainly, as though he were opening and closing a safe containing precious things. The man he was shooting at was difficult to follow, but, despite the fact that the man was using smokeless powder, the man in the cabin could always tell where the other fired from last but never where he would fire from now, never where he was now. He could always see the two Indians, despite the fact that they kept changing their seats. They always seemed to select something on the rock balcony that gave them a perfect view no matter to which window he went. He had been tempted early in the fight to fire at least one shot close to the Indians simply because they were wherever he looked and because wherever he looked for the white man they were there, complacently, as though there were some law protecting them— two wild things out of season, or two people buying into this incident without payment. Now a shell was too expensive to waste on them. It was a silly idea anyway. Do people always get silly ideas when they are weak? Was it getting dark outside, out there, or was the weakness making everything turn to darkness?

"Son." His voice sounded weak and strange to himself. "Son, remember this." Or was the boy too small now to remember anything of this later, remember ever? "Son, remember this. Are you listening?"

No one answered him at all and then a bullet came through the window and made a strange sound as it slashed through the table.

The man who fired that shot wondered, now that the shooting had slowed down, whether that would hold things for a while, whether he might even now be able to get away, but a shot whee-ed near him as he moved quickly to new cover. He rested the New-Texan 35-caliber short-barreled Marlin saddle rifle between his knees and looked down on the house where he could see no one and wondered whether he would have to wait for darkness to escape with his animals. It was showing no signs of darkness yet. He looked hard at the windows to see if he could see someone there and then he looked up at the Indians who were always there. It would be nice to shoot at them, to do something with someone you could see. He toyed very briefly with the idea of firing at the Indians because they were there so damn comfortably as though they were two civilians inquiring the time in no man's land at the Battle of Gettysburg. Are people this curious? Indians are, I guess.

"Do you think it's right of us to do this?" the taller Indian said.

"Why not?"

"Watching?"

"Why not?"

"It's none of our business."

"Why not?"

"You're doing awfully well with the why nots."

"I don't think it will matter at all. I know it will not matter at all. It will come out the way it's going to come out whether we watch or not. It would not have made any difference whether anyone was watching when the whites drove us out."

"We're still here."

"I don't think we are. We're not Indians any longer."

"What are we then?"

The shorter Indian took his eyes off the battle a moment and studied his army surplus shoes. "I don't know," he said.

"Sure we're Indians."

The other Indian put his hand to his mouth and made a warwhoop noise like the one he had heard white children make in the streets of Albuquerque. "Indians! Here come the Indians!" he said.

"We speak Navaho."

"We're speaking it now."

"Then we must be Indians."

"Sure," the shorter Indian, whom the trader called My Prayer, agreed. "Sure we're Indians." And then for the first time he said something in English. "So what?" He ran it together so it sounded like some Navaho word. So whah. Sowhah. Sowah.

"I will tell you sowah," the Indian called President Taft said. "Do you know that, outside of a moving picture, they wouldn't even bother even to shoot at an Indian now?"

"That's perfectly all right with me."

"You don't understand. To them we have become nothing."

"Sowah?" the Indian called My Prayer said.

The white man who had come up fast and tired on a horse one hour ago to draw the first shot observed from his new position that he was close to the Indians. That was all right. If something happened they could testify in his favor. By moving up and over slightly to his right he could join them and find something out.

"Hi!" he said as he moved in ahead of the Indians' rock, still keeping the sage between himself and the house.

"Hello," the Indians said. They could speak four languages, through necessity: Navaho and Apache, which have the same root,

291

Spanish, which most of the settlers were, and English, which was increasing all the time, and Zia Pueblo, which came in awfully handy in this location. That makes five languages actually, but two of these languages they spoke poorly, so they counted them as one. English and Pueblo were the two foreign languages that counted as one.

"Hello," they said in one of their poor languages.

"Hi," the white man repeated.

"It's a nice day," one of the Indians said.

"Hace buen tiempo," the other Indian tried, not so sure of the white man's nation.

"No, it's a nice day," the white man said.

"It sure is," the Indian who had been correct said.

"Yeah," the white man said.

"You think it will rain?" the Indian who had been wrong said.

"It could," the white man said.

"You think it could not rain?"

"Sure it could not rain." The white man wondered what language he was speaking.

"You think it could snow?"

"Hardly, at this time of year." The white rider felt on firmer ground now.

"Yes, it could snow very hardly this time of year," President Taft said. The white man thought it would be nice if they could start all over again.

"We have been wondering what all the firing is about," the taller Indian said.

The white man pulled down on his cowboy hat. "So have I."

"Isn't it true," President Taft said, "isn't it true about all wars?"

"Isn't what true?"

"That no one knows what they're about?"

"No, it isn't," the Indian called My Prayer said. His partner, he thought, had a habit of trying to be wise by being very simple. "As long as people are involved they're about something."

"Now, that is a bright remark," the other Indian said. His partner, he thought, would go a lot farther if he did not try to be

292

so stupid that he appeared solemn. "I can tell you what this one is about."

"What?" The white man parted the rabbit brush.

"Well, you wanted to water your cattle."

"And?" The white man picked up his gun, held the brush, and looked down on the house.

"Do you have to fire that thing here in front of us?"

"I have to fire back."

"Why?"

"So I can get away with my cattle."

The two Indians looked at each other. "All right," My Prayer said. "Fire away."

There was a soft click in front of the Indians.

"What happened?"

"A misfire."

"Try another bullet."

"The empty shell has jammed."

"Let me see the gun."

The white man below the Indian on the rock passed the gun up to My Prayer, who passed it on to President Taft, who broke off a greasewood twig and inserted this in the ejector while he hit the side of the cartridge case with the big palm of his right hand. The misfire fell out and he levered in another shell and passed the gun over to his partner, who passed it down to the white man.

"I think it should work all right now."

"Thank you," the white man said.

"It's perfectly all right. We're enjoying the show."

"But it's nice, decent of you, to take sides."

"But we're not."

"No, we're not," his partner agreed.

"You mean you'd do the same for that other—?"

"Certainly. Why not?"

"Yes, why not?" his partner said. "After all, why not?"

"I want you to try and remember who started this," the white man said from the brush. "It could be very important and I want to tell you that I don't like this at all."

"You've lost your nerve?" one of the Indians asked.

"I don't want to hurt anyone down there."

"Then why are you firing the gun?"

"So he does not fire at me."

The two Indians looked at each other.

"Oh," they said.

Below, the man that the white man above, talking to the Indians, did not want to hurt was hurt badly. But not quite so badly that he had not noticed the Indian on the rock fix a gun and pass it back down to someone in the brush. So the Indians had taken sides. Now at last he could fire at someone he could see. He raised the gun and rested it on the back of a piñon chair and got the bead right between the eyes of the tallest Indian. He could not pull the trigger. He wondered why. He tried to pull the trigger again and failed. He still had that much strength. He tested his trigger finger in the air. He still had that much strength all right. He lowered the gun and wondered why he could not shoot an Indian. He felt dizziness now and he wiped his forehead and looked around for the boy.

"Son!" he called. He could not remember now where he had put the boy. It was getting very dark. He had better light a lamp. He felt that the Coleman gasoline-pump lantern would be too much for him, so when he saw the tall, glass-chimneyed kerosene lantern, and so close too, he lighted that. He knocked the glass chimney on the floor, where it smashed, but soon he had a tall yellow flame going. Now he remembered where he had put the boy—under the bed. He had something important to tell him. He wanted to tell him to flee, run, get out, go southward again, but then, later on—finally, when he had grown, become a man—to reconquer this, to regain this—this island. This darkness. He waved the lantern weakly but it made no light. Where were all the green fields and the fresh water? Where was a small light to see the big West?

He slipped on something now and went down, the whole glass lantern smashing now where the fragile chimney had smashed before, the kerosene spreading out ahead of small pennants of flame and then licking up the walls, illumining in soft orange the books, the endless row upon row of books; tall books, wide books, thin and fat and leather books, green, red and paper books. The room, the house seemed made of books. Books, stacks of them building new rooms of books within book rooms. The flames eating upward now on books. The man on the floor wanted to tell the boy many many things but all he could say was, "Come back. Come back."

"He seems to have lighted a light."

"Yes, he's lit the light," the other Indian agreed.

"To read those books."

"What books?"

"Just books."

"What for?"

"They say he's a little crazy."

"He's got books of records too. Maybe he lit the light to play them."

"Why?"

"They say he's a little crazy."

"A houseful of books and records in the Indian Country. What's the world coming to?"

"They say he's a little crazy."

"Maybe that's why he took a shot at the white man. Maybe he thought someone was coming to do something about all those books and records."

"Yes. But I've been wondering. I been wondering why he doesn't take a shot at us."

"Why should he take a shot at us? Aren't Indians supposed to be a little crazy too?"

"I mean I fixed that gun for the white man right here in plain sight. He must have seen it." Both Indians dropped off the rock now, down behind the rock where they were out of sight. Now the white man came around the rock.

"The house is on fire!" he hollered. "Here, hold this gun. I suppose somebody's got to go down and try to get him out."

"Why?"

"God, you Indians are lunatics." The white man thrust his gun on them and took off on a long running lope down toward the burning house.

"I wonder what he meant by that?"

"Well, everyone that's different—"

"But our hogans aren't stacked with books and records."

"No, but we're Indians."

"Yes, that's true. We're Indians."

They watched as the white man rapidly approached the house and they both gave a jerk of surprise when he threw open the door and flung himself in. A wide sheet of golden flame leaped out when he opened the door but he went in anyway. Everyone was very strange today.

When the white man went in the front door the Indians noticed something run out the back. It was about the size of a good dog but it ran upright and very fast and soon it had disappeared out of sight over a small rise.

"Maybe we better catch it," the taller Indian said.

"Yes," the other Indian agreed, rising quickly. "It may be all there is left, all we have to prove to ourselves we're not absolutely —anyway, after an absolutely crazy day."

The Indians finally ran it down. They twisted and ran, twisted and ran until, at last, going up a long butte and after losing it and retracing it again and going up and down three arroyos and two mesas, they finally ran it down and carried it all the way to their wagon and put a tarp over it where it would be cool and started up their mules and were off to Canyon de Chelly.

"It's a he and he is black," the taller Indian said. "The man in the house was black so this is a black boy." He touched the tarp as the wagon bumped over a prairie-dog mound.

"Yes. And he is all that's left at the end of a very crazy day."

"We're left."

"Yes, that's true," the shorter Indian said.

"Do you think the white man is left?"

"There are plenty more."

"Yes. But what was it all about?"

"Haven't you seen a movie at the trader's? This was the same thing."

"You mean it was about nothing?"

"Not exactly. It means something to them."

"We've got to be generous."

296

"And understanding."

"Yes."

"I think this was about water. I think it was important to us before the white man came and the same thing is still the same and everything else is still the same."

"It's weird." He used the Spanish words, *"Es sobrenatural."*

"Yes."

"This is still the same," he said, motioning to the rocks and sky and sage around them. "And even this," he said, bending and allowing his hand to run through a wave of orange flame they rode through. "What do they call this flower?"

"Cowboys Delight."

"They call everything by a different name but it's the same thing. And they call everything by a different time but it's the same time. Everything repeats. It would be no different if everything in every language and every time was called Cowboys Delight."

The taller Indian realized that the shorter Indian still oversimplified a very complex thing to appear wise. Nevertheless, there was not much arguing with the idea that if a thing can happen it has happened, that if anything can go wrong it will, and there's nothing *sobrenatural* about this if you realize that there's a law governing everything, including Indians, and it's called Chance, sometimes God, but, according to this Indian, it might just as well be called Cowboys Delight.

"That makes sense."

"Does their shooting it out back there make sense?"

"No. But maybe it makes sense to them."

"Now that they've taken it from us they'll fight over it with each other?"

"I hope there'll be some war surplus left over for us."

"There is," the Indian said, touching the bulge beneath the tarp.

"And I hope everything takes the pressure off us."

"It will," the Indian called President Taft said, staring away. "It's taken the pressure off us for quite a while now."

"Yes, that's true," the shorter Indian said.

The name of the shorter Indian was Walking Across A Small Arroyo, called My Prayer, and the taller Indian was Water Running Underneath The Ground, called President Taft. More important to them, they were going to Canyon de Chelly, but still more important, everything happened on a bright, shining, Western day, a clean, ordinary happy, New Mexico afternoon. Even now, as the bright Indian wagon made its way through the rocks, the whole weird warp of the landscape, the entire gaudy, scintillant pattern of the West was still with them, changing yet unchanged, ending but unended. Recapitulant.

"All very well," Taft said. "But what will happen now to the Circle Heart?"

"What will happen to the Circle Heart should not happen to an Indian."

"The Circle Heart?"

"Yes. The children of the Circle Heart."

They went over a hiding undulation in the rolling sage and rock. They could see the Coyote Pass ahead, and the huge fire behind them became only a lingering pattern against the quiet blue sky.

TWO   **T**wo years to the week after the wagoned Indians had trailed through Coyote Pass, after the Circle Heart had trailed through the pass, another man trailed through here going in the opposite direction.

Lemaitre was coming back. The native returns. Now he was a city bronc man. Now he was a city cowboy riding out of the East back to the West. From his high mountain road he looked down at the bright red country below, at the incarnadined earth interset with jewels of green alfalfa, green jewels upon a red plain within the dark mountains round. From his high mountain road, red too, his eye could not separate the red adobe-built northern New Mexico town of Coyote from the valley it was made of. He could only see the yellowish, new wood construction of the rodeo grounds; the maze of fence, corral, and tower, virgin but faded—alien to a bright country.

Lemaitre got back in his car—a powder-blue Chrysler Imperial pulling a regal, air-conditioned horse van done in quiet gold, and small-lettered, in caliph flourish, LEMAITRE. He took one last look at the judges' tower rising below before he slammed the door.

The tower of the judges' stand was built of number-five raw timbers, two by twelves that, according to local wisdom, shrank one inch a year. Since this was only the second year of its life the tower still had ten years to go. The corrals surrounding the judges' tower were built of the same timbers, and out in front of all this was an arena one hundred yards by fifty, enclosed by an eight-foot-high hog-wire fence. Behind this were the pickup trucks and the

Indian wagons, and in front of these, their faces pressed against the hog wire, were the watchers—the cowboys and Indians and Spanish-American farmers, caked already with the red dust, watching the prisoned animals in the corrals around the reddening tower, watching particularly the chutes, the final pens from which the animals and bronc people were shot into the arena.

Near the tower a small boy made for the wire fence. He was dressed in a miniature cowboy outfit and had soft, wide-apart, wild blue eyes the color of the sky. His hat was red and his spurs were handmade from finishing nails. His red belt bore the black brand of the Circle Heart.

The first time Sant had heard of the bronc people he was seven. Now, the first time he saw them, he was seven and a week. He crawled between the Indian wagons and under the fence and watched as the announcing man made the announcement.

There was a hush over everyone, as if a fuse had been lit. The big gate of the chute swung open. There was an explosion, and out shot the rider without the horse. They tried it again; the announcing man made the announcement, a hush fell. There was the explosion, and out shot the horse without the rider.

"In case you, some of you, ain't never been to a rodeo before," the announcing man announced, "they was supposed to come out together. Watch again," he said, and someone behind that barricade must have lighted a third match and after the explosion the horse and rider came out together but only for an instant, only for the half second it took the horse to nucker into the earth and sling the man against the fence. The bronc man attempted wildly to land on his face, failed, and crashed all in a heap next to Sant. Slowly he unwound himself from his own wreckage until he reached a sitting and face-stroking, hard-thinking position.

"Why, the bastard!" he said.

Sant leaned over, inquiring with all the profundity of children into the burning red face of the bronc man, "Is it fun?"

Now the announcing man had something else going—the steer-wrestling contest. It seemed the object in this one was to see who could get killed first. A square steer shot out of the chute and made for the other end of the arena, chased by one of the bronc people on his blue quarter horse. Another bronc man rode on the other side of the steer so that the steer ran down an alley formed by the bronc people. Then one of the bronc men fell on the horns of the steer and wrestled him to earth, tied him up, and walked off proud. The next time it happened it seemed it was the man who was tied up because it was the steer who walked off proud. The bronc people retrieved the man, gathered him up as if he were a sordid, soiled, discarded pile of old cowboy clothes, and threw him, not without tenderness, behind the bull chute. Sant found him there reminiscing to himself of better days and ways.

"Isn't this," the bronc man said, "isn't this a hell of a way to make a living?"

"Is it fun?" Sant insisted.

Sant now climbed the board barricade that surrounded the judges' stand until he could look down at the corral maze below. He walked the fence maze, looking down on calf pen, bull pen, steer pen, horse pen, Brahma pen, cowpen, and, yes, here was a pigpen. Whatever did bronc people do with these?

What they did with these was to put a clutch of pigs in a pickup truck out at one end of the field, then all the horse-mounted men came hell for leather, dismounted, grabbed a greased pig, remounted, held the flashing object high, like Montezuma's men the golden mantle, like offerings to the god, the animals flashing and screaming, fighting along the arms, upward to the sun.

Sant could not see from his position above the maze what they did with them finally. Maybe et them, he thought, or put them someplace first and won a prize.

He had now reached the tower where the judges sat, way up in ultimate wisdom. They pulled on their chins and stroked their thighs and squirted down wild brown juice on lesser heads, as wise men will.

Sant slowly twisted and twined his way up the tower by the ladder the timbers formed to the seats of the judges. One of the judges leaned forward with solemn weight and raised a finger. The chute was flung open, the watchers yelled, and out plunged a Brahma bull, twisting to catapult the bronc man on its back. The watchers froze. The judge stroked his elk ring and placed a square

301

of tobacco in his jaw before his ice-blue eyes, narrowed hard in awe, froze too.

"If Arturo Lucero Cipriano de Godoy is determined to get hisself kilt—" one of the Anglo judges said and rubbed his horny hands together in a working gesture and finally relaxed as judges must.

By climbing the boards in back of the judges' stand Sant gained the top, the roof, and he looked out at the new world below, feeling within as small boys do, as Cortez did upon that peak.

"Oh Lord! Stay with him, Arturo Lucero Cipriano de Godoy!" Sant shouted.

Away from the arena, toward the mountain, a plume of dust rose from the scar of road to the east. It was the arrival of Lemaitre, king of the cowboys—of the pulp novels anyhow, one of the judges thought, watching it, expecting it, although no one had had the courage to bill it. No one had had the credulity to believe Suds Lemaitre, his cousin—the cousin of Lemaitre the King, whose plume now feathered in the east.

"He said he might make it up on his way, iffen he had a mind to, on his way to see the president," Suds had told them.

"President of what?" someone asked.

"The United States," Suds said.

"Then why would he stop here?"

"We're kin."

"I see. Then he'll stop here when the only place can afford him is Madison Square Garden, the Cow Palace, and the Court of Something?"

"Saint James, he said," Suds said. "But we're kin."

Sant watched the plume increase to tornado size as the entourage neared. Then the plume of fairy-red dust collapsed as the caravan paused, revealing the powder-blue Chrysler and the horse van.

A loud hush fell over the arena as Lemaitre pulled in and parked his caravan, got out and stretched.

"Cousin!" Suds said. Suds was standing at the end of a long line of pickup trucks and he advanced on Lemaitre as a committee of one.

302

"This way, Cousin," Suds said and he conducted him among the abruptly silenced world—even the animals now—to the board ladder that reached to the judges. Sant watched down as the big winged orange hat mounted toward him. Then the face tilted up to check its progress. The clean, hard, slanting jaw of Lemaitre. Big as an ax, so close Sant could reach out a small monkey hand and touch it. The face of Lemaitre.

"Howdy, Pardner." The voice of Lemaitre.

Sant stared back without speech.

The man bent down, entering the seats of the judges.

The rear end of Lemaitre.

Sant, safe now in the center of the roof where he had retreated, moved a miniature grimed hand over an equally grimed face and whispered secretly, "Howdy, Pardner."

The judges, now feeling judged, stood up and fumbled, embarrassed, for cigarettes and whisky. At last a judge who was selected to judge because he read books and had no friends among the contestants—among anyone—leaned forward in sincere diffidence.

"How, sir—" he said. He stared at the man in the bat-winged orange hat, the two-hundred-dollar alligator boots, and the green phosphorescent shirt that lit up at night and in the daytime too. "How, sir, are you?"

"Right smart," Lemaitre said, and he took the judge's seat, sprawled down into the chair, placed the alligators on the railing, and splayed his jeweled hands, the hands that whipped a thousand broncs, on the rough pine arms of the judge's seat.

"Right nice of you to ask," Lemaitre said.

The crowd now had recovered enough to go off, to explode, to stampede, knock their children together, and toss whisky bottles in the sun. The crowd settled into a rhythmic roar, "Lee Mater Lee Mater Lee Mater!" The gaudy man finally rose from the rough pine seat of the judge, approved of what he saw, bowed in brilliant humility, and sat down with a nod that said that whatever they had been doing before he arrived they could continue to do it now.

Sant could watch the gods without leaning over the edge. The two-by-twelve roof boards had sun-crept apart, so the structure was more a lattice than a roof, and he could look down on the shadow-striped gods with ease through the interstices and hear them, if not understand.

One of the judges who did not read things but was awfully social leaned forward and said to Lemaitre, "Sam Tollerfield wants to get hisself kilt. I hope he's no kin."

"All men are kin," Lemaitre said.

God, the judge who read books thought, our hero's a philosopher too.

Lemaitre's eyes narrowed on a palomino that looked fancy. The palomino knocked down the first barrel in the obstacle contest.

"Yes," another judge said. "Yes. We are all everyone's children."

Lemaitre winced and winced again when the palomino touched the second barrel.

"Now, when you meet a king—" one of the judges said. "Now, you are a man who has met many kings. Now, what do you say when you meet a king?"

"Hello," Lemaitre said.

"Now, I mean, do they talk as we're talking now, say the things we say—presidents and kings?"

"Yes," Lemaitre said.

"Well, but you're kind of a king yourself," another judge said. "King of the cowboys. What would they say if they was to meet ordinary people like us?"

"Hello," Lemaitre said.

"I mean if they was to meet us the second time—we'd already had this conversation and they was to meet us the second time—what would they say?"

"Hello again," Lemaitre said.

"What we're getting at," the tallest judge said, "is you mean that if you met us again—" Lemaitre was trying to follow the palomino. "If you was to meet us again all you'd say was hello again? You'd treat us like dirt?"

"Yes, yes," Lemaitre said. "Anything."

Sant retired from his crack to the middle of the roof self-consciously and scratched his ear. They should show more respect for Lemaitre.

Now Sant watched the horses that were swimming in the tight corral below. They had whipped up a circular motion and flowed loose, intertwined and clockwise, without touching the boards, the crimson dirt fluid and spraying out, redding the judges' stand, with a stud's mouth sharklike leaping out and up toward the blue sky, then falling back into the pool of red and flowing horses, as if a fish had been wounded and turned the water thus, the horses churning, still-white teeth snapping and bright in the overwhelming sun, the quiet, whipped dust settling upon Sant from the vortex beneath his feet, his eyes trying to count and failing. Now he selected a white mare and lost her as she was dyed the same pink in the mad, churning, deep aquarium of horses.

"Zowee!" Sant said.

And now the announcing man, whose name, STACEY, was written on his shirt, announced that his father had driven a stage through this country way back when times were desper-*ate*—a stage without wheels, without any wheels, folks. And how was it held up, folks? Well, it was held up by bandits.

"Now," a judge said, "wouldn't Stace go over big in New York City, New York?"

"In New York City, New York. Yes," Lemaitre said.

Sant watched, below, some gaudy-rigged cowboys beginning to work on the killer. The killer horse was not in the aquarium with the other horses but prisoned in a heavy cell of logs that fitted him exactly. They had brought him off the mountain yesterday with seven ropes and twelve horses. He had never been ridden. Rumor had it he had killed five men. Actually he had killed one and crippled another. The killer had been brought off the mountain once before, last year, to sell to a city rodeo, but the city man, the buyer, said, "Hell, that's not a horse, it's an electric chair. It would be an execution, not a bronc ride. Keep the down payment and wait till my truck gets five miles away before you turn him loose."

No one knew where the horse came from. He had suddenly appeared on the mountain one day, full, enormous, black. All the people and half the dogs from Coyote had climbed up to see him.

The mangled, bloodied remains of an ancient, high-backed Spanish saddle hung downward around his belly, and a man, quickly killed, went toward him with a rope.

On Spanish fiesta days, when the town was lighted with provoking torches for the feast of San Antonio, the killer was sure to come off the mountain and tear through the streets, scattering the pilgrims and sending the dark-robed people retreating back into the church. Caballo de Muerto? Or He Alone Who Was Free? All the people and half the dogs of Coyote wondered.

The crowd at the rodeo knew what was up. The crowd had quietly turned into a mob, no longer going off in individual shouting, whims, and directions but all intent now on helping the men with the ropes and poles and pickups strain and inch the killer into the chute.

"The great Lemaitre will now favor us country folks with a ride," the announcer said flatly and evenly, and he removed his hat.

Sant looked through the cracks. Lemaitre seemed to have collapsed. He seemed to be holding one hand on the other hand to keep it from moving, but only for an instant. Then he placed the bad hand in his pocket to make it behave and with the good hand he reached slowly up to the Bull Durham label drooping from his electric shirt, removed the sack, and made a cigarette with one hand. He blew out a cloud of smoke and removed the bad hand and it seemed good again. He looked, narrow-eyed, down at the mob and nodded his head.

The bright-crested, swearing, pushing men were trying to work the big black forward into the chute. A fenced alley led from his prison to the chute beneath the judges' stand, but he would not go. They prodded and heaved him forward with ropes, squeezing and pulling until they reached parallel posts at four-foot intervals in the alley, then they placed a log through the fence on the forward side of the post, so the big black could not retreat, and then they swore and heaved him to the next post. In this fashion they finally got him to the chute, whereupon he smashed the log they held him with and backed back to his prison, where he waited. They began again, this time with a larger crew, larger log, larger cussing, gayer hats, and this time three men with three horses pulled ropes from out in the arena until the big black was safely chuted; cussed, sweated, pulled, and prodded until the gates at both ends of the chute were sealed.

"Now," one of the judges said, "we are all ready. We can commence as soon as they get this strap tied around his back you can hold on to." The judge paused. "Like as not they'll try us for murder, and yet it was they"—he indicated the mob—"asked for it. Demanded it."

"Listen," the fattest judge said, "I can raise my finger, turn him back. It will be all right with them. They'll all laugh and go home happy. They'll have had their joke." He watched Lemaitre.

Lemaitre was slumped down in the big pine chair in advance of the judges, slumped there between the people and the judges. To catch the eye of the fattest judge he had to roll back his head and look partly upward and into the face of Sant. Their eyes gripped together a full instant. Then Lemaitre leaned far back and caught the judge's eye, hesitated, then said quietly, "No. No, it's all right."

"You think the people care?" another judge said. "They don't care. They'll take their satisfaction either way."

Sant ceased looking down, looked up at the overpowering sky, and scratched his head.

Lemaitre began to roll another cigarette. "Maybe, maybe not," Lemaitre said. "Maybe we got to do what we're expected to do. The horse is ready, expecting me. The people are expecting me." He looked down. "Particularly the horse. To keep the horse waiting—" he fretted the cigarette and placed it in his mouth—"it wouldn't be polite."

Below, the men were trying to get the surcingle around the horse. Sant watched as they slipped the strap through the crack in the boards beneath the horse's furious belly. The man on the other side of the chute reached in, cautiously, deliberately, to intercept the strap. The horse fired out his hoofs like a shot, and the man fell.

"Who fired that shot?" the announcing man demanded. "He'll be all right, folks," he said as they pulled the man beneath the shade of an Indian wagon, waved fans in his face, and applied things to the slow trickle of blood.

"Here's the horse what did the shooting, fired that cannon, folks. Well—" the announcing man paused—"let's have a moment's silence in memory." The announcing man sat down, and Sant watched as Lemaitre worked on the bad hand again, held it to keep it from moving, then finally placed it in his pocket, blew out a huge cloud of smoke and waved it away with his good hand, leaned back and winked up at Sant.

Now another volunteer rushed forward, uncoiled a long piece of baling wire, and fished down between the boards and beneath the great horse and speared the strap and passed it up to the man atop the barricade and above the horse. The man above the horse reached over to the other side of the barricade to receive the other end of the strap.

"Folks, he shouldn't have done it," the announcing man announced.

The horse had fired again, rising up in his chute to twice his height. He jackknifed and shot the man clean over two Indian wagons, a pickup, twenty bales of hay, and a Coca-Cola stand. The man landed and bounced twice in the red dust and then, without ceasing his movement—he was running now—he made toward the hills, followed by his wife, an only child, and an old Indian retainer who chased zigzag and kicking like an antelope, as though pursued—all four of them shouting and shouted to, distant and disappearing, hushed at last in the far hills a mile and one half from where the black horse stood contained, recoiled again, and trembling for other victims.

"Well, folks, that wasn't nice." The announcing man paused and watched Lemaitre. "Maybe we shouldn't ask a man with a city reputation to ride a country horse."

The people laughed.

The announcer seemed to be reconsidering, tapping quietly with a stick on the railing in front of him. "No, folks, I mean this. Let's go home, call it off. You've had your fun."

The crowd booed.

"I wash my hands." The announcing man stepped aside and the show seemed over. People began to move toward the trucks and wagons.

"One moment." Lemaitre stood where the announcing man had stood. "One moment. We got one more rider." Then Lemaitre began to climb down the judges' stand toward the chute. The crowd paused, not going to their trucks or back to their wagons but hanging there watching.

Sant beat Lemaitre to the chute, swinging down the tower like a monkey. As Lemaitre neared he saw Sant talking to and stroking the head of the horse. When he got to the chute Sant was down there below the horse someplace, disappeared beneath the barricade, beneath the big black, among those hoofs, still talking soothing horse gibberish. Now Sant passed up both ends of the strap to Lemaitre waiting above the horse. With the same movement of taking the strap, Lemaitre grabbed Sant's wrist and gave it, not a pull or even a jerk, but a flip that landed Sant on a pile of hay ten yards away.

"The horse might get bored with your conversation. We don't want to push the luck."

Now the horse gave a high gyrating lunge that shook the stands as Lemaitre tightened the surcingle and Sant regained the barricade. Some other volunteers, too, now crept up to the barricade with advice.

"Don't," they said in chorus.

"Oh," Lemaitre said, looking down on the horse. "It's too late."

What happened next fixed in Sant's mind as a dream, unconcluding till ever. Not till another country, even, or another land, ever. Not even to the big death of Little Sant. Never.

The horse with one great series of furious kicks was toppling the barricade. As the barricade fell, dissolved in huge splinters, the men leaped clear and Sant remained standing in the air. Lemaitre on his way down to gain the horse plucked Sant and, with no leverage to fling him clear, kept him in his right hand and grabbed the surcingle with his left. Together they shot straight upward into the nearing sun, Sant held even farther upward like some trophy, up and up until they seemed to stall at leaving the earth and glide heavy downward and hit to rise up again and again and again, like some wing-broken bird failing above tree height. Now the horse in huge bird fashion laid a serpentine pattern in the sky so that those on the occasional ground on which he hit fled under the trucks and wagons to watch safely the three up there that all came down together in unexpected places. Like an unexpected dream.

The horse now tried the earth, careening like a mad jet, earth-bound, at sudden right angles and with awful breaks to fling the riders over the mountain. But they seemed now part of the horse, even as they left the arena, flew over the fence like Pegasus, and made toward town. The audience emerged to watch the three nailed together tear around through Coyote before threatening them again with their return back over the same fence to make one final flight in the air. Then the horse quit. The dream seemed over.

Lemaitre stepped off, still holding Sant high and precious, as though they were leaving a rocket to the moon. The mob was still stunned, noiseless, as Lemaitre led the horse with a nose hold into the quiet, gold, air-conditioned trailer and bolted the door with a combination lock, placed Sant in the front seat alongside him in the powder-blue Imperial, and drove off. But the dream was still not over.

Lemaitre held the wheel and made a cigarette with the other hand. Then he looked at Sant.

"We won him," he said.

They rode hushed between huge yellow rocks in the red earth, smelling the pure New Mexico air, feeling the huge space around them, sensing a roof now as they entered beneath cottonwoods at the sulphur springs, then passed between the low clay mounds which looked like melting elephants, then emerged finally, climbing and gliding into bright hills the horse had known.

"He'll get used to being a bronc horse," Lemaitre said. "Fed regular every day and such, catered to and primped. He'll get used to the aquarium." Lemaitre paused. "You think he earned his freedom then. You think we should turn him back loose. You think with all the catering and feed and primping there is nothing worse than not freedom." Lemaitre studied the lost cliffs in the pure distance and dropped the twisted Bull Durham stem into the ash box.

Sant stared ahead in childish blankness with his dream. Then he said as though absent, "I was studying—"

"Yes," Lemaitre said. "But first I'm driving you home wherever you live."

"The Circle Heart Ranch, on your way back to Albuquerque."

"Yes, maybe so," Lemaitre said as though listening for another voice. "Yes. I guess maybe that's it. I guess that's the worst there is."

"The Circle Heart?" Sant said.

"No," Lemaitre said, and he stopped the car and got out and fiddled with the combination lock on the trailer, and then there was a great noise, kind of a smooth rushing of wings into the high hills, and then Lemaitre got back in and said, "Not freedom. That's what it was. That's what *I* was studying."

They rode now through the darkening hills in their shared secret, their mutual conspiracy, as though together they had broken jails for strangers. They had released him who had tried to murder them; against justice, against all man-laws of not freedom, they had conspired together and were linked as one in the act.

"That horse, that's what you were studying, isn't it?"

"Not that horse particular," Sant said.

"My card," Lemaitre said, proffering Sant a small paper. "Maybe one day—you never know—maybe one day you'll want to join the bronc people. Look me up. Lemaitre's the name."

"That's what I was studying all the time. Sant's the name," Sant said taking the card.

The car paused in front of the gates marked the "Circle Heart." Sant got out and watched the Imperial caravan pull away down the long road to Albuquerque.

"Sant's the name. Sant Bowman," Sant said.

The boy started down a cow-trail short cut to the main house, the path beaten hard by the passing herds and the punishing sun. Now he entered a grove, a thicket of tamarisk trees and greasewood brush, and came upon a sudden deer. The buck paused, staring in wild disbelief before he turned, and whipped imperiously off. As the buck leaped he flashed his white card of tail. Now the two, shocking each other in sudden encounter, were fled as quickly as they were joined.

As Sant began to enter the house gate his mother came fluttering.

"Where've you been, boy?" Millicent Bowman, always called Millie Sant, was small and sudden in all her movements. "Where've you been?"

"Up there," Sant said, pointing to the tough sun, the clean distant sky.

"Come, boy," she said, still fluttering. "Where you been?"

"Here," Sant said, taking out the small white card and passing it to her. "Up there," he said still pointing. "Up there where I've been telling you. And I've got that paper," he said, watching the card she examined. "I've got that paper to prove it."

THREE   **M**illie Sant listened to a wide catalogue of soft music. That is, she had subscribed at one time or another to every religion in the book and some she had made up. The one she liked best, the one she stayed with the longest, was Theosophy.

"Isn't that the same as Christian Science?"

"No, it is not. Theosophy is the one where you face reincarnation in the form of something maybe you et, so it's important to eat nothing but vegetables. Otherwise you might be a cannibal. If you kill an ant even, you might not be, but you just might be, killing your own grandmother. Murder then."

A refinement on this led her to believe, and support with small money, a man who lived, loyally, in Darkest Africa and played loyally on an organ and was kind to the birds and very careful not to tread on ants and had religious qualms about killing cattle. But he did not have qualms about taking Millie's money to repair that organ in Darkest Africa. Millie dropped the loyal African in Darkest Africa with the ultimate realization that her husband made his living selling cattle in Brightest New Mexico. She even wrote a letter to that loyal man in Darkest Africa (which he must have read, bemused, by candlelight between Bach fugues) asking why he drew a line that discriminated against her husband. Millie had her loyalties too. He did not answer. The hell with him.

Millie's husband, Big Sant, watched her now scurrying with all the inside work that has to be done on a cattle ranch in Brightest Northern New Mexico. He believed in cattle. His hobbies were collecting land and butterflies. But Millie was no butterfly. She

313

grew up in the wide country where women swearing was as acceptable as women forming clubs in Albuquerque. Big Sant collected real butterflies and very real land. Big Sant wore the red-flowering brand of second-degree burns, a brilliant splash of color on an otherwise clearly hacked and wind-leathered face. The Circle Heart was run by a branded man.

Millie was all very pretty, from her carved, tiny face to her neat, unruined figure. Her ability to have any more children had been ruined by a disaster on a horse, but it did not show. The thing that showed most in both of them was open ranching—ranching, ranches, and more ranches, way back on both sides since the day the first settlers came.

Big Sant did not think it fair of him to muse, as he had been musing, to be unfair, as perhaps he was being unfair, about Millie's religions. After all, she wanted children, more children, and what's a woman going to do with all that is pent? What was he going to do with all the land he had got? Little Sant? Wrap him up in a huge education. Get him to forget he had been born to the cows. Get him to forget the tragedy of this land by books, a good education. The tragedies of the Greeks. Sophocles, Aeschylus—there must be a good one there. And then modern nuclear physics. Little Sant could study that one. If he himself had had, he thought, watching Millie, the advantages he could give to Little Sant, northern New Mexico might be all as bright as it appeared. Things would be as nice as cowboy stories, where no woman lives and cowboys are as facile as larks and no man grieves and wooden men gallop across a purple page pursued by wooden Indians. Right proud to meet up with you, ma'am. Do you reckon the future will reckon anyone lived here? Do you reckon they will?

Christ, Big Sant thought, wiping a heavy hand over his scar-flowered face. Oh Jesus Almighty Christ.

Zen, Zoroastrianism, I AM, Theosophy and the reincarnation of the living Buddha all passed in formidable pageant against the grim forces of reality. Beef at fourteen cents a pound on the hoof—down twelve cents. Incidence of fatal Blackleg and ticks among the cattle, 3.2—up 1.2. Which meant fifty-two of his cattle dead this year. The calf drop was nine per cent down, which meant the calf crop was off, which meant there were twenty-six less calves born this year than last. All this, according to Big Sant. According to Millie it became unimportant. Anyway the blows were much softer to her when she was supporting with trivial but important sums the reincarnation of the Living God, Krishnamurti. All the tragedy of ranch life became bearable, including the erosion, the deep wide arroyo that ran through the Circle Heart and became wider with each flood. Including her husband's ever need for more land, including the bright, burning bloom of changing hues of purple that got darker each year and extended down to the loin of Big Sant. Including all the forces of death in life. She had her armed pageant.

She had her periods of transition though, when she just swore. Big Sant could always tell when she was changing armies to oppose fate because she just swore. Curses not loud but deep, explicit and exact, genuine coins minted in the Old West and uncounterfeit.

Millie was even now deciding on battalions.

"If I can't have any more kids and if our one kid—" She threw a ball of dough on the board and stared out the window in a reflective gesture to where Little Sant was seated on a hill. "If our one kid does not become something other than a cowboy— A doctor perhaps. Dr. Bowman will see you when he emerges and he will emerge when he is G-o-d-d-a-m-n well ready."

Fresh legions for old foes. She felt better now and slammed the dough, then kneaded it with new courage. New strength from old wells. Old cesspools marshaled to fling in the face of new droughts—a new dying off of half the herd perhaps—the widening of the arroyos—the deepening scar on Big Sant's handsome body. Come what would come, she had new armor.

"Yes," she said, watching out the window at the boy. She had a clean, boyish, handsome profile.

"Yes what, Millie?"

"Yes, I feel better now," Millie said.

Millie looked out the window again at Little Sant standing on a big butte. He was not much more than a speck of color, and if he was doing or saying anything up there, they would never know. They could not see him staring at the house with his hands on his hips, a miniature statue on a pinnacle of sandstone, a monument of reproof, a memorial statue with a small voice.

"Who says I'm not a really cowboy?"

Sant was nine and he wore the cowboy's shirt, the boots and the chaps—shirt, purple, chaps, orange, boots, bright, and spurs scintillant, flashing the New Mexico sun in a sharp glint from his heels. He called out again from atop the pinnacle above his father's Circle Heart Ranch. He had just had a fight with his mother. He had brought home a dog belonging to someone else and she had made him turn it loose.

"Who says I'm not a really cowboy?" He threatened the house again with his high voice from atop the rise.

"I bet I'm a really cowboy!"

The last dog he had brought home was not a sheep dog and his father had said, "What good's a dog if it's not a sheep dog?" and his mother had said, "It belongs to someone else anyway."

Sant now got bored with threatening the ranch house, and anyway nobody paid any attention. The thing to do was to find some kind of treasure and show them all up and things like that. There wasn't any telling what kind of special treasure to get. Something, maybe, like uranium or gold. He knew where there was plenty of gold, but grown-up people called it iron pyrites even after it looked more like gold than gold did. People want to give a different name to things that they don't find their own selves, so that they can keep people from being really cowboys and things like that.

Sant began to look very carefully for things now from his vantage point on the mesa. He saw the juniper that makes good fence posts, the scrub oak that makes poor fence posts but is easier to get, and the sage and lemita that make no kind of fence posts at all. Now he sat down and decided to look for no kind of things at all and just let his father and mother suffer if they wanted to find him. It didn't do any good to look for anything because if you find it they said it wasn't gold anyway or they said it's not a sheep dog and no kind of dog is good if it's not a sheep dog. Anyway they made you turn everything loose. So why bother to make discoveries and find things?

"We found something new," a voice behind him said.

Sant knew it was a Navaho Indian speaking and he knew what kind of Navaho Indian it was and he knew his age, not much more than Sant's own. He even knew his name, which was even more than the Indian himself knew. That is, the Indian threw out a lot of names to confuse everybody, so that he didn't know his own name sometimes, which was Afraid Of His Own Horses. And he must be with The Other Indian. That was some name even for an Indian—The Other Indian.

"What did you find new?" Sant said.

The two Indians came around from in back and sat in front of Sant.

"We found something real new," The Other Indian said. "A white boy that's black."

"Yeah. Cheese and baloney," Sant said. "What do you think I am or something? I don't believe that."

The Other Indian seemed to take this pretty calmly. He sat there with his hands across his knees and stared at Sant with liquid dark eyes. His American name was The Other Indian because they had left him unnamed for such a long time and called him simply The Other Indian for such an eternity that they finally settled for The Other Indian permanently.

Afraid Of His Own Horses is an exact translation of an Indian name and it means afraid of his own horses.

"Sure it does," Sant said.

"What?" Afraid Of His Own Horses said.

"I was thinking."

"You go right ahead."

"A man's got to think."

"Sure he does," The Other Indian said.

Navahos believe that they should send the stupidest boys to school and leave the intelligent ones to take care of the sheep. It was a long time before the Anglos found out (the Spanish-Americans knew it all the time) that by the stupidest the Navahos meant the ones who learned English the fastest. According to the Navahos, Afraid Of His Own Horses and The Other Indian were about the

stupidest Indians to come along in a lot of moons. They had to go
to school.

"Yeah, you sure did," Sant said.

"What's that?"

"I'm thinking."

"But what about what we found?"

"What about what we discovered?"

"Well, I don't exactly trust Indians."

"Neither do we," Afraid Of His Own Horses and The Other
Indian both said.

"Neither does me," Sant said, but he had been plenty confused by the Indians. They always did manage to outsmart him.
That wasn't because Indians are naturally smarter than whites and
things like that, but because (Sant took off his turquoise ring from
one finger and put it on another finger; he looked at the new finger
now), but because they always had two Indians just against his
own self.

"Show him to me," Sant said.

"You got to pay something," The Other Indian said.

"What?"

"Two arrowheads."

Sant took out one arrowhead from his clip-shirt cowboy
pocket, spat on it and shined it up with his dirty hand and passed
it to Afraid Of His Own Horses. Afraid Of His Own Horses took
it and The Other Indian said, "That will be two arrowheads, sir."

"That's all it's worth."

"A white boy that's black?"

"Yeah. That's all it's worth."

"If you give us two we'll count it as a down payment if you
buy him."

"I'll give you all my share of the gold."

"That, sir, we've got," The Other Indian said.

"I'll give you my father and my mother."

"That, sir, we've already got two of," Afraid Of His Own
Horses said.

"All right," Sant said and he removed another arrowhead

318

from his clip-front cowboy shirt and without bothering to spit on it or shine it up in any way he handed it to The Other Indian.

"Remember that counts as first payment if I buy."

"Aren't we very nice?" The Other Indian said taking the arrowhead.

"You got both of my arrowheads."

"I still think we're very nice," Afraid Of His Own Horses said. "Who else outside of us two Indians would do this?"

"I guess you're right," Sant said.

"You want to get on the back of my horse and ride there?"

"Where?"

"That's the secret."

"I guess I do," Sant said.

The Other Indian and Afraid Of His Own Horses mounted their horses they had staked in back of a piñon, and Sant jumped on the back of The Other Indian's horse. He didn't have to put his arm around The Other Indian. He didn't have to hold on to an Indian.

"Why don't you Indians get some saddles?"

"Because we're cowboys."

"Well, you look like Indians to me," Sant said. "Where are you taking me to anyway?"

"No, we are not taking you to Anyway," The Other Indian said.

"No, we haven't been there in an awfully long time," Afraid Of His Own Horses said.

"Not that we have anything against the place."

"No."

"It's just that we've decided to take you to Somewhere for a change."

"I think you'll like Somewhere very much," Afraid Of His Own Horses said.

"Anyway is overrun with tourists now," The Other Indian said.

"Somewhere is the only place to go," Afraid Of His Own Horses agreed.

"Oh, Indians are cards," Sant said, annoyed and bracing

himself on the flank of the Indian's piebald horse. "Indians are cards."

"Indians," Afraid Of His Own Horses said, swinging his horse through the rocks, in the lead, "Indians don't like to be run all together. We're Navahos."

"Then Navahos are cards," Sant said.

"No, we're Indians."

"Well, here's where I get off," Sant said.

"Never get on an airplane at all or get off a horse that's moving."

"Is that an Indian saying?"

"Now it is," The Other Indian said.

In the lead, Afraid Of His Own Horses was twirling a rope for no reason at all, but he was also following an arroyo and inspecting the sides carefully for a very good reason. He was looking for a way down that would work. There are many ways down an arroyo in Indian country but there are very few of them that will work. That is, an arroyo is always cutting and there are very few paths down that last very long before they are undercut by flood waters that tear down every time it rains. Sometimes you get halfway down a steep, two-hundred-foot, narrow path before you realize, or the horse realizes, it is not safe and you have to get off the horse and try to keep the horse from panicking while you attempt to turn it around on a one-foot path. It is something like trying to maneuver an elephant on a two-by-four. These paths are always started by sheep or cattle on a slope that has begun to stabilize on the angle of repose and to build up protection for itself of greasewood, rabbit brush, and sage. Then the arroyo swing begins to make an S and undercuts all that nature has done to recover, all the cattle have done to get a drink, and it foils this small cowboy and these two Indians from finding their treasure. Another thing about the sides of an arroyo is that horses and cattle will never even start down an arroyo path that is undercut if left to themselves. But if left to themselves horses are obviously quite useless. They might go around in circles or squares but they won't go down in an arroyo, and that is why Afraid Of His Own Horses watched for a path which he thought would be a working path to force the horses down.

After rejecting many he finally turned into one and spurred the horse down followed by The Other Indian and, of course, by Sant, who shared the horse with The Other Indian. Sant had to grapple with The Other Indian now, and the Indian's sun-catching *concha* belt burned his hands as they went down the slope. They went all the way down without any trouble. Here the bottom of the arroyo was fed by springs, and to follow the arroyo they had to keep crossing and recrossing the stream that refused to stay in the center but kept swinging from one side of the bank to the other. Sometimes the horses would refuse the soft sand crossing and the Indians would drop down and pull the horses over. Sant never got off the horse. He sat on the horse and told the Indians how to do things. "The customer's always right," he said.

"Well, supposing the customer got pushed off the horse and got drowned?" The Other Indian said, pulling on the horse and knee deep in water.

"The customer would still be right," Sant said. "Right is right. Of course I might not ever buy the treasure anyway. Particularly if I'm not shown any respect."

"We'll show you plenty of everything," Afraid Of His Own Horses said.

They were all on the horses now as they began to wind up out of the arroyo. The lead Indian had on a straw orange cowboy hat above a paint horse. Sant wore his purple cowboy shirt, and The Other Indian had yellow chaps, so that, at a distance, they seemed a flamboyant bouquet, a slow-moving riot of color, strange and tropic, moving through the dry sage to the hills.

"I can't make too great a trip at this time of year," Sant said. "You wouldn't be taking me to New York City, New York?"

"Is that in Indian Country?" the lead Indian said.

"No," Sant said. "The Indians sold it off."

"What do they grow there now?"

"Very tall buildings, I understand," Sant said.

"If you got plenty of water you can do anything," the lead Indian said.

321

"And the wit and the will and the wisdom," Sant said.

"What's that?"

"Well, it's what you learn at school."

"Well then maybe it's a good thing we never showed up. Can you eat it?"

"No, and you can't ride it," Sant said.

"Well then maybe it's a good thing we never showed up."

"Will you take me to New York or not?"

"No."

"What's the matter with New York?"

"Do you like it?"

"No. I just asked what's the matter with it?"

"Do we have to put up with this for just money?" The Other Indian said.

They were out of the arroyo and had moved across the chico and rabbit-brush country and were well into the piñon when Sant began to sense that the Indians were lost. If you have never seen a lost Indian, remember that very few have. Even these special Indians may never have been lost before. It had probably happened because the lead Indian had been thinking of other things. Of course he blamed it on Sant, the fact that Sant kept bringing things up, but the Indians had kept bringing things up, too, and thinking of other things besides where they were going. Maybe they had stayed down in the blind arroyo too long, maybe not stayed down long enough. Anyway down there you can't see where you are going and when you should come up. But maybe it was because the lead Indian was not much of a lead Indian today. When you are trying to sell something at a high price you don't remember where you are.

"Do you remember where you are?" Sant said.

"I know where I'm going," Afraid Of His Own Horses said.

"But do you remember where you are?" Sant said again.

"But we know where we're going," The Other Indian said.

"But if you don't remember where you are how are you going to get to where you're going?"

The lead Indian stopped his horse. "Is that what they teach you in school?"

"Yes. Part of it," Sant said.

"Then it's a good thing we never showed up," The Other Indian said.

"Well, it's common sense as well," Sant said.

"How did you get all those wells in there?" The Other Indian said.

"It's because," Sant said, "I was using a preterit pluperfect clause."

Afraid Of His Own Horses looked up into the pine country and scratched his head.

"You know," he said carefully, "the boy is absolutely right."

"Well, I was only guessing," Sant said.

"Yes, you are absolutely right," Afraid Of His Own Horses said. "We are lost."

"I was only guessing," Sant said. "It is nice of you to admit it."

"Oh, forget I ever mentioned it," Afraid Of His Own Horses said. "I'm just a nice Indian."

"A lost Indian," Sant said.

"Oh, I'm that too. I'm a little of everything," Afraid Of His Own Horses said.

"Maybe if you could tell me what he looks like I could find him—find what we're looking for," Sant said.

The Other Indian looked over at Afraid Of His Own Horses.

"I'd say," Afraid Of His Own Horses said, "he looks particular."

"You mean peculiar," Sant said.

"Yes. A little like that."

"Something like that," The Other Indian said.

"Well, how does he sound?"

"Like this," The Other Indian said. " 'My name is Alastair Benjamin. I presume you are red men.' "

"Well, that's particular all right."

"That's what we been telling you all along," Afraid Of His Own Horses said.

"Yes. What is presume?" The Other Indian said.

"That's both particular and peculiar," Sant said.

"Yes, I don't know what it is either," Afraid Of His Own Horses said.

They walked their horses around for a while in great circles, the Indians looking off in all directions but never coming up with anything except comments on the weather, the very low price of wool, and why the sun gets out of the way in the night. This was nothing original, they were both quoting their fathers and it had nothing at all to do with the treasure they were supposed to be looking for, on which Sant had already paid half.

"Listen," Sant said. "Why don't we scatter the way cowboys and Indians do in the movies. We'll cover more country that way. I'll meet you up there at that big white boulder."

"Where do they scatter to in the movies?"

"Just anyplace."

"Well, we know where that is."

Sant slid off the horse. "Well, I'll see you," he said.

After Sant had gone a way he turned to watch the Indians gallop off in all directions.

When Sant got up to the big white volcanic boulder he sat on top of it a while thinking, his shirt a sharp glint of purple, a bright jewel set in a dazzling rock. Looking out over Indian Country he could see Arizona and if he had been higher on the mountain he could have seen Colorado. Two hundred miles in each direction, that is how clean the air is in Indian Country. He could see Cabezon not too far away and all the other cores of the volcanoes that had helped to make this mountain and he could feel the fast wind in his face that was helping to make this part of the mountain disappear. He could feel and especially see an awful lot of things from here but he could see even no hint or suspicion at all of what he was searching for. He could spot some sheep way out there in the purple-blue haze and some hogans, because he knew how to look for them, and he could spot his own ranch house because of the sudden violent green of the cottonwoods that went around it. But he could spot no speck of anything black. That is a color that never appears in Indian Country. There are all kinds of colors but not that. In Indian Country black is rare, exotic, prized.

Sant slid down now off the rock and wandered, searching,

into the piñon and juniper forest. Piñon grows straight and short, a stalk of pine in miniature. The juniper twists and turns nowhere, shooting out branches in grotesque attitudes, attempting to fight for space with the overreaching pine that crowds in. Sant walked through this short, dense, dry jungle, stopping suddenly after ten paces to listen and catching only the high, sharp cedar smell of the juniper and the very far-off, distant caw of an unhappy bird. Now he stepped abruptly into an absolutely circular clearing, man-made over a thousand years ago by some pre-Pueblo, basket-making wanderers who always built by digging circular holes thirty feet across and three feet deep with a high center post and thatch over this, now long since rotted. But the circle of earth is so beaten down it is never receptive to trees again. Sant walked to the center of the gently sunken clearing and stood there with hands on hips and studied the tight crowd of trees that pressed around.

"Who says I'm not a really cowboy?"

The crowd of trees made an excellent audience so Sant tried again.

"Who says I'm not a really cowboy?"

"Me."

Sant saw that from nowhere had come someone who stood quietly there in the juniper jungle, a miniature man of very coal black, dressed in rags and pieces, the whites of his eyes immediate and demanding from the quiet shade of the forest. He stood there as though he belonged, as though he were part of it, part of something distant and enduring and native there before the white man, before any man came. And yet there was something comic, too, in this ragbag of color he wore which seemed to belie, seemed to give an audacity, to the somber crowd of forest through which he had pushed to the fore. Now he waited patiently and, despite his size, almost majestically beneath the juniper jungle. He finally made a quick gesture, as though to speak for all, then he started to move into the clearing, extending a small black hand from out of his rags.

"I presume," he said, and there was a sudden flash of white from the mouth of the dark face, "I presume you are searching for me."

325

"I presume," Sant said. He did not know what this meant. He had bigger words for later, when he had time to think, but meanwhile he would not be caught off guard. "I presume," Sant said.

"My name is Alastair Benjamin," the small, dark, gay-clad figure said. "I sent two natives to search, to find me another— another white. I sent out two Indians to look."

"Oh?"

"Yes. They are very reliable, alert, not presuming, active—I am in need of food. I will sell them. Will you buy them?"

"I presume," Sant said.

"Then give me anything, something. They're yours."

"I presume no," Sant said.

"Oh," the dark, tattered miniature that called himself Alastair Benjamin said. He said it suddenly, "Oh," as though he had been bitten. Then he sat down and began to rub his huge almond eyes, and Sant realized that he was crying.

Sant looked around at the forest for some kind of idea. Some kind of big word maybe that, used well, would make the raggedy stranger feel better.

"I remit to say that I am king of the Indians," Sant said. That didn't seem to stop the raggedy stranger from crying so Sant thought he would try one of the stranger's own words.

"I presume to be willing."

That didn't work either so he looked around at the forest and said, "I'm a really cowboy."

That seemed to work better. The stranger almost stopped crying and said, "That's why I ran away, why I came up here, because that's what I am too."

"Well, the first presume we got to do is to eat," Sant said.

That did something. The sobbing finally came to a gentle halt and Alastair Benjamin stood up.

"Maybe we can become partners," he said.

"Partners?"

"Yes. Don't cowboys have partners?"

"Yes, they do," Sant said and he stuck out his hand, and Alastair Benjamin took it and the forest seemed to press, lean forward a little to get a better look.

326

Farther down the slope the two Indians who had scattered were working the badlands, those deep, eroded clay formations with alleys and sudden towering castles in the clouds like a huge undiscovered city. They searched this bright magic maze of legerdemain until they were certain there was no Alastair Benjamin there, then they went back to the rendezvous and from there tracked Sant to the clearing in the forest.

They both slid off their horses, and Afraid Of His Own Horses said, "Well, I see you found him first."

"I presume," Sant said.

"Yes," Alastair Benjamin said. "And I've decided not to sell you at all."

"Sell us?" The Indians looked at each other.

"Yes," Alastair Benjamin said. "I've decided we should all become partners."

"Partners?"

"Yes," Alastair Benjamin said.

"Indians don't have partners," The Other Indian said.

"That's how much you know about Indians," Sant said.

"Well," Alastair Benjamin said, "then we can become enemies."

"We always have been enemies," Sant said. "That's how much you know about cowboys and Indians."

"Yes, that's how much he knows about cowboys and Indians," The Other Indian said.

"I know enough to know that we can't be good enemies," Alastair Benjamin said, "if you got all the horses and we haven't got none."

"You know," Sant said, "he's right, I presume."

"He could be right, I presume," Afraid Of His Own Horses said.

"Then if the other Indian will get on the back of your horse—" Alastair Benjamin said to Afraid Of His Own Horses.

The Other Indian did this, and Sant and Alastair Benjamin crawled on the vacant horse and rode off, leaving the two Indians in the middle of the clearing.

327

"I wonder how he knew your name," Afraid Of His Own Horses said.

"I don't know," The Other Indian said. "But I think he's got us all presuming too damn much. Where did they go?"

"Oh, they're gone now."

"With my horse."

"I presume," Afraid Of His Own Horses said.

Sant and Alastair Benjamin rode down, hidden, through the long mountain forest, then appeared, visible in the scrub oak, until finally they entered the chest-high sage—a study in grand color on a paint horse.

"Where are you from?" Sant said.

"From the Amenoy Orphanage in Albuquerque," Alastair Benjamin said.

"What's an orphanage?"

"That's a place."

"What kind of a place?"

"Well, it's a place where rich people's kin go."

"And you don't mind associating with me?"

"No. Hardly at all," Alastair Benjamin said.

"Is that the way rich people dress—the way you dress?"

"They dress every kind of a way," Alastair Benjamin said. "That's how you can tell they're rich."

"How does it feel to be rich?"

"It feels okay when you eat," Alastair Benjamin said.

They took the short cut back through the badlands, that other world on earth. You always go down into badlands and then, when you look up, you are hit with another world, a world of battlements and gay cathedrals in the sun—nature bizarre, nature weird, nature at its brilliant best. A gallery, a museum unseen, where you always go down, a city in the southwest, a cellar in the sun.

"An orphanage," Sant said. "Do you have to have a lot of rich kin people to be at a place like that?"

"Yes."

"Is it good, a place like that?"

"They say it is."

328

"Why did you leave a place like that?"

"Because I run away."

"Why did you run away from a place like that?"

"Because I want to be a cowboy."

Sant was neck-reining the great paint horse through the secret way home, the marked labyrinths of the badlands.

"I'm a really cowboy," Sant said.

"I could have told you that the second I saw you," Alastair Benjamin said.

"Then why didn't you?"

"Because I thought you had already presumed it."

"Well, it's always nice to have it presumed out loud by somebody new," Sant said.

"Yeah, I guess it is," Alastair Benjamin said.

Sant was beginning to thread the paint horse now up out of the painted badlands. Sant turned halfway on the horse and faced Alastair Benjamin.

"Why are you black?" Sant said. "You're the first one I ever saw."

"Rich people are black," Alastair Benjamin said.

"Were all your kin people black?"

"I don't know how rich they all were," Alastair Benjamin said. Alastair Benjamin tightened his hold on Sant as they began to go up. "Does a cowboy have to be white? Could he be another color?"

"Sure," Sant said. *"Cómo no?* Why not? With a horse, an Indian, anything, what difference does a color make to a really cowboy?"

Sant felt Alastair Benjamin release his hold, go easy behind him as they climbed the final rise and left the badlands behind them.

"Why were you coming up this way?" Sant said.

"Because this is where I came from."

"Before you were rich?"

"Yeah."

"How do you know this is where you came from?"

"Because I remember they brought me down there by taking

me down alongside this big, long mountain. So that's the way I came back. I just followed the mountain back."

"But whereabouts did you come from alongside the mountain? How did you know where to stop?"

"I remember the earth was red where I came from so I stopped here where the earth began to get a little bit red."

"It's a little bit orange here only."

"Well, that's getting close."

"Yes, I guess it is."

"I kept asking people where the earth was red and they kept pointing up this way."

"Maybe you only wanted to get as far from where you were and become a cowboy."

"Maybe."

"Is that all you remember about the place you were—that the dirt was red?"

"That's all I remember now."

"Maybe you only wanted to get away from all those rich people and become a cowboy."

Alastair drew his hand carefully over his face in thought.

"Yes, maybe. They didn't treat me so good there," Alastair said.

"That's my house," Sant said, pointing to the cottonwoods.

"You mean you got a whole house for just you and your kin people?"

"Yeah. Don't rich people have that?"

"No, they don't," Alastair Benjamin said.

"Cowboys always have it."

"That's why I want to be a cowboy."

Sant made a great circle of the house, always keeping the cup of the hill between the riders and the house. When he had circled the house twice he dismounted in a grove of tamarisk.

"You wait here," Sant said.

"Don't I get to go no farther?" The stranger wiped a dark arm across his face.

"I just don't know," Sant said and he walked off toward the

house, leaving Alastair Benjamin alone on the top of the paint horse hidden in the tamarisk, which is purple in June.

Sant walked into the kitchen that was thick, adobe-walled. It had been calcimined pink; and his mother, in a powder-blue, Sears best house dress, was taking the bread out of the oven. Her face was good, uncalculating, easy, open, and interested.

"Where've you been?" she said.

"Looking."

"Looking for what?"

"Things."

"What did you find?"

"Somebody from an orphanage."

"Do you know what that is, somebody from an orphanage?"

"Yes."

"What is it?"

"Black."

"Well, not always," she said.

"Well, they always got rich kin people then," Sant said.

"Not ever," she said.

"Oh," Sant said. "But can we keep him? All alone I haven't got anyone to be a cowboy with."

"Orphan," she said. She tapped a brown loaf to test it. "Well, that's all right. Black. That's all right, I guess." She walked to the window. "But it's never done," she said. She watched out the window. "Your father has discovered him. He's driving him away, I think. Here comes your father now."

Big Sant looked very tired and he came in and sat heavily in the chair.

"I put the boy in the barn. But we can't take him in, Millie."

"Of course we can't. I know that."

"Of course we can't. But we've got to, Millie."

"Why?"

"He's been beaten, very badly beaten, with a two-by-four across the back. We don't do that to animals. We've got no choice, Millie."

"Well, no, I guess we haven't. But then still—you still better call the authorities. I'll go out and talk to him."

"I've already talked to him."

"That's why I want to talk to him. I want to find out what happened to you. You call the authorities."

"All right," he said.

When she came back, in five minutes, she said, "Well, did you call?"

"The line's not working."

"Well, there's no hurry," she said. "I've got to fix him some clothes."

Big Sant got up now and walked over and sat on the chair Little Sant had just left to go out to the barn. But Big Sant still kept his eyes on Millie Sant.

"He's never been able to keep anything yet. There's nothing he's brought home yet we haven't made him turn loose. And now this. He's certainly not a sheep dog either. He may be absolutely no account at all. Still," he said, "still—" Then he said suddenly, "So he talked you around too?"

"No," she said. "He could never do that. Impossible. It's just that—well, it's simply that, well—" She was tossing around Little Sant's clothes now, holding things up to the light to examine them, to find something that would fit. "Well," she said, "you know what he's like."

"Yes," Big Sant said, placing his cowboy boots on the table and staring at the ceiling. "By now, after seeing, talking with him, we all, everyone knows, I presume."

Big Sant was silent a long moment, watching out the window.

"I wonder if it could be the boy."

"What boy?"

"There were some Indians who said there was a boy in that cabin." Sant stroked the broad purple flower on his face.

Millie jerked her head suddenly toward him as if to swear but then, just as abruptly, her expression became calm and beatific.

"Om mani padme hum. Oh the flower in the heart of the lotus, Amen."

"Amen," Big Sant said.

FOUR There was never a place or time when time was not involved. It had just fled by—three years. Time had cut deeper the huge arroyo through the center of the Circle Heart. It had caused Millie to accept and reject the idea three times (now it was rejected) that Alastair might have been sent to them as the Living Prophet. Time had not cut the arroyo, though, as much as in former years and Alastair had only been rejected as divine the more he filled her earthly yearnings.

And there was always the brilliant land, the wide country, uncharted and unknown, unlike the seas, unplumbed and undiscovered—unsung. The land with island mesas rising from the gray sea of sage and falling away into the long canyons of the night. The land, towered and pinnacled, sculptured by the fine hand of the wind, painted red with iron and green with copper, fired in the sun. Raging in the sun, quiet in the moon.

And the people of this far country: the gentle Indian, the drunken Indian, the begging and the proud and the last Indian, the Indian who will not be here tomorrow, the final Indian. A nation displaced by a baseball team, a V8 with twin pipes, the sixty-four-thousand-dollar question, a strange god, a wad of bubble gum, and you.

And the cowboys. As long as there are cowboys there will be alive the legend and the dream, the frontier, the hardihood and the hardness, the independence and the myth, the iron line to fall back on. And as long as there are cows there will be cowboys. So the secret, and the miracle, of America lies in the bull. Save the bull

333

and save the country. Nurture the legend. Remember Big and Little and Millie Sant, the keepers of the bulls. Remember our triumphs and our tragedies and remember our humor, the coin that makes both bearable.

Remember the Indians. Turn out the lights. Have we forgotten anything?

You will never have forgotten a long day in northern New Mexico. It is not a memory you lose easily. There are all the strange sights and sounds and sudden beauty.

And there are adventures. Nothing like Camelot. Nothing like the Siege of Troy or What is he to Hecuba or Hecuba to him that he should weep for her. But adventures on a high, dry mesa in northern New Mexico. Like this day, today, as Little Sant watched Alastair coming toward him on a white horse—pale horse, dark rider.

Alastair wore a turquoise Navaho bracelet that matched the New Mexican sky and now, as he dismounted, the crude silver caught the sun and glared.

"You're nonchalant," Alastair said. "What you cogitating?"

"Cogitating?" Sant said. "I've been practicing roping and bulldozing all morning. Is that what's called cogitating?"

"What you got?" Alastair said.

"This," Sant said and he took out a dead lizard.

"You had that last week. What else you got?"

"I got this." Sant took out the card with the name of Lemaitre that had cellophane pasted on both sides of it. "The cellophane is to preserve it," Sant said.

"I seen it," Alastair said but touching it with his finger.

"The cellophane is to preserve it," Sant said. "What you got?"

"Information."

"Information about what?"

"Information about an Indian attack on us whites."

They were both huddled now against the old sod front of the house, the section that had been built—mostly dug out of the slope—by Grandfather Bowman. Sant stared at the yellow pickup truck parked near huge sandstone boulders, again yellow, that formed a corral.

334

"But," Alastair said, "I don't know whether exactly if this attack is speculative or manifested."

"Manifested? How manifested?"

"Killing us whites."

Sant knew he must remain nonchalant.

"How is this manifested?"

"You're being very nonchalant," Alastair said.

"How is it being manifested and all?"

"Throwing rocks down on the secret canyon house."

"You told them they could join?"

"They said they don't want to join no white outfit."

"You told them you were, for example, black?"

"Yes, but they can see different. They know, for example, the way I live, speak the language and all. It's hard to fool an Indian."

"You can't fool an Indian, but you can ambush them." Sant reached for a stick of rabbit brush and began to trace in the hard dirt. "When they start tossing rocks down on the secret canyon house you can bet an Indian will be close to his horse. No chance to ambush them. But when they hunt piñon nuts on the Peña Blanca Mesa later in the afternoon you can bet they'll be what you call nonchalant and you can ambush them. And I bet if you didn't read all those books you could speak English."

"What are we going to do with them after we ambush them?"

"Never scalp an Indian before you catch him." Sant got up and began to catch a pinto horse called Temperature 99. He waved the horse with gentle movements into the corral corner and removed a bridle from the side of the barn. He held the bridle behind his back with his right hand as he talked to the horse and slowly eased the bridle over the horse's head, gently.

"Temperature 99 is dangerous," Alastair said.

Sant threw on the double Navaho blanket woven like a United States flag but with only five stars, and then he threw on the Monkey Ward saddle.

"Not if you ambush him," Sant said. Sant tossed the reins of the horse over the hitching post to keep Temperature 99 from nipping back as Sant pulled hard on the belly strap.

"You got to ambush him first," Sant said.

Under the floor of the secret canyon house there must have been two tons of gold. The fact that it was not gold bothered no one at all. It looked like gold. Also at the secret canyon they had a secret language to confuse the Indians. The fact that no one else spoke it was of no importance. They spoke it. They spoke some Navaho, too, and plenty of Spanish, as did their neighbors, but Alastair Benjamin spoke no black, only white and this secret language which the Indians knew Alastair had made up out of his own head, which still made Alastair a white. You can't fool an Indian. Everyone was white or Indian, sometimes Spanish, but that was all there was. You couldn't pull another kind of people out of your hat and fool an Indian.

"Which makes us," Alastair Benjamin had said one early morning while shooting a cornsilk cigarette out of Sant's mouth, "the only white people here." He had lowered the gun and touched a very white handkerchief to a coal forehead. "And I just come awful close to my being the only one left."

When they had got the horses swinging easily and together in a nice lope through the mouth of the wide Baca Arroyo and were approaching the narrow neck of Wetherill Canyon, big, towering, orange and clean up to the sky on both sides, Alastair Benjamin looked up at the slit of hard blue above.

"You still going to be a bronc man when you get grown up?"

"I'm grown up."

"I mean when you get paid for being grown up."

"When I get paid for grown up—yes sir!"

"How much will you charge for a bronc show?"

"Forty hundred dollars or so. I don't know."

"Them movie cowboys aren't really cowboys."

"No sir!"

"They shoot sixty shots from a six-shooter."

"Yeah."

"And they ride through brush country without chaps. That would tear a cowboy's clothes all off."

"Yessir."

"They say Tom Mix and Zane Grey were real cowboys."

"That's because they're dead."

"Is Zane Grey dead?"

"I think he is."

They were moving deep into the dark canyon now. The bright walls all became gray on the shadow side. They moved easily at the bottom of the long crack that led even deeper into the heart of the wild mountain.

"You take an Indian," Alastair Benjamin said. Alastair Benjamin ran his arm along the neck of his white horse to reassure the animal against the darkness of the canyon. "You take an Indian," Alastair Benjamin repeated, his soft voice knocked back sharp from the close rock. "Why won't an Indian join our outfit?"

"It's a white outfit," Sant said.

"Will the Indians always be our enemies?"

"I guess so."

"Why?"

"Well, what would there be to do for example if they weren't?"

"Yeah."

"Indians are just naturally Indians."

"And there wouldn't be nobody to fight if they weren't. For example, there'd be nothing to do."

"That's right. I wonder what they do in the city, where there are no Indians."

"Nothing I guess."

"Oh they probably do something."

"I guess they do."

Now the canyon began to widen and let in more of the sky, which allowed the rock to resume its varicolors again, still towering but vivid now and visible, shone upon and shining back, greeted and greeting back, all lighted and lighting in pyrotechnic reds to the abrupt sky.

"You like this better?" Alastair Benjamin asked his horse.

Sant began to work his eye along the sheer face of the left canyon wall to pick up the geological fault that, as they rode on, would become wider. It would always remain about two hundred feet up but soon the slipping formation beneath would become a narrow ledge that a man could walk on, then it would become so wide you could set down a house, which the Old People had done before the white man came. Even before the Navahos came. Alastair Benjamin had been the first white man to see it and Sant had been the first to climb up to it. Climbing up to it was quite a trick. The Old People had used handholds and yucca fiber ropes that they pulled up after them at night or when being chased by the people who must have finally caught them.

"There she is," Sant said, pointing. They both pulled in their horses and their eyes followed the great distance up the side of the wall to where the secret house sat on a secret ledge. Actually part of the house was in a natural cave, but even that part had a roof and wall and window openings, and part of the house was a tower like those that the same people had built in the flat open country. In other words, it seemed as though these people didn't give up a style easily. When they built in the cliff they built the same way they had always built. They weren't going to give up something simply because they were hiding.

"Who you think they were hiding from?" Alastair Benjamin said.

Sant looked away from the house and to the top of the cliff two hundred feet above.

"New people, I guess."

"But what did the new people have against these people?"

"They was here."

"That's all?"

"I guess that was plenty," Sant said and he moved his pinto horse down the gentle slope, and Alastair Benjamin followed on his all-white.

After going up a steep path they arrived now at the spot where they made the two-hundred-foot climb straight up the face of the cliff. The Old People had chipped handholds in the flat rock most of the way up but the earth from the bottom of the cliff had eroded down ten feet since then, or they had used their yucca fiber ropes at the bottom. Anyway there were no handholds on the first ten feet of the climb, so it was necessary for Sant to stand tiptoe on the pommel of his saddle to begin his climb. As soon as Sant's weight left the saddle the pinto moved forward and began to graze, and Alastair Benjamin moved his horse in and followed Sant.

They worked their way up and up the flat burning face of the cliff. They could have waited until the sun left the cliff but then it would have been in shadow—more comfortable but more dangerous—much easier then to mistake a weathering on the face for a true handhold. Shadows hide and they deceive too. But, most of all, shadows come before the darkness of a fall. So they sweated and burned upward in the sun, rapidly like quick monkeys against the moving of the sun. Before the dangerous arrival of the shadows on the sheer face, they went upward like quick monkeys moving fast.

"There," Sant said. "Look down there."

Alastair Benjamin turned his head cautiously downward and saw two Indian boys leading away their horses.

"Now, why would they do that?"

"Because we're here," Sant said between his teeth, and clinging.

They reached a ledge soon where they could sit down. Above them the handholds ceased and they would have to use a rope— the lasso that Sant had carried around his neck.

"Yeah," Alastair said, sitting and watching down, "I been cogitating."

"You been thinking too," Little Sant said.

"Yeah," Alastair said watching the Indians move down canyon with their horses. "I been thinking that the universe is not moral, that things fall upon the just and the unjust equally almost."

"That's what my dad says, but Ma doesn't agree."

"Yeah."

"What does it mean?"

"Big Sant says it covers everything," Alastair said.

"Does it cover us ambushers being ambushed?"

"I guess it does."

"What else do you know?"

"We come a fur piece."

"I know where you got that. From the movie cowboys."

"Yeah."

"Like us, they got a secret language too."

"Yeah, I guess they have."

They had reached the point now in the climb where they had to cross a wide fissure in the rocks. It was about ten feet across. When the Old People built the house the crack might not have been there, or they had used the yucca ropes. Anyway now it was a ten-foot gap with almost one hundred feet of nothing beneath to the floor of the canyon. Sant rose, uncoiled his rope, adjusted the loop, and began swinging it around his head. There was not too much room and it was difficult. He kept his eye on a pinnacle of rock twenty feet above. The thing was to lasso this pinnacle, which was part of a formation that, up there, hung over the middle of the void. You lassoed this and then swung over the ten-foot gap. Sant caught the pinnacle on his first try and winked back at Alastair Benjamin.

"Lemaitre," Alastair Benjamin said.

Sant moved to the edge of the gap now, pulling in the loose rope and coiling it around his wrist.

"Okay," Sant said. "Shove me off."

Alastair Benjamin moved in behind him and gave him a push. Sant swung out over the void and when he reached the other ledge he touched it with his foot and pushed back hard with his leg. Back he came across the gap almost into the arms of Alastair Benjamin. Alastair Benjamin gave him another push, sending him again out over space, and this time he had enough momentum to drop off on the other side. He held the rope. He made a coil of the loose rope now and shot it back to Alastair Benjamin. Alastair Benjamin caught the rope and advanced to the edge of the big drop, coiling the slack rope and tensing himself to jump.

"Be nonchalant," Sant shouted.

Alastair Benjamin wiped the sweat off his forehead and said, "I'm coming." Then he came. Sant was ready for him and shot him back across the gap. The second time he came back he still did not think he had the momentum to land safely.

"Again," he said, and Sant gave him another shove out over space. "Again," Alastair Benjamin said when he came back.

"Land this time," Sant said.

"Landing," Alastair Benjamin said and he landed on top of Sant and they both went down.

"There," Sant said from the scramble and looking down below. "There go the Indians with our horses."

"The ambushers been ambushed," Alastair Benjamin said.

"The bushwhackers been bushwhacked," Sant agreed.

"We can't go back down."

"So we got to go up."

"Who was it stole our horses, can you see?"

"Indians."

"But what Indians?"

"Bad Indians."

"But what's their names?"

"Including the middle name their names is Awful Bad Indians."

"I think one of them is Afraid Of His Own Horses. He's wearing a red baseball cap this season."

"And instead of stealing second an Indian steals horses."

"That's not a very good joke, Santo."

Sant looked up at the cliff above and back down the void where they had come. "I guess it's not too funny," Sant said.

"Afraid Of His Own Horses always hangs out with The Other Indian."

"The Other Indian's a pretty good guy. Are you saying he'd try to break up our outfit?"

"Yeah."

"Yeah, I guess he would all right."

"Shall we get started up?"

"Yeah, I guess we better get started up."

The old handholds resumed again now and Alastair Benjamin went first. They had left the lasso rope dangling. They would retrieve it when they reached the pinnacle twenty feet above.

"I got a feeling," Alastair Benjamin said, "that the shadows are coming on."

"Keep going, Alley," Sant said.

"I don't know whether the next one's a handhold or not."

"Keep moving, Alley."

Well, that one was.

"They've got to be. We can't back, we've come too far and

341

we can't get caught on the face now. We would be lost in five minutes. The only way now is up."

"I don't know—what do you think about this next one?"

"Just keep moving, Alley."

The next one was okay, but what now?

"Just up, Alley. Always up. We stop and it's all over."

"I think I'll rest."

"You can't rest here, Alley."

"You should have gone first again."

"I can't pass you now, Alley."

"I guess I'm finished, Santo. My hands have gone dead."

Sant looked at his own hands and realized he could not feel them or control them at all.

"Alley?"

"Yes, Santo?"

Sant was quiet long moments and then he said from the now-lengthening shadows, "Alley, I've got hold of a mountain mahogany bush. I've moved over to the right and have got hold of a mountain bush. If you keep moving up I can see the handholds get much larger. If you fall you'll just land in the bush. Get started up, Alley."

He heard Alley move up above him in the shadows. He could not move himself; he would have to hang here and think of another trick to get himself moving, but he could think of nothing, only feel the pain in his deadening arms.

What does a bronc man do? What does a real bronc man do?

Now he felt something brush his face. It was a rope. A bronc man has friends in high places.

Above, when Alastair Benjamin had made it over the ledge, he got the rope and dropped it down to Sant. Now he gave the final heave that pulled Sant up on the ledge too.

"Not that you needed any help," Alastair Benjamin said.

"No. I was okay," Sant said.

They sat a long time resting and recovering and finally trying to capsulize all the wisdom of the ages into one good sentence that might last. The best they could do was: In this country it never rains in June and almost never in August with the exception, anyway as far as last August is concerned, of last year and maybe the year before that. They couldn't remember.

"Anyway, Santo," Alastair Benjamin said standing, "let's get moving."

"Cómo no?" Sant said. "Why not?"

It was easy going now along the wide ledge that ran to the cliff house. When they got to the cliff house the first thing they did was go in and see if the gold was okay—iron pyrites they had dug off the side of the ledge that looked more like gold than gold did.

"The gold is okay, Santo," Alastair said.

"Yeah," Sant said, running his hands through it. "It sure is handy to have a lot of gold if you ever want to run away or something."

"Yeah," Alastair said. "Like the trader, Mr. Peersall, says, it sure gives you a lot of mobility."

"What does that mean?"

"It covers about everything, I guess."

"I bet it does. I bet gold covers about everything, I guess. Alley, let's speak our secret language."

They spoke the secret language now, the one that Alastair had invented.

"Santo," Alastair said finally in English. "Let's get out of here."

"Yeah, but how?"

"The easy way."

"You want to take the easy way?"

"Don't you think we've had enough of the hard way for one day?"

"Yeah, I guess we have."

First they checked the house thoroughly to make sure that everything was okay. The house was divided into apartments with woven willow reeds over cedar logs for the roofs. To get from one apartment to the next you had to go through the low doors in a stooping position, so the Old People could dispose of you quickly if you didn't belong. Also you always had to go through another apartment to get to your own, which must have made for interesting living. The whole thing was built in about the tenth century,

343

when the Old People had been pressured off the flat country to down here in the middle of cliffs to make a final stand. There was a cesspool-like hole in the front of the building, called a kiva, where the religious rites were held and restricted to men. They must have gathered down there every evening to ask for something they thought important, but the New People finally got everything anyway.

"They sure built nice buildings," Alastair Benjamin said, staring up at it.

The house was made of flat rectangular stones the Old People had gathered above on the top of the mesa and lowered down here. They were mortared with adobe, but the fact that they were worked perfectly and fitted exactly accounted for the building still standing after one thousand years. Around the building were scattered large pieces of pottery with abstract colored pictures, painted with freedom, which signified nothing except maybe that a thing called art is a deeper part of us than we suspect.

"Well, I guess we better get moving before we get attacked."

Alastair Benjamin allowed his eye to climb above the shallow cave where the building lay and to go all the way up, which was about another twenty feet, to the top of the cliff.

"You think they're going to attack us from up there?"

"Well, you know Indians."

"Yeah."

"Indians never miss a chance."

"Why are Indians that way?"

"Because they're Indians."

"It's not because we're white men?"

"Oh, it's that all right."

"Before you said it's because we're here."

"Well, I guess it's a little of both, but we better get started up."

They followed the ledge until a deer path branched off that led quickly to the top of the mesa—that is, it always had. Now they came to a cutback and the path was gone.

"Indians," Sant said.

"Yeah."

Here the sandy bank was very steep and below fell off abruptly at the stone cliff. The sharp, small hard feet of deer had begun, and maintained by continuous use, a path here; but now someone with a sharp instrument had destroyed it, and to try to walk it would send you sliding and then falling to the canyon floor three hundred feet below.

"Indians."

"Well, I guess we better get started back down."

"Yeah."

When they got back to the Old People's building they sat down next to the hole where the men who lived there used to think, and that's what they did too.

"I wonder," Alastair Benjamin said, "what the women did while the men thought."

"Made these pots," Sant said.

"I guess so. Have you thought of anything yet?"

"Yeah," Sant said. "From here we got to throw a lasso over the top and climb up that way."

"We've done it before."

"But not with Indians up there."

"That's true."

"You think when we got started up they would unhook the lasso?"

"Well, you know Indians as well as I do."

"I'm afraid I do."

Alastair Benjamin looked all the way to the top, shading his eyes. "What makes you think the Indians are up there?"

Sant thought a while and then he said, "Well, I know Indians. I may not know nothing else but I think by this time I should know a little about Indians."

Alastair Benjamin rubbed his nose and tried to think of an interesting way he could contradict Sant. And then a rock fell.

"I guess you do," he said.

They retreated back into the part of the cave that overhung the building but the rocks continued to rain down anyway.

"Just to show us they're there," Sant said. "Just to show us how smart an Indian is. And an Indian's awful smart."

345

"If they was smart they'd pretend they weren't there and when we started up they'd unhook our lasso."

"Well, an Indian ain't that smart."

"I wonder if this is the way they killed off the people that lived here."

"Maybe not killed them. Maybe just got them out of here. This same kind of pots"—Sant touched a pile with his foot—"I've seen at the pueblos where people live right now."

"But why didn't they kill them all off before they got away?"

"I just don't know."

"You mean you don't know everything, Santo?"

"Yeah. Not everything, I guess I don't."

"Now the rocks have stopped raining. You think they gave up?"

"Yeah. The Indians don't stay with an attack very long."

"You sure it's safe now to throw up the lasso?"

"Yeah," Sant said, uncoiling the rope. "Maybe I don't know everything but I should know Indians by now."

"I hope you do," Alastair Benjamin said.

Above, the two Indian boys sat near four horses under some piñon scrub, waiting for the rope to come up. They were giggling. Sant's mother had said that Indians, especially Navahos, were the gigglingest people she had ever met.

"You think they'll be fools enough to throw up that rope?"

"Well," The Other Indian said, "if they don't I don't know my whites. And if I don't know my whites I don't know anything."

"Well," Afraid Of His Own Horses said, "there is a bunch who claim you don't know any—" A rope landed near them. "And another bunch who claims you do."

Before they could grab the rope and make the boys below think they had caught something solid the rope was dragged below again.

"You want me to try this time?" Alastair Benjamin said.

"Yeah. Okay. Try to make her land flat and hook one of those tree stumps we've seen up there."

Alastair Benjamin whirled the rope twelve times around his head before he let her fly.

"That puts mojo on it," he said, but it didn't do any good. The rope fell back.

"This way," Sant said, twirling and pumping the loop with a snap. "Like Lemaitre. It puts style into it." He flung the loop with quick grace. "Style," Sant said.

Now he pulled the slack in and the rope went taut.

"I think I've caught something solid," he said. "You want to feel?"

Alastair took the rope and pulled. "It's okay."

"You sure we haven't caught an Indian?"

"Yeah."

"How can you be sure?"

"By the feel."

"How does an Indian feel?"

"With his hands."

"Boy, you're in lousy shape today. I better go first."

Sant took a good grip on the rope, and The Other Indian above dropped the loop on the saddle horn of the horse they had stolen below.

"Something happened," Sant said.

"Yeah, you lost your nerve."

"No, something happened."

"Yeah, you lost your nerve."

"All right," Sant said and he started up. When he got up a way, Alastair Benjamin started up too. Sant turned his head and looked back.

"Don't you feel it's kind of giving?"

"Yeah. Like the tree is bending."

"It feels funny."

"You sure we didn't catch an Indian?"

"Pretty sure."

"Now it's only pretty sure."

"Well, as sure as a man can be. Anyway it's something bigger than an Indian."

"Is it bigger than the both of us?"

"It's funnier than you," Sant said and he began to climb again rapidly now to get it over with.

347

Above, Afraid Of His Own Horses watched the stolen horse brace himself.

"You think he can hold them?" The Other Indian said.

"That's what we're going to find out."

"Maybe we should back the horse up a bit closer to the edge. Make it more interesting."

"Why not?" The Other Indian said.

Sant looked back down. "The rope seems to be stretching."

"If it don't stretch it breaks. You learned that in school."

"We should have stayed there," Sant said and he climbed hard trying to make up for the stretch.

"Well," Afraid Of His Own Horses said, "we can't back the horse any farther without it going over the edge."

"Is that bad?"

"It sure is. Then we couldn't steal the horse again."

"Then why don't you try running the horse forward?"

"Why didn't I think of that?"

"Well, you're not very smart," The Other Indian said.

"Does it strike you that the rope is getting shorter?" Alastair Benjamin said.

"Yeah," Sant said. "What they say about that in school?"

"Indians. We roped an Indian," Alastair Benjamin said, and they both held on as they flew upward fast.

Sant and Alastair Benjamin ended up all in one heap on top of the mesa alongside the tree that they were trying to rope and beneath two of the "gigglingest people"—even for Navahos—that ever lived.

Sant unwound himself to a sitting position and looked carefully at Afraid Of His Own Horses.

"You crazy Indians. Don't you know you almost—?"

"We didn't though, because—well, because—" Afraid Of His Own Horses looked at The Other Indian.

"Because, why, because," The Other Indian said, "if we did that—"

"Let you fall," Afraid Of His Own Horses said.

"Yes. If we did that there wouldn't be anybody left to fight."

"We had that figured out all the time," Alastair Benjamin said.

Sant looked down on the building of the Old People below and then on down to the far canyon floor beneath, blue with distance. Then he removed his small finger from his nose and examined it.

"Yes, that stopped us a lot of times too," Sant said.

FIVE   Indian Country has still got living a real, live Old Indian Fighter.

"I've lived from the age of the horse to the age of the rocket, from the age of real animals to this age of toys. I've—" Mr. Peersall seemed about to deliver a peroration against missiles, an antimissile missive, but he paused. "I don't want to bore you, son."

"Tell us about the gun-slingers of the Old West," Sant said. "Who had the fastest gun?"

"The silliest gun was had by Billy the Kid, the most ridiculous gun was had by Mr. Hickok. Doc Holliday shot number-seven birdshot from a shotgun—he never missed. Mr. Earp lived in Hollywood, died in Frisco. That should finish him. They got those guns now, all of them, preserved in a museum, guns that were never fired, owned by people who didn't exist. Why, they're trying to make heroes out of people claiming they shot themselves into history. They was only, most of the time, trying to shoot their way out of a whorehouse without paying the fee."

"What's that?"

"A place where Navvyhos buy tobacco."

"Oh?"

"Yes. I guess there was only one hero."

"And that was you, Mr. Peersall."

"How did you know, son? Yes, I was the only hero. I was the only hero because I had the only kind of courage that counts. When the Texans in Tularosa wanted to throw all the Mexican kids out of school to protect the white children's pure Texas asses I said

I was a Mexican and would be studying in first grade for a while myself and I would try to see that none of us got bothered. Moral courage. Nothing happened. Moral courage is the only kind that counts. Remember that, and remember, Sant, always hold your hands lightly when you ride, back straight, but always forward. Control the horse with your legs. If you're not part of the horse you're not riding."

"I'll remember, Mr. Peersall," Sant said.

Alastair seemed bored. Every time they went to see Mr. Peersall he was bored. Mr. Peersall never talked about books.

Mr. Peersall claimed that maybe you can get attached to things outside of books—the world. And you can get attached to things that have nothing to do with the world—Indian Country. On Jupiter they say it's so big people can't see each other—never meet up with each other. On Mars it's somewhat different. There are no people to bother you at all on Mars, and you can walk freely about saying and doing pretty much as you please. This is what Mr. Peersall, who ran the trading post and who was actually so old he had fought Indians, said the day before yesterday. This was all apropos of why he stayed in Indian Country since almost infinity—because he couldn't get to Mars, he said.

"Haven't got the time, the money, or the experience, son."

The "son" he had been talking to was Millie Sant. But the old Indian fighter was old and tired and his eyes were bad and he lied a lot because people made him and that's why he called Millie "son." He called people all sorts of odd things. And he threatened the "Navvyhos" still, which the Indians found droll. Alastair anyway said the Indians found it droll. Little Sant found it trying. Big Sant found that he spent all of his time with the cattle and did not have too much time to think about anything much. He brooded down there, Millie said. He brooded darkly, too much.

Up on the vast Martian spaces of the mesa, gay-colored horses moved rapidly, skimming across the wide, flat mesa so that at a distance they seemed borne in the dust they created, seemed part of the heavy white clouds and even the blue beyond. Close they were a roar—four plunging horses tearing the mesa in attitudes of blind speed, splitting the awful silence up there, with jacks jumping

351

up ahead and the buzzards tightening their circles above in anticipation of something happening there below, on a weird, dry, moon mesa of the planet Earth.

"Nonchalant," Sant said between his teeth. "That's all we need."

Sant, straight, white, and wind-burned, rode out in front followed by Alastair Benjamin, who was followed by a red boy, followed in turn by another Indian, The Other Indian. Sant was close to thirteen now, and the others were about that age except Afraid Of His Own Horses, who was fourteen and a half and who was mad now because no one else would do what he wanted to do.

"Don't you think he's crazy, Alley?" Sant said to Alastair Benjamin, turning on his horse.

"Yeah."

"Seeing someone in a shack counting it and knowing where it's hidden, like in a book."

"Even in a movie," Alastair Benjamin said, "would they be giving the Indians two hundred thousand dollars, even in a movie?"

"Yeah, that's right," Sant said.

"Even in a movie it's an original conception," Alastair Benjamin said.

"And they're being nonchalant."

"Oh, Indians are always nonchalant. That doesn't mean anything. Indians are always nonchalant," Alastair said, and Sant increased the speed of his horse and they all, including the Indians, leaped forward suddenly.

"Nonchalant," Sant repeated again. "That is all we need."

They had gotten their other words from Alastair Benjamin or the radio commercials, but this one, nonchalant, they had gotten from an old sign that an Indian had stolen from Route 66 to make a door for his hogan. His door had read: BE NONCHALANT— LIGHT A MURAD. So that Indian family was always known as Murad. And the boy, the son of the father, Sant and Alastair had captured once throwing rocks at their secret house and they had tied him to a stake and lighted a small fire, scattered by Sant's mother, but not before they had lighted a Murad. And he wasn't very nonchalant, Alastair Benjamin had said.

352

"You think, Santo—" Alastair Benjamin had his blue-dyed straw cowboy hat pulled hard over his forehead so that he could barely see and be seen—"you think they could maybe—our Indians, I mean—you think they could maybe not even have two hundred thousand dollars?"

"Yeah."

"But if they have it and we maybe don't get any of it at all? That is, supposing they just ride off and eat it or something all their selves without us?"

"That's what they'll do if we're anxious. We got to be retiring."

"We sure do."

"We got to pretend like we got more than that. That is, we got to act up to our own gold and all."

"Yeah."

"We got to be very uninterested in two hundred thousand dollars or so. Indians can tell when we whites bite too hard."

"When they got us hooked."

"We got to be indiffident."

"You can say that again."

"We got to be indiffident."

"Okay, that's all. What you think, Santo, you think the Indians are listening?"

Sant lifted his hat and half turned in his saddle and watched the following Indians. One of them, Afraid Of His Own Horses, had on his red baseball cap and a white tie over a blue T shirt. He wore stovepipe cowboy boots with white eagles in inlaid leather. He was quite an Indian. The Other Indian was dressed identically except he wore a yellow straw cowboy hat with a high roll and he had no tie on at all. The Other Indian was some Indian too. Both of the Indians rode bareback and rode very well.

"Well," Sant thought out loud to Alastair, "you can't tell about Indians. An Indian could be listening or not listening and no man could say amen."

"Amen."

"An Indian could be dead or alive, breathing or not breathing, fighting or fooling—"

353

"Amen."

"What I mean is we'll both forget about their two hundred thousand dollars."

Alastair Benjamin pulled his blue hat even harder down on his black forehead. "I won't."

"I mean, Alley, we got to pretend to be indiffident."

"Yeah. But you sure you got that indiffident pronounced right?"

"Yeah, I got it right all right."

"Because if that's what we're going to be—"

"I got it right all right. Anyway you know what it means. It means we're not interested in their two hundred thousand dollars."

"You're not."

"Alley, are you with me or with the Indians?"

"Do you want to make it red or white?"

"Yeah."

"Then I'm with us."

"You'll never live to regret it."

"I always have."

"That's not fair."

"Well, you said I'd never live to do something and I said I always have."

"I never thought of it that way."

"Santo, you think there's any danger going with our Indians?"

"Well, if there is my name's not Sant Bowman."

"Well, if it's not Sant Bowman what is it then?" Alastair Benjamin said.

"I don't know, Alley. I just don't know."

"But you don't think we should be worried?"

"Worried? Worried about what? Certainly not whites in front of Indians."

"You mean we shouldn't lose noses?"

"Faces. Or face, I guess it is."

"How about our lives?"

"Well, you've got a point there."

"I didn't want to make a big point of it."

354

"You go right ahead and make as big a point of it as you want."

"Oh, forget I ever mentioned it," Alastair Benjamin said.

"No, you're entitled to your ideas too."

"But not to the aforesaid exclusion of your say."

"Oh, I'll have my say."

"Yes, I guess you will," Alastair Benjamin said.

On the other side of the mesa two men stood on the path that cut through the sagebrush, holding sawed-off shotguns. They were dressed like hunters in plaid woolen shirts and caps and high-top leather woodsmen's boots, but everything was too new and fit too well and the shotguns were sawed off. Three days ago they had robbed a bank in Durango.

"I really don't think the Indians will come back, Mike."

"You think he'll believe that story about us being government men here to distribute this money to the Indians?"

"Well, if you'd been here instead of mailing that Mother's Day card maybe you could have told him something better."

"I never got it mailed. I told you that trading post was closed."

"Then we can forget it."

"No, we can't. The day after tomorrow is Mother's Day."

"And you don't think they'll trace the address?"

"By the time they do that we'll be across the border and into Mexico."

"Why don't you send it from Mexico?"

"Then Mother's Day will be past."

"Did you ever think that of the three guys you murdered they had mothers too?"

"You talk like a cop."

"I only want to talk you out of mailing that letter."

"No. If Mother didn't hear from me on Mother's Day she would go crazy. But I've got an idea. I've been thinking about it. We can run a trip wire from the door of the shack to the trigger of a shotgun that will fire on the person opening the door. That way the Indian and his friends will get a blast in the face."

"And Mother will get her card on Mother's Day."

"Can you think of something else?"

355

"Yes. Forget your mother."

"You don't know my mother."

"Oh?"

"She's not like other mothers."

"I believe you."

"You really don't believe me. It was just your way of getting me to go on this job." The man's voice now rose like a woman's and he began gesturing with the gun.

"I tell you I believe you, Francis."

"Very well, if you believe me then let's go and mail the letter. The trading post should be open now."

"You don't trust me alone with the money?"

"Well—"

"All right. I'll go along. But why don't we take the money with us and make a run for it now?"

"Because they'll still have a roadblock."

"Then why don't we take the money with us to the trading post while we mail the letter?"

"Because a large bundle like that might look suspicious."

"All right. Let's go."

"But first we got to fix the sawed-off shotgun."

"Of course," the other man said. "After all, soon it will be Mother's Day."

On the mesa, Afraid Of His Own Horses (he wasn't really; it was a family name) raised his arm the way Indians do in the movies and said, "Look. They're leaving."

The group stopped between two huge orange sandstone boulders and watched the two men below. One of them was sitting in the jeep waiting while the other man was doing something carefully to the hogan door. What the two men had called a shack was actually an abandoned hogan. The door was another sign borrowed several years ago from Route 66 and it said: REPENT. THE KINGDOM OF HEAVEN IS AT HAND. JESUS SAVES.

"They were good signs," Afraid Of His Own Horses said.

"Yes. They don't make them like that any more," The Other Indian said.

"What does it mean, Santo?" Alastair Benjamin stroked his horse to keep him silent.

"They made good doors," Sant said.

"I mean what does the writing mean?"

"What it says, I guess."

"There's a good one over there," Alastair Benjamin said, reading it aloud. "MOTORISTS WISE SIMONIZ."

"No, it's not a very good one," Afraid Of His Own Horses said.

"No. They don't make them like they used to any more," The Other Indian said.

Alastair Benjamin allowed his horse to move up a little.

"Why does he keep fooling with the door? Is he trying to lock it?"

"Yeah, but he can't."

"But for two hundred thousand dollars you try."

"Yeah, I guess you do. What we going to do with all that money?"

"I guess, like they said, we'll give it to the Indians," Sant said.

"Why?" The Other Indian said.

"Well, you can buy things and all," Sant said.

"What?"

"Rolls-Royces, for example."

"What's that?"

"A foreign car."

"Have you seen one?"

"I've seen pictures."

"Are they good?"

"Oh, they're very good."

"Then I guess I'll have one."

"*Cómo no?* Why not?" Sant said.

Below, the man waiting at the jeep with the other sawed-off shotgun, pressed the horn and hollered, "Hurry it up. For God's sake, get the lead out, Francis."

"Don't get me nervous. You know how I get when I'm nervous." The man called Francis had walked over to the jeep but he didn't get in.

357

"All right. Take it easy, Francis."

"You know how I get when I get excited."

"Then take it easy."

"I killed those men when I was nervous."

"Then take it easy."

"I'm not responsible when I'm excited. You know what I've done, Mike? You know what you made me do with your hurry, hurry?"

"No. But take it easy, Francis."

"You made me leave my Mother's Day card inside. And the door's triggered to the shotgun."

"Well, that's a laugh."

"I could kill you."

Mike, the man in the jeep, suddenly sobered and stroked the steering wheel.

"Yes," he said. "I guess you could." They were silent for almost a minute and then Mike looked over carefully at the hogan. "There's a hole in the top of that shack," he said. "And it's got curved sides. A man could crawl up the sides and drop down in and get that letter without opening the door."

When the man came back with the letter the other man revved the engine and put her in four-wheel drive but he did not let out the clutch.

"If we take it easy—if we learn to take it easy, Francis, everything will work out."

Now the man called Mike, who looked very worried, released the clutch and the jeep moved forward. Soon they had disappeared in the far red hills.

The boys on their horses watched the two men go off in their jeep.

"Well, what do you think, Santo?"

"Well, I don't know, but the Indians think they're very courteous people."

"Why courteous people? They look like very city people to me."

"Courteous because it's a hogan where Indians died and you

358

know no one's supposed to go in a hogan after that's happened."

"So they went through the roof."

"Yeah."

"Well, I guess that's courteous all right."

"You sure that's why they did it? They don't look like that kind of people to me."

"Well," Sant said, beginning to move his paint horse forward, "it just shows you can't judge nobody by their looks."

"Yeah."

"My dear sir," The Other Indian said, "shall we get the money?"

"Where did you get that dear sir?"

"Isn't that the way rich people talk?"

"Yes, I guess it is," Sant said, and they began to wind their horses down the bright mesa. The mesa here was eroding away in five giant steps that descended down to the floor of the valley where the abandoned hogan lay. Each of the five steps clearly marked about twenty million years in time. In other words, they had been laid down twenty million years apart, and were so marked by unique coloration and further marked by the different fossil animals found in each. It took the four boys about twenty minutes to descend these one hundred million years but they didn't think that was very good going.

"We'll be all day at this," Alastair Benjamin said.

"The money will still be there."

"Easy," Afraid Of His Own Horses said. "Don't force my horse. Money isn't everything."

"It's a Rolls-Royce," The Other Indian said.

"Well, then, we'll slide down this one." They were on the west sandy edge of an Ojo Alamo formation, vaguely striped in red and orange. Afraid Of His Own Horses, riding without saddle, suddenly turned his horse into it and went straight down. The others waited to see how he made out. When they saw he was down there in one piece waving to them, The Other Indian followed.

"It's easier to do that without no saddle," Sant said.

"It sure is."

"But they'll get all the money."

359

"Well, they earned it."

"It was going to be distributed to the Indians anyway."

"And we're not Indians."

They turned their horses in eights, pacing the ledge and watching the Indians below.

"They're waiting for us."

"Let them wait."

"It's hard to have Indians for buddies."

"Yeah."

"They expect you to kill yourself."

"Over two hundred thousand dollars."

"Is that how much it is?"

"Yeah."

"It would take you a long time to make that much money at a bronc show. That's what you're still going to be, isn't it?"

"Yeah."

"How much they pay for a bronc show?"

"Forty hundred dollars or so. I've told you that before."

"But you were never so exact."

"Well, now I'm being exact."

"Well, money isn't everything."

"That's what the Indian said."

"They're still waiting. I guess they think we're chicken."

"Well, I guess we better try it."

They went down together and at once, creating a storm, a tornado of ageless dust, a hundred million years in outrage, that followed them all the way down to the level of the Indians.

The two men carrying the letter saw the plume of dust as they entered the trading post.

"I wonder what that was," the delicate-looking one said. "It seemed near the shack."

"Don't get nervous," the man called Mike said. "It was probably a tornado. Don't get nervous."

"Do they have tornadoes here?"

"Sure they do. Small ones. All over."

"What kept you so long?" The Other Indian said as Sant and Alastair became visible in the dying dust.

360

"Well, it's a lot easier for Indians. Without saddles, that is," Alastair said.

"Sure it is," The Other Indian said. "Well, there it is," he said, pointing. "It was nice of those city people to go through the roof."

"Does it make it okay if you go through the roof?" Sant said.

The two Indians looked at each other. "Yes," Afraid Of His Own Horses said. "We guess it does."

"Then we better go through the roof, I guess," Sant said.

"Everyone else is doing it. I guess that's the thing nowadays," Alastair Benjamin said as he started his all-white horse down the final gentle slope.

The Other Indian shinnied up the side of the hogan first. It was not too difficult. The hogan was built octagonal-shaped of eight-inch cedar logs woven, interlaced, so that the final shape was like an igloo, complete with center hole for the smoke. It was as though these people, Navahos, had made it down from the north a long time ago but had never forgotten their houses, only now they built them of wood, instead of ice. The door, which had always faced east, and still does, was formerly of hides. Now it was usually a stolen sign—SAVE AT THE FIRST THRIFT AND LOAN COMPANY or something like that. This one said, JESUS SAVES.

"I don't know," Afraid Of His Own Horses said as he saw The Other Indian drop through the roof hole. "I don't know whether it's all right really."

"Well," Sant said, "if it's not all right really this is a fine time to think of it. He's already in."

"I don't know really what the Navaho book says."

"It will be okay," Sant said.

"The book is in the minds of the old people and I don't know what it says. I know it says we should never enter the house where a Navaho has died, but you don't enter a roof. You fall in."

"It will be okay," Sant said.

"Oh, that's easy for you to say. You're not an Indian."

"It will be okay," Sant said.

"It was very nice of those city people to remember the book."

"Oh, awfully nice. Shall we join the others?"

"My dear sir, why not?" Afraid Of His Own Horses said.

Alastair Benjamin got down off his all-white horse and joined them, looking up. He removed his powder-blue straw hat. It matched his turquoise bracelet and looked grand and gaudy against his dark skin.

"Well," Alastair Benjamin said, "those city people. I don't trust them. It's a trick. I don't trust them."

"My *compadre* is not the trusting type," Sant said.

"My dear sir," Afraid Of His Own Horses said, "just because a man is from the city—"

"Yes," Sant said. "Just because—"

"Well, all right," Alastair Benjamin said. "But who goes first?"

"My dear sir, my brother is already in there."

"Then you go first," Alastair Benjamin said.

At the trading post the two city men dressed like hunters walked up to the counter and the delicate one dropped the letter in the box.

"Well, Mike," he said to the other man, "that's over with."

"Are you the two men living in that Torreon hogan?" It was the trader, Mr. Peersall. He wore a large Stetson over a big, sunken face and he wore a heavy leather jacket.

"Now we just might be," the man called Mike said. "Which one?"

"Jesus Saves," Mr. Peersall said.

"We just might be," Mike said.

"Yes," Francis said. "We could be."

"Well, I think you better move out." The trader took off his hat and looked at them carefully. "A Navvyho died there. No one is supposed to enter a hogan where a Navvyho died."

"Why?" Mike said.

"Evil spirits are still there," the trader said.

"Do you believe that?" The man called Francis had already walked to the door once impatiently. Now he came back.

"Do you believe that?" His voice was very high.

"I try to go along with their traditions," the trader said.

"Oh, you do?" Francis said. "Well, that's interesting."

"Don't get him nervous," Mike said to Mr. Peersall.

362

"I don't care if I do," Mr. Peersall said. "I'm not busy now."

Francis was biting his lip and turning very white.

"Just don't get him excited," Mike said to the trader.

"At the moment I've got nothing else to do," Mr. Peersall said.

"Come on, Francis," Mike said.

"Don't touch me. Just don't you ever touch me," Francis said.

"Come on, Francis."

"Listen," Mr. Peersall said. "If you people don't want to behave, if you want to stay on in that hogan, I don't have to deliver that letter you just dropped in the box, to the mail pickup at Coyote."

Francis had begun to reach under his coat toward a very bulging long object but now he buttoned his coat again.

"All right," Francis said. "I suppose—I suppose an Indian's got as much right to be a fool as the rest of us."

"Sure he has," the trader said.

"Come on, Francis," Mike said.

The two city men dressed in the new red wool plaid of hunters went very quietly out the door.

"City people or Martians or Plutonians, somewhere from outer space. City people, I guess. City people. They're not bad people for city people," the trader said to the Navahos lined along the far wall beneath the hanging and dusty festoons of hides, saddles, harness, and lanterns.

The Navahos did not respond to this saying of the trader. Then Mr. Peersall abruptly realized with that sudden knowledge you get when you have lived with people who do not communicate much with words, that instinctive learning a trader must have to be a trader—to be in Indian Country at all—he suddenly realized that the two city people had drawn a perfect blank from the Indians, that they had ignored the city people absolutely.

"Well, then, the city people never existed," the trader said. He removed the letter and tossed it into the burning fireplace.

"If they never existed, don't exist, why should we confuse people with their mail, if they don't exist?"

The Indians grunted and their women made a quick shuffling

363

sound with their feet to assure him he had made a bright saying and they went back to ignoring even him now.

What the trader had done was not an outrage—the tossing of the letter in the fire. It was simply that in this part of Indian Country mail was a thing that had never become a habit, a vice. They had not yet become addicted to a thing that had not as yet traditionalized through long custom. It was still the part of the world where you could tell a person what you thought about him to his face without making magic against him on paper.

The letter burned with a tall cool flame within the dark room, and the Indians enjoyed it very much.

The two small cowboys and the two small Indians were down at the bottom of the hogan counting the money.

"Well, it's all here," Sant said. "Two hundred thousand dollars—such as it is."

"What do you mean," Alastair Benjamin said, "such as it is?"

"I mean that it's patent that it's phony money."

"What do you mean, patent?"

"Just what I said."

"Then what do you mean, phony money?"

"I mean," Sant said, "take, for example, did you ever see money all pressed and in neat packs like this, all crisp and clean? That's not right. That's not money."

"Well," Alastair Benjamin said, "I guess you're right. It must be patent money okay."

"And it's phony too," Sant said.

"Then what shall we do?"

"Burn it," Sant said.

"Wait a minute," The Other Indian said. "What about my Rolls-Royce?"

Sant tilted his porkpie-shaped cowboy hat and thought carefully, closing his eyes to make sure he missed nothing in his judgment.

"Well," he said finally, and still keeping his eyes closed, "the trader man says you got to pay a big price for everything you get out of this world, or something."

"Well," The Other Indian said, "if his saying is going to take

364

away my Rolls-Royce then he better buy me another kind of car."

"That's fair," Sant said.

"Shall we burn the money?"

"My dear sir, please do," Afraid Of His Own Horses said.

"You don't have to talk like a rich man any more," Sant said.

"Okay, then start the fire."

"I thought I heard a jeep."

"You sure it wasn't a Rolls-Royce?"

They all laughed and then Sant began very solemnly stacking the two hundred thousand dollars in a pyramid shape. "The better to make it burn."

"Imagine that," Sant said, "trying to make fools out of us with their phony money and all. I don't even think they're hunters. Why should government people come dressed like hunters when they can wear government clothes? I don't even think they're nothing."

"That's right," Alastair Benjamin said.

Sant put the final sheaf of money on the pyramid.

"Sure it is. Do you want to light it up?" he said to The Other Indian. "Or maybe you, sir?" he said to Afraid Of His Own Horses.

"I'm only a poor Indian again," Afraid Of His Own Horses said.

"Go ahead, light it anyway," Sant said. Sant passed him a pack of matches but it was The Other Indian who took them and lighted the fire. Two hundred thousand dollars makes a pleasant small fire but it smokes a lot.

"Always remember this," Sant said, "in case this happens again. It smokes a lot. Let's get out of here."

Sant bent over and the other small cowboy and the two Indians jumped on his back and crawled out the smoking hole. Sant was still trapped down there until, as an afterthought, as they were mounting their horses, the others decided to go back and get him. The Other Indian crawled in with Alastair Benjamin holding his ankles and they pulled Sant out that way.

When they got on their horses Sant was still rubbing his eyes and he said to Alastair Benjamin as they started off, "Always remember, Alley, how much money smokes."

"Yeah," Alastair Benjamin said.

The two city men who three days ago had robbed a bank in Durango of two hundred thousand dollars and were now dressed as hunters drove their jeep through the square pass, the window in the cliff of La Ventana Mesa. La Ventana means the window in Spanish. The Spanish were the first people here and gave all the mesas their names. They didn't bother to name the valleys because that is where they were standing when they named the mesas and didn't think it was important to name where they were seeing from but only what they saw.

As the jeep rode through this window in the mesa Mike said, "Look, there's somebody in the shack. She's smoking."

"Well, tear down there," the other man said. "The gun's gone off and that's the dust."

The driver drove down the incline toward the hogan as fast as he could go.

"We must have killed an Indian."

"It serves him right."

The driver jammed on the brakes and they both leaped out of the jeep and ran through the door of the hogan as fast as they could go. There was a big roar as both barrels of the shotgun went off. One of the men dressed as a hunter threw up his hands and collapsed immediately and never moved again. The other man was blasted backward and began to stumble blindly through the sage and yucca and greasewood as though he were drunken and searching for something. Then he, too, collapsed and never moved again. Above, in the very New Mexican blue, the gentle, far buzzards began to tighten their circles and move down.

"You hear that shotgun go off?" Sant said. "Maybe those people were hunters, after all."

"I don't think they were," Alastair Benjamin said.

"Then what you think that shotgun blast was? You think they're shooting their own selves?"

"Yeah," Alastair Benjamin said, trying to be difficult.

"My dear sir, why not?" The Other Indian said, trying to be impossible.

"*Cómo no?*" Afraid Of His Own Horses said.

"Yes, why not?" Sant said. "If all the rest of you are crazy, why not me? The hunters are hunting their own selves. The killers are killing each other."

They all guessed that this was true or something and then they began racing their horses down the valley as fast as they could race. They went through the window on La Ventana Mesa flying fast, and then they scattered, each trailing off to their different homes way out there somewhere in the nowhere, in that endless New Mexican country that must go on and on in its bright infinity even after they had sped over the horizon, individual specks now, and disappeared completely.

Now the gentle buzzards came on, waving in on a long concentric glide and lighting big and alone in the exact center of the awful silence, and the sky assumed that huge and violent majesty of color it always does in the mesa country as the day, before quickening into dark, gives her grand and splendored welcome to the night. Finally only a hushed pillar of smoke rising from an abandoned hogan gave any sign at all.

PART II

SIX Indians believe that inanimate objects like a stone, a leaf, a bridge, or even a tree have the ability to move. They notice that this remembrance is borne out with proof when they are walking across a bridge path when drunk. When you fish them out of the water, as Big Sant did once at Blanco Crossing, they will say, as this Navaho said, "The bridge walked away from under me." Or when a wrecked Navaho pickup shows up at Sauter's Garage in Cuba, the Navaho will explain that he was driving along drinking quietly when this tree walked up and hit him.

Whites near Navaho Country have even stranger convictions backed up with even stranger proof. For example, they explain to the Indians that the whites own all the good land, the only land with water on it close to the mountains, because when—way back when—the land was surveyed the Indians demanded the worst land. As proof of this there is a signed treaty.

"You mean a tree hit us then too?"

"No," Big Sant said. "The bridge must have walked out from underneath you."

The Indians had a strange belief, too, about the unsolved death of the bank robbers. They said the bank robbers' own guns had fired off and killed them. Indians will be Indians.

There was an even stranger belief held by both whites and Indians around Indian Country and that concerned the Gran Negrito. The Gran Negrito had settled in Indian Country during very strange events about twenty-one years ago. He acquired a ranch called the Circle R, which became known as the Gran

371

Negrito, and built on it a red adobe house, filled it with records of odd long music and books without pictures, ran fifty head of mother cows into three hundred, and held the key to the Circle Heart. When the government springs numbers one and three dried up, the Circle Heart, lying on the long flank of the Circle R, could not trail to its summer mountain pasture without water trouble; so the Gran Negrito on the springs of the Circle R controlled the beat of the Circle Heart.

Now the Gran Negrito was gone. The Circle R was gone—it all belonged to the Circle Heart. The strange belief held about this by both whites and Indians was that, like religion and politics, it was not to be discussed. And the proof of this was that the last time it was discussed someone ended up dead—the Gran Negrito.

Big Sant today was very much alive. He rode his horse all in one with the horse, like a centaur. He carried his brilliant scarred face like a flag. When he rode, it seemed as though he were continually returning from some conquest, carrying this branded face stiffly like a pennant of victory, as though a train of more horses were to follow bearing prize. On closer look there was something wrong. The splash of color repelled. What was triumphant at a distance was now tensed into the tight, reflective face folds of defeat.

Today Big Sant dwelt on secrets and touches.

The secret in creating anything new seems to lie in borrowing all you see and hear about you and adding one small touch. Big Sant's one small touch in cattle ranching was always to carry wire cutters on his saddle string and always to cut the fence rather than go round. He would repair it quickly and it sometimes saved ten miles. No one else did it. It was his one small touch.

Another small touch of Big Sant's was to collect butterflies. No one else in Indian Country did it. He was doing it now. It was another small touch. A lot of other people had gathered new land in strange ways but who in Indian Country gathered butterflies in any way? It was a pretty big touch.

Now he pursued the mighty monarch. Not at the expense of his cattle time. He had already, this day, spent eleven hours pursuing cattle and he was done. He was done for this day anyway. Big Sant would have liked to chase in the direction of home, the

Circle Heart, seventeen miles west, but the great monarch fell in huge circles from cactussed hill to tamarisk. (From morn to noon he fell, from noon to dewy eve, a summer's day.) He fled before the stumbling Big Sant and his faltering horse in every direction but home; he wandered through every ranch but the Circle Heart. Big Sant kept on with the knowledge that, although the butterfly belongs to the same order as the moth, unlike the moth, the butterfly is diurnal, not nocturnal. You have to catch them while the day lasts. They differ from the moths also in having antennas club-shaped, those of moths being fine and threadlike or featherlike; in resting with the wings folded vertically, the moth folding them over the abdomen. Butterflies are not only found close to the Circle Heart. Forty separate species occur within the Arctic Circle. What else? That's all for now, except remember you catch them while the light lasts. They only belong to the same order as the moths, not the same phylum. Sant nevertheless sat down. His feet and legs belonged to the order of man and the same phylum, too, and they got very tired.

You are supposed to be a cattleman anyway, and what do you know about them? The principal beef brands are the Angus and the Hereford. Every schoolboy knows that. Cattle are not native to America but were brought by Columbus on his second voyage. The Western range cattle are in part descendants of the cattle of the early Spanish settlers. Wealth of primitive man consisted chiefly of cattle. The word "pecuniary" is derived from the latin *pecus*, cattle, and the words "cattle," "chattel," and "capital" are related. He did not want to think about that any more. He had better get back to chasing that damn butterfly.

But the butterfly was gone. He had marked the monarch on a Spanish bayonet yucca but now it was gone. All right, he would try the word "cowboy." Cowbird, a small terrestrial or semiterrestrial bird of the hang-nest family, native to the new world. No, I want cowboy, not cowbird. All right, cowboy. The name given Tory marauders, adherents to the British cause in the American Revolution who infested the neutral grounds in Westchester County, New York, and plundered their patriotic opponents. Not many school-boys know that that's the way the word "cowboy" began. But how about cowboys like you are and Little Sant wants to become? He wants to become a bronc man. All right, but you start by being a cowboy. All right, we'll do cowboy. Name also given to mounted men employed as herders on cattle ranches of the western United States. They were more important and picturesque in the days before the vast ranches were fenced, when their duties consisted of driving cattle to pasture and water, branding them at the roundup, protecting them from wild animals and thieves, and driving them to the shipping point. At the present time their duties are not as dangerous as formerly but cowboys are still fearless and expert horsemen, skilled with the lasso and in all the details of their work.

Well, enough of this encyclopedia word game. You'd better get on your horse and get back to the Circle Heart. Except this—a cowboy never calls that thing a lasso, he calls it a rope. And he doesn't call it a roundup. It's a gathering. And except this—why don't you think about your own life? Why do you have to pick on words? Why do you have to pick on butterflies?

Big Sant rolled a cigarette carefully while watching the Spanish bayonet.

Because I have an interest in things scientific. Because I never had the courage to leave the ranch. I guess that's it. Or maybe it's because my brother didn't have courage to stay during the big drought. Anyway I've always done the work of two men. Little Sant will have an education. He will stay at my brother's when he's getting it. That's the least my brother can do. And speaking of brother, he left when I bought the Gran Negrito, not during the drought. Face it, boy. It wasn't the big drought, it was the big steal, the big murder.

Big Sant removed the cigarette from his mouth. No, it wasn't. It wasn't murder. It was an accident. Two Indians testified to that. And it wasn't stealing. I was just there with the highest bid when it was auctioned, that's all. Another accident. Why didn't you tell the boy then—Little Sant? Because he's not old enough. He might not understand. Murder, stealing? Murder, stealing? All nonsense. It was all legal. And no one knows who Alastair is really. That's not true.

374

He crushed the cigarette in his bare hand until he felt the sharp burn, then he threw the mess on the ground.

"All legal," he said out loud. "Come on," he said to the horse. "It's got me talking to myself."

As he rose, the great monarch took off from the underleaf of the Spanish bayonet and Big Sant followed. He did not pay much attention to the direction it was taking but plodded after it steadily, clutching his net. A cowboy will not carry a canteen, perhaps because he's afraid someone will take him for a Boy Scout, but a butterfly net—there's no law against that.

Big Sant smiled. His mind was getting on to better things now. The great monarch had lofted over the ridge and fluttered down into a green grama valley. Big Sant followed it up and down and over to where it lighted on a pile, a broken and charred pile, of adobes. Sant stopped the horse and stared at the burned house. Now he mounted the horse and turned back toward the Circle Heart.

"That butterfly might take us into the next county," he told the horse. "It might take us clear to Texas and there it would become three times as big as it is now and we might not get it in the net. That's a joke," he told the horse.

Now he spurred the horse, sticking great rowels into the horse's flank. He took two wire fences going as fast as the horse could go.

"It was all legal," he reminded the horse. "All perfectly legal. Oh Christ."

The horse's name was Indian Country and Sant loved the big horse and was annoyed with himself for having caused him to lather badly on the quick trip home. He rubbed the horse down before he went inside and into the bathroom and stared into the mirror over the medicine chest. Indians have a medicine chest, too, but they don't study their own reflection in it. Sant saw in it forty years and a bright brand—forty Christian calendar years. Sant got out the shaving soap and remembered that the Navaho year is divided into twelve months because a coyote questioned the wisdom of having twenty-four. That is, the Navahos recognize only two seasons, winter and summer, and the coyote questioned the wisdom of assigning twelve months to each. You can find all kinds of information like this if you bother to ask an Indian. It helps if you speak the language. Big Sant did. He didn't speak coyote. Very few do. Even coyotes seem to have a tough time with it. If you listen to them carefully in the darkest night you will notice that they repeat the same cry and keep repeating it as though they were not getting through.

Big Sant brought up a coyote once from a pup. Everything was fine; that is, the coyote behaved very much like a dog for one year and everything seemed to be going splendidly. Big Sant always knew the day would come when the wild coyotes would begin calling her from the close ridges. She was a bitch. Then he realized that, growing up in isolation like this, she would not speak the language, and he let her out of the house quite freely, knowing that she would not understand at all what the coyotes were talking about when they called. They might just as well be giraffes up there hollering down. But when the coyotes called from the near ridge Sant's coyote was gone immediately and never came back. The only moral Big Sant could get out of this was that giraffes are different from you and me. Coyotes, too, I guess. She was a bitch all right.

Navahos believe that sickness is due to the magic influence of some divine power and that chants have been ordained for its removal. The first chant may not prove effective in every instance; then a second medicine, found in another chant, becomes imperative, a process that is repeated until the disease has been correctly traced to its source and the medicine will eventually, of necessity, prove effective. The chants can go on all night. They can go on all week.

It could be a very long drink of medicine, Big Sant thought. There must be some simpler way of keeping those he loved closer.

Sant's mind wandered on these touchstones because he had been brought up close to the Navahos, and very close to coyotes, too, for that matter. The Indians and all the animals were very close. People were kind of distant. People were complicated. Unlike coyotes, people have the damndest difficulties understanding each other. He wanted to get close to Millie and help her. He wanted to get close to the boys and help them. He wanted to get close to himself. He had even tried growing a beard but the brand still showed through and people seemed to know what he was up to. He tried cutting it off and defying them. Nothing worked. Millie said she never noticed it. He owed her a lot. He should be afraid of nothing, he told himself as he wiped the razor foam off his chin, watching himself in the mirror of the medicine cabinet which held no chants. Now he hung up the towel and went into the living room.

Millie was reading a copy of Zen, which she put down.

"What's happened to the boys?" she asked.

"They'll be in," Big Sant said. He went over to the shelf and took down a copy of the *Ethnological Dictionary of the Navaho Language*. He was still working on it. He spoke the language rather well but he was interested to see what it was made of.

"They've been planning for some time now to go where they remember. Wherever that is," Millie said.

"That sounds silly," Sant said, sitting down with the book, but he didn't look at the book.

"I thought it sounded silly too," Milly said. "Still, Navahos are silly. We're silly. That dog of ours is quite sensible." They had acquired a sheep dog.

"Yes, as we get older I guess we don't remember what we sounded like when we were kids," Sant said.

"I thought we'd go to Gallup next week," Millie said. "Dr. Graham is going to speak at the Civic Auditorium."

"I was by the old Circle R today," Big Sant said, putting the book aside.

"What do you say about Dr. Graham Saturday?"

"Going where they remembered," Sant said. "They can't remember any place."

"I thought I'd get tickets for Saturday."

"They can't remember that place."

"What place?" Millie said. She paused. "What place would you like? We can get close up for two dollars."

"Get close up," Sant said, taking the book again.

377

SEVEN **W**hat do you remember?"

"When my grandfather was a kid," Little Sant said, "my grandfather ate buffler meat."

"Tell me more."

"My father eats butterflies." The two boys just stood stock still for a while. "I remember," Sant said, "there was this big horse."

"What big horse? You mean the killer horse?"

"Yes. The horse that I rode."

"I remember," Alastair Benjamin said, "there were all these books."

"What all books?"

"The books that burned."

"Tell me about it," Sant said.

"Tell me about yours again first."

"Well," Sant said, "nobody could ride this horse, but I did it."

"After this fire I was rescued by the Indians."

"Yeah. Cheese and baloney," Sant said.

"Cheese and baloney to your story, too, then," Alastair said.

"Well, I'll believe yours—"

"If you'll believe mine," Alastair said.

They were both all of fourteen years old now. They held the reins of their horses as they sat beneath the shade of a piñon tree and looked out over the bright Indian Country.

"It all began," Alastair said, "I was hiding under a chair or a bed or something like that. Then these spurs came in the room."

"Spurs?"

378

"Well, there was somebody in them," Alastair said.

"Who?"

"This man who kept shooting a gun or something like that."

"Well, was he shooting or wasn't he?"

"He had been shooting I think."

"And then what happened?"

"Then one of those spurs came off the stranger and the room was filling up with smoke and I ran out. Then some Indians rescued me."

"You expect me to believe that?"

"Well, what happened to you?"

"Well, we were at this big show and nobody would ride this horse. It was a wild horse, a killer horse."

"But you rode him, or so you always say. With Lemaitre. You and Lemaitre were partners."

"Yeah."

"You expect me to believe that?"

"I see what you mean," Sant said.

"We both got to co-operate more when we listen."

"Yeah," Sant said. "We certainly do."

They both began chewing thoughtfully on the horse reins they held as the horses watched them and they watched out over Indian Country.

"They certainly gave the Indians a lot of sorry land," Alastair said.

"Oh, it's not sorry land, Alley," Sant said.

"No water."

"Oh, I guess the Indians like it that way. They call it *Năhoké*."

"What does that mean?"

"The land."

"Well, they certainly gave the Indians a lot of sorry *Năhoké*."

"Nobody gave it to them. It was always theirs."

"Always?"

"Almost always."

"Who had it before they did?"

"Other Indians, I guess."

"How did they get it from the other Indians?"

"Shot it out."

"Even before there were guns?"

"Well, that's a very good question," Sant said.

"Well, I didn't want to make it too good."

"You make them as good as you like," Sant said. "I guess I asked for it. . . . Do you intend to eat that rein all up?" Sant asked after a minute as he watched where the horses stood. Alastair took the rein out of his mouth and the horse looked away.

"Did you know," Alastair said, "that the Navahos believe they always had horses?"

"Didn't they?"

"No," Alastair said. "The white man brought them."

"They brought the guns too."

"Do the Indians know this?"

"Yeah, they know about the guns," Sant said.

"And the t.b.?"

"They know where that came from too," Sant said. "Are you enjoying the rein?"

"What rain?"

"The rein you're eating up."

Alastair dropped the rein from his mouth and continued to stare out over the Indian Country.

"Boy, this country could use some rain."

"So could your horse," Sant said.

"Yes," Alastair said. "We both got to co-operate more when we talk."

"Yeah," Sant said. "We certainly do."

Alastair fished around on the rocky slope without moving until he found two rocks about the same size but of different colors. He placed one rock between his legs and began trying to drop the other rock exactly on top of it.

"I remember it vividly," Alastair said.

"What does vividly mean?"

"It means most well."

"What do you remember most well?"

"The gun fight."

"Oh, that again," Sant said. "Was it before the white man brought the guns?"

"No."

"How do you know?"

"Because there was a lot of noise."

"Other things make noise."

Alastair tried to line up the colored rocks exactly over each other before he dropped the high one this time.

"Blood too?"

"Sure," Sant said.

Alastair dropped the rock but he missed again.

"I guess so," he said. "It's all kind of vague."

"I thought you said it was vividly," Sant said.

"They both mean nearly the same thing," Alastair said.

"Oh," Sant said.

Alastair reached over and plucked a blood-red Indian paintbrush.

"Where did all this happen?" Sant said.

Alastair pointed with the Indian paintbrush. "Out there."

"Out where?"

Alastair was gesturing to infinity with the poison-bright flower. "Out there."

The movement took in the world. From what they could see it took in La Ventana, the Puerco, the Cuevo and the Perro and the Madrid Mesas. All appeared aflame this time of sun, and it took in the deep shadowed land in between. It took in the giant Jemez Range and the quick streams coming down and it covered nicely all the unending sage that wandered south and down to the Arizona peaks rising from their solid foundations like blue, distant, dim cities of a strange faith.

"All that?" Sant said, following with his eye the slow swing of the poison paintbrush. Sant put the rein back in his mouth and talked around it. "Well, that certainly narrows things down."

Alastair put his rein in his mouth, too, picked up the colored stones. He still held the bright Indian paintbrush in his free hand so that he appeared a small, heavy-laden, black, bridled and bitted conjurer preparing to startle the world, amuse anyway the mesa, for money and fame.

"I only want to tell you where I come from, where I first remember," Alastair said.

"Well, you certainly narrowed it down," Sant said.

"I remember the boots," Alastair said. "The boots and the spurs moving from one window to the other window, suddenly and mixed up, and I remember the shots."

"Do you remember the house?"

"I remember it was made of mud. Adobe."

"What color?"

"Blood color."

"Red," Sant said. "That's the red country. Gallina, Capulin, and Coyote. Iron."

"Iron?"

"In the soil," Sant said. "It turns everything blood red. That's where I made my first appearance. That's where I remember too."

"First appearance?"

"Yes. Where I rode that horse."

"Then you've been back?"

"No."

"Why not?"

"Because my parents want me to be a gelologist."

Alastair dropped the rein from his mouth. "You mean geologist."

"Is that good?"

"Wonderful," Alastair said.

Sant looked up at the horse and then over at Mount Taylor. "I been thinking," he said. "We could go our own selves."

"Where we remember?"

"Where we remember," Sant said.

"Would they mind us going?"

"They might mind me going," Sant said. "You know they don't want me to be a bronc man. They don't want me to remember. But I can't think of any reason they wouldn't want you to go there."

"No. It's only where I remember."

382

"Only where we remember," Sant said, getting up.

"Well, you can't very well go," Alastair said.

"That's true. I'll just follow you."

"I guess that's legal."

"It won't hurt anyone."

"How could it hurt anyone, going where we remember?" Alastair said rising.

They got on their horses.

"Which way we got to go?" Alastair said.

"We got to follow the Jemez all along the base."

"Even where it makes the U?"

"Yes."

"Why don't we just go over the top there? It would save time."

"No, they got her all fenced off. They got a secret city up there."

"Secret city?"

"Yeah."

"Los Alamos?"

"Yeah."

"To blow up the world?"

"Yeah. It's before somebody else does it."

"Well, that's the way everybody on the outside is," Alastair said.

"You're sharp today. How is everybody on the outside?"

"Very well, thank you. How are you?"

"Crazy now."

"No, today you are very perspicacious, Santo."

"Maybe. But I feel perfectly all right, Alley."

"It will catch you up later in the day, Santo."

"*Vamos a ver.*"

"What's that?"

"We shall see, Alley, what we shall see."

They could not go over the hump of the mountain because that's where the secret city lay and it was fenced off. But they could save some time by going over the Valle Grande. The Valle Grande is a huge cup, maybe twenty miles across, the largest extinct volcano crater in the world. For the last one hundred thousand years it had been the home of thousands of elk; now it was the home of the New Mexico Cattle and Timber Company Incorporated, Keep Out.

Before they got there, though, they had to climb way up. They had to get up on a hogback ridge where they could look down on the Navaho and the Apache country, the Santa Ana, the Zia and the Jemez country. The Navaho country ran way on west and farther even than they could see, on all the way through New Mexico over the horizon into Arizona, Utah, and even into Colorado. They could see all of the Apache country, about six hundred thousand acres of piñon, sage, and cedar fringing the mountain. The Santa Ana and the Zia and the Jemez, why, you could drop a handkerchief on each of them from up here and seem to cover each. They were all pueblos, Pueblo Indian people who never had more land than they could cultivate and they never cultivated more in the old days than the Navahos and the Apaches could steal. The Pueblos remembered in the dim and distant memories of the race how they were destroyed once upon a time by the Navahos and the Apaches, how later they were destroyed by the Spanish. They did not remember what was happening now.

"What do you know about Indians?" Sant said, beginning to twirl his pigging string.

"Well, you take those Pueblo Indians," Alastair said, "that live in these mud apartment houses."

"Yes?"

"Well, when they first saw white men it was the first time they saw horses too."

"And?"

"And they thought they were part of the horse."

"Which part?"

"Yes," Alastair said. "Well, anyway, the Pueblos drew a line about a hundred yards in front of the pueblo and told the white people with signs that they better not cross it."

"And did they?"

"Yes, they did."

"What happened?"

384

"It was terrible. Later they killed all the missionaries and burned all the churches."

"Why?"

"Because they wanted it the way they remembered it, I guess."

"What else?"

"Nothing else. What is that one?" Alastair said pointing down to a square of mud, broken into cubes.

"That one's Santa Ana."

"It looks deserted."

"It almost is."

"What happened?"

"They don't remember."

"How about that one down there?"

"Zia. They're doing all right."

"And that one there?" Alastair said, pointing east.

"Oh, they're putting up a good fight too. That's Jemez."

"What are they putting up a good fight about?"

"I don't know. To keep it, I guess, the way they remembered."

"How do they remember it?"

"The way it was."

"How was it?"

"The way they remember, I guess. Or maybe it was just a lot of baloney."

"That reminds me," Alastair said, "I'm getting hungry."

They were riding through a dense growth of short thick scrub oak now and for a while, as they rode, everything was hidden from their view. Now they emerged on a sheer flat table rock and everything in the world opened quickly before them and below. They were silent a while watching.

"Let them have it," Alastair said.

"Let them have what?"

"What they remember."

"That's big of you."

"What is it they remember exactly?"

"Things."

"Things like what?"

"Things like the world started right here and grew out."

385

"What else do the Indians remember?"

"Oh, things like the world began in fire and smoke."

"It probably did."

"Yeah."

"What else?"

"That it will end suddenly in quietness."

"Will it? You think it will?"

"I don't know, Alley. I really don't know."

"You don't remember."

"Yeah, that's right. I've got a bad memory."

They sat on their horses very quietly, for a long while resting their horses and looking down over it all.

"Where do we go from here, Santo?"

"Onward and upward, Alley."

"On what and up what?"

"You see that red pinnacle up there with the yellow top?"

"Yeah."

"We don't go there. Now you see that other one on the other bluff, the green one that looks like the tip of a Mexican church?"

"You mean Spanish-American."

"Yeah. We don't go there either. That's copper."

"What is?"

"The green."

"Yeah, I know. We don't go there either. But where do we go?"

"Like I said, Alley, onward and upward." Sant touched his horse and led the way through a trail that seemed to have been hiding, hidden by the sage at the entrance to the scrub oak.

"You can tell about how high you are when you lose the sage, Alley. And we just lost it. That's the last of it. Then you can tell about how high you are when you lose the oak. Then you can tell how high you are finally when you lose the pine, the ponderosa pine."

"*Pinus Ponderosa.* How high are we then?"

"Then we're in the clouds."

"That's where I am now," Alastair Benjamin said.

"Actually, Alley," Sant said, breaking off a brittle white twig from a budding grove they entered quietly, "you're in aspen."

"*Populus Tremuloides*. How high is that?"

"It's funny. Sometimes way down, sometimes higher than a kite."

"You are too," Alastair said. "We're supposed to be going to where we remember."

"But I remember all this."

"Yes, but it's not relevant."

"Not what?"

"It don't count," Alastair said.

They went over a piece of ground that gave them the feeling that they were riding over the edge of something, and then, there it was—the Valle Grande. The Great Valley, an enormous, perfect bowl of something, empty and green, twenty miles across in each clean direction.

"Well now!" Alastair said.

A sign posted on a barbed-wire fence said, NEW MEXICO CATTLE AND TIMBER COMPANY, INCORPORATED. KEEP OUT.

"Back to the old wire cutters," Sant said as he got down off the horse and unfastened them from his saddle string.

"I remember this country," Sant said, "when you could ride from the Chama to the Rio Grande without hitting a fence."

"Impossible for you to remember that."

"Someone does and I come from someone and that makes it all one and the same thing."

"Your logic escapes me."

"I'm sorry if something of mine got away from you," Sant said, busy cutting. "Why don't you help me? Maybe you wouldn't be losing all those big words."

"I'll stay up here and watch—stabilize the situation."

"You do that," Sant said. He had the fence open now, and Alastair Benjamin rode through majestically, as though re-entering his kingdom. Sant pulled his own horse through and then repulled the fence. It was hog wire, a sheep repellent with two strands of barbed on top for the big cattle. Wire cutters are a very fancy and valuable tool. They've got gadgets on them for cutting, pulling, turning, and stretching. Sant did all this while Alastair thought important thoughts from atop his horse and idly twirled a pigging string.

"Did anyone see us?" Sant said, regaining his horse.

"Yes," Alastair said, looking up at the sky.

"I mean some human being," Sant said.

"Yes," Alastair said, looking toward the center of the bowl. "That too."

Someone was making toward them, skimming the green grass as fast as his white horse could come. Sant watched the rider coming in on them fast. Indians always stand their ground. Cowboys too.

The rider was coming so fast he had to circle them once before he could stop. He got off his horse in bright Spanish rigging, including yellow tapaderos. He was a tall Spaniard in a black hat and he looked the way a descendant of the conquistadors should. He had a clean, tough, burnt face with small blue eyes watching out. As he got off his horse he removed one of his orange pigskin gloves.

"What passes?" he said.

"*Nada*," Sant said.

"*Pues*," the rider said, "then who tore up the fence?"

"Let me first introduce my *compadre*," Sant said.

"Make it fast."

"If you want to be impolite."

"I'm sorry."

"This is my *compadre*, Alastair Benjamin."

"Very pleased to meet you," the rider said. "Why in the hell did you tear up the fence?"

"If you want to be impolite," Sant said.

"I'm sorry," the rider said, turning to Sant now. "Then why in the hell did you tear up the fence?"

"I can see we're not getting anywhere," Sant said. Sant thought a moment, puzzled and trying to help the rider out. "Aren't you," he said finally, "Arturo Lucero Cipriano de Godoy?"

"Yes."

"Didn't you ride at the Lemaitre rodeo in the red country?"

"Yes."

"Well, I happen to be the one who rode the killer horse."

"That was the Anglo, Lemaitre."

"Well?"

"He was a big Anglo."

"He had me in his hand."

"Oh, maybe he had something in his hand, but it wasn't a person."

"It was me," Sant said.

"It was I," Alastair corrected.

"You mean he carried the both of you?"

"No. I'm a grammarian," Alastair said.

"Pleased to meet you," Arturo Lucero Cipriano de Godoy said. "A little while ago you looked like a fence buster."

"If we've got to be impolite," Sant said.

"I don't care, I only work for the corporation. I don't want my fence busted."

"That's a *non sequitur*," Alastair said.

"I don't care."

"We can't very well allow wild statements."

"You see," Alastair said, "you can't very well work for a corporation that we assume owns the fence and then in the same sentence say that it was your fence that we busted. We can't allow both these statements, can we, without having a *non sequitur*? Can we?"

"I don't care."

"I think you should answer his question, Arturo."

"I don't care."

"We can't very well allow wild statements."

"Not very well," Sant said.

"I don't care."

"I think he may be verging on hysteria. You better let him go."

"You can go, Arturo."

"*Mil gracias,*" Arturo said, taking off his hat. "I thank you from the bottom of my heart for wrecking my fence and then letting me go."

"Let's not be bitter," Sant said. "It's only a corporation."

389

"Only a corporation is not a fair statement," Alastair said. "After all, a corporation is people."

"Sure," Arturo said.

"All right then, maybe we shouldn't let you go," Sant said.

"I don't care," Arturo said, tired and putting back his hat.

"But you should care," Alastair said. "After all, they pay you."

"But I don't care," Arturo said, smiling insanely.

"How much do they pay you?" Sant said.

"Two hundred dollars a month," Arturo said, sobering now under a sober question.

"That seems fair," Sant said. "Why don't you ride with us to the other rim?"

"All right," Arturo said and he got on his horse and turned it in to theirs.

"What," Alastair said, "what exactly are you supposed to do for the two hundred dollars a month?"

"Please," Arturo said, raising the orange-gloved hand alongside his black hat. "Please."

"That's fair," Sant said. "It has gone far enough. He has more than earned his money. It has gone far enough."

"It's more than true," Alastair agreed, and they rode down the slope toward the center of the vast and very silent, green-carpeted volcano in a small, tight, quiet bunch. Soon they were gone in space. From anywhere on the rim, nowhere could you see anyone, anything. There were clumps of trees down there unseen, and somewhere out there three thousand head of cattle, fifteen cowboys, seven jeeps, twenty-eight horses, five chuck wagons, three bunkhouses, nine corrals, and one stream—all lost, all hidden in pure space like the stars, to be caught only at night when lantern-lit. Now bright daylight hit.

"You can't see nothing," Sant said.

"Anything," Alastair said.

Arturo Lucero Cipriano de Godoy tilted up his black hat with a straight thumb.

"I remember how it used to was."

"How was it?"

390

"*Más que* regular."

"More than ordinary. Go ahead," Sant said.

"A man could have a place, a small place."

"Now?"

"Only a place in a big place."

"What else do you remember?"

"When a man did not have to learn a foreign language."

"*Como Inglés?* Like English?"

"*Sí.*"

"What else?"

"Education."

"That's bad?"

"Very bad."

"Why?"

"Because it takes you someplace else."

"And that's bad?"

"Yes, it is."

"Now that you're in a profound mood," Alastair said, "do you have any bright saying that might solve all the problems of the world?"

"Yes."

"What is it?"

"*No me pregunte. Qué lástima, qué cosa, Dios mío.* I have said it."

"What did he say?"

"Don't ask questions," Sant said.

They were at the bottom of the enormous green bowl now and they watered their horses in the stream that ran there. They all got off and drank with the horses. They took off their big hats as they bent over, holding the hats with bent wrists at a certain angle, bodies pitched forward so that they appeared at prayer. The horses jerked up first, looked around askance as though surprised to find themselves so far from home and down at the bottom of something from which they might never get out. The other drinkers with quicker memories nevertheless looked with awful wonder at the great green cup. When they got up and even on their horses they still watched.

As they started up the other side Arturo Lucero Cipriano de Godoy, leading with a strange hat, a strange horse, wove his arm in a big circle signal and the other horses caught up and passed and they all charged into the hill and up, but not for long. The gallop died into a canter, the canter soon died into a trot, the trot very soon into a walk.

"It's very important really to remember what you remember, Arturo," Sant said.

"Why?"

"Because Alastair and I remember things that nobody won't admit."

"Like what?"

"Like my bronc ride. The one you won't even admit."

"He maybe had something in his arm—a bomb, some gold cup he won, one of them shoats."

"But why not me?"

"Why you? What would he be doing with you?"

"The barricade fell when his horse struck it. I was on it. He snatched me to save me, couldn't toss me away, had to take me on the ride."

"Oh?"

"Something like that," Sant said.

"No, I don't believe it. And what does he remember?"

"A gun fight."

"Yes," Alastair said.

"Who won?"

"We don't know."

"I don't believe it," Arturo said.

"That is, I don't know exactly."

"I don't believe it anyway," Arturo said.

"Would you believe it if I had proof?"

"No, I don't believe I would," Arturo said. "After all, I'm a man. I don't have to believe things."

"What does that mean?" Alastair asked.

"He's speaking English now."

"I don't believe it," Alastair said. "I wouldn't believe it if—"

"If he had proof?"

"Yeah," Alastair said.

"Well," Arturo said, getting off his horse in front of a gate. He opened the gate. "Well, good-by."

"Well, good-by," Alastair said as they rode their horses through.

"*Adiós,* Arturo Lucero Cipriano de Godoy," Sant said.

"Don't go to the right," Arturo hollered. "You'll run into the Los Alamos barricade."

"What did he mean by that?" Alastair said as they went through the thick brush bearing to the right.

"Los Alamos means the cottonwood trees."

"Is that what the barricade is made of?"

"No. That," Sant said, pointing to a heavy steel-mesh cyclone fence that suddenly appeared. "That's what it's made of."

"I wonder what those people in there, in the secret city, remember," Alastair said.

"Secrets," Sant said.

They started away from the fence and when they got well into the forest the brush got thicker and the long shadows became solid. They both ducked a very dangerous branch they could not see but only sensed was there somewhere in the deep shadows as they worked their way through thick aspen and alder. The aspen you could always see because it was white and neat like sudden columns of chalk; the other trees gave you trouble. But it was not very long before they were out of the darkness of the forest and they both felt very much better. And it was not very long after that, as they were riding across a blue field of mountain grama, that Alastair said, "Didn't you find him intriguing?"

"Kind of," Sant said. "But he wasn't buying any of what we remember at all."

"Not one bit," Alastair said.

"People are weird."

"Strange," Alastair said.

"Maybe we just attract especially odd people."

"Not that we're odd."

"Oh no," Sant said. Sant twirled his pigging string. "*Un poco, tal vez.*"

"What's that mean?"

"A little maybe," Sant said.

"But only to other people."

"Only to other people," Sant agreed.

They approached now an open escarpment in the hills, a bleak torture of giant tangled boulders fallen down from the sleek walled Mesaverde formation above. The yellow Mesaverde, scattered here on the pitted floor of the red-and-yellow-striped Kirtland, allowed only an alley through which you could pass.

The two boys rode across scrambled time now; all of the rock formations that were so clean and stark down below had been uplifted and had fallen all around them here so that even an expert, by reading the formations, could not tell what time—how old the earth was here. Their horses moved silently among all the welter of varicolored confusion until they got on the stable earth cover, the bright blue-and-gold and green-shooting and silver-treed slope of the Jemez watershed and entered a deer path, sudden with wild roses and heavy with honeysuckle that garlanded, tight and bright, the dark branches that roofed the trail; entered a quick deer tunnel on a quiet day, and did not say anything at all to each other until they came out on the other side.

On the other side there was a stream, the small beginning of La Jara, which was the last water that fed the Rio Grande and the Atlantic. In a mile now they would be over the Divide and the water would go to the Pacific. But now they allowed their horses to drink, to still rob the Rio Grande and the Atlantic. In another hour of riding they would take from the Colorado and the Pacific.

"It tastes the same no matter which," Alastair said.

"No matter which what?" Sant said, drinking.

"Yes," Alastair said, speaking from the stream. "No matter which way we go we all end up in the same place."

"You're a big philosopher, Alley. Let's get moving." But Sant just sat there alongside the stream.

"Like you say, Santo," Alastair Benjamin said, crouching alongside the stream, too, and staring down intensely at his own reflection in the water. "God, I'm a handsome son of a bitch!"

"Your mother's side, I presume," Sant said.

"No, I get it from all sides."

"You got some mule too?"

"Yeah. I'm thinking of making a study of it," Alastair said. "A study of where we come from and how."

"Intercourse," Sant said. "Mr. Peersall said that, and even the missionary admits it."

"Yes, but there are all kinds of intercourse. Social, for example."

"Yeah, but that don't count."

"All right, but we agree that two cells come together?"

"Aren't you skipping a bit?" Sant said.

"All right, but we agree two cells come together?"

"Yeah."

"Making one cell."

"Yeah."

"Then isn't it a fair assumption that the cell that started it all is a cell that is composed of tiny particles of the man's body that started it all?"

Sant began tossing pebbles in the water so that their reflections, their exact images, spread outward in quick waves. "No, it isn't true," Sant said.

"Why isn't it true?" Alastair said, watching the destruction of his image in the water.

"Well," Sant said, "when people have this nonsocial intercourse— Wait a minute," he said, throwing a whole handful of pebbles in the water. "It's got to be social. After all, these people have got to have met each other, been introduced anyway."

"You've got a point there," Alastair said. "I'll tell the missionary it's got to be social. They've got to have met before, I hope.

"Sure," Sant said.

"But what about my statement not being true?"

"Well," Sant said, "if this cell is composed of tiny particles of the body of the man that started it all, supposing the man had lost an arm in battle or something, would the child be born with only one arm? I don't think it would."

"Maybe you got something," Alastair said. "I've got to do some more thinking."

"You certainly do."

"Maybe," Alastair said, beginning to toss pebbles into Sant's reflection now. "Maybe the cell remembers. Maybe it remembers to remember everything the way it was before the battle where he lost the arm."

"Maybe."

"I wouldn't want to have to rework my whole theory."

"You can always get facts to fit anything," Sant said.

"But I wouldn't want to mislead the world," Alastair said.

"Oh, they've been misled before."

"But they don't give medals for that."

"I think they have," Sant said.

"But it would be on my conscience."

"I can't help you there."

"No one can," Alastair said. "No one can. I have got to follow the truth where it leads, to take it where I find it, even if it's against me."

"Sure," Sant said. They both watched their perfect reflections in the water.

"That reminds me," Sant said. "I'd like to find something to eat."

Alastair stood up and looked down on the wide country beneath the clouds that were below them, floating above the long blue mesas like lambs or small puffs of smoke. Each mesa was an island above the earth and each large island was very sufficient unto itself. Each had its own mule deer, a large amount of juniper, jack pine, sage, ground scrub oak, and each its own foxes—red foxes. Some of these islands above the earth had coyotes; the long blue mesas are the last refuge, the final sanctuary, of these beautiful, light-running creatures that the government is determined to exterminate and the islands above the earth are determined to hide. The coyotes with these mesas are winning now because the coyotes are too smart to come down and the government men too lazy and too clumsy to get up.

"We got to get to the top of one of those one of these days," Alastair said.

"We been."

"It doesn't look possible from up here, does it?"

"No, it doesn't. But we been."

"When we going again?"

"When we feel like it."

"We can do anything."

"Anything," Sant said.

Alastair allowed his eye now to follow all the many clouds that lightly flowered the sky in each direction. One of them must be darkly shadowing the place where he remembered.

"Let's get going," Alastair said.

Soon they were cutting down the slope sharply but moving blindly through the trees. Then they hit an old and worn, narrow, one-way cattle path that followed along the wide bench of the Jemez. They must have followed this for about five miles or close to one hour, until they came to a clear opening on a sandstone slab escarpment where they could look straight down to sudden green fields below. The green was bright against the red earth. A protective ridge of gray sage sprinkled with the orange of Cowboys Delight and the blue of lupine circled all around the green place in the red earth.

"That's ours," Sant said. "It's part of the Circle Heart."

"This is where I remember. Where we had the gun fight," Alastair said suddenly.

"No. It's ours. It's part of the Circle Heart."

Alastair touched his horse and sped down ahead of Sant. Sant just sat there and watched him go down. He really could not see Alastair for the dust but he could see him finally as he opened the gate to the green pasture and stood holding it for Sant. Sant rode down slowly and went through the open gate very slowly. Alastair fastened the gate quickly and was gone again quickly on his horse, racing the animal to a burned mound in the middle of the green fields. When Sant got there Alastair was sitting on some burned adobes near a rusted iron bed.

"This is where it happened," Alastair said carefully and studying it all. "The gun fight. Where I remember."

"No. It's ours," Sant said. "It's part of the Circle Heart."

"Wait," Alastair said. "Over there. That's where the Indians were watching from—those rocks. And here," he said, "here is the bed and alongside the bed, look—shell casings."

"No. It's ours," Sant said. "It's part of the Circle Heart."

"But for how long?"

"As long as I remember," Sant said.

"Here," Alastair said, moving, then standing. "Here's where the window was."

"That orphanage where you were at," Sant said. "There must have been a lot of lonely nights."

"Yes," Alastair said.

"Where a guy could dream of cowboys and Indians."

"I guess so."

"And even of being one himself."

"Maybe. But I remember this."

"Oh," Sant said. "I bet you do."

"You mean you think—?"

"Yes," Sant said. "In the orphanage there must have been a lot of lonely nights."

"Then how about your bronc ride?" Alastair sat down now on the burned and rusted bed. "What about what you remember?"

"Oh that," Sant said. Sant was still mounted. "But this," Sant said, "this is ours. This is part of the Circle Heart."

"You mean that what we remember isn't any good now?"

"That's right," Sant said. "What you remember isn't any good."

"Just because this is yours?"

"That's right."

"Well, I didn't mean to pick on yours."

"Then why did you pick on the Circle Heart?"

"It's what I remember."

"Why didn't you pick on the New Mexico Cattle and Timber Keep Out? They can afford it and it's a nice place too."

"It's not what I remember."

"You see, Alastair," Sant said, speaking down from his horse, "whoever controls this controls the Circle Heart. Two hundred permits on the Peñas Negras. Without this water halfway between we couldn't drive to our summer pasture. If we didn't have this we'd have to get it. It's the heart of the Circle Heart."

"What do you mean you'd have to get it? Wasn't it always yours?"

"I think so."

Alastair picked up a blackened brass shell casing and tried, by aiming carefully, to drop it on another shell casing lying there. He hit it easily every time he tried. Now he began tossing shell casings over the hunk of burned adobe wall with an easy swinging motion of his arm.

"Maybe, Santo," he said, "maybe I should have picked on the New Mexico Cattle and Timber Keep Out. I don't know what got into me, picking on your place."

"Your place too," Sant said. "We adapted you."

"Is it adapted or adopted?" Alastair wondered.

"I don't know, Alley. But it's your place too."

"I don't know what got into me, Santo. I must have been crazy."

Sant got off his horse and sat down on the burned bed alongside of Alastair and looked over with him toward the great rocks.

"No, it's just that it's very lonely in an orphanage."

"Yes, I guess so," Alastair said.

"Alley, let's go where I remember."

"Today?"

"Yeah."

"Don't you think we've had enough today?"

"Maybe so. Then let's go back to the Circle Heart."

"*Cómo no?*"

"You're learning Spanish."

"I've learned a little bit every day."

The horses had drag-reined over to the distant fence. Sant was standing now. "I'll get both of them," he said, starting off.

Alastair Benjamin kicked around in the rubble of the burned house looking for treasure but he found nothing. He picked up a few burned books and let them drop. Then he decided to help Sant catch the horses. Sant was trailing them along the fence, careful not to move too quickly, but the horses were very careful to stay just ahead of him. Sant quickened his pace and the horses broke into a small trot. Sant stopped, placed his hands on his hips, and said, "Bastards."

Alastair began to trail the horses as they came across the field and Sant doubled back. When Sant got to the burned house he could see that Alastair had caught the horses in the far corner so he kicked around in the rubble looking for treasure but he found nothing either. Except this, he thought, bending over and picking up a spur that barely showed in the adobe. He wiped off the thick, hard mud and put the spur in his pocket. Now he took it out again and examined it carefully. Near where the sharp Spanish rowel was welded onto the heel piece there was some kind of a brand. Sant wiped it again with spit. It was a circle. Sant wiped it again. Inside the circle was etched a heart. Sant put it back in his pocket as Alastair came up with the horses.

"Any treasure?"

"No treasure," Sant said.

Alastair watched the sky. Big, anvil-shaped black clouds were tumbling in over the mountain already impinging quietly on the gentle blue.

"We got to make a run for it," Alastair said.

"It's too late, we're caught," Sant said.

"Yes," Alastair said, feeling the beginning drops. "But we'll make a run for it."

"All right," Sant said, mounting.

They got out of the green pasture as quickly as they could and put back the gate. Soon they were making rapid time through the dark forest with the rain noisy against the leaves.

"You said something about spurs," Sant said. "You remembered spurs."

"A silver spur. The man lost one silver spur," Alastair said. "But remember from now on we're going to pick on the New Mexico Cattle and Timber."

"Keep Out," Sant said.

400

"Yes, that's better," Alastair said. "It's a corporation, not a person. You don't stir up things."

"Yes. You don't stir up nothing," Sant agreed.

"Then we'll drop it," Alastair said.

"All right," Sant said.

"I'd like to find a cave where we can hide," Alastair said.

"Yeah. Someplace out of the rain," Sant said.

They got their horses out of the forest and made along a stone ledge between two cliffs. Somewhere along here were caves and they began watching the rock wall. What had been gay with vivid colors before was now all dull with rain, and the heavy clouds moved in beneath them as well as above them, blanking out the long valley below so that they moved between two layers of darkness alongside the even darker cliffs, but they continued to watch for a cave, without the protection now of the forest with its noise of the rain. Now there was only a big silence here as they walked their horses seemingly between the dim-lit sandwich of heaven and earth.

"There," Alastair said. "A cave."

The cave was not only large enough for them but great enough for their horses too. But the horses were not having any. They balked at the cave so the boys tied them to each other to keep them from drifting and sat themselves at the mouth of the cave looking out at the forlorn horses and the dark clouds that seemed to be ascending from below.

A deer tripped by with that easy ungainly going-in-all-directions, long-legged clumsiness deer have when they are not running. The deer did not spot the horses till he was among them; then he did not panic but seemed to stare them down as he moved through them and on into the cloud. Actually the deer must have been occupied with something else in which horses did not figure so that the horses did not register yet. Later, in a cloud, the deer might suddenly panic. The deer was a doe. Now there came a buck, a very wide-antlered, businesslike-looking animal except for those antlers. They must give him trouble moving through the heavy brush, but now he moved through the clouds well enough and with the haze around his feet he seemed diaphanous, before vanishing again and cloud-lost.

"They did not pick up our scent," Alastair said.

"No, I guess they didn't."

"I've got a thing about deer."

"What's that?"

"How there got to be different kinds of deer—mule deer, white tails."

"How did there get to be different kinds of deer?"

"Well, they got separated by a river or something. They had different kinds of country, different problems, so they became different."

"But deer could swim that river."

"I know," Alastair said. "For deer I need something bigger than a river."

"Yes, you do," Sant said.

"Maybe oceans," Alastair said. "Oceans separating the land for a while and then letting it join millions of years later. That would do it."

"It sure would," Sant said. "If you could move those oceans."

"Maybe they moved themselves. I'm not going to give up."

"That's right, don't quit, Alley."

"I won't."

"Jesus, I wish the rain would stop," Sant said.

Alastair began to collect a bunch of stones.

"You know, Santo, if a man waited at the mouth of this cave long enough the whole world would go by."

"Yeah."

Within the darkness of the cave Sant and Alastair were getting very low, sitting and watching the rain.

"But if we sit here long enough the whole world will go by," Alastair said.

"I'd rather go out and meet it," Sant said.

"Very pleased to meet you."

"How are the twins?"

"Yeah."

"I'm going out."

"In the rain?"

"Yeah."

"Did something happen back there, Santo?"

"No, I guess not. We better get going."

"In the rain?"

"Why not?"

"Cómo no?"

When they got to the place where the tunnel of flowers ran alongside the mountain they decided against going the way they had come. Everything was all wet and dripping in there and what had been bright and alive, riotous, before, was now only gaudy and wrong in the rain. They went up on top and trailed the ridge on an old deer trail. Up here you could sense the first break in the weather. Up here you could look out and over the whole weird, awful land and be in a nice position to enjoy it if anything good happened. They continued to ride the ridge that seemed the top of the world. Up here the two of them were alone and together. Maybe it would be nice if they never had to go down.

"Let's ride her all the way in," Sant said.

"The ridge?"

Alastair touched his hand along the mane of his white horse. "That would be nice."

Now his horse followed a Z in the trail that led him up even higher. He was lost a brief second before Sant spurred his paint and then again quickly they were joined.

"That's the secret-city fence," Alastair said, pointing. "But I don't see any guard and I don't see our tracks. I suppose you've always got to watch out for a trigger-happy guard."

"We're hitting the fence at a different place this time," Sant said. "We'll have to follow the fence down."

The rain clouds were breaking up, dissolving in wraiths and then reforming in less weight, less darkness; but a very quiet, small rain still fell in the manner of rain that will go on falling and has fallen already past remembrance.

"Oh," Sant said. He thought he saw the guard up ahead. Sant and Alastair turned their horses into the brush and disappeared.

"Like Indians," Sant said. "We just move off and leave the white man. That's the way Indians always were, you know. Maybe they'd be with a white party two or three days and then suddenly they had left."

"Maybe they remembered something."

"It could have been that."

"Then let's go where you rode the bronc horse."

"Another day."

"If it's because of those crazy people like Arturo Cipriano de Godoy, remember there's always your father."

"Yes, there was always him."

After four hours of steady riding they were heading down off the mountain now. The rain had eased to be almost nothing, yet the sky was a very deep gray and all the country below was somber in shadow and wet without glisten, green without color. They rode in silence down to the mouth of the long valley. Way up ahead, but visible, were the beginning fences, five barbed-wire strands, horseshoe-nailed to juniper posts, going all around the Circle Heart.

"Yes," Sant said as they brought their gay horses into a trot, "yes. My father eats butterflies."

"You intrigue me," Alastair said. "Tell me more."

"Tomorrow," Sant said. "Today we've had plenty. Tomorrow. I'll remember more tomorrow."

EIGHT   **M**illie Sant began working in the kitchen early and by ten o'clock she was finished with Zen. Zen did not seem to fit too well into New Mexico, but to Millie this bright morning made her feel generous and she could not leave any religion without saying some good word for it. She removed from the shelf from between the butter and the beans a copy of Zen Buddhism. She wanted a good word to quit it on. She read from Zen to find a good word.

"When Hui-neng declared, 'From the first not a thing is,' the keynote of Zen thought was struck. This keynote was never so clearly struck before. When the masters who followed him pointed to the presence of the Mind in each individual mind and also to its absolute purity, this idea of presence and purity was understood somehow to suggest the existence of an individual body, however ethereal and transparent it may be conceived. The philosophy of Prajnaparamita, (wu-i-wu) which is also that of Hui-neng, generally has this effect. To understand it a man requires a deep religious intellectual insight in the truth of Sunyata. When Hui-neng is said to have had an awakening by listening to the Vajracchedika Sutra (Diamond Sutra) which belongs to the Prajnaparamita group of the Mayahana texts, we know then at once where he has his foothold."

Millie put the book down.

"He has his foothold in—well, I guess, bull turds," Millie finally decided. That was about the only apt word that ranch life in northern New Mexico had given her to quit the yogis on. Not

405

bad for a young yogin with a high Zen education trapped in the west.

Not too bad, Millie thought, replacing the beans on the shelf and putting Zen in the trash.

"Not bad. It's the best religion I've read in a long time. You can quote me on that," Millie said as she went over and sat on the window box, touched her index finger to her small face, and stared out.

The kids have got to have a religion though. Yes sir, she thought, watching them. They've got to have a religion, some real religion. None of this Zen stuff. Come to think of it, though, they've got to have one of the big three religions so they will fit in with other people and not use bad words and so they'll have a place to look forward to when they die, up there with the big three. Me, when I die, I'll come back to the ranch. I like this ranch very much. Those kids, though, must do things properly. If I had done things properly I would be married to George Hutchinson and working in his dress shop in Gallup. I beat that rap. Big Sant has his problems and only his will to face them with—and there go I. So be it. God save us all.

It was a crystal day at the Circle Heart, a dense clear blue with no clouds at all. Little Sant was working in the corral when Alastair came up.

"He really does," Alastair said. "He catches them anyway. He's catching them now."

"He eats them," Sant said above his pounding on the stock-branding chute. Now he ceased his pounding and cocked the hammer behind his ear. "He eats them."

"Well, he catches them anyway," Alastair said.

"He eats them too," Sant said and he resumed his hammering.

Alastair went back to the hill above the barn where the speckled squirrels had a lookout and where he had been watching from before, and watched Big Sant lumber about in the fields below catching butterflies.

"Eats them?" Alastair wondered.

Later, in a small, dim-lighted room in the great house, Big

Sant had the day's catch neatly impaled on a board in front of him with bright pins.

"Can I come in?" Alastair said.

"I suppose so, but I'm very busy."

"Are you going to eat any?" Alastair said.

"Not any of these."

"Aren't those any good to eat?"

"It's not necessary."

"Is it necessary to eat some of them?"

"Yes."

"Why is it necessary to eat some of them?"

"So as you can tell what they're up to."

"Oh?"

"So as you can tell why their color is useful. Most butterflies resemble their surroundings, that is, they have got a protective coloration. But some butterflies challenge their surroundings with big crosses and stripes that holler, Look at me, look at me, look at me now! These are the bitter, nasty-tasting ones. Once a bird has eaten one of these he will never eat another so he keeps looking for those loud markings to distinguish what he should not eat and the bitter-tasting butterflies who can be told by loud markings are safe. Now this system has worked so well that some sweet-tasting butterflies have adopted this kind of loud coloring and it has confused the birds very much."

"I've been adopted."

"Yes. We adopted you."

"Why?"

"That's a different subject. Now we're talking about butterflies."

"Why do you have to eat some of the butterflies?"

"So I can prove that some of the loud butterflies taste good and so I can put down exactly which ones they are."

"Who for?"

"For people who are interested."

"I hope you get some pay for it?"

"No. It's science."

"Don't scientists get paid?"

407

"Not if they haven't gone to school."

"Why didn't you go to school?"

"Because somebody had to work this ranch. My brother had something more important to do."

"You mean it wasn't very important?"

"Yes."

"But you would have liked to have gone to school and become a real scientist?"

"Yes."

"All of those butterflies adopting all those colors and then your adopting me."

"Yes, we adopted you, and that was because, way out here, we figured Little Sant needed someone his own age to be with. Now we have two sons."

"I've got a thing about deer."

"What's that?"

"That we get different kinds of deer because at one time there was one kind of deer and they got separated and then, in a trillion years, naturally they became different."

"How did they get separated?"

"I'm thinking about that."

"It's a very good thing to think about."

"It all began when I was thinking how I got black. We must have got separated from the people who were white."

"It's better when science is impersonal. Try to think about the deer."

"All right. I'm sorry I interrupted your work on the butterflies."

"That's all right. It's fine. I like to see it. I wish Little Sant took some interest."

"You going to send him to the university?"

"Yes."

"He wants to be a bronc rider."

"Yes. We hope he'll get over that."

"He never asked you why you eat butterflies?"

"No, he hasn't."

"Well, I'm sorry I asked you what you wanted him to ask."

"You're my son, too, Alastair," Big Sant said and he slid over a new tray of bright varicolored butterflies that were impaled like the others on a stiff burlap cloth. "That's all right. And you go right on thinking about the deer."

"Well, I was thinking about the old Circle R too. We were up there." Alastair looked around. "I see you've got some burned books."

"Yes. But you go right on thinking about the deer," Big Sant said. "Always try to follow through on important things that might affect your future."

"Okay," Alastair said and he left.

Big Sant buried his flowered face in his hands and stared down at the bright butterflies all impaled there.

Later on in the day, when the big, deep, clear, total blueness of the sky had collected a few high clouds, Alastair and Sant were going around the yellow overhang of the Cuba Mesa on a mission, a mission to a mission. That is, they were supposed to deliver a message to Mr. Sanders at the Torreon Mission from Millie Sant. But they had thought of a better mission of their own which was to go where Little Sant had ridden the killer horse at the rodeo. And now this mission had been sidetracked for a still better mission, which was to trap the trapper. The government trapper was laying out poisoned meat to kill the coyotes and they had just spotted him going up a draw that led to the top of the Cuba Mesa.

"How are we going to trap a trapper?" Alastair said. "We're supposed to be on some other kind of mission anyway."

"We can still do our mission to the mission and go to where I rode the killer horse, too, but we may never get a chance to trap the trapper again."

"It's a unique opportunity."

"Yes. And we may never get a good chance again."

"Yeah."

The government trapper was actually a government poisoner; that is, he did not carry traps but poisoned meat in his saddlebags. Cyanide of potassium was mixed in the meat, which he placed wherever he saw signs of coyotes. It caused violent convulsions in the sleek gray animals and, in not too long a time, they were dead. There are not too many left. The ranchers at one time complained that the coyote was killing their sheep, but now most of them are in cattle and they have stopped complaining but the government has still got the habit of killing coyotes. It's a war. There was one government trapper who used to work the region whom they called Unconditional Surrender Rothrock. He killed eight hundred and fifty-two. A very brave chap. He quit to take a more interesting job at Yucca Flats. Some said he was too lazy to climb the mesas where the last of the coyotes were, others said he got bored killing coyotes and wanted to try something more challenging. Anyway the man below was Unconditional Rothrock's replacement. His name was Charles Enright and he was determined to do his duty; that is, he would climb the mesas. That is, he would go where the coyotes were regardless of the terrain or lack of challenge. As Enright climbed, pulling the horse after him, he would occasionally stop, go back to the saddlebags on the horse, and drop a bait of meat; and the two boys, Sant and Alastair, following at a cautious distance, would on every occasion retrieve the bait and put it in their own saddlebags for later use. The one thing the boys noticed about Enright was that he was not as smart as Unconditional Surrender Rothrock. He did not take the precaution, as did Rothrock, of looking back with field glasses to make sure no coyote lover was following and picking up the meat.

"He's pretty dumb," Sant said, putting the bait in his saddlebag and regaining the horse.

"He didn't go to poisoner's school," Alastair said.

"Do they have that kind of schools?"

"They got every kind of school."

"You know, Santo," Alastair said, "I've been watching him."

"All right, what did you notice?"

"That he's examining the rocks. He seems more preoccupied with the rocks than the coyotes."

"What does preoccupied mean?"

"You know what that word means. You just think I'm using too many big words."

"Sure you are. And the danger is that pretty soon you won't be able to use small words."

"Are they better?"

"Sure they are."

"That's very perspicacious of you."

"Sure it is."

"Well then, I've noticed he's interested in the rocks."

"I've noticed that too."

"Well, why didn't you agree with me before?"

"Because you wouldn't speak English."

"Santo, you're a snob."

"What does that mean?"

"It means that you're probably right, that I like to practice big words."

"Well, practice them on your own time."

"When no one's looking?"

"That's right. Sometime, Alley, when we're not trapping the trapper."

"We're supposed to be on a mission to the missionary."

"Missionaries can wait."

"There's something profound in that statement that escapes me."

"Me too. Notice, Alley, our friend is examining the rocks again."

"Friend?"

"Well, studying the rocks is not a good way to catch coyotes, according to Rothrock."

"Well, maybe this is a new way to kill coyotes."

"I never thought of that."

"An innovation."

"I did think of that but I thought it sounded silly."

"Okay, Santo. But it's got me why rocks have got anything to do with coyotes."

"Me too, Alley."

As the trapper, Charles Enright, climbed he marveled that he had come where even the famous Rothrock was unwilling to go, scattering the meat as he went. Now he sat down to study something carefully and he nibbled on the meat bait as he sat. But he spat it out. It didn't taste very good uncooked. The coyotes didn't seem to mind, or the foxes, who must get some of it too. The coyote, he thought, belongs to the dog family. There are several species. Man is only one species. He hadn't remembered this from school, he had looked it up before he applied for the job, thinking they might ask him something. They asked him nothing. Yes, they had asked him if he was willing. He was willing. Charles Enright was one of the few ranchers in the area that still ran sheep. The government thought they knew exactly why he was willing to kill coyotes. Charles Enright owned thirteen hundred and twelve sheep according to the latest tally that his two Navaho shepherds had made on their tally sticks, and six goats to do the leading. Maybe five now. The Indians ate goat when they felt like eating goat. But, Enright thought, pulling on the reins to bring the horse up close to where he was sitting, according to my observations from below I am supposed to be sitting just about exactly where the Nacimiento rock divides from the San José. But now that I am up here I'm not so sure. The San José was sedimentary, laid down about sixty-five million years ago and the Nacimiento around eighty million, but right here the formations seem to have faulted. That is, when that mountain rose over there it pressured the scarp into a down tilt and right here the San José seems like a card cheated into the wrong position in the deck. If I could find a fossil in this lens I am in doubt about, I could send it to the American Museum and they could tell me exactly where I am. Where I was.

"Where is he now?" Sant asked.

"He has just begun to climb up into the San José."

"What is that?"

"That's a formation. Don't you ever read any of your father's books?"

"No. I told you, I'm going to be a bronc rider."

"Well, I'm not so sure he's in the San José myself. There's a bad fault there. She could be out of place."

"Then books don't help much."

"They make you curious if they pose the right questions."

412

"Well, Alley, I wish you'd be curious about the question at hand."

"Doing the trapper in?"

"Yeah."

"Well, we could shoot him."

"Yeah, we could."

"We could dine him."

"What do you mean, dine him?"

"Well, all this poison meat he's been dropping for the coyotes we got in our saddlebags. We could circle ahead of him, cook it up, and invite him to eat with us. Feed him what he's feeding the coyotes."

"Couldn't they give us the electric chair for life for doing that?"

"Not if it's not premeditated."

"What's that mean?"

"If we don't think about it, it's okay."

"Then we won't think about it. We'll just do it."

"All right. Let's circle ahead of him without thinking."

"And cook up the poison meat without thought."

"Yeah."

The danger is, Enright thought, resuming his climb, that those two boys following me don't know that I know they are trailing me. The danger is they might do something silly. They could do something with the meat that would lose me my job. From the looks of them they are the boys from the Circle Heart. The Circle Heart is a queer bunch. The father catches butterflies. Still, maybe my outfit's a queer bunch too. I catch rocks. Maybe every outfit's a queer bunch if you really know enough about them. I think, though, that maybe the Circle Heart is a queerer bunch than the rest. After all, where did the dark boy come from? At the inquiry, after the fire at the Circle R, it was brought out that the black had no son. Yet President Taft says there was a boy, says he rescued the boy from the fire, kept him several months before the boy ran away—to get back home, that he must have been picked up by the police somewhere and put in an orphanage. Yet Bowman, who was at the fire too, who fired back when he was fired at, says he saw no boy; and who would take President Taft's word against a respected white Christian? And yet the boy they adopted is very dark. Coincidence? Conscience? Maybe he thinks bringing a dark boy into the outfit will make himself easier to live with after he bid in the Circle R so cheap at the tax sale. Maybe he suspects that there might have been a boy in that fire that the Gran Negrito never wanted anyone to see, by some woman he wanted no one to discover. Maybe. Maybe this and maybe that. Maybe I should mind my own business. Maybe, he thought, halting the horse he led and getting down on his knees. Yes, maybe this is the San José. It's too bad they don't have a blood test for these rocks or that I can't find a fossil so that I could be certain of the identification. Bowman has the same problem and I don't mean with rocks and I don't mean with butterflies. But maybe we should mind our own business.

Enright began scattering meat to the right and some to the left. He threw meat above the path and below. This would show all the citizens and fellow taxpayers following how efficient he was. Just as good as Unconditional Surrender Rothrock.

"And my opinions are just as good as President Taft's. I only wish I knew more about these rocks and why the boys are following me. But maybe even President Taft wouldn't know exactly."

"You suppose he knows we're watching him?"

"I think he does."

"Why do you think he does?"

"Because he's acting. He's throwing the meat with more verve than Rothrock."

"Verve?"

"Style. You know I got a theory."

They climbed their gay horses, an Appaloosa and a paint, through even gayer rocks to higher ground beneath a brighter sky, went through a sea of brighter blue beeweed that did not belong at this altitude. Now they gained a deer path that twisted, tortured its way around great stones in a punishing sun.

"So no one is interested in my theory. All right," Alastair said.

"All right, what is it?"

"He is acting."

"Oh."

414

"Yes. He's not throwing the meat the way your father catches butterflies."

"They're two different operations."

"But here there's something acting."

"You mean, as the missionary would say, his soul ain't in it?"

"Maybe. But I still say style."

"Alley, why do you have to contradict everybody including Mr. Sanders, the missionary?"

"Did I?"

"You just did."

"You mean I contradicted him?"

"Before we got there."

"Well, now," Alastair said.

The deer path they followed began to straighten out as they neared the top of the Cuba Mesa. Like all deer paths, this one took the longest distance between two points, but as it neared the top of the mesa the deer decided to cease the game and the path made quickly to a close cover of scrub oak. And so now did the boys on the paint and the Appaloosa.

"Well, now," Alastair said, stroking the paint beneath a juniper, "this looks like as good a place to dine as any."

"Yeah," Sant said, taking the meat they had collected out of the saddlebags. "Yes, it does."

From way up here they could look down on all the land between the mesas and see the sheer sides of many other mesas. They both knew that mesa means table in Spanish, and that's exactly what they looked like. Alastair had found out that they did not rise there in the forming of the earth but that they remained there, these tougher tables in the clouds, when the rest of the land had water- and wind-eroded away. Some of the land that was formerly there between the tables is now in Old Mexico, some of it may be in Madagascar, more of it is at the bottom of the ocean.

"Yeah," Alastair said.

"Yeah what?" Sant said. "Why don't you help me with the fire?"

"Yeah, soon this mesa will be gone too. It's disappearing

before our eyes." Alastair was still atop his horse. "In another hundred million years there will be none of this mesa left."

"Oh, that's terrible," Sant said. "Now you have got me worried. The way you're dreaming up there on the horse it may be gone before we get this fire built."

Alastair got down and gathered some dead piñon and brought it to Sant, who was cradling a small beginning flame.

"Alley, we got to stop worrying about tomorrow and get this nice dinner cooked."

"I wasn't worried about tomorrow. I said it would take a hundred million years."

"As a matter of fact, Alley, it will be only a few minutes before he gets here."

"All right," Alastair said, and he got the frying pan and the bread out of the saddlebags. Sant took the pan and held it over the fire.

"Now get the meat," he said. Sant took the meat, made it into patties with his quick, grimed hands, and settled each patty carefully in the pan he held over the piñon flames. "Now we're in business," he said.

"What we going to use for a table?"

"This whole thousand acres we're on top of is a table. That's what you been dreaming about, isn't it?"

"But supposing we get caught?"

"They can't do nothing because we haven't been thinking about it. We been thinking about something else. We been thinking about tables. We haven't been thinking about poisoning poisoners."

"Yeah, I really have been thinking about something else lately."

"Good. You'll make a good case. Pass me more of the meat."

Alastair passed another ball of meat. "I've been thinking lately that we can't do this."

"We're doing it. Watch."

"I mean even if we don't get caught. We got to live with ourselves."

"Were you planning to live with someone else?"

"I mean our conscience."

416

"Put it in the pan."

"You know what I mean."

"If you can't put it in the pan I don't know what you mean."

They both huddled around the pan watching the meat fry.

"It's about done, Alley," Sant said. "Now we can throw it away."

"Throw it away?"

"Yeah. I scared you."

"Yeah, you did."

"Then that's all. I sure would like to think of some way, though, of keeping him from killing the coyotes."

"Me too."

"Some way we could live with our own selves and someone else too."

"Me too."

Sant cocked his arm to throw the dangerous meat into the brush. "Well, here goes his dinner."

"Wait a minute! Don't throw good meat away, boy." The trapper had come over the top pulling his horse. Now he advanced on Sant and took the pan Sant held. "Don't throw away perfectly good meat," he said, examining it.

"We've already et more than we can hold," Sant said. "We're all finished."

"But maybe someone else. I haven't eaten yet." Mr. Enright wore a big, squared roundup hat above a small, red, inquiring face.

"Oh," Sant said.

"Yes, oh," Alastair said.

"You wouldn't begrudge a man?"

"No."

"Oh, no," Alastair said.

"Then I'll dig in."

"No," Sant said.

"Oh, no," Alastair said.

"Why?" The man went over, still holding the pan, and got out a fork from his saddlebag. "Why not?"

"Because it might be poisoned," Sant said.

"Who would want to poison meat?" the trapper said.

"Some people."

"Sure. Some people," Alastair said.

"Well, I don't think so," the trapper said and he forked a piece of the meat.

"I wouldn't do that," Alastair said. "Like I said, some people."

"Some people such as who?" the trapper said.

"Such as you," Sant said. Sant stood up from his crouched position over the fire.

"Yeah," Alastair said, getting up too. "Such as you."

Enright sat down on a juniper log as the boys stood up. "You think I'm another Rothrock?"

"Another Unconditional Surrender Rothrock," Sant said.

"Well," Enright said and he ate some of the meat, ate it all the way down.

"You're on your own," Alastair said.

"On my own," the man agreed and he ate another piece of the meat.

"All the way down," Sant said to Alastair.

"Yeah, I noticed that too," Alastair said.

"Have you noticed me tossing out the meat too?" Enright asked between bites.

"Yeah."

"Did you notice me mix any poison with it?"

"No."

"Then why should I be afraid to eat my own meat?"

The boys now both sat down on the juniper log with Enright.

"The government," Enright said, "told me to take care of the coyotes."

"That's right," Sant said.

"They gave me the poison and the meat. It's good meat."

"Is it good?" Sant said.

"They didn't tell me to mix the poison and the meat."

"They're not very good about instructions."

"No, they're not," Enright said.

"Still," Alastair said, leaning and looking under the log, "your instructions were tacitly implicit. Is it ethical of you—?"

418

"Yes, it is," Enright said.

"What's that?" Sant said.

"He means I knew my intentions all along and I had no right to take the job."

"Then why didn't Alastair say that?" Sant said.

"The same reason the government didn't," Enright said. "Didn't say it to my face, 'Go out and kill all the coyotes because we have already killed almost all the big cats that prey on them and after you have killed all the coyotes then kill all the rabbits because when the coyotes are gone the rabbits will, of course, explode, and after the rabbits are gone whatever they feed on will be all over the place and then you exterminate that and then the next and the next until we are the only animal alive!' "

"Then you're the opposite of Unconditional Surrender Rothrock."

"You might say that."

"But then that evades the law," Alastair said.

"But there was another law before we ever got here."

Alastair moved a stone with his foot. "What law was that?"

"Nature," Enright said. "The law of nature. It keeps everything nicely balanced. No animal got out of hand."

"We got out of hand," Alastair said.

"Yes, we did," Enright said, and he finished the last of the meat, wiped his hands on his horse that stood by. "Isn't it a beautiful day," he said, looking out. "It was a beautiful trip up here and I think I found out where the San José and the Nacimiento divide."

"Then you're not taking the government money for doing nothing," Alastair said.

"No. I think I've made a contribution they can use."

"In more ways than one," Sant said.

"I hope so, son," Enright said. "Thank you, son, for the dinner." And Enright was off across the mesa, tossing meat above the rocks and below the rocks, around and over the logs, wherever the coyotes might lurk. Just like Unconditional Surrender Rothrock.

"Yeah, I don't know why he did it," Sant said.

"Did what?"

"Took the job."

"To save the coyotes, like he said."

"But, like he said, he's got sheep."

"You mean the rabbits that the coyotes used to keep down are eating his grass."

"That's right."

"And that's why he wants to bring back the coyotes, don't want another Unconditional Surrender Rothrock to get the job."

"Yes, maybe."

"But maybe he is an idealist about bringing the coyotes back with no personal gain at all and maybe you're a cynic."

"Yes, maybe. And maybe, like Mr. Peersall says, I'm a realist."

"And maybe, like the missionary says, realism is a corruption of reality."

"Oh," Sant said, getting on his horse and looking out over the country below. "The missionary said no such thing. He speaks English as good as the rest of us."

"Well, where to now?" Alastair said, mounting.

"Home."

"Where the woodbine twineth."

"Yeah. Where my old man catches butterflies."

Alastair led off down the slope. "Where the woodbine twineth is just a phrase."

"Where my old man catches butterflies isn't."

"Santo," Alastair said, allowing his paint to pick and choose in jerky fashion down the slope, "Santo, you've got to be more tolerant."

"If you mean I catch his butterflies, okay if he'll catch my horse.

"Santo, you mean he doesn't give you any encouragement about being a bronc rider."

"That's right. And moreover, he's *dis*couraging."

"Well, you don't encourage his butterflies."

"I try to, Alley. I've worked at them, but somehow I don't follow the train of his mind. Butterflies."

"It's a science. He'd like you to take an interest in science."

"Butterflies," Sant said.

They rode across the very level mesa with Sant roping a rock or a stump when he saw one that was right for roping. They rode mostly through piñon, a tree that produces nuts. They are very irregular in their production and if the Navahos can make a good gathering every three years the Indians are doing very well. Although the Indians don't gather them exactly, the squirrels gather them. The Indians find the nests of the squirrels and rob the squirrels. The same Indians who robbed the pueblos now rob the squirrels.

They rode, too, through an orange sward of pentstemon, then a burst of golden goldeneye and blue bluebells, desert phlox, gilia, and four o'clock, but nearby it was filaree—filaree and yucca. Yucca boiled makes a good soap and the Indians didn't have to rob anyone to get it but the Navaho women had to gather it all by themselves without help from the squirrels. Squirrels aren't concerned with soap.

"Look up ahead there, Alley," Sant said.

"What?"

"See the rainbow?"

"No."

"Well, I'll rope it for you." Sant threw a long rope into the clearing ahead and pulled it in carefully. "There," he said, "I got it."

"Jeez," Alastair said. "You're roping things now that don't exist."

"That rainbow was the Madison Square Garden rodeo, Alley, and I'm going to make her."

"With pluck and luck."

"And practice."

"Even on rainbows?"

"Even on rainbows."

"That don't exist?"

"That don't exist yet."

"Look out!" Alastair dropped his horse off the mesa onto a narrow trail that led below.

"Can we make it down that way?" Sant called.

"You can make her down any way," Alastair said, not raising his voice. "When all else fails you can always fall."

"Down, you mean."

"Well, you can't fall up."

"That's why I keep practicing, Alley."

"You're still on the bronc kick."

"I always was, always will be." Sant joined Alastair now down on the narrow ledge below. "Did you mean that as one of your pure laws when you said you can't fall up? Is that another Benjamin law?"

"Yeah."

"What are some other Benjamin laws?"

"Well, for example, your grandfather can't be your descendant."

"You mean I can never be older than Grandfather?"

"That's right."

"Well, I never did worry about that law. Is there another law that says black people can never be white and vice versa?" Alastair didn't say anything. "Well, I never did worry about that law either," Sant said.

"Follow me," Alastair said, "and don't worry about anything."

Sant allowed his horse to creep along the narrow ledge after Alastair's. "I didn't say anything that annoyed you?"

"No," Alastair said. "This is just a short cut."

"What do you know about girls?" Sant said.

"Very little," Alastair said. "But I'm going to study them."

"And you'll let me know?"

"I'll let you know," Alastair promised.

After one half hour of very slow descent during which they continued to discuss very important things and only the horses worried, they finally made it down to the flat sage and bloom of yucca country where the big arroyos cut in weird angles up ahead.

"Older people seem to take more of an interest in girls than we do," Sant said.

"And it's not an academic interest," Alastair said.

"Yeah."

422

"No, I don't think it's an academic interest," Alastair said.

"Me neither," Sant said.

"But we don't want to condemn before we know more."

"That's right."

"What's right?"

"What you said."

"Yes, I think it's true, don't you?" Alastair said.

"Yeah. Look, I just remembered something."

"What?"

"There's the Circle Heart."

"So it is."

"And I just remembered that we were supposed to be on a mission to the missionary. Instead of that we trapped the trapper."

"So we did."

"And here we are back at the Circle Heart."

"So we are."

"What do we do?"

"Bluff," Alastair said. "Just ride in looking like we been to the mission."

"How does that look?"

"Kind of solemn, I guess, and serious and put in our place."

"All right."

They rode into the yard now of the sprawling adobe house, looking all of those things. Millie Sant stood there in front of the pump house with a dustpan and a piece of bridle in her hand.

"You boys been to the mission?" she called.

"We're going there now," Sant said.

"Yes, we're taking this short cut," Alastair said, and they both rode through the yard and out the other side.

"Lord!" Millie Sant shrieked and retreated back into the house.

"I guess we didn't look solemn enough or serious."

"Or put in our place," Sant said.

When they were absolutely certain they were well out of danger they halted their horses to figure out what to do.

"Did it ever occur to us that the thing to do," Sant said, "is to deliver the message?"

423

They were hidden in a bunch of loose-waving tamarisk along-side a broad saline wash that whitened the dry bed of its course as far as they could see.

"Wouldn't that be too obvious?" Alastair said. Alastair broke off a piece of the bitter tamarisk and ate it. "Yes, too obvious."

"How do we know?" Sant said.

"Read the message."

"Will that tell us?"

"It should," Alastair said.

"Well, it says here," Sant said.

"Where?"

"Well, I haven't found it yet. Have you got it?"

"No. You got it."

"Here it is," Sant said. "It says here."

"That's an odd way to start a letter."

"It says here: 'Dear Mr. Sanders, I'm sending you my two boys.'"

"You see, it is obvious," Alastair said. "That is, it will be obvious to the missionary when he sees us standing there."

"It says here," Sant said, "'Dear Mr. Sanders, I'm sending you my two boys—'"

"She's being redundant."

"What's that?"

"She's repeating herself."

"No, that was me."

"Well, don't interpolate. Just extrapolate."

"What's that?"

"I really don't know, Santo."

"It sounds pretty good."

"Yes it does. But don't put in any more of your own lines."

"All right. To continue. That means I'm going to start where I left off."

"Did she say that?"

"No. That was me again."

"You better let me read it, Santo."

"All right."

Alastair took the letter and then removed gold wire spectacles

424

from a red leather case, looked at the horse to get the range. The horse looked back and Alastair returned to the letter.

"Now, where were we?"

"I didn't get that far," Sant said.

"Oh, here we are."

"A very interesting letter," Sant said.

Alastair picked up a rock as he examined the letter.

"Okay," Sant said.

Alastair removed the letter as far from his eyes as he could reach but evidently he still couldn't see anything.

"Where did you find those glasses?" Sant said.

"Alongside Route 66. Don't you think they become me?"

"Sure."

"Make me look academic?"

"Sure."

Alastair had the letter turned upside down now. "She doesn't write clearly."

"If you'd take those things off you could see."

"Do things have to be functional?"

"No, but they should work."

"A point," Alastair said and he removed the glasses, held them at arm's length, and looked at the horse through one lens. The horse looked back in unbelief and Alastair returned the glasses to the case and then read the letter all the way through.

"Read it again," Sant said.

Alastair read the letter again, this time out loud.

" 'Dear Mr. Sanders, I am sending you my two boys. The trouble with them is, one of them reads too much and the other never reads at all. The other trouble is, both of them are never home and when they are home one ropes and the other reads. But the trouble about sending them to you is religion. They don't have much, maybe because I don't have any, but everyone else should. I mean everyone else does. And I don't think they should inherit my religion, that is, none. Their father isn't any good either at religion. He is worse than I am. I think these boys should get some religion. Not too much because that's what maybe happened to me. I got too much too young and now can with a good mind sub-

425

scribe to none. For a while I subscribed to the *Christian Science Monitor*. That's a religion where you subscribe to their newspaper but you don't subscribe to doctors. But after a horse fell on me at Gallina I gave it up. But I think the boys need something to make them more like other boys in case they go to school, where religion is taken for granted. Not that I want everything they do to be taken for granted but I do not want them to be taken for freaks either. What do you say to this? Give them enough religion to make them respectable but not so much that they end up with none. I think you have just the right amount. You help the Indians but you don't make a fool of us in front of them. What do you say to this? Feel them out, my two boys, that is, and see if you can use on them what you use on the Indians. All the Indians in your territory seem nice and one of them, President Taft, seems respectable. Not that the others aren't respectable too. It's just that I don't know the others as well as I know President Taft. If you could make these boys like you made President Taft that would be a fine thing and I thank you. The darkest one is the one that reads books. Sincerely, Millicent Bowman.' "

Alastair tapped the letter with the spectacles. "A good letter," he said.

Sant now had taken to eating tamarisk. He had his cowboy hat pushed back and was leaning foward critically from his seat in the speckled shade and eating tamarisk.

"Was the grammar okay?"

Alastair snapped the lid of the red spectacle case, shying the horses.

"Just about," he said. "When we speak of how a thing is said we aren't concerned actually with grammar. We are speaking of style."

"Are we?"

Alastair touched the spectacle case against his knuckles. "By style one means the ability to communicate emotionally, sentiment but not sentimentality. Sentimentality is the failure of emotion. One frequently uses a symbol to express an unexpressible emotion. The primitive symbol of God is still extant in our civilization. But one finds exceptions."

426

"Does one?" Sant said, feigning sleep.

"Yes. With you it's a horse."

Sant looked sleepily at the horse.

"With me it's truth."

"Oh," Sant said, embarrassed. "I thought it was memorizing books."

"Do I sound silly?"

"Just very young," Sant said.

"I'm older than you."

"Most people are," Sant said. "But they can still sound silly."

"Yes, but because you win an argument doesn't mean you are right."

"Big words don't either," Sant said.

"Listen," Alastair said. "This isn't getting us to the mission."

"Boy, you are so right," Sant said.

"How did we get off the track?"

"I asked you if the grammar was okay."

"No."

"Good," Sant said.

They both lay now in the dappled shade, hidden here against the overreaching sun; even the horses were nuzzled into the tamarisk against the sun and now they began to nibble on the shade above Alastair.

"What I say is," Sant said, "let's go see Mr. Peersall instead."

"Okay."

"You know he fought Indians."

"He's very old. He could have."

"Yes, he could have fought Indians."

"Did he?"

"I think he did, Alley. His stories add up pretty good."

"That's what you would have done."

"Fought Indians?"

"Yeah."

"I guess so."

"Sure."

"And you would have written about it."

"I guess so."

"That's what you got to watch out for, Alley. That you don't end up by being just a writer."

"I guess so. But what's so wrong with that?"

"Nothing, I guess, except you don't do nothing."

"I guess so. But what's so hot about Mr. Peersall?"

"He fought Indians."

They both broke off a twig of tamarisk before the horses got it all.

"Where does he live?"

"Just a piece."

The horses had now eaten away a good deal of the shade.

"What I say," Sant said, "is let's go see Mr. Peersall before our horses make us perish in the sun. There's a word for you."

"All right," Alastair said, rising and hitting the horse above. "Well, anyway it's my own horse," Alastair said.

They got on their horses and Sant took the lead in the direction, he said, of the *casa* of Mr. Peersall.

"*Del hombre* who fought the Indians. *Luchaba contra los salvajes,*" Sant said, allowing his horse to move well ahead.

NINE　　　**M**issionaries and traders—the mercenaries and the missionaries—have one thing very much in common, Big Sant held. They are both exploited by the Indians. Cowboys and Indians know this. Sometimes it will take a trader a whole lifetime to realize that he has spent his life working twenty-four hours a day for the Navahos. Sometimes missionaries will spend all the loose money in Kansas, half the tithes of Salt Lake City, before they realize they have clothed and fed one fourth of the Navaho Nation and haven't got true convert number one. Mr. Peersall, who fought Indians in his youth and should have known better, spent his old age waiting on Indians in the delusion that he was making money, for which he had absolutely no use. Mr. Sanders, the missionary, according to Charles Enright, had spent fifteen years now carrying water, which gave him little time to spread the gospel, if he indeed remembered now what it was he was supposed to spread.

If you keep the white man busy he's quite harmless, the Indian Nice Hands held. The trouble is that there are not enough missionaries being sent to the Navaho Nation. Things are not getting done. Soon there will not be enough water. Soon the Indians will have to go to work. Soon the Indians will lose a little dignity. Soon the differences between the red and the white will only be in the legend.

Mr. Sanders was still a missionary. God bless him, the Indian Nice Hands said.

Mr. Peersall had quit being a trader. "What are we going to do for someone to haul the groceries?" the Indian My Prayer said.

"You realize that one day our children will maybe be reduced to trade?"

Now Mr. Peersall, the ex-trader, and Mr. Sanders, the missionary, both lived beneath Luna Mesa. Mr. Peersall had quit the trading post now, more from age than from the realization that he was taken in. He ran a very small still now, the results of which he shared only with a few pet Indians. Rumor had it, according to Big Sant, that the missionary, Mr. Sanders, was behaving queerly now, as though he were pulling out too.

Mr. Peersall was exactly one hundred and one years old. He did not realize who Alastair and Little Sant were sometimes. Sometimes they were his cavalry, sometimes they were hostile and sometimes they were friendly Indians. Sometimes they were arresting officers coming to take him back to Missoula, Montana, where he was born. Cowboys and Indians didn't follow him too well now. None of us follow too well the imaginary life of a very old man. But some cowboys and Indians have an inquiring mind.

"Is it possible," Alastair called, "for a man to still be alive who fought Indians?"

"Sure," Sant said.

"I don't personally know exactly when the last Indians were fought," Alastair mused to himself.

Sant had paused up ahead on the ridge in wonderment at a kit fox and Alastair caught up.

"He's gone now," Sant said.

"Well, I was beginning to figure he was very very old."

"No, he was a young one."

"He was?"

"Yes. I could tell."

"You must mean someone else."

"The fox."

"Was there a fox here?"

"Yeah."

"How old is your Indian fighter?"

"A hundred or better."

"Well, I guess he could have fought Indians."

"Sure."

430

"He could have fought Indians easily."

"Fighting Indians wasn't easy."

"That's true. But in front of grownups, like the missionary, we've got to make sense. They're not very subtle."

"How do you spell that?"

"Sub-tel. It's got a b in the middle."

"That's what I thought," Sant said. "More nonsense. Let's piss up a storm with these horses."

"You mean—?"

"I mean what I just said. Have you got better English?"

"No. Just more acceptable."

"Are we trying to get accepted to each other?"

"No, but we're going to see the missionary."

"We're going to see the Indian fighter."

"I forgot," Alastair said, and they both touched their horses and fled suddenly toward the purple distance in a moving dark cloud of their own dust, kicking a steady storm of flowing weather in their wake. Just as Sant had said.

"I think that's it up ahead."

"That shack?"

"I think we better start to slow down."

But they could not stop fast enough, and the Indian fighter, standing out in front with a hand shading his eyes, watched them fly by and wondered why he had not been warned of new trouble. They circled slowly as they came back.

"What's up?" the Indian fighter said.

"It's us," Sant said.

"They should have warned me," the Indian fighter said. "I could have hid out."

"I'm General Reno and this is my scout Colonel Benteen."

"They should have warned me," the Indian fighter said, "and I could have cooked a batch of candy. Come on inside. I've got a plan of battle all drawn up."

They hitched their horses to the real hitching post and went into a dark logged house of one room and sat at the rough, only table.

"First of all," the Indian fighter, Mr. Peersall, said, touching a greasy beard and staring at them through the gray cataracts of his eyes, "no quarter."

"Not fifteen cents," Sant said.

"No quarter," the Indian fighter repeated.

"Not ten cents," Alastair said.

The Indian fighter leaned back and surveyed the scene. "What do you want, Love Nests or Oh Henrys?"

"Oh Henrys," they both said.

The old man drew quickly, faster than their eyes could follow, two bars of candy from a drawer and handed them each one. He placed both hands splayed on the table and turned to study in their direction with his clouded eyes.

"There's hardly a man that's now alive that remembers what I remember."

"That's why we're here," Alastair said.

"First off," the old man said, looking up at the ceiling, "they made the wrong alliances."

"What?"

"Well, we made the wrong arrangements. We fought the wrong people. We should have joined the Indians, fought the whites, the Easterners. That's why we come here, mountain men, the plainsmen, to escape all that. And then we joined them to fight the people who were the same, who wanted to live like us—the Indians. I don't know why we did it except we were confused by the color of their skins, the Easterners' skins, their language. Because they were the same color, spoke the same language, we must have been confused into thinking, into forgetting we had come out here to escape them."

"Oh?"

"Yes, we fought the wrong wars against the wrong people. We won the wrong battles, lived, some of us, to see the wrong victory."

"What's it got to do with us?" Sant said.

"Does it have to have—? Yes, I guess it does," the old man said. "All right, supposing you were born free, as some of us were, as some people must be still being born free, what land is there to go to now? What are you going to do now?"

"Vote," Alastair said.

"That's about it," the old man said.

"Become a bronc rider," Sant said.

"Yes, that's about it," the old man said. "We lost the wrong war."

"How about this," Alastair said, leaning. "Civilization. You fought for that."

"No," the old man said with thought. "We weren't thinking. We were fighting. We were all young."

"But you accomplished—"

"We defeated ourselves. We—" The old man was tired and paused. "We lost—defeated ourselves. All lost. We got confused." The old man mumbled something, confused again.

"What we want to say is," Alastair said, "we don't blame you."

"Yes, we don't blame you," Sant said.

"It was a logical mistake," Alastair said.

"To confuse civilization with highways and trains and airplanes?" The old man examined his knuckles. "No, we knew about that all the time. We never made that mistake. I tell you I was young. Too young. Too full of piss and vinegar."

"Not Coca-Cola."

"Not then," the old man said.

"How was it, fighting Indians?" Alastair wondered.

"Cruel," the old man said. "They never had a chance. They never had a plan. They fought when they felt like it and quit when they felt like it." The old man fumbled under the table and brought out a Sharps rifle and put it on the table and felt it, no longer trusting his eyes. "It was like you were playing baseball and they had you fifteen to two and then they never bothered to show up for the fourth inning. They felt like doing something else now. They were bored."

"That's no way to fight a war," Sant said.

"No it's not," the old man agreed.

"To what do you ascribe your being out here like a hermit?" Alastair asked.

433

"Money. The lack of it," the old man said, getting away from the rifle and touching his beard.

"Didn't you make any money running the trading post?"

"No, but I didn't lose any either. The Navvyhos always saw to it that I always came out exactly even, that I'd never have any excuse to quit, that I never lost money."

"Remembering what you remember you could go on TV or the movies," Alastair said. "Remembering what you remember."

"No. I remember the wrong things. Fighting Indians. The Indians were hungry and dirty and there weren't many of them and it was like shooting people. Poor people."

"It would be undoing everything they have done on the TV and the movies."

"Yes," the old man agreed.

"They couldn't charge people for remembering what you remember," Alastair said.

"TV don't charge anyway," Sant said.

"You think not, son?" the old man said.

Well, Sant thought, anyway he hasn't said yet "I've fought too many Indians." He always said this in answer to any kind of question when he became very tired or bored with talking about himself and wished the people to leave. He would suddenly cry in answer to something, "No, I have fought too many Indians." It is the prerogative of the famous and the very old, and he was something of both. Now the old man said, "Never shoot a man in the back— his brother may be walking behind you." The old man fingered the rifle and looked at the ceiling and smiled. "Always question authority. It's the way the ignorant have of covering up. Always carry a loaded gun in Albuquerque and they'll treat you nice."

"I never met a man before," Alastair said, "who fought Indians and television both."

"Never go to a fandango without at least appearing to be drunk," the old man said. "Never listen to an old man because his experience is no substitute for intelligence or the lack of it. People being as different as horses there is no use in telling them anything except maybe listen to the wind, watch the stars, observe the moon, feel the sun, notice the animals, smell the fields, hear the birds,

434

listen to what is alive. Alive without talking to excuse or apologize for being alive. My talking's not a very good noise. Here's a good noise." The old man paused and soon a meadow lark tweeped. "There. That's a good noise." The old man paused again. "I must find that bird and thank him for being so damned prompt." The old man lifted the rifle slightly and dropped it as though it were some signal to himself to cease.

"Let's talk about the Wild West," Alastair said.

"No, son. I've fought too many Indians."

Sant rose. "Well, I guess we better be going."

"Go in beauty," the old man said.

"We're going to the missionary's."

"Even there," the old man said.

They got on their horses, and the old Indian fighter leaned feebly on the open door. "That's all this country's got now, missionaries and mercenaries."

"What's that?" Sant said as his horse moved off.

"I said head them off at the pass," the old man hollered.

"We will do," Sant said, and they moved off suddenly, clouding the old man's already clouded eyes in a dark version of the last rider, the last dust, the final memory.

"Wait," the old man thought. "I must thank that damned bird."

Now the boys rode into a sinking sun that oranged and pearled the purple and green-hued clouds in refracted tricks of strange and violent wonderment.

"He said," Alastair said, "something about Albuquerque."

"Who said?"

"The Indian fighter said carry a loaded gun in Albuquerque and they'll treat you nice."

"So he did," Sant said.

"That's where I was in the orphanage, Albuquerque."

"So you were."

"I've got to find out more."

"What more?"

"For example, exactly where I came from."

"Didn't your teacher tell you?"

"I mean where *I* came from."

"It's all the same," Sant said. "As you get older you'll realize that."

"I think I'm a little older than you."

"A little is not a lot," Sant said.

"Are we going in the right direction for the missionary's?"

"Any direction's all right," Sant said. "He's all over the place."

"I mean his house."

"Yes. It's hiding behind that mesa," Sant said pointing ahead.

"What we going to tell the missionary?"

"We won't tell him nothing. We'll just give him the letter."

"You mean he knows everything?"

"Yeah."

"Still, he strikes me as a pretty nice fellow."

"Oh well, tell him hello, good-by—things like that," Sant said.

"You suppose he'll want to listen to what we remember?"

"No."

"No one does."

"That's right."

"Let's not be bitter, men."

"That's right. There he is now."

The missionary was standing with a bunch of something in his arms near a New England, saltbox house, clapboarded and wooden-shingled in the style of another country, the house standing too straight alongside the straight-standing missionary, below the huddled, long mesa, the leaning gray sage. The missionary watched the boys approach, clutching tighter the bunch of something in his arms, watching with the cold glint of a warrior the two enemy horses approach.

"A warrior who no longer believes in the war," Alastair said.

"What makes you say that?"

"He looks defeated."

"No, they all get to look that way."

"Out here?"

"Out here for sure," Sant said.

"Hello, boys," the missionary said. He was dressed in army

khaki clothes with open shirt beneath a keen and florid face. He had on white canvas sneakers and a red pith helmet of the kind and shape, if not the color, the missionaries must have worn in the old days. "Hello, boys."

"What you got there?" Alastair said, pulling in his horse.

The missionary looked at what he held. "Wood," he said.

"It looks like rock to us."

"Fossil wood," the missionary said and he put the hard blocks down alongside the white and plastic-green New England house and sat on them. Now he took off his red pith helmet and stared around the world he had made until his eyes lighted on the boys again. "How can I help you?"

"This," Sant said and proffered the letter.

The missionary read it quickly as the boys waited in front of him, holding the reins. The missionary seemed to read it at a glance. Now he glanced up.

"You've come to the wrong person."

"Why?"

"You came to the wrong person, that's all."

"Well," Alastair said, not wanting to push it. "Well, let's see. We admire your tenacity."

"You lasted a long time," Sant said.

"Sixteen years," the missionary said. "Since before you were born."

"Where did you come from?"

"New England," the missionary said.

"That's part of the United States, isn't it?" Sant said.

"Yes it is. It was. I suppose it is. Of course it is. Why not? Yes, it is part of the United States."

"Can we help?" Sant said.

"To what do you ascribe," Alastair said, "to what do you ascribe your desire to convert the Navahos?"

"Damn foolishness," the missionary said.

"Well," Alastair said, uneasy, "well, I mean the underlying —that is, when you were a young man."

"I was just like you."

"Can we—can we help?" Sant mumbled, honestly concerned.

437

"I mean," Alastair said, talking against his uneasiness, "I mean you can't leave the Navahos alone."

"Can't I?"

"Who would—?"

"Who would do their work, be their servant, haul their water, bring them medicine, feed them, clothe them? Who would they have to laugh at, order around?"

"If we can help," Sant said.

"Yes," the missionary said, "you can wait on them a while."

"I mean read the Bible, things like that."

"They are not interested in the Bible, things like that."

"Perhaps patience," Alastair counseled.

"Sixteen years," the missionary said. "I've run out."

"To what do you ascribe," Alastair said, "the lack of interest in religion?"

"Common sense."

"Don't be blastemous," Sant said.

"Blasphemous," Alastair said.

"Common sense. Is that blasphemous? Maybe it is. Report me to the pope."

"Are you Catholic?" Alastair asked.

"No. But report me to him anyway." The missionary looked around at the New England cottage. "Maybe it's just that I've been out here too long."

"Sure," Sant said. "If there's anything we can do to help."

"Yes there is," the missionary said. "Just give the Navahos in this area a little sense of courtesy. A little consideration that I exist as something other than their white slave."

"We understand," Alastair said, "that you did a splendid job on President Taft."

"President Taft is an alcoholic," the missionary said. "He would be respectable, even splendid, to get a drink."

"Ours not to reason why," Alastair said and he nudged Sant. "Say something. Try to help."

"I gather you read the letter," the missionary said. "What did you think?"

"A good letter," Alastair said. "A fine letter."

"Did you read the part where she says see what you can do—do for them what you did for President Taft?"

"That was good, I thought," Alastair said.

"You know, before I came here President Taft never touched a drop."

"Well, that wasn't your fault," Sant said sympathetically.

"He means," Alastair said, "you have got nothing to do with anything."

"Did I?"

"Sure," Alastair said. "Now the missionary was saying—?"

"I was saying that my coming here imposed on the Navahos a cultural dichotomy."

"Oh, no," Sant said.

"A contradiction," the missionary said. "An impossible choice between life and death as they had known it, understood it for centuries, and now, something radical." The missionary paused, put back his red helmet. "What am I doing confiding to children?" he wondered aloud.

"If we can help," Alastair said. "If only to relieve your mind, to talk to another white."

"Yes," the missionary said, staring up at Alastair. "Yes." And then he said quietly, "I suppose so."

"We're here to help if we can," Sant said.

"But you must be—you must try to be rational," Alastair said.

"I suppose so," the missionary said.

The clock of sun told them in silent splendor of another lost day, told them in a change of abrupt and quiet magic. The sun wavered there in a final call, in penultimate moment, in impatient finality and pause before Finis. The mesas and sage were all in shadow and the New England house in gloom. The boy Sant raised his arm in gesture. The missionary touched his chin. Somewhere off there a coyote sang. Alastair Benjamin touched the ancient stone upon which the missionary sat and said, "What you going to do with this, now?"

"Now, with this wood, I don't know," the missionary said. "Later."

"Later what?"

"Build a house that belongs here," the missionary said. "Something that's native."

"How about adobes?"

"Adobes are good too," the missionary said.

"I have a theory," Alastair said.

"What's that?"

Alastair tossed pebbles, pieces of rose quartz, in an embarrassed gesture, toward a sagging cedar.

"It's that when people hurt you you've got to get revenge," Alastair said.

"That's brilliant," the missionary said. "What else?"

"What I mean is," Alastair said. "What I mean is, nothing else."

"Oh, you are brilliant today," the missionary said.

"Yes, he is," Sant said.

"What I mean is," Alastair said, ceasing his tossing and stroking his cheek. "What I mean is, if the Indians or someone hurt you, or even if they hurt your father, if you didn't do something to even it up you would get to think you were crazy or—"

"Or what?"

"Or reasonably adopted to ignore it."

"Adapted is the word," the missionary said.

"No, I'm not getting those words mixed up now. What do you think of the theory?"

"Very little," the missionary said.

"Not much," Sant said.

Alastair put one of the stones in his mouth and talked around it. "But it is a theory."

"No," the missionary said. "Actually it's an observation."

"Is there a difference?"

"Very little."

"Not much," Sant said.

"As long as you don't call it an opinion."

"Maybe that's it. Maybe that's what it is."

"Sure," Sant said.

Alastair looked concerned.

"What I want to know," the missionary said, "is what the hell are we talking about?"

"Do you always use words like that?" Sant said.

"Only lately," the missionary said. "Since I was saved."

"Saved?"

"Saved from being a missionary."

"That's sacrilegious," Sant said.

"No, it's the truth," the missionary said. "It came as a revelation. The revelation that I was about as qualified to be a missionary as President Taft. It came while I was walking the top of the Luna Mesa."

"A revelation is only the culmination of experience," Alastair said.

"I tell you a revelation is a revelation. This was a revelation in reverse, that's all."

"Is that possible?" Alastair wondered.

"Anything is possible," Sant said.

"Well," Alastair said, "but we need a missionary here. You suddenly can't—you suddenly can't walk out on us."

"My mother would say we done it," Sant said.

"You suddenly can't walk out on the Indians," Alastair said.

"Can't I?"

"You suddenly can't walk out on yourself then," Alastair said. "After all these years."

"We change."

"But the truth," Alastair said. "The truth doesn't change unless the evidence changes. And nothing changed."

"That's right," the missionary said. "Nothing changed. The Indians, everything's the same since I came."

"Patience," Alastair said.

"Patience your own damn self," the missionary said.

"Temper, temper," Alastair said. "One doesn't want to do what one would regret later."

"One doesn't care. This one," the missionary mimicked Alastair.

"My mother would say we done it," Sant said.

441

"Let's go into the house and talk this over quietly," Alastair said.

"I won't go into that house any more. That Puritan house," the missionary said. "That New England house."

"Come, come, it's a nice house," Alastair said. "A nice house."

"It doesn't belong here. I don't think I belong here."

"You come along quietly," Alastair said, "and we'll see what we can do to help."

"Leave," the missionary said.

"But we can't leave you in this condition."

"My mother would say we done it," Sant said.

"You leave me as you found me," the missionary said.

"I guess that's all right then," Alastair said, mounting his horse.

"I don't know," Sant said. "My mother will say—" But he mounted his horse anyway.

The missionary rose from his stones and handed Alastair the letter. "You have been a help," he said. "Just talking to someone, it's been a help."

Alastair put the letter in his jacket. "I'm the dark one she mentions. The one who reads books."

"I gathered that," the missionary said. "You come back."

"Good-by," Sant said.

"The both of you come back."

They rode on a way before they looked back. The missionary was sitting on his stones now but he was still waving.

"Doing anything alone for sixteen years is hard on a man," Alastair said.

"Very true," Sant said. "He does this about every five years. After all, you can't expect anyone on this earth to put up with being the slave of the Indians without revolting occasionally."

"Has he been revolting long?"

"I don't know. But he'll get over it."

"As long as he doesn't burn his place down."

"Or the Indians don't. They've done it before. If it gets dull they might do it again."

"Why would they do it though?"

"Oh, they can still revolt too."

"You mean three hundred years ago they burned all the missions down."

"They burned one down not too many years ago."

"Yes, I guess they can still be revolting then. I was intrigued," Alastair said, "by what he had to say about Albuquerque."

"He didn't say anything about Albuquerque."

"It was somebody else?"

"It was the Indian fighter."

"I certainly would like to know more where I came from."

"Get off it," Sant said. "Please get off it. If you get off it I'll tell you an old joke that's pretty good."

"Okay."

"Well, this guy from here whose father I know was in Mazatlán, Mexico, in a *cantina*. That's Mexican for a bar. This Mexican was saying that in the United States they give a foreigner everything free. A free bed, a free breakfast in bed, free nice things to wear, even free jewelry. 'Have you ever been there?' the guy from here whose father I know asked the Mexican. 'Have you ever been to the United States?' 'No,' the Mexican said. 'But my sister has.'"

"All right," Alastair said. "But why don't you want to talk about *my* father?"

They eased their horses around the final bend of the Peña Blanca Mesa. The land toward home would be all flat now save for the old volcano cores that stood as though on a strange planet, and an occasional rise where the antelope watched and sometimes a lonely juniper and sometimes pine, sage and, rarely, a willow weeping downward to an arroyo. The moon rose cold and they became a small army in shadow, multiplied and moving homeward along a trail that had shadowed Coronado too, Billy the Kid, the plumed Indian, and all the great shadows of the buffalo. All gone, shadows into final shadows without any sign on the land, any mark at all. Now Sant made a gesture in the air to quicken the pace.

"All right, Santo," Alastair said. "It's not a bad joke. But I'd still like to know—"

"Tomorrow morning," Sant said. "Everything can wait until tomorrow morning."

443

TEN   One week later it was a very nice morning, a New Mexico morning, a crisp and sage-smelling and San Juan flower, red-blooming morning, a morning all alive with every growing thing; the gilia, the Cowboys Delight, the filaree, the Indian paintbrush, the *añil del muerto,* and the fireweed, the evening primrose, the verbena, and the desert pentstemon, all exploded, all coming around to the opinion to bloom at once and all of a different opinion on what color the morning showed—all in sudden riot.

"You know—" Big Sant was having an opinion too. The two boys were seated on the adobe porch beneath him.

"You know, I don't know," Big Sant said. He tilted back his broad hat from a broad, bright-splashed face. "I don't know where you came from. Is it so important?"

"Yes," Alastair said. "I think so."

Big Sant looked out over all the flowers growing wild out there, all scattered out there by seeds borne on an indifferent wind, growing in an indifferent earth, fed by a could-not-care-less sun, but watched now by careless but caring blue eyes.

"Yes, I guess people care about where things, especially people, especially their people, come from. That's all right, but—"

"But if you know, I'd like to know," Alastair said cautiously.

"I don't know," Big Sant said. "That Indian, President Taft, he did claim to know when he was alive. He did claim to know there was a boy in that house. It's not impossible it was you. Still it's not impossible it was any one of a million unfound boys—if there was a boy."

"When he was alive? Who?"

"President Taft."

"He's dead?"

"Yes. He was sick for quite a while before he died. Whisky."

"You're sure he's dead?"

"Pretty sure. They're going to bury him today."

Alastair scanned the sky in seeming abstraction, the sky in big blue, big solid, pure blue absence of anything. Alastair now joined this absence in seeming absence, watching the vacant sky vacantly.

"Well," Alastair said, "will there be any of his friends there at the funeral?"

Millie Sant emerged now and sat in the middle of the silence, sat up above Sant and Alastair and looked down on them from where she sat even with Big Sant.

"There is no life, truth, intelligence, nor substance in matter. All is infinite mind and its infinite manifestation for God is all in all," she said.

"Will there be any of President Taft's friends there at the funeral?" Alastair insisted.

"President Taft didn't have too many friends toward the end. After he took up Christianity," Big Sant said.

"Ye shall know the truth and the truth shall make you free," Millie Sant said.

"Will it?" Alastair said.

"The Indians tend to isolate the different," Big Sant said.

"Whose truth?" Alastair said up to Millie Sant.

"What do you mean?" she said.

"You just said that the truth would—"

"Oh," she said. "That's just some saying left over from my Christian Science days. I was just kind of not thinking out loud. Whistling."

Little Sant whistled low. "Alley wants to find someone who knows something about him."

"My Prayer will be there," Big Sant said.

"Who? Where?" Millie Sant said.

"My Prayer, the Indian, will be at the funeral of President

445

Taft, the Christian; at the missionary's who doesn't know which way to jump."

"That reminds me," Millie Sant said. "Did you two boys get to the missionary's last week?"

"Yes," Alastair said. "And we're going again today too."

"The Indian fighter should be there," Big Sant said.

"What do you mean the missionary doesn't know which way to jump?" Millie Sant said. "You boys spoke to him last week. He was all right, wasn't he?"

"He didn't know whether to build of adobe or petrified wood," Little Sant said.

"Something wrong then. What's wrong with his fine New England house? We need a Christian structure here."

"He said it didn't belong here."

"All right, all right," Millie Sant said. "So he's quitting too. Because the rest of us don't wear shoes is no reason the shoemaker should quit. Or I guess it's as good a reason as any."

"It's the Indians who let him down," Big Sant said. "A missionary can be living among one million heathen in New York City and yet they come out here to convert fifty Indians."

"They are the exotics," Alastair said. "The Indians."

"Yes," Big Sant said. "They are the trip around the world in a fourteen-foot boat. They are the elk a New Mexican hunter will pursue in Alaska when he could shoot one out of his own window."

"The exotics, I presume," Alastair said.

"You said that," Big Sant said.

Alastair took off his hat and scratched his ear. "I was trying to put it cogently," he said.

"How many of my books have you read, Alastair?" Big Sant asked.

"All of them twice. Including the ones that are partly burned."

Big Sant winced, then looked over at Millie Sant, and then down at Little Sant. "And you?"

"None of them. Twice."

"Wouldn't you like to talk like Alastair?"

"Like Alley?" Sant mused. "No. I'd rather be understood."

"But after a while, when he grows up he'll get over those big words and he'll still be smarter than most," Big Sant said.

"I'd still rather make sense," Little Sant said.

"He's got a lot of his great-grandfather in him," Millie Sant said. "He was a mountain man."

"I'm going to be a bronc man," Little Sant said.

"Well," Big Sant wondered out loud, "I wonder what happens to a bronc rider after he's thirty-five?"

"What happens to a mountain man after he's thirty-five?"

"Yes." Big Sant took off his hat and tapped it reflectively on the adobe step. "Yes. You are like Great-grandfather."

"Who am I like?" Alastair said.

A dove, an Inca dove with white wing tips and mauve breast, landed in a close cottonwood, one of the chain of cottonwoods that ran around the house. The dove called furtively in a sharp, clean trill until another dove landed too. Now the Inca doves measured each other in silence until a swarm of Inca doves, the whole covey, made a circle in the sun and alighted on a near long branch. Now all of the doves eyed the people sitting on the steps of the adobe house.

" 'From the first not a thing is.' But of course that would leave out my children. It would leave out this wonderful ranch. It would leave out those doves," Millie said.

The Inca doves zoomed off at some secret signal, made a flowing turn in the sun before they were lost in the sun.

"What about me?" Alastair said.

"Yes, well," Big Sant said. "At the funeral My Prayer will be there and he was there."

"Where?"

"At the fire."

Sant extracted a burned spur from his pocket and passed it up to Big Sant.

"Yes. I was there of course," Big Sant said, fingering the spur. "But I saw no child."

"Who fired the first shot?" Alastair asked.

"He did."

"And the last?"

"I did."

"Why?"

"Fear, I guess," Big Sant said. "Isn't that why every shot is ever fired? But I think his was directed at the whole human race. I was only firing at him."

"And you hit?"

"I must have."

"And your books in there?" Alastair said. "Were some of them his?"

"Yes," Big Sant said. "Those slightly burned or those that smell of burning."

"The one that has written on the flyleaf 'Revenge is the only certain thing you can ever get—the only sure thing'?"

"Yes, that was his."

"Why didn't you tear that flyleaf out?"

"Because I had no right."

"It was written on the burned flyleaf of Mr. Shakespeare's *Hamlet*, wasn't it?"

"I think that's where it was written," Big Sant said.

The air turned crisp now, as it will in New Mexico on a sunny day in October when a cloud obscures the sun. They sat there in the deep shadow in the sudden cool of October as the Inca doves again circled close in the autumn warning of winter. Soon the doves' circle would become greater and even greater until the last wide final circle of fall before they shot south for Old Mexico and the fleeing sun.

"As I said," Big Sant said, "they will all be there, everyone who ever remembers anything about it; and all those who made something up, they'll be there too."

"All those that made something—?"

"Yes," Big Sant said. "Everyone had an opinion."

"Well," Millie Sant said, "you mean you're going to let those children—?"

"Go to the missionary? Isn't that what you wanted?"

"Last week," she said.

"What's wrong with today?" Alastair said.

"I hear tell there's a man dying there."

"He's dead," Big Sant said.

"You mean President Taft has passed away?"

"President Taft is dead. I told you that."

"Well, I wasn't listening," Millie Sant said. "Well, I suppose everyone should ought to go to President Taft's funeral. Except me."

"Except you?"

"Yes. I don't believe in funerals. I gave them up."

"Oh?"

"Yes," she said. "Dead is dead."

"You used to believe this was the biggest thing that ever happened to a man."

"Yes," she said. "But now dead is dead."

"Well, Millie," Big Sant said. "How many religions have you gone through?"

"One."

"I thought it was five."

"They were all the same. All one."

"Maybe it's better when you've got one."

"I have," she said. "Respect for other people's religions."

"But where's the poetry and the mystery?" Alastair said. "It says that women need that."

"I used to need it."

"I wish you would go to the funeral," Alastair said. "I need people to help me with things."

"How do you expect," Big Sant said, "how do you expect the missionary to carry on if you don't support him, Millie?"

"Carry on what?"

"Well, he tried to help our country."

"All right," she said. "I'll go to President Taft's funeral. Yes," she said. "All right. I'll go."

And she went, riding in the front bucket seat of the Willys jeep alongside Big Sant with the boys in the back and the dogs chasing them till they crossed the cattle guard, where the dogs gave up.

Millie Sant hung on, and the jeep took off over the hills following a very dim wagon trail.

"What does it mean for me?" she said, raising her voice for Alastair. "What do the Dead Sea scrolls mean for me?"

"Well," Alastair said, leaning his chin forward on her bucket seat. "The Dead Sea scrolls are ancient religious documents whose recent discovery in a cave in Transjordan throws a new light on scholars' interpretation of the Old and New Testaments."

"What do they mean for me?" Millie Sant had to holler above the noise of the grinding jeep as it went into four-wheel drive. "What does it mean for me?"

"Well," Alastair said loudly in her ear, "it's the most important discovery in many centuries. The Dead Sea scrolls may completely change the traditional understanding of the Bible."

"Well, does it have anything to say to me?" Millie Sant hollered.

"Well," Alastair said in her ear, "it's directed at all those who are concerned with religion and archaeology."

"And what?"

"How people lived before we were born," Alastair said. "And it's valuable for both the scholar and the layman."

"Which am I?" she hollered.

"Yes, who am I?" Alastair said.

"I can't hear you," Millie hollered.

"No one can," Alastair said.

"Where did you get all that information?"

"The trading post. *The Dead Sea Scrolls,* paper bound. Signet Mentor, thirty-five cents."

"Thirty-five cents. That's cheap enough," she said. "Where are we going?" she hollered to Big Sant as the jeep went up an almost vertical cliff, heaved and groaned finally over the top.

"Is it a good book, Alastair?" she said, quieter now.

"I don't know," Little Sant said. "I don't know whether we're going the right way."

"Well, for one thing," Big Sant said, "you don't follow the wagon trails. You navigate. In the night you can use the stars but in the day you line up landmarks. If you follow an Indian wagon trail to someplace, you finally begin to realize the Indian wasn't going anyplace."

"Just a Sunday drive," Little Sant said.

"Yes," Big Sant said, using the small levers alongside the transmission box to shove her back into two-wheel drive. "You got to remember to use the four-wheel drive as little as possible. It's hard on everything."

"Horses is better than jeeps," Little Sant said. "They're in four-wheel drive all the time and they don't mind it at all. And another thing about horses," Little Sant said, "if you're lost and you drop the reins they'll take you home."

"If I let this steering wheel go, how do you know this jeep won't go back to the factory?"

"Or the war it remembers."

"Which war was it?"

"The Second World War."

"I wish we'd make this conversation more relevant," Alastair said.

"Like how?" Little Sant asked.

"Like talking about what we're going for."

"Getting there first is more important."

"The first thing I'm doing," Big Sant said, dodging the jeep between five junipers, "the first thing I'm doing is lining up with Cabezon Peak. About halfway there is the Indian fighter's shack and then we'll bear due north to the missionary's."

"There's the Indian fighter's shack now," Millie Sant said. "Maybe he'd like a ride to the funeral."

When they got in front of the shack Big Sant stopped the jeep and Millie Sant got out and went inside the shack. It was hard for her to see at first but then she could make out the dim form of Mr. Peersall sitting up straight and formal in a cowhide chair, watching a small still percolating whisky in the corner.

"I thought you might like to ride with us to the funeral, Mr. Peersall," she said.

"I am at the funeral, Millicent."

"Taft's funeral, Mr. Peersall."

"Did the president die? Why, the old son of a bitch, dying before me."

"Yes."

451

"You know, in the old days I shot him several times. It never seemed to bother him a bit. Now, finally, I got him with whisky."

"You fed him whisky?"

"Yes. We drank together in the evenings and talked about old massacres."

"You're only trying to shock me," she said. "Now come along to the funeral."

"I'll take along some ammunition, Millie. You never can tell." He slipped a half-pint in his leather jacket. "You never can tell what sidewinder will show up at a formal function like this—a fandango like this. Wars and rumors of war," he said as she led the way through the door. As he hit the blinding sun he nodded toward the jeep. "Who assassinated the old gentleman? The function will be hopping with secret-service men." As he finally seated himself in the jeep and signaled to shove off he said, quietly, "He was a good Indian and he made a great president."

"You're only trying to shock me, Mr. Peersall," Millie said.

"Maybe I am, but maybe my memory isn't so good."

"Your memory," Alastair said. "Can I ask you a question, Mr. Peersall?"

"Yes, you can, son."

The jeep faltered and skipped and then began to settle in some loose sand that had drifted in the bobtail cut, a narrow canyon east of Cabezon that took you up on the escarpment where the mission was. They went into four-wheel drive and they all felt on firmer ground as the jeep moved forward steadily again.

"Can I ask you a question, Mr. Peersall?"

"I said you could, son."

Alastair wiped his chin in thought and studied the dashboard where it said DO NOT EXCEED FIFTY MILES PER HOUR IN HIGH GEAR. DO NOT EXCEED FIFTEEN IN LOW. DO NOT EXCEED THIRTY MILES PER HOUR IN THE INTERMEDIATE.

"Well, Mr. Peersall," Alastair said. "What do you remember about me?"

"Stop this thing," the Indian fighter whispered to Big Sant. The jeep stopped.

"Up there," the Indian fighter said in a husky whisper, "up

there and to your left, standing in front of that red concretion. Antelope."

They all watched the delicate animals cautiously, as though staring hard might frighten them.

"They'll pick us up in a second now," the Indian fighter said. "Then they'll come down here. They are the curiousest animal that ever was."

Soon the antelope did notice the new object on the bobtail cut and soon they were down examining it. The people in the jeep had to remain motionless, almost without breath, so the Indian fighter could study the animal which was as curious as himself.

"All right," the Indian fighter said. "Blow the horn." At the blast of the horn the antelope exploded away, gone in sudden nuclear magic.

"Beautiful animals," Mr. Peersall said to everyone. To Big Sant he said, "Proceed." And turning to the two boys in the rear he said, "What were you saying?"

"The Wild West," Little Sant said. "What was it like? What were they like—the bad men?"

"The bad men?" Mr. Peersall mused. "The bad men? Well, the West was unorganized, not much law. When there became law and organization the bad men went into business. Now they've become presidents of banks and medical doctors. Now they're legal."

"You're only trying to shock us, Mr. Peersall," Millicent said.

"Now they've got Elks, Rotarians, instead of the Prescott gang. Look. You see that signal?" The jeep had made the top of the mesa and Mr. Peersall was pointing to the rear rumps of the fleeing antelope. On all of the rear rumps of the fleeing antelope there had suddenly appeared huge white targets. "That white spot the antelope cause by contracting their muscles. It makes the white rear hairs stand on end and flicks a danger signal to all the other herds. Soon all the herds on the mesa will be running."

"A telegraph," Alastair said.

"What, boy?"

"I want to ask you a question," Alastair said.

"Go ahead, son."

453

"What do you remember about me? Where I came from?"

"Where's your brand?"

"Where's my what?"

"Without a brand it's very hard to tell. Even then it can be faked."

"How?" Little Sant asked.

"Well, you can easy see how you could make an N into an M or a heart into a circle heart, things like that. Don't you read any pulp novels? Of course if you cut off the hide you can tell by the marks underneath that the brand has been changed. Haven't you seen any Western movies? However—" Mr. Peersall paused as though about to render a decision—"however, we had a boy worked for us on the Hashknife outfit who cut a piece of hide off the cow where the brand was and sewed the hide back together again before he put his own brand on so that, even by skinning the animal you couldn't tell he stole it. Now, when people will go that far, and that's a fact, how can we ever trace humans? They're running around loose without any brand at all."

"Loose?"

"Yes. And even when branded it was not unusual to see calves of certain brands following cows of different brands."

"What about me?" Alastair said.

"What about the Hashknife?" Little Sant said.

"It was one million acres of land the railroads got free from the United States government to build a railroad. They got bored with the idea of a railroad and decided to run cattle instead. When they talk about a free country they're serious."

"Wait," Alastair said. "Don't you recollect anything President Taft might have said about me?"

"He was given to earth-shaking platitudes."

"About me?"

"About you?" The Indian fighter had to think about this now and he pulled his mustache.

"What about the Hashknife?" Sant said.

"Well," Mr. Peersall said. "Then every cowboy stole from the Hashknife, even those that worked for them. That's how most of the ranches in the West were begun. So when they talk about a free country they're serious."

"All right then," Alastair said. "So it's a free country."

"That's right, son."

"But that still doesn't answer my question."

"But it explains how the West began."

"But it doesn't explain how I began."

Mr. Peersall didn't know what the dark boy was up to so he retreated back to the West, where the other boy lived.

"Actually," he said, watching the West go by, "actually, they got free not one million acres but two because on the grant along where the tracks were supposed to be they were given alternate sections, and as there were no fences at the time, and as and whereby the company objects most strenuously to entry upon its lands of any herds or droves which must necessarily occur when they cross from section to section, we must preserve this land of ours against all comers. And so the freedom was compounded. They took all the land. The land of the free became the freest land in the world."

"More," Little Sant said. "But put some action in it. No more speeches."

"Yes," Mr. Peersall said, trying to recollect where he had left off. "No, it's not that those antelope were curious. It's just that, as well as being the fastest hoofed animal in the world, they also have the best eyesight. That's why they come so close to us. They only trust their eyes, nothing else."

"But what about Wyatt Earp and the Ringo Kid? What about all them?"

"They only trusted their eyes too," Mr. Peersall said. "Nothing else. Those who thought stayed back East."

"And who was the fastest gun in the West? Hondo?"

"Me," the Indian fighter said and he laughed quickly. "Blue-eyed Billy Peersall. Me."

Little Sant reached up and touched the gun arm of the old Indian fighter.

"Me." Blue-eyed Billy Peersall laughed a bit louder now as the jeep went down the western slope, the wind and dust making everything dim. "Me," he said again quietly beneath the din of the jeep, conjuring up all the dim memories of the wild and slandered West. "Me," he said. "Blue-eyed Billy Peersall. Ask any girl at Alice Boardly's old fandango in Taos. Ask them if they remember Blue-eyed Billy Peersall and the fastest gun in the West."

Alastair gave up and settled back against the rear of the front seat and watched the country retreat. But Little Sant was not going to be put off the track.

"Tell us about—"

"No," Mr. Peersall interrupted. "I've fought too many Indians."

Sant now was quiet and settled alongside Alastair, watching the West disappear.

ELEVEN Navahos will gather at the drop of a dollar. That is, they will gather for most anything. They do not appreciate a dollar as much as they should—there's no respect there—but they will even gather at the drop of a dollar. The Navahos love a gathering. They will not gather for a funeral; it's too late, the damage has been done; they should have gathered sooner. Still, if a man was a Christian, as President Taft was, we should gather. It's a chance to show we're broad-minded. It's a chance to study a primitive culture. It may even be an opportunity to get drunk. Let us gather. And on the third day they gathered and there was never such a gathering as this in the history of the Checkerboard.

They danced the sweetie sweetie. Sweetie sweetie was the local, Checkerboard, name for a *yebechai*. My Prayer was an older Indian who did not dance the sweetie sweetie any longer. He was at an age in life when a Navaho becomes a member of the orchestra, while the young Indians who pay dance the sweetie sweetie. To dance the sweetie sweetie you need to be young and have ten cents. A girl touches a man and, if he does not dance, he must pay ten cents, or if he accepts her command, he pays ten cents. The sweetie sweetie costs ten cents no matter what you do, if you are young and have ten cents.

My Prayer, as a member of the orchestra, arrived early and was reinforced with three and a half bottles of Four Roses to stay late. He had on blue wrangler jeans and a red-and-green-striped pajama top and his hair was done up in a bun in the back of his neck, as a man's should be. Many of the young men, My Prayer observed, had their hair cut very short in the manner of Navaho delinquents. They would also, he knew, by moving slowly, try to slow down the beat of the chant in the manner of Navaho delinquents. In the old days this would have got them a bullet up their ass and they wouldn't be Navaho delinquents any more. Now My Prayer watched the reservation police watching him from the periphery of the great circle and he knew there was no opportunity now to save the youth of America. Let them go to hell anyway, My Prayer thought. I remember my grandfather telling me the day will come when we can't shoot any more whites and we'll all go to hell. My Prayer did not think the word hell. He used the Navaho word *hajinai,* which is identical and frequently used at sweetie sweeties.

My Prayer gave a few bangs on the drum as a gesture of impatience as he waited for the Indians who were still streaming across the mesa toward the mission. This was only the second time they had played for a sweetie sweetie at the mission. Still, this was the first time a Christian Indian had died from the Checkerboard area. The Checkerboard area was an extension of the Navaho Reservation. It was every other section of land near the Jemez Mountains that the railroads didn't get, that the Jicarillo Apaches didn't get. The Apache Reservation was close. Some of them would probably try to horn in on this sweetie sweetie. My Prayer gave the drum a big whack and all the close Indians jumped back a little because they knew this was not the start of the sweetie sweetie but My Prayer annoyed with somebody—probably the Apaches. Actually My Prayer had just glanced at the missionary's house. The New England clapboard, green-and-white, three-story monstrosity made him bang the drum. Inside the house, he knew, rested the body of President Taft. President Taft was a very old friend of his. He had known him when. He had known him when he was only Water Running Underneath The Ground. He had known him before the old trader at Torreon had made him President Taft. The trader had made two other Indians presidents at the time, to keep down hard feelings. He had made one Indian from the Heeka clan President Lincoln and another from the Dohi clan President Washington. Washington was killed in a brawl in

Gallup many years ago, but his wife survived to have a child by Abraham Lincoln. All the presidents had always been friendly. President Taft had survived to become a Christian and get drunk without fighting. Evidently the Christians do not believe in fighting unless it's properly organized into a war.

My Prayer banged the drum again to frighten those that had jumped before, to wake up the prairie, maybe put a little life in President Taft, but mostly to applaud himself for all the very bright things he was thinking.

Now you take the missionary. He's a pretty nice fellow. It's a shame that he's thinking of giving up this Christian business. What's a man going to do when he's put his whole life into something? What's he going to believe, and will the whites take him back or are we going to be stuck with him? They say he is going to build a hogan or something from adobe, that he'll burn down the tall wood house. He's been here fifteen years converting one Indian. Now that Indian's dead. It's too bad. More of us should have signed up. We Indians are too damned independent. It wouldn't hurt a bunch of us at all to sign up, to say we're saved or saving something, whatever it is they want us to say. We Indians are too damn unco-operative. He thought this in Navaho but he banged the drum now in a universal language of protest that everyone understood—banged it against all the Indians who didn't become Christians. Imagine having to write back to this Boston or someplace, after fifteen years, "Nothing doing yet. Hold on. Be patient. Send more money." Imagine what the other Indians would do to me if I was away for fifteen years to convert the whites and showed up again with only their President Taft.

My Prayer beat out a little Navaho rhythm now on the drums to buck himself up and to dismiss his idle thinking. He didn't get into anything solid yet, it was too early. After a few riffs he put down the drumstick to examine the early arrivals. Of course all the Indian ladies, and especially the young squawlets, were examining My Prayer. My Prayer was very famous for banging on the drum. As with Arturo Toscanini among the whites, age did not diminish My Prayer's attraction; genius, as well as being universal, is timeless. Banging on a drum, besides being noisy, is virile—to an Indian lady. My Prayer shrugged off the soft eyes fastened on him. Fame is not so much fleeting as too late, not so much a spur as a bit. It kept all of the men watching you too. My Prayer watched back at the new arrivals. Now a jeepload of whites arrived. My Prayer shook his head, annoyed.

One of those getting out of the jeep, he thought, is Blue-eyed Billy Peersall, the old Indian fighter. As an old white fighter, I respect him. I wonder if he lies as much as I do about the old days. Well, if you tell the truth you can't compete with the moving pictures in Gallup. Cowboys and Indians were supposed to have done certain things, I guess, and if you tell the little Indians you didn't do them they think you were not much of an Indian. The other white following out of the jeep is Sant Bowman. He is the one Taft and I watched having a gun fight before the cabin burned down. It would make a good movie. Then there's the boy, Little Sant, and the wife, Millicent, of Big Sant. It would make a good poem. Now there's the black white boy, Alastair, who wonders whether he is the boy we picked up after the cabin fire. Black white boy, Alastair, he repeated. He thought again, I've got to stop thinking that if you're not red you must be white. There can be other kinds of people and Alastair is one. But if he's not white why does he talk and act like one? No, black is just another color of white. After all, he doesn't speak Navaho, he doesn't speak Apache; he speaks and dresses white and so did his father and so did every black man I ever saw. I never met a black white who spoke Navaho and I never met one who spoke Apache. I hope they don't bother me today about the gun fight. President Taft has already said all we know about it. Almost everything. What we didn't say is not what they would want to hear. It wouldn't make a good movie. It wouldn't make a good poem. It's not what they would want to know. They always would blame me for telling the truth. I suppose the old Indian fighter has learned that, but I must tend to my music. My Prayer began to bang the drum slowly.

The missionary stood erect alongside the straight house that stood on a slight rise, and looked down on all the people arriving. It looked from here as though the Indians were trying to start a sweetie sweetie. What else could My Prayer be doing with the drums? It was part of Prostitution Way, an Indian rite that always began with a sweetie sweetie. He had President Taft's body in the house. It was probably, he thought, the last time the house would be used for anything. He felt badly that the final use of the house would be as it had begun fifteen years ago, with a sweetie sweetie. The failure of a mission.

It looked from here as though there must be trouble. It looked from here as though people are different. It looked from here as though Navahos might have trouble if they went to New England, built a hogan on the commons and tried to convert people to Navaho beliefs, and it looked from here as though the opposite were true. It looked from here as though the thing that made the New Englander believe what he believed never happened in Indian Country. You could buy a few, bribe a few, but, he thought, the thing that loaded a very proper Bostonian with guilt only made an Indian question your sanity. Take My Prayer, banging on that drum. He wants to help. He probably feels sorry for me. He is organizing the sweetie sweetie because he feels it's the correct, the proper thing to do. He just doesn't know what's proper in Boston when a person dies. He doesn't know there's any other way than a sweetie-sweetie way. Indians are tough and they know they're not in the center of Boston but in the heart of Indian Country and they're going to make it stick. Mr. Sanders wondered, watching down, whether he had been a complete failure, as he had wondered unceasingly for many dark nights now, sleeping outside the New England house. Out here it made a problem without a cellophane wrapper, without a crush-proof box, without tail fins, without anything to help that helps others.

Now he watched the party of whites unwind from the jeep. Perhaps they would help him stop the sweetie sweetie and make the Indians pass in front of the bier properly. And then maybe they had problems of their own. The whites that were brought up among the Indians didn't seem to take the Boston kind of problem seriously. The problems they had of their own seemed to have something to do with that black boy, and maybe they would feel that having the Indians stop the sweetie sweetie and pass in front of the bier wouldn't help anything at all. The missionary looked up at the

461

high house he didn't like to enter any more. The failure of a mission.

Down below, the word had been passed around by the faithful, or, rather, something said had been passed around, and distorted in the repeated saying, that beer was going to be passed around. What had originally started as a command by the missionary to stop the sweetie sweetie and pass before the bier had been corrupted by wishful-thinking Indians into, The missionary is going to pass out beer if we stop the sweetie sweetie. All the Indians began to move toward the New England house, and the missionary, wondering what someone had wrought, stepped inside the house to maintain order in the line. Inside discipline.

The Indians entered the kitchen door and entered the living-room door and the whites stood by the living-room door wondering what was up.

"They've got a dead guy in there," one of the Indians said.

"No beer," another Indian said, and they drifted back unhappily toward the stamping ground of the sweetie sweetie.

My Prayer continued to bang the drum loudly. He had not capitulated to the bier-beer rumor; he maintained his dignified beat. Anyway he was a Four Roses man. He was an Indian Fighter man too. That is, he drank the old Indian fighter's home-made liquor, which was called Old Indian Fighter. President Taft had turned out a batch of the stuff once they called Old White Fighter but it wasn't any good. The failure of a still.

My Prayer nodded to the other orchestra members as they moved in and began their practice chants. The orchestra consisted, as all Navaho orchestras consist, of one or two drummers and as many male chanters as were sober. They were in excellent voice, My Prayer thought. They must have been to Gallup recently. My Prayer thought that if a man fornicated enough he could do anything well. It was his *mystique*. My Prayer was the poor Indians' D. H. Lawrence without the consumption but with the coterie, the cult. Even religion was on his side. That is, three medicine men said that fornicating, or *edesh il,* does no harm. My Prayer took this as a solid endorsement of his theory. It was his letter from Rome, his cachet, his diploma in dentistry, his argument with the missionary. They had apparently passed a law against it in Boston which had passed through all the white kingdom; but, my children, you are not in Boston now. *Edesh il*. Forever *edesh il*. Most Navaho words sound as though they were formed by wind rushing around their back teeth.

Yes, My Prayer concluded. But he couldn't conclude anything when someone was chanting off key. My Prayer pointed his drumstick at the weak Indian and it was better now. Yes, My Prayer thought, but the youth corrupt early. Of the young perhaps those two over there were the worst, the ones with the short haircuts, Afraid Of His Own Horses and The Other Indian. They leaned coyly against the post in secret dream while watching the girls. They had associated too much with the whites. They were always hanging around with that Little Sant and that dark Alastair and there was no telling how far they were gone in white nonsense. Soon they might even take an automobile and kill themselves.

The orchestra seemed ready now and My Prayer touched the side of the drum for their attention. This was not quite necessary because My Prayer always began the sweetie sweetie with a long solo on the drum that would drown out Niagara Falls. All watched and waited with respect—awe. My Prayer was an old Gallup man. What New Orleans was to the blacks and whites, Gallup was to the Indian. If you got your start in Gallup around the turn of the century under old Twenty-three Burros you were pure and true and clean in your drumming without any falseness, any of the frills of the northern reservation people. My Prayer was a galloping Gallup man and he was driving now real good.

The missionary stepped out of the New England house and up to the band of whites.

"I wouldn't mind," he said, "I wouldn't mind their ceremony so much if they'd take care of this first."

"What?"

"The burial."

"Why?"

"Why—well, it is the proper thing."

"Why?"

"Why—well, it is, that's all. You know that. You're white."

Young Alastair pulled up his pants and nodded in agreement but no one said anything.

"And well—," the missionary said, and then he faltered.

"And well what?" Big Sant said.

"And well he's beginning to smell," the missionary said.

"All right," Big Sant said. "How deep do you want it?"

All the whites pitched in to dig the hole. They were told to dig it deep enough so the coyotes wouldn't get it and Blue-eyed Billy Peersall set the depth at seven and three-quarter feet and stood alongside the hole measuring while the other whites dug. After two and a half hours' working below in the darkness where they could hear the distant Indians chanting about something else, they finally satisfied Billy Peersall that the grave was coyote-proof. Now those at the bottom were pulled out with ropes and they went up to the mission-house porch to receive a cool glass of water, except the Indian fighter, who drank from his own bottle because he was very tired from measuring. Now an Indian from Cabezon by the name of Almost Never Talking came up and said that a drunk Indian had fallen in the grave and the side had caved in somewhat and there was no way to get him out and furthermore he seemed very happy and quiet down there after fighting above and why bother him. Why bother?

"Was the drunk Indian President Taft?"

"No. It was another drunk Indian. This one was alive."

"We were saving the grave for a dead Indian. President Taft," Mr. Peersall said, putting down his bottle.

The whites trooped back to the grave with their rope, and the Indians began to troop over too. It seemed another rumor had started. This time the rumor was that the missionary was trying to bring President Taft back from the dead. They could all see the whites hollering down into the grave and dangling the rope. So the rumor was not false. They could see the attempt being made with their own eyes.

"Let him alone," one of the Indians said to the missionary.

"It's drinking that caused it," the missionary said. "And he's got to be helped."

"It's a little late," the Indian said.

464

"We will do what we can to save him," the missionary said.

All of the Indians knew or had heard second hand or third hand that the head of the missionary's religion used to bring people back from the dead and now they guessed the missionary was going to try his hand at it. The least they felt they could do was to show respect for the other religion by remaining silent, which they did now while carefully watching the missionary and the other whites do their damndest.

First the whites tried dangling down a rope and hollering, "Grab this." Of course nobody grabbed it and the Indians shifted their weight on the other foot and waited for what next.

Next, one of the whites fell in the hole. He was trying to see to the bottom of the hole and the loose edge gave way and he fell in. Now they dropped down two ropes and told him to tie one to the other man. When they pulled the body up the Indians inspected it. The man was alive all right but it wasn't President Taft. It was another Indian. They all went back to the sweetie sweetie annoyed.

Alastair Benjamin, the dark white boy who had arrived with all the other whites, came over now and sat beneath My Prayer. My Prayer looked up at the pure sky and tried to lose himself in his beat. An artist has got to be different from other people—he's got to have more talent. A rich man has got to have more money than other people and an artist has got to have more talent.

So, My Prayer thought, beneath this baton is not only the dark white boy and a hundred loyal Indians but a thousand sleepless nights that every genius knows.

Now Little Sant went over and sat next to Alastair Benjamin beneath My Prayer and watched up at the man above the big drum.

"If I'm not," Alastair began between beats, "if I'm not being—" after another beat—"I'm not being—" after a loud bang—"if I'm not being too inquisitive, who am I?"

The song ended. He could have waited. My Prayer acknowledged the stamping of the crowd with a raised arm, as though he had completed many scalps, a gesture without humility, without recognition, even, that they were there. He could have been alone on the mesa with his kill and his gods.

The big Bowmans were off comforting the missionary, and

Mr. Peersall had taken a stand on a small rise overlooking the wide flat mesa and all the scene. If he had had his Sharps repeater he could have been mistaken for a picket, for a guardian of the rite and the right. Nothing that he saw had changed much in the almost century since he had first seen it except that damned house. The house appeared set down in rudeness, in contempt—in rudeness of everything that appeared there and in contempt of everything that was believed there. A house set down in righteousness and accompanying blindness, set down to affirm The Truth, not a truth. A house rampant with gold crosses and palm-leaf clusters, alien to this moon.

"Wait a minute," Mr. Peersall told himself. "They've got a right. The Christians have got their rights. Just because I'm not a Christian." When Mr. Peersall acknowledged he was not a Christian people wondered whether he was a Jew. Indian blood then? Or maybe a Unitarian or a Buddhist or something?

"No, I'm just Blue-eyed Billy Peersall. I've tried to be all of that and I've helped people without the need to sell them what I believe and I'm William Peersall, which is quite enough, quite a job right there, quite a bit to cope with still on this earth without making a bad guess at who occupies the universe."

Mr. Peersall brushed a fly off a beaten but unbeaten face. "Blue-eyed Billy Peersall, sometimes known as. Hell, what I'm getting at," Mr. Peersall said aloud, "is, if they want to dance, let them dance. They're not changing money in the temple. They're not—" Mr. Peersall paused and removed something from his pocket for the stomach's sake.

Mr. Bowman and Mrs. Bowman, Big Sant and Millie Sant, were close to the house trying to comfort the missionary.

"I only thought," the missionary said, "I've only been thinking that I'm leaving anyway. I'm getting out soon. They know this. That is, I think it's known. You'd think on this last occasion— No, it's not respect I want. I've never demanded that. I was careful to remember always, careful to remember I had no right to demand anything. Now, you'd think on the last occasion they'd pause before rubbing it in, if they were human. You'd think they'd allow themselves to forget for a few of these last minutes anyway that they're Indians."

"Can you forget Boston?"

"No," the missionary said. "But can't we all remember we're human?"

"They'll quieten down," Millie Sant said. "Maybe, if we ignore them."

"Listen," the missionary said. "You can't ignore that. The end of the world. Listen."

"The children, Sant and Alastair, seem to be enjoying it," Big Sant said.

"Children, yes, they'll enjoy the end of the world. That's always been known." The missionary took off his red sun helmet and drummed on it, unconsciously following the drumming of the Indian drummer. "Always been known," he said, drumming with the drummer.

"There," Little Sant said, looking up at My Prayer as the chanters took over. "That was all right."

"Very all right," Alastair said. "You know, do you mind, Mister Indian, if I ask you a question?"

"Don't call him Mister Indian," Sant said. "You wouldn't want him to call you Mister White Boy."

"That's true," Alastair said, still watching up at the big face above the drum.

"Call him Water Running Underneath the Ground."

"How about My Prayer?"

"That's okay too."

"What other names has he got?"

"Well, he's got a secret name, a war name. All Indians have outside of their Indian name and their white name; they've got a secret name."

"What's his?"

"I said it was a secret."

"I heard someone call him the Galloping Gallup."

"That's just another white man's name," Little Sant said.

"Well, how do I get his attention?"

"This," Sant said and he picked up a rock and dropped it, not too hard, on the Indian's toe.

The Indian looked down.

"Who am I?" Alastair said. "That is, now that President Taft is dead you're the only one left who was there at the fire after the shooting. Am I the one you rescued?"

My Prayer looked down quizzically and annoyed and curious too.

"I don't know," My Prayer said. "All white people look the same to me." And he resumed his drumming, began to bang the drum grandly over the heads of the two boys and in front of all those Indians.

"You know," the missionary said, "I think he's saying something."

"Who?"

"The drummer. I've lived here long enough to know he's saying something. Telling the Indians something with his drums."

Mr. Peersall came up in back of the group that was seated around the open grave. "Yes, he is," Mr. Peersall said.

"What is it, Mr. Peersall?" the missionary said, turning quickly, his abrupt movement sending dirt into the open grave. "What is it? I've got to know."

"It's too late. They've done it."

"Done what?"

"Moved the body. Taken it from your house to his hogan."

"Oh." The missionary turned back to the grave, his motion sending a small rivulet of sand into the hole the whites had dug. "Yes, I should have known better." He looked over at the hogan, cut logs and mud, hexagonal and almost camouflaged against a short tower of rock a thousand yards away. The hogan his retainer, his convert, had built to be near the Word—or the handouts, the missionary wondered. Yes, he thought, I should have started right, begun properly, made him face that door west as missionaries have always made them do, always started by making them give up that first Indian superstition that the door must face east in the direction of *their* gods. I made my first mistake fifteen years ago. But maybe I made it twenty years ago when I became a missionary. Maybe, perhaps, then this was all inevitable.

"Well, don't worry," Millie Sant said. "They're not going to eat it. They're not cannibals."

"They're going to burn it," Mr. Peersall said. "Along with the hogan, they're going to burn it."

The missionary purposely now pushed a little sand into the grave. "A heathen rite," he said.

"Their rite. Their right," Mr. Peersall said, wondering up at the sky.

"I hope they're not doing this to shock us," Millie Sant said.

"Or to finish me off," the missionary said, wondering into the ground as the Indian fighter had wondered into the clouds. Parting is such absolute sorrow, such dirty work.

"Patience," Millie Sant said. "Wait and see what they do first. Patience. Watch and listen."

A big solitary bang came from the drum, an alone bang preceded and followed by silence. All the Indians now moved toward the hogan with the door facing east.

The Indians grouped around the hogan in the manner of flies settling, groups of them here and there in bunches and singly; in large groups and in ones, twos, and threes; in laughter, some of them, and others in expectation, and most in wide, pointed cowboy hats and in narrow pointed cowboy boots; many, including the men, in squaw boots and bright headbands. All of the Navaho women had rubbed iron oxide from the sand cliffs into their cheeks, as Navaho women will for a celebration—a wedding or a death or spending borrowed money. They looked like painted china dolls. They looked very pretty to another Indian.

Mr. Peersall realized now that the Indians were going to do this right. He knew they believed that when an Indian dies there are two ghosts to be coped with by the Indians who are left. One of the ghosts, the good ghost, goes up into the sky and that is okay, but the other ghost hangs around and can be very annoying. It helps if you burn the hogan and it helps if you burn some of the things with the hogan that the dead man loved. The ghost likes that. Burning a live hunting dog with the Indian helps because then he can go hunting. However, Taft never did go hunting much lately. Now that you could buy corned beef in a can at the trading post there wasn't much point to hunting. The Indians are not romantics. Then burning a live woman would help. As every Navaho knows, it keeps the ghost from sleeping with your wife, which is nice. But for a long time now the Navaho women have objected to being burned alive to sleep with a ghost. The Navaho women seem to take their religion with a grain of pemmican. Burning an Indian body in his own hogan too will give the dead Indian's bad ghost a sense of where he lives, a sense of belonging. Of course he will always try to follow the Indians home after a funeral, but if the door is quickly slammed in his face there is a good chance the ghost will go back to where he belongs. That is why it's ideal to burn a real dog and a real widow or something nice along with the Indian. It's especially ideal, the old people claim, to burn a woman. But Mr. Peersall knew the Navaho women were no longer keen on this. Mr. Peersall wondered what the modern Indian would go with to make the ghost feel better, to make him stay at home. Now he knew. One of the Indians went slowly up to the door and dropped a full quart of old Four Roses inside. It was old My Prayer. He understood. He would understand. My Prayer felt certain now that the bad ghost would not follow him home. Everything that must mean anything to the ghost of President Taft should be inside the bottle that would always be full in the afterworld.

Take the way they are piling brush up now around the hogan. That is to keep the bad ghost inside the hogan until all the Indians can get safely home without being too closely followed. Two things are distinctive about the Navaho. (Mr. Peersall wished he had his Sharps rifle to lean on while he was thinking; he felt naked.) One thing was their fear about death, this continuous fear before and after the event. And the other thing was their continuous unfear about sex before and after the event. A Navaho boy will, if he is normal and healthy—there are queer Indians—but if he is normal and healthy he will *edash il* a Navaho girl any chance he gets. When she is going for water is a good chance and it's a very good chance when she is tending the sheep. So cowboys are likely to

470

find, all over the prairie and anyplace on the mesa—particularly near the bubbling springs or the amazed sheep—Navahos *edash iling* until they are blue in the face. Navahos seem to like to do this very much.

Mr. Peersall leaned on a scrub oak in lieu of his Sharps rifle but it wasn't the same. Nothing was quite the same any more. He liked to remember that he was able to remember everything as it was.

The two Indian boys still sitting near the orchestra—the drum had not moved, still played on—they liked to remember everything as it was going to be. They could not live in the past because they had no connection with it. They could not live in the present because no Indian had any connection with it. So they liked to remember everything as it was going to be. Everything was going to be a big blank, so they lived from hour to hour, drifting from dying week to hopeless month through unrecorded and unremembered years. They did not know what the older people were up to, burning down the hogan. They didn't much care. They didn't know what the white people were up to with their rites. They didn't care at all. They were caught exactly in that hiatus between the death and the resurrection of a race. That maybe was the blank, the big blank, in the minds of the two boys lolling there, physically equi-distant between the red group at the burning and the white sad knot at the missionary's. With, not, and for neither, unwanted and unbothering—uncaring. Their names were Afraid Of His Own Horses and The Other Indian.

"Who am I?" Alastair Benjamin asked.

The Other Indian looked up and down at Alastair Benjamin. "The hell you say," he said.

"What I mean is," Alastair Benjamin said, "what I mean is, My Prayer was there but he won't say. You haven't heard him say anything, have you? Something he maybe wouldn't tell a white man?"

All Alastair got was that big blank from both of the boys.

"What I mean is," Alastair said, "now they're having this burning it could have been the same thing. What I mean is, it could have been the Indians also that—"

Alastair was still getting the great blank and he finally turned away.

"The hell you say," Afraid Of His Own Horses said.

The Other Indian watched Alastair Benjamin diminish. Another white problem like a white-school problem—if you have eight apples and John has four apples. No one really had any damn apples at all. Why was Alastair—anyone—worried about the past when there was no damn future. Yes, there was this nice blank. There were those nice girls over there now and there would be a nice blank tomorrow. Afterward did not exist and they hoped Alastair Benjamin would recover some of his marbles tomorrow and not go around mooning Who am I? Hell, you're a white man, aren't you? What more is there? What more would he want to know?

"He is, though, an awfully odd color, don't you think? For a white man?" The Other Indian said.

"They come in assorted colors."

"Parece," The Other Indian said. "It seems they do."

"And they got weird problems. In assorted flavors."

"It seems," The Other Indian said.

They both strained to see some kind of a ghost pop out of the burning hogan and they both remembered, as all the Navahos grouped around did, *not* to remark the ghost. A ghost will sometimes take the form of a coyote or a bear or even a snake. Sometimes even a— My Prayer beat heavily on the drums. My Prayer knew what other forms ghosts could take. He had seen it happen. A ghost running from a dead man's pyre can take the form of Alastair Benjamin.

The steady bang of the drums increased in a rolling and mounting objection to thought—a furious and inchoate beat that lost the listener in a new world of other gods.

"Like I have been trying to say all along," Big Sant said. Big Sant was standing near the white house with the other whites. "Like I've been trying—"

"It's not Christian Science," Millie Sant said.

"What?"

"What those Indians are doing." Millie Sant watched. "No,"

472

she said. "What those Indians are up to is no true religion. It's not written down, not financed."

"Not financed," Mr. Peersall agreed.

"Like I been trying to say all along," Big Sant said, "it's not whether it's written down or whether it's financed, it's simply that we're outnumbered two hundred to one."

"At least," Mr. Peersall agreed.

The missionary, Mr. Sanders, took out his ballpoint and wrote on a close rock while thinking of something else—ARCHIBALD SANDERS.

"What I've been thinking is," Mr. Sanders said, "does might make right?"

"Outside of a speech hall, it generally does. Yes," Mr. Peersall said. "That is, when we had the Indians outnumbered two hundred to one we always noticed some difference in the result."

The missionary wrote YES on the rock and then crossed it out.

"I always had the faith," he said, "that right makes might and in that faith I would always do my duty as I saw it. Does that sound silly now?"

"Yes," Mr. Peersall said.

"You're a bully," Mr. Sanders said.

"No. I just have trouble sometimes figuring out what's right."

Mr. Sanders wrote YES again on the rock and then he crossed this out and wrote ARROGANT BULLY.

My Prayer banged on the drum and watched over at the white people. He saw one of them writing on a rock. Most Indians, wrong or right, contend that writing is the white man's way of laying a ghost. An Indian will quell a ghost by building a neat pile of stones, the dog will plant his ghost by pissing on it, and the white man by writing on the queer pile of rock KILROY WAS HERE. Actually the ghost the whites planted most on the rocks of Indian Country was JESUS SAVES. The Indian will probably always go with his neat pile of rocks, maybe with marked trees, the white man with his written business, and the dog will always piss on all three. If there was some moral, some *anaji,* here My Prayer could figure out none. He got back to planting his own ghost with his drums.

Big Sant watched from the group of whites with more especial

473

concentration than anyone else. He thought that nothing extra, nothing but flames would fly out of the hogan. But after what the Indians claimed, after the last burning, it would do no harm to watch carefully.

My Prayer watched for the match expectantly because an old friend was in there and they had both been through this before when they were both on the outside. None of the whites believed what happened then and he was happy to see there were many watching now. In case something happened now there would be many witnesses.

Nothing happened. The hogan burned with a long, high, bright flame as tall as a ponderosa and lighted all the Indians into silhouette, but nothing happened.

"Something happened all right," the missionary said as the flames began to retreat back into the ground from where they seemed to rise.

"What happened?" Big Sant said, concerned.

"The Indians had their way, that's what happened," the missionary said. The missionary, Mr. Sanders, worked his hands together in thought, watching the quieting blaze. "I guess we had better cover over that grave with logs before an Indian falls in."

"We can throw back the dirt," Big Sant said. "Make it permanent. I guess no Indian will ever use it."

"This Indian maybe," the missionary said carefully.

"Why is everyone trying to say something shocking today?" Millie Sant said.

"No, this Indian won't," Mr. Sanders said, still speaking carefully, and dazed. "Maybe this Indian won't. Maybe he'll go the way of all Indians." Mr. Sanders threw a helping twig toward the fire. "In a nice blaze."

"You see," Millie Sant said, "when you go back to Boston everything will be all right again."

"Yes," Big Sant said. "They'll all be exactly like you. No problems."

Mr. Peersall fingered an imaginary Sharps. "Exactly like you," he agreed. "That's all right," Mr. Peersall corrected himself. "There's not nothing necessarily wrong with people being like you." Mr. Peersall still did not think this sounded generous. "We got to be tolerant," he concluded.

"When you get back there," Millie Sant encouraged, "your faith will be restored. You'll get real Bible back there. No body snatching. There's real Bible back there."

"Where?"

"Boston. Boston Bible. Isn't that where you come from?"

"Yes," Mr. Sanders said bleakly.

"Why you can go to a ball game every day if you want," Big Sant said. "Any time you want."

"The Braves have moved to Minneapolis," the missionary said.

"Then you do know what's going on," Big Sant said hopefully. "I thought something might have happened to you—been out here too long."

"Oh, I know what's going on," Mr. Sanders said. "Watch the Indians dance." Watch the Braves dance had been his first thought. "Watch the Navahos dance and howl their chant. I know what's going on. I know what's happening. That's where all the difficulties lie."

"You'll see," Millie Sant said. "In a little bit you'll find yourself."

"It will take a little time," Big Sant said. "Let's cover up that grave before an Indian falls in."

All the whites went down to cover up the grave except Mr. Sanders. He just sat there studying the fire. Now he was joined by Alastair Benjamin, who sat alongside him and studied the fire too.

"We've both got the same problem now," Mr. Sanders said.

"What's that?" Alastair said.

"Finding out who we are."

"You too?" Alastair asked.

"Me too," Mr. Sanders said and he tossed another twig toward the fire.

At the grave everyone worked very hard. That is, Big Sant worked very hard filling it in now that there was no body. Everyone else watched. No one to help, Big Sant thought. Even some Indians who were bored by the fire came over to watch. The sweetie

475

sweetie was still going on, the drum continued, but these watching Indians were too old for sweetie sweeties now. Mr. Peersall stood as straight as a very worn ramrod addicted to whisky above the grave watching down at Little Sant beneath him, watching up.

"What's a good book to read on the Wild West, Mr. Peersall?"

"Andy Adams' *Log of a Cowboy*."

"Nothing else?"

"No. That's all."

"Who was the best bronc rider that ever lived, Mr. Peersall?"

"Mr. Peersall."

"Anybody else?"

"No. That's all."

"If I try very hard can I become a great bronc rider, Mr. Peersall?"

"Not necessarily."

Little Sant made a big circle on the loose ground with his foot. "Why not?"

"Talent. The lack of it," Mr. Peersall said.

Little Sant wiped out the circle again with his booted foot. "Oh," he said and then he drew a cross with his foot. "What would you say distinguishes you most?"

"Lying."

"I mean very truly, Mr. Peersall?"

"I was all right at busting horses," Mr. Peersall said. And women, Mr. Peersall thought. Blue-eyed Billy Peersall said, "Yes."

"Yes what?"

"Yes, horses," Mr. Peersall said.

"Who was the best horse buster that ever lived?"

"Lemaitre."

"I rode with Lemaitre," Sant said. Sant fumbled quickly at the lips of his pants pockets as though drawing guns. He drew from this a dirty card.

"Sure you did," Mr. Peersall said.

"And I got this to prove it," Sant said, passing it up to the man above.

"Sure you did," Mr. Peersall said, examining the card that could have been given away with every box of Cracker Jack.

476

"I got that Cellophane on to protect it," Sant said.

"Sure you did," Mr. Peersall said, returning the card that could have been given for sending in five whisky tops. "Sure you did."

"Nobody believes me," Sant said.

"So you rode with Lemaitre," Mr. Peersall said.

"Yes, I did."

"Sure you did," Mr. Peersall said.

Little Sant strode away, not making circles or crosses or anything any more, just kicking the dirt as he went. When he got to the first two people who looked the way he felt he sat down beside them within the noise of the music and all the shadows the dying fire made.

"They have no souls," Mr. Sanders said finally.

"No, they haven't," Alastair agreed.

Sant noticed that without any shoes it was obvious that the Indians didn't need any, but he was in such a mood he went along anyway. "Very true," he said. "Yes, just bear in mind that I'm better than fourteen years old now and I don't have to look up to Mr. Peersall or anybody else."

"Very true," Alastair agreed.

"And I don't have to do nothing but ride a horse proper."

"That's all," Alastair said. "Nothing happened."

"What do you mean, nothing happened?"

"Nothing ran out of the hogan."

"Did you expect somebody would?"

"I didn't know."

"Let's dance."

"What about the missionary?"

"Forget the missionary," the missionary said.

"Will you join us?"

"Why not?" Mr. Sanders said.

"Look," Millie Sant said. "Look over there. The missionary. He's going to dance. Oh my God," Millie Sant said.

Mr. Peersall sat down on a grama clump near the edge of the unused grave. It was the first time he had sat down since the sweetie sweetie began. "It's all right, Millie," Mr. Peersall said.

"Big Sant," Millie Sant said. "Darling, Mr. Sanders is going to dance. A pagan dance. My God," Millie Sant said.

"It's all right, Millie," Big Sant said, sitting down alongside Mr. Peersall. "It's all right, Millie dear."

"By God, that's a crock of crap," Millie said quietly. "By God, I still know right from wrong."

"What's up?" Mr. Peersall said.

"He's betraying us," Millie Sant said, still thinking about it, still trying to figure it out.

"You can't betray someone who never believed in you, Millie," Big Sant said.

"Yes, that would be a crock of—" Mr. Peersall was interrupted.

"Don't be so vulgar. Do you have to be so vulgar?" Millie said, her voice rising.

"You said it, Millie dear."

"It makes no difference," she said sincerely. "Do you have to repeat like children every damn thing you hear? Men! Oh my God, men," she said quietly now. "It's all right if I said it. It's all right if I said it, I guess, but don't be like children—vulgar to be vulgar. Men are like children. He's betrayed us, and don't say that, just because no one believed in him— That's a crock—"

"Millie dear."

"All right. Very well," she said.

At the stand for the band, a small rise on the flat mesa hung over with juniper and surrounded by silver sage flowering in gold and smelling sharply and pungent always, My Prayer played on without pause, emitting his beat that wafted with the wind, prevailed with the prevailing breeze, loud, and when the wind went wrong his beat carried into the canyons, lost.

Yes, My Prayer thought, watching out above his boom, as long as I can make great magic, as long as I can keep a good beat, I will have the world, this little world, firmly held by the *ziz*. I don't know why one kind of magic must always give way to another kind of magic, why the missionary and I can't live together, why the red man and the white man can't live in the same world without speaking to each other. As soon as we spoke, the day we spoke, that was the beginning of the end. That was the day the white man began to love the Indian to death. A white man can never commit a crime and forget it. When we stole this land, when the Navaho stole this land from the Gallina people, the Navaho forgot it. Except for some rather pleasant memories of the war, the Navaho forgot it. When the white man stole this land from the Navaho Nation he has got to compound the crime in order to forget it. He's got to love us to death. Love is their way of not giving back something they have stolen. Take that white man over there, Blue-eyed Billy Peersall. He is the only white man ever known who hasn't tried to love us. He doesn't even like us—he tolerates us. I wonder if the white man will ever learn that that is all any defeated people ever want—to be tolerated. To be allowed to be different. Love is their way of intolerance. Love is their gentle way of grabbing you firmly by the *ziz* and twisting until an Indian hollers Uncle Sam. The whites never did anything wrong that wasn't made up for by this love. Their love is like a gentle *ziz*-twisting thing. Their love.

Now My Prayer got back to the sweetie sweetie, the dance, the reason for being. He would try hard now not to go back over all those reasons for not living. He would stick with the true love, the dancing, the music, the sand painting, the *edesh il,* the stars in a very black sky, and the way the world looks in the very early morning in Navaho Country and in the evening and at noon. All these true things which were mostly music. That is my true thing anyway. Now he gave a series of awfully good bangs and the Navaho people felt it in their beings and showed it in the movement of their bodies, their feet. Even the whites were beginning to circle in now—even the missionary. Go easy on him, My Prayer thought. He's got a life to lead.

My Prayer turned over the drums to an assistant, a boy who had never been to Gallup—Paris—a boy without sufficient training to release his creativity but with sufficient knowledge to imitate genius. My Prayer turned over the drums to him—his name was Andy Alltogether—and slithered through the Navahos until he got to the missionary, Mr. Sanders.

"I wouldn't do it," he said.

"What?"

"Dance."

"Why not?"

"I wouldn't do it," My Prayer said.

"Why?"

"You've got a life to lead," My Prayer said.

The whites were standing at the periphery of the circle watching the serpentine pattern of the dance. They all seemed unconscious of My Prayer; even Mr. Sanders, who was supposed to be talking to My Prayer seemed unconscious of the Indian in their midst.

"Why?" Mr. Sanders said again.

"Because you've got to live with your people, not with my people," My Prayer said.

"Do I?" Mr. Sanders said.

The Indian in their midst looked perplexed.

"So is your old man," Mr. Sanders said. This was a phrase from his childhood, Mr. Sanders thought. This was something he had not said since 1922. "Says you," Mr. Sanders said, and then he said carefully, looking closely at the face of the Indian in their midst, "Yes, we have no bananas." That was his childhood, 1920 maybe, long before he entered the seminary. "Yes," Mr. Sanders agreed.

"Yes what?"

"Yes, we have no bananas," Mr. Sanders said carefully to the Indian.

Well, My Prayer thought, something has been added to the brew. Have I got to cope with a nut?

"Have you got all your arrows okay?" My Prayer said.

"Have I got all my marbles?" Mr. Sanders said, translating. "Have I lost some of my marbles? Maybe I did for the last fifteen years. Maybe I did lose some of my marbles but now I'm beginning to collect them again. My Prayer, I don't want to go into all this. My Prayer, I simply want to dance with your dancers."

"No good," My Prayer said.

"What My Prayer's trying to indicate is that it's a question of your loss of status pattern among the whites."

Mr. Sanders looked down, looking for Alastair. There he was looking up. There, too, alongside, was Little Sant and the old Indian fighter.

"Yes," Alastair said, "he's worried about your loss of symbol status among your own people. It would be traumatic in the context of white mores for you to accept, by dancing, a primitive symbol pattern other than the cross—other than the Christian."

"It's legal," Little Sant said. "He got it from a book."

"He said it very nicely," My Prayer said. "What did he say?"

"No good," Mr. Sanders said. "In his childish way he said exactly what you said. No good."

"In a very vulgar way from where I stood," Millie Sant said. "Do men have to be vulgar for the sake of being vulgar? Where's that small dark crock—" She reached over to give Alastair a jerk but he had retreated safely in back of Mr. Peersall. "But he's awfully cute," Millie said. Now Millie turned on the missionary. "You can't dance that heathen dance," she said. "If that's what My Prayer said, he's right."

"That's what I said," My Prayer said.

"And if that's what Alastair tried to say, he's right," Millie said.

"That's what his book said," Little Sant said.

"You see," Millie said quickly into the face of the preacher. "You do see, don't you?"

"Yes, I do see finally," Mr. Sanders said and he left for the dancing with a dusky Indian girl who had been tugging on his arm all this while. But first he paid ten cents, as was the Indian custom at sweetie sweeties.

"I see," he said.

PART III

TWELVE Inca doves that for weeks had been building quick and wide circles around the Circle Heart were now at last ready to shoot south. The young that were still young could at last keep pace with the flight. Not too well; they faltered and got out of line and sometimes they tried to take the lead when they were too young to take the lead. Sometimes the small Inca doves would not join the practice flights, as though they had no intention of leaving here at all. Nothing wrong with the Circle Heart. But they went finally. The young doves could not survive to come back to the warm summer of the Circle Heart unless they fled it during the long winter. One day they were gone. Gone so they could come back stronger to the summer of the Circle Heart.

"The cottonwoods have not lost their leaves so early this year."

"That's because we've had some good rains."

"I'm going to go away," Little Sant said.

Apropos of nothing, Alastair thought. He is so full of *non sequiturs*. Well, I have got a few myself.

They were both sitting, hanging, on the corral fence on a pleasant Sunday morning two years after the funeral of President Taft, and Alastair thought he would continue the conversation by branding with a pencil on the fence board $E = mc_2$.

"Is that going to be your brand?" Little Sant said.

"It's going to be the brand of everyone in the twentieth century unless I do something about it."

"So you're going to save everybody?"

"I guess so."

"With your education you're going to save everybody."

"I guess so."

"That's some of what I'm running away from."

"What?"

"Education."

Alastair had to think about this for a while, had to try to imagine somebody that would run away from an education. He couldn't.

"I can't," Alastair said. "I can't even imagine anyone hypothetically."

"Who said hypothetically?"

"I did."

"Then you run away from it. I am running away from an education."

"Why?"

"Well, that's better," Sant said. "Well, I'll tell you exactly why. Because I am."

"Why?"

"Because I am a bronc man."

"That's just a saying."

"Well, I got something to prove it."

"Everybody's got to have an education," Alastair said.

"Now that *is* just a saying," Sant said.

"Oh?"

"Yes. If everybody spent their time studying and nobody doing, what would the studying people be studying?"

"Oh? Yes. But I'm still going to get an education."

"Yes, it's right for you, Alley. Some people are not fit for anything else. It's not the way they were brought up or who their parents were, it's just that they're kind of all thumbs and they can't do anything so they have to say I'm educated. Nobody can do anything to help them, they are just the way God made them—helpless. Yes," Sant said, "like Reverend Peavey of the Holy Rollers said when he was against putting a sewer system in Cuba, 'If God wanted the people to have sewers he would have put them

486

there.' Yes," Sant said, "if God didn't love education he wouldn't have invented so many helpless people."

"You think God's got a sense of humor?"

"I can think of no other explanation."

"Don't talk about this to grownups. They'll say we're getting out of line."

"Don't worry. You can't talk to them exactly."

They thought about this for a while and then both wondered what they were thinking about, exactly.

"Well," Alastair said finally. "When exactly are you going to leave?"

"Tomorrow early."

"What's going to happen to me?"

"You'll get educated."

"I mean me without you. I can't imagine it."

"You'll get used to it."

"I don't think I ever can."

"In time you can. I'll write."

"I don't think I ever can."

"I'll write."

"I don't think I ever can get used to it."

They both sat sadly on the fence thinking about it. Alastair retraced the brand, $E=mc_2$, but he was not thinking about that.

"Why exactly do you have to leave so suddenly, Santo?"

"It's not so suddenly, Alley. I have been planning and thinking about it a long time now."

"Ever since you got that piece of paper from Lemaitre."

"That's right. But it's what's behind a piece of paper, Alley."

"That's right. You know, Santo," Alastair said, turning on the fence toward Sant, "I think what's indicated for you—"

"What?"

"I think what's indicated for you is that you've got to have a go at this running away, ride at bronc shows and find out that what was behind that piece of paper is a lot of baloney."

Sant thought about this.

"And what's behind your piece of paper, your diploma they'll give you for studying—that piece of paper? What's behind that piece of paper is a lot of books written by somebody else."

"Maybe. We'll see."

"Don't you think, Alley, if a man tries hard enough he'll make it?"

"That depends."

"Then you don't think there's any justice?"

"Only the justice we make."

"Another book?"

"No, that's my own reckoning."

"I'm still going to leave tomorrow early. Alley, is there something you want to say to me before I go?"

"Yes, there's a lot I want to say. But nothing in particular."

"Nothing particular about my father and your father?"

"Nothing particular."

"How your father died?" Sant said.

"He was killed by your father. But it was an accident."

"You're sure it was an accident?"

"It's always an accident."

"You mean it always is? Even war?"

"That's right. And don't forget your father had a jury trial."

"Yes," Sant said, and then he looked around at everything before he said, "But there weren't any black people on the jury."

"No, but there were some red ones."

"What's that got to do with it? You mean the reds will see that the blacks get justice?"

"No, not necessarily."

"It's a pretty good theory."

"Yes. But that's not what I know."

"What do you know?"

"I'd rather not talk about it."

"I tell you, Alley," Sant said. "I can't leave unless I talk about it."

"Then stay."

"I can't stay, Alley, unless I talk about it."

"Then leave."

"I can't do nothing, Alley, unless I know."

"All right," Alastair said. "The black took from the red by accident and the white took from the black by accident."

"What do you mean?"

"I mean my father, the one they call the Gran Negrito, came out here and he needed land and a wife. He had a gun and a legal book. There was a dead Indian and in the end the Gran Negrito had land and a wife, Indian land and Indian wife. Then it all died, first my mother, then the land, and the Gran Negrito himself. Us. Like we got it, we lost it. All an accident again. The law proved it was all an accident, the same as the way we got it."

"How do you know?"

"That's the story the drums told at President Taft's funeral."

"How do you know?"

"I followed My Prayer home. I would not leave his hogan. He said I was a ghost; he had seen me flee from a burning hogan way back—and I must leave. I told him I would leave forever if he told me all. I would never harm him again. Then he told me how I came out of the burning hogan like a ghost and how they hid me from the other Indians who might destroy a ghost until they made a long trip in their wagon and left me on the steps of a white orphanage because I was not red. And he told me how my father stole the land by accident. And I told him I would not haunt him any more, and I left."

"Alley, are you going to haunt us?"

"No. I have decided to try to bury the dead, as your father decided to try to bury the dead by taking me in. I walked all that night, when I left My Prayer's hogan. I walked like a ghost, thinking of all the accidents ghosts can cause, wondering what caused my father to do it, wondering what happened to him to make him do it—why he had to do it. Then I realized it would never end, that ghosts would haunt ghosts forever, that accidents would never end. Then I suddenly realized that there was nothing I could do about it, that I had to have revenge, as my father must have had to have revenge, that I could not walk in the daylight any more, couldn't look in the mirror any more, until I had revenge. I got your father's gun and went into his bedroom."

"Yes?" Sant said.

"He woke up and saw me standing there with the gun and he said he understood."

"Understood what?"

"That there had to be another accident."

"And then what?"

"Then I told him I couldn't do it."

"And then what?"

"Then we decided to kill his horse."

"Did you?"

"Yes."

"So that's what happened to Indian Country. I thought he traded him. What did killing Father's horse do? Did it help?"

"Yes. It ended something."

"It was a beautiful horse."

"I suppose they were all beautiful—all those people the accidents happened to. I don't remember."

"Do you want to?"

"No. I don't have to remember anything now. Something is ended. I think I can take on what comes now okay."

Sant reached over and touched Alastair on the back.

"Yes, I think it will be okay now, Alley."

THIRTEEN **I**n the middle of the night, a moon-filled New Mexican night where the owls can see Old Mexico and wild animals move gently and call suddenly, something like the coyote calling will happen or the departing bugle of an elk from on top, moving down country, will happen and shock. In the middle of a moon-filled New Mexican night there are all these arriving and departing sounds to quicken, to startle you.

"What was that?" Millie said.

"Little Sant," Big Sant said.

"Where is he going this time of night?"

"I guess he's moving down country."

"What do you mean?"

"He's leaving us."

"What do you mean?"

"He's going to hunt on his own. He's sixteen now."

"What do you mean?"

"He's leaving."

"For good?"

"For good or for worse. That's what he's got to find out."

"We've got to stop him."

"No, Millie, he's got to find something out."

"But we've got to stop him."

"We can't stop him, Millie. We can only be here if he can't make it there."

"Where?" she said, rising on her elbow and staring down at the face of the reclining figure. "Where?"

"Cortez."

"Why Cortez?"

"That's where the rodeo is."

"And why didn't he tell us?"

"Because it's none of our business."

Millie relaxed back into the bed and stared up at the viga-beamed, moon-lit ceiling. Now she sobbed gently. Big Sant took her hand that lay limp on top of the gray four-point blanket.

"A boy has got to cut out something new, Millie. A boy has got to try."

"Like you did. Cut out something new."

"I made it, Millie."

"You're making this worse," she said.

"I made it, Millie, the only way I knew. Maybe he doesn't like my way, maybe this land is wrong for him. Education's wrong too. We've got to let him go."

They both lay there silent now save for a quiet sobbing.

"I put fifty dollars in his wallet, Millie, last night. I saw this coming. He kind of told me in a silent way. He can always make it back here with that money."

"But supposing—" Then what she said was lost again in the sounds of her grief.

"He can always make it back," Big Sant insisted.

Now the boy moved down valley on his horse, his movement joining in with all the other gentle moves on the slope. On his flank a prong-horned elk was moving unseen and downward too. His horns were at the straight stage before they branch out, at a stage where it is legal for hunters to kill them but at a phase in the development of their fighting antlers when it is difficult for them to make it on their own. But for this elk there was nothing else to do. He picked up the horse and man scent now and paused to let them get down to the low country first.

Sant touched the horse with his heel to quicken it. He would ride as far as the missionary's, leave the horse there, and go on to the Greyhound stop on the highway by foot.

Now a tall burst of flame lighted in a glare all the country ahead. The fire had not suddenly risen—the horse and rider had just topped out over a hogback ridge of jack pine and there was all this brightening country below. The wild animals, making their final move before dawn caught them exposed, made a wide, frightened circle around the fire. The horse and rider made toward it, it was directly in their path. As a matter of fact, Sant realized suddenly, it was their destination. The fire was at the mission. The mission was on fire.

Sant tried to speed the horse by rein-slapping his flank but the horse was not having any. He was broken enough to go toward a fire if he had to but no horse is ever busted sufficiently to move toward a fire quickly. If the Indians have done this, Sant thought, it is not a very nice thing for the Indians to do. As Alastair would say, Sant thought, burning down the mission is not a very subtle way to say something. I hope the missionary got out alive. It is supposed to be funny, Sant thought, burning a missionary. That is, cooking him in a pot so you don't waste anything. According to the cartoon jokes in the magazines it's supposed to be quite funny. Alastair would have the cause for humor in the fact that no one invited the missionary to come—he invited himself and if he insists he might as well come to dinner and bring his own dinner, or, to keep things neat, *be* the dinner. But Alastair wasn't here any more. It was all over with Alastair now and he must begin to figure out things all by himself. The way to figure this was that it wasn't funny at all. Mr. Sanders had come here with the best of intentions. I wonder if the best of intentions excuses an invasion—if you can violate any nation's—the Navaho Nation's—beliefs with the best of intentions. Alastair would like the word "violate." He would like the whole phrase "violate a people's traditions." To hell with Alastair. I think that you can't violate another nation's traditions. You can't and expect to get away with it. But here you have got a mitigating circumstance. You've got the missionary's best of intentions. "Mitigating" is good. To hell with Alastair. To hell with all those phony words.

Sant tried to get the horse to move faster by kneeing and heeling and turning his ear, but it wasn't any good. A fire is still always a thing an animal doesn't like very much. So they proceeded

493

toward the burning mission at the horse's pace. You could tell it was the mission now. It made a beautiful fire. It was built of foreign materials, thin clapboard, and it was three stories high, higher than anything in Indian Country. The three stories would give the fire a splendid draft, and nothing burns better than New England kindling wood. Nothing burns better than two-by-four studs, joists, and rafters on sixteen-inch centers, that the New England building code calls for. It calls for the best fire Indian Country ever had. It is too much of a temptation for a poor Indian. You cannot tempt even an Indian too much. Even a Navaho. No, Sant thought, they should not have done it, but if they had to do it I hope they let him out of his New England house first. It seems only fair. I wish this damn horse would get a little bit of a move on. What's he scared of? What are we all scared of, I wonder?

Now as the dark horse and young rider got closer you could see clearly the giant sage and the scrub oak and weird cholla cactus all emblazoned against the black sky. It made a much better fire than the Indians were ever able to build for a *yebechai*. The mission was going out in a blaze of gory. Glory, Sant had meant to think. He dropped off his horse and made toward the blaze. It was very hot against his face and when it got unbearably hot he began to circle, watching for some kind of opening to dash in, but the fire was going good all the way through and up, crowning and billowing and easily sixty feet above the house. Sant began to retreat now. If the missionary was in there there wasn't any hope at all. God damn those Indians. What did they think it was—1840, 1860 or what? Indians aren't supposed to behave this way now. All the money the government has spent to civilize them. All the money the government has stolen from them to spend on them to civilize them. Do they still think they're savages or what? Indians will still be Indians no matter what you steal from them to civilize them. Maybe they all ought to be rounded up and put in a camp where they can be civilized and watched, but that was tried once. I guess there's nothing you can do about Indians.

Sant sat down on a burned log a safe distance from the fire and was joined by his horse, who finally arrived. "I guess there's nothing can be done with Indians."

Sant realized he was sitting on a burned log from the old hogan. The whole place was burned down now—there wasn't anything left at all of the mission. "I wonder if there is anything left of the missionary."

Now Sant could make out some activity in back of an enormous rock that his circle of the fire had been too small to observe. There were people arriving. Indians. There were many Indians arriving and all going to say something to a man standing there, protected in back of the rock. It was the missionary, Mr. Sanders. God protects the protected. Sant edged in close and so did the horse. The horse was very brave now. Sant could hear that the Indians were all saying the same thing and all with a touch of awe in their voices. Where there had been a touch of contempt before now there was a touch of awe in their voices.

"Why really, this is the tallest fire. Oh, why really, this is the fire that very well, really, might end all fires. We have really never seen such a fire and none of our ancestors have either. Really, they haven't."

There was awe in their eyes, too, as they stepped back from congratulating the missionary. They looked at him with an awe-filled expression. Sant knew that there is nothing an Indian respects more than a man who is responsible for a good fire and this one was the finest fire the Indians had seen, including their ancestors and their children and their children's children. Who else would or will ever trouble or afford to import the makings of such a fire? Build a house and have such a respect for fire as to burn it down? That was why the awe was in the Indians' eyes. Here was one man who, why really, understood, and he was a white man. A white man who beat the red man at his own game. Their own religion. Why really, this is some white man. Why really, did you say he was from Boston? Why really, what a loss to the nation of Boston, his coming here was. To a red man this fire was what a globe-circling satellite would be to a white, and put up by a private individual and not one containing a mere dog, but a satellite ringing the earth, containing a herd of elephants. That's what the missionary's fire was to the Indians. That's about it, Sant thought. The man, I guess, is a kind of genius, Mr. Sanders is.

Sant went back and sat on his burned hogan log until the fire had died down to a respectable pile of glowing coals and there was nothing left standing but a very respectable and straight New England, kiln-brick chimney, the only thing that had withstood the outraging fire. The tall black chimney of foreign and manufactured stones was the only thing brought that would stay, all that would endure.

"I suppose," Sant said, sitting alongside the missionary after all the Indians had gone, "I suppose in a couple of days they will pull that down too."

"What?"

"The chimney. All that's left."

"No," Mr. Sanders said, watching it. "They allow things to fall of their own weight, their own absurdity."

"Oh?"

"Yes," Mr. Sanders fanned himself against the heat with his pith helmet, then he tossed that into the glowing fire with a large gesture. "Yes," Mr. Sanders said. "Their own contradictions. I remember," Mr. Sanders said in a tired voice and yet looking around him with a kind of glee, "I remember at Concord, at the Bethlehem Seminary—that's where I studied in my youth. My youth." Mr. Sanders stared into the fire. "My youth. Well," Mr. Sanders said, snapping out of it and looking up suddenly. "They gave a course—Mr. Perklers—a course on the understanding of the red man, on our problems with our savage brothers. Are you interested?"

"Kind of."

"Well, the main part of the course was based on a diary, a book called *Brother Smelzer among the Indians*. That title for Brother Smelzer's diary didn't sound so foolish then. The Rover Boys and Teddy Roosevelt were very popular then. You were always among somebody or up some river then. Well, anyway—" Mr. Sanders caught himself suffering total recall and got to the point. "Brother Smelzer's diary among the Indians was four thousand pages long. He must have written half of each night in that jungle among those savages by lantern up some lost tributary of the Amazon, I'm sure it was. Anyway, only a fourth of it had been

496

printed by the Society, which was a lot. Mr. Perklers, who gave the course, told us to go to original sources. Maybe I was the only one who did or maybe I was the only one who ever read to the end of the four thousand pages. You know what the last words in that diary were?"

"No."

" 'I must get downriver before they convert *me.*' "

"Wow!" Sant said.

"Yes, that's the only word now," Mr. Sanders said. "In my youth I didn't understand. I thought maybe it was insanity, that Brother Smelzer had gone insane. Now I will always wonder."

"Wonder what?"

"Whether they did."

"Did what?"

"Converted him," Mr. Sanders said. They both sat silent a long time looking into the dying fire. "But I suppose you have your own problems," Mr. Sanders said.

"I sure have," Sant said.

"What?"

"Some place to leave my horse."

"Leave it here at my place."

"You haven't got a place," Sant said.

Mr. Sanders looked around slowly at the cactus and sage; holding on to one he raised back from his sitting position. "I never thought of that before."

"You always had a place before," Sant said.

"No, I never had a place before," Mr. Sanders said. Mr. Sanders looked more intently now at the surrounding country in this first cold light of morning. "Now I have got a place. Until now I've been moving around a piece of Boston. Now I've got a place." Mr. Sanders motioned at Sant. "You can leave your horse at my place."

"Thank you," Sant said.

"Por nada," Mr. Sanders said. "For nothing." They both sat silently watching the morning break.

"What do you know about women?" Mr. Sanders said.

"Very little," Sant said. "Next to nothing."

497

"Where are you going?"

"To join the bronc people," Sant said.

"Where are you going?"

"Cortez. They're in Cortez now, the bronc people. They've got a show in Cortez. The rodeo's in Cortez."

Mr. Sanders watched the fire. "And you know nothing about women?"

"Next to nothing," Sant said.

"Me neither," Mr. Sanders said.

Mr. Sanders fished around in back of where he was sitting until he came up with a box. "You know what this is, son?"

"It's an adobe form. You make adobes with it," Sant said watching.

"The Indians just gave it to me," Mr. Sanders said. "I thought it was very nice of them."

"Yes, it was," Sant said, waiting for his chance to leave politely, watching the gathering day.

Mr. Sanders laid down the adobe form gently. "You say you know very little about women. How little?"

"Very little," Sant said.

"Do you know what an affair means?"

"No, but I guess Alastair does," Sant said.

"You mean Alastair's had an affair?"

"Very little," Sant said.

Mr. Sanders looked impatient and tapped the box again. "An affair means intercourse."

"I've had that with a lot of people," Sant said.

"You still don't understand," the missionary said. Now he looked at the sky in thought. *"Edesh il,"* he said.

"With Indian girls, yes," Sant said. "Does that count?"

"Yes, it does," Mr. Sanders said. "Was it good?"

"Very good," Sant said.

"Good," Mr. Sanders said definitely. "I'm not a dirty old man. I only want the facts of life. I'm a child. I am the child in this conversation. I know the words but not the facts, not the acts. I was a puritan, now I've seen my first morning and there's nothing dirty about it. There was something dirty about the puritan but

498

there's nothing dirty about the morning." Mr. Sanders picked up the box, the adobe form, and examined it carefully. "I'm sorry you had to be the first person to come along, that I had to pick on you."

"That's perfectly all right, Mr. Sanders," Sant said.

"I'm sorry that the puritans had dirty minds."

"That's perfectly all right, Mr. Sanders." Sant wanted to get on with his own business but he could not resist the last statement. "What do you mean, had?"

"Why did we make God a dirty-minded puritan?" the minister said.

"That's very strong language," Sant said.

"Well, eighteen years in a cast is a long time. I would use stronger language but I'm very poorly equipped with my New England background. But I'm sorry you had to happen along."

"I tell you it's perfectly all right, Mr. Sanders. And I came here on purpose to leave my horse."

"Okay," Mr. Sanders said.

"I presume you'll take him back to the ranch."

"I presume I will. Yes, of course," Mr. Sanders said.

"If you'll turn him loose he'll go back by himself."

"No, he might roll off the saddle. I'll take him back. I promise," Mr. Sanders said. "What ever happened to Alastair Benjamin?"

"He's going to get educated."

"Worse things could happen. Did Alastair ever resolve what happened to him?"

"Yes. And he thinks things will stop happening now."

"Why? Has he forgiven everything that happened?"

"No. He killed my father's horse."

"Well." Mr. Sanders thought about this a moment, watching the last fire. "Yes. That's all right. That could stop the chain letter of killing people. That could finish the old West, the old revenge."

"Alastair feels so," Sant said.

"Well, if he feels it, doesn't presume it, I guess he will make it now."

"I believe he will," Sant said. "I think maybe we can all make it now. But I want to ask you about my trip."

"What about it?"

"You think I'll make it as a bronc rider?"

"No."

Sant looked around at everything and then back to Mr. Sanders.

"Because if you don't know, who the hell does?" Mr. Sanders said.

"Well," Sant said, "you see, I've arranged it so I've got no way to come back. I've got only enough money to get there."

"You could crawl back," Mr. Sanders said.

"I don't think I can," Sant said.

They both rose now as though at a signal, as though the sun, finally appearing now after faking a long false dawn, as though this were a signal, they both got up. Mr. Sanders rose, still holding the adobe form the Indians had given him, and Sant went over and unloosed the cowhide suitcase from the horse.

"I'll flag down the Cortez Greyhound on La Ventana Hill."

"You do that," Mr. Sanders said. "And never a borrower or a lender be, and above all things, don't get killed."

Sant winked at Mr. Sanders.

"By the time you get back I will have learned to walk," Mr. Sanders said. "I have got to learn everything from the beginning as though I were born yesterday."

"I hope it works out," Sant said.

"It will be exciting," Mr. Sanders said.

"I mean, I hope the Indians don't hand you a line," Sant said, slinging the cowhide suitcase over his shoulder.

"Well, I guess if anybody can hand out a line I can."

"True," Sant said, striding off.

Well, Mr. Sanders thought, watching Sant move off, he didn't have to be quite so definite. By God, I was never that bad.

Mr. Sanders sat down now to figure out how the adobe forms worked, to figure out how you make bricks without straw.

FOURTEEN   Sant found the suitcase much heavier than
a suitcase should be and the Tex-Tan saddle, which weighed about
thirty-eight pounds, much heavier than thirty-eight pounds ever
was. Altogether he was lugging one hundred pounds, give or take
ten, up and down every rise and fall in the slightly tilted escarpment that was the eleven miles that stood between the mission and
the road. Every now and then, actually at the top of each rise, he
would set it all down and sit on top of it and contemplate the things
that Spinoza thought about but from a more "really" point of view.
That is, how far are the stars and how near the moon; but mostly
he wondered if someone had moved the highway farther over toward Santa Fe. Take during antelope season, he had hunted this
distance easy in this same country but then he was carrying a 1903
Springfield with a Weaver four-power scope which would add up
to maybe nine and one half pounds. It's funny what a difference
ninety pounds makes. It's funny, too, what a difference it makes
whether you're riding a horse or not.

I hope they never do away with the horse permanent, even
if it's only kept for what its ancestors have done. Never in the
history of affairs have so little done so much for so few—or something like that. Anyway let us start a Save the Horse Week. Anyway
let us try to make it on this last hill. There she is—the highway.
Now, that's nice, they haven't moved it so awfully much at that.

Sant pulled down to the highway, dragging the suitcase until
he reached the edge of the pavement and a lemita bush, then he
put the saddle on top of the suitcase and then sat on this as though

he were horsed and watched down the highway for the Greyhound.

I wonder if the Greyhound will stop. I wonder if there's a regulation against it or I wonder if maybe the Greyhound just can't be bothered to stop for one little stove-in cowpuncher. I wonder if maybe the Greyhound will think I'm a highwayman and not stop. I wonder if the Greyhound will think I'm a gun-slinger. No, the Greyhound will think I'm too little to be a gun-slinger. Still, Billy the Kid was very little too. I wonder what I could do to make myself look less like Billy the Kid. I wonder what Alastair would do. I wonder what Lemaitre would do. I must see if Lemaitre will keep his promise. I wonder if he will remember me and what he promised. I wonder what I could do to make myself look less like Billy the Kid to the Greyhound.

While Sant was figuring this the Greyhound loomed suddenly on a rise and bore down quickly, began to roar and run to make a hill, then jammed on all the air and came to a stop just in front of Sant. Sant lugged all his stuff on board and then asked the Greyhound man how much.

"Where you going?"

"Cortez."

The driver looked around at the country. "How far north are we from the Tinian Trading Post turnoff?"

"About twenty-five miles," Sant said.

The driver thought a while. "That makes it eight ninety," the driver said.

Sant paid him and got his change and the Greyhound started off but Sant didn't move.

I've got two twenty-dollar bills and a ten here in my wallet I can't account for. My father could have slipped one of them in and maybe it was the missionary who gave me the other. But how could he have done it? Maybe it was Alastair. Do they think I won't make it out there?

He looked for some place to toss the money and then noticed that people were staring so he put it in his wallet and looked for a place to sit. He pulled his stuff down the aisle looking for a familiar face but he didn't see one till he got to where the Indians sit in the back. Indians always sit in the back. Now he saw a

502

Navaho he had seen around and he threw up his stuff on the rack above Tso.

"Where you going, Tso?"

"Anyplace."

"No place in particular?"

"That's right."

"Well, you're sure to end up some place." Sant sat alongside Tso.

"That's right."

"You know you're going north."

"Thanks," Tso said.

"Do you want to go north?"

"I wanted to go north since I was this high."

"What will you do when you get there?"

"I'll go see the Hurry-down boys," Tso said.

"Who are they?"

"They're always on the trader's radio," Tso said. "They want everybody to hurry down to their place. They want us all to hurry down while there's a few days left. Ever since I was this high the Hurry-down boys have wanted me to hurry down. Now that I'm going north I guess maybe while I'm there I'll hurry down to the Hurry-down boys."

"Don't forget the Tomorrow-for-sure boys."

"Hurry down tonight, tomorrow for sure. No, I won't forget them."

"You got to give them all a chance at an Indian who's sold his sheep."

"They're all equal."

"What do they charge, Tso, to carry an Indian?"

"Interest? Six per cent a month."

"That's seventy-two per cent. The Hurry-down boys are charging you Indians seventy-two per cent a year."

"The Tomorrow-for-sure boys too?"

"I guess so."

"Well," Tso said, putting a brown finger on his high cheekbone, "is that good or bad? Does it mean the season is open or closed on Indians?"

"Open season."

"Well."

"I guess the season will always be open on Indians," Sant said.

"Well." Tso seemed to be thinking about this as he adjusted the band around his head, but he wasn't. "Where you going, Santo?"

"I'm going to work the shows."

"What does the rodeo pay?"

"Casey Tibbs already made two hundred thousand dollars. I guess Lemaitre made about half a million in his lifetime."

"Is Lemaitre dead?"

"No, he's just resting up."

"I heard he was dead."

"No."

"I heard he got hurt so bad so many times he's about dead."

"No. He's just resting up."

"I hear he can't walk."

"How do you know that?"

"We got Indian guys who follow the shows, get all those show magazines."

"The rodeo magazines don't know what they're talking about. I take them too. It's just an opinion."

"They say he's paralyzed."

"You get paralyzed, well, you can get unparalyzed. Everything else is an opinion."

"They say Lemaitre will never ride again."

Sant got up and walked to the front of the bus and looked out at everything going by up there and then he walked to the back of the bus and checked everything that was going by back there. Then he returned to his seat and looked over at Tso.

"He will ride again okay," Sant said and he looked over at Tso. "He'll ride again okay," Sant said. But the Indian was asleep.

Everyone except the sleeping Tso got out to rest when the Greyhound made a rest stop in Cuba. There was one Zia Indian, though, that got out but he didn't rest inside the hotel. He just walked around to the rear of the Greyhound and when Sant passed him on his way to the hotel the Zia was directing his stream of rest

504

against the hood of the rear Greyhound engine, which cooled the Greyhound and made it steam nicely.

Inside the adobe and log hotel a lot of Indians, Navaho and Apache mostly, were sitting on the circular steps of the sunken fireplace, not speaking. Piñon logs were burning in the fireplace and gave the adobes and the hanging Indian rugs a good smell. Mr. Boker, the ancient Anglo owner of the hotel who knew everything that happened, was better than a newspaper for Indian Country because he didn't consider the advertisers, didn't consider the outside world.

"Well, Mr. Bowman," Mr. Boker said. "You going someplace?"

It was the first time Mr. Boker, anyone, had called him Mr. Bowman. It felt all right.

"Cortez maybe," Mr. Boker said, looking at the posters on the wall.

"Yes," Sant said.

"Well, I hope you do all right."

Sant nodded. Mr. Boker looked at him carefully. "You hear your friend Lemaitre got his?" Sant nodded again. Mr. Boker took out a pencil and began making meaningless scratches on the register.

"Right here in New Mexico. He starts right here in Indian Country, goes all over the world, presidents and kings, New York City, New York, Paris, France, a million dollars, and he come right back here where he started to get it."

"Where was it, Mr. Boker?"

"Ratón."

"Is it bad?"

"Murder." Mr. Boker paused. "The horse murdered him. An older horse too. Tricked him off and then stomped him to death. They couldn't pull the horse off."

"Is he dead?"

"The papers say he's alive. They call it living."

"Was it a local horse?"

"Local horse, local boy," Mr. Boker said. "Imagine Lemaitre starting right here in Indian Country, goes all over the world,

presidents and kings, New York City, New York, Paris, France, a
million dollars, and he comes right back here to get it. It's as
though the horse were waiting—waiting to claim him for where
he belonged. Waiting to trap him here finally where he belonged.
Indian Country," Mr. Boker said.

"Was it the horse—? Was it from Coyote?"

"Yes," Mr. Boker said. "Local horse, local boy. Wait!"

"I can't keep them waiting," Sant said.

Back in the Greyhound Tso woke up as they went over the
Cuba bridge. "Are we there yet?" Tso said.

"Where?"

"Anyplace."

"No, we're not anyplace yet," Sant said.

Tso watched up at the ceiling of the Greyhound and Sant
watched out at the land. It had snowed in the high country during
the night and everything above seven thousand feet was scintillant
in the early sun. The deer now would work their way down to the
mesas where they would try to make it during the long winter. The
elk would move down too, but not so far. They would drift down
to where the big mountain benched below the sharp-white granite
tailings, where the mountain spread out before it fell off into the
long valleys. You could make a living there.

"Tell me, Tso," Sant said, "what ever happened to Afraid Of
His Own Horses and The Other Indian?"

"They drifted out of the country."

"Oh?"

"Yes. One of those government projects to relocate the Indians in Chicago."

"Then they're gone?"

"No. They drifted back again."

"Wasn't the feed any good?"

"The feed was okay but it wasn't here."

"Wasn't the money any good?"

"The money was okay but it wasn't here."

"How you going to please an Indian?"

"Leave him alone," Tso said.

Sant looked out again at the land. The highway leaves the

foothills of the Jemez Mountains not too far north of Cuba and now they were in the wide flat country of the Jicarilla Apaches. The Jicarilla Apaches work sheep mostly and they live in tents. Now the tents had all been folded and the Apaches were working their way back to the Indian agency at Dulce where the railhead was, where the government was, where the Department of the Interior was handing things out. You could make a kind of living there.

"Tso, have you seen this year's new horses?"

"They're too big," Tso said.

"Then they've brought the new horses into the agency?"

"Yes," Tso said. "And they're too big."

"It's about time the Indians got some new breeding horses."

"Maybe," Tso said. "But these are too big."

"The Indians' horses are too small."

"Maybe," Tso said. "But the new ones are too big."

"You mean they can't make a living here?"

"Not the both of us," Tso said.

"They burn too much hay?"

"And they won't fit our stalls," Tso said.

"I didn't think the Indians had stalls. I thought they left them under the trees."

"They won't fit under the trees."

"Or between them either?"

"That's right," Tso said.

"Then the horse trader will have a bad year."

"I hope so," Tso said. "Santo, do you have to go out and break your neck in this rodeo business?"

"It's what I want to do."

"Break your neck?"

"I want to work the shows."

"But you're going to see Lemaitre first?"

"I'm going to get off in Durango to say hello."

"I'll settle for that," Tso said.

"You must think he's in awfully bad shape."

"I know. I know what big horses can do," Tso said.

When Sant got off the Greyhound at Durango, Tso was again asleep. The first thing Sant had to do was find where Lemaitre was. The man at the Greyhound depot in a green eyeshade told him to try the Saddle and Bar.

"Where's that?" Sant asked.

"Mountain and Fourth. You're at Mountain now."

Sant went up Mountain Street toward Fourth feeling trapped. Durango, Colorado, lies within the deep fold of a mountain. The business section of town is on faulted rock. It moves slightly each year. But it was not this that Sant sensed. He sensed the oppression of the overwhelming mountains. It was a place where you couldn't see out. You had the feeling, without ever being able to see the horizon, that this was it, that if you couldn't see it you would never feel it, never know anything more than Durango. He had had the same feeling at the bottom of deep canyons on hunting trips. City people must have it always. It makes no difference that people are close. You are lost.

Sant watched into the windows of all the cowboys' shops, making a note of all the things he needed to buy at the Tomorrow-for-sure, at all the cowboy Hurry-down boys, shops he passed, all the important, unessential things a small triumph in the ring could buy. If Durango were not so mountained in there'd be other dreams of other worlds a small triumph could buy.

Now he was at the Saddle and Bar and he pushed in before reflection. Any thinking at this point he knew would send him back to the Greyhound, so Sant pushed in and found himself in a nice, clean, simple room with a very long bar with saddles for stools. Down where the bar made a short L there were two cowboy gentlemen watching the bartender, who was watching the ceiling. It was very quiet.

"I would like to see Lemaitre," Sant said.

The bartender walked down to the middle of the bar where Sant was and leaned over and slightly down and said, "Lemaitre's not seeing anybody." The bartender had a crew haircut.

"It will do him good to see people," Sant said.

The bartender only smiled.

"Tell him it's a friend."

The bartender smiled again and winked down at the two cowboy gentlemen at the L of the bar. They made no sign. Their expressions were frozen. They were very fancy-dressed. They must have had many triumphs.

Sant unfolded his arms. "Tell Lemaitre it's me. Tell him it's Sant." Sant removed his wallet and passed a card up to the bartender. "Sant Bowman."

The bartender went into the back of the room and then into another room through a solid oak door with a horseshoe on it. Sant folded his arms again and waited. The two cowboy gentlemen watched Sant with the same expression they had used in watching the bartender—nothing.

The bartender came back wearing a surprised look.

"Lemaitre will see you," he said.

Sant went through the oak door and the two cowboy gentlemen looked at each other very surprised.

Lemaitre was seated, propped up, in the dealer's chair in front of a huge and round green card table. The only light came from a fierce shaded lamp that spotted the table and nothing more. Sant was in the room a whole minute before he saw anything more of Lemaitre than his hands.

"Sit down," Lemaitre said.

Sant took a seat at the opposite of Lemaitre's at the concentric green stark table with the hard light.

"What is it?"

"Do you remember that?" Sant said, pointing to the worn white card that lay on the green table in front of Lemaitre.

"I remember," Lemaitre said.

Now Sant saw more than Lemaitre's hands and it was awfully bad.

"You promised."

"I know," Lemaitre said. "But—"

"But you promised," Sant said.

"To let you break your neck?"

"That's what I want to do."

"Break your neck?"

"I want to work the shows."

Lemaitre didn't say anything.

"Was it fun?" Sant said.

Lemaitre made a cigarette with the fingers of one hand without moving his arm, flashing an emerald as big and bright as an arena. He dipped his head and snatched the cigarette quickly, then swung back his hard, taut, pained face and blew out perfect blue rings, concealing the jewels of Ophir, the memories. Some distant night, a knight—a knight dying, felled in Samarkand.

"Yes," Lemaitre said.

"Was it worth it?"

"Yes," Lemaitre said. Lemaitre paused and drummed his fingers on the green table, the only movement he seemed able to make. "But don't tell anyone." He paused again. "They'll lock us up."

Twenty minutes later Sant got on the same bus. He had expected he would have to take the next bus but the same bus was still there. So was Tso.

"Tell me this, Santo," Tso said. "What did he say?"

"Well, he said they'd lock us up."

"And they should too," Tso said. "What did he say next?"

"Lots of things," Sant said. Sant watched the bus try to make its way through a town that was caught in the crevice of a mountain.

"You can tell me all," Tso said. "I'm just another Indian."

"You mean no one would believe you?"

"That's right."

"Tso, it was very funny."

"Funny?"

"Tragic."

"Tragic?"

"It was weird."

"Funny, tragic, or weird?"

"Weird is the closest."

"Then it was weird."

"Not exactly. He's got dignity. *Dignidad*."

"How did he get that?"

"He was born with it, I guess."

"Is it good or bad?"

"Very good, Tso."

"I never went to school."

"It's when a man can take a funny tragic weird situation and still remain a man. A guy can be smashed and remain a man."

"Is that dignity?"

"Yes."

"You seem very sure of yourself."

"I'm sure of myself now."

The bus began to wind through a Mormon town now. You can always tell a Mormon town by its name. It has no style. When a Western town has a name like Farmington, Fruitland, Kirtland, Peachblossom, it's probably Mormon. Names without style. Not Aztec or Cuba or Tierra Amarilla. These names have style and were not named by Mormons. You can tell by the buildings too. If they're kiln-fired red brick, two stories, ugly, with the ring of money, you just went through Peachton. Capulin is slash and adobe, falling down in style. Coyote, too, it has style.

"He's still got style."

"Who?"

"Lemaitre."

"This town hasn't, I guess."

"What was it?"

"Blockton."

"No, it hasn't at all."

"What good is style if he's falling to pieces?"

"Oh, it helps an awful lot," Sant said.

"It got him into it."

"And it will get him out."

"How will it get him out?"

"It will, that's all," Sant said.

They rode up now a rich green valley with snow above them on both sides.

"I wish you would think it over, Santo," Tso said.

Sant was quite a while watching out the window at the high snow on both sides before he said, "No. It's all right now, Tso."

On the outskirts of Cortez they both got off the Greyhound

where all the cars were turning off the asphalt into the very dusty road that led to the rodeo ring.

"Why did you get off here, Tso?"

"This place looks as good as any place."

"Do you want to carry the saddle?"

"Sure, I'll carry the saddle."

They lugged all their stuff down the road that sprayed them with a continuous fall of dust from a steady line of cars going toward the stadium. Sant carried the cowhide suitcase and about every hundred yards he would sit on the suitcase and Tso on the saddle and rest.

"I've ridden at Dulce and Windowrock," Tso said. "It wouldn't hurt me to try again."

Sant spat out some of the dust and looked over toward a sign that was beginning to appear through the haze.

"I see they got Jim Shoulders riding here."

"Who's he?" Tso said from his seat on the saddle.

"He'll be the next all-around champion."

"What about you?"

"It takes time, Tso."

"You know what George Washington said?"

"I don't care, Tso. Let's get moving."

They got started down the road on the last lap.

"This George Washington's an Indian," Tso said.

"All right, what did George Washington say?"

"George Washington said the next champion would be you."

"I'm sure George Washington meant well," Sant said.

They went around to the back of the stadium where the riders and the animals made their entrances and their exits, where they had all the stock corralled and penned and tied. Tso minded their gear while Sant looked around for someone who seemed important. He found a man finally who wore a tight, small, snap-brim black hat and a bow tie.

"I've come to ride," Sant said.

"I've got enough troubles," the man said.

"I've come from Lemaitre."

512

"I told you I have enough troubles," the man said and he continued to hurry, disappearing into the dust and horses.

Sant went back and sat next to Tso.

"Did I ever tell you what Thomas Jefferson said?" Tso said.

"I don't care," Sant said.

"This Thomas Jefferson was an Indian. He's dead now."

"I know Jefferson's dead," Sant said.

"He got killed in a rodeo in Salt Lake," Tso said. "They brought him back to Penesteja before he died. Do you know what his farewell address was?"

"I don't care."

"What Jefferson had to say?"

"Someone probably wrote it for him," Sant said.

They both looked quite sad and both quite forlorn there, sitting in the middle of all that motion alone and gathering dust. Especially Sant, the white boy, seemed to show more dust than the red boy, who seemed to take dust better, and Sant seemed to look much more forlorn than the forlorn Indian. As a matter of fact, the Indian was taking their defeat fine. They sat in the middle of all the commotion and falling dust for maybe twenty minutes watching out quietly but not seeing anything. They came but they could not see, and Sant was wondering whether anything would be conquered now.

"Who the hell wants to ride?"

"Me," Sant said. It was the man in the snap-brim black hat towering above where they sat.

"Who the hell said you could ride?"

Sant undid his wallet and passed up a letter.

"Lemaitre," the man said. "It's his writing all right." The man tapped his knuckles with the letter. "I'm short of riders." There was a lifting of the dust now and they could see two cowboys lying recumbent. "Are you ready?"

"Yes," Sant said.

"The other boy?" the producer said.

"No. No, I don't think so," Tso said.

"You came to ride, didn't you? Didn't he?" the producer said to Sant.

"Yes, but—"

"Yes, but what?"

"Yes, but he's a Jeffersonian."

"I've got enough trouble," the producer said. "You, boy, follow me."

"Yes, sir," Sant said.

"What's the name?"

"Sant's the name. Sant Bowman."

"Never heard of you."

"You will," Sant said.

"I've got too much trouble already," the producer said. "Are you ready."

"Is the horse ready?"

"Of course."

"Then we shouldn't keep him waiting."

"Oh, God!"

"It wouldn't be polite," Sant said.

They were moving through the darkness of the passageway that ran under the stadium toward the arena.

"I've got a tough one for you to go with," the producer said up ahead in the darkness. "I can't help it."

"A local horse?" Sant said.

"Yes. A local bastard."

"Local horse, local boy," Sant said.

There was a sudden burst of violent daylight as they hit the arena and a sudden burst of awful noise.

As they made the turn for the chutes the producer grabbed a telephone from a red box marked "Private" while Sant knelt down in the sand of the arena to buckle on spurs.

"I got one," the producer said into the phone while watching up at the press and announcer's box that jutted out high over the stadium. "I got a Sant Bowman next on Flamethrower. Where from?" He spoke down to Sant.

"Indian Country," Sant said. "Same town as Lemaitre." Sant made the final tie on his spurs. "Say I'm riding for Lemaitre."

The producer repeated this on the phone and Sant trotted across the big open stretch that had suddenly gone very quiet and tight. He made a quick leap to the top of the chute that was ready and held Flamethrower. Flamethrower was a big black and trembling to go.

"What are we waiting for?" Sant told the restraining cowboys. "Let him go!" and Sant dropped onto the horse, twisting the points of the razor spurs behind the shoulders of Flamethrower and as deep as he could sink them. The horse shot out. Flamethrower was both a shooter and a twister. He took several long shooting leaps and then went into a sudden twist. It never failed. It failed this time.

"Always go relaxed," Lemaitre had said across the poker table. "Become part of the horse."

Flamethrower was a shooter and a twister and a scraper. When he failed at all else he would tear you off against the boards.

"Let him know who's the master." This was not Lemaitre. Sant had figured this himself.

Sant shoved in the spurs brutally as far as they would go and the horse went into a tight spin. This was not the technique of Flamethrower, only an agonized attempt to kill the thing on his back and, like everything without technique, it failed and the horse began to give out. Sant gave it one more final spur that set the horse gyrating straight up, and then Flamethrower was finished. When Sant realized the horse was about to fail he gauged the distance between himself and the catching horse and rider but instead of allowing the catcher to help him he placed his hand on the rump of the catching horse behind the rider and vaulted over the horse and came up running on his own feet alongside the running horses. He gradually came down to a trot and pulled up at the railing. He still had on his hat.

The stadium was making an awfully loud noise now. At the other end of the stadium the producer was on the phone again.

"Sant Bowman," he said.

Now above all of the noise of the stadium the loud-speakers were trying to say "Sant Bowman."

Outside, the waiting Indian could hear it too. He kicked into the dirt and then looked up into the wide sky.

"That's our boy," Tso said. "Sant Bowman."

515

FIFTEEN Alastair Benjamin had been gone now from the Circle Heart three weeks. He had been sent away by the Bowmans to be educated. They missed him very much. The house was empty. The house was quiet. The whole ranch was without sound. This morning they had gotten a letter from Big Sant's brother, to whose house Alastair had been sent to stay while he got educated. The letter had said that Alastair had disappeared. They had gotten a note from Alastair one week before this saying, "This is not an education, it's a war. This is not a school, it's a battlefield."

"We should not have sent him there," Millie Sant said. "There were other places to send him. We could have sent him to Albuquerque."

"We had to send him where we could afford to send him."

"Did it have to be there?"

"That's where my brother was."

"Will he come back now?" Millie Sant was sewing on a sock but now she quit. "Will he come back here now?"

Big Sant was on his knees putting a log on the fire. "I don't know," he said.

"Well, isn't there something we can do?"

"We're doing it," Sant said, and he dropped the log, cracking the hearth, making the only noise that had been made in the house for a long while now.

"Now I've done it."

"It can be fixed," Millie said.

"We'll see."

516

"He'll come back."

"We'll wait and see," Sant said and he began to wrestle again with the log that had broken the hearth.

When he got off the train Alastair Benjamin had decided to walk the very long distance from Albuquerque to the Circle Heart. It was not that he had run out of money. He had that much money. It was that he had run out of something else. He had run out of the ability to go home. Like any soldier in defeat he would have liked it very much if there were a long interval of nothing. If several years would run by quickly so that he might find something that he had lost before he went home. The thing was, he had reckoned, the thing was that no one had ever let on there was a war. The war that must have been on since forever had always been concealed from him in this corner of New Mexico. They had always kept this war very carefully undeclared here.

Now he topped a rise in the cattle trail he was following and there was Cuba, the heart of the country where war was undeclared.

He had been rolled back now, he figured, almost five hundred miles and it was a very queer thing that all along the way everyone along the way seemed to sense they were talking to, or watching, a man who was running from something. He seemed to be carrying his body, moving along, like a flag of failure.

He was careful to follow the cattle trails that went around Cuba. He did not want to meet anyone from there now. He did not want to see anyone yet. Maybe he had been hoping he would have walked it off before he got to Cuba. That he would have forgotten what happened and it would not show like a flag when he got this close to the Circle Heart.

The mountains around the town looked black now and much taller than when he went away only a few weeks ago. The snow always makes pines look black at a distance and the snow always makes mountains appear taller, but something else made them look tall and black now, and he wanted it to go away but you cannot remove a mountain by thinking about it. You could not remove the black trees either, the pines in funeral rows that led up into the clouds.

517

The animals were not talking, coming up from Albuquerque— the wild animals he had seen while walking the back trails that ran along the west base of the Jemez. He had met quite a few animals that seemed surprised to have met him. "Very surprised to meet you." They had all bounded away quickly. The animals were not talking. Take another time, take an ordinary time, take the average time when the hunting season is well over, and you walk this much distance in the back trails of the slippery Jemez and you will find animals to watch while they watch back. They ordinarily have a healthy animal curiosity about such a weird animal as you. But today the animals were not talking. It is a comfort to have a rapport with animals without the report of a gun. It is a comfort when you are very lonely to see wild animals who seem very lonely too. Alastair wiped his cheek in the immemorial gesture of sweating something out and sat on a juniper log and watched the sky whiz by, the white clouds moving rapidly across the all blue. Animals should not have feared him. Alastair broke a twig. You can always marry a Pueblo girl, but then you can't live in the pueblo. They have a law against it. No whites are allowed to live in the pueblo even if they marry a Pueblo girl. We Pueblos have got a restrictive covenant leveled against everyone but us. This includes any shade of white at all, including black. The Navahos are okay and Apaches are okay too and maybe Utes. With Utes it never came up. But everyone else can take a flying jerk for themselves. This is not nice but it is the American the Pueblos have been taught to talk and I suppose it's nice that a Pueblo can talk at all, bad words and restrictive covenants falling where they may.

Alastair stood up and dismissed all this. After all, he was not trying to crash a pueblo and he had not either been trying to crash the white world. He did not want to sleep with their white daughters. He only wanted a small education.

Alastair stretched his arms and tried to think more relevantly. A relevant way of thinking would be to decide where he was going. It's always nice to know where you are going even when you are retreating. But of course the main thing about a retreat is that you are going nowhere. The very name must derive from nowhere.

Obviously he was making toward the Circle Heart, but a while ago he was making toward Cuba and he had gone around that. Now would he go around the Circle Heart?

"I don't know," he thought aloud, and he lifted the suitcase to his shoulder.

He could have gone around Cuba by swinging west out into the Indian Country, the trading-post country, the flat country, the country without water that they gave to the Indians. The chances were he would meet someone out there who was not interested. The trader would be trading and the Indians would be resting against the work their wives were doing. But instead of swinging west he had swung east. With luck he would meet no one at all on the trails that ran along the foothills of the vast mountain. The trail that had been crowded before with the footmarks of the wild animals, the doglike paws of the coyote and the smaller same paw of the fox and the cloven foot of the deer and the same larger foot of the elk now gave way to the mark of cattle and the hoofprints of the shod horse. He was close to civilization. He was on the ranchers' trail where the cattlemen brought down their stock through the Señorito cut. There was danger now of meeting someone.

"What passes, friend?"

Someone, Arturo Cipriano de Godoy, had ridden up soundlessly from the rear and waited now alongside.

"*Ninguno novedad,*" Alastair said, putting down his load. "Nothing much. What with you?"

"Nothing at all," Arturo said.

"How is the cattle business?"

"Terrible, you wouldn't believe it." Arturo used this phrase interchangeably with "Wonderful, you wouldn't believe it." Not depending on business, which was unimportant, but on his morale.

"Remember we met in the Valle Grande," Arturo said.

"We met in the Great Valley," Alastair agreed.

"New Mexico Cattle and Timber Keep Out."

"Yeah."

Arturo made a cigarette. "I decided to let them go broke on

519

their own." Arturo finished the cigarette with a flourish and applied the sharp end to his mouth.

God, he's dressed gaudy, Alastair thought.

"In the Great Valley you were with Sant Bowman." Arturo lit the cigarette with a large match. "You were very young, *muy joven,* and I lied to you because I did not want him to get killed. He wanted me to remember that he had ridden with Lemaitre and I remembered it well but I lied to him because I did not want him to go out there to some other place and get killed. There is nothing more dangerous than the broncs and I thought I would save his life. But I was wrong. He has made a life."

"Made a life?"

"Yes. Don't you read the papers? He is defeating all the broncos. Yesterday he had an enormous success in Salt Lake. Back there in the Great Valley I didn't know what big courage he had."

"I've got to be going, Arturo."

"Some of us have it and some of us don't."

"I've got to be going, Arturo." Arturo had worked his huge brown horse across the path.

"Some of us talk big and some of us act."

"I've got to be going, Arturo."

"Some of us use big words to hide the word coward."

Alastair reached up to grab the bit of the big brown, and the horse wheeled, frightened and violent, striking Alastair as it rose and pivoted. Alastair felt his own suitcase hit him as he fell down through the white aspens into the ravine. He lay there a while, not moving, listening to the Spanish horse and Spanish rider thunder off. They both seemed out of control.

Alastair got to a sitting position now and felt the blood, gentle and warm, running down his face. He wiped it off with a sock that hung on an aspen twig and then began with crippled motions to gather all his stuff and put it back in the suitcase. When he finished he sat on the suitcase a minute, not thinking, before he started the stiff climb back to the path. Thinking does not help much. You have got to do something. You've got to climb back up. It's a long way up. It's strange how easy it is to come down. You come down without thinking and I guess that's the best way up. Thinking doesn't help much I guess, unless, as Santo would say, you are climbing at one and the same time.

From where the Bowmans sat they could watch all of the vast Jemez, clear almost from Coyote to San Ysidro. They were sitting on a leather couch made from Angus steer hides, black matching the black-and-white Indian rugs, and looking out through a five-by-five window encased with heavy timbers in the three-foot-thick adobe and mud wall which gave out on the Jemez, turning all red now. Even the long white reaches of the thick-with-snow Mimbres Haunch that ran all the way down into the Vacas were burning in the thin bright shadow of a dying New Mexican day.

"A wild Spaniard runs through here on a wild horse and wants us to believe he saw Alastair on the Jemez." Big Sant shook his head. "I tell you, Millie, what would Alastair be doing wandering the mountains when, to reach the Circle Heart, he only has to follow down the Señorito cut?"

"It's getting dark," Millie said. "He could have hit a box canyon. Hunters get lost on the Jemez every year. There's not a year goes by a hunter doesn't die on the mountain, and it's getting dark now."

"City hunters," Sant said. "No, we got a message from a wild horse, wild rider. Arturo has not been quite right in the head since he got fired by the Keep Out outfit."

"I think Alastair's lost," she said.

The sun went out. Darkness comes suddenly in northern New Mexico. Now all the light was gone on the Jemez. The lighted stage of mountain they were watching through the wide proscenium of mud bricks darkened quickly until there was nothing to watch. Just before this happened they could see the dark groves of pine following the deepest folds of the mountains lighted all the way to thirteen thousand feet. This display was different from any other. Each night something new happens because the mountain is always lighted differently. Each night the mountain gives a different performance.

"I will put some candles in the window," Millie said. "Because Alastair is lost up there." And she went about doing it.

"Wild horse, wild rider," Sant said. "You can't trust Arturo since he got fired by the Keep Out. Did you ever see such an outfit like he wears?"

"He wore that outfit when he still had his senses." She lit the candles. "It's his *pasó por aquí* outfit. With that outfit everyone will know that Arturo Lucero Cipriano de Godoy passed here."

"They certainly will. Do you think your candles will do any good?"

"Certainly."

Sant knew that the dim yellow light of the candles could not be seen for more than a few hundred yards but he said nothing. There was nothing to watch now but the candles and neither had anything to say so they watched the faint yellowness glistening against the blackness of the window and said nothing for a long while.

"You presume—you think Alastair got himself purposely lost?"

Sant touched his chin in the faint light. "Why? Why would he do that?"

"Yes," Millie said. "Why?"

And they both were silent again as they looked out at the silent and dark mountain.

"Why?"

Why is anything? Why is everything so much the exact total of what we do? Why is so much black and white and why is it the mountain always says things so well, silently, and we in a whole lifetime of brilliance only manage to level the wrong gun at the wrong bird in the wrong season? And on the wrong mountain, Sant thought. Why? The candles flickered as though they might go out, and Sant and Millie Sant wondered as Alastair wandered the mountain they had just seen go out.

"Maybe," Big Sant said, "Alastair could not quite make it back here now."

"The snow?"

"No. Something else."

"What else?"

"Unfinished business," Big Sant said. "I think before he

522

comes home he's got something to finish. Something we'd want him to finish. Something he wants to finish."

"In our country?"

"No. Another country," Big Sant said.

Alastair made it back up the steep aspen-clogged ravine into which he had fallen but when he reached the path it was black dark. Alastair felt his way quickly along the path in the matching darkness. He did not like the feeling, the knowledge now, that the path was slanting up the mountain. The strategy would be to turn down the next ravine and hope that it would follow all the way down and not box, not dead-end into a high ridge of stone, not slant sideways finally instead of down, not lose him up there in the beginning snow. The ravine he was in boxed quickly and it took him a good hour to climb up the saddle of the ridge in the now thickening snow. Just one more mistake like that, lugging the suitcase with absolutely numbed hands up the sheer frozen cliffs in a now hard-driving snow, just one more impossible climb to reach the saddle of one more barrier ridge, and he knew he would have had it. He would then know exactly why he had come home. He would have come home to do something he could have done just as nicely where he had been. Where had he been? He had been involved in some nightmare. He put down the suitcase and clung to a thin pine with his arms to keep the wind from toppling him down the cliff below, the cliff that began two feet from his left foot. He had been to the outside world and now he was near home. It does not seem that nightmares are restricted to the outside world. I bet nightmares can be had in heaven. I bet that all of the natives here who swear they know this mountain as well as they know the palm of their rear end could, in a sudden snow, find themselves, or someone else could find them here, frozen to a pine tree on the next bright morning. Where? No, they would find him in some frozen attitude of movement. He would keep moving here, walking, climbing, crawling, over every mountain between here and the Pacific Ocean. *Pasó por aquí,* Alastair Benjamin on his march to the sea.

Alastair had not been many hours on his march to the Pacific

Ocean when he topped out over a crest of wind-screaming oak and saw ahead and below a fire swirling high into the night. He might have lost his mind now. He was not certain he was seeing a true fire. But you might as well walk toward an imagined fire, toward a crazy glare. A crazy fire is better than none. He approached the fire now, down a barren hogback ridge. The fire still swerved up madly, and now, out of the clearing where the fire was, there rushed a bearded madman. Mad because he grabbed Alastair and carried him like a board toward the warm fire. Mad because he was white and did not belong to a mob. But mostly mad because Alastair had fixed in his mind a march to the sea. *Pasó por aquí,* Alastair Benjamin on his march to the sea.

The white man who was all alone—imagine a white man all alone—had him wrapped in blankets and was bringing some feeling into his arms and legs by rubbing and now forced something to his mouth.

"Drink this."

Something scalding went down through his insides and he saw the fire again. It was not such a big fire now and the man was not so mad. It was Mr. Sanders, the missionary.

"Try to move those arms and legs," Mr. Sanders said.

Alastair sat up and Mr. Sanders screwed back the bottle top. "Something I got from Mr. Peersall."

"I saw them go by up there," Alastair said.

"Who?"

"The bank robbers. The ones that got killed that robbed that bank in Durango. They went by. They were lost."

"Where?"

"On the mountain in the blizzard when I was holding onto the pine tree."

"You had a hallucination," Mr. Sanders said, unscrewing the bottle again.

"Is it a hallucination that we all seem bent on killing each other off?"

"No, that's not a hallucination," and the former divine took a quick drink.

"And I saw the death of Sant."

524

"How was he killed?"

"In an arena. They bore him out like a Roman hero."

"That was a hallucination again." Mr. Sanders tapped the bottle. "He's still going very big."

"But they wanted him killed."

"Now you're talking normally again." Mr. Sanders touched back Alastair with ruthless kindness. "Keep those blankets on."

"And I got to figuring," Alastair said, "that you can't solve anything by killing a man's horse."

"Yes, you can if you think you can," Mr. Sanders said.

"Aren't you practicing religion any more, Mr. Sanders?"

"Yes, I'm practicing it now," Mr. Sanders said. They sat there hushed for a while with only Mr. Sanders' tapping on the bottle audible.

"There are still some hunters lost on the mountain," Mr. Sanders said. "I'll keep this fire going until they report in someplace. It could be they've topped down over the Los Alamos side and are already saved."

"Saved?"

"For this season," Mr. Sanders said. Mr. Sanders looked into the darkness. "Starting next month I'll be able to ship three carloads of adobes a month to Boston."

"Why Boston?"

"They got me into this and now I'll get them out."

"It doesn't make sense," Alastair said, and then his eyes seemed to awaken. "Let's not be bitter, men," he said. The former divine remained quiet, seeming to be studying something out in the darkness where the adobes must be stacked.

"I pay the Indians a dollar ten cents an hour and I've organized them into a baseball team. They like to call themselves the Braves. The Boston Braves. And who am I to raise my hand against them?"

"Who indeed," Alastair said. "But then you're not practicing religion any more?"

"You can take the missionary out of the mission but you can never take the mission out of the missionary. But you can't storm the Indians and you can't ambush them."

"Can't ambush them?"

"No," the missionary said. "You've just got to quietly appear in their midst as just another Indian."

"Just another Indian?"

"That's right," Mr. Sanders said thoughtfully. "But we'd better be getting you home."

"Home?"

"Yes. I gather you're running away back home."

"Not exactly. I was on the mountain."

"Well, you can stay the night here and sleep on it," Mr. Sanders said.

Alastair rose at the first false dawn to a world of adobes. The adobes seemed stacked high and wide to infinity. Actually they covered four good acres in the middle of the sage. Mr. Sanders had built another mesa alongside a true mesa.

"Boy, you certainly can sell adobes, Mr. Sanders," Alastair said over *tortillas* and eggs.

"No," Mr. Sanders said, "but, by God, those Indians certainly can make them."

They quickly finished their *tortillas* and eggs and Alastair studied Mr. Sanders' mesa of adobes again.

"Actually I sell two truckloads a day in Albuquerque and one in Gallup," the former divine said. "The rest I'm stockpiling for Boston."

"You certainly are going to get even with Boston."

"Yes, I am," Mr. Sanders said. "Did you figure out last night where you're going?"

"I figure I better see Mr. Peersall first," Alastair said.

"Mr. Peersall is dying." Mr. Sanders rubbed his chin. "I don't think he can help."

"I think he gave Sant something."

"Mr. Peersall is dying," Mr. Sanders said. "I don't think he has anything more to give."

"Well, *vamos a ver.* We'll see," Alastair said, rising in a corridor of adobes and raising his suitcase to his shoulder. Alastair put out his free hand. "I hope your Braves have luck."

526

"They'll need it," Mr. Sanders said, rising and taking the hand and then releasing it. "They play lousy ball."

"They'll improve with age," Alastair said, walking away through the brick maze.

"We'll all hope" were Mr. Sanders' final words.

When Alastair got to Mr. Peersall's log shack Mr. Peersall was sitting in the sun tending his weeds. The weeds of the West are cactus and sage and such as this that grow violently everywhere where there's not much water. An Anglo and a Spanish-American will usually plant a rug of lawn and surround the rug with things that won't grow here—tame roses and other Eastern exotics that do not want to live in a strange country. Mr. Peersall cheated somewhat. He brought up lower desert plants to his high altitude in spite of the experts.

"They told me she would not bloom at seven thousand feet," Mr. Peersall said, pointing his Sharps at a red-blooming cholla. The three-foot plant seemed one of nature's experiments with abstract art. It was composed of sausage-shaped balloons stuck together at weird and odd angles with extruding needle and razor points to discourage the critics—and the cattle that want to eat it up, Alastair thought.

"But I've come about something important," Alastair said.

"Sit down," Mr. Peersall said, pointing to a rock. "Now, what is so important about your running away back home? I ran away from my first battle—my first fracas is a better word. You're very aware of words, aren't you, son?"

"I was, but I found they're not much help."

"Well anyway, I ran. Like you, I ran."

"You believe everything Arturo de Godoy says?"

"I believe this. I recognize the symptoms."

"Well, you don't know what it was like."

"Maybe I don't then."

"You mean I should have stayed in there?"

"I don't know who else is going to fight your battles, son."

Mr. Peersall used his Sharps rifle like a hoe and from his sitting position nurtured a small bur sage.

"I guess you think you're quite a sage yourself," Alastair said.

"I've learned a good deal." Mr. Peersall had gotten so good he could turn over a leaf or twist a bloom toward him with the forward sight of his Sharps.

"Well, I guess you gave Sant something."

"I didn't give Sant anything. I guess maybe that's what I learned, that you can't give anyone anything. You maybe can hint at what they've got that they can try to give to others. And that's about all."

"What have I got to give, Mr. Peersall?"

Mr. Peersall had sharpened the back edge of his forward sight so that he could yank off dead wood with it. He did this now to a failing twig and then put the gun across his knees and looked at Alastair.

"Nothing," Mr. Peersall said. "I suppose you've got nothing to give yet." Mr. Peersall removed the bolt.

"But you gave Sant something."

After Mr. Peersall removed the bolt he looked through the bore.

"When you talked, Sant would always listen. I was always thinking of bigger things."

"This thing's a better plow now than it is a weapon," Mr. Peersall said, watching through the bore.

"Am I boring you, Mr. Peersall?"

"No, son. It's simply that Sant—well—" Mr. Peersall paused.

"You mean I've got to do it alone?"

"Yes."

"But the missionary used to say no man is an island."

"Well, he is."

"You think he just got that from another preacher?"

"Yes."

"We've got to go it all alone?"

"Yes, we do."

Alastair thought about this while Mr. Peersall waited patiently. Then Alastair thought some more, watching down the valley, rubbing his neck and looking down the long valley.

"So you want me to go back to where I just came from. Do

you know where my father came from, Mr. Peersall? You knew him as the Gran Negrito."

"That's how we knew him."

"Well, I found out from Big Sant's brother where my father came from before he came here and stole the land from the Indians—drove them out."

"Yes?"

"Well, my father was driven out from down there. 'A smart book nigger.' They drove him out down there and when he got up here he did the only thing he knew, the only way he'd been taught —he drove an Indian out."

"Yes," Mr. Peersall said. "And now they've got you afraid. They've got you afraid to claim the education that belongs rightly to you. The circle has begun all over again just when the Circle Heart thought they had it stopped."

"Belongs rightly to me?" Alastair rubbed his chin in thought about this. "Belongs rightly to me?" Alastair looked straight at Mr. Peersall. "Well, I guess we can't let the curse start all over again just when we thought we had it stopped with Mr. Sant's horse." Alastair picked up some stones and stared down valley. "Well, I don't know but I think I'm ready to try it again, back where it all began—catch it back there before it gets loose again, Mr. Peersall."

"All alone?"

"Yes."

"Well, it will take me a little time to get ready," Mr. Peersall said.

"But you just said—"

"I said we had to go it alone, but I didn't say there would not be others. Other fools to join the battle too. And old fools as well," Mr. Peersall said.

"Don't try to get up, Mr. Peersall."

"I *am* up," Mr. Peersall said, leaning on his stick of gun. "Now, in which direction does the smoke of battle lie?" Mr. Peersall exchanged the stick to the other hand. "Where's the trouble, son?"

After one hour of scurrying around they both got started off together. Mr. Peersall took the lead and set a very good pace. Then Mr. Peersall ended all at once. He faltered, stumbled only half a minute, and then went down all at once like a shot deer. He had time to mumble in Alastair's arms that he had had only a few more days left to tend the weeds in his garden, that he had been only waiting around for the last weeks for an opportunity to quit the world like this—to quit it going somewhere and to be taken from behind and quickly. Like a fallen wild deer, to go quickly.

Alastair found a kind of plaque for the tomb of gathered rocks that he put the body under—large field stones to protect the body from wild animals. When Mr. Peersall had faltered and fallen they had just topped the crest of the Piedras fault, a jutting Mesaverde formation that outcrops coal. After Alastair finished with the grave of Mr. Peersall he pried a piece of coal from a pure-black ledge and wrote these words on the flat sandstone concretion plaque:

WILLIAM PEERSALL. WHO WILL MOURN HIM?

Alastair tried again on another concretion.

PASO POR AQUI BLUE-EYED BILLY PEERSALL ON HIS WAY TO JOIN BATTLE. 186- —1958. IN BELOVED MEMORY.
ALASTAIR P. BENJAMIN.

Alastair got up from his job and began moving down. The P.—the Peersall—Alastair had just added to his own name on the plaque made him feel that he had a great deal in back of him now to go on—a great deal, he guessed, to kind of live up to. Indian Country. A wild free country. *El pais de los broncos*. The country of the Bronc People.

Alastair picked up the pace, passed beneath a tremulous aspen shattered brilliant with light, walked beside a mesa brushed in fiery cloud, then descended into a long valley that led to another country.

Portrait of an Artist with
Twenty-six Horses

ONE

WITH EYES WET and huge the deer watched;
the young man watched back. The youth was crouching
over a spring as though talking to the ground, the water
pluming up bright through his turquoise-ringed hand,
then eddying black in the bottomless whorl it had sculptured neat and sharp in the orange rock. The rock retreated
to a blue then again to an almost chrome yellow at the
foot of the deer. The deer was coy, hesitant and grease-
wood-camouflaged excepting the eyes that watched, limpid
and wild. The young man called Twenty-six Horses made
a sweeping arc, raising his ringed hand from the spring. The
deer wheeled and fled noiselessly in the soft looping light,
and now all around, above and far beyond where the youth
crouched at the spring, the earth was on fire in summer

solstice with calm beauty from a long beginning day; the sky was on fire too and the spring water tossing down the arroyo was ablaze. The long Sangre de Cristo range to the east had not fully caught; soon it would catch; not long after, in maybe half an hour, the world would be all alight.

Now there arose from down, far down the arroyo, seeming from the earth itself, an awful cry, terrible and sibilant, rising to a wavering and plaintive call; but not a plea, not even an anguish, more a demand, peremptory and sharp before it faded, died back into the earth from which it had arisen. Here, directly here above this sea of sage and straight up in the hard blue New Mexican sky, a huge buzzard hurtled and wheeled toward the planet earth—monstrous and swift.

Twenty-six Horses rose from his crouch over the spring and slung on a pack roll. Before the world was all alight he would have to go some distance. He could waste no more time talking to the ground. The earth he heard had made a noise but it was no sound he knew, no language spoken, a distant anguish from below, addressed to no one and everyone. Now he heard the cry again, human, but it was still nothing he knew, more a harsh shadow than a sound, more a single note of retreat, a mellifluous oboe ending the world. But he could waste no more time talking to the ground.

To the east, but still at a height of 7500 feet, ran the village of Coyote. It was a collection of adobe shacks on the long wobble of asphalt going someplace else. A dark and handsome Navajo woman, the mother of Twenty-six Horses, disguised in the costume of city people, was stirring outside a restaurant labeled The Queen of Coyote

534

City. She was hanging a sign that began "REAL LIVE WHITE PEOPLE." The Queen of Coyote City finished hanging the sign and went back inside. All of the sign said: REAL LIVE WHITE PEOPLE IN THEIR NATIVE COSTUMES DOING NATIVE WHITE DANCES.

"I don't think that's funny," James said. James was her husband and the father of Twenty-six Horses, but he never came around the restaurant much. James had a rough and weathered face and he had a purple ribbon which knotted his hair in back of his head, a custom that the young Navajos had abandoned.

"You can't compete with people by imitating their ways." James sat at the end of the counter and looked unhappy.

The Queen of Coyote City and the mother of Twenty-six Horses had begun her restaurant by excluding Navajos. That didn't seem to do much good so she refused service to Christians, Jews, Seventh Day Adventists, Apaches and people from Albuquerque in about that order. Two weeks ago she had put up a sign: WE RESERVE THE RIGHT TO REFUSE SERVICE TO EVERYBODY. That didn't seem to help business either.

"They don't put up those signs to help business," James had said. "They put them up because they're sick."

"I'm not sick. I want to make an extra buck," The Queen of Coyote City said.

"An Indian who wants to make an extra buck is sick," James said.

"I should go back to those hogans a hundred miles from nowhere and die?"

"And live," James said. "An Indian dies in the city."

"An Indian can learn to live here," she said. "Soon the hogans will not be a hundred miles from nowhere. What you going to do then?"

"Come back home and we'll figure it out."

"I got a business," she said.

A customer came in and James went back to looking unhappy sitting at the end of the counter.

"That's a good sign you got out there," the white man said, and then he ordered a hamburger. "Did you ever see the sign: Your Face Is Honest but We Can't Put It in the Cash Register?"

The Queen of Coyote City was frying the hamburger and she didn't hear the white man so the white man turned to James and said, "Did you ever see that sign: Women Don't— Oh, you're an Indian," the white man said. "I was trying to explain a gag to an Indian," the white man hollered back to The Queen of Coyote City. James got up and walked out.

When The Queen of Coyote City brought the white man his hamburger the white man said, "He doesn't speak any English I hope. I hope I didn't hurt his feelings."

"Not much," the mother of Twenty-six Horses said.

"You let Indians in here?"

"That was my husband."

"I'm sorry," the white man said, putting down the hamburger gently and examining it carefully. "You look white. You talk white. I hope I didn't hurt your feelings."

"Not much," she said. "I'm trying to make a buck."

"Oh," the man said relaxing. "And you will, too." He bit into the hamburger and swallowed a mouthful. "You've got what it takes," he said.

On the outside of The Queen of Coyote City Café, Ike Woodstock was standing near the steps talking to Rudy Gutierrez about uranium, and Evelyn and Tap Patman were standing in front of their service station beneath a sign that said GULF PRIDE MOTOR OIL and between the STOP-NOX and BE KIND TO YOUR ENGINE signs. Across the street Arpacio Montoyo was talking to the priest beneath a CLEAN REST ROOMS sign. They were talking about how many angels could stand on the head of a pin.

James looked around for his horse but a car was standing where he had left it. Mr. Patman came over and said, "I put your horse around back, James. Out here it's liable to get hit."

"What did you tell James, Tappy?"

"That I moved his horse. Liable to get hit."

"It got hit."

"By what?"

"That sixty-one Olds."

"It's a sixty-two."

"When I can't tell a sixty-one from a sixty-two!"

Evelyn and Tap Patman walked over and identified the car as a '61 with '62 hubcaps.

"There now, what is our world coming to?"

James saw at a glance that the horse was favoring his left hind leg. He examined the leg carefully, going down on one knee while the horse swung his great neck to examine James's head. The leg was not too bad, nothing broken, but James would have to lead him home, twenty miles through the back country. Not too bad.

James had ridden into Coyote every week now for the last four months and at first he thought it would not be too bad. She would come home. Each time he was certain she would come home. Both of them had been certain too that their boy would come home, come home the first time, and he had—slightly damaged, but he had come home. He had stood around the hogan a few hours, afraid to sit down on the rugs as though the bugs would get him. He kept standing in the middle of the hogan as though looking around the wall for windows, around the rough room for chairs and tables, a radio, a bed that stood on legs, a familiar white face. And then he was gone for Gallup. Outside the hogan he had taken a big deep breath, stuck his head back inside the hogan heavy with smoke, repeated something pleasant in English and then was gone for Gallup. He left, the mother of Twenty-six Horses said, because an artist can make a living there. "We got to make a living for him here," she said.

When James's wife came to Coyote the first thing she did was refuse to speak Navajo. She leased the restaurant next to the Gulf Station from Tap Patman—sixty-eight dollars a month plus five percent of the gross—hired four Spanish-Americans, fired a slovenly Anglo cook who was supposed to come with the place, stippled the rest rooms with neon, hung out a lot of white man's signs and concentrated on not speaking Navajo.

"You speak Navajo and soon the place is full of Indians. Indians haven't any money and they come in and play chants on the jukebox, look under things, ask what the signs mean, bring their wives in to show off their jewelry, make big talk about the kids their wives stack on cradle boards along the counter, make jokes about the Whites— and they haven't any money. I left the reservation, I came to Coyote to open a restaurant, because it is a white man's world and you have to make it the white man's way. Anything else is talking to the ground. The white man came, saw, stole; the Indian smiled. Okay, make a joke, but the white man is Chee Dodge. Even if the white man wanted to stop pushing us under the table, and sometimes he wants to stop, he can't. All right, so our boy came home the first time. What is he? A weaver. All right, he is the best weaver on the Checkerboard Area. All right, on the reservation too. All right, he is what the trader calls him, an artist. But listen, James The Man With Twenty-six Horses, by the time it takes our boy to set his loom, listen, the white man has a thousand rugs. Listen, the white man has a machine. All right, the trader says the machine has the white man but that's Indian talk. The white man has a machine. Maybe he can't stop it, Man With Twenty-six Horses, but he has a machine. Any way else is talking to the ground. It's a white world."

The Man With Twenty-six Horses had walked in front of his horse to the edge of Coyote. Now no one would call him James. It was all right to call him James. James was a good machine name, that's the way he made his mark in the government book. The Man With Twenty-six Horses was the name the People had given him when he had twenty-six horses. Now he had twenty-four, twenty-five, sometimes—once—he had thirty-four, but when they gave him the name he had twenty-six horses. That was a good name. It meant he was a big Chee Dodge. Actually his son's name was The Son Of The Man With Twenty-six Horses. The Indians named his wife The Queen of Coyote City when she moved into town and refused to speak

Navajo. It was not a good name; it meant she was worse than an Apache—a Pueblo almost.

James had got the horse now to the top of the hill that overlooked Coyote. So they said his boy was an artist. Artist. What does their calling him an artist exactly mean? They meant nice by it he could tell by the tone, but it certainly had something to do with not being able to sell what you do. That was clear. It had something to do with not wanting to sell, too. The white trader at Nargheezi, George Bowman, had gotten the boy an order from a nice tribe of Whites called the Masons. The Masons had even drawn the picture for him and left a ring with the same picture on it. Orders would follow from other nice tribes, the Kiwanis, the Elks, who wanted to help. They pay big. No, the boy had said, I do not feel it. James felt the Mason ring and he could feel it. Here, the boy had said, touching just below his chest.

So an artist is a person who feels things just below his chest. All right, but he must feel something below that in his stomach too. Maybe that was why the boy left. Maybe his squaw had been right. Maybe his son wasn't looking around the hogan for a TV set or a bed with legs. Maybe the outside had gotten him accustomed to three meals a day. Maybe an artist on the outside can make three meals a day.

"Can an artist on the outside make three meals a day?"

James had come upon a fat white man leaning on the side of his car on Coyote Hill and he figured he might as well ask him as another.

"No," the fat white man said. "Tell me, what town is that?"

540

James told him it was Coyote.

"You're an Indian, aren't you?"

"Yes," James said.

"Well, I can tell you I paid ten thousand dollars for this car," the man said. "It's got nearly four hundred horses. I've been busting to tell somebody but on the outside you're not supposed to tell anybody. I can tell an Indian I guess."

"Ten thousand dollars! I didn't know it was possible," James said. "Four hundred horses?"

"Since last month it's been possible," the man said. "The Caddie people did it. Tell me, are you going to sell some paintings on the outside?"

"No, my boy," James said.

"That's too bad," the man said. "If there's anything I can do to help, outside of buying one—?"

"I guess not," James said.

"Buying a picture would make it worse," the man said. "He'd only go through life under the delusion that he'd sell another."

"Maybe," James said.

"Everyone," the man said, "has been sane at one time or another in his life. He wants to create something, then he sees the way the world is going and decides he better go with it."

"Not even three meals a day?"

"Three meals a day is a lot of meals to give a man who will not go along."

Now that the man had made his speech James pulled on his horse.

"Wait," the man said. "I can tell this to an Indian.

Keep your boy here in the world. Don't let him get out there on the big white reservation. Out there we think we're on the outside looking in, but it's just the opposite; we're on the inside looking out. We are out there seeing who can be the biggest failure and we got a system of checking. We can always tell who wins. It's the man with the biggest car, the biggest house." The man leaning against the car hesitated. "Did you ever see a child's drawing?" the man said. "We have all got it and we all give it up."

The man had made two speeches now and James felt he could move on without being rude. He did, going on down the Coyote Hill pulling the horse after him.

The man continued leaning against the car watching the flowing sun behind the purple rocks. He was one of the many vice-presidents of an oil company that was working the Navajo Country. He always stopped where he could enjoy a beautiful sight like this. Now he got back in the car and started her up. It was good to sound off. It wasn't often you got a chance. It wasn't often you could find someone like an Indian. And it would never get around. No one of his friends would ever suspect for a moment that he was sane.

James continued on down the hill and wondered how a man like that was permitted off the big reservation. It can only be that, like many others, he never tells anyone.

But the news about his boy was bad. I wonder how you go about looking for someone out there? James had seen a television play in Arpacio Montoyo's bar. He had made his can of beer last to the end. It was about a girl who left

542

home and the ending was that you should buy this soap. The man kept holding the soap up and hollering about the soap. It made a kind of exciting ending and probably a lot of sense too, if you grew up on the big reservation. The play might have been a solution to his problem. Certainly, James thought, if buying the soap of the man who was hollering would get his boy home he would buy all that man's soap the trader had. James was very worried about his own son, The Son Of The Man With Twenty-six Horses.

James had reached the bottom of the north side of the Coyote Hill and started up the slight rise that had the only aspen grove at this altitude that anyone had ever heard of. The aspen leaves had ceased budding out and were waiting to fly into Ben Helpnell's porch when the wind blew. Ben Helpnell was working on his new Monkey Ward pump beneath his abandoned windmill. The new pump was the latest thing, later even than the piston pump. It worked on the theory that "it is easier to push water than it is to pull it. It is a hermetically sealed, self-contained unit, and without any fuss or bother or expensive plumbers or electricians, you just drop the whole thing in the well." Ben had done that yesterday and since, he had been looking for it.

Ben saw James coming up and said, "I'm well shut of the damn thing." Ben was a horse and cattle trader and he saw now that James's horse was limping. But he must work around to the subject gradually.

"I'm just as well shut of it," he repeated, but his heart had gone out of it. It was in James's horse.

Suspecting a trade, James said nothing.

"Your wife's got some good signs on her restaurant," Ben said.

James did not want to talk about that.

"I ain't seen you by for a time," Ben said.

"My boy is gone," James said.

Ben studied over this for a while, looking down the well, then he looked over at the horse but his heart was no longer in the horse. It was involved now with James's grief.

"I tell you what, James," Ben said, studying the well again. "Take a horse, leave it off when you come back through."

Another day James would not have taken the horse first off. He would have hunched down, snapping sticks with his fingers and drawing pictures on the ground until they made a trade. It would have taken four or five hours, and Ben's wife might have changed clothes two or three times to impress the Indian. And James would finger his turquoise jewelry from the saddlebags to impress everyone and Ben would do a dance he picked up in Chihuahua that impressed even horses—all this to relieve the tension of the dealing when the excitement or the danger of closing the transaction became too real.

But now James's grief was in all their hearts and Mary would not want to change clothes three times, Ben would find no joy to do his dance nor James to show his jewelry. They would have only stumbled through a city deal with nothing to show for it except the grieving that James had brought.

"Take the blaze mare," Ben Helpnell said.

James transferred his saddle to the little blaze in the

544

near corral while Ben Helpnell continued to stare down the well to figure the meaning of a lost pump.

"I should of tooken it back," he said. And finally standing up, "It's nothing against Monkey Ward. I must of done something wrong."

"You chunked it down the well," Mary said from where she watched behind a screen door.

"It said in the book—" and then Ben ceased, knowing that women will even contradict the book, and walked over to James at the corral.

James was weaving the cinch strap through its final gyrations before pulling good.

"Lots of horse," Ben Helpnell said. James swung into the saddle and started off leading his own horse with a rope in his dark right hand.

"When you get home he could be there," Ben Helpnell said.

"He could be there," James agreed, but he was not heard. He was already going up the road that led past the sawdust-rotting remains of Girt Maxey's sawmill.

Two hours later he was going up the trail that led past the Bowman trading post, a long, low log and adobe building with a small blue hogan huddled nearby, and then on up to the top of the piñon- and pine-studded mesa that looked out on his own hogan below. His hogan was smoking.

"He could be there."

No. He would shut his eyes and take another look. When he opened his eyes again a thin stream of blue cedar smoke still poured a fine column straight up from the middle of the conical hogan. He touched the horse and both of his horses flew off the mesa bearing straight down at the hogan with the long blue smoke.

No. This was not good. It would be pushing his luck too fast. He swung his horse in a great circle around the hogan and then stopped. Both of his horses were breathing hard and the long blue cedar smoke still came out of the hogan. Now a quiet wind started and bent the long blue smoke until it curled heavy around James and the two horses. It was real smoke. But it would not do to go straight at the hogan. If luck was there it might be surprised away. Perhaps to call gently? James made a cup of his hands and called the boy's name toward the smoking hogan. Nothing happened but he did not want anything to happen so suddenly. He patted the blaze horse and looked back at his own horse at the end of the string.

"He could be there."

Now James cupped his dark hands again and called just a little more this time but still gently. And then he dropped his hands and watched quietly, careful that no move was made to disturb anything. The horses were very quiet too, as a hand pushed back the sheep flap at the hogan door and his boy stepped outside.

James waved. The horses began to move and the boy held both hands above his head.

The boy and James ate meat, coffee and bread for a long time. When they had finished the meat and coffee and bread they had some more coffee with James not saying much, not wanting to push any of his luck away. The boy had been talking all along at a good pace without saying anything but watching the heavy wooden loom on which he had begun to weave a picture. Finally he stopped and said after a big pause and in English, "There now, what's the world coming to when an artist won't settle for twenty-six horses and a Navajo loom?"

"No English spoken here," a voice said in Navajo. "The trader saw the smoke and sent a message that someone was home. I took down my signs in my restaurant and threw away the key. I finished with the restaurant. What's the world coming to when an Indian won't let the Whites fight each other?"

James did not think it was time to recognize his luck but he looked around the round room and recognized everything in it that was all gone yesterday and all here now. And outside too there were twenty-six horses.

"What's wrong with talking to the ground?"

This, James knew, was his wife called Married To The Man With Twenty-six Horses talking. It was not The Queen of Coyote City.

"What's wrong," the woman repeated, "with talking to the ground? The Navajo People talked to the ground before the white man came. We could do worse than to be with our own people even when we are talking to the ground."

James knew now that Married To The Man With Twenty-six Horses and The Son Of Twenty-six Horses had all made their speech and were waiting for him to say the end. The end, he knew, must have some style. It must not be the endless speeches of the white man. It must have style. It should be about three words. It should be in the best manner of the People. He looked over at the powerfully simple mountains and rocks, abstracted in quiet

547

beauty, woven on the big loom. And yet the People seemed to be worried about talking to the ground.

"The earth understands," The Man With Twenty-six Horses said gently for the end.

TWO

GEORGE BOWMAN, the white trader, had a long hard slant face that appeared whiter than it was in Indian Country, and more credulous too than could survive in Indian Country, so that you had to watch hard before you saw that somber clouds in running shadows arrived and departed over the broad slant plains of his face beneath a hand that worked his jaw in constant annoyed outrage at the Indians. Now he looked steadily at the Indian and said slowly, "I've got a premonition."

"Sell it," Rabbit Stockings said. "You're pretty good at that."

"A premonition that something's happened."

The Indian, angelic-faced and innocent, sat down on the bench next to the trader and they both watched out over the wide country. "The arroyos are deep, but when you've been an Indian as long as I have—"

"Cut it out, Rabbit Stockings."

"I was only trying to confuse."

"I just thought—"

"Don't," Rabbit Stockings said. "That's what started it all."

"Thinking?"

"Yes."

"Progress?"

"Don't you agree?"

"Of course I agree," the trader said. "I never argue with an Indian. I'm just telling you that pretty soon we are going to look for Ring."

"I've tried that."

"Don't give me any of that Indian talk. I mean look for him now."

"You're saying that he's lost."

"Now he is."

"And that he hasn't been."

"That's Indian talk again," George Bowman said, watching other Indians enter the post. "My son Ring is strange, that's all."

"Does that mean funny?"

"No, it means strange," the trader said. "Will you give me a hand with these Indians?"

"We're not going to look?"

"Later."

"Business first?"

"It's not that," George Bowman said, moving away. "It's

simply that I never—I don't—I never had any idea where to begin."

The sound that Twenty-six Horses had heard at the spring in the beginning day, the voice the young Indian traveling called Twenty-six Horses had heard was a cry from the dark bottom of the canyon. Ring Bowman, the son of the white trader, was caught in quicksand where the vast arroyo deepened and shadowed, where no one ever went.

"I went. No, my horse Luto went. Why?"

The big sky of morning, bright and swift and empty, began on the face of Ring and it seemed to Ring that this long beginning day must be another cunning stroke by the enemy, for it had been announced by his father this morning that this was the day of the summer solstice—another trial shared now by a black horse beneath a blue window, a vacant sky, bright and huge and empty.

He had, three years ago, lying beneath the long eaves of the trading post, tried to arrest time by stopping a cloud, holding it fixed with his eye, not allowing it to move, in his inner eye transfixing it for long seconds, but then it joined battalions of clouds, commingled and was lost so that his medicine, his hex, would not serve even a pastime to pass this endless day. But there was all of a short, long life. There was the bird on the mesa, a poet on the moon, a small blue hogan and that portrait above me by Twenty-six Horses. Can you figure out that painting, Luto? Or what Nice Hands held? I'll tell tales. I've got battalions too.

Two hours before, Ring Bowman had begun to cross the turbid arroyo stream on his great black horse and the animal had refused. Ring got off and tried to pull the horse, but Luto stood rooted on the edge. Ring did not notice that he himself was going down, he did not realize it was impossible to move until the rein broke and the horse moved back to firmer ground. "All right," Ring called to the horse. "You're a strange horse, Luto, a strange horse. I never bought you, Luto, you just showed up. Why, Luto? What made you choose me?" But the young man was already descending like a slow elevator. It was not until the quicksand reached his chest that Ring realized that Luto might go forever unpunished. What had the horse done? Behaved sensibly, that's all. Why doesn't he go back to the corral with his empty saddle so they will know that something has happened to me? Because I did not train him; but no one could train Luto. That's the last time I'll own a black horse. Yes, it may be the last time you'll even think about it.

Ring splashed the water with his arms as it flowed around him on its way to the Rio Grande. The sun was fire hot on his face but he had to lie back in this position to present as much body surface as he could to the fluid sand. At times he could relieve his burning face with his wet hands but very quickly because he had to use them as oars, swinging them gently to stay alive.

And then he thought, yes, Twenty-six Horses is an artist. Maybe that explains everything. When he passed me up just now he was coming back from the outside world. I hope he did well. He left the reservation a few months ago and now he's coming back and when he stopped to drink he did not hear me because he's got a problem. Maybe his problem is how to spend all the money and all the fame he made out there. No, I don't think that's the problem.

There's one—not a problem, but there's one of Twenty-six Horses' paintings up there where the cliff slants down. Maybe it's supposed to be something but it's only the suggestion of something. The running bones of something. I don't think anyone would understand. It's done in quick strokes of red ocher against the white sandstone—spattered blood. This water is killing me. I remember when Twenty-six Horses painted the picture he said it was for anyone dying here. And I said, not me. Maybe for the medicine man. Remember that old fraud, that old tricker, that mad medicine man with eleven wives who died above here? Remember him? Noble and great and wonderful and still a hypocrite and still noble and still a son of a bitch and still great. Listen, Luto horse, we got to start, we got to start to find out why I'm marooned here, why I am alone. If we can figure the way I got in we can maybe figure the way out. You remember the old fraud, that wonderful big man. Jesus, boy, you were there. Twenty-six Horses was there. There could be a clue there. Oh God, everyone was there. That's when it first started, the day the medicine man died, the day you discovered that people stop, the day everything really began, the day Tomas Tomas went down to the spring at the bottom of the canyon and came back dying.

Tomas Tomas, behind his round, cracked face and shallow-set, quick lizard eyes, was one hundred years old, or he

553

was chasing one hundred, or one hundred was chasing him, no one knew, least of all Tomas Tomas. But early one morning nine months ago Tomas Tomas had gone down to the water hole in the arroyo and had come back dying.

It was cold for a September in New Mexico. The old Indian medicine man, Tomas Tomas, would never see another, warm or cold, and now he knew he would never see the end of this diamond-hard and dove-blue New Mexican day—he sat dreaming in front of his log and mud conical hogan; he sat dreaming that the white man never happened; he sat dreaming death never came.

His hogan was on a small bald rise beneath a fantastically purple butte. His home had not always been here; he had lived all around the Nation called Navajo Country. He got his name, Tomas Tomas—he had others—while a small boy and before he went to the United States government concentration camp at Bosque Redondo, when they rounded up all the Navajos during the last century to protect the settlers that were stealing Navajo land. That's the way most of the Navajos saw it, but Tomas Tomas thought and said very quietly otherwise. "We stole it," he said, "from the Anasazi People who built those cliff houses up there and the big houses in Chaco Canyon. Killed most of them. At least the Whites, at least they let us live to see the bug and iron bird arrive." Automobiles and airplanes he meant. "The tin bugs were not male nor female. We got under the big bugs and had a look. We know now they are made by people, like you make an axe or like you make a picture, or make noise, not like you make children. Although there is a clan among the Navajos who live

554

mostly around Shiprock, the Red Stick Clan, who believe that children are sent by the child spirit and making love accomplishes nothing, or very little. That it's just funny, or fun. Exercise," Tomas Tomas added, not wanting to leave out some purpose to love-making entirely or altogether.

The other Navajo Indians had been expecting Tomas Tomas to die off and on for a hundred years. He was always being mortally wounded by a person or a horse and this day when he came back dying was not the first time that it had come to pass that Tomas Tomas was dead. The initiation rites into manhood of the Navajos in the Checkerboard Area kill an Indian boy so that he may be reborn again, reborn again even with a different name. The boy is killed in pantomime with a stone axe by the medicine man. You die and are reborn again by the medicine man, then all of the dream time is played out and the boy is shown all the magic that no woman knows, and in this manner and rite the boy dies and is reborn again as a man. But only after he has slept all naked in the night with a young girl, and that's important. If this is not done the boy is not reborn again and can never die. He is condemned to live forever in some form. Tomas Tomas did this very repeatedly and successfully and on his first night became a man among men, and now he could die.

When a Navajo dies he can have all his wives again in heaven. There is prosperity, joy and wit and wisdom in Navajo heaven. Navajo heaven is not a solemn gray high refuse heap for humble failures.

So when Tomas Tomas came back to his hogan dying he was not sweating cold in fear of judgement. He had been judged and found with much wisdom, many wives, three hogans all in giant circles, and enough turquoise and silver to founder a horse, enough pride to have killed four plundering Whites, enough magic in his medicine bag to confound the universe and a long, never quite out of fashion turkey bonnet festooned with bright parrot so long it dragged the ground.

One of his wives must catch a horse, Tomas Tomas thought with his arms grabbing his chest to contain the awful pain of death—also to keep the death from spreading before he got to the mountain. A Checker Clan Navajo must die on the mountain, that's what mountains are made for. Mountains are for dying.

Tomas Tomas knelt down painfully in front of the Pendleton, yellow-striped blanket door of the hogan and made a cigarette; it was time to be calm and appraising. Death comes very seldom to a man and it must be taken with dignity and carefulness. It must be arranged, if it can be arranged, so that there is no messiness, no blood, no dreaming, no raving out loud so that everything is undone that was properly done in your life.

That's why the ascent of the mountain is so valuable at the end. Occupied instead of preoccupied. Gaining ever new heights in spreading splendor, not the visit of fading visitors between coming-together walls.

What was that? A horse. It was nice of the white man to send his horse. A black horse, but still a horse. Maybe he didn't send it. Maybe the horse just got away. Well, it's a fine horse for the occasion. That is, I always thought he'd make a good mountain horse. Luto—I think that's the name they call him. But some call him that black son of a bitch. That's a nice name too. Pretty name. "Come here, Pretty Name," Tomas Tomas called in White language to the white man's black horse. "Come here, you pretty black Luto son of a bitch," Tomas Tomas called softly.

Now the medicine man finished making the cigarette and licked the paper carefully, eyeing the horse and seeing into and beyond the old familiar place. The Navajo Nation had been an old familiar place for a long time. Tomas Tomas did not want to go to any unknown place, but things were beginning to repeat themselves here. The medicine man had traveled a great deal in his practice, into foreign countries as far as Arizona. His wives did not like travel, or they did not like horses, it was difficult to tell which. Someone should find out if the Whites' women would travel if they had to travel on a horse. What am I doing dreaming about such rubbish when I've got to be on the mountain to see another world before the sun goes down? I never saw such an accommodating horse, come all this way here to help me keep the appointment. I never saw the hogans and the piñons and the fires all around them and the great yellow rocks above them so fixed before. It is as though it will never change, like a drawing on the rock or a picture on a pot. It seems stopped forever now in this last time. Only she moves.

"Where do you go, Tomas Tomas?" one of his wives said.

"To the mountain now."

"Why, Tomas Tomas?"

"For the last time."

"It's growing cold up there."

"That's all right."

"Soon it will be winter."

"Yes, I know."

"Whose horse?"

"It belongs to a White."

"It's black."

"Yes, but it belongs to a White with red hair and blue eyes."

"And a green nose."

"The Whites are funny enough without making anything up."

"Look, Tomas Tomas," this one of his wives continued. She was Spotted Calf with a soft face and curling a huge orange blanket around her youth. "Look, why go to the mountain?"

"Because it's best."

"Why not here in comfort?"

"Because comfort is not best. The mountain is best."

"I will bring you some soup before you start."

"No, I just want to look from here at everything. Here is for the last time, which is like the first time. The last time and the first time are really the only time we ever see anything."

"Shall I get the others?"

"No. I remember them."

"Shall I get your magic, Tomas Tomas?"

"No, I leave my magic to the world. Wouldn't it be something to arrive there with my medicine before the Big Magician? But I don't know. I have no good medicine."

"What, Tomas Tomas?"

"I will not take my magic. It's not much medicine."

"Are you sure, Tomas Tomas?"

"Yes!" That hurt him. It made a sharp axe sink deep within his chest to speak so firmly and it hurt Tomas Tomas around the heart to speak so sharply to Spotted Calf. "No, I will not take my magic," Tomas Tomas said quietly. "You get me packed up now, Eleventh Wife," Tomas Tomas said quietly in his pain. "And my empty medicine bundle."

"Yes, Tomas Tomas," and she disappeared into the hogan.

If I only had one piece of respectable medicine, the medicine man Tomas Tomas thought. Certainly He cannot object if I show off a little too. And there are a few things I want to find out. Why was I sentenced to earth? What will the white man's position be up there? Will the Whites have all the good land there too? But, more important, why is all God's medicine a failure now? At one time I suppose He had very good magic and then He began to lose interest. He found the Indians no longer interesting. Something else I can bring up quietly with Him on the mountain: Why is the white man frightened of his God? What did his God do to him that makes the white man scared? "Do you know, Luto?" he asked towards the horse. "What is the white man afraid of? Is he afraid his God is not there? Where is my watch?" Tomas Tomas asked himself. The watch could not tell time. Tomas Tomas tied the watch around his wrist for fetish. The sun could tell time. "I must go to the mountain on time."

Tomas Tomas looked out over the long slow fire of the Navajo Nation that had been his home for so long and that now he was going to leave. The Checkerboard Area was shaped like a great horn, a horn of nothing. The wide open mouth of the horn lay along the flat Torreón and Cabazon country that was pricked with sharp white volcanic cores. The horn of volcanoes. The heavy middle sweep of the horn was checkered with flat high green-capped, copper-hued mesas that gave you the feeling that the world was on two levels, which it is in the Checkerboard. The horn of many levels. Here at the narrow tip of the horn the land was drinking from the narrow, quick, crazy mountain streams that cough past and were called the La Jara, Los Pinos and San Jose, and finally all became a great—dry in most seasons—wash called the Puerco which crossed under Route 66 at Gallup and entered the Rio Grande among spider cactus at Hondo. The horn is a dry river. Not really, Tomas Tomas thought. The horn is none of these things. The horn is home. Home is where you breed and leave other persons to take your place.

Nature is no longer interested in a person past the breeding age. That's true, Tomas Tomas thought. The rest of the body begins to quit and you die. But it's also true that a man can breed a long time, longer than a wolf or a coyote or a goat. Because he drinks alcoholic drinks? Smokes cigarettes? Lies? That's it. He does it longer and lives long because he lies, Tomas Tomas thought. Although I may be an exception. Tomas Tomas allowed his weakening but still hawk-severe eyes to roam the faint-in-the-hard-distance Cabazon country. "Every man is an exception," he said.

"What, Tomas Tomas?"

"Have I been a good husband?"

"Best," she said in clear Navajo.

"Where are the other wives?"

"They went to wash in the Los Pinos. Shall I get them?"

"No," Tomas Tomas said. "I like arriving to people but not going from people. The wrong things are said when there is nothing that can be said. Don't bother to drag out the saddle. A saddle blanket will be enough. I didn't need a saddle to come into this world and I don't need one to leave." Indian, Tomas Tomas thought to himself, you're getting silly. But I still don't need a saddle, he thought. That Luto horse has a wide comfortable back. That horse was by no horse bred. A strange horse by no mare fed.

"Just a saddle blanket," he repeated and his youngest wife again disappeared into the hogan. "Listen, horse," he said to Luto, "why did you come? All right, I know why you came, but you're only taking one—me—and it took you a long time—a hundred years. You're only taking one, and for every one you take we breed three or four, sometimes five or six. A person like me, who knows how many? I guess about a hundred. You don't believe it? Possibly more. It's not important. The important thing is we Indians don't waste anything. We have enough wives. Do you know how many Navajos there are now? Eighty thousand. When I was a young boy there were only six thousand. Soon now millions. That's how we're going to defeat the Whites. One day there will be no room for the Whites. If you can't fight them off our land, ———— them off. Would you like to see our secret weapon? That's a joke." Tomas Tomas used the Navajo word which sounded like laughter—adeesh. "Haven't you got a sense of humor, horse?"

While the medicine man was leaning over in pain on

561

one knee waiting for his youngest wife, Tomas Tomas tried to think something more that might be funny to work against this pain. It was a great pain. It was a new kind of pain deep in the chest as though something had entered him, something that had never been inside him before and only came once. No, he couldn't think of any joke to make against it but he could make this: Death will never get us all because the tribe has got something that the White hasn't got, a belief in the earth and in the world inside everyone, and like a bear or a coyote or an elk, the Indian is still part of the earth. And this, Tomas Tomas thought: Any Indian, me and every Indian I know in my clan, goes through a big time of his life believing it never happened. That's the only way an Indian can live. An Indian must spend a big time of his life in front of his hogan in the north part of New Mexico believing that the Whites never happened, that the white man never came.

Who are those two young white idiots coming towards me below the butte on those silly speckled horses? They are the magicians. Why can't they let an old Indian medicine man die in peace? No, I shouldn't say things like that. I should say, Who are those two silly speckled Whites coming towards me below the butte on idiot horses. Why can't they let an old Indian die with a little excitement of his own?

The medicine man watched the door of the hogan for his youngest wife to appear with the saddle blanket. The black horse would not wait all day.

"Something big is happening to me," Tomas Tomas said as the riders pulled up.

"Olá, Tomas Tomas! We were looking for Luto."

"Some horse," Tomas Tomas said.

"We were trailing Luto and we trailed him to here."

"Don't bother. I'm going to use him now."

"For the mountains?"

"Yes."

"Already?"

"Already. Don't you think it's time?"

"But you've been here forever, Tomas Tomas," Ring said.

"Yes, I have."

"But not forever and ever?"

The young white man who asked this was accompanied by an Indian of about the same age. The medicine man knew the young white man's name was Ring Bowman and his father owned a ranch and the White Horse Trading Post. His Indian partner's name was The Son Of The Man With Twenty-six Horses.

"I was thinking," Tomas Tomas said, "we could not beat the white man but we can wait slowly and patiently like a woman and in time tame the Whites. In time."

"But now it's your time, Tomas Tomas."

Tomas Tomas looked out over all the staggering bright land that was forever lost. All the opportunities that would never come again. Where did the Indian make his mistake? In being born. Partly that. Partly that and partly not dying, staying around too long, trying to hang on to life when there was no life. The White is a knife. I have known some good Whites, but I have also known some good knives, some good looms, a good hatchet and an excellent rope. But it's not the same as people. We were conquered by the knives. We defeated the Anasazi People and then we were defeated by knives. That's all right because there's nothing we can do about it but it would have been nice if I could leave the world to people. If people still peopled the world. "Do you agree?"

"Sure, Tomas Tomas."

"I was thinking how nice it would be in leaving it if people still peopled the world."

"Yes, Tomas Tomas."

"You think I'm an old medicine man with too many wives and cow shit talk."

"You leave the world in good hands, Tomas Tomas. Your world will be in good hands."

"Give me your hand." The medicine man took the white boy's hand and looked at it carefully. "Chalk hand. What do you expect to get done with this?"

"Nothing."

"That's right. You will get nothing done. It's not a hand that can make any magic."

"Did you hear that, Twenty-six Horses?"

"Yes, I heard it," Twenty-six Horses said. "Does that mean you are going to kill me?"

"Yes, it does."

"Right here?" Tomas Tomas asked.

"Yes," Ring said. "There will still be a lot of magic after you're gone, Tomas Tomas. I'm going to kill Twenty-six Horses right before your eyes."

"Yes, he is," Twenty-six Horses said.

"That's not magic," Tomas Tomas said. "Anyway you're not Twenty-six Horses, you're The Son Of The Man With Twenty-six Horses."

"Just the same," Ring said.

"Now, if you could kill twenty-six Whites that would be a trick."

"You're bitter, aren't you, Tomas Tomas?"

"No, I'm an Indian," Tomas Tomas said. The medicine man was still hunched forward in pain and he could not figure why the two young men did not understand that he had some very important business to take care of. "You should understand," Tomas Tomas said, hoping that he had picked up where he left off. "You should understand that I don't have much time. I must arrive on the mountain before it is too late."

"It will take just one shot to kill Twenty-six Horses."

"Believe him, it's true," Twenty-six Horses said.

"I believe him," Tomas Tomas said, raising his voice. "I believe that he can kill you, Twenty-six Horses, in one shot. But what is great magic about that?"

"The great magic, Tomas Tomas, is that I bring Twenty-six Horses back to life."

Tomas Tomas tried resting on one hand to ease the pain. "I know the missionary says the same thing. There was a man who died and came back again by magic, but no one saw it. I never met anyone who saw it. The missionary didn't see this magic. Did you?"

"No, but we can do it," Ring said.

"The both of you die?"

"No, just him," Ring said, hooking his thumb at Twenty-six Horses.

Tomas Tomas looked over at the hogan. "Ihda!" Tomas Tomas called toward the hogan door.

"The saddle blanket must be in the other hogan," Tomas Tomas' youngest wife called back. "I will go there and look."

"Hurry," the medicine man repeated in a guttural whisper. Then to the magicians, "Now?"

"Now," Ring said. "Twenty-six Horses will stand there on the rimrock."

"No," Tomas Tomas whispered.

"At about ten paces I will kill him."

"No, don't."

"Then bring him back to life."

"Sure?"

"Positive."

"Could you bring me back to life? Don't answer. I am going this time. I'm all prepared to go and I'm going. But if you have some good magic I would like to take that magic with me. Can I take it with me in my medicine bundle?"

"Yes," Ring said. "Now stand over there on the rimrock, Twenty-six Horses."

"Something I can take with me," the medicine man repeated. "I would like to take some good magic with me when I go and I go to the mountain now."

Tomas Tomas saw the young man called Ring who was tall for his age and hard blue-eyed withdraw from the saddle holster on the patient speckled Appaloosa a Marlin carbine.

"Just an ordinary thirty-thirty," Ring said to the dying medicine man, Tomas Tomas.

"Yes."

"Now I put the cartridge in the chamber. You notice it has a red tip."

"Why does the bullet have a red tip? Does it have something to do with the magic?"

Ring did not answer but slammed the shell home with a swift solid swing of the lever action.

The medicine man watched the young, arrogantly young, white man named Ring Bowman—who came from a near ranch with water and green grass that sleeked the cattle and the young man's cheeks and demarked the boundaries of the Navajo Nation—raise the gun slowly and carefully until the bronze-tipped front sight was perfectly down in the V of the rear sight and the front sight was exactly on the heart of the Indian called Twenty-six Horses.

"Now I will kill an Indian," Ring said.

"Wait!"

"Why?"

"Well, I have decided I don't need to take any magic with me."

"Oh, you'll need magic up there, Tomas Tomas, won't he, Twenty-six Horses?"

"Yes, you will, Tomas Tomas."

"All right. If Twenty-six Horses is willing, go ahead and kill Twenty-six Horses with one shot." The medicine man was annoyed.

"One shot," Ring said and began to squeeze the trigger slowly. The roar was terrific, the noise came back again and again from the mesas and the dark canyons and Twenty-six Horses toppled down dead like the very dead and bled red from the stomach all over the ground.

"Get up!" Ring shouted.

The dead got up.

"Now give me the red bullet I fired."

Twenty-six Horses raised his bronzed hand to his mouth and spat out the red bullet.

"Now here is your magic to take to the mountain," Ring said, taking the red bullet and placing it in the quavering hand of Tomas Tomas.

"Do I dare? Sure I do," Tomas Tomas answered himself. "I will try it on Him as soon as I get to the mountain."

"Who is him?"

"The one who allowed the Whites to defeat us."

"You mean an ancestor?" the dead-alive and standing Twenty-six Horses asked.

"Yes," Tomas Tomas said, standing with great effort. "An ancestor. That's a good name, ancestor. Where's the horse?"

When Twenty-six Horses and Ring brought Luto over to the hogan Tomas Tomas was ready. His youngest wife placed the white saddle blanket on the very wide-backed black horse and Tomas Tomas mounted painfully by himself. Now she passed Tomas Tomas up a small dark bundle and Tomas Tomas placed the red bullet inside.

"If it does not work," the medicine man said down to the young men, "you will hear from me."

"Where you are going it will work," Ring said.

The black horse started slowly toward the easy foothills that began the big climb of the mountain. "Goodbye," the medicine man waved to his youngest wife. "It has been good. Marry rich. Die old. Bring magic. I will see you. I

568

will see you all. I climb dying. I climb dying. Something big is happening to me," Tomas Tomas called.

"We should have told him how it works," Twenty-six Horses said, watching the medicine man disappear.

"That there were two blank red bullets, one in my gun and one in your mouth, and catchup in your pants. No. No, it's not necessary because they will believe him."

"His ancestors?"

"Yes, Twenty-six Horses. Haven't we always believed he had eleven wives instead of five?"

"Yes."

"Well, if he wanted to believe eleven, then his ancestors will want to believe anything."

"I suppose," Twenty-six Horses said. "Let's get some more catchup."

"And bullets," Ring said.

In a few hours all the Navajo Indians from the Checkerboard Clan had gathered around Coyotes Love Me who held a spy glass loaned to him by the trader.

"Where is the medicine man, Tomas Tomas, Coyotes Love Me?"

"He is on the Vallecito."

"Is he steady?"

"No, he seems sick in the saddle, as though he will fall."

"How is he now, Coyotes Love Me?"

Coyotes Love Me steadied the long scope. "Better. The black horse is trying to help. He stops and tries to steady Tomas Tomas, but I do not think Tomas Tomas will make it."

"If you would take the metal cover off the end of the telescope you could see better, Coyotes Love Me."

Coyotes Love Me took off the cover, petulant, then he looked through the scope surprised. "You can see everything! Well, it's just like I said only worse. I don't think Tomas Tomas will make it."

"Let me see." Afraid Of His Own Horses took the scope. "It's worse than Coyotes Love Me said. No, Tomas Tomas will never make it. The black horse seems very tired. The black horse cannot make it up and over the Gregorio Crest. Well, that's too bad. I guess the medicine man will fall off and die on the way up. It's a terrible thing, he won't make the mountain to die, but we don't have any magic for this."

"No, we don't," Coyotes Love Me agreed.

"I've got some," Ring said. "Will you hand me the rifle again, Twenty-six Horses?"

"Nothing will work now. There is nothing anyone can do now at this distance," Coyotes Love Me said.

Ring raised the gun very high, much too high most of the Indians thought, but a half second after the shot the great black horse, even at this distance with the naked eye, could be seen going over the top in furious desperate leaps as though fleeing a battle. The medicine man, Tomas Tomas, was on top. Home.

Afraid Of His Own Horses put down the scope and looked at Ring. "That was good magic."

"That was a good, while no one was looking, far-off long-distance kick in the ass," Coyotes Love Me said. "White medicine."

They found the body of Tomas Tomas two months later near a spring on the exact top of the mountain above a live oak knoll near the Las Vacas ranger cabin. There were tracks from where Tomas Tomas had dismounted, gone down to the spring, come back to the top dying and finally died.

There was never found any trace of his medicine bundle containing the red bullet. Twenty-six Horses and Ring went up to search all around the Las Vacas one day, spent the night and came down bright the next morning, but they never found the red bullet either.

"Do you suppose—?"

"No," Ring said. "You've got to realize, Twenty-six Horses, that dead is dead."

But Twenty-six Horses, besides being a Navajo who believed in magic in the afterworld, had been shot dead many times in this one, so all the way down the mountain and even after they had passed the hogan of Tomas Tomas in Navajo Country, Twenty-six Horses kept saying, "Do you suppose?"

And Ring kept saying, "No I don't. I guess I don't."

Which is a good place to leave it, where we left it, Ring thought, a place where the world has always and will always leave it. Ring rode ahead on Luto carrying the gun and Twenty-six Horses followed on a small paint. The horses slipped down obliquely into the wide flat far-lost beauty of the Indian Country and disappeared in the hard purple and wild mesas that fell in steps through a fierce color continuity that was not dying, a fabulous and bright Navajo Nation that was not dead, the hushed song in the land, disappearing and faint but still an alive and still smoldering Indian incantation against white doom—singing that the white man never happened, chanting death never came.

"Yes, Ringo," Twenty-six Horses said from atop his bright paint in the dim dawn. "It takes all kinds of medicine, Ringo, and even a medicine man gone. Do we go home now, Ringo?"

"No, I don't."

"You don't like home much, do you, Ringo?"

"I haven't exactly got one."

"A trading post, that isn't a home?"

"That's right. A trading post where things are traded, near a blue hogan. Let's go to the mesa and look for that heifer that's going to calve."

"On Luto?"

"Why not?"

"I don't much like your horse, Ringo."

"Well, maybe he doesn't like your painting."

"My painting on the side of the Sleeping Child Mesa? How can Luto resist?"

"He can try," Ring said. They sat in stiff silence for long seconds, then Ring said, "Can you hear an airplane, Twenty-six Horses?"

"Yes, somewhere above my painting on the cliff."

"No, above the Sleeping Child Mesa," Ring said.

THREE

THE SLEEPING CHILD MESA rose through the clouds like an atoll. From above there was nothing more to see, nothing, no land or life, not even water or sand anywhere, nothing, only this mesa in all the universe—nothing more.

"Jesus Christ," Ring said. "Jesus Christ, what's anyone doing out here?"

The two on horseback below the mesa could hear the airplane in those clouds shrouding the mesa, the roar going round and round like a distant high whining toy held on a long twirling string by a child. Now they wondered when the airplane would run out of gasoline and sink to earth.

"It's been about an hour now."

"Yes. He must have been short of gas when he began to circle. I bet he can see the top of the mesa; why doesn't he land there?"

"Because he'd never get down from the mesa."

"That's true. Not without us."

The two young men on horses could have been sitting here on horses a hundred years before. That's the way they were dressed, in blue hard pants, rough shirts; and this land of northern New Mexico looked still raw and unshocked too, still virgin and bright, with gray-green sage and mesas that rose like undiscovered islands in the clouds.

"He must have all the gasoline in the world."

"He'll come down."

"We've got to be patient."

"It really doesn't make any difference to me. I've got all the time in the world."

"The heifer can wait."

"Boy, can she wait!"

They both watched up from atop their nervous cow ponies to the thick, ugly, dark, swirling-in-gray, slow-moving clouds above, where the heavy hornet buzzing of the plane was inconstant as it whirled, unremitting and mad.

"What would an airplane be doing out here in nowhere?"

"Oh, this is somewhere, Twenty-six Horses. The most important place can be nowhere."

"Like the heifer we're following who's going to calve. She's going nowhere to do it."

"Yes, or that plane up there above the mesa."

"I wonder what they're up to that they came here to nowhere."

"Well, we're close to the Mexican border; they could be trying to smuggle something across."

"Like what?"

"People."

"You mean Mexicans? They can cross the river at night."

"They've got a high fence on this side now. This way they are flying them over that fence."

"To this mesa? It's a long way over."

"Yes, it is, Twenty-six Horses."

"You know, Ringo—" Twenty-six Horses let the rein fall on the fabulous horse. "You know—how do you know there are people up there?"

"Well, it's not a bird above the mesa."

"That's true," Twenty-six Horses said.

Yes, there were people above the Sleeping Child Mesa, but right now there seemed only one, the man at the controls of the old, gaudily painted DC-3. The soft light from the fantastic and myriad panel of instruments lit only the bony jaw outlines, throwing the face and brow in hard relief. It was the face of a murderer. There seemed no one else in the ship.

"You can come out now," the pilot said, almost to himself, and then again, "I said you could come out. Venga!"

"Okay, okay, okay," a man said, getting off the floor, and then nine others rose. The Mexican up first leaned over the pilot and said, "We there?"

"No," the pilot said. "The weather's been bad all the way. We're going to have to land down there." He pointed. "It looks like a flat-top wallowing in the ocean, doesn't it?"

"A what?"

"An aircraft carrier."

"You were supposed to land us near Albuquerque," the Mexican said, annoyed. He was the only one of the ten Mexicans who spoke English and he did all the negotiations with the gringo who had agreed to fly them into the States of the United States for three hundred dollars apiece.

"Are we in the States of the United States?" a wide peasant-faced Mexican asked in Spanish.

"No," the tall, thin-faced spokesman who leaned over the pilot said. "We're over an aircraft carrier."

"Actually a mesa," the pilot said.

"*Una mesa*," the spokesman explained to the others.

"Can we get down off it?"

"I never heard of one you couldn't," the pilot said, adjusting a large red mixture knob. The interpreter translated this and all the Mexicans seemed satisfied except the wide-faced peasant who thought about it a while and then touched himself and said, "Yo, sí."

"What's that?"

"He says he has," the interpreter told the pilot.

"Well, we're going to land on the top of that mesa anyway," the pilot said, and he touched back the throttle and he thought: I can land there all right. It's long enough to land. I don't know about taking off again with this load. I don't think so. The thing to do is land and conserve gasoline and when the weather clears I will take off again without the Mexicans. I'm very sorry, but I have fulfilled my contract. I told them I would land them someplace near Albuquerque. I'll be sorry if they can't get down off the mesa. If they can't get down off the mesa then no one will ever find out I brought them in. After a reasonable time, when this bunch is dead, I could bring in another bunch. It could work forever. I guess half the people in Mexico would like to come to the United States. The top of that mesa is the United States. Well, anyway you could get away with a few more loads. This is quite a discovery, a new island entirely surrounded by clouds.

The pilot felt like Magellan or Balboa, but lighted by the yellow deep shadows of the instruments he looked more like a pirate, a well-dressed, successful and even bow-tied Captain Kidd. But no one walked the plank, just that mesa, he thought. The pilot kicked the plane into a long glide towards the high flight strip, the steep sides of the mesa, raked by long combers of clouds breaking in on the scrub oak and piñon and then sweeping back into the turbulent big sky. Now the port engine sputtered. The pilot listened and then the pilot heard, really heard, the engine sing perfectly again and he began to let her down. The Mexicans got down on the floor and held onto each other. She hit, then hit again and again, and then a hard, awful once more, before she held the ground and rolled to a perilous halt on one leg.

Ring leaned back and touched the crupper of the horse. "Whatever it was, it lit."

"The bird's on the mesa," the Indian said.

"And they can't get down."

"Maybe they'll take off again."

"If it could fly it would not have landed."

Twenty-six Horses tried to think of something wrong with this proposition but he couldn't so he confounded Ring. "Do you know what, Ringo? We've never been on that mesa. Why do they call it the Sleeping Child Mesa? I think it's because at a certain angle the mesa is shaped like a sleeping child."

"You sure?"

"Sure I'm sure. But maybe my forefathers—"

"Do you know what forefathers means?"

"Indians?"

"No, it means you had four fathers. Now which one of them was looking at the Sleeping Child Mesa?"

"Does it make any difference?"

"I don't suppose it does. Did you hear that? It sounded as though the engine, the bird, started again and then quit."

"I like another idea now."

"What's that?"

"That they're smuggling dope in that airplane, or running arms."

"What's running arms?"

"It's an expression."

"I like our first idea best."

"Running people?"

"Yes. Running people is better than running arms. Running legs would be more apt."

"Apt? Apt? Listen, do you hear the bird again?" There was a faint mechanical coughing on the mesa and then silence. "The idea of running people is ridiculous when you think about it." The Indian sat his horse straight and felt secure in his judgement.

Ring swung around backwards on his saddle and looked over the long country, then up at the dark ceiling where the bird had lit. "Ridiculous when you think about it, yes," Ring said. "But so is Twenty-six Horses."

"What?"

"Don't think, Twenty-six Horses," Ring said.

The man on the mesa, the pilot, was thinking into the overcast. The Mexican illegal entries tumbled out when the plane came to an awkward stop. The front right wheel was off the ground, the left leg of the plane was in a hole. The Mexicans were under the shadow of the wing and waiting for the pilot to come out and tell them where to walk to get to Albuquerque.

"First we better get this plane out of the hole, then I'll show you how to walk to Albuquerque," the pilot called from the open hatch of the cockpit.

The interpreter got the Mexicans pulling and lifting on the plane and soon they had the purple-with-blue-wings and red-tailed bird that had brought them so far sitting alertly on a yellow apron of sandstone surrounded by low junipers.

The pilot turned on the radio to try to get a weather report while the Mexicans began to scout the mesa for a way down and out to Albuquerque, excepting the Mexican with the thin mustache. He stayed put beneath the wing.

The pilot could not call in for weather information because he had, of course, filed no flight plan. He had left a small field with his live cargo outside Guaymas, Mexico, five hours ago and he had hoped to land at the foot of the Sandia between Bernalillo and Albuquerque and get rid of the illegal Mexicans, then fly back to Guaymas for more if all went well. The radio told him nothing but loud squawking so he turned it off and watched the sky boiling around him to figure when he could take off. It was too bad he would not be able to take the Mexicans but he had gotten them to their States of the United States and that was all he was hired to do. There was a hole in the weather now towards the east so he started up the engines and let her idle to be able to get off quickly if there was an opening. It would be best to get off while the Mexicans were looking for a way down. There was no way down.

"Shut her off!"

"What?" the pilot called down to the Mexican interpreter.

"Shut off the engine. You're not going anyplace without me."

The pilot killed the motors and the propellers finally coughed to a jerky standstill.

"You're not going to leave me here to die. I could see from up there that there wasn't any way down off this mesa."

"Let's not be melodramatic."

"What?"

"Let's make a deal."

"All right." The interpreter seemed relieved. This was the kind of language he was used to interpreting. He had made a deal to be flown along for half fare if he would do

580

the interpreting. But he did not want to die for half price on this mesa. "What's the deal?"

"Keep the others in ignorance and I'll fly you off with me."

"What you want me to keep them inside of, did you say? Speak more clear."

"Keep them occupied when they get back."

"*Ocupado*. Keep them busy when they get back. It's a deal."

"It's a deal."

"Remember, the deal is we go off together."

"That's the deal," and the pilot wondered how he was going to get rid of this Mexican who seemed more than willing to interpret his comrades out of their lives. The sandstone landing strip was about twelve hundred feet long and he doubted very much whether the ship could make it off the mesa with both of them—it would certainly be critical. Why take chances? There was not only the risk of not getting off, there was the risk of another living witness if you got him off. Why risk double jeopardy? Wait. I think there was a real break in the clouds. I think I saw some blue.

"The *muchachos* are coming back," the interpreter called up. "Can we take off fast now?"

"Not quite now," the pilot said down quietly. "You'll have to placate them."

"Are you sure you're speaking English?"

"Con them."

"Okay." The Mexicans came up and circled the plane with folded arms, their legs wide apart. They stared at the

581

plane with small dark eyes, with somber and certain knowledge. They all wore loose-fitting, once-white clothes, but not the enormous wide hats you see in the cartoons and the movies. They didn't have any hats at all and their hair was very black, cut short and stood up like coarse dark wire in continuous amazement, and now imminent attack, like the hackles of a bear.

"What did you find?" the pilot asked down calmly from his perch above the blue wings.

"*Es una isla.*"

"It's an island," the interpreter repeated.

"Yes," the pilot said surely. "But it's in the United States and it's near Albuquerque. What more—?"

"*Qué mas?*"

One of the Mexicans reached out a great arm and broke off a thick branch from a juniper tree and tapped it on the ground. "*Este.*"

The translator did not have to translate the word "this" for the pilot. The pilot understood the weapon and he thought, Well, I didn't want to produce my Smith and Wesson, but a thirty-eight is very small and there are ten of them, but here goes because it is the only language that any of us seems to understand, the only communication we've got left, and he reached under the seat and felt first with his fingers to feel if the clip was home and then he brought the blue gun over the wheel and pointed it down over the big blue wing straight at the faces of the marooned Mexicans. "*Mira,*" he said, using one perfect Spanish word and shaking the automatic. "*Mira!*" Then he said more quietly to the interpreter, "Ask them, ask them in Mexican, how they want to go." There was a great silence.

The clouds, the ocean of solid clouds around the mesa began to shift and, if not yet to break up, then to allow the first white light to beat down on the quiet tableau around the big blue bird on the high island mesa.

Now the pilot fired one loud echoless shot to cow the Mexicans and lend himself courage.

"I think we been up on this Sleeping Child Mesa," Ring said.

"When?"

"When we chased the polled bull."

"No."

"When we lost the bronc."

"No."

"When we saw into Old Mexico."

"Not then either."

"When was it then?"

"We were never on this mesa, Ringo."

"Then this will be the first time."

"No, someone else just made it."

"The first time for us then."

"If there is a way up."

"Well, there was a way down."

"If there is a way up," Twenty-six Horses repeated.

They stared at each other from their glaring horses. The horses wore identical yellow látigo hackamores; they had twin crazed ceramic eyes and now both pawed the red earth in furious frozen attitudes of Greek bronze and cow horse impatience.

"We should ought to find that heifer first."

"One heifer in three will need help having her first calf."

"So we should ought to find that heifer first, but—"

"Take this heifer though, I bet it's the two in three that don't need help. It's like you said, I think, about my forefathers."

"No, it's nothing to do with that, Twenty-six Horses. It's that you're right about it being the two in three. Why didn't I think of that?"

"You were distracted by the bird on the mesa."

"Yes. How are we going to get it down?"

"How are we going to get up to get it down?" Twenty-six Horses looked around wisely and then up at the heavens. "She's beginning to break up."

"Yes, the bird will escape. Let's see if we can find a trail up."

They couldn't. They walked, then trotted, cantered, finally ran their horses around the tall mesa, examining carefully the steep crenelated sides that rose like a Roman temple in the west, but forever and up into the once blue, now pressing sky, the mesa punching through and hidden up there, hiding and hidden and itself concealing—what was it? That noise, the big toy whir of a new bird on the mesa.

"I thought I saw—"

"What?"

"I thought I saw a way up."

"Where, Twenty-six Horses?"

"There. That cave."

"It's dark."

"And it goes in, not up."

"And it's dark, very dark. You're right, Twenty-six Horses, it goes in, not up."

584

"I guess that's it." Twenty-six Horses placed his hands on his hips and looked around solemnly. "If we can't get up we better locate that cow."

"That heifer before it becomes a cow."

"If we don't it may never live to be one."

"I said it much better," Ring said. "Don't always try to improve on what I say."

"After all I'm only an Indian."

"It's okay to be an Indian, Twenty-six Horses, it's okay, but remember the war's over. Don't still try to count coup."

"What's that?"

"Take scalps."

"Keep me filled in on all the Indian lore, Ringo."

"I'll fill you in with a rock in your head," Ring said. "Now what are we going to do?"

"Chase the heifer."

"All right, we'll chase the heifer, but I hate—"

"Me too."

"It's only a plane that got lost. Soon it will take off and go home."

"Me too."

"No, no, Twenty-six Horses, see if you can pick up a track of the heifer. That's what Indians are supposed to be good at, but in my experience they tend to confuse things."

"You only know a few Indians, Ringo."

"Oh, that's plenty," Ring said. "Now please see if you can pick up the heifer's track, won't you, Twenty-six Horses, like a good Indian?"

"The bird will escape, Ringo."

"That's too bad."

"You had them smuggling dope, arms, people, legs, everything."

"It was a weak moment."

"No, no, no," Twenty-six Horses said and he swung his horse in repeated half circles to pick up the track. "No, that's good, Ringo. It shows imagination. Why, in a little while, if you keep your nose to the—grindstone, is it?— why, soon you'll know as much about crime lore as Indian lore, if you rub two criminals together—"

Ring hurled his black horse into Twenty-six Horses' paint and they bumped and swayed, pitching and tossing across the sage; then a shot rang out. They pulled up their horses and stared around, then up at the mesa.

"If we can't get up, there is nothing we can do," Ring said.

"Look," Twenty-six Horses remarked, pointing. "There's the heifer."

It was the track of the heifer and they followed it. It took a circuitous, wandering, faltering route, stopping and searching for something, the way a heifer will, to find a perfect spot for her first calf. The animal is afraid, confused, worried and alarmed, but proud and secretive too and wanting a high dry sanctuary.

"Look, it's making for the mesa."

"The cave in the mesa."

"It might go up after all."

"It's very dark in there."

"You shouldn't be afraid of that, Ringo. Follow me. Follow the Indian."

They tethered each horse to its left stirrup with its own

rein. The horse thinks it's tied. These did. Ring followed Twenty-six Horses and Twenty-six Horses followed the heifer tracks until the light got dim, but the cave was narrow now and slanting upward so that the animal could not be avoided.

"We're going up, Ringo. Follow the Indian."

"Did you hear that?"

"Another shot. Don't be afraid, Ringo. Follow the Indian."

I'd rather beat him in the head, Ring thought, but he followed the Indian, followed the faint dry noise, smelling old dust and cheap hair oil you bought at the trading post, smelling of secret places and Twenty-six Horses.

"Can you see anything?"

"Not yet, Ringo, but we're going up fast."

"If you can't see anything—"

"Don't worry, Ringo, follow the Indian."

Above on the mesa, leaning out of the great airplane, the pilot with the long piratical face repeated down to his illegal cargo of Mexicans, but particularly to the interpreter, "Ask them how they want to go." While the interpreter translated, the pilot waved the blue gun for attention.

The pilot waving the small blue gun, who was very shortly to be killed, had now lived almost exactly thirty-four years. Three weeks short. His name was Peter Winger and his friends, when he had friends, called him Wingy. Peter Winger had been born and lived his early life in New Haven, Connecticut, until he was turned down by the Air Corps because of chronic conjunctivitis, whatever that

587

means. Peter Winger found out what it meant, but he didn't tell anyone else what it meant. Peter Winger learned to fly but couldn't get a commercial license in the United States so went to Old Mexico where he could not get a legitimate job either and was now hauling illegal immigrants. But he never thought he would have to use this gun. There seemed no other way out.

"Do they understand? Tell them to get out of the way. Tell them I am going to turn the ship around."

"Yes, but don't forget me," the translator called up.

The pilot, Peter Winger, started the engines and the great bird made a terrible roar as she began to pivot in a circle. "I won't forget you," Peter Winger called down to the translator from the still open cockpit. Now he slammed the window and began to taxi the huge, awkward, slow-moving bird towards the other end of the mesa for take-off. The translator screamed something at the other Mexicans and they all ran after the slow waddling DC-3 and one after another threw themselves on the tail of the plane, flat, and held on so they were all lying and holding on to the horizontal stabilizers as the plane trundled slowly down to the take-off point.

They are like flies on my tail, Peter Winger thought. How could they be so stupid? I've not met people so stupid since those doctors who turned me down for the Air Corps for poor vision. My vision is not so poor that I cannot see them trying to get off this mesa on my plane, and my eyes will not be so bad that I will not see them brush off like flies when I get up some speed.

The pilot, Peter Winger, now had the DC-3 all the way down at the far edge of the mesa where he had so perfectly hit while landing. The sky was clearing nicely now and in a few hours he would be back in Guaymas. Peter Winger applied full brakes and gunned the engines. He could see the Mexicans on the tail begin to flutter and stream like old rags, their eyes and tongues pop out when the giant raging wind from the backwash of the roaring eighteen-cylinder engines hit them. But there's more to come, Peter Winger thought. Wait till I get this thing up to two hundred miles an hour. There will be no more Mexican flies on the tail. As a matter of fact they will be off before I get fifteen feet. As a matter of fact, there they go now.

The Mexicans could take no more punishment and they were fleeing the plane. Now they were all off. A few of them picked up sticks and rocks and hit the side of the tinny bird, making a hard tinny noise, but even they now had fled from the great wind as Peter Winger made the engines roar still more. Peter Winger tried the ailerons and the rudder and checked out all the instruments. He could see the instruments fine and everything was okay. He was heading into the wind. He released the brakes and the great bird leaped forward for a perfect take-off, except that the heifer now moved into the middle of the runway. The heifer moved into the middle of the runway. The heifer moved into the middle of the runway: everyone said that a thousand times afterwards. Peter Winger would never live to say it to anyone. Now he was saying everything is perfect, I'm going to get off, I'm going to get off. But he wasn't. He could see to a point of piñon and he knew when he passed this point as he thundered down the strip that he could no longer abort the take-off, the plane then was committed to fly, and if something went wrong and she could not become airborne, then neither could she be stopped and the great DC-3 with Peter Winger, who could not quite see the heifer, would go skidding off the edge of the mesa and smash on the rocks nine hundred feet below on the desert floor. Now he gave the twin engines full throttle and the plane leaped down, down the runway, speeding past the rock and cactus like a hurtling horizontal rocket. Now it reached the point of no return, the point of piñon, and at this exact second Peter Winger saw the heifer where it had emerged from a motte of scrub oak, where it stood and gazed around at the high big blue world. Peter Winger killed the engines and touched the brakes and the hurtling bird lost all its grace and purpose and began to careen drunkenly at a wild speed as though it were being torn apart.

"Oh!" Peter Winger saw the edge of the world coming up. "Oh, the damn cow. Oh God, the damn cow. How did a cow get up in the sky? Oh, the damn cow."

The plane bucked now on one wing, then began to skid at a ridiculous cruel angle and make a terrible cracking noise as it fled to the wrong side of the mesa and then flared out over the edge and dropped, wingless, flightless, like a house in a hurricane, to the great rocks below.

"The cow. I never saw. I never saw. I never saw that cow in the sky," were Peter Winger's last words on the mesa and on earth. Peter Winger repeated them over the broken wheel as the plane fell; he mumbled with stubborn, pathetic repetition as though he had seen a ghost. And yes, was Peter Winger's final thought, no one will believe, even with perfect eyesight, that there are cattle in the air after storms on the island mesas of northern New Mexico.

Ring and Twenty-six Horses peered out of the scrub oak after the cow just as the plane went over the edge.

"We missed it."

"No, there it is. The heifer."

"I mean the bird. It just flew."

"No, fell."

They both silently agreed about this, then looked around the high island mesa in wonder.

"Look, Ringo, your heifer is going to become a cow."

And it was too, and all the Mexicans appeared from nowhere with advice and wisdom. This was something they understood and knew a great deal about, something that was not shocking, mechanical, different and indifferent, but was the same in Mexico as it was, as it obviously is, in the States of the United States.

The calf flew out now from the heifer, suddenly and quickly, like a dolphin, a copy, a miniature replica of the cow, and the flat-faced Mexican dropped his weapon stick and reached in quickly with his hand and broke the caul and the calf careened its head and breathed air, was alive for the first time on earth.

"*Es un buen torito.*"

"What?"

"He said it's a fine little bull," the translator said.

"Yes," Ring said. "And Twenty-six Horses here is an Indian. He doesn't look too Indian but he's an Indian, and you gentlemen I presume are all Mexicans," Ring said portentously, "trying the hard way over the border fence. Well, no matter. We came up here looking for an airplane, a big bird we heard—"

591

"That rhymes."

"Twenty-six Horses is conscious of poetry, being a painter," Ring continued to the Mexicans. "He— Never mind. Follow me down. We—after all the noise, the shooting, we expected something terrible and we found life on the mesa. Life as we know it on earth. How am I doing, Twenty-six Horses?"

"Terrible. You should have quit while you were ahead."

"Twenty-six Horses doesn't understand," Ring called back to the others as they emerged from the tunnel.

"I'm only an Indian."

They marched down to the wreckage of the blue plane where Luto was grazing near the cockpit. Ring laid his hand on the withers of the big black horse and looked up at the huge, lonely Sleeping Child Mesa that was all visible now.

"God never," Ring said, "nature never, I mean people were never meant to fly. If we were I guess we would have been born with wings. Ask Luto. Luto knows."

The Indian didn't seem to be appreciating this. Then Ring quickly mounted the high horse and said proudly, "Certainly people shouldn't fly without passports, not on Monday."

The interpreter translated this and the Mexicans scratched their black stiff heads and shrugged their shoulders and watched the boy on the black horse. "*Quién sabe?*"

Now the procession led by the great black horse wound through the bright cliffs that Twenty-six Horses had painted, the Indian-painted section of Indian Country, followed by the heifer, now a cow. The lead Mexican right behind the horses bore the calf beneath the gaudy cliffs. He carried the calf as if the new life were a thing of great portent, a redeeming and saving angel that by some mysterious mission had arrived in the sky at a zero hour to return them safely to these bright rocks and these beautiful, odd inhabitants of these States of the United States.

"Look," Ring said to Twenty-six Horses, pointing upwards. "Look, from this angle down here your painting looks like a threat."

"What?"

"All red and angry."

"No. It's a monument."

"To that flyer?"

"Anyone."

"Not me."

"Anyone, Ringo," Twenty-six Horses said. "Anyone at all. Anyone who dies here."

"Not me."

"Okay, not you," Twenty-six Horses said.

"Because you would save me."

"Would I?" Twenty-six Horses asked.

FOUR

THE SUMMER SOLSTICE. The longest day in the year. A long day dying. Me, too, in the quicksand. There is no way out of this. Yes, there is. Yes, yes, yes. If I could get the cooperation of Luto. Luto, please. Please, Luto. All right, all right. Okay. Standing there in the dappled shade, the coffin shade, you've got a mission. Everyone has got a mission. Everyone has got the co-operation of someone else. God. Goddamn.

Ring stared up at the feckless and hard and guilt-pure sky. Okay, Luto, I'll tell you a story about our tame poet. No, I won't, Luto. I won't tell you a damn thing. I'll tell you about the trading post and the blue hogan. No, I won't tell you that one either.

Ring felt he was not welcome at the trading post when the blue hogan was occupied. He thought of more and more excuses to stay away from the post. The blue hogan was his father's business. He could do anything he wanted there. He could keep anyone he wanted there.

"You can't run your father's life, Twenty-six Horses," Ring said.

"You've got one of your own?"

"Yes. Did you ever think of painting the blue hogan, Twenty-six Horses?"

"Someone has."

"I mean a picture of it."

"I don't think it would make a good picture."

Ring pulled down on a branch of cedar tree that dangled above him. The thing, Ring thought, is to forget it. The reservation is divided into three parts. That's not too interesting. I wonder how many parts, I wonder how many rooms the blue hogan has got. I was never inside. Try to think of something else. You are in the Cabazon country now where there are extinct volcanoes. Try to think of that. There is a writer, a hermit, a poet or something that lives near here. Why don't you try to think of that? A poet should know something about blue hogans; blue hogan is poetic. Why don't you ask him? Because I don't want to.

"Twenty-six Horses, why don't you want to paint the blue hogan? All right, I'll quit. What are you trying to say in your paintings?"

"I'm not trying to make a speech, Ringo."

"But will an Indian get heard off the reservation?"

"I said I'm not trying to make a speech."

"Will he get looked at?"

596

"Oh, an Indian will get looked at, but will they look at what he does?"

"That's the question."

"It's a good question, Ringo, but I am thinking of something else."

All Indian Country is divided into three parts, Twenty-six Horses thought, and the Checkerboard Area is the most forgotten piece, certainly the most unmagical, Winding Water says. But neither Winding Water nor his friend Many Cattle are big Indians; that is, they carry no weight in the clan. So little weight, Twenty-six Horses said aloud, that when Winding Water and Many Cattle enter a hogan you feel that several Indians have just left.

"That's perhaps why they want to start a volcano."

"No."

"Then why do they want to start a volcano?"

"I don't know," Ring said, raising his voice. "I'm a poor student of Indian culture, but it seems it could be dangerous."

"That's your way of saying you know it all," Twenty-six Horses said.

"I know more about Indians than you, Twenty-six Horses."

"Because I'm an Indian."

"No, but because you don't read or think logically, Twenty-six Horses. Like any artist you have prelogic— emotion—that's all."

"But I'm not an artist, I'm an Indian."

"That makes it worse," Ring said. And to make it much worse, Ring thought, Twenty-six Horses belongs to a Navajo sect or clan called the Hundred Fires. The Hun-

597

dred Fires Clan, according to Navajo custom, have the right to steal. They have other rites and rights they don't use much any more, but they don't have the right to secede from the Navajo Nation. They fought a war about that in 1840 with the rest of the Navajo Nation and lost, and now some Indians say the Hundred Fires devote their time to embarrassing the other Navajos by mixing with the Whites.

"It's true, you know, Twenty-six Horses," Ring said, thinking out loud. "It's true that you do hang around a lot with me."

"I don't care, Ringo," Twenty-six Horses said. "I simply don't care."

"You Hundred Fires Navajos don't have any racial prejudices."

"Not much," Twenty-six Horses said. "Very little. But let's just say we Hundred Fires don't get along too well with the other Navajos."

They were sitting cross-legged under the awkward gyrations of a sharp-smelling cedar tree and smoking kai which is the dried bark of a willow. Although Ring was white and Twenty-six Horses was red the kai was turning them both green.

"You say the Burning Bear People are going to start a volcano? How?"

"If I knew I'd be a Burning Bear person."

"You're not in their secrets?"

"I'm not talking," Twenty-six Horses said. "The best thing all us Hundred Fires Navajos can do now is to lay low. Unless you can think of some greater magic."

"Yes, I can," Ring said.

"Oh?"

"Kill you."

"We've done that. And supposing the last half of the trick, the bringing me back to life part, doesn't work some time? Something goes wrong?"

"Twenty-six Horses," Ring said carefully and raising his hand-made and fragmented cigarette to the awful blue unintimate and infinite New Mexican sky, "Don't you trust me? After all, the world is built on faith."

"Unbuild it."

"I like to think of myself as a friend of the Hundred Fires People."

"Go ahead."

"Then you'll trust me?"

"No, I won't," Twenty-six Horses said.

The willow bark tobacco rose in a personal black cloud over each young man and hung there as a dark omen might or visible gloom on a bright day.

"Sawing a woman in half."

"That's old stuff."

"Sawing an Indian in fifths."

"It all depends on the Indian."

"I had you in mind, Twenty-six Horses."

"I appreciate the thought, Ringo. Why do you smoke this stuff?"

"It's cheap. And Indians have always smoked it."

"I'd rather be sawed in fifths."

"Would you really, Twenty-six Horses?"

"No. What is this thing about you sawing me in fifths?"

"Simple."

"Could I do it to you?"

"It's not that simple."

"Then I guess we better forget the whole thing."

"And let the Burning Bear People get away with their bringing a volcano to life?" Ring dropped the wilted bark cigarette. "All right."

"I don't care really," Twenty-six Horses said. "Magic is for children."

"Kids." Ring looked down to the volcano country in the blue-mesaed distance below San Luis.

"Children," Twenty-six Horses said. "The Burning Bear People are children. How do they do it?"

"They go up to the dead volcano craters at night with junk tires. They set a slow yucca-made fuse to them and then come down and hold the volcano dance. Their predictions always come true."

"Let's expose them."

"No, we've got to make better magic, Twenty-six Horses."

"Can't you think of some magic that doesn't involve sawing me in fifths or shooting me?"

"The bullet trick."

"No," Twenty-six Horses said. "There must be a better way to get ahead. No. What about sawing an Indian in fifths?"

"I haven't worked that out yet."

"Good," Twenty-six Horses said, jumping up quickly.

They both rose and mounted their sheen-glared horses.

"Let's go to the white man's house."

"He doesn't want to be bothered, Twenty-six Horses. He wants to be left alone with his shame and his wounds."

600

"Shame and wounds is good," Twenty-six Horses said. "What is he?"

"A poet."

"Do poets have shame and wounds?"

"They are the white people's magicians. They were. Now I guess the white people haven't any use for poets, else what would he be doing here?"

"Neither do Indians," Twenty-six Horses said. "Magic is for kids. Why doesn't he become a scientist and go to the moon?"

"You think if the white people went to the moon it would solve all their problems, don't you, Twenty-six Horses?"

"No, it would solve all ours," the Indian Twenty-six Horses said.

"Wait! Why don't we tell him we just got back from the moon?"

"The poet?"

"Yes. I think he'd like to know these things."

"Keep in touch?"

"If he's any kind of a poet at all he would be concerned. We could be moon people who just got here. We like it on earth fine. Planning to send for my relatives."

"I'm taking the next rocket back home."

"You haven't liked it on the reservation."

"No. I guess I'm just an old moon-body," Twenty-six Horses said.

They rode now in high color through the sharp accent of the blooming sage as they entered a saddle of the Continental Divide below Ojo del Padre where the world fell away in absolute space to Mount Taylor, Gallup and Grants.

"There's the poet's house."

"Do poets live in houses?"

"This one does."

"We shouldn't patronize poets."

"We might want a poem some day?"

"We shouldn't patronize poets anyway."

"What's the world coming to when we can't patronize poets? What's it mean?"

"It means they've got a patron who doesn't pay. If you buy something at my father's and don't pay, that means you're patronizing him."

"Do poets have a lot of people like that?"

"I guess they do, Twenty-six Horses."

"Then no wonder poets want to go to the moon."

"Who said?"

"Well, living out here. Isn't this the moon?"

They allowed their horses to sift down through the delicate lacing shadows of juniper, wither- and cannonbone-high, in blue grama perfumed, the high wide equine nostrils lofting above the gray chamise, plunging in feathered step past all of time, the eroding Todilto formation, the yellowing Wingate and today's earth too, precarious and in almost fluid suspension on a steep hostile slope.

"I can tell time by the rocks."

"Keep your eye on the poet, Ringo. Keep your eye on the poet."

Now they entered a dry glade, a neat cup bereft of life, an old sheep bedding ground that would take two centuries to recover. They went swiftly down, then steeply up its

602

perfect sides. Here, from the top, they could see the cabin where the poet lived. There was an absolute and perfect silence, a dead lack of movement, the weathered cleanliness of a grave. The cabin rose stark like an obelisk and there was a bunch of lean-as-paintbrush paloverde weeping toward the east for epitaph. You could see a battered Stetson on the step if you looked close.

The man called the poet, with an aging, skeletal and harried face, was seated at a rough table among a chaos of books and watching toward the wide window. I wonder where? I wonder where. Yes, I need it against this sun. I wonder where I put my hat. No matter. All Indian Country is divided into three parts and the part I like best is this moon. Down there toward Cabazon and the volcano peaks it looks exactly like the moon. A poet on the moon. It's about time the Burning Bear People started their volcano. There's still time for magic on the moon. But that's not why I came here. Why does a person go to the moon? He's unhappy on earth? He's curious? No, a person goes to the moon to find something. To make a discovery. To find the person within. That's not true, the only person within is what you put there. The inner self is all too shallow and obvious. The mystery is not mysterious. I guess you're a pragmatic poet. Why then didn't I stay in the world as vice-president of the Lincoln Casualty Insurance Company? I was their first casualty. One day the vice-president didn't show up. That's not being very practical. What about the wife and kids? Martha has taken care of me for twenty years now and the kids can find someone else to milk too. Kids are not bad, it's just that they are not human. Wives are all too human. They should have passed a law against them but they never did. It's too late now, all the laws have been passed. All sorts of clever sayings like this are not going to find my hat. The ex-vice-president of the Lincoln Casualty Insurance Company cannot find his hat. Maybe they haven't missed me. A modern corporation gets along very nicely without human beings. They get in the way of the computers. They get in the way of getting things done to other human beings.

Martha will realize there is something missing between her club dates, and the kids will now be free to burn down the house. My colleagues at Lincoln Casualty should have become suspicious when I didn't become an Elk, a Lion, a Mouse or member of some other service organization. Service the world. They never realized when the world began to bore me; then I began to send off poems that were published. Fortunately no one reads published poems. It's the best way of keeping a secret. Only the poets are private. Only the moon is safe.

Phillip Reck was the name of the poet who was going to commit suicide. But why did he want his hat? He wanted his hat out of habit. He always had his hat when he walked outside, and although now he was going outside to walk off an Eocene cliff, he still wanted his hat. Phillip Reck gazed all around the room with a claimsman's eye. Phillip Reck was about fifty-seven. He had waited a long time to retire, to have all the time he wanted to write, to say all the things he wanted to say. But now, after two months here on the moon, he found out he had nothing at all to say. Nothing at all, not even one small poem. Nothing, not even an involved pun poem on his own name that came to

604

nothing—Oedipus Recks. "Time was—" He sat his long, lean frame on a rough board. "Time was, between actuarial charts, you were free to escape, but now there is nothing to escape from. All my life was to culminate right here. Like the Indians and their volcano, we Whites are a strange tribe too. I was going to erupt in a pyrotechnic display of talent that would shower the world with my genius. But after I lit the fuse nothing happened. My used tires never burned. A person dies every one point four seconds. There is a suicide every ten point four hours. I never thought that the vice-president of the Lincoln Casualty Insurance Company would be reduced to a digit in his own statistics. Where's my hat? No matter. I don't need a hat."

Phillip Reck, hatless and in an Ivy League striped coat, his sparse hair streaming in the wind from the same gust that blew fraud volcano smoke up Devil Canyon, walked smartly out the door and with quick purpose to the edge of the smoky canyon whose bright, hard floor glittered three hundred feet below.

Phillip Reck did not hesitate. He had been involved in enough huge business deals to know that he who hesitates is not lost and he was still enough of a poet to appreciate the success possibilities of a determined failure. "Sheer o'er the crystal battlements," Phillip Reck repeated as he stumbled forward. "From morn to noon he fell, from noon to dewy eve, a summer's day." The edge of the abyss came up before it should and Phillip Reck shut his eyes and someone shouted, "Wait, sir! You forgot your hat."

And so he had, Phillip Reck thought. But what a time to bring it up, and what a voice. What a sight. Two huge beasts mounted by smaller beasts. Now one of the riders hurtling past the cabin swept down and retrieved Phillip's hat, then pounded on towards Phillip Reck, brought the horse up terrifically at his feet. "Is this yours?"

"Yes," Phillip Reck said.

"We'd like to speak to you if we may."

"What about?"

"Did we interrupt?"

"Yes, but go ahead."

"This is Twenty-six Horses. He got the name because his father has or had twenty-six horses. A local Indian. A painter."

"Yes?"

"Also a Hundred Fires."

"All right."

"We heard you did magic, Mr. Reck."

"No."

"Oh?"

"I'm not interested," Phillip Reck said.

"We're sorry if you're not interested."

"I'm sorry too. Now, if you'll excuse me I've got a life to lead."

"Have you, Mr. Reck? Aren't you Phillip Reck?" Ring said down from his horse.

"Yes."

"We've got a proposition," Ring said.

"Have we?" Twenty-six Horses asked.

Phillip Reck, the poet, looked at Ring the cowboy and Twenty-six Horses, the Indian. I guess that's what they are, Phillip Reck thought, some kind of bridge with the past, back into ancestral and pioneer times, and the Indian before that, back to the primordial womb of America,

606

the world, an extant and live bridge of flesh and blood that lived in the earth before the white man invaded and still lives in that dirt hogan of earth, but maybe will live to see his dirt, his race, vanquished. This Indian then no damn symbol—wait—but still nature alive, the only nonmechanical man, and I'm a tin witness to this last— "All right, I was busy," Phillip Reck said. "Let's see now, what do you want?" Phillip Reck questioned as though not certain of his own identity and willing to be judged by children.

"We've got a proposition," Ring insisted, dismounting from his great black horse.

"You had better get rid of that horse," Phillip Reck said.

"It's only Luto," Ring said, touching the horse.

"Yes," Phillip Reck said, taking his hat and eyeing the wild white limber eye of the dark stallion. "It's another link with the past, but that stallion is a fateful one. Get rid of—Luto, did you call it?"

"I forgot."

"What have you forgotten?"

"That you're a poet, Mr. Reck."

"Everyone has. I'd forgotten it myself."

"It's perfectly all right, your being a poet, Mr. Reck. You can be anything you like."

"You're very young."

"That is, being a poet is your business."

"It's not my business."

"Well," Ring said, confused.

"You better pay attention to Ringo, Mr. Reck," Twenty-six Horses said, touching his head. "Ringo's got a lot of stuff up here—no brains, but a lot of stuff up here."

607

"Well, I guess we better be going," Ring began to pull on the horse.

"Don't!"

"Why not? We interrupted what you were doing, Mr. Reck."

"What I was doing was not important."

"Oh?"

"It can be put off till another time."

Two horses and three men close to the edge of a precipice in the high Checkerboard Country of northern New Mexico, the sun white-hot, invisible over an aged invincible earth, torn by barrancas, canyons, livid scars, color-muted by eons, the people on the edge no violence to the totality—the vast breathless tranquility of time.

"Being a poet we thought you might—"

"Yes?"

"Make some magic."

"No. You see, that's not—" Phillip wondered about this, wondered aloud at the young men. "Not now. You see, the scientists, now it's not the religious or the poetical—"

"I like that word."

"But not even the scientists. No, it's— Now it's—" Phillip Reck struggled there at the edge. "Now the magic is in being alive."

"Alive?"

Yes, Phillip Reck considered to himself, science will never solve all of that magic, not with their twenty-eight chromosomes, their RH factor or their genes. Being alive, I mean. Oh, here's a trick to end all magic, being alive. But it gives me an idea. "I might do one more small magic," Phillip Reck said aloud. "I've got an idea."

"Good."

"For a poem."

"Oh dear."

"Yes," Phillip Reck said, moving away from the edge. "But what was it you boys had in mind?"

"Well, I was going to kill someone—"

"Is that magic?"

"And then bring them back alive."

"You just did," Phillip Reck said.

"I mean seriously."

Phillip Reck sat down on a rock where he could survey the deep canyon below and began to sweat. "Ah, seriously," Phillip Reck said quietly. "All Indian Country is divided into three parts—*y tenia optar por la luna.*"

"What does that mean? Does it have anything to do with the blue hogan?"

"It means 'and I had to choose the moon,'" Phillip Reck said.

"Don't be discouraged, Mr. Reck."

"We're moon people," Twenty-six Horses said.

"Yes, I know," Phillip Reck said. "You live here."

"We're not just visiting, but we like it."

"I'm just visiting," Phillip Reck said. "I suppose if I told you I made sixty thousand dollars a year you wouldn't believe it."

"Why not?"

"Or that I was a poet."

"Tell us a poem."

"I haven't written one recently." Phillip Reck pondered about this, reflectively wiping a thin hand over a long face. "Not lately."

"I guess you're not a moon-body either. Why don't you join us?"

"Yes," Ring said. "Throw in with us."

"What do you do?"

"Saw a poet in fifths."

"I was leaving," Phillip Reck said. "As you came up I was just leaving."

"Then come with us," Ring said. "We'll show you the long way down."

The long way down, Phillip Reck thought, looking out over the wild endless country. The long way down. All the long way down. Yes, there has got to be a way down and out, and I guess it's always the long way. There are no short cuts. A man can't, no man has the right. Failure must always be part of trying. You can't escape. You've got to go all the long way, every bit of the way. It will be quite a time before a man can escape to a real moon. I don't want a ticket. I don't want a ticket ever, because you can't buy one that takes you away from yourself. That's the kind of magic no Indian, no man, is any good at. And until they have that kind of magic I will write my own. No one need know. Only the poet is private. Only the world is safe.

"Yes," Phillip Reck said, turning. "All right, gentlemen, the long way down. But I've learned something."

"Yes, Mr. Reck?"

"I've learned that the earth is a beautiful world peopled with creatures wonderfully from way back. There's still poetry—being alive. That's poetry with you, isn't it? A mystical involvement with the country, that's your magic. It could be the only magic that counts. But I owe you something."

610

"What for?"

"A summer," Phillip Reck said. "That pillar of smoke. For saving— For saving—" Phillip Reck began again, but he could not get it out, so he said, "For saving my hat."

"That's all?"

"Very well," Phillip Reck said, drawing a thin hand over his forehead. "Very well. For saving my life."

"It was nothing."

"Perhaps," Phillip Reck said. "But how do we know?" Phillip Reck shook his head slowly and pondered emptily into the long perfect space of Indian Country. "How can anyone be absolutely certain?" Phillip Reck watched the pillar of smoke explode soundlessly into a gray canopy shrouding the earth. "Yes, gentlemen, you can show me the long way down."

Far in the west the Burning Bear People led by Many Cattle and Winding Water had finished their job on the volcano and they waited huddled in groups for the effect to spread over Indian Country. They would all be great shamans. And yes, their Indian logic did go back to a kind of prelogic, a world where all objects and animals, even effects, have a feeling, a mind of their own. Before they left for the volcano the Burning Bear People had carefully built a taboo of pyramidally arranged rock alongside each of their hogans to keep the Hundred Fires People from stealing from the houses while the Burning Bear People were making their magic. Now, as their giant black cloud drifted toward Gallup, putting all the land in the shadow of the Burning Bear, Many Cattle and Winding Water, forming a group of their own beneath a lesser volcano, noticed a party of three going over the Continental Divide; the one trailing in the rear, by his weird walk, was obviously a White. "Yes, it's strange," Winding Water said, "when he entered our country you felt someone had just left."

"And more strange," Many Cattle said, tending the volcano with his eye, "now that the white man is leaving you feel that someone has just arrived."

The magical black cloud of many spirits widened over all parts of Indian Country, darkening the trading post and the blue hogan, hiding the bedizened earth past the volcano country, encircling Mount Taylor in a grand cape, high over Route 66 to the south, softly, gently sheltering, shadowing blue- and red-ocher-faced hogan dwellers to the north; and at the Continental Divide the cloud hid the walking white man in sudden darkness; reoccurring, he appeared and reappeared in the somber recapitulant magic of the Burning Bear. Now the walking white man departed the two on big horses and tumbled down toward Route 66 all alone, but quickly, to join the flow of tin cars. The first white man—the last poet—on the moon.

"Did I interrupt a thought, Twenty-six Horses?"

"No. I was only thinking."

"About the poet?"

"About my painting down there at the top of the arroyo. That flat spot up on the sandstone is a good place."

"No one will ever see it."

"Poets and painters can't worry about that," Twenty-six Horses said. "The watcher not only can't figure out what it is, but this time he won't even know where it is. Let him worry." Twenty-six Horses stared down into the awful abyss of the arroyo below the sandstone wall. "Yes, Ring, we'll let him worry."

"Don't you believe," Ring said, "that two people can be together all the time, trust each other like Hundred Fires People but more than that, be blood brothers?"

"Blood brothers?"

"More than that. Not have to be all alone like the poet."

"Sure, Ringo, sure. Sure, why not? Sure." Twenty-six Horses stopped the Appaloosa horse he rode. "But a man has got to paint his own pictures, paint his own blue hogan." He allowed his horse to move off. "Every man has got his own pictures," Twenty-six Horses said.

"Not like the poet, but more—like The Prince?"

"Yes, more like The Prince," Twenty-six Horses said.

FIVE

THE PRINCE CAME to Indian Country when his world fell. His title was no accident of blood nor fantasy nor imaginative appellation of some trader in the area. The title had been conferred on him by all, earned by him for doing something better than anybody in the world. He blew a horn. He blew the horn better than anybody in the world. His kingdom in the South had been overrun, but the defeated were unvanquished. They left the South, New Orleans mostly, for nowhere when their world fell, when corruption rode in on a slick facile beat infecting everywhere. They left the South but they remembered, they endured, until they died in some hovel. They endured, their gold trumpet still there, their sceptre still borne in the dust, and sometimes singing.

The Prince wandered to Indian Country to die in an unclaimed hogan. Before death Twenty-six Horses, who lived hard by, could hear the quick jerk of sweet music flow out over the quiet land, rhythmic and gay and sometimes sad.

The Prince had been on his way to Denver he thought, from Albuquerque, but he was on his way to nowhere. He was one of the dispossessed, the unwanted, the wanderers over the unsinging land.

"One of those who had secret dreams. He would not corrupt. One of those who knew who he was," the trader George Bowman said.

"Yes, of course," the city man who had come so far said. "But I don't want any philosophy. I'm paid to get the facts. Did he die of starvation?"

"Why?"

"We're making a TV spectacular of his life," the man said.

"Maybe."

"Maybe," the man who had come so far and dressed in city clothes said. "Maybe. The producer won't settle for maybe. I got to get the facts. I pay well."

"That may very well be," the trader said. "Maybe he did die of starvation. What would that be worth?"

"I'm going to level with you," the city man said. He wore a pork pie hat with a narrow brim snapped down over a harried, small-featured baby face. "I'm going to level with you." The baby-faced city man stared around the trading post at the goods and the Indians against the wall. "We'll pay what it's worth. If he died of starvation for example and you gave it to us, we'll send you a check for what it's worth."

"It's worth nothing," the trader said.

"All right," the city man said. "I'm going to level with you. I want to succeed."

The trader, George Bowman, was dressed like the Indians in tight Levi's with a big Stetson pushed back above a long and slanting face. Absent-minded in back of the long counter and leaning forward he waited for the city man to continue his sentence.

"I want to succeed," the city man repeated. "That's all. I want to succeed. Offering you money doesn't seem to work so I'm giving it to you straight. I want to succeed."

"Congratulations," the trader said and he went back to Ring, telling Ring to turn the black horse out.

"But I've failed," the city man said.

"Congratulations anyway," the trader said, turning back.

"Listen," the city man said. "I was going to bluff it through. This is my first assignment but I was going to act like an old vet, toss some money around and things like that. Did I hurt your feelings?"

The trader shook his head no.

"I'd like to get back to Albuquerque and call the wife and say, Look, look who succeeded."

The trader was mixed up with Ring again, telling him that if the black horse was claimed by no one there must be a good reason, but the city man interrupted.

"The company flew me out here in a DC-8 Mainliner and they put me up at the Albuquerque Hilton, rented me a Hertz Drive-Ur-Self car, no questions asked. Today I'm dead. You sure I didn't hurt your feelings?"

617

The trader shook his head no.

"You mind if I talk to the Indians?"

"There's no law against talking to the Indians."

"Do they speak English?"

"They speak some of all foreign languages, Apache, Pueblo, English. Yes, they speak English," the trader said. "But don't tell them you want to succeed."

"Thank you," the city man said.

"And talk to the one on the end of the bench, the one with the turquoise ring. He was his friend."

"Did you know The Prince?" the city man said to the Indian, without any niceties.

"Yes," the Indian said.

"Did he die of starvation?"

"Maybe," the Indian said.

"My name is Winterhalter," the city man said.

"Congratulations," the Indian said.

"I've come a long way," the city man with the pork pie hat said, "to get the scoop on The Prince. And all I get is maybe. The producer won't think much of that."

"That's too bad," the Indian said.

"The Prince is a famous man now," the city man said. "They're playing his music again. Everyone wants to know about him. I've come a long way to find out. You might say I represent a hundred million people." The city man paused and watched the Indian for the effect. "Yes, I might say it—"

"Say it," the Indian said.

The city man got up and walked back to the trader.

"I'm not getting anywhere. I'm dead," he said. "Just

618

tell me, did The Prince come out here and starve to death?
I can build from that."

"Work on that Indian you just talked to," the trader
said. "They call him Twenty-six Horses. He's an artist.
They were friends, The Prince and Twenty-six Horses.
They were artists."

"Yes, but I can't build on that. I'm interested in The
Prince," the city man said. "The Prince must have come
into your post."

"Yes."

"Did he have anything to trade?"

"No, nothing."

"What do the Indians trade?"

"In season, wool. Most of the year their turquoise jewelry. I keep the jewelry until they redeem it."

"He had a trumpet," the city man said. "Why didn't he
pawn that?"

"Because I wouldn't take it," the trader said.

"Why?"

"Because I figure with the Indians the jewelry is their
wealth, their beauty. With his trumpet—"

"It was his life," Winterhalter said.

"Maybe," the trader said.

"But you loaned him money without taking the
trumpet?"

"Some."

"Listen, I'm doing all right," the city man said.

"You always will."

"I mean I'm getting somewhere," Winterhalter said.
"Now, did he finally die of starvation?"

"Maybe."

"That's no help."

"He came a time ago."

"We know that."

"It was a rainy night. I don't know how he got here. Some salesman gave him a lift I guess, who went back to Albuquerque. He hung around the post till it closed. I couldn't see him standing out on that muddy road with no cars. It was dirt then."

"It still is."

"No. Gravel."

"Gravel?"

"I took him to a hogan. He was a tall, bent man with small alert eyes, graying hair under a wide preacher hat. Carried a brief case with socks, new shirt and such. He was a clean old man. In the other hand he carried the instrument. It was in a black case. I knew that's what it was because when I left him there, and had only gotten away maybe fifty yards, it started."

"What was that?"

"This thing he had in the case. I just stood there in the rain, maybe fifteen minutes, listening, not knowing I was soaking wet. Then I realized I was surrounded by Indians listening too."

"Then he did die of starvation?"

"No. Not then. That is, he became a thing with the Indians—his music anyway. They fed him for months, almost years, and then he had a hogan—a house—for the first time in maybe ten years. Then one night the Indians burnt it down."

"Then he didn't die of starvation. He was—"

"No," the trader said.

"But why burn his house down? Oh, of course," the city man said. "I see."

"What do you see?"

"He was a Negro."

"No," the trader said. "I mean, the Indians didn't know that. They thought maybe he was some new kind of a white man. They'd never seen a Black before and they thought he was some new kind of a white man."

"And you never told them?"

"What was there to tell them?"

"I see," the city man said. "I'll accept that. But what did he die of? You say he didn't get burnt in the house."

"No. He played on that thing while the hogan burnt, helped them start the fire, then played on that thing while the house burned. Then they built him another."

"What was wrong with the one they burned?"

"A Navajo had died in it. Evil spirits. That's why it was vacant, why it was available for him to move in and why it was burned."

"I see. Then he didn't die there?"

"No," the trader said. "He became a thing with the Indians, played at all their yebechais. He was their new kind of a white man. The first white man they had discovered who was black. They knew he was a white man because that's the way he acted, dressed and the language he spoke, but they knew he was a new kind of white man because he was black—"

"And made sweet music."

"Yes," the trader said.

"He was a genius. We know that now. A little late."

"A little late."

"But the Indians knew it because they too were primitive, could understand the clear, simple, honest note—"

"You reach," the trader said.

"Maybe we don't reach enough," the city man said. "Anyway they'll take care of that in the office. But what happened then? When did he die of starvation?"

"Who said he died of starvation?" The trader moved down the counter.

"You didn't deny it," the city man said, following.

"I didn't say it either," the trader said.

"You mind if I try the Indian again?"

"Go ahead," the trader said.

When the city man sat down Twenty-six Horses got up and went over to the window. His round dark face was without expression.

I'm projecting the wrong image, Winterhalter thought. My company wants a certain image and I guess I just don't have it. Maybe I'm a human being. The company psychologist told me how to relate to the nonurban guy but I'm dead, the city man thought. You can't approach an Indian. You can't approach an Indian or a king or a genius. You can't get anything out of those kinds of people. They got a world all of their own. Why did they have to send me on this kind of assignment to the damn Indians? I'm dead. I'll never succeed. I wonder how The Prince got close to the Indians. I guess he had something they wanted to buy. Well, they won't buy money, I found that out. What did he have, what did The Prince have they wanted to buy? Art? That covers too much. That means nothing. That's awful vague. Better, it was his music that got around all

622

languages, all differences. What have I got? Nothing. I'm dead. I'll never get around them. I'll never succeed.

The city man thought a bit about all the money the company had put out to send him here to the end of the world. I must have something. The wife says I've got something. The company says I've got something. Well, it certainly isn't brains and it certainly isn't good looks. Well, what else is there? Will power. That's what I got—will power. If God forgot you on everything else you can always pick up plenty of will power around the place. And stick-to-itness and perseverance, keeping my nose clean and hitting the line hard. That's what I got. I got nothing.

The city man turned to the Indian next to him. "Yes, I have. I've got patience, that's what I've got. Patience."

"Congratulations," the Indian said.

Twenty-six Horses, who had gone over to the window to avoid the city man, looked out over the far country and thought: How can you tell it to a man like that? How can you tell him about the man who knew who he was? How can you tell him about The Prince? Who but another artist would understand the loneliness and the separateness of wanting to belong but needing to belong in your own way? Who would understand? Who would understand that he had to live at the end of the world because the end of the world was the only place people understood. Now it's different; from what the city man says some people understand now all over the world and they want to make something about him now. But who understood back there? No one understood back there. That's why people have to go to the end of the world because people don't understand in the middle of the world. Well, why not change? Why not come down to earth? I guess it's because the earth's not right. When the earth is right people like The Prince will come down to it. How did he say it? Peace. That's what The Prince said. That doesn't sound much like a prince talking but he said it just that way. He said other things too, like, Give me some skin, Indian. The city man wouldn't understand that but the city man wanted to know about starvation. Yes, The Prince starved to death but maybe not in the way a city man would understand. He wants the facts, but what good are the facts without The Prince?

"Listen," the city man said. "I've got a proposition." He had joined the Indian at the window and he pulled down on his narrow-brimmed oval hat. The Indian noticed that the city man had a green and red feather in the band from no bird that ever lived.

"My proposition is this." He reached into a green leather brief case and brought out strings of bright beads. He placed the bright beads along the counter, draping some of them so they hung down over the edge in all their gaudy glass brilliance. The city man stepped back away from them to admire them and envy the ones that were going to get them and wonder whether he could afford to part with them and furrowed his brow at the terrific expense of giving away this chief's ransom. When he had used up all these expressions and more he said, "I give you these in return for the facts about The Prince."

The trader translated to some of the Indians that did not follow and all the Indians mumbled among themselves for a long minute.

"I'm waiting," the city man said. "Is it a deal?"

624

The Indians ignored him, continuing to mumble.

"I've got to have a decision," the city man said.

The Indians stopped their conference now.

"Well, what is it?" the city man said.

"They want to know where you got them."

"It's a collection formerly owned by a man named Woolworth. That's who I got them from."

The Indians mumbled again among themselves before the trader announced their decision.

"They say for you to blow the whistle on that guy Woolworth. He sold you a pile of glass."

"Well, that's what I read," the city man said.

"Manhattan Island," the trader said. "New York City maybe, but nothing they think worth while. Not for glass."

"All right, you win," the city man said. "But I've got another proposition. My proposition is this," the city man said. "I've got patience. I'll stay around here for years if necessary, badgering you people. It's the big weapon. I hope you people don't make me use it."

The Indians were silent.

The city man took off his hat, examined it, flicked his feather and put it on again. Then he watched the Indians a long moment before he went over to the counter and came back with his green cowhide briefcase from which he withdrew a book with the title *Hommes et Problèmes du Jazz*.

"I've got another proposition," the city man said. "You understand that?" He held up the book. "You understand what that says?"

"Yes," Twenty-six Horses nodded from a hooded glance.

"Oh," the city man said. "You're not supposed to. I was going to translate what this man said about The Prince's music in exchange for your facts."

"I learned a few words at Indian boarding school," Twenty-six Horses said. "Not too much."

"Enough probably to correct me. No, I've got another proposition." The city man took off his hat and drummed on it, then he touched the bright feather of no bird with a preening motion. "Supposing I could bring The Prince back—back to life. Would you give me the facts then?"

"Yes," Twenty-six Horses said, knowing he was risking nothing. "I buried him."

"And I shall make him rise again," the city man said.

All the silent, invulnerable Indians who looked straight ahead into infinity, seeing and hearing nothing, all smiled now. All tapped their feet and moved their eyes and all the squaws sitting under the counter shook their heads and winked and touched each other, looked at the city man and then away again, embarrassed.

"He shall rise again." the city man repeated.

"When?" Twenty-six Horses said.

"Now," the city man said. "Follow me."

All the Indians trooped out in file after the city man with a feather. They followed him to the car while he got another case, a red one this time. Now he had a green and a red case in either arm and a green and red feather in his hat.

"Where did he live?" he said.

Twenty-six Horses pointed to the hogan under the purple brow of a near blue mesa. The Indians followed the bright feathered hat of the city man through the gray sage and stark greasewood, past a pale blue hogan surrounded by beavertail and cholla cactus. Now they went through the piñon, clumped and huddled, the line of file of the Indians swinging with the lead of the city man. Now they were in the flat country, the land of grama and sand and infinity and occasionally this.

"What's that?" the city man said.

"Arroyo," Twenty-six Horses said. All the Indians and Ring stood at the edge of the canyon that separated them from the hogan.

"Impossible to cross here," Twenty-six Horses said. "We can cross five miles down."

"Then it might be too late," the city man said. "Might lose the tip."

"The what?"

"The audience," the city man said. "Follow me." He crossed his green and red cases in front of him and got down on his rear and slid down the bank. At the bottom he got up running. When he reached the opposite bank he ran right up it, full at it, then he fell and scrambled, clawed his way to the top, the red and green cases finally flung over the top and the man following, slowly pulling himself up on a greasewood root.

"There," the man hollered loud across the arroyo. "Don't just watch. Follow me."

The Indans settled for just watching, standing there along the edge of the canyon. If he was going to produce The Prince they could see from here.

"All right," the city man said, and he turned and walked toward the hogan, entered it and soon reappeared without the red and green cases and without The Prince.

"Now," the city man said, and he kicked the hogan and out came The Prince, not in the flesh but as the Indians remembered him.

The Indians piled down the bank now and ran up the other side, not even scrambling but running upright on the impossible angle. Now they stood panting, listening, in front of the city man. The city man took off his hat, drummed on it and preened the feather.

"It's a phonograph," Twenty-six Horses said.

"But it's him, The Prince." The city man put on his hat. "He's come back," he said.

Twenty-six Horses listened now to the long solid wail of an alone trumpet blasting clearly and big through the long Indian Country.

"Yes," Twenty-six Horses said. "It's him."

A note hung now, wavered and then blew loud and clear.

"Yes. Yes," Twenty-six Horses said.

"That's all a man is," the city man said. "What he does. This is what he did. This is The Prince. The Prince had patience."

"Yes," Twenty-six Horses said.

The music started to walk now and sing, led by the big trumpet, then hushed, muted now before it exploded brilliantly, colored glass shattering in the sun.

"A man doesn't die now," the city man said. "Not some men. They can always come back when the world is ready, when the world is right. Patience."

The music shifted now to a weird, steady beat, the trumpet sliding in and out tenderly, then suddenly clean and brave.

628

"Some people don't die any more." The city man took out a pack of cigarettes and offered them around but the Indians and Ring were listening. "If he has patience he can come back. He can live forever."

"Yes, yes," Twenty-six Horses said. "But listen."

"Do I win?" the city man said.

"Man is more powerful than death. Yes. Anything. But listen."

"Thank you," the city man said.

Late that afternoon back at the post the city man gave Twenty-six Horses a large album of records marked "The Prince."

"Keep these," he said. "And the machine too. You can bring him back any time you want."

"I didn't think there were any records of his."

"Not for a long time," the city man said. "But you've only got to find some busted old ones in New Orleans, piece them together and make a million copies."

"Is that what they did?"

"Two million," the city man said.

"That's nice. That's very nice," Twenty-six Horses said. "Thank you."

"And now, did he die of starvation?" the city man said.

"Yes," Twenty-six Horses said. "It was a long hard winter, that winter. There wasn't much a man, an Indian, could do against such a long hard cold winter. But he played against it and he was winning as far as we were concerned. But he couldn't stand it. With all the hunger he had seen in his own people he had never seen anything like what happens to an Indian in a long hard cold winter. He sold his trumpet to a trader from Aztec, bought food

629

from him and fed us all. Not from our trader. Our trader was out of food, but he bought food from Aztec and fed us all. Then he starved to death. You understand how a man with food could starve to death?"

"I think so."

"Without his trumpet to blow. It was his life."

"Yes."

"Is that enough?"

"I think we can build with that."

The city man rose now, put on his pork pie hat and proffered his hand towards Twenty-six Horses. Twenty-six Horses looked at it and then up to the ceiling. The city man pulled down on his hat then held out his hand again. Twenty-six Horses took his hand slowly now, but he took it. They stared into each other's eyes a brief second, the pressure between their hands increasing.

"Peace. Now I go," the city man said, turning and walking to the door. Before he closed it he said, "See you later, alligator."

Twenty-six Horses went into the back room where the sheep hides hung and where the Indians, the trader George Bowman, and his son Ring were listening to the record. Twenty-six Horses had a whole album of the records in his arms. He walked out of the room again, conscious of his riches. Twenty-six Horses went over to the window and raised the album to his lips. Then he watched out the window as the city man's car, running beneath the big mesa became a speck of almost nothing soon to disappear. "Yes, all right," Twenty-six Horses answered toward the nothing, and smiling. "In a while, crocodile."

SIX

AT THE BOTTOM of the arroyo where Ring lay, all the time was running out. All the time was running out and all the strength, but not all the love. He could feel the body, all of his hard, young and tired, very stiff and tired self go gently down, gently, gently, but down, down to a bottom, and there was no bottom. There was no other place. There is only this place.

And I want to say this, Ring thought up at the blinding sky. Indian Country is a good place; it is an all right place. It's a feudal place, the trading post—a castle and subjects, I guess, like in the Middle Ages. My old man said—What did my old man say, horse? Luto stood black and solid and quiet in the silent shadows.

My old man said a place where the only law is love and

the only occupations watching sheep and making love—
a community of nature. Do you like that, Luto? But we
get invaded. We get invaded by Texas and countries like
that. I'm trying to keep my mind occupied, Luto. Help
me, Luto. We get invaded by Albuquerque and cities
like that.

Ring wiped the watery sand from his lips. The Portales
Mesa. We get invaded by ourselves, people like that.
They come from all over with a problem: the poet, the
pilot, The Prince. Indian Country is a solution for my
father, the poet and the pilot and The Prince. This water
is a solution. Digging in the ground and burying someone is a solution. Just digging is good. The Prince had a
problem he brought to Indian Country. So did those three
men we met on the Portales. Don't they know we got
problems here too? That death comes to Indian Country
too?

There was a brooding silence at the mouth of the prehistoric cave on the Portales Mesa, a slow ballooning of
hushed time on the Portales, because at this point, now,
here, a stasis had arrived on the mesa so that this day,
hour, this second did not flow but remained fixed without
a continuum in any time or even place; although this
tableau of the near-naked young men at the mouth of the
cave site was now, the scene could have fled back in
prehistory to join the other fancies scattered here in mural
haste on these savage walls, or the polychrome abstrac-
tions on the smashed pots at their feet; because they too
were frozen in the same sort of enigma, in search of some
exact kind of paradox, such as: Why are some personality

types more prevalent in certain groups than others? Why is the Navajo word for corn the same as the Pueblo word for food? Why does the Navajo expression for planting mean "snow sprinkled on the ground"? And why is the Navajo phrase for a bad spirit "He Who Brings Darkness Back To The Canoe"?

"I swear I don't know, Ringo."

"It means you Navajos originally came from the north."

"How far north?"

"We suspect Siberia originally, don't we, Luto?" Ring said to his horse.

"You do?" Twenty-six Horses said.

"We can date your habitation here now by carbon nineteen."

"You can? Habitation? You can?"

"Yes. Organic matter you used in building, such as timbers, degenerates at a constant rate and that change can be measured to give us the time it's been here. It's a clock."

"It is?"

"You don't care, do you?"

"Not much."

Ring looked around at the site, the mouth of a huge cave on the west slope of the Portales Mesa. Well, anyway this is getting me away from all the superstition about my horse Luto. Luto is okay. When people can't see what's bad in themselves they blame it on a horse. They get another superstition.

"Superstition is a word we use to describe someone else's religion," Ring said.

Twenty-six Horses looked around the site puzzled.

"In spite of our worship of gadgets and rockets," Ring said, "we Indians, and I mean all Americans—"

"You do?"

"We are innocent of science, especially artists are, Twenty-six Horses, of the beauty of the everlasting hunt, the excitement and gusto in the never-ending chase of truth. It is depersonalized but humanized. That's what makes it unique as a religion."

"Is that what does it?"

"Yes. All other religions are an escape, if I can repeat myself, from our uniqueness."

"You can repeat yourself all right," Twenty-six Horses said.

"But it's not getting on with our dig, is it?"

"It's not our dig, it's your dig."

"Yes, Twenty-six Horses," Ring said. "Your Navajo culture lag is greater than I imagined."

"Thanks," Twenty-six Horses said, looking in back of himself. "Thanks."

"Yes, and oddly enough," Ring said, "we have only one case of a patrilineal society becoming matrilineal, which means descent through women. You Navajos are matrilineal."

"That's nice," Twenty-six Horses said. "Are there some people who don't use women?"

"Women are always indispensable we've found," Ring said.

"Me too," Twenty-six Horses agreed. "And another thing, you can't get along without women."

"As an artist you're not as unscientific as I thought."

"And I've got pretty teeth too," Twenty-six Horses said.

634

"But my eyes tell me there are two men over there forcing another man down into a break in the rock."

"Where?"

"Just above the rimrock on the Portales."

"I don't see anyone."

"Below the piñon."

"Yes. Is that people? But there are only two."

"Yes, just two now. They've got the other man down in the big crack. His hands were tied behind his back."

"You're imagining things, Twenty-six Horses," Ring said.

"Indians don't have imaginations, remember?"

"Let's go over and find out."

"I think we better stay away," Twenty-six Horses said. "It looks like bad business."

"Do you want to go on with the dig?"

"No, I guess we better go find out."

"It's all the same thing," Ring said. "One and the same thing—curiosity. Science is curiosity."

"Tell it to the horse."

"Science is curiosity," Ring said to the horse Luto as they rode off in a confused dust.

Not quite at the top and not quite at the widest place on Portales Mesa, but on a wide, high, flat ledge near the top, the two men in city clothes stood with their hands on their hips and looked down into the great three-foot wide fissure in the clean rock.

The two men over the fissure had taken a third man prisoner from in front of his house early this brittle, blue New Mexican morning. Now the third man was down in the crack. The two men standing there were Morris Lennie and Lou Adler. The man down below was a German named Reinhardt Haupt, a Nazi, a former Nazi, who now read the Bible. Every day after work at the Rocketdyne Corporation he read the Bible. It helped him to forget.

Morris Lennie and Lou Adler were Germans too, but not Nazis—refugees. They could not forget. They did not want to forget. They had planned this kidnapping for a long time and this morning they had brought it off. Morris Lennie was now a surgeon who lived in the snob suburb of Albuquerque called Ranchos de Bernardos and Lou Adler taught music at Albuquerque High and lived in a crackerbox tract called Princess Jean Park on the Heights near the airport and Rocketdyne. But they both loved revenge. They had planned this kidnapping for a long time. They had planned to throw Haupt over the cliff, but neither quite had the heart for this, so they forced him down this fissure instead.

"It's really crueller this way, Morris," the tall bony man said down to the wide, sweating doctor. "He will suffer more."

"Will he, Lou? And can you stand it?"

"Of course I can stand it."

"We will see if you can stand it, Lou," the doctor said looking up. "When we didn't follow the original plan I wash my hands."

"This is better. He suffers more. For the suffering he caused, he suffers more."

"But can you stand it, Lou?" the doctor insisted.

"I can stand it. I can stand it, Morris. But where is he?"

"Haupt? Down there," Morris said, wiping his pale, wet face with a white linen handkerchief. He tapped his foot. "You saw him go down?" They conversed in questions.

"But look?"

"But why should I look, Lou? Tell me why I should look?"

"Are you afraid to look, Morris?"

"Tell me why I should be afraid to look? Tell me why?"

"Because I think he's dead."

"No?"

"Yes. I don't hear anything."

The man called Morris got down on his knees and looked. "He's not dead. He's not even down there."

"He didn't come up, Morris."

"He may have fallen further down. We'd better get a rope."

"Get a rope? Why should we get a rope?"

"Can you sleep tonight?"

"Where can I get a rope?"

"We'd better get a rope before he dies."

"That's a Nazi, Morris. We planned this very well. We were going to kill him. Now you're worried."

"Maybe he wasn't a Nazi."

"We checked and rechecked everything carefully, Morris. He was a Nazi."

"Yes. Was." Morris was down on his hands and knees staring. "But what good does killing one more person do?"

"He's not a person, Morris."

"Where have I heard that before?"

The man standing, called Lou Adler, raised his arms in impatience. "I haven't got a rope, Morris, to save your Nazi, but I've got a light to see him." Lou Adler removed a pencil flashlight from his pocket and passed it down to Morris Lennie.

"Lou!" Morris called, and then he got up and began to run. "Follow me! Haupt got out the lower level! The Nazi got away!"

The two men in loose city clothes bounded over the flat rock with surprising speed. When they got to the ledge they jumped down the seven or ten feet to the next level without fear in their desperate haste to catch the man. They both sprawled on their faces when they fell but got up almost in the same movement and were running. They ran down the long haunch of the Portales Mesa in the direction of a piñon forest they had seen the man enter. When they got to the forest they were running heavily, breathing like spent animals, but they pushed themselves on. Now they had pushed right through the forest and the sheer edge of the mesa loomed up, but there was no man ahead.

"Where did he get to?"

"We must have lost him in the forest."

They both pulled up and turned back into the trees, moving quickly despite the big strain on their city hearts. After searching the forest tiredly Morris sat down.

"He got away."

"You let him get away."

"I let him get away?"

"Before, you wanted to save him with a rope."

"How do you know I didn't want to hang him?"

"Did you want to hang him, Morris?" the other asked sadly.

"Not then, but now I would."

"Would you, Morris?" Lou Adler had small, liquid, light eyes and he spoke to Morris as though the doctor were very important. "Would you actually, Morris, take a life?"

"His, yes," Morris Lennie said.

They were both spent and sweating dismally into the ground, watching down forlornly into the cool earth.

"Look, Morris," Lou said, going down on his hands and knees. "A beautiful potsherd," he said, holding it up.

"Lou," Morris sang in a low, high-pitched voice. "You're supposed to be looking for the German."

"He can't go any place, Morris. Look, I've found the mate. You see, the pieces fit perfectly together. This is pre-Navajo work, Morris. Prehistoric."

"Pre-Nazi," Morris said.

"Just help me find the rest of this pot, Morris. It won't take long. We may never find this site again."

"No," Morris said.

"Then I'll find it myself. Here, I've got the bottom of the pot. Notice the design."

"Here's a piece of the top," Morris said, leaning over. "And the handle."

"That's not a handle, Morris," Lou said, adding it to his pile. "It's an imperfection in the pot."

"It's a handle."

"Any student of archeology, anyone who handled artifacts, would recognize this as a thumb mark."

"It's a handle," Morris said.

639

"I've got the rest of the bottom."

"And here's the lower part of the top."

"Look up, Morris! Look up!"

Morris did not have to look up. He could see the shadow of the man in the trench coat on the ground by his hands. He could also see the shadow of the boulder the man held aloft. "Go ahead, throw it," Morris said "There are a few of us you haven't killed. Finish the job."

"We are hopeless," Lou said. "When we are supposed to be killing a person we dig our graves at archeology."

"We deserve everything we get," Morris said. "We behave like human beings in a world of animals. There is no place for us. No place." As a final gesture on earth Morris Lennie, under the great dark shadow that was over him, fitted together the lower puzzle of the pot.

"No, Morris," Lou said. "That's not a handle. You've got this part upside down."

"It's a handle." Morris said what he thought were his last words as the shadow above moved violently and the great rock was flung, but away somewhere, and Morris stood up in time to see the man in the trench coat, which was the heavy gray color of dark shadows, disappear in the trees to be replaced by two young men on horses.

"What's this?" Morris asked up at the young men. "Where did you come from?"

"We were watching you," Ring said.

"Will you help us catch that man?"

"What for?"

"We want to kill him. He has murdered many people."

Ring looked down at the heavy sad sensitive faces of the city men and thought about the other face, particularly the manner and bearing of the man who had held the great rock over their heads and had just run. "Yes," Ring said down from his horse. "But can you do it?"

"Of course."

"Why didn't you?"

"He got away."

"While you were digging in the ruins?"

"No, before that. Digging in the ruins had nothing to do with it, did it, Lou? This is Mr. Lou Adler. I'm Dr. Lennie."

"I'm Ring Bowman," Ring said. "This is Twenty-six Horses."

"You're just the man we need," Morris said.

Twenty-six Horses looked down at the two men hard. "Why are certain personality types more prevalent in some groups than others?"

"Twenty-six Horses memorized that," Ring said.

"Why," Twenty-six Horses continued. "Why is the Navajo word for seed 'snow sprinkled on the ground', and why is the word for a bad spirit 'He Who Brings Darkness Back To The Canoe'?"

"You Navajos must have originally come from the north where the Indians used canoes," Morris said.

"He's heard this before, Ringo."

"No, he figured it out from the evidence, Twenty-six Horses. That's science."

"Say it all again," Lou Adler said. "And say it slowly."

"I'll say this slowly," Morris Lennie said. "We'd better find Haupt before it gets dark. After two thousand years of darkness we are going to have some light, some revenge. With the help of these two with horses we can't lose."

Morris Lennie and Lou Adler exchanged glances of mutual certainty. This was the crowning moment of all their plans. In a little while now it would all be over. Twenty-six Horses and the boy on the black horse would help. No one had said this was so but Lou Adler and Morris Lennie wanted to believe it was true. They wanted to believe as they watched the sky in an explosion of color below the mesa that this was the end of Haupt's road. There would be an inevitability about events now that would keep them from bungling again.

"Rope him!" Morris hollered.

The man called Haupt broke from his place of concealment in the trees and ran for the edge of the cliff.

"Don't let him escape! Stop him!" Morris shouted.

Without command Luto leaped like a horse speared after the fleeing man who ran with a loose drunken abandon now in his desperation to reach the edge. Luto followed him as he would a steer; the horse, anticipating the quarry, moved in sudden jerks of speed to get alongside the man so the rider could put a rope on the scurrying, dodging man animal. Ring began to swing his rope and then shot a small compact loop that caught the man perfectly. The horse stopped instantly and the man was thrown down with terrific force. Now Luto, again without command, began to drag the man back to the trees.

"No!" Morris shouted. But the horse was already tumbling the body back over the rough, sharp, cutting rocks.

"No! No! No!" Morris rushed out of the trees with his arms outstretched. "Don't! Don't! Don't!"

Now the horse finally stopped, but the man it was dragging did not move.

Morris Lennie went down on both knees and ripped open the man's shirt and listened for the heart beat. "We'll have to get him to a doctor."

"What, Morris?"

"We'll have to get him down where he can have treatment. He's in shock. Possible internal bleeding. Now if you boys will help. Can we make some kind of stretcher?"

As they were working the improvised stretcher down the mesa to the automobile Morris Lennie kept repeating, "There isn't any. It doesn't exist."

"What, Morris?"

"Revenge. There is no revenge," he said, halting. "None, none, none. Nothing. Always remember that. You've got to think of something else."

"What, Morris?"

"Well, you've got to learn to put a pot together properly."

"You'll never be an archeologist, Morris."

"That I don't know," Morris Lennie said. "But what I do know, what I learned today, unlike that black horse there," he said, touching the stretcher, "and unlike my patient here, I'm not a killer."

"That's good?"

"It's neither good nor bad, Lou," Morris Lennie said. "It's knowledge."

"As I was telling Twenty-six Horses before you came along," Ring said, "that's science."

As they placed the heavy patient in the car Morris Lennie touched Ring and said, "I don't know. I don't. But there is nothing can be done so we'll call it science, call it valuable, because, well, I'm a doctor. Maybe before

643

I'm a human being, certainly before— No, it's not true. He wasn't worth—"

"Worth what?"

"He wasn't worth killing," Morris Lennie said and slammed the car door. Now he looked out the window at the two young men on huge horses alongside the low car. "But I've marked this spot. I'm coming back here to try again."

"Revenge?"

"Yes," Dr. Lennie said, starting the car. "Revenge on that damn piece of pot that's missing. I'll find it and put it in its place."

The car moved off in low gear and they watched it waver off into the sun and sage toward the asphalt highway.

"Like I said, Twenty-six Horses," Ring said, "you couldn't do it either."

"Well, I thought about it. I almost could have. Then your horse—"

"You're almost smart too," Ring said. "But you're not. You're an artist. And those city people when they come back, they'll never find the rest of that pot and that's fine because they'll need another reason for living now that there's no revenge, and there's no better reason for living than to be searching for something that can never quite ever and completely be found, discovered for certain, without reservation, never quite. Although I suspect that thing, that person, that animal or bird in Navajo prehistory, He Who Brings Darkness Back To The Canoe, is probably an owl. I'll never know, and their piece of pot will never be joined, but that's the whole joy."

644

"Then it's damn foolishness."

"No, Twenty-six Horses, it's science," Ring repeated as though this were a religious paeon spoken, sung, into the bright earth, a phrase inviolate, unalterably preordained on the infallible and fabled rock of this mesa. "It's science. Yes, but more, the love of life. Anything alive, living—anyone, anything at all alive, must be sacrosanct."

"What?"

"Sacred," Ring said.

They allowed their horses to march down the bizarre slope. "You mean that in the sense of that man who moved like a dark shade?"

"All men," Ring said.

"We all got something we want to get rid of."

"Maybe," Ring said. "I don't know."

SEVEN

"But no one is sacred to quicksand." Ring splashed his hand in the quicksand at the bottom of the arroyo and looked for the horse that had broken away. Luto still stood in the shadows of the tamarisk, brooded in the checkered shade.

"I was just thinking, Luto, of everything that could be important, everything that led to this. Tell me, Luto, have we all got something we want to kill? Why do you want to kill me? You don't, Luto, it's just a white man's superstition. Maybe I got into this myself. I'm too smart to let you cross here, Luto. I know this arroyo too well. Why did I let you cross here? Sometimes we want to get out of something too much and there is no way out. This is a lousy way out. Twenty-six Horses says everyone has

647

something they want to get rid of and I guess maybe sometimes the first man is yourself. Wow!" Ring hit the water again.

"Twenty-six Horses and I were together all the time. Where is Twenty-six Horses now, Luto? I never told you all about the blue hogan, Luto, because I want you to wait, but you won't wait much longer, will you? I will tell you now. All right, Luto, good. You are coming out of the tamarisk. Do you want to hear or are you coming for something else? You look like a demon shadow, Luto, dark and soiled, like the man that ran on the Portales. Wait, Luto, I've got something to say. Wait, I've got something to tell you first. Wait, just for this. Hold off till I tell you about the blue hogan. Don't come closer, Luto. This is important to tell."

Listen, the blue hogan began with the Legion, and Twenty-six Horses was great on advice. He said of the Legion Club that it was a retreat. Everyone wanted to escape. He said we wanted to live in the past. Everyone wanted to do that. In the Legion we wanted to go back to our mother.

"It's a place to play poker," Rabbit Stockings said.

"No," the Zia Indian, Tom Tobeck said. "We build a Legion Club because we don't want to face being Indians."

"I'm no God damn Indian," Ralph Clearboy said.

"I mean we're all Indians," the Zia said, "in the way I mean."

Philosophy. We have a great deal of time for philosophy out here. Or let's say we talk a lot. It's a long time between branding and the fences are good.

Once Rabbit Stockings had a plan to hold up the bank. On horseback. Hide in the hills where the old whisky still still was in the Largo country, impossible to reach.

"It's regressive," the Zia said. "Like our Legion. Everything you guys think of is regressive. Holding up banks is conforming to a regressive pattern if I ever heard one."

"And you can get shot too," Twenty-six Horses said.

The Zia, Tom Tobeck, had been to school, Utah Agricultural College. He still had the Utah Aggie sign on the T shirt and he usually wore a cigar and talked a great deal about everything but agriculture which bored him.

It was the Zia Indian's idea to start the Legion Club and it was his idea to keep all the Indians out.

"You are an Indian yourself," Ralph Clearboy said. Clearboy broke broncs, followed the rodeos and appraised you like a horse.

"Yes, but other Indians tend to be dull," the Zia said.

So we started the Legion Club between Torreón and my father's White Horse Trading Post, the Zia, Ralph Clearboy, Rabbit Stockings, Twenty-six Horses, all of us. We were refused a charter by the National Legion because some of the guys had not been in a war. To have eliminated the guys who had not been in a war would have been sad and to change the name of the club, as Tom Tobeck the Zia Indian said, would be conforming to outside pressure groups.

"And letting other people run our lives," Twenty-six Horses said.

The club was built on the property of a man named Three Ears Of An Elk, a Navajo, a Navajo Indian who believed in progress. At the cornerstone laying the son of

Three Ears Of An Elk said, "Jesus Christ!" But Three Ears Of An Elk hoped to see the day when they had elevators like in Albuquerque. Our mud hut was a start—adobe mixed with straw. Tom Tobeck directed the operation because Zias build of mud—Navajos, no. Navajos build of chinked cedar posts, igloo shaped. The Legion was something else—a cube in a round country. You felt a long way from home.

The first idea was to raid the surrounding country using the Legion as a base of operations, but this idea never got off the ground. I think the second idea was to drink a lot. This must have fallen through because of lack of money. Rabbit Stockings wanted to grow surplus crops and collect from the government. I don't know what happened to this idea but we did acquire a breeding herd of sheep that we ate. There were other more practical ideas that fell of their own practicality, and gradually there was a vacuum into which the Zia stepped. Fell.

I think the Zia had the idea from the beginning. That's why he got the thing built. Don't forget, Luto, he had been to Salt Lake, Denver, Socorro, Utah Agricultural, and he always said the Legion had to have a point. "It has got to have character, purposefulness and a point."

The Zia's point was difficult. At the beginning I suspect he had none. That is, I think his meeting with the Navajo girl, Nice Hands, was accidental. I think his speech, "The partnership in brotherhood of all Indians," was thought of afterwards. But it has always been a fact that a Navajo can't marry a Zia. Can't, as a matter of fact, have anything to do with one. Of course at a Navajo yebechai, what we call a sweetie sweetie, you may see a Zia or a Santa Ana or

650

even a Jemez sitting there coy, but that's about it, that's about all. I don't know about the rest of the reservation but it's true in the Checkerboard. An Apache is different. I've seen Apaches dance at sweetie sweeties and more, but then the Apaches and the Navajos were once the same tribe, speak almost the same language. A Zia is a Pueblo Indian like a Santa Ana and a Jemez and a Taos, and you can't get much lower, you can't get much closer to a white man than that.

Our Zia, Tom Tobeck, met the Navajo girl, Nice Hands, at a sing at Star Lake, which is between Tinian and White Horse, and he brought her back to the clubhouse and she never left.

At first we thought of Nice Hands as a liability, then she began to think of us as an intrusion, then things started to level out and we took each other for granted until we began to notice her more—her sand painting, her excellent coffee, her eyes, her nice hands. She would sit there maybe making a rug for the Zia, Tom Tobeck, in back of her loom, her sharp and sculptured face etched in back of the woof and warp as though the face were a pattern her shuttle would soon weave.

"God is a unicorn. The only problem is exploding populations and dwindling resources. I know I speak too much of Beethoven but Beethoven, my friends, is a universe." The Zia, Tom Tobeck, was off on something else before you got what he had just said. The dwindling resources thing was kind of a half answer to Clearboy's statement that the Zia was in real trouble with the Navajos by taking up with Nice Hands.

"No. Exploding populations and dwindling resources.

That's the trouble, remember. And neglected geniuses. Remember that."

The Navajos knew that the Zia had been to college and in their heads it excused a lot. The Navajo is a gentle race but suddenly vicious. In the depths of the reservation, law and order is on their own terms and even here in the Checkerboard death can be violent.

"The way I see this—" Clearboy said. We were sitting in the clubhouse, the one high window gave a fairy light. Nice Hands was working at the loom. The floor was never finished and a foxy dust always rose and settled gently on all and on the pieces of furniture: a loom, a bar, seven empty tomato juice crates, a wine press and a diamond necklace. The wine press never worked and was shattered. I don't know where it came from. The diamond necklace was glass and was a present from the Zia to Nice Hands and she hung it on the wall for all to see.

"Yes, the way I see it," Ralph Clearboy said, "the Navajos will burn our clubhouse down or worse. After all, Nice Hands's father is a leader."

Being a leader in the Checkerboard gave the Navajo absolutely no authority but enormous prestige. A leader has a great deal of face to save.

"What do you think?" Clearboy was directing his question at Nice Hands. "What do you think your old man will do if you marry a Zia?"

Nice Hands did not speak English too well and did not seem to understand it too well unless the Zia, Tom Tobeck, was speaking. Now she just seemed to concentrate on the loom more and the shuttle went a little faster and there was that kind of primitive, embarrassed half smile on her face that a Navajo will frequently give a White as though the white man always spoke in dirty words.

"Nothing," the Zia, Tom Tobeck, said. "It's a civilized country. Nothing. No Navajo can do anything about it."

It would have been dramatic if the shots had been fired then, exactly then, like in a movie at the mission. But it was about five minutes later when there was the zam zam zam, until six shots, exactly what a lever-action Winchester will hold, were emptied off at the clubhouse.

Everyone froze until all the shots were over and then went quietly and innocently outside in time to see a distant and unrecognizable figure get into a blue pickup and slowly drive off. He, she or it didn't use a horse, but the bullets were real. The Zia dug one out of the adobe and tossed it on the ground.

"A thirty-thirty."

Everyone began to wonder now what Nice Hands held. What she believed. What she would do about this. Love is an enormous word. Sacrifice and Love are quite a pair and we didn't expect the Zia to use them but he did. Outside the Legion he got them in somehow. But we still didn't know what Nice Hands held.

Inside again the Zia glanced at the work on the loom and said, "Art is a universe," and lit a cigar. I swear that outside he said something about sacrifice for love, but then all of us at the Legion were being shot at too.

Twenty-six Horses tried the quiet and gentle approach. He sat casually on a tomato crate and said, "It's simple. We send her home."

Actually the Zia and Nice Hands were using the club as a home so Twenty-six Horses' point was lost even on me.

653

Marriage? Marriage rites the Indians find embarrassing, funny, and I guess needlessly expensive. The only thing they understand is that the woman owns everything. She puts his saddle outside when she's finished with the man, and the mother-in-law is never permitted to show her face or be seen.

Outside of that Utah Aggie shirt and the cigar I don't think the Zia owned anything. Yes, he had a Tex Tan saddle that was always with him. He took it even to Utah Agricultural College. He used anybody's horse and, with the Zia mounted on top, the horse became the horse that smokes. The saddle, I think, was the Zia's touchstone for reality—what he was. After all, though genius is neglected and art may be a universe and populations explode all over the place as natural resources melt before our eyes—can you ride these things? Use them as a pillow? Can you say, there rides the smoking Zia on his art? Dwindling natural resources? No, a man to be a man must have a saddle on which to sit.

The Zia sat on it now and ignored Twenty-six Horses. He withdrew the cigar politely and addressed himself to Nice Hands.

"What are all these guys doing in our house?"

Well then, let him fight his own battles. However, on second thought, it was our clubhouse and then too it was our war. Most of the cowboys and Indians (for that is what we all were) had not been in any war, so our Legion was not going to back away from this one. Rabbit Stockings, I guess, had had the most interesting war experience. He had been bumming around California when the war broke, he tried to enlist but was rejected as not being right in the head, not integrable they called it. He tried to get a job in a Western movie as an Indian but was rejected again. They finally gave him a small part as a soldier in a war picture. I guess at the Legion we had heard every detail of his war experiences a million times.

"We're not going to pull back," Rabbit Stockings said. He always talked in military talk.

I watched Nice Hands. She had a great deal of poise, like a wild deer, the kind of poise that comes from doing anything you're about exceptionally well, but she still had the impossible problem of marrying a foreign Zia, the problem of the bullets that had just been fired. Nice Hands stopped the shuttle and looked back at the Zia.

"I want to die with you."

How would the Zia take this? Could he rise to the occasion of death? How great a word was his love? We knew he would "Sacrifice for Love," but was it a love that passeth all understanding of a 30-30 caliber Winchester? The Zia tapped his cigar on the saddle, looked at the wine press as though seeing it for the first time and then back to Nice Hands.

"We are a speck in the universe and all temporal relationships are ephemeral."

I don't know why none of us at the time were able to translate this into: the Zia is looking out for number one—himself. And that when he said "Sacrifice for Love" he was talking about someone else's sacrifice. It just shows how we wrongly take the meaning of something for granted. But then none of us had been to Utah Aggie.

The Zia got up then, slung the saddle over his shoulder below the cigar and above the T shirt sign.

"I'll get that bastard's scalp," he said and went out the door. In a few seconds he was back, kissed Nice Hands on the forehead, examined her work and then disappeared.

Disappeared where? Nice Hands, after a few quiet minutes at the loom, got up and tied a leather lariat rope from one wall of the hogan to the other about six feet up. The Navajos believe that as long as the leather rope remains tight their loved ones are safe. Clearboy suspected that the rope would remain tight if the weather remained dry. We kept our mouths shut on all those things. I was suspect enough already being the son of the trader despite the fact that we also ran cattle. Clearboy had handled enough horses to keep his mouth shut. Nice Hands went back to her loom. The rope remained tight.

After a while we went outside and left Nice Hands alone with her rope to watch. We were in the habit of getting out and leaving Nice Hands and the Zia alone. Navajos all grow up in one small hogan room. They are accustomed as children to their parents' love-making. Love to a Navajo is not a long series of forbidden things, shocks, as it is to Whites. It is a natural, pleasant and beautiful thing to them. Nevertheless the rest of us were in the habit of leaving and sitting outside at their Legion home.

We smoked a cigarette and looked around but we couldn't see the Zia anyplace. He must have lugged his saddle somewhere in search of a horse to look for the shooter. The Zia wasn't in sight.

"Let's track him," Twenty-six Horses said.

You don't have to be an Indian to track a man. Anyone who has run cattle on a big place can. It's the only way you have of locating them. A man carrying the weight of a saddle is easy to track even if he tries to fool you.

Even if he tries to fool you. This did not really sink in to any of us until the Zia used four or five tricks to throw us off his trail. First he took out over a ridge of hard Lewis shale and it took us a while to find where he came off, then he walked all the way through the Ojo del Espíritu Santo Grant keeping to the middle of the shallow Rio San José. He crossed the Puerco below the Grant where he mingled with some fresh horse tracks but he didn't catch a horse and four of those six horses were catchable. We recognized them and they recognized us without moving off. Now the Zia topped out over the Portales Mesa. He must have been moving fast because when we topped out we could not pick him out on the Valle Grande valley floor below. But we knew now from his direction that he was headed for the highway, the blacktop, so we stepped up the pace. Now all of us were suspicious and curious. What friend of his had fired those shots at the Legion and why?

When you get to the top of the red Chinle formation that is the true southern end of the Rockies, Route 422 flows beneath you, a narrow black ribbon making its way through Indian Country down to Texas and other improbable places until it empties somewhere into the Gulf of Mexico. Up here you have an endless airship view of the white man's dirty trail to the sea, and right below us on the asphalt was the blue pickup waiting for the Zia.

"Wait a minute," Clearboy said. "It's a woman."

I don't know why we had all expected, taking it for granted, that it was a man that fired those shots from that pickup.

657

"A woman. An Anglo woman," I said.

How were we going to explain this to Nice Hands? I think that's what went through all of our minds. How would we let her down with a gentle lie?

The dark ribbon of road, Route 422, is visible from the Portales Mesa all the way almost to the Sandia Peaks. We watched the Anglo woman greet the Zia with a kiss, then the Zia started to throw the saddle in the back of the pickup, seemed to change his mind and tossed it in a near deep arroyo instead. Then they got in the pickup and drove off rapidly and desperately, burning rubber as criminals, children, police and lovers will.

I said that from here you could see the Sandia Peaks. You could certainly see with ease all the way down to the San Ysidro Motel where the blue pickup stopped and the Anglo woman and the Zia got out and went in and must have closed the door and here it was only high noon.

"They couldn't wait," Clearboy said. "Couldn't wait to get to New York City, Socorro or wherever out of Indian Country. They couldn't even wait till it got dark, didn't even eat or have a drink."

"Or marry up."

And then too there was Nice Hands. Nice Hands waiting back at the Legion and watching, watching that rope. Watching that rope in the manner and custom of the old people who believed that as long as the leather thong remained taut, did not go suddenly slack, their loved one was safe. Safe from everything, and this certainly meant, and with proof, wolves and bear and, if the rite went back far enough into their dark past, the saber-toothed tiger and other strange beasts including us. But was the reckoning of the rope ever with women? Anglo women?

We found out. Not that it was. No one could ever claim that. The rope, the leather rope found around the neck of the Zia, still taut above the T shirt, might suddenly have gone slack in the hogan minutes, maybe only seconds, after the motel door slammed. The door closed and in the first fumbling seconds of their lover lust, those first anguished, taut seconds, the rope went slack in the hogan. No one claimed that, mentioned it. A rope slack, a lover lost.

However it was that same leather hogan rope. And how did Nice Hands know or get there within those few hours? She got there by tracking the same way we got there. But the reservation police called it suicide as police will when they figure any other verdict is more trouble than it is worth. When you don't have a jail. The adobe jail dissolved in '98. Then, Tom Tobeck was an Indian anyway. Finally then, an Indian despite the T shirts, neglect of genius, exploding populations, dwindling natural resources and the universe of art. A dead Indian.

The Legion finally dissolved. Remember it too was built of adobe. We will never know whether the old people's magic works, whether the rope went slack and Nice Hands knew, or whether someone like Twenty-six Horses ran back to the Legion and then Nice Hands knew. But of one thing we are very certain. We were always puzzled at the magic and in awe and wonderment at what lay behind the nice face of Nice Hands. What did she think in back of this? Believe? What did Nice Hands hold? We know now. Nice Hands held a rope.

They buried the Zia at the adobe Legion and Rabbit Stockings said something good at the burial about neglected genius, the universe of art, exploding populations and dwindling natural resources, but he couldn't resist working in his own war experiences which had nothing to do with the dead Zia, and once during the services he did look hard at the wavering Nice Hands and say, "We can't pull back now," which, although military talk, did seem to buck her up. Then she picked up something from her lap and Rabbit Stockings went suddenly quiet as he watched the rope that Nice Hands held.

Along with our adobe Legion and the adobe jail the Zia's tombstone has since dissolved. Everything was made of mud.

And I remember during that whole burial Twenty-six Horses was staring at Nice Hands and the thing she was toying with—something that seemed alive like a snake. And I was staring at the rope too, Luto—the rope that Nice Hands held. And do you know what? Nice Hands still carries it around in my father's blue hogan. My mother quit this country when I was a child, went back to New England or someplace before I remember. Not many white women can take Indian Country. Maybe there was more to it, I don't know. It's my father's business. But is it just my father's business when he moves Nice Hands into the blue hogan?

From the bottom of the arroyo Ring could hear a bird trill three separate measures, parading quick notes into a dying day. The bird trilled again. It was far off in the direction of Sleeping Child Mesa. Again three separate notes repeated in a telegraphic insistence of code, distinct and implorant but faint now from the far mesa.

"Yes, maybe it is my father's business, Luto, bringing in Nice Hands to take my mother's place. My father has a lot of businesses. He thinks he's here to save the Indians. That's quite a business in itself. But of all the Indians why did he have to pick on Nice Hands to move into the blue hogan? Nice Hands was our business too, Twenty-six Horses especially I think, and me especially. Why did my old man have to compete in our business? Why did his body have to be the next figure her shuttle would weave? The next one that Nice Hands held. I know, I know, I know. Who would not want to be the next victim? No, I don't want to be funny. It wasn't funny having her there close in my father's blue hogan. I went away, left, took off, fled to someplace out there on the big reservation, Colorado, someplace. I don't know. Twenty-six Horses fled someplace too, the city, someplace too. I went straight north, straight north with Clearboy.

EIGHT

TWO BRONC RIDERS and one clown were sitting in a café four miles out of Montrose, Colorado, all watching another bronc man, Ralph Clearboy, watching and listening, listening but not quite catching until Clearboy removed a battered cigar, replacing this to a bright cut lip with a clear bourbon; then he held the fragmented cigar and the empty bourbon glass in either hand and confronted the others with a pure blank stare.

"What was you fixin' to say?" Willard Moss said.

"We'll take him."

"Who?"

"Ring. He's done left home. He and Twenty-six Horses quit the reservation. We was all on the reservation.

663

Twenty-six Horses went on to the city but Ring come with me."

"Why?"

"Ring's got a problem."

"Where?" the clown said.

"No matter. We'll bury it for him."

"Where?" the clown said.

"We'll bury his blue hogan in the Black Canyon of the Gunnison."

"What else was you fixin' to say?"

"A white Lincoln," Clearboy said.

"What about it?"

"I bought one," Clearboy said. "I bought a white Lincoln."

"And what is the moral of that? What does the Good Book say about that?"

"I wonder."

"Wonder no longer, my boy. We are off."

"Where to?"

"To Gunnison," the clown said. "Where else? The rodeo's at Gunnison." The clown stood up. He had a sign on his back and he waved his arms over Ring as though he might fly away but before he took off he would make a speech. The clown pounded the table for attention and embarrassed everyone in the café.

"And we will pay a visit to Maria's joint. We will be the first cowboys to ride from Montrose to Gunnison in three hours including a two-hour stopover at Maria's. The first."

Clearboy remained seated. "In a white Lincoln," Clearboy said quietly.

664

The clown was talking to Clearboy. A clown seems to be only the comic character that entertains you between the rodeo acts but actually his main purpose in the arena is to entice, cajole or pull the Brahma bull or the bronc horse off the rider after the rider has been thrown, to keep those sharp raging hooves of the bronc or the needle horns of the bull from killing the cowboy. The clown is, of course, a contract man, different from a bronc rider. A bronc rider shows up at any show he shows up at and if he shows up at no show it makes no difference. It is only his entry fee that allows him to compete for the money anyway, his entry fee and his card in the R.C.A., the Rodeo Cowboys Association. The cowboys got a union too.

"Do you know this cowboy's got a sore ass?"

The clown did not say this. They were in the white Lincoln now, where you go over Blue Mesa just before Cimarron between Montrose and Gunnison, and Clearboy, Ralph Clearboy, said it and stuck one foot out the window whilst the white Lincoln was going one hundred miles an hour. The clown never said anything funny. His name was Morg or Morgan Beltone and all the stuff he said and did at the show was written for him. What was most appealing about the clown was that as a contract man he drew a regular salary. The white Lincoln used a great deal of gasoline, Hi-Test Flite Fuel, forty-one cents a gallon in Aztec. At these prices you can't ride with a better man than a contract clown.

Four riders and Ring on a trip to Gunnison in a white Lincoln, including a colored cowboy and a clown. The colored cowboy's name was Willard Moss. Moss is the only colored cowboy who belongs to the R.C.A. outside of Marvel Rogers. If he draws a good horse Marvel is worth the admission price. Willard Moss, the colored bronc man who rode in the rear seat of the Lincoln, is not so good as Marvel Rogers but Willard Moss is very good.

Ralph Clearboy was the best. He drove and owned the Lincoln and was the best. Together with the finance company he owned the Lincoln, but he was still the best.

"We're doing one hundred and ten miles an hour," Ralph Clearboy announced to Ring sitting beside him in the front seat.

"I don't get paid for this," Willard Moss said.

"You don't get paid for anything if we don't make Gunnison in time," Abe Proper said. Abe Proper sat near the right window alongside the clown and Willard Moss in the back seat. That made five cowboys in the car plus a saddle that couldn't fit in the trunk with the other saddles. They all wore tight Levi's and tight bright Miller shirts and twisted Stetsons and Justin boots. Except the clown and he had a sign embroidered on his shirt back announcing Lee Rider Wear.

Abe Proper made a cigarette at a hundred and ten miles an hour. He was the only cowboy in the bunch who rolled his own, maybe because he was brought up in New York and found making them exotic, an accomplishment, a badge. Proper had not gotten into bronc riding until he was fifteen, nine years ago, but he was pushing Ralph Clearboy for total points or total dollars earned for the All Around Champion Prize. Actually Abe Proper was ahead right now since Montrose where Abe Proper took first money in the second bareback go-round. But no one expected it to last. Proper did not expect it to last.

"One hundred and twelve miles an hour," Ralph Clearboy announced.

The white Lincoln mounted by Ring and four cowboys from the Spanish Trails Fiesta at Durango, from Colorado Springs, from Butte, Montana, and Cheyenne, from the Rodeo de Santa Fe, from the Monte Vista Roundup and back to Durango and then Albuquerque and now bent for the Cattlemen's Days at Gunnison. Four cowboys in batwinged hats, orange and red shirts, mounting a white Lincoln, their flowing chrome horse a high, white streak on dark Blue Mesa above the Black Canyon of the Gunnison.

"Like as not—"

"Like as not what?" Abe said.

"Like as not," the clown said, "we'll make it into Gunnison okay."

"If we don't make it into the Gunnison."

"One hundred and fourteen," Clearboy said.

"The turn!" Willard Moss said.

"Too late!"

The white Lincoln did not even try for the turn, did not even seem to know its front wheels were turned, but continued to go straight, even to gain some altitude, to zoom out in flight, hang there in the quiet high sky an endless moment before it began to fall off on one tail fin, not as though the car were not made to fly but as though the pilot, the cowboy at the controls, had quit and lost control, and she went into a long slanting dive down the mountain, began to clip clip clip the pointed spruce trees with an awful whack whack whack, and then the white car fell off on her left tail fin, crump crumped into some scrub oak, made a weak attempt to become airborne again, then slithered to final rest in weird and abrupt silence at the exact edge of another black cliff where there was a fall to infinity to the river, the last slide down into the Black Canyon of the Gunnison. The white Lincoln hung there.

"I was just fixin' to make a cigarette," Abe Proper said. Proper wiped the blood and tobacco from the side of his face.

"Is everyone here?" Clearboy said.

"I think the clown stepped out," someone said.

"Without a chute?" Clearboy felt around for the saddle.

"It's back here," Willard Moss said. "And I've found the clown under the saddle."

"Did I make a good ride?" the clown said.

"We're not even at Gunnison yet."

"I reckon we missed. We missed a turn on the road," Clearboy said.

"Again?" the clown said.

"You'd think I made a practice of trying to fly this thing."

"One of us should take lessons." Willard Moss discovered now that the Lee Rider ad on the back of the clown's shirt was being vandalized with blood, Proper's blood. He ceased suddenly however his attempt at humor as he made another discovery. Now he said gently, "No one move."

"Why?"

"No one even talk."

"Why?"

"Because this thing is balanced on the edge of a cliff."

"Oh?"

"Yes," Willard continued gently. "Any movement, even vibration—"

"If we could," Clearboy whispered, "slip out each door without almost breathing."

"But the clown's in the middle," Ring whispered.

"Then suddenly. All climb out suddenly."

"I think it's beginning to move."

"She's moving."

"She's going."

"Everybody out!"

They all tore out and fell into the oak brush except the clown. He stayed put. The car moved slightly then hung, delicately, on the final edge, balancing lightly, waving there, a seesaw with the clown sitting in the car on the pivot, reading something.

"Get out!" Willard Moss hollered to the clown. "She's going to go!"

The clown looked up from his reading. "I can't seem to move," he said.

"You mean you're hurt?"

"No. I seem frozen."

"Something broken?"

"No, scared. Kind of frozen. Scared."

"Then relax. Forget where you are. The car has just drove up to the front of Madison Square Garden. They're waiting for you in there. Get out."

"No," the clown said. "I can't get out."

"Listen," Willard Moss said. "The car has just drove up in front of Maria's joint. They're waiting for you in there. Get out."

"No," the clown said. "I can't get out."

"If you don't get out you're a dead clown."

"I can't get out."

"You yellow?"

"I still can't move. If I move the car will go."

Ring now tried to think of something. "We will all grab the car and try to hold it."

"Don't! Don't touch the car!" the clown said. "If you touch the car the car will go."

The clown and everyone else were silent for a while and then the clown said, "Clearboy was driving fast because he didn't want to get to Gunnison because he knew Proper would take him at Gunnison like he took him at Durango, like he took him at Santa Fe," the clown said evenly. Everyone was quiet and then the clown said, "Clearboy lost his nerve at Santa Fe when War Paint nearly killed him but he didn't know he'd lost anything till Proper took him three in a row. He didn't know he lost anything until suddenly he was going one hundred fourteen miles an hour and he didn't really know what he was up to then, didn't know he was trying to cash out the easy way because he'd lost his nerve. Clearboy's got a problem."

Clearboy was down on one knee searching for his hat. Now he found the remains of a hat and looked up at the clown. "No, Ring's got a problem, and if you've got any nerve," Clearboy said, "just get out of that car before she goes."

"I never had any nerve," the clown said. "That's why I

670

never took up bronc riding, never thought of riding War Paint. Jumping off a building either. Never thought of riding War Paint."

"You started riding me in Montrose."

"I started riding you in Durango," the clown said. "I started riding you when you stopped riding horses." The clown could not resist adding, "Properly."

Abe Proper got up now from a scrub oak and said, "For God's sake get off Clearboy and get out of the damn car before she goes."

"She's going," Ring said.

And she was too, very slowly at first as though the see-saw car were being tilted downward by an invisible hand toward the invisible void. Now the car picked up a light momentum, then it hesitated before it made the long slow bounce down the cliff as though in a dream. The clown in a white car down a black canyon as in a dream or a very slow motion film with no reality at all except that finally now the car and the clown were gone. The three bronc riders and Ring were left standing there on a lonely slope horseless—carless anyway, and without the clown—clown-less and breathless too.

"I was just saying—and there I was left talking to the air," Willard Moss said.

"I saw the car enter the water," Clearboy said.

"And like as not," Abe Proper pulled down the shapeless remnants of a cowboy hat. "Like as not— Well, I can't believe it."

"Believe what?"

"That the clown would do it."

"He didn't."

"Oh, yes he did."

"I mean a purpose."

"I don't care how he did it, he did it."

"That's true."

"He was quite a clown."

"Yes, he was."

"What do you mean, was?" Clearboy said. "I am fixin' to go down and get him."

"That's impossible."

"It's impossible that anyone can call me a coward." Clearboy knelt down to study the canyon wall. "And die to get away with it."

They all thought about this a while.

"You mean he's still alive?" Ring said.

"Of course he is," Clearboy said. "I've seen him dive off a high platform without a river into only fifty gallons of water, without no river at all and without a car, without any car to protect him." Clearboy looked down carefully into the dark shadows of the canyon. "Without my car," Clearboy said, and then he spit and said quickly, "I see a path down."

"He didn't call you a coward, Clearboy."

"He said I lost my nerve. It's one and the same thing."

"Well, you have been looking bad lately."

"I been drawing bad horses."

"But why don't you spur them out of the chute?"

"Because I don't want to make bad horses look worse."

"Oh?"

"Yes," Clearboy said.

"You want to take all the blame?"

"Yes," Clearboy said. "And yes, well maybe I'm not

doing too good myself but that's not why I tried to kill the clown."

"All of us."

"Well the clown thought I was trying to kill him particular." Clearboy paused. "Because he was riding me. I was not trying to kill nobody. I was only trying to get to Gunnison on time."

"He said you didn't really know it. It was your sub something," Willard said. "Your problem."

"Your subconsciousness was driving the car while he was riding you," Abe Proper said.

"It's all those books the clown reads," Clearboy said. "And he's reading one of them right now," Clearboy stood up. "In my car."

They all followed behind Clearboy until he got to the path he had spotted and then they continued to follow him but far back and cautiously. After fifteen minutes of awful descent, lost down there, hidden from the blaze of noon above, Clearboy suddenly halted and they all bunched into him.

"This is as far down as the path goes," Clearboy said. "The deer or whatever made it must have quit here."

"Or committed suicide."

"Yes," Clearboy said, invisible and canyon-lost, his voice quickly lost too in river noise.

"Out there and down there," Clearboy said louder. "The car. My car."

They could make out, after studying ahead and down, a white car shape all right.

"But we can't get to it," the voice of Abe Proper said.

"It's only about a fifteen foot drop," the voice of Clearboy said from somewhere. "He made it sixty feet in my car."

"But you can't."

There was a rushing noise and then a splash.

"But he did," Willard Moss finished.

"I reckon we better get back up."

"Yes," Willard Moss said. "We better get back up and hold some kind of a funeral or something."

"Yes," Abe Proper said. "Something nice. Something to—" Proper paused, invisible and hushed, climbing up ahead somewhere to the sun. "Yes, a funeral," the voice of Abe Proper continued. "Something to make it legal."

"We didn't have to jump to prove anything," Ring said.

"No."

"All we've got to do," Willard Moss said, greeting the torch of day with upturned face, "is to hold something to make it legal."

They lay down on the mesa top as though thrown there on the dark igneous rock, three bright-costumed and beaten cowboys beneath a wild sun. Abe Proper tried to pull his remnant of Stetson over his eyes.

"And, oh God—" Proper said weakly.

"What?" Willard said.

"I just remembered."

"What?"

"Both of our saddles are buried down there."

"Oh," Willard Moss said and then he said, laying a dark hand on darker rock and wincing quickly, "Amen."

When Ralph Clearboy hit the water he hit just above the car and allowed himself to drift down to it. He went through an open door, felt all through the car including the front seat. He felt a saddle, nothing more. No clown. He went out through the open window of the other door and got up on the roof, which was well above water, to think. Where was the clown hiding?

The clown was not hiding. He was sitting on a sand bar fifty yards below the car holding the unreadable remains of a book. He had made it down okay by wedging himself in a ball between the front of the rear seat and the back of the front seat before the car took its first bounce. He was banged up quite a bit and was bleeding red from the ear but the clown was okay. The book he held was an awful mess.

"Down here!" the clown hollered.

"Where?"

"Down here!"

Clearboy started to drop off the car and drift down to where the clown was sitting but the car moved until it got stuck again on the clown's sandbar.

"Well, you haven't lost your nerve then, Clearboy," the clown said, watching Clearboy dismount.

"And you didn't lose your book," Clearboy said, only now barely able to see the clown.

"I didn't know I had it," the clown said, letting it drop. "It was only something to hold on to, I guess."

"I guess," Clearboy said, his teeth chattering from the icy water. "How do you reckon we're going to get out of here?"

"I've fished below here," the clown said. "It's not too far down to a boat landing near Maria's place."

675

"I guess you've done everything," Clearboy said, still iced and chattering.

The clown thought about Maria's place and then he looked up toward the tall canyon wall he had come down. "Now I guess I have," the clown said. The clown paused and added, "Except—"

"Except what?"

"Ride War Paint."

"You still riding me?"

"No, I'm not," the clown said, standing up. "You will ride War Paint. Let's get down to Maria's place."

"You think so?"

"Of course we'll get to Maria's place," the clown said. "Follow me."

And Clearboy did and regretted it. Even when they were sitting on the dry boat landing he still regretted it. He regretted following a crazy clown. The moral is, you don't follow a crazy clown to prove nothing. The moral is you ride a horse when you have to ride a horse but you don't invent a ride to please a clown. Until he met War Paint again Clearboy would settle for this. War Paint and himself would make it together, uninfluenced by nobody.

"I wonder what happened to the other three cowboys?"

"Willard and Proper and Ring?"

"Yes."

"They're probably having a funeral over us."

"Well," Clearboy said, beginning to warm in the sun, "the next guy who has a funeral over me when I'm having bad luck is going to be tied to War Paint and throwed in this canyon, then you will be the first dead clown to ride

676

down the Gunnison River on a horse. Do you understand? Ring's got a problem; Nice Hands, Abe Proper, Twenty-six Horses, everybody's got a problem. God's got a problem. I haven't got a problem. Do you understand?"

"I think I understand," the clown said weakly.

They sat there on the dock in the sun, resting and nursing their wounds.

"Look," the clown said. "There's the car. The current must have freed it and brought it down. That makes us the—" The clown paused and stood up. "That makes us the first two cowboys to go down the Gunnison River in an automobile."

Clearboy remained sitting and watching with a blank, enchanted fixity where the clown watched, watching as children must watch an empty gondola emerge from the tunnel of love.

"Anyway I reckon we was the last ones down in a white Lincoln," Clearboy said.

The clown thought about this a long while without being able to top it. The clown had a button nose and small red cheeks and now, standing all oozing wet with his Lee Rider ad running red, he pointed his finger to the sky.

"Someone's been praying for me. Here I am all alive because a cowboy got the nerve to jump down a canyon to rescue a clown."

"To rescue—" Clearboy got up, placed a yellow square of tobacco into his square, hard face still blued from the water and began to wade out toward the huge, slow-turning object. "My white Lincoln," Clearboy finished.

The clown, Morgan Beltone, watched Clearboy guide the white car onto the beach. He decided no help was needed and moved off towards Maria's place.

"Here you are," Maria said across the mahogany bar. "Here you are supposed to be at the rodeo in Gunnison and here you been swimming. Where's Clearboy? Where's Proper? Where's Moss? Where's your partners?"

Morgan Beltone wiped some water off his face. "Clearboy found a boy with a problem so we decided to fly the car to Gunnison this time and we came down near here a little bit ago," the clown said. "Will you give me a drink?"

Maria, her wide Spanish face puzzled, poured the drink.

"To all the bronc men I saved from getting killed in the arena and never got no appreciation from. To all those cowboy heroes and to progress," Morgan Beltone said, raising the glass. "Today I have pioneered a new route in a new kind of machine, cutting off half the distance across Blue Mesa. Why, perhaps some day I will be appreciated very much."

The clown drank the drink down and looked plaintively through the window at all the big world he had not conquered. A clown—and so wrongly so, Morgan Beltone thought—had never been loved or appreciated very much. "Who's got problems? It's very rough all over."

"Honey, save it for the show," Maria said. "You want another drink?"

Ring came in but he stood near the door looking tired, hot and small. The clown watched him.

"If that little son of a bitch thinks he's got a problem—"

"Honey, you want that drink?"

"Why not," the clown said.

NINE

THE NEXT DAY Ring sat under a paloverde tree and watched the people enter the Café Wilderness and he watched the dark heavy small elephant clouds pass over the paloverde in sudden shadow and go someplace else. Probably the rodeo grounds again. It was the wrong season. Clouds build up here and then go someplace else. Over at the rodeo grounds they'd got a very heavy rain that ruined everything. Down here by the river in front of the Wilderness it was all parchment dry. Blessing is given to those who don't need it, have had it too often, don't want it. Hate it.

Ring had slept that night at the fairgrounds, outside under the high dry stars, until the rains came. Then he went inside the horse barn and slept standing up with the horses. Several other potential performers without the price of anything had scattered under something too when the rains came, but not in the horse barn. They had been around longer than Ring. Ring was new.

There was a gray, hard-faced woman inside the horse barn, from Montrose, Colorado, who stayed up all night with her three horses that would run in the cheap races next day. She said it was necessary. She showed Ring weird, ghostlike, blurred pictures of her horses finishing sixth, seventh and second at the cheap races at Gunnison and Raton and asked Ring if he would stand in all night with a nervous gray who kept circling within a too large stall. Offered Ring four dollars. Ring could not figure why she did not halter-tie the horse. Ring did not ask. It was a living for the night. Maybe she loved those horses, figured they needed human love. Love will pass over many cities, many towns, a blue hogan, even a ranch house near Montrose and finally descend within a horse barn at the fairgrounds, scatter itself in a stall. Ah love!

Ring had these four dollars. It was not enough for his entry fee to ride the broncs which was what he had recently determined to make his life, his work, his new dream. But he had enough money now to go to the Wilderness, a very nice bar near the river where all the greats would come. All of the artists. All of the bronc riders who were doing very well indeed: Casey Tibbs, Jim Shoulders, Clyde Morning. Well, maybe not those greats at this rodeo, but certainly the lesser greats who were willing to settle for a five hundred dollar prize would enter the Wilderness tonight. Ah Wilderness!

Picture the Wilderness, a log and chinked, very large

cabin set in a conifer forest down by a silvered and flashing Colorado mountain stream near where the aspens are, the golden aspens. The Wilderness was set down here oddly and wrongly enough because this was the heart of the dude ranch country: oddly enough because the dudes never entered the Wilderness, wrongly enough because they tried.

Each night someone fought in the Wilderness. It was a way of life for the proprietor and Mrs. Jason, his wife. It was the reason for living for most all the bloods between Montrose and Ouray. The Wilderness was famous for this, surviving for this; in this it had found its niche in the struggle to survive. A strange log house in a high and beautiful place with all the men who fought inside waiting for the final hour, waiting for the other contestants to arrive. They all came in the guise of buying a drink or wanting to make love, but they all had a secret dream. Each had his thing he had to work out. Some men in some places will work it out in the very nicest of fashion. Here in the Wilderness set in a wild forest near the silvered stream by golden aspens, they fought. This was their sword, their Cloth of Gold, their Armageddon, a bright Excalibur, their odd way of Gethsemane. Fighting in the Wilderness.

"My name is Bretta," she said.

"I haven't got any money," Ring said.

Bretta was a very young girl, the daughter of two dudes from St. Louis who were here for two weeks.

"Why do you imagine," she said, "why do you suppose they have to fight?"

They both sat beneath wide shadowing paloverdes and ponderosas, outside the Wilderness, by moon-struck aspen and by a moon-shattered stream, and watched the Wilderness, watched and waited, listened to the Wilderness. Even as she smoothed out her Levi's, even as she spoke, both watched.

Ring did not yet reply, "What?" but looked now at the girl who had quietly come and sat beside him. She looked too young to be here outside the Wilderness but she fitted her tight Levi's just right so maybe not too young, but too—what was the word? Too like the fresh growing aspens, golden too on top and all bending easily with grace and nicely fresh. But aspen was not the word. What was the word?

"What did you say?" Ring said.

"Why do you suppose," she repeated in a voice too poetic for the Wilderness, "why do you suppose they have to do this?"

"What?"

"Fight," she said.

"Men are different," Ring said.

"Ah yes," she said.

"It's true," Ring said.

She stuck a piece of grass in her mouth to think.

"But dudes don't fight. I've noticed that," she said. "The dudes that come here from the city, they don't fight."

"Dudes are different," Ring said.

"But they're men."

"Kind of men." Ring stuck a piece of grass in his mouth

682

too. "They're kind of men. Now you take a cutting horse—"

"Ah men," she said.

Ring removed the grass from his mouth and moved his boots embarrassed. It was like a woman to try and get things personal. Very personal. Unlike men, they could never take a subject like a horse and discuss that. It had to be very personal like you. Ah women!

"My name is Bretta," she said again.

"I haven't got any money," Ring repeated.

"Do you have to be rude? What do you take me for?"

"Bretta," Ring said.

"So you'd rather fight than—?"

"I guess I would," Ring said.

"Than go with me?"

"Where?"

"I like gentle men," she said. "Why can't you be a gentle man?"

"Why then did you come to the Wilderness?"

"Because— why, because—"

"Nothing is wrong that's natural," Ring said. "Unless being dishonest about it."

"Fighting is not natural," she said.

"Nothing is wrong that's natural." Ring wondered how he got stuck with this sentence. It did not seem a good sentence, not a sentence anyway that was worth always ending up on.

"Sometimes a man's got to fight," Ring said.

"Then why aren't you inside the Wilderness?"

"Why because— Well, because—"

"Well, because what?"

"Because a man gets scared, I guess."

"Certainly," she said.

"You think I'm scared?"

"No, I wouldn't say that."

"Well, I guess I did," Ring said.

A bright blue cold moon shook through the riverside aspens, exploding the fragile trees in sudden light, shadowing the Wilderness and torch-lighting the flashing stream to a sinuous glare of silver, then ceasing; from nowhere going only here—the moon, all here and all theirs, unshared, nailed safely for an infinity, shadowing the Wilderness, lighting them.

"Like I say," Ring said, reaching for a new piece of moon-bright grass. "Like I want to say, you've got an awful good shape."

"There," she said. "You said it like a gentle man."

A stark white Lincoln drove up and parked in the tall moon shadow of the Wilderness. The brand-new white Lincoln appeared to have made its last journey without benefit of roads, as though tossed off several cliffs along the way and proceeding here finally via the river and unknown and unexplored peaks. All the bumpers were gone off the brand-new white Lincoln and she was fenderless and almost paintless too.

"That's Ralph Clearboy and Abe Proper getting out and going in the Wilderness," Ring said. "And that Negro with them is Willard Moss, and the clown with them is Morg or Morgan Beltone."

"Who are they?"

684

"Bronc riders."

"How do you know their names?"

"Everyone knows their names. Ralph Clearboy and me grew up together. He is the one that will fight tonight."

"How do you know that?"

"Because he's doing lousy at the show."

"Does doing badly at something make a man want to fight?"

"It seems to," Ring said.

"Dudes don't fight."

"Maybe it's because they do everything badly."

"Dudes don't fight, they sing. Why don't those men sing? Singing is better than fighting. Promise me you won't fight."

"Well I can't sing," Ring said.

"You're not logical," she said.

"It's not natural," Ring said. "Singing does not come natural in the Wilderness."

"If you want to go with me promise me you won't fight."

Ring looked into her very earnest, very innocent, very beautiful face and said nothing.

"If you want to go with me promise me you won't fight."

"All right," Ring said.

"They're fighting now," she said, listening and watching fascinated. "They're fighting now. And me only—" She suddenly caught herself.

"What is it?"

"I'm a dude," she said. "I really am a dude. I'm from

685

St. Louis on vacation with my family. I'm only a dude. Nothing but a dude."

"That's all right," Ring said.

"Did you suspect it all the time?"

"No," Ring said. "Because it's not true."

"You mean I'm not from St. Louis?"

"I mean you're not a dude," Ring said. "A dude can grow up on a ranch in the West. A dude is just someone who doesn't belong wherever they are."

"Oh," she said.

"It's true," Ring said. "I didn't belong where I was."

The fighting suddenly ceased. The noise stopped. The Wilderness went all quiet, kind of weird like a brawl in church. The Wilderness was all still and as silent as the moment before a bomb is to be detonated or a prayer said.

"Like I said," Ring said, "it was Ralph Clearboy fighting and now he's found no one to fight."

"Promise me you won't fight," she said.

The door flew open and Ralph Clearboy stepped out of the Wilderness and stood silhouetted in the cold moon.

"Promise me you won't fight if you want to go with me. If you want to go with me."

"All right," Ring said.

"What was that?" Ralph Clearboy said. Ralph Clearboy moved his cold moon shadow till it shadowed them. It seemed there were two Ralph Clearboys. They could see his moon-hit face now. "What was that?"

Ralph Clearboy's face was almost a dishonestly drawn, honest Anglo-Saxon-vacuous, immaculate and magazine-cover and motion-picture face, except for a cruel tension, except for a trickle of blood, except for the rasp of, "What was that?"

"What was that?" Ralph Clearboy said again.

"I said all right," Ring said.

"Ring, I could kill you by looking at you," Ralph Clearboy said.

"All right," Ring said.

Ralph Clearboy marched into his own shadow until he stood over them.

"Dudes," Ralph Clearboy said and then he retreated from his own gorgon image on the ground, withdrew his moon-self, withdrew his wide-hatted, bowlegged, pointy-toed and long curve-heeled and antic moon-self slowly back towards the waiting Wilderness, towards the waiting door.

"You going to let him get away with that?" she said.

Ralph Clearboy removed, redented and then replaced with formal boredom but quick style his gay green wide hat and then touched forward tentatively for the darkened door.

So there was no one outside for his lover lust, no one out there to hit, only Ring. Ralph Clearboy stepped inside and joined the three ladies of the Wilderness at the bar. There he leaned backward, elbows on the bar, watching the men in the darkened long room, ignoring the ladies of the Wilderness.

It would be good to hit Abe Proper, Clearboy thought, Abe who had been outriding him in the arena now for weeks. But you can't because he has a hex on you. If you could beat him in the arena you could hit him here, and you can't do that either. It would be good to hit the clown but no one hits the clown. It would be awfully good to hit Willard Moss but you couldn't hit him unless he started it because he is a colored man, in fact he is a colored rider, but some dudes don't know the difference. In fact he was a good friend and should be very hitable.

The thing was to get Willard Moss to swing on you so you could hit him as a human being. Ralph Clearboy had already kicked unconscious two men but the lover joy for fight was still hot and tense and had to be got out somehow and he smashed his fist into his empty palm alongside the ladies of the Wilderness.

Now in a very self-pleased low voice seeming to come from beneath the floor, Willard Moss began to sing:

> *Since when did a rider own all the world?*
> *Since when did he buy it?*
> *How much did he pay?*

So Willard Moss was going to insult him by singing. A surge, a tinge of hot joy went all through Ralph Clearboy.

"There's no singing in the Wilderness," Ralph Clearboy said suddenly.

"Knock it off, honey," a black-haired, green-eyed lady of the Wilderness said slowly to Ralph Clearboy. "Knock it off and grow up."

> *Since when did a rider own all the world?*
> *Since when did he buy it?*
> *How much did he pay?*

688

"No singing in the Wilderness," Ralph Clearboy announced. "Isn't that right, Jason?" The proprietor had hidden. "Isn't that right, ladies?"

"Knock it off, little boy," the dark-haired, green-eyed lady said to Clearboy without looking from her drink. "Knock it off and grow up."

"Mr. Jason don't allow no singing in here," Clearboy hollered again. Willard Moss rose slowly, a great, black giant who never seemed to stop rising from the chair, but before he touched the low ceiling he hunched down, his right fist cocked, his smile beckoning, his whole huge body continuing to sing, and Clearboy sprang off the bar at him like a lover cat.

Abe Proper got in Clearboy's way and he knocked Abe Proper down. The clown got in his way and he knocked the clown down. The boy from outside, the moonlight lover, Ring, got in his way and he had to knock him down. Too bad. Now Willard Moss hit Clearboy and the Wilderness exploded on Clearboy's jaw. Clearboy went down hard. Too bad, too awfully bad, and so dark, so awfully quiet dark.

Ring was the first to revive and one of the dark-haired, sloe-eyed ladies of the Wilderness sat him in a chair at the table of Willard Moss, and the proprietor, Mr. Jason, came out of hiding and set up two free drinks for Willard Moss. Willard Moss seemed embarrassed at his prestige and he pulled his great hat down over his broad face. It was so misshapen it looked like a farmer's hat.

"Is it all right to sing in here, Mr. Jason?" Willard Moss said.

"Yes, and fight too," Mr. Jason said. "We've got to have some kind of—some kind of a—"

"Floor show," one of the ladies said.

Ring felt very good with the ladies of the Wilderness and the bodies of the performers all around him and Willard Moss there beside him.

"Would you help me put these gentlemen in the white Lincoln?" Willard Moss asked.

"Certainly," Ring said.

"You upset his timing," Willard Moss said. "He was going to lead into you with his right and cross me with his left. He had it figured perfectly. He has been doing that all evening. He's a beautiful fighter. But he saw you were small and tried to hold up on his swing, you know, like a baseball player tries to hold up at the last second on a bad pitch. Well, so I hit him because his timing was off when he tried to cross me with his left. I hit him very good because you had him off balance. But he's a beautiful fighter and, as you know, one of the best performers we have."

"He sure is," Ring said.

"Even though he's my roommate it's still the truth."

"That's right."

"Ralph's in a losing streak now. He's been riding badly but I think his losing this fight will help."

"It sure will," Ring said.

"I mean getting something knocked out of you can help a man to get back to work." Willard Moss drank both of the free drinks while talking.

"I bet that's true," Ring said.

690

Willard Moss put down the glass. "Well, you want to help me carry these gentlemen out to the white Lincoln?"

The small dude girl, Bretta from St. Louis, watched in wide-eyed awe as her wild-eyed hero helped place each victim in the long white Lincoln.

"It's better that they wake up in our Lincoln or back in our motel room," the dark, invisible-in-the-darkness Willard Moss said. "It could be frightening to wake up in there, in the Wilderness."

"Yes, but—"

"But what?"

"Yes, but why are you going back in—in the Wilderness?"

"Because I got to finish that song. Remember we was— I was interrupted."

"You sure were," Ring said, but Willard Moss the giant black man was gone. Ring saw him once again visible in the fiery doorway, his huge bulk suddenly re-entering the Wilderness before he was gone for good.

"I didn't mean for you to fight," she said.

Ring sat upon the moon-spilled grass to recover. She touched alongside him. "I didn't mean for you to fight."

"Then what did you mean when you said are you going to let him get away with that?"

They both watched up at the huge bold moon, cold and wide above the conifers, not nailed, not entirely theirs—it had moved somewhat since last they watched it. The inconstant moon.

"Well, I didn't mean for you to fight," she said. "Not entirely."

691

"Well," Ring said, "that settles that. I can see that I don't know where I am at. Maybe I'm not even out of the Wilderness."

"Not entirely," she said. "You want to go with me? Take me home?"

"Not entirely," Ring said.

"Very well," she said and she stood up.

"All right, I'll go," Ring said.

They got as far as a new-mown field of blue grama that overlooked the distant sinuous stream, conifers, aspen and dim-lighted Wilderness, and now they were joined as they lay in the soft blue grama by the hard, following moon. Lighted in amber.

"Oh," she said, "it's good to get away from that awful place. Awfully good."

Ring felt the warm little dude alongside him and then he reached his hand from her and felt his cheek, bruised where Ralph Clearboy had hit. Oh, that felt good! Now he heard way down below them, below the aspens and the conifers and way beneath the flashing stream, the clear, heavy and deep voice of Willard Moss singing in the Wilderness. Ring touched his cheek again and again he felt all that joy, all that awakening, all that remembrance of things happening in a wild place beneath an inconstant moon, waxing and then waning above the house below of dubious battle. He reached for her waist again, dreamt of the place again, felt of her warmth again.

"I was okay," he said.

"Yes."

"And now you beside me."

"Do you hear the singing in the Wilderness?"

Felt of her waist again, back to her warmth again, his lips to her lips again. Ah Wilderness!

After Willard's deep distant song, after five minutes of lying in amber beneath the following moon on the soft blue grama, Ring sat up quickly. "I am very sorry, Bretta, but I've been thinking."

"Oh?"

"That I've got to finish my song."

"What?"

"Like Willard Moss I've got to go back and finish something. Like Twenty-six Horses—he's got to go back and finish something."

"But—"

"Yes," Ring said. "Sometimes maybe something *is* wrong that seems natural. Maybe they drive cars off cliffs—maybe they came here to fight because they didn't fight somewhere else—couldn't face it somewhere else."

"Where?"

"Home. A loom, a picture, a place, that's what it was with Twenty-six Horses."

"Twenty-six Horses?"

"He couldn't make it at home," Ring said. "And with me it was a blue hogan."

"You're talking queer or something."

"No," Ring said. "Not now I'm not. If a man can't understand a blue hogan how will he understand anything? If he can't make it there, he will have to fight here. They've all got a blue hogan."

"What's that?"

693

"Something we walked out on," Ring said.

"But you can't leave me now—go back to a blue hogan now."

"I don't know, Bretta," Ring said, standing and watching down over the Wilderness. "I don't know. But watch me try."

TEN

"THERE'S THAT goddam bird again, Luto."

Ring had spread his short Levi jacket like a web, a bat's wing, to keep floating in the sand, and from above the arroyo, somewhere out in the world above, came the same three separate chants, recapitulant and exigent, as though the singer, the signaller, were not being heard, as though the world were going on above but there was indifference to each voice. Now it ceased and Ring lay over in the viscid pool and glared a baleful blue eye up at the empty sky.

"Luto, come over here and look up at the cliff. You see that picture by Twenty-six Horses up there? What was he trying to say? Maybe nothing, but everything you do is part of yourself. We leave our imprint everywhere. When you die someone finds it. Maybe they don't find it but it's there. We are all painting a picture. Up there on the rocks is a picture of an artist with twenty-six horses. But mine is someplace too. Everyone paints a portrait of himself someplace—every place—an unfinished picture. A remembrance of himself.

"Look up there. It just came to me. I can see for the first time. I have been trying to see with my eyes and eyes are not for seeing—they are only a small part of seeing. You have got to feel. Now I see up there because I feel it, because I am beginning to understand and feel. I see up there that all those strokes add up to twenty-six horses— not twenty-five—twenty-six—all running across the cliff. He did it. My friend left a mark. I guess I never made it. I have not left anything. Wait. If that's all the mark he made he didn't leave much either. But he left a lot of other things. He did a lot of other things. He left his mark on me. That's quite a lot. He affected another person. That's small but that's quite a lot. And I buried a medicine man. I rescued a poet, saw the end of a flyer and brought animal life into the world, lay with a girl and knew what Nice Hands held. Small things but maybe they affected this world—left a mark. I was here. Never quite reached my old man but I stretched and his hand was not there. I tried. I tried everything I could. Twenty-six Horses and I did what we could together, but Twenty-six Horses says a man's got to paint his own pictures and I guess I was really doing it all the time. I just never realized I was doing it myself. I was all alone out there. Yes, I left a small picture too. Ring Bowman was here.

"But there is a time in a man's life when he has to decide what kind of mark to leave. That's the big problem

—what kind of mark to make out there. Wait. Think. What kind? I guess most of us never decide. We run off our lives, never think what kind. I've had a little chance to think down here and I am going to try to reach further, to reach further toward other people, to not be afraid, to never be afraid of their not being there when I reach toward them. The Man Who Had No Fear—that would be a good Indian name. It would not make a bad picture. That could be a pretty good picture of myself—without Twenty-six Horses."

The bird above, the only contact with the world outside, the mad telegrapher signalling nothing so beautifully in a sharp, mechanical sweet rapture, turned off.

"Jesus, Luto!"

Two shots were fired off above and a piece of the cliff rained down.

"Hello! Hello!" Ring raised up in the ooze and hollered again. "Hi!"

But there wasn't any answer. The world above was a big loud hush again save for the bird which commenced now making the big quiet above seem more noiseless and empty.

"They did not hear me. Jesus, Luto. Jesus, Jesus, Jesus—What's going on up there?"

Above in the bright-shot world the unending sun of the summer solstice, slanting under the eaves, beaming through the broad window interstices, wondrously impaled in its mote-heavy beam the Indians and the trader where they stood in rayed splendor among the dangling sheep-hides, intestinely-draped harness and the dust of all time.

697

The trader, the father of Ring, seemed to be staring vacantly at a group of gaudy, blanket-hooded Indians.

"But then," the trader said evenly, "Ring went away from me. What happened? Did anything out there make sense? I want to put it together."

"What?" Rabbit Stockings said.

The trader watched the Indians leave and then pretended to be adding up some figures. "I was never able to get close to him. You know him better. Did Nice Hands—? Was there anything that—?"

"You mean Ring?"

"Who else?"

"Well, Twenty-six Horses knows Ring better than me."

"I'm not interested whether Twenty-six Horses knows you better than he does Ring."

"I mean ask Twenty-six Horses."

The trader put down the pencil. "You know Twenty-six Horses went to the city too."

"Did he?" Rabbit Stockings said. "Of course he did. It serves him right."

"There's worse things," the trader said, going back quietly to his figures. "Like believing in Navajo ghosts."

"You don't believe Luto is someone else?"

"He looks like a horse to me."

"City people look like men," Rabbit Stockings said. "But have you ever noticed—"

"I'm worried about Ring," the trader said. "He should have been back five hours ago. Where shall we look?"

"I'm only an Indian," the Indian said.

"Yes," the trader said, looking down at his account books. "Yes, Rabbit Stockings, you owe three hundred and ninety-five dollars and thirty-two cents, but we'll forget that and remember you're only an Indian."

"How much credit I got?"

"How much more?"

"Yes."

"To infinity, I guess."

"Is that enough for a pair of Levi's?"

"Not quite," the trader said. "We're going to find Ring. Will you catch the horses? Wait! Did you hear that? Who fired those shots?"

Bearing down on the trading post was a bright New Mexican day and tooling towards the post was a bright car, bright driver, bright passengers. All was bright. The woman driving the car was from Dallas, Texas and she was driving between Aztec and Cuba, New Mexico and she had a small automatic stuck down between her good breasts. All three women in the car were from Dallas. They were all school teachers but the lady driver was the only one who had an automatic in a secret place, but they all knew about it. Millie Hopgood, who threatened children with mathematics and home economics, was squeezed in the middle of the front seat. Millie thought the pistol a good conversation piece—nothing more. She was pressed in between the two fat ones and now she said, "My God, we haven't passed anything for a hundred miles but those dead arroyos."

"That's why I've got the gun," Doris Bellwether said. Doris Bellwether was fat and strong and she taught physical education but she had read the books, seen the TV and knew all the dangers of the Indian Country. "Not that the normal chronological pacification hasn't reached the Navajo," she said, "but, my God, we are three unprotected girls among—how many?—fifty, sixty thousand Indians."

"Eighty thousand by now," Tiddy Sutton (sociology) said from the door seat.

Doris Bellwether raised a delicate hand to her pistoled chest, "Rapine!" They all emitted blasé giggles because Dallas, Texas is about as sophisticated as you can get unless you've got in mind some other Texas town like San Antone.

They had all gone up together to the Neiman-Marcus store on the Friday afternoon before vacation and bought clothes that would befit an expedition west of Texas—red and blue cowgirl outfits of gabardine and white Stetsons. Doris Bellwether's husband had made her take the gun—he didn't suggest the hiding place, he lacked the imagination and the courage. Doris' husband was a shy, retiring man, embarrassed and self-conscious, a timid, small and self-effacing man who seemed to have finally found his niche assembling the trigger section of the hydrogen bomb at the Sandia subassembly plant in Lubbock. As Doris Bellwether examined the long empty stretches of the Indian Country from her position above the wheel the pistol seemed to give her that little something that her analyst had worked so hard to achieve.

"A gun is a gun," Doris Bellwether said. She took a corner too fast. "It's also a gun."

"We in sociology are against guns," Tiddy Sutton said. "I don't know, it's a matter of principle I suppose. Then too, I think guns are silly."

Doris Bellwether made a face and touched her fat, deli-

700

cate hand to the spot where the gun lay. "I bet those missionaries we read about in the paper that were killed by those Indians the other day in Ecuador wished they had had a gun like ours."

"Yours," Tiddy Sutton said. "A gun like yours. I want no part of it. I think it was arrogant of the missionaries to try to force off what they believe on those Indians. The Indians there responded in the only way they knew how."

"And a very pretty way," Doris Bellwether said, tromping down on the gas to miss a bounding jack. "You do defend the queerest people, Tiddy Sutton."

"I suppose we, with our atom bomb, are a lot prettier, a lot more civilized."

"I've only got a small pistol," Doris Bellwether said. "Only a small pistol. It's my husband that's got the bomb, works on it. Of course he is timid enough to use it but we'll never give him the chance. But I've only got this small pistol."

"You really think there's a possibility we might use it?" Millie Hopgood said.

"Use what? The bomb or the pistol?"

"The pistol."

"With a gun one shoots, one shoots, one shoots," Doris Bellwether said.

"But all that aside, what do we do?"

"One shoots," Doris Bellwether said. Now she stopped the car and withdrew her pistol. "You see that red spot towards the top of the arroyo? It looks like a picture. Watch." There was a blasting noise in the car as she fired off two shots.

"You missed it a mile."

"Practice," Doris Bellwether said, driving off and putting the gun back where it seemed to belong.

"You're a bully, Doris," Tiddy Sutton said.

About three miles up the road from where the white women from Texas with the gun to protect them from the Indians sped, four Indians sat in front of the trading post and watched the road.

"And I don't think we should be afraid of tourists," the Indian on the end said.

"Yes," the second Indian said. "It might discourage them from coming out here, then our medicine man wouldn't have anyone to convert."

The very young and willowy medicine man, dressed brighter than the others and sitting on the far end of the group, looked up annoyed.

"I don't want to convert anybody."

"You're beginning to talk sad," the first Indian said. "I don't think I'll send my boy to your sings."

"It would be sad getting your kid out of a tree to send him any place," the medicine man said.

The white trader, dressed like the Indians in curled hat and riveted form-fitting pants, had come out of the post after having sent Rabbit Stockings for the horses to find Ring, and stood in back of the Indians and listened to the Indians talk in Navajo which he understood.

"Didn't you hear some shots?"

"No," the first Indian said. The Indian looked around as though searching for something else to discuss. Instead he found a bright agate in the sand and tossed it in the air. Then he picked up a sagebrush twig and broke it.

"Any of you Indians seen Ring?" the trader asked.

"No, Sansi."

"He's been gone a long time."

"Maybe he went to the blue hogan."

Will they ever get off it, the trader thought. "Well, I'm going to check the slope of the mountains. My God, look!" the trader whispered. "Here comes trouble."

Doris Bellwether played the car down the final slope to the trading post. When she spotted the Indians in front of the trading post she touched her hand to her breast where the pistol lay and said, "Hang on, girls."

"How silly can you get," Tiddy Sutton said.

"Oh, Doris can get awfully silly," Millie Hopgood said.

"Since when is there anything silly about self-defense?" Doris Bellwether said. Doris Bellwether began to slow the car down.

"You're not stopping here in front of those Indians?" Tiddy Sutton said.

"When you've got plenty of self-defense you can stop anywhere," Doris Bellwether said.

The Indians and the trader watched the car pull up in front of the post but the Indians did not move. The trader walked over.

"Dr. Livingstone, I presume," Doris Bellwether said and the other two girls giggled.

The trader looked worried. "Did you see a young man on a horse—a black horse?"

"Nonsense. We want some gas," Doris Bellwether said.

The trader watched them giggling, and Doris Bellwether, who, the trader guessed, was running the outfit,

703

pointed to the red pump with ten-gallon glass bottle on top into which gasoline, when there was gasoline, was pumped up by a big hand lever.

"Gas. Gasoline. Gasolina," Doris Bellwether, who, the trader had already guessed, ran the outfit, said. "Now." Doris Bellwether began moving her forearm up and down with her fist clenched to suggest a piston. She blew through her lips to suggest a carburetor emitting fuel. "Gasolina!" she said, slapping her hands against her big thighs. The other girls giggled because they were embarrassed and because, in the strange situation, they were scared. So they continued to giggle.

"A young man on a black horse," the trader repeated. "If you just came up the highway—he was riding a large black horse. Why— Well, get out, madam, I'll fill this thing up."

Doris Bellwether slid out and motioned the girls over towards a huge red rock that began a razorback formation into the eroded, varicolored badlands beyond. From the huge red rock the girls could watch everything that went on and yet not be in any danger at all from the Indians or the strange, tall and slim, wide-shouldered white man who was talking now to the Indians in their own language. The trader looked rough.

"God save us," Tiddy Sutton said.

The trader had gone over to the seated row of Indians and now he was telling the Indian on the far end that there was no gasoline in the tank below the glass-topped pump.

"Drive the car around in back and fill it out of the gravity tank in back of the post."

The Indian's name was Trujillo. He had a lot of other names too, some Indian, but the trader used Trujillo because the Navajo had been in a Spanish mood lately.

"Okay. Sure," the Indian, dressed like the others in Levi's and gaudy shirt, said, getting up and moving toward the car.

"Look!" Doris Bellwether said, watching the Indian get in the driver's seat of her car. "One doesn't get in a car to put in gasoline."

"No!" Millie Hopgood said, frightened.

The Indian started up the car to drive it around in back of the post to where the gasoline was and Doris Bellwether reached in delicately with her tiny right hand between her breasts and came up with the gun which she pointed at the Indian and quickly fired. The Indian threw the thing in gear and swung the car around the post to remove the target.

Doris Bellwether put the still warm gun back where it came from. The trader watched from the door of the post as the leader of the oufit, Doris Bellwether, wormed her girls up through the rocks taking cover when they could.

"Quickly, girls, quickly," Doris Bellwether said, crouching down behind a rock. "I have five shots left," she said, touching her breasts. "We don't want to get excited or do anything silly that would waste ammunition or expend energy. And there'll be no help for us from that tall white man among those Indians. Any white man that would live this far from the fruits of civilization is probably all man. Not like my husband. This one will fight."

The two other girls were too excited to talk yet but

they were both conscious of the coolness and deliberateness of the leader of the outfit, Doris Bellwether.

"They have the car," Doris Bellwether said. "The only plan we can have is to follow the cover of these rocks along this ridge up here until it works down to the road and we can flag a passing car. I will only fire when I have to. We have only five bullets left and we must make them count."

Millie Hopgood had stopped panting now. "Did you kill that Indian?" she said.

"I think so," Doris Bellwether said.

"No, you didn't," Tiddy Sutton said.

"Why didn't she kill him?"

"Because after she fired our car went around a corner."

"Well," Doris Bellwether said, thinking about this as she peered around the rock. "Well, they've got all kinds of gadgets on a car nowadays. They will drive themselves."

"I see a Navajo," Tiddy Sutton said.

"What?"

"An Indian."

"Where?"

"Over there." She pointed.

"Don't point," Doris Bellwether said. "Where?"

"If I can't point I can't show you."

"Just tell me where."

"Right there beside the tall cactus by the road."

"Oh," Doris Bellwether said. "It's a child. I don't kill children."

"Well, they evidently don't draw the line at women," Tiddy Sutton said.

" 'Women and children' is a phrase used by white

706

males to keep women down," Doris Bellwether said. "I refuse to accept it. But I don't kill children personally. I only have a normal, healthy hatred for kids. I'd never shoot one intentionally."

The other girls seemed relieved that she did not kill children. They seemed pleased too that "women and children" was no longer an accepted phrase, even though it might cost them dearly.

For example, Tiddy Sutton thought, the child might be a scout used by the men below to ferret out the position, knowing the ladies would not shoot. Still it would have to go as a considered risk. Tiddy Sutton would not alarm the others by telling them of the possibility of the Indian child being a scout. Then too, Tiddy Sutton thought, there was definitely the possibility that the child had been sent out as a decoy to draw their fire and reveal the position. Any way you look at it, she thought, I should keep my mouth shut and let Doris Bellwether lead. She seems to have been born for war and such.

"I tell you," Millie Hopgood said, "if the boat is sinking I won't particularly resent the phrase 'women and children first.' "

"You should," Doris Bellwether said, touching the barrel of the automatic against her chin in thought. "Yes, Millie, you should," Doris Bellwether said.

The trader was inside now, leaning against a stack of brilliant trade goods when Rabbit Stockings ran in.

"They took a shot at me, Sansi. I guess they thought we were trying to steal their car. Many Cattle and Winding Water followed them into the high rocks. The danger is the women might kill each other with that gun."

"Yes," the trader said sadly and moving over to the door, "But I sent you to do something more important. We've got to find Ring."

"But," Rabbit Stockings said, "don't blame the white women. This is kind of an unusual happening. Just one of those weird things that happen through a misunderstanding."

"Maybe civilization is based on a misunderstanding," the trader said. "The misunderstanding that if you asphalt the whole world, replace nature with chrome, do everything and get everywhere ten times as fast as before, then you got progress."

"Don't be bitter, boy," Rabbit Stockings said.

"I know a place," the trader said, thinking. "Chico Verdad. No road. You got to get in by packing."

"On the Sangre de Cristos."

"How did you know?" the trader said.

"You've said it so often the whole tribe has memorized it. The medicine man works it into his sermons."

"You're kind of a bright Indian," the trader said.

"Soon even your—how do you pronounce the place?"

"Chico Verdad," the trader said, looking up on the rock where the teachers had fled. "Chico Verdad," he pronounced carefully.

"Yes. Soon even your Chico Verdad will be—"

"Doomed. You're kind of a bright damned Indian," the trader said. "You want to go with me?"

"Follow the Whites up in the rocks?"

"I guess we got to," the trader said. "I could use Ring now. I'm supposed to be looking for Ring. I believe that

708

life is one continuous interruption. I only wanted to find out if they had seen a young man on a black horse."

"Watch," Doris Bellwether said. "See there below? Two more are chasing us. The white man, he's in on it now too."

"Maybe there's a misunderstanding," Tiddy Sutton said. "Maybe they're not chasing us."

"Ho ho," Doris Bellwether said.

"Well, Tiddy Sutton could be right," Millie Hopgood said. "It could be a misunderstanding."

"Hee hee! Hoo hoo!" Doris Bellwether said.

"Oh Doris," Tiddy Sutton said.

"Hey hey!" Doris Bellwether sang. Doris Bellwether was standing, exposing her head above the red rock while the other girls cowered behind it.

"Seriously, girls," Doris Bellwether said, crouching down between them. "Of course there's a misunderstanding. They expect us to behave like women, cowering, begging, pleading, feminine, weak. Ho ho," Doris Bellwether said and she stood up again and sent off a shot in the direction of the men that ricocheted off the big rocks. "Hey hey!"

"Oh Doris," Tiddy Sutton said.

"Ho ho!" Doris Bellwether hollered again and waved her gun at the men. "Hey hey!"

"Duck, Sansi," Rabbit Stockings said.

"We don't hide behind rocks," the trader said. "That would be silly."

"Yes," the Indian said, joining the trader again. "But a ricochet could hit us."

"We could be hit by lightning too," the trader said.

709

"I suppose you got it in the back of your head that they should have told you whether they saw a young man on a black horse."

"Maybe," the trader said.

"Couldn't this happen in your Chico Verdad, Sansi?"

"No, because it's too far from Texas."

"One day everything will be closer to Texas. What are you going to do then, Sansi?"

"I don't know," the trader said. "But you Indians sure can worry."

A bullet whistled between them and from high up on the rocks a voice screamed, "Hey hey!"

The three Texas women were figuring out now their position in relation to the men moving up and they figured it was time to withdraw. Doris Bellwether figured this, anyway. Tiddy Sutton hedged, Millie Hopgood was indecisive, but Doris Bellwether was definite, decisive and willing to sacrifice all on the turn of a card or a cliché.

"We must show our mettle, girls. Texans."

"True-blue," Millie Hopgood said in a tired voice. "If we must act like this let's not be banal."

"Is there something banal about true-blue Texans, teacher?" Doris Bellwether asked.

"Yes, but more subtle, there's something banal about showing our mettle."

"What do you want to show, honey?" Doris Bellwether said. "Hey hey!"

"No, you don't understand," Millie Hopgood said.

"I do understand, honey," Doris Bellwether said, touching Millie Hopgood on the knee. "And I've kept kids

710

after school for less—knocked my husband down for less." Doris Bellwether looked soulfully and thoughtfully out over the weird rocks and desert hills. "The little jerk," she said.

"I've got a secret," Millie Hopgood said.

"You have no secrets," Doris Bellwether said.

"Look," Millie Hopgood said, and she drew out a pint of tequila from her purse.

"Give it me," Doris Bellwether said. Millie held on to the tequila. "Give it me," Doris Bellwether said.

"I don't know where you picked up the affectation of leaving out the preposition. It's actually lower British middle class."

"Give it me," Doris Bellwether said.

Millie Hopgood held the bottle of white liquid marked José Cuerva Tequila next to the miniature alligator immobilized on her handbag.

"When I was being equipped at Neiman-Marcus the salesman said I might need something to drink. He gave it to me."

"Give it me," Doris Bellwether said.

Below, Rabbit Stockings, who was cresting a hill with the white trader, paused. "I'm a little beat," the Indian said. "I had a bad night last night."

"You and your yebechais," the trader said. "Why don't you Navajos find a religion that is easier? They're selling a lot of quiet religions around the reservation."

"Too quiet," the Navajo said.

"The Pueblos buy them," the trader said.

"They're a quiet people."

The trader leaned against the rock with the Indian.

"The Navajo's got to be a pretty tough guy. He's got to keep up with the myth."

"The story. That's right, Sansi. You got a cigarette?"

The trader offered a pack of cigarettes. "So the Indian hides behind a rock."

"From some women," the Indian said. "From Nice Hands and white women, that's all."

"The Navajo's pretty tough."

"He's not crazy, Sansi." The Indian took a cigarette. "Sorry to disappoint you, Sansi, but I'm not crazy."

"You mean you draw the line at bravery where some women are concerned?"

"That's right."

"Well, I don't," the trader said. "Not this bunch anyway. Let's get going."

"You first, Kit Carson," the Indian said. "You know, Sansi," the Indian said seriously and drawing a careful lungful of smoke, "I think you been away from the white people too long. Living out here alone among these Indians can do things to you."

"I only wanted to find out," the trader said, "whether they saw a young man on a black horse. Me first."

"I'm with you," the Indian said, following. "I've lived out here a long time myself."

Doris Bellwether was leading her girls along the ridge and she had the bottle now.

"It steadies one under stress," she said as she took a quick drink and passed the bottle to Tiddy Sutton as

712

she came up. Tiddy Sutton took a drink, at the same time watching the trail below them. She passed the bottle to Millie Hopgood and wiped her face. "Ish good," she said.

"It makes a man of you," Doris Bellwether said. "Hey hey!"

"I don't want to be a man," Tiddy Sutton said.

"Of course you don't," Doris Bellwether said. "You're like my husband. That worm."

"Why don't you divorce him then?"

"Because it would embarrass me to recognize that he exists. Hey hey!"

"Perhaps I've had too much to drink. I don't follow you, Doris."

"You'd best follow me. Walk this way. They're gaining fast." Doris Bellwether started off with a slight limp and the other two girls imitated the slight limp when they were told to walk this way.

"He assembles the hydrogen bomb." Doris Bellwether had the bottle now. "He assembles the hydrogen bomb and paces the bedroom dreaming of all his power, his big explosion. The worm. I could squash him like a bug."

"I know," Tiddy Sutton said. "You don't because it would embarrass you to recognize that he exists. But those men following exist and we'd better— Maybe they really only want to find out whether we saw a young man on a black horse."

"I hear hoofprints," Millie Hopgood said, sitting down. "It's not good. They're upon us."

"It's hoofbeats."

"I hear those too," Millie Hopgood said. "Pass the bottle."

713

The trader and Rabbit Stockings climbed up the dull burnt rocks through the high wild world of burnished mesquite and grama and occasional cactus and dazzling lime formations. Now there was a fissure to cross. Again and again the strewn boulders made the going slow and tortuous and always the sun was heavy on them but now the pistol shooting had stopped and they climbed on and up in the big silence with only the sun shooting and gay, but no "Hey hey!"

"There," the Indian said.

The trader looked where the Indian pointed. The three ladies were lying sprawled behind the natural fortress of red rock with an empty tequila bottle in the center where they could all reach it before they passed out.

The trader and the Indian climbed over to where the ladies had made a last stand. The Indian leaned down and felt the pulse of the very heavy lady who still had the pistol in her tiny fat hand.

"Could squash you like a bug," she said, but did not open her eyes.

"They're okay," the Indian said. "But how are we going to get them down?"

"Roll 'em down," the trader said.

"Well get some blankets at the post and make stretchers," the Indian said. "Let's go."

The trader stared at the ladies a second before he followed the Indian.

"You worm," the trader thought he heard someone say as he followed the Indian but he could have been mistaken. He could have been mistaken too in his hardheadedness towards progress—towards the stream of asphalt,

714

studded with chrome, infecting everywhere. He could be mistaken about these things. It was one man's opinion. As the Indian told him, maybe he'd been out here too long. Maybe asking whether they'd seen a young man on a black horse was asking too much.

"Hey hey!" he heard someone shout. He did not want to ask the Indian if he had heard it too because the Indian might disqualify himself by saying he'd been out here too long himself.

They went all the way down to the post, gathered up some Indians and handmade stretchers, went back up the hills and gathered up the ladies.

The trader went over and leaned on the blue hogan where he could be away from it. Let the Indians run things, they seem to know all.

Soon Rabbit Stockings came over to the hogan. "Get with it," the Indian whispered to the trader. "The women have all been waked up now. They're in the car and ready to go. Look cheerful."

The car swept away in a cloud of everything that was on the desert. Soon it was speeding down the highway as fast as it could go. Now two shots rang out from the car, a bullet ricocheted off the tin roof of the post and a woman screamed, "Hey hey!"

The Indians scattered for cover. The trader tried to look cheerful. The Indians were right, maybe he'd been out here too long.

"Cheerful does it," he thought. "But listen to that."

Somewhere in the distance an Indian shrieked, "Hey hey!" The trader paused now, his big arm frozen in movement towards his curled Stetson as a final bullet bounced off the dirt roof of the blue hogan. He completed the gesture now, pulling the wide brim down over his burnt, slanting forehead to protect him, not from the sun but that from which there could be no escape even out here among the Indians. The Indians, he thought, who not only accept outside nonsense but abet it, compound it, or anyway twist our attitudes into some kind of burlesque to make damn fools of us. And me too? the trader wondered. He struck a match on his tight pants and illumined briefly there in the shadowing blue hogan a twisted cigarette and a hard but confounded face.

The trader abandoned all thought as he relaxed back against the blue door with the smoke going straight up. "Oh God!" he shouted into everywhere, into nowhere.

George Bowman waited for the echo to come back from the rocks. It was good that Ring was on the mountain for the horses. Anyway he wouldn't get shot. But Ring had been away ever since he got home. Ring had really never come home. He had simply been there. The boy has a problem he has to work out all by himself and then I guess he will come home, really home. He's got to put things together. Maybe I can help. It's something we have to do all alone.

He threw away the cigarette and entered the dusky interior of the blue hogan. There in the center of the circle room was the beautiful faint shadow of Nice Hands at the shadow of the loom.

"Why was so much noise?"

"Texans," George Bowman said.

"Has Ring come back yet?"

"I'm going to look for him now."

716

"Take Twenty-six Horses. He should—he should be back now. What's an Indian going to do for very long on the big reservation?"

"He could be a civilizing influence."

"What?"

"Why should I take Twenty-six Horses?"

"Because they were always together. Twenty-six Horses would know where to look."

"Of course. Yes. I never knew where to look."

"Don't talk like an Indian. You knew where to look for me. You know how to look."

The trader sucked in a deep breath. "I've got to push my luck."

"Luck nonsense," Nice Hands said. "Just get on a horse and look. Luck nonsense."

"You think I've been out here too long?"

"Not long enough," Nice Hands said. The shadow of her shuttle began to move again on the cool surface of the dirt floor followed by the shadow of her hands. "Not long enough," she repeated in soft Navajo. "Now when you get back it will be better because then you will have been here longer."

"Rabbit Stockings has gone to get the horses."

"Good," she whispered. "Every second that goes by you will have been here longer."

He leaned over and kissed her cool forehead and felt again all the warmth and all the being of her secret dignity.

The Indian appeared in the doorway. "Well, if we're going to look for Ring we better get started."

"Of course, Rabbit Stockings."

"We're always getting interrupted."

717

"Every time an Indian takes off his feathers and leaves the reservation . . . Every time a picture is painted on the loom . . ."

"What?"

"Yes, we'll get going, Rabbit Stockings."

ELEVEN

THE TRADER WAITED at the corner of the adobe warehouse stacked high with Navajo trade goods and wool, waited for the Indian to bring the horses from the corral. The Indian would prefer to use the jeep but they might not be able to go where Ring had gone, using the jeep. Maybe the boy had left home again. Maybe he and Twenty-six Horses had gone to look for a better country. Maybe Ring had gone to look for Twenty-six Horses. They were always close. Indian Country is hard on white women but a man should be able to make it here. A man should make it here better than anywhere in the world. Soon it will be the only place a man can make it, the only promise left. Women don't want promises, but it's all a man can live by. The promises we live by.

719

"Ring!" There's no use my shouting his name here. When he was standing directly next to me Ring never heard me. I never spoke plain enough. He spoke another language. I can speak Navajo and English pretty good but I never learned to communicate with Ring. Twenty-six Horses did. The secret language. How will I ever find him if we can't talk? Just the quiet invisible smoke signals of despair.

George Bowman glanced up. "Rabbit Stockings, I said we weren't going to use the jeep."

"You can have the jeep or the horses."

"Thanks."

"Sure you don't want the jeep?"

"Sure."

"It's not that I don't want to be seen on a horse."

"I know."

"It's just that Luto is faster than any horse."

"He's faster than the jeep too."

"You don't believe that?"

"Now, Rabbit Stockings, I am ready to believe anything. I am even willing to believe that the Indians think white men are people."

"Don't go overboard, Sansi. Wait right here, I'll have the horses in seconds."

"That's all the time we may have," the trader, George Bowman, said.

When the Indian came back with the horses Rabbit Stockings said, "They don't want anything to do with us."

"They? Who is they?"

"The people. The white people on the big reservation."

"Where's Ring, Rabbit Stockings?"

"On the mesa."

"Which one?"

"Sleeping Child Mesa."

"Sure?"

"Or the moon," the Indian said. "That's the thing now for white people on the big reservation."

"Is it?" the trader asked. "You haven't seen him then?"

"Early he said he was going to get the cattle."

"On the mountain?"

"By way of the mesa."

"Or the moon?"

"Sometimes," the Indian said. "Did I ever tell you about the poet on the moon?"

"Yes."

"But what did you mean, every time an Indian puts on all his feathers and leaves the reservation?"

"Rabbit Stockings," the trader said quietly, "it's simply that a man leaves his home to try to make it someplace else."

"There's no money here?"

"It's not money."

"I'd leave here if I could," the Indian, Rabbit Stockings, said. "But an Indian can't make it off the reservation. An Indian has got to stay on the reservation."

"Else what's a heaven for? Follow me, Rabbit Stockings, we'll try the foothills."

"I know how to find Ring," Rabbit Stockings said, riding alongside.

"Good."

"I know how to find a bear. Maybe we could do it the same way."

"I don't think so."

"You've got to have a telescope, a tweezer, a white man's book and a medicine bundle, but a tobacco box will do. Any small box."

"Rabbit Stockings!"

"You take all this stuff up to Pedernal Mountain where there are bears and sit on a rock and read a white man's book. It is so dull you will be asleep in a few minutes, then a bear will come out. Bears are very curious animals, right?"

"Right, but—"

"So curious that the bear will come up and read the white man's book. The book is so stupid the bear will be asleep in a few seconds. Now you wake up because you went to sleep first. You take the telescope and look at the bear through the wrong end. The bear looks so small that you take out your tweezers and place the bear in your medicine bundle or your pocket and go home. You've got a bear."

"But we haven't got the boy."

"And soon we'll have Ring," Rabbit Stockings said. "Remember, 'all is lost,' the captain shouted as he staggered to the deck, but his little daughter whispered as she took his icy hand, 'Isn't God upon the water just the same as on the land?' "

"The Indian mission school?"

"They're trying to make us Christians."

"Yes, but we'd better hurry," the trader said, spurring his horse by a glittering and scintillant limestone slope. He rode alone along a hogback of greasewood and sage until they were beneath Pedernal Peak and he felt the Indian alongside, then he said, "Purity, loyalty, honor and devotion to noble ideals. They don't work. They are not enough."

"Who said they were?"

"I was thinking out loud," the trader said. He was riding again in advance of the Indian.

"All right, I say they are."

"I said I was thinking out loud and watching the country for sign."

"I shouldn't hold what you think against you. But why don't they work?"

"Because they never fit any real situation."

"Did you learn that at Yale?"

"I didn't learn anything at Yale."

Rabbit Stockings rode lightly and watched the cliffs. "Why do you think Twenty-six Horses made those bright marks all over the cliffs?"

"Some superstition," the trader said. "Now we call it art."

"You do?" Rabbit Stockings said. "Now you call it art. That's good," Rabbit Stockings said, annoyed. "Well, they were put there as a protection."

"Yes," the trader said. "To protect everyone who is at the mercy of everybody."

"That's not bad, but we shouldn't feel sorry for ourselves, Sansi," Rabbit Stockings said.

They topped out on a layer cake of striped sandstone and looked down over the lost country for a sign.

"Why would a man," Rabbit Stockings asked. "Why would you leave all that for this?"

"That for all this? Exactly why we do things, who knows? Don't you think it's the most far—the most beautiful country?"

"It's okay," The Indian said.

They started down the west slope of the layer cake butte.

"The only real escape left. The only sanity."

"What?"

"The only island." The trader tilted back his Stetson, slanting back from a slant face, hard and marked. "The only reservation left. Have you seen any sign?"

"Nothing," the Indian said.

"We'd better work higher."

"You've been in the clouds a while now."

"It's just that I don't want to face—"

"You won't have to face anything. We'll find Ring," the Indian said. "Tell me, when he got back did he mention it?"

"Did who mention what?"

"Did I take your mind off business, or is business just a game?"

"No, not a game, Rabbit Stockings. The trading post is just a way of survival. I mean, it keeps me here," the trader said.

"Service to the Indians. Why don't you start one of those Gallup service-minded clubs here? I wouldn't mind being an Elk. Start an animal club."

"Do you see anything?"

"Start an animal club."

"I'm watching for Ring."

"I wouldn't mind being a Lion. If I were a Lion—"

724

"Keep watching."

"If I were a Moose—"

"We've got a job to do, Rabbit Stockings. I'm worried. Keep your mind on Ring."

"I tried to ask how long he was gone."

"You know as well as I do. Four months."

"Was it right after Nice Hands—"

"Yes, it was."

"How does a thing like that happen?"

"I don't know, Rabbit Stockings. Try to keep an eye open. Do you see anything?"

"No, nothing. I don't see—I can't seem to make out anything at all," Rabbit Stockings said. "As I said, I can't seem to make out anything at all."

"But when Ring left you were there, Rabbit Stockings."

"Yes, but I still don't know why he went."

"Yes," the trader, the man on horseback, the father, said, pulling short and sliding off his Appaloosa, dropping to the ground to examine fresh tracks. "Yes, why did Twenty-six Horses, Ring—?" Without using the stirrup he leaped back into the saddle and sat upright and said into the clear day. "Nice Hands."

"But she is in your blue hogan."

"Yes." The trader pulled on his slant hat over the angular burnt face. "Yes. Yes." The trader, the father and the lover now worked his face with his big hand. "After the funeral Nice Hands came running, almost naked—"

"Naked?"

"Yes, and bleeding, and I took her in, picked the cactus spikes out of her—"

"That's why Twenty-six Horses left?"

"And put Nice Hands in the blue hogan."

"And Ring left?"

"Ah, yes," the trader said, trader and slave to the damn Indians, lover, animal, victim. "Yes. Everyone wants to help, but the only way back is home, and they ran. We spend our lives fleeing as fast from everything the human heart wants, demands. Maybe it's that. We are afraid, in deadly fear of, not each other, but ourselves, and we blame fate, a black horse," the trader said.

"But Ring's here."

"If he was, Rabbit Stockings, we'd be back at the post," George Bowman said.

"You mean since Ring went away he never really came back?"

"He's still away."

"If I could tell you where he went—?"

"That would not help."

"If I could tell you where he went when he left home then maybe we could figure where he is now."

"It would not help."

"You never can tell," Rabbit Stockings said. "And—" Rabbit Stockings stopped his horse, arrested it suddenly and patted the great neck while looking out. "Look over there. Do you see who's standing over there by his hogan?"

"Twenty-six Horses!"

"Yes. I'll go get him. I'll look after his sheep. With Twenty-six Horses you'll find Ring. He knows all their secret places."

"All our secret places. Yes, Rabbit Stockings. Thank you very much."

726

TWELVE

QUICKSAND. Ring tried to remove the word from his thoughts. Quicksand, a viscid, unsubstantial whorl—phantom. Neither is quicksand fluid nor solid; neither can you stand nor swim. Quicksand, the stuff a nightmare and the rest of my life is made of. But try to think of something else; try to think of something pleasant to pass this short time left. Think of your Indian friend and the day you said to Twenty-six Horses:

"How many chiefs are there in that summer wickiup?"

"It's not that wickiup, it's my home."

"How many chiefs are there?"

"Plenty. You know, Ringo, you've got to stop thinking like a white person."

"That's going to be difficult."

"You've got to try. You know the Whites are going to be extincted."

"What's that?"

"Blown up. Isn't that what they are trying to do?"

"Are we?"

"Sure. And when you're all gone and then you try to come back again we Indians are not going to be so nice next time."

"You Indians are not going to let the next Columbus land?"

"That's right, Ringo."

Ring thought about this odd, unimportant conversation. He had had a great deal of time to think this day so he let his mind wander over all of his short rich past, because he had tried everything to keep from sinking but nothing worked. The thing that seemed to work best was to lie backward and try to float on the cool boiling sand. That seemed to work best, but each long alone hour that passed he was getting in deeper. It's a grave. That's it. It's as though the earth wanted you, decided to take you now, and when you have tried absolutely everything else and there is no way out, then you try resignation and courage. Quicksand is heavy water in which swimming is impossible and it's as if the drain below were open and you were being sucked down into the earth. Ring had been struggling alone down at the bottom of the lonely arroyo for eight hours now.

Eight hours to relive one life. One life is composed of about ten separate incidents that you remember. Each separate. Not like a play where everything flows smoothly like a stream, but more like a spring pulsing beneath the sand. Finally I suppose it begins to flow smoothly. Somewhere it joins and runs steady to the ocean. But I can't figure how. I can't figure where what happened to me ever got together. Now, you watch Twenty-six Horses make a painting and you see what I mean. It all quickly comes together. That one up there on the rock above me —I saw Twenty-six Horses paint it and it always made sense. You always felt everything in it belonged together. That's not my life. Something big is happening to Twenty-six Horses when he paints. He has good medicine. But when he weaves a rug it takes time and there is always a big piece unfinished standing there on the loom. A rug takes time and is made of threads of a different color. Each day something separate takes place on the loom, but on the last day it makes sense. And on this last day maybe my life makes sense even if it was made up of separate threads. A life is an endless rug that ends all at once. That's my life. Luto! Luto horse, tell me what that portrait by Twenty-six Horses up there above me on the cliff means. That's too big an order for a horse to understand. All right, I'll use simple horse language. Luto, you are bad medicine. Luto, are you waiting to take me to the mountain? Luto, aren't my sounds, my noises making any sense? Isn't my music any good? Luto, boy, what's happening to me?

On the great haunch of the Sangre de Cristo Mountains that rose like another planet above the flat arroyo-cut land the two riders appeared like centaurs at a distance.

"Twenty-six Horses," George Bowman said, "it's a superstition or something you dreamed up, I don't know which."

"I just have this feeling that Ringo did not go to the mountains yet."

"But feeling is not enough, Twenty-six Horses."

"I have this feeling that he went the other way. Something happened to him."

"What happened?"

"He drowned."

"In the small stream from the spring in the arroyo? It would be quite a trick."

"Well, I've got this feeling. He could be in that quicksand," Twenty-six Horses said.

The trader couldn't take this Indian seriously about his son at the bottom of the arroyo. The Indian religion was part of their way of life that the white man had not been able to make a dent in. The Indians still insisted on getting their inspiration from their guardian spirit. Sometimes it was a bear, an elk or even a certain pine tree isolated and clinging to a ledge on the mesa which they would watch from below each day. Sometimes it was only a rock, a large yellow concretion about to tumble from a ledge, threatening and high.

"Where did you get your information, Twenty-six Horses?"

"From a snake."

"I thought so. We will continue up the mountain." And he touched his horse to increase their pace to a trot, the Indian keeping up on his matching Appaloosa that had to work hard to maintain the pace. They had been traveling for about an hour now.

Indians are alarmists, the trader thought. Ring was overdue about eight hours on his trip to the mountain to gather the cattle. But what happened to the boy? What had happened to Ring? Probably his horse went lame. Don't ask Twenty-six Horses. Indians are alarmists.

"You didn't tell me what makes quicksand," Twenty-six Horses said.

"It's caused by water rising from below a table of sand. This causes a turbid—"

"What's that mean?"

"Something that is neither water nor sand, Twenty-six Horses. You can't swim in it, neither can you get any purchase on it to get out. You founder and die."

"There's nothing down there pulling you below? Nothing that wants you? Something that says, now is the time?"

"No, Twenty-six Horses. It's like your snake again. There is nothing to it."

"Nothing to it," Twenty-six Horses repeated, bouncing on his smaller horse. "Nothing to it. Another Indian superstition. Well, maybe you're right," Twenty-six Horses announced suddenly. "After all, Luto didn't show up in fire and smoke."

"Try to remember that, Twenty-six Horses," the trader said.

Ring, sinking into eternity at the bottom of the arroyo, was looking up at the soft gray-green slopes that led away to the world and thinking small thoughts to fight the insidious and larger thoughts as he lay dying.

Another thing about Indians, Ring thought, another thing about Indians is they don't plan for the future. I remember Twenty-six Horses touching his head and saying, the future is here. In other words, the future isn't. It's

731

another idea. That true? Yes, I guess it is. So why should an Indian waste time with the future if it doesn't exist? Progress is part of the future, so that's a waste of time too. Right? Words, words, words. Now, your snakes. Snakes exist, don't they? Bears, deer, elk, coyotes—they're real, really real. Right?

Really real. Right. Anything you say, Twenty-six Horses. And then the young man with the red hair in the quicksand at the bottom of the long deep lonely arroyo cried suddenly up into the big empty space, "But get me out! Find me if your magic works." It was a quiet cry with no attempt to reach anyone, a cry to himself and the quiescent spirit of the rocks and sage, yucca and gray sad tamarisk that wept toward the Rio Grande. But there is no one, Ring thought. There is no spirit, no life, no death—no death outside this one right here. It's only a word until it happens to you. Where is the horse, Luto? I can see him there in the half shadows. Luto seems waiting for me to get it over with so he can carry me away. Was he in on this too? Was this the exact time and place, absolutely and perfectly arranged to the second? Luto is all black, a pure black horse. I never did like that horse waiting there in the quiet shade of the tamarisks. But there was an understanding, there was always an understanding that he was the best horse in the country, the fastest, the quickest and the best cow horse in the country. We were never friendly. We never spoke. And I never bought him; that day he just showed up, unbranded, little more than a colt, but he knew everything, wasn't even green-broke but he behaved like a ten-year-old. I wonder where he came from and where he will go back to now.

Ring felt himself sink a little more into the heavy fluid sand. He waved his slim arms, fluttered them like a wounded bird, but he could feel himself being pulled down deeper. No, no, no, he told himself. You are behaving like an Indian, thinking like a Navajo. You've been around them too long. Like father says, you should associate more with white boys. But why does Luto wait there in the solemn dappled shadows and where is he going soon?

Ring ceased all movement and Luto emerged out of the shadow tentatively, the black horse bringing the shade, the darkness with him, a shadow interlaced among the shadows in the tamarisk.

And it wasn't my idea to cross this arroyo at this point, it was Luto who pushed down here in that steady stride and it was again Luto that flew almost airborne down Blind Wolf Canyon to bring us around in back of the ranch so that not even Twenty-six Horses would select this arroyo as a place to search. And it was Luto with terrific almost deathless delicacy who had been able to cut out a calf from its mother, a colt from a stallion, and charge from cover and then whip a mule deer to the mesa and in the snow gambol like a puppy with a jack until the rabbit, wraithlike in the matching frost, would founder in abject capitulation to the dark mountain that moved like a cougar. The sudden darkness of Luto ascending, then descending, the pine-feathered slopes of the Sangre de Cristos like a writhing storm, somber and wild. Yes, Ring thought, Luto, yes, Luto is alive. Luto is the best horse, queer, yes, but Luto is the best damn horse.

Luto, the shadow, has moved out of the tamarisks'

shadows, moving catlike, moving over here; because I have been silent, ceased to struggle for seconds, now Luto is moving in. I will wait and when his tail passes by I will grab it and hold on. I will foil the horse. I will make it out of here.

Ring did not believe this, he had been settling in the quicksand for too long now to have grand hope. Ring's helplessness had long since turned to hopelessness but against utter despair he told himself, *I will make it out, I will make it out,* as the horse nuzzled forward, fretting its monster nose toward the young man in long sweeping casts, treading delicately in the beginning soft sand, trailing the broken reins like a shroud. Then Luto jerked up his head in discovery and wheeled to escape as Ring's arms rose to catch the flying gossamer tail. He had the horse tail in his hands. It was like threads of ice, new-forming fragile ice that slithered in his grip, and Luto was gone. Now Luto came slowly back, then stopped ten feet away—Luto staring out of the beginning darkness, merging again into the shadows, spectral and huge.

"Luto!" Ring called weakly. "Luto!" Ring felt himself settling more into the quicksand. "Luto, boy, what's happening?"

I'll tell you one thing that's happening, Luto. Luto, I'm fighting away the bigger thoughts. Did you notice, Luto, I never told you anything about the ranch? Nothing about home. All about the Indians. Big talk. But I never told you the truth about Nice Hands and my father and me. Did I want Nice Hands myself? But it was my father . . . But we secretly blame it on ourselves. A white woman is all alone in this country, Luto. My mother was all alone.

734

We made her alone. This country invites a man out and we go. And when we are gone and women are alone something pulls them to the mountain. Men are always out and so women are pulled away toward the hill city. Believe me, Luto, it's true. It's true. Come here, Luto, so I can touch something firm. I've been playing with a puzzle, Luto, trying to put things together so I can go home. I am sinking home. I am trying to remember everything that ever happened so I can finish, understand that picture by Twenty-six Horses up there on the cliff. I think I've got all the pieces together now, Luto. I thought it was a picture of Twenty-six Horses; it could be that it's a confused picture —a picture of us all. In the terror, in the loneliness of my father, in the loneliness of the beautiful land, we were all in love. We were all alone, but we were all lovers, Luto. I think that's true. I know I am very tired. I'm tired of fighting sand. Take me home, Luto. I am all ready. I'm all finished. Take me home. It's all right. It was okay. If you loved something, loved anyone, you were never alone. We are never alone. Take me home. Black horse, it was good. Black horse, it was wonderful. Black horse, tell them I didn't beg—tell them I didn't cry.

The pair of horsemen moving fast up the precipitous slope merged with mountain mahogany, then fled between brakes of aspen, trampling columbine, mariposa lilies, found a trail strewn red with gilias that led straight to the peaks, then entered a lowering and ominous cloud.

"Do you know what day it is, Twenty-six Horses?" George Bowman asked.

"Shrove Tuesday? The day after tomorrow? The day before yesterday? Ass Wednesday? What other days have you invented?"

"Today is the day, three years ago to the day, we got Luto. I remember because it's the summer solstice."

"What's that?"

"The twenty-first of June."

"I mean what's the summer solstice."

"It's the longest day and the shortest night of the year."

Twenty-six Horses thought about this as they cantered through bowers of ponderosa, then debouched into a quiet explosion of orange cowboy's delight ringed with high wavering Indian paintbrush midst the gaunt and verdigrised collapse of a homestead, a monument to unhardihood and puerile myth; but some eastern hollyhocks rose in towering weedlike formidability from out of New England ruins in the yellow New Mexican sky. Twenty-six Horses plucked one as he passed and placed the garish New England flower in his black Indian head knot.

"You see," Twenty-six Horses said in sham Indian solemnity, "I've been thinking about your summer solstice. It could be the twenty-first but it could be the twenty-second because it seems to my thick Indian head that both days have got that shortest night."

"Yes," George Bowman touched his head and blew out a forced breath annoyed, and the Appaloosa horse started in sympathy. "Yes, but it was the twenty-first we got Luto." Then he said, flat and peremptory, "Twenty-six Horses, you should be a scientist."

"Yes," Twenty-six Horses said. "But I am a weaver."

"They tell me, Twenty-six Horses," the trader said, "that

736

an Indian can tell, that is, his religion gives him some secret insight into animals."

"That's not true," Twenty-six Horses said.

"That, for example, a horse like Luto, do you suppose—? What do you suppose? I've always felt that Luto was too damn cooperative, that it had some ulterior purpose."

"Ulterior?"

"That there is something wrong with Luto I mean."

"What do you mean?" the Indian asked.

"If the Indians believe that each person has a guardian spirit like a rock, a stone, a snake, could it be a horse?"

"I guess it could."

"Would the guardian spirit take care of everything?"

"Except dig the grave," the Indian said. "And sometimes that."

"What do you mean?"

"Well, if it were quicksand," Twenty-six Horses said.

"Why have you got this thing with quicksand, Twenty-six Horses?"

"Because it's the only way a horse could kill Ringo."

"Oh?"

"Yes. Ringo is too smart for horses with the usual tricks."

"And why would Luto want to kill Ring?"

"I don't know. I'm only a poor Indian. I only work here."

"Do you have a guardian spirit, Twenty-six Horses?"

"No, I don't," Twenty-six Horses said. "Or maybe I do, but it doesn't count because I don't believe in it, not all

737

the time. It's difficult to believe in anything all the time. You see, if you don't believe in your guardian spirit he can't help you."

"Or hurt you?"

"That's right. If Ringo doesn't believe in the horse it can't hurt him or help him. If Ringo's time had come and he didn't believe the horse was anything but a horse, then the horse would have no power."

"Well, I think there's something wrong with Luto. As I said, Luto's too perfect for a horse. What can we do?"

"It's probably too late now," Twenty-six Horses said. "All we can do now is continue up the mountain. I guess your way is as good as mine."

"I'm sure it is, Twenty-six Horses. A horse is a horse no matter how perfect a horse."

"My guardian spirit is a snake."

"When we get back," the trader said, "we'll have a drink to the snakes."

"Look!"

The horses plunged back, rising to enormous height on their hinder legs in blurred Appaloosa furious fright before the dice—a hard clean rattle in the sage ahead.

"There!" Twenty-six Horses hollered and the diamond-back rattler exploded toward the plunging and furious motions of the horses, some grenade or antihorse weapon planted in the innocent sage, lashing out with sidewind perfect accuracy to the falling mark and missing the falling-away Appaloosa, but recoiling, re-arming itself before the rapt and cold stricken-eyed terror of the horse as George Bowman slid off and seized a log and hefted it in a vast surging motion above his head to crush the snake.

"Wait!"

"Why?"

"He's trying to tell us something."

"Yes, that's true, Twenty-six Horses. I got the message."

"You don't understand."

"Oh, I do. I understand rattlesnakes perfectly and they understand me. Get out of the way before the snake kills you."

Twenty-six Horses stepped deftly and quickly as the snake exploded again and then quickly again and then again, the snake in surly dusty diamonds flinging itself at the mad Indian before the Indian gained a high boulder in an unfrantic graceful leap, resting and looking down from there at the snake, his arms akimbo.

"Well done, Twenty-six Horses! Now can I kill the other half of the act?"

"Why do you—why do you have to kill things?"

"Rattlesnakes."

"Still?"

"Rattlesnakes. Oh, yes." From his safe distance the trader let down his trunk of wood and sat on it. "Or is this one a friend of yours?"

"No."

"Your guardian spirit maybe telling you to go back?"

"I don't know."

"Some Indian nonsense like that," the trader said. "Still, if you want to check the arroyo instead of the mountain we will check the arroyo instead of the mountain. Anything you say. Anything your snake says, any opinion a rattler holds. If you don't kill 'em, join 'em. What do you think?"

739

"We will check the arroyo." Twenty-six Horses said.

"Not that I hold with snakes," George Bowman said as they quickly mounted the trembling, subdued Appaloosas, "but I'll always go along with a legend, a good Navajo myth. Look, Twenty-six Horses, your snake has called it quits."

They scattered down the mountain, their horses tumbling in mad pursuit of home, wild and uncontrolled, the riders allowing their horses to plunge downward in furious gyrations, careening and bouncing with abrupt speed like some kind of huge bright chunks of ore hurtling downward from a blast above on the high, still snow-coifed in June, scintillant far peaks of the Sangre de Cristos, flashing down down down in twisting horse rapture to the sage fields of the flat earth.

"The La Jara Arroyo," Twenty-six Horses hollered to the trader, beginning now to direct the horse. "That's where Ringo must be. That's where the quicksand is. The La Jara Arroyo."

"Yes," George Bowman said quietly to himself and the horse. "Yes. Yes, at my age I'm taking orders from a fool Navajo Indian and a snake; a guardian spirit Twenty-six Horses called it, but you and I," he told the still raging horse, "you and I saw a rattler. Wait! This way," and the trader went the way of Twenty-six Horses, both fleeing now between yellow plumes of yucca and among a bright festooned desert carpet of the twenty-first of June.

At the bottom of the arroyo nothing moved where Ring Bowman had been struggling. The water ran serene now, limpid and innocent. Where the two spent riders watched from their horses atop the great canyon their searching eyes could see all the way to where the La Jara joined the Puerco, but no sign, no clue of Ring, only the dusky, burnished copper fire sky above the arroyo heralding the slow end of a long day.

"We should have continued to the mountain," George Bowman said.

Twenty-six Horses slid off down the sleek sweat of his speckled horse and stared from the ground with uncomprehending disbelief at the vast empty cut one hundred feet deep, bottomed with a thin thread of water feeding the Rio Grande and becoming bronze now as it refracted in quick shimmers the maddening and molten sky. Twenty-six Horses crawled forward on the hard earth up to the sage-sprinkled lip of the arroyo, then he thumped the earth with the palm of his small rough red hand. "Yes."

"Yes, what?"

"Yes, they crossed here, Ringo and Luto. Look, this is Luto's hoofprint."

"Yes, that's Luto. But where did they go?"

"Down," Twenty-six Horses said, capping his vision and staring across. "But I don't see where they went up." Twenty-six Horses continued to search all along the arroyo while George Bowman sat frozen. "But there's something moving down there in the tamarisk," Twenty-six Horses said finally.

"Hello!" the trader shouted "Who's there?"

"It's me!"

"It sounds like Ringo," Twenty-six Horses said. "That you, Ringo?"

"Yes," the voice of Ring called up. "But don't come down. Please don't come down."

But George Bowman had already started his Appaloosa in a steep dive down the slope. Twenty-six Horses tried to arrest him with an upraised hand but the trader was already hurtling halfway to the bottom, horse and rider commingled in a vortex of riotous earth.

"Me too!" Twenty-six Horses shouted as he gained his horse and catapulted it in one great leap out and down, the horse sprawling as it hit and never quite recovering, cavorting crazy to the bottom where it righted itself on all four scattered legs and stood amazed and triumphant.

"Don't come!" Ring shouted toward them both. "Don't come over here!"

"Why not?"

"Because I'm telling you why not."

"Go ahead."

There was a long silence from the tamarisks.

"Because there's a snake here, a dangerous rattler. He killed a horse. The snake killed Luto."

"Where's the snake?" Twenty-six Horses dropped off his horse and moved into the thick interlacing tamarisk. "Where's the snake, Ringo?"

"He's gone. The snake was coiled there, where you're standing now. He's gone."

"What snake?" The heavy voice of the trader moved into the tamarisk. "What snake? Another snake? Where's the horse? Where's Luto?"

"Luto's dead. Luto went down in the quicksand." Ring stood up, a small tower of mud. "I was stuck in the quicksand and Luto just stood here and watched. Then Luto was struck by this big snake. I could see the snake strike Luto, then Luto panicked into the quicksand, got stuck, but I was able to get out using Luto to crawl up, but Luto got stuck worse and began to go under and there was nothing I could do. Luto's dead."

"No," Twenty-six Horses announced. "Luto's not dead."

"I saw Luto die."

"No, you saw Luto sink in the sand, that's all. Luto will be back, you'll see."

"Oh, you bet I'll never buy a horse that looks like that again."

"Luto won't look like that again," Twenty-six Horses said. "Remember Luto can be a beautiful woman behind a loom, for example."

"Well, I'll never just buy a beautiful woman for example."

"Get up in back, Ring," George Bowman said, reaching down from his horse. Ring was lifted up easily on great arms to the back of the horse, then fell forward, limp like a doll, clasping his muddied hands around the big form in front. He touched his father and his father was there.

"And another thing," Twenty-six Horses advised in his advising tone. "Never do anything on Shrove Tuesday."

"It's not Shrove Tuesday, it's the summer solstice," George Bowman said.

"All right, be careful of that too," Twenty-six Horses advised. "Now that we don't have any medicine bundles, now we have to be careful all the time."

As they passed the stream in muddy file Ring pointed at the spot. "That's where it almost happened."

743

Twenty-six Horses turned in his saddle. "That's where it did happen."

"I mean to me."

"You're not the center of the world."

"I suppose the Indians are."

"That's nice of you, Ringo. I've always supposed they were too."

The horses bounded now in furious great leaps out of the fast-darkening arroyo and they gained the wide and endless undulating country gilded in light, all of them in the big sunset.

"Well, I'll tell you," Ring said, "it was terrible, my almost and then Luto's death down there, but outside of that—" He stared from behind his huge father with muddied eyes at the Indian. "Outside of that, I figured what the picture above me on the cliff meant. It's a picture of all of us."

"A picture of everyone," the father said, "who is at the mercy of everybody. Could it be something like that, Twenty-six Horses?"

The Indian, Twenty-six Horses, trotted forward in a wild rhythm on his dazzling pony and pointed his luminous arm up at the faltering fire going out. "This was the day of the white man's summer solstice, the longest day of the year."

"Yes," Ring Bowman said. "The artist won't talk. Yes." Ring watched the somber shock of Indian Country, the wild eclipse of a Midsummer Day. "Another thing, Twenty-six Horses, you passed me while I was down there in the quicksand."

"You mean I passed you there at the arroyo without seeing you, without hearing you?"

"You were coming home."

"Yes, I was coming back from the States of the United States. The big reservation."

"Yes," Ring said. "We passed each other coming home. We both passed our portrait on the rock on this long day, coming home."

They flew lightly and all together up a gaudy-thrown profusion of raging color and the sharp high scent of Indian Country until they topped out on the end of a day, on a New Mexican sky infinity of burnished and dying gold.

ABOUT THE AUTHOR

WILLIAM EASTLAKE was born in New York City and spent his early years in Liberty Corners and Caldwell, New Jersey. He served in the Army from 1942 until 1946 and after the war spent three years studying and traveling in France, Italy and England. Upon his return to this country, he purchased a ranch in New Mexico where he now lives with his wife. His chief interests are good cattle, good horses, and the plight of the Navajo Indians.

Mr. Eastlake's other novels are *The Bamboo Bed* and *Castle Keep*. He was the Vietnam correspondent for *The Nation* in 1968, and his short stories have appeared in *Harper's*, *Hudson Review*, *Evergreen Review*, the *Saturday Evening Post* and other magazines, and have been reprinted in various anthologies.